<BW>

Acknowledgments

I knew getting Burning World out of my head and onto paper wasn't going to be a quick or easy affair. What I didn't know at the time was that it was going to require the kinds of sacrifices that I alone could not make.

Thank you, Joanie, for your patience and support and for being the best mother and friend anyone could hope for. Thank you, mom, for providing me a safe space to chase my dreams and for encouraging every one of my endeavors. Thank you, Chris, for setting the example on how to put your nose to the grindstone and get sh*t done. Thank you, Sarah, for investing in this dream early and for never letting me quit. And for my departed brothers Emmett and Sean, thank you for your inspiration and for constantly reminding who I am and why it's important to never lose sight of the big picture.

Miriya, when the going gets tough, all I have to do is think about you holding my hand, dancing your crazy dances, or laughing at my dumb jokes. Daddy loves you forever and ever and ever-ever.

Lastly, to the beta testers who dove into this universe before the paint dried. Your feedback helped make this crazy fantasy a reality.

The Burning World Beta Testers:

OhJinAh!
AHeinen
Hannah
BigGreeezy
AlleyCat
KatieL

And a special thanks to Claudio Pilia for bringing Burning World to life visually.

1

00: Prologue

"What doesn't get better by chance gets better by change."

- Some yoga website

Marine Corps Sergeant First Class Emmett Byron approached the Major as advised: slowly, confidently. The Major sat on the shoulder of the toppled statue of the chief justice of North Korea's Central Court. Surrounding him were his Phoenix, his commanders. They were all grinning, reveling in the victory, all but two: Battalion Specialist Blake Turner was not smiling, largely due to the fact that his jaw had been shot off in the Tokyo counteroffensive, and the Major was not smiling, largely due to the fact that the Major *never* smiled.

As Byron approached, the only person in the vicinity not wearing the stark colors of the Phoenix Battalion, he could not help but feel foreign, even though his entire company and many soldiers of the Marine Corps of the United States occupied the shattered streets of Pyongyang.

Among the Major's Phoenix, he recognized the soldier called "Pops." This wasn't hard, considering the old soldier's physical mass and former status as Phoenix Battalion commander. He also recognized the Phoenix lieutenant called

"Legion," a swarthy woman with orange hair and an exposed exo-skeletal spine that somehow made her even more attractive, at least to Sgt. Byron.

His steps were slow, measured. He held his head up, and he was careful to make eye contact with the orange-clad paramilitary faction. As though stepping out in front of a crowd, he pierced the Phoenix Battalion's inner circle.

Major, sir! he rehearsed internally.

"Major, sir!" he tried to say aloud but croaked.

"Major, sir!" he finally managed in a voice that was sturdy, if a bit shrill.

The Major, who was nursing a cruel shrapnel wound in his right cheek, turned to face him, silencing the giant Pops mid-sentence with a glance.

"Major, sir!" Byron repeated, standing at attention. "General Maecht has instructed me to notify the Major that we've detained a POW, sir!"

"Taking prisoners is a part of war, soldier," the Major replied, in a voice that was beyond anyone's years. Looking around, he added, "I'd say this prisoner is rather fortunate, all things considered."

The sergeant glanced nervously at the Major's retinue. Soldiers, but not part of the Corps or Army, the Phoenix Battalion were mythical among the Allied forces participating in the invasion. They moved with and between militaries of the Alliance with impunity, and represented the first boots on peninsula soil. And, unlike their enlisted counterparts, every

4

soldier in the Phoenix Battalion was a "MOD" — a man-machine hybrid.

"Major, sir, perhaps it'd be best if I could deliver the remainder of the general's message in private."

The Major's silver prosthetic hand fell away from his face — taking with it a red wad of gauze — to reveal a spider's web of deep, fresh wounds. The cuts degraded even further the wreckage that had already been the Major's face. Looking at the gauze, the Major sucked his teeth irritably. "There are no secrets among the troops you see here, Sergeant First Class."

With a gulp, Byron delivered the remainder of the general's instructions. "You'll find the captive in the general's quarters, sir."

"General's quarters, you say?"

"The prisoner was caught when your team toppled the Communications Ministry. She appears to be a Sodang officer," Byron continued, referencing the North Korean special forces unit. "Sir, the intel this captive supposedly possesses is for your ears and your ears alone. He — the general, that is — says you'll know what to do with it. General's explicit instructions."

It was then that a strange expression swept over the face of the man many of his peers credited with crushing North Korea's Special Forces. The expression was almost boyish behind the trauma and betrayed a seemingly authentic curiosity. The Major leapt down from the statue and approached, his metallic arm creaking as it swung at his side, his boots grinding on the grey debris of what was once North Korea's Ministry of Justice building.

Despite his best efforts, as the Major's immense presence and horrible visage came to bear down on him, the Marine sergeant could not help but quail a bit.

The Major, clearly recognizing his discomfort, placed the heavy metal hand on his shoulder. His expression softened, as though his face was not in shambles, as though the pain he must have felt didn't matter. "How are you, soldier?"

"Sir, I don't follow, sir!"

"Don't look beyond the obvious, Marine. How are you?"

The question, though simple, banal even, stalled something in Sergeant Byron. Tokyo and the horrors he'd seen, the horrors that stole his sleep. He tried to enunciate how he "was," truly, in what people believed were the final days of the war, but found that the words carried with them emotions that he could not and would not burden the Major with.

"Forget it, soldier," the Major said after a moment, as though reading his mind. "Our general was wounded — concussed, to my understanding. Any updates on his status?"

"General Maecht, sir, was medevaced and is on his way FOB Liberty. The men are praying, sir."

"Do that," the Major said dryly, slinging a bloodied tarpaulin poncho over his shoulders. "Pray."

The Major, blood still dripping from his face, dispersed his unit with a series of harsh commands, never once using

6

their God-given names. As he strode past, hand resting on that odd blade he carried, he paused. "Fret over the things you never had control over later, soldier. Mourn your brothers and sisters for now and revel silently in your own survival."

Sergeant Byron saluted, but the Major had already passed, his poncho leaving behind it the smell of death and fire.

1: Who's the Boss?

"Violence begets violence begets media attention begets shoe contracts begets fame and fortune begets parties begets drinking begets violence begets violence. You see, it's cyclical."

- Unit One Sgt. Alec Jefferson "AJ" Moore

Sergeant Alec Jefferson Moore checked himself before crossing the quad. His jacket was crisp and clean, having been recently dry-cleaned, and his shirt was pristine white. There were tiny bits of blood splatter around the knees of his jeans, but he doubted anyone would notice. Comfortable with his appearance, he descended the steps into the plaza and began pushing his way through the crowd.

Some folks recognized his face from TV and pointed him out to one another. These were mostly the civvies: party-goers, consumers and the like. Others recognized the weapon he carried. These people eyed him suspiciously, as they should. And they were the drug dealers, the pimps, the black-marketers, and the drug-dealt.

Regardless of classification, all recognized the jacket he wore. It was black, high-collared and adorned on the back with a white delta: the symbol of the State Defense Consortium's elite task force, Unit One.

[Other end of the plaza, AJ, up the stairs. She's standing in front of the Indian restaurant, by the patio. She's got two others with her.]

AJ's partner "spoke" to him through neurotrigger: a "system-to-system" communication protocol that — among other things — rendered frontal lobe activity as digital speech. It was the primary means of communication in the State Defense Consortium, as agents and soldiers could relay information in physical silence, over networks that were, for the most part, State controlled.

"You sound terrible, Rena."

[Thanks.]

The channel she'd chosen was likely full of beat cops struggling to keep a weekend-bound Sun City from imploding. The throttled bandwidth made her sound like artificial intelligence, or the public service recording that reminded you not to urinate on the skyrail.

[Sorry about that,] Rena replied. *[The unmonitored SDC channels are full. I thought using a police channel would be better.]*

Rena refused to use monitored communication channels, which was ironic, considering one of her job functions included monitoring communication.

"It'll have to do, I guess," the sergeant replied, his voice carrying an authority that he did not possess.

[Keep straight ahead, AJ. You're closing on the target.]

"You do know that this will make three on the day?"

[Collars?]

"Well, two collars and a frag. Up about six grand, thanks to the new Queue spiff structure."

The fragged suspect had lobbed a grenade at AJ's feet. Fortunately, he'd played a little soccer as a kid and still had a decent return.

[So, you're sitting pretty right now.]

"Not too shabby."

[Neat-o.]

AJ sighed. "I can tell you don't care."

[Oh really?]

"Yeah. You say things like 'neat-o.'"

[I noticed you skipped a few perps in the Queue to get to this guy,] Rena said. *[You're supposed to pull targets in order. That's more of a rule and less of a suggestion. Otherwise, we're going to end up with a Queue full of international terrorists and mob assassins and empty of chem brewers and kidnappers.]*

"The others may be lazy, Rena, but not me. I'd take out Changgok himself if the name came up."

[So why cherry-pick now?]

"Call it part of a larger project."

[Is this your Luther Gueye theory?]

AJ could hear her smile. She was mocking him, just like Chris and Dice had mocked him. For some reason, it bothered him a lot more when she did it.

"Just you wait, Rena. One day you're going to say the words, 'AJ, you were right. You are the smartest, most dashing, bravest, best-dressed agent in all of Sun City.'"

[I'm going to say that, am I? Verbatim?]

"Just you wait…"

[Do I have to? Though I suspect your need to impress people is the result of some very personal self-doubt, AJ, you don't have to try and impress me. You really don't. Also, you really can't.]

"Heh."

His sneakers were custom, produced by Skyy Shoes as part of the "Unit One – Street Justice" product line. His shoe, as in the shoe designed specifically for him by the product team at Skyy Shoes, was called the Stalker. They were black-and-silver high-tops with a rubber tread and magnetic ankle strap. They had a flat tread that, when wet, morphed to produce ridges for traction. They could be worn lace-less or with laces, rope-style or wide, depending on the person's tastes, of course. The toecaps were paramagnetic and would shift in color to match that of the jeans you wore. At present, the shoe-tips were gunmetal grey, a shade that played nicely with the washed black, low-waist jeans he wore.

Skyy Shoes paid him four hundred dollars a day to wear the shoes and three thousand for every high-profile collar made wearing them. And this would be collar number two on the day.

11

It's a shame they don't pay for frags, the sergeant thought.

[She should be visible now. You're practically on top of her.]

"Gross. I've seen her mugshots."

[Jesus, you're such a child. You know what I mean.]

AJ slowed his approach. "I see her."

[And?]

"She's a lot bigger in person."

[Fat-shaming now?]

AJ grimaced. "Not fat, Rena, and I'm not sure muscle-shaming is a thing."

The weapon he carried had been named "Deadbolt" by his brother, who, at the time, insisted that all good weapons should have a name. Long and pole-shaped, it housed a blade of heated, single atom–tipped graphene, four feet in length. When fully heated, Deadbolt was capable of splitting concrete. The scabbard, too, was an essential part of the weapon and served two purposes. First, it heated the blade when sheathed, and second, it acted as a gas-powered firing chamber. When the sensors on the hilt detected his grip, a flip of the switch on the hilt would fire the blade from the scabbard. The contained explosion within the pole/scabbard ejected the blade with a tremendous force, resulting in an otherwise impossibly fast sword stroke. Like his shoes, it was a one-of-a-kind custom, built for him and him alone.

AJ shoved his way through a cadre of loitering clubbers, slapping a beer from the hand of one.

[Pretty sure that's assault.]

"Don't hate, Rena, it's unbecoming. Besides, there are strict policies against public consumption."

As he passed the congested retail shops and over-stuffed media arcades, smart-ads offered him products based on his biometrics and internet search history. For him, they flashed images of hip-hop albums and online dating apps in split-second sales pitches that left burns on the brain like staring at a light bulb.

He quickly mounted a low flight of steps and could feel his heart rate begin to climb. The sensation before a fight was a bit like falling. And he knew he was in for a fight. In three years, he'd never arrested a Titan without a fight. And in three years he'd never arrested one the size of two football linebackers conjoined at the hip.

The target's name was Diedre, and she was a corner boss for the Titans. Corner bosses were mid-tier drug dealers, typically assigned a small section of the city. The better the territory, usually the more influential the boss. Her territory was a three-block stretch of Section Seven that hugged the border of the red-light district. She wasn't all the way big-time yet, sitting on that territory, but she had aspirations. That much was clear by her rap sheet. Diedre stood well over six feet and, at present, had her massive, diamond-shaped back to the center of the quad.

13

"Garcia's gonna get all silverback on that ass," she was telling her cohorts. "Fight won't go two rounds, right? But I got two thousand on what's-his-nuts just in case. Them odds are too good to sleep on, right? What's his opponent's name again? I should know. He wins, I'm a rich woman! No more corner-standing with you broke gig-runners."

Typically, a bonehead like Diedre wouldn't end up in the Unit One–monitored Queue. She only had two homicides on her rap sheet, while there were killers with nearly a baker's dozen still outside the Queue. Diedre was special because she apparently had no luck. One of the homicides of which she was suspected just happened to be the son of State Defense Consortium chairwoman Diane West's sister-in-law. Needless to say, a few strings had been pulled to get Diedre off the Sun City Police Department's plate and into Unit One's Queue. And that suited AJ just fine. As far as he was concerned, it was open season on Titans. And it was quite personal.

No place felt the brunt of the cartel's presence in Sun City like Section Seven. And Section Seven was the district from which AJ hailed.

He came to a halt directly behind Diedre, one hand on Deadbolt, the other in the pocket of his jacket.

"Way I see it," she was saying, "if the guy — the other guy — gets lucky, with them odds, I might as well retire and get the fuck outta Sun City. You know, go someplace like Maui, Fiji, or Hawaii. One of them sandy places where dudes got like flowers around they necks, and oiled-up pecs."

14

"Maui is in Hawaii," one of her men corrected.

"So what, you like an archeologist or some shit now?" Diedre laughed and it boomed over the median raucus of the quad. "This stupid runner can't even trim his goatee without it coming out all spotty."

Diedre's cadre joined her in mocking the man.

"The shit around his lips looks like bat fur! Right?"

AJ shook his head, waiting patiently for them to notice him. When they didn't, and several minutes of misguided gambling counsel and mean-spirited soul-dampening had passed, he rapped the metal end of Deadbolt against Diedre's heavily muscled shoulder. The massive woman wheeled around with frightening speed.

"You're Diedre, aren't you? Diedre Smiley?"

The giant woman wore a long, green pleather coat of faux-crocodile, and a yellow-and-gold silk shirt unbuttoned to reveal a tattooed chest and perplexingly muscular bosom. A diamond-encrusted chain around her neck hung down to her navel and carried a white gold medallion in the shape of an assault rifle. On either side of her, men — fairly large goons as well — served only to accentuate her mass, like moons.

"Aw hell," Diedre said. "Sergeant Moore, right? You're the joker on the TV. What can I do you for, Officer?"

"Well, it's 'agent' technically. I ain't no cop. But I do have a couple of questions before I drag your big ass back to the station. First and foremost, where's el jefe? Where's that scumbag Luther?"

15

Diedre cocked her head and gave a half-lidded, dead-eyed stare.

"Let me guess: he's uptown getting his wingtips polished while you and the rest of the Titans peddle coke and poppers to school kids."

[Don't antagonize her, AJ. Just make the collar.]

"Who's that? I don't know nobody by that name."

"'Who's that?' You heard me. Luther Gueye. Man, I swear he's got you guys programmed. It's okay, though, Diedre. His luck will run out one day, just like yours has."

She looked to her men and made a bunched-up expression of disbelief. "This guy…"

The Titans were drug dealers mostly, moderately organized, and typically not deadly. However, they were numerous, so numerous as to make them the largest gang in Sun City. They shipped their narcotics up from South America using the NASCO super-corridor, and primarily the superhighway 101. This was problematic, as the 101 was Sun City's aorta. That was why, of all the cities in the Pacific State, Sun City had to bear the brunt of the Titans' presence.

AJ had formed a theory some time ago as to the identity of the Titans' boss. Over time, his hypothesis had solidified through bits of information obtained throughout his personal campaign against the Titans. Whispers and gossip here, a murmur or mention there. One could only hear a thing on the streets so many times before one had to give it credence. And now, after years of striking at the limbs of the city's largest

16

criminal network, he was certain he'd finally uncovered the root. Their boss, as far as AJ was concerned, was none other than Luther Gueye: a Togolese expatriate and billionaire philanthropist. Of this, AJ was certain, and yet, much to his frustration, no one in the SDC cared to entertain his theory. Worse, they all just kind of laughed at him. Well, technically no one *actually* laughed at him per se, but he could feel their skepticism and it irked him.

AJ pulled a magnetic bracelet from his belt and offered it to Diedre the way a dolphin trainer might offer fish: dangling it in front of her. Maglets, as most in the SDC called them, were used to subdue suspects. They were easy to deploy and intelligently reactive, so much so that it was probably possible to *throw* one onto a suspect. Throwing one was on his list of things to try one day. His "Fuck it" list.

"Do the smart thing, Diedre," he told her, "go ahead and cuff yourself. Behind the back, please. If you need an extra bracelet, I've got you covered."

"You ain't got nothing on me," Diedre replied, her expression cooler than that of an employee talking to their supervisor on their last day.

AJ shook his head. "You've multiple warrants out, in multiple sectors, Diedre. I'm here because you are wanted in connection with a shooting that left a man dead. And before you deny it, know that we saw your dumb ass on camera fleeing the scene. We even saw the murder weapon. A chrome semi snub-nose, firing depleted uranium rounds. Looked like a six-shooter."

"Oh, you can tell all that from camera footage, huh?"

"You betcha!" AJ replied giddily. "Now let's get those cuffs on. I've got shit to do tonight."

Diedre took a step back. Behind Diedre, her men, silent up to this point, were whispering to one another. They then fanned out.

Titans always fight, AJ thought. *And that is why I love them.*

The plaza was thick with onlookers, some already hooting and catcalling at the promise of spectacle. Above, amid the radiant glow of Section Three's skyscrapers, he could hear the drone of SCPD hover units like bees, probably already headed their way.

"You ain't even a real cop," Diedre spat, somehow making herself even taller. "All you Unit One snitches are phony. Like soap-opera phony, right?"

AJ, assessing the terrain, chose the optimal position for a melee. "Is that so?"

Diedre growled to her men, who now flanked her on either side. "Let's take his head back to the boss and get paid!"

AJ swung Deadbolt down from his shoulder and brought it to his waist. Taking a wide stance, he offered one last warning. "Blah blah blah, 'we don't have to do this.' Blah blah blah 'I don't want to hurt you.'"

18

Diedre drew her gun quickly, expertly. Of what AJ caught before the flash, it indeed appeared chrome.

The Unit One sergeant triggered Deadbolt's release, even as he contorted at the sight of the gun. The blade burst free in a bolt of steam and lit up the quad in a red-hot arc, parting the gun in two.

Still holding half a firearm, Diedre pulled the trigger repeatedly. The results were wickedly dangerous and inept explosions of gunpowder and shrapnel. In disgust, she cast the weapon aside. "That gun cost more than you probably make in a decade." She waved at her men. "What the fuck are you waiting for!"

As her men descended on AJ, Diedre turned and took to heel.

"Better run, punk!" he yelled after her.

Diedre's men rushed him with clumsy brawler's strikes. He slipped a punch, sheathed Deadbolt's blade for a moment, only to trigger the ejection chamber, firing the sword's metal hilt into the face of the first attacker. The sword rebounded off the man's skull and re-sheathed itself, where the firing chamber soon clicked ready for use again. Meanwhile, the force of the blow rocked the man's head back and sent the knit cap he'd been wearing spiraling into the air. His body crumpled to the ground on knees now made of rubber.

When sheathed, Deadbolt was really just a heavy metal pole, and this AJ swung at the shin of his second attacker. The man jumped to avoid the swipe and was met in mid-air with a

19

pair of Stalkers. As the man struck the ground on his back, the sergeant slammed the pole down on him in a woodcutter's motion, finishing the fight.

The citizens who hadn't fled the scene offered raucous and gladiatorial cheers at the violence.

"Rena, have the SCPD pick up these two." He collapsed Deadbolt down to its "carry" length of roughly one foot and allowed it to magnetically snap to the base of his spine, a convenient combination of the tool and a nanofiber-reinforced vertabra. He then broke through the semicircle of onlookers to sprint after Diedre.

[Clean strike on the firearm, AJ. Impressive.]

"Thanks."

[Next time, take the arm to be safe.]

"Too many people watching, kids too."

[Wouldn't have mattered. Diedre is more bootleg MOD at this point than woman. You knew that, didn't you?]

"Sure I did, Rena, at least partly. The way her hips moved, especially when she ran off... she was either a 'typo' or Captain of the Posture Police."

The sergeant himself was a Deckar Applied Sciences Type-A MOD. "MODS" were the recipients of a biomechanical augmentation kit of one kind or another. The Type-A classification was military grade. Type-A MODS were specifically outfitted for close-quarters, hand-to-hand combat. To accommodate this very specific function, his spine and chest plate were encased in a nano-fiber-woven layering, capable of absorbing small-arms fire. Other, more fallible, parts had been replaced outright. His lungs, much of the muscle fiber in his arms and legs, his stomach, kidneys, and liver were all synthetic. These upgrades came in packages, like fast-food combos. Most common among the State Defense Consortium were Type-A MODS which were basic combat kits. Then there were the Type-R MODS like Technical Detective Rena Bryant, the strategic voice in AJ's ear. Her kit focused less on combat and more on reconnaissance, including an access port for deep web immersion. And there were others. Deckar Applied Sciences was steadily pumping out new kits and upgrades for the Consortium to snap up. Black-market MODS like Diedre were given the moniker Type-O, as in "typos." These were people whose bodies consisted of a hodgepodge of black-market prosthetic brands. They were cyborg mutts, whose components ranged in quality from "premier prototype" to "what-the-fuck-is-that?"

Because of the severe penalty for black-market prosthetics possession, some typos went to great lengths to cover up their illegally acquired parts. Many wore spray-on epidermis or simply bundled up. Others, like Diedre, flaunted their contraband, essentially daring the SCPD or Unit One to do something about it.

Hordes of people, an infinite stream of vehicles, and an evening of soaring decibels greeted AJ as the chase left the Merchant Maze and took him through the Section Three market district. Exhaust, tobacco smoke, and the partisan scent

21

of ethnic food caressed his cheeks and clogged his flaring nostrils as he sprinted after Diedre. Storefronts sandwiched street-front apartments, delis, clubs, pubs, dens, shelters, and shops. Hover units zigzagged overhead, their spotlights fencing in the night, playing off the cobalt black spires to jab at the stars.

Diedre was fast, but weight, technique, and the quality of AJ's augmented legs made him faster. He bolted up Market Street at an unnatural clip, enjoying every bit of the chase. He could see Diedre up ahead, her hulking frame a foot taller than most, and knew that he would overtake her soon. With a glance back at him and what could only have been a moment of calculated acceptance, Diedre began throwing her wares into the air. Thick bags of powdered MDMA, stem vials, PCP inhalers, and sandwich bags stuffed fat with pills, nanobots, and spacial encryptors or "blackouts:" devices that emitted enough magnetic interference to throw out most forms of technical surveillance. These discarded wares hit the pavement, spilling everywhere, and a crack-shot photojournalist could have stacked their portfolio with the human chaos it created. People dove on the jetsam. The result was a manic scrum that brought a city block of pedestrians colliding into one another like zombies over a fresh corpse. Men and women in suits dove at the ground like football players scrambling for a fumble. People left their cars abandoned in the street, and storefronts emptied, as virtually all of Market Street fought for the chance to get high.

Diedre's ploy had worked to perfection, as now AJ found himself caught in a riot. Up against a frenzied wall of people, he could only watch helplessly as Diedre threw a driver to the pavement and hopped into their vehicle. With an almost charming grin, she showed him the finger and reached into her overcoat once more. This time, rather than drugs, she removed something round and roughly the size of a baseball.

AJ's heart leapt in his chest. "Rena!"

Diedre underhanded the spherical object into the crowd and sped off, the door of the car still ajar.

All AJ could do was wrap his arms around the person in front of him and fall to the ground.

The explosion rocked the avenue and sent people reeling, many of them falling on top of one another like flattened trees in the face of a hurricane. After the initial shock and the sound of falling glass ceased, all AJ could hear were cries for help and car alarms.

The sergeant released the person he'd dragged to the ground, and got to his feet, relatively untouched. The folks caught in the blast were mostly moving, and the lack of carnage came as a tremendous relief.

"Diedre just threw some kind of low-yield concussion grenade! Not seeing any casualties but we've got wounded!"

The citizen he'd shielded was a woman in her late twenties or early thirties. In her arms was a girl of about two. They looked up at him, wide-eyed. The woman looked as though she might speak, but her lips only trembled.

"You're ok," AJ told them. "Stay right here. Help is on the way."

[Emergency services are en route.]

"Stop her, Rena!"

[On it.]

Moments later, every traffic light for several blocks went to red. Intersections not already halted by the blast quickly became quagmires. The sound of screeching tires and collision sounded in intervals off into the distance.

For a moment AJ thought they might trap her, but was soon disappointed, as Diedre took the stolen car onto the curb.

[Well, that backfired.]

"No shit! Is this scumbag online?"

[One sec... Yes! You can get to her through a neurotrigger dating channel or I can try and put you through to her mobile. She also has a gaming profile, but that won't hel—]

"Something quick, please!"

[Dating channel.]

He shook his head. "Pathetic. Put me through to Diedre, and" —he paused, not wanting to say the words— "see if Chris is available for backup."

[Probably a good idea at this point.]

Chris was also a Unit One agent, and the two of them were responsible for the lion's share of Queue arrests. It was no secret that their relationship was immensely competitive, especially when it came to the Queue. The idea of asking his rival for help made AJ nauseous.

Seconds later, the sound of Diedre's breathing filled his ear against a backdrop of vehicular mayhem.

[I can't chat right now!] Diedre was yelling. *[Attach your message to my profile, right? And I only talk to men with nudes. No swingy, no ringy!]*

"Why are you running?"

[The fuck? Oh, wait...]

"Why are you running, coward!"

[I ain't running, pig! I've got places to be!]

"Stop now and you might live to see central booking!"

AJ could hear her work the clutch and downshift, and the gallop of six recently highjacked cylinders. Up ahead, he could see the stolen car swerve back onto the street and veer dangerously into traffic. Still chasing her on foot, AJ had taken to running in the street to try and keep up. His shoes, though fashionable, were revealing themselves not quite up to the task. The flat soles were hell on his heels, and he wasn't getting nearly enough spring in his step. The result was a pain that crept up his shins and coalesced in the lower part of his knees. The sensation — a bit like bone on broken glass, nagged him to throttle his pace.

"Diedre! Stop the car!" the sergeant demanded.

Too late, the fleeing Titan corner boss slammed into the back of a sedan, sending it careening into the side of a building.

Her car rebounded from the impact and weaved, yet again, back into the street.

AJ watched the mayhem unfold and could hear Commander Williams' voice as clearly as if the Unit One Deputy Chief Constable was standing next to him. "*AJ,*" the voice said, in the boss' menacing, autocratic drawl, "*you destroyed downtown and didn't even catch the {insert_chewing-tobacco-muddled_expletive}! You're fired!*"

AJ shared his terror and frustration with its root cause. "Diedre, you're dead when I catch you!"

[What?] she replied, *[I honked!]*

"Insufficient, asshole! Right now, you're looking at six years minimum in Supermax, assuming, of course, none of the people you just threw a grenade at or drove over die." AJ took a deep breath before continuing. "Pony up for a half-decent defense attorney and you'll be out in two. But if you make me run you down, I swear to God, I'm gonna slice you up like potato wedges. The checkered-looking ones!"

[Big talk, Moore! Do you know what you are to us? A clown! The Titans laugh at you. With your dumb hair and stupid commercials, you're a joke. You're a mascot, Moore! A mascot, and no one takes you seriously.]

[Ouch,] Rena added.

AJ sputtered an incoherent response before replying. "My hair isn't dumb."

The sergeant's legs were pumping and every signal in his body warned of impending failure. Soon, he would have no

26

choice but to comply. Above, hover units were banking to pursue the stolen car, and the very real possibility of losing his mark to the Sun City Police Department loomed.

[AJ, Chris is en route.]

The bittersweet confirmation of support did little to assuage the damage to his pride.

"Thanks, Rena. If I lose this moron, I'll never live it down."

His lungs were designed to carry twice the oxygen of their God-given counterparts, but they, too, were now fading. Soon AJ's run became a labored jog, then a powerwalk, and finally a frustrated, hands-on-hips stroll. What had started off as a very productive day was quickly becoming a disaster.

Not arresting Diedre was bad, but spooking her into a vehicular rampage was much, much worse. Deputy Chief Constable Williams would have his ass, wholesale.

Hands still on his hips, chest heaving, AJ looked down. A black, oily streak ran over the toe of his left shoe and across the once-white, extra-fat laces.

"Rena, I'm going to cry."

A holospot, an immersive hologram commercial, swam around him in the shape of a mermaid holding a bottle of overpriced bourbon. It wasn't helping.

"Where did I go wrong, Rena?"

[Grade school, probably.]

"Where is she now?"

[Heading for the 101, looks like.]

27

He could only shake his head.

[Don't take it so hard, champ. Emergency services are on site at the blast. Looks like there aren't any casualties. So, there's that.]

"That's good, but beside the point. She would have tossed an incendiary into the crowd if she'd had one. I'm certain. Diedre's a menace."

[Well, the uniforms aren't close to pinning her down yet. So technically, there's still hope for a Unit One save. Oh, wait... What's that I hear?] She was laughing.

It was then that AJ heard it too. Behind the wind, behind the drone of traffic, it began as a murmur: a kind of druidic hymn. Horns, music, and the cadence of a city of thirty million people fell away. Soon, all sounds were lost to the roar of twenty-eight hundred cubic centimeters of motorcycle engineering.

Took you long enough, AJ thought bitterly.

The bike sprang from traffic like a panther from foliage and slid to a halt in a rank, bluish cloud of tire smoke. Great swaths of boiled rubber trailed behind like a signature. As the whine of the engine and squeal of tires died, it gave way to the guttural rumbling of a bike not made for idling. The rider wore red tinted goggles, a bandana, and a black jacket identical to his own. On his sleeve were the same three chevrons embroidered on AJ's own left arm.

AJ's fellow Unit One agent dropped a booted foot to the ground with a gravelly crunch and addressed him without looking. "Problems?"

"Hey, Christian," AJ greeted.

"You know I hate it when you call me that," his partner replied dryly.

"Of course, Christian."

Chris wasn't exactly cocky, he just had an air of confidence about him that rubbed a lot of people the wrong way. A Unit One agent by day and a literal rock star of some renown by night, Sergeant Christian Calderon took the traditional expectations of a government law enforcement agent and smoked them curbside. Where AJ was famous for his role in Unit One, Chris was just plain *famous*. This was part of what irked AJ the most. Chris didn't need this. He didn't need the money or the status, he just did it because he could; because he was bored.

"You want help or not?" Chris asked him.

With a clenched jaw, AJ detached Deadbolt from his belt and climbed onto the bike. Sensing the added weight, the bike produced a high-backed sissy bar that he could lean against.

The bike was a custom cruiser and, like AJ's shoes, netted Chris advertisement kick-backs. Matte black with crimson brake calipers, the bike was Chris' pride and he called it Revenant.

"She's a mile up the boulevard, headed for the 101," Chris said, over his shoulder.

AJ knew his partner was getting updates on Diedre's location in real time from Rena. "You should hold on."

With a throttle and a roar, Revenant sprang forward and was off, tires screeching. The bike groaned and jerked as it transitioned through the gears, steadily accelerating. As their speed climbed, the suspension lowered them, until the bike seemed to swim in the street. They left the market district as though ejected and swung up the 101 on-ramp, onto the great elevated superhighway.

From his seat, AJ could touch the pavement, so low to the ground they were. Soon his frustration seemed distant, and the excitement of the chase invigorated him once more.

SCPD hover units, large, potbellied quadcopters, highlighted them annoyingly with spotlights that made the night feel like day. AJ knew that the presence of SCPD units meant network helicopters and drones were on the way. Network choppers would mean a televised arrest, and a televised arrest would net him three thousand in Skyy Shoes sponsorship money. He whipped Deadbolt to full length, holding it aloft like a cavalry saber, and howled.

Evening traffic on the 101 was moderate for a weekend. The Section Three span of the superhighway was nine lanes wide and carried traffic high above the street where the pollution of non-electrics could not be smelled and the noise of supertankers could not be heard. Instead, from street-level, the

30

traffic rumbled overhead like some great oil pipeline, spilling out periodically in the form of off-ramps. Security checkpoints dotted the 101 throughout its route through Sun City, the largest of these being at the city's border where the 101 passed the Rampart line.

Deidre won't attempt to cross that checkpoint, AJ thought, *so she's not leaving Sun City. Rather, she'll exit in the Veins, where Libra coverage is weak and she can disappear in any one of a thousand alleyways. We've got to stop her before that.*

Chris swerved to pass a semitruck two lanes wide and, as they did so, Diedre's stolen car came into sight. AJ patted Chris' shoulder and pointed. His partner acknowledged with a nod and throttled. The bike, already pushing the one-hundred-mile-per-hour mark, accelerated further and with ease. They roared past another lumbering semi, its chrome wheels so tall he could see his reflection among the tennis ball–sized lug nuts that spun like the blades on a blender.

Putting an empty lane between them, Chris pulled alongside the speeding cab and slowed Revenant to match the cab's pace. Deidre hadn't noticed them yet.

AJ propped himself up against the sissy bar, standing on the passenger foot pegs. The wind felt as though it would tear his jacket free or send him tumbling to a violent demise. His thighs, fighting to keep him balanced, quickly began to burn from the strain.

Diedre appeared to be working the car's radio. When she finally turned and saw them, her eyes grew wide. A cigarette fell from her lips, and a chrome object that could only be her gun rose from her lap. The muzzle flashes confirmed, as she fired twice at them through the window.

For them, she might as well have been snapping photos, as the rounds sailed harmlessly into the night.

That's it! Let's end this!

AJ couldn't resist the urge to return the middle finger to her, as the bike swung across the lane. With a press of the trigger on Deadbolt's hilt, the blade tore out of its sheath and lit the night like dragon fire before striking the cab at its engine block. The blade ripped through the hood and the engine, and put a gash on the pavement several yards long. The force sent AJ's arm flailing behind him painfully like a whip.

The result of the strike was devastating.

The front of the cab pitched forward and rolled, where it became lodged beneath itself, folding the vehicle in two. Sparks lit the highway in orange waves as the cab slid, tumbled, and tore to pieces.

The sergeant dropped back into his seat and patted Chris on the shoulder once more. They rode alongside the tumbling wreckage for a quarter of a mile. When it finally settled in a smoking heap, Chris braked hard and brought Revenant sliding sideways to a halt on the shoulder.

AJ hopped from the bike grinning. Firing Deadbolt from a moving vehicle was a first.

32

What was once a taxi now was unrecognizable. Pieces lay strewn about, as though some great invisible thing had stubbed the vehicle out like a cigar. What was left of the compartment sat smoking against the highway's noise barrier.

"Rena, tell me you recorded that!"

[Don't worry, AJ, that bit will be on the twenty-four-hour news cycle for a week.]

AJ spun the blade and sheathed it, very aware of the network drones buzzing overhead. He collapsed the weapon down to a foot in length and slapped it into place at the base of his spine in a flurry of motions. Next, the sergeant pulled on the hem of his shirt to remove any wrinkles and tugged on his pant legs to make sure that the hems fell over the mid-point of the laces on his shoes. It wouldn't do to have shoelace knots showing. He brushed a hand over his platinum-dyed curls.

"Showtime!"

As he got close to the smoking heap, he could see movement. Diedre was upside down and pinned by what might have been the dashboard or the floorboard. Her arms were trapped somewhere in the wreckage, as were her legs, and blood flowed from her forehead. Despite all of that, remarkably, she was alive.

AJ approached with his hands in his pockets. "'Sup?"

"S-son of a bitch!" Diedre tried to move but only came away wincing. "Moore, you goddamn pig!"

"Now, now, you did this to yourself."

"I'm not going back to prison. I've got enemies there."

"So, what? You're like nine times the size of most women."

"Funny." She was upside-down and her mock smile caused a stream of drool to stretch out of her mouth toward the ground. There was blood in it. "I'm not talking about women's prison, you fuck! I got bodies on me. They'll send me back to Supermax."

She was in Supermax? Jesus…

Supermax was a coed mega-prison north of Sun City. It could get by being coed because every cell was solitary confinement. Twenty-four hours a day, seven days a week. It was Hell on Earth.

"Well, if you don't want to go back there, help me out, Diedre. I've been hunting the kingpin — or queenpin — of the Titans for three years and my patience is tapped. So, answer one question for me. Who's the boss of the Titans?"

The Titan corner boss shook her head. "Shit, man…"

"'Shit Man?' That's an unfortunate name."

"Fuck you, Moore! I can't tell you that. They'll kill me, or worse."

"What's worse than death?"

Diedre laughed. "Lots of things are worse than death."

"Like a tiny-ass cell and forgetting what sunlight looks like?"

AJ could tell by her face he'd struck a nerve with that. He pressed. "You just said you're not going back to prison.

Well, this is your one and only chance, Diedre. Who's the boss of the Titans?"

A breeze tugged at the column of smoke coming from the wreck and scattered it momentarily. For a moment, all that could be heard were the whooping copter rotors behind the incessant buzzing of drone propellers.

"What about witness protection?" Deidre asked solemnly.

"Sure."

[Strange... her neurotrigger just went offline.]

"Not now, Rena."

The sirens were close now. Behind the constant stream of vehicles, many of whom slowed to view the wreckage, a pulsating horizon of red and blue could be seen. Once the SCPD arrived, there would be no negotiation. He told Diedre as much.

AJ was desperate now but he could sense Diedre wavering. Her eyes darted around, searching for a way out when there was none. "Tell me and I'll get your charges dropped. Once they've patched you up, I'll even sneak you out of the city."

[Ha!] Rena's voice was mocking. *[You'll do no such thing, Sergeant.]*

"You won't do a day in Supermax," he lied. "After that, you're on your own. I hear Harbor City is nice this time of year."

35

Diedre shook her head, her shoulders bouncing in a grotesque laugh. "Fuck it… I'm screwed either way."

[AJ, something's wrong!] Rena's voice had changed.

"What is it?"

[She's gone totally offline.]

"Big deal. She was just in a car crash."

[That's not how neurotrigger works. It doesn't just shut off.]

"You're pretty smart for a toy cop," Diedre told him. "But you still don't get it. He sees and hears everything!"

"Who does? Who sees everything? Who's the boss, Diedre?" AJ pressed, snapping his fingers impatiently. "Who runs the Titans?"

"One man runs the show, Moore. And his name is L—"

Diedre's eyes went wide and her mouth gaped. A moment later, a piercing scream forced him to put his hands to his ears. Her head began to twist and pull as she struggled to free herself from the wreckage.

"What the hell is happening?"

The Titan contorted as though being electrocuted, her massive frame breaking itself against the car's warped chassis to get free. All the while she howled in what could only be agonizing pain.

"Diedre! Stop it! Help is on the way!"

She clenched her jaw and shook her head furiously, clearly in agony. She bellowed.

"AAAAAAGGGGGGGHHHHHHHHH!"

A massive arm tore free of the wreckage, at a great physical expense. Bleeding from several deep gashes, she bashed at the dashboard of the vehicle and looked set to free herself.

"Diedre, calm down!"

Screaming her voice hoarse, and still stuck by a leg inside the vehicle, she clawed at the pavement and then her head.

"OH GOD! OH GOOOOOOD!"

Diedre reached into her coat and withdrew what appeared to be another grenade.

"Diedre, no!" AJ lunged at her to kick the grenade free of her grip, but before he could, she jammed it under her chin.

"THIS IS IT! OUROBOROS!"

[AJ, get back!]

AJ was struck hard, but couldn't be sure from where. He saw the cab disappear along with the freeway wall behind it. Beyond, he saw the lights of Section Three for an instant, as he became weightless. Suddenly, he was not next to the cab, but rather quite far from it. Fire engulfed him from all sides, and something like pain froze time. He raised his arms to shield himself, only to watch them come away in pieces. The rest was a nonsensical display of colors and sounds, but for a moment, he thought he saw a shoe — scuffed across the laces — fly up into the air and turn to a cinder.

Once dirtied, laces can never really be restored. Washing them ruins the integrity of the stitching and, after that, it's impossible to apply a decent straight bar lacing. Fuck.

Rena was screaming something in his ear and a feeling, somewhere removed from the pain, pinged him. It was regret. Regret that he never—

2: The Men Who Never Sleep

"In the game of Chō-Han, you have two teams betting on odds and evens. Losers pay out to the house. Sometimes, to keep a game going, winners will front losers. Hell, the house fronts losers all the time because what's important in the end is the game. It's communal, the game. Now compare Chō-Han to craps, a Western game. In craps, it's every man for himself. Everyone's trying to beat the house — the system — in whatever way they think is best. This ideology — the 'every man for himself' way — is flawed, you see, because without guidance, without the instruction of another person with a shared interest, people eventually, inevitably, lose. If enough people get knocked out, eventually the table dies, and the game dies.

This is the situation now with the yakuza: order versus chaos; the old way, the gokudō way, versus the new way, the Western way... the dog-eats-dog way."

- Unit One Deputy Informant Daisuke "Dice" Yamazaki

Section Seven gripped the westernmost inner coast of the Bay of Sun. A port district, Section Seven's fate was inexorably tied to that of pan-Asian trade and, by extension, the war. When the war ended and America began to decouple almost a century's worth of trade with China, the Port of Sun went into spiraling decline. Once the Pacific's second leading port in tonnage, it now shipped less in one month's time than the amount of goods received by Sun City via superhighway 101 in a day. As a result, Section Seven's unemployment rate sat somewhere near sixty percent and its crime rate nearly doubled that of Sections One to Six combined.

Today, Section Seven was home to Sun City's red-light district and a network of illegal casinos. Titan drug dealers manned the corners all hours of the night, and alleys were lined with men and women left with no choice but to sell themselves. Much of the district sat immobile, grown over with weeds and rusting, and sometimes it seemed the only cars still capable of motion were the sleek, black sedans of yakuza den lords.

It didn't help that the Section Seven borough itself was in a state of gross neglect. Its streets were old-timey narrow, unkept, and crisscrossed in a shattered-glass array of avenues and lanes that gave law enforcement of all stripes fits. Also, a wrong turn was often fatal, as it was home to the single most dangerous neighborhood in the state and quite possibly the country: the Veins.

On this day, in the Bondi blue of pre-dawn, the Veins lay brooding. Its sagging skyline steamed like some defective machine, ready to bring down the whole of Sun City.

In an alley chipped away from Market Street, men gathered in huddles, their breath filling the air like Victorian chimneys. They clustered in front of a windowless, four-story building, talking in low, rapid exchanges. When they were done conspiring, they went inside, pausing only to confirm their innocuousness once more to the man acting as security. As they entered, others exited, only to cluster up, smoke, and reenter. Like this, men and women fluttered about, but never far from the lightless building. This was a den for the restless. This was a Minowara house of cards, a yakuza casino.

Standing alone, Daisuke ground his cigarette into the pavement with the toe of his dress boot and followed the latest group inside.

Open around the clock, these casinos pockmarked Sun City, concentrated mainly in the blue-collar or poverty-stricken sections of the city. Safeguarded by lifelong Minowara yakuza, these casinos exploited the SCPD's depleted resources, blatantly disregarding the statewide ban on unsanctioned gambling.

Inside this particular casino, The Lady Nō, a gem in the Minowara network, it might have been Saturday night for the crowd and ambiance. Men and women of all pedigrees hunched over felt-covered tables. Waitresses, in their shimmering and impractical dresses, moved through the packed mass of people with the efficiency of synapses, trays stacked high with drinks and packs of complimentary cigarettes. Private rooms held private games whose stakes were made clear by the stern-faced men who manned their sliding doors.

You would find no windows or clocks in The Lady Nō, and only the faintest sound of music could be heard over the

41

incessant ringing of slot machines, shuffling of bets, laughter, groans, and spattered cheers that came with gambling.

Daisuke checked his watch but for some reason didn't register the time. He checked it again. It was just shy of four AM.

"Yama-kun," a voice purred.

She wore the kind of dinner gown most reserved for special occasions, and it hung from her loosely. The gown looked pulled-on and showed signs of spilled alcohol.

"Good morning, Maggie," Daisuke greeted, turning back to his cards and the stale hand he held.

With a finger, Maggie took his chin and turned his head to face her. It was the kind of over-familiar violation of personal space that irked him to no end. But he let it slide, as he did with most things involving Maggie. Besides, from the look of it, she was well past tipsy. Her tongue rested exposed between two pouting lips as she stood over him, goggling him like the last piece of fish at a banquet.

"Here, sweetheart," she said, holding a lit cigarette out to him.

With his cards pressed face-down to the table, Daisuke took a pull. He shook his head to the others at the table in subtle apology.

"You're looking well," he lied.

"How come you don't come around so much no more?"

"Not everyone here is as happy to see me as you, Maggie." Daisuke tapped his cards on the table and the dealer slid him another. The card put him at eighteen. He waved away and the dealer began dealing himself. "Are you still working?"

She was leaning heavily on his shoulder now, her breath oppressive. "I got off a looong time ago, Yama-kun." Fingers gripped his earlobe awkwardly. "How come we don't hang out?"

Daisuke looked up at her and frowned. There were so many reasons.

"Twenty-one," the dealer announced solemnly, before deftly cleaning the table of cards and bets.

"Aww, that's too bad, Daisuke. Go again. The next hand is yours for sure."

Daisuke ran a hand over his hair irritably and took a cigarette from his inner coat pocket. He wore two coats, a very heavy overcoat that touched the floor from the stool he was perched on, and beneath it, a high-collared black jacket whose white delta was best left hidden in a Minowara gambling den.

"Give me a light, Maggie, could you?"

She lit his cigarette with her own, dropping ash onto him in the process. He batted the ash away, leaving a dark grey streak on his white overcoat.

Maggie was young and her skin was a shade lighter than the other cocktail waitresses. She was a second-generation Ukrainian who'd had the misfortune of growing up in the Veins. Her father had sold her to the Minowara yakuza a few

43

years back in exchange for clemency on a debt unpayable. A student and aspiring actress once, Maggie had slowly retarded over the course of her tenure with the Minowara. Like the other unfortunate women in their indentured employ, she was slowly being chewed up and the process was slow and tragic. Daisuke reached back into his jacket pocket and produced a wad of notes. He peeled off three hundred-dollar bills and slipped them into her hand covertly.

"What's this for?" Maggie slurred.

"Services rendered."

She chuckled. "What services?"

"Lighting my cigarette."

Maggie took the notes and dropped them lazily into a beige leather handbag under her arm.

New cards were doled out. Daisuke took a glance. Twenty-one.

Fucking finally, he thought.

"Maggie, have you gone back to school yet?"

"Not yet. I can't get the days off. A girl's gotta work, you know?" She was pressed against him now. And her fingers were tracing the seams of his coat.

Maggie's contract with Minowara had to be ending soon. A girl of her... *caliber* was worth at least thirty grand a year. Her old man's debt couldn't have been more than that, considering the man was still breathing.

"Mizoguchi," Daisuke called out, turning to the dealer, "get Maggie a cab home, would you? On me."

44

The dealer raised a neon-lit baton, now blue, a passive signal to security. You didn't want to be around when a red baton went up.

"Maggie," Daisuke said with a smile. "Tell your papa I want to talk to him. Is he still washing dishes at the Golden Leaf?"

"How'd you know that?"

"I know everything. It's how I stay alive."

She threw her arms around him and planted a sloppy kiss on his cheek. He could smell marijuana and something else, something burnt and synthetic.

Dammit, Maggie.

As Daisuke's winnings were pushed to him, a suited bouncer walked over and politely extended an arm for Maggie. She took it and Daisuke watched attentively as she was escorted out.

If Maggie's father was still gambling, it was possible that his increasing debt was simply being appended to her sentence, and likely unbeknownst to the damned. If that was the case, Daisuke would bring charges of human trafficking against her father. Maggie was old enough to avoid being taken into the meat grinder that was State juvenile services, but fending for herself in the Veins in her current state was another kind of death sentence. Whatever the solution, the whole affair would have to be sorted out in a way that the Minowara found acceptable. And that would likely mean a barter of some kind.

They were not the kind of people to forgive a debt of any amount graciously.

Just what I didn't need, he thought, shuffling the chips in front of him.

Balancing the laws of the State with the laws of the yakuza was his day-to-day as deputy informant for Unit One. Daisuke walked a very fine line between mole and snitch, and yet had managed to create a system that benefitted both the State Defense Consortium and the Minowara crime family — no small accomplishment, even by his own standards.

Daisuke signaled a waitress over and ordered a whiskey and lime. Meanwhile, an older man had come to stand uncomfortably close to him, pining for his seat, no doubt. Daisuke contemplated giving it to him. It had been an expensive night and an even more expensive morning.

I'm going to get my drink first, he thought. *Calm down, old man, the casino will get your money eventually.*

In the meantime, the table continued on without him. As Daisuke spotted the waitress in the crowd, returning with his order, a familiar face intercepted her. The man took the drink from her, seemingly ordered another, and approached. With the table full, the man patted the gambler sitting next to Daisuke on the shoulder. The gambler, an elderly Chinese man, recognized the newcomer instantly and got off the stool as fast as his old bones would allow. With hardly a glance back at the chips he'd left on the table, the old gambler disappeared into the crowd.

"Kyodai," the man said, greeting Daisuke as brother. He extended to him the drink he'd taken from the waitress.

The man's name was Raizen Minowara, and they were all sitting in his casino. Raizen was a senior advisor to Oyabun Minowara, but, as the name might suggest, was much more than that. He was Boss Minowara's only surviving son, and heir to the Minowara syndicate.

Raizen slid forward several healthy stacks of chips left by the old man. The dealer responded by deftly firing a pair of cards his way. Raizen placed two fingers on the cards and waited for his drink. As the action at the table ground further to a halt, the dealer waited patiently and silently, as did the others at the table, most of them with their heads down. Several awkward minutes later the waitress came, practically running, and bowed as she handed Raizen what looked like a whiskey sour, and not the same kind with too much ice and watered-down ingredients being served to everyone else.

Raizen held his drink in the air, and Daisuke returned the gesture to the man who had been his friend since childhood.

"To Shibuya," Raizen said, toasting the borough in Tokyo from which they hailed.

"To Shibuya."

Raizen flipped his cards. "Blackjack."

I bet, Daisuke thought sarcastically.

The dealer deftly measured the stacks in front of Raizen and paid him one and a half times the wager, leaving a little over four thousand dollars' worth of chips.

The yakuza prince's response to winning was the reaction one had when finding a letter in the mail that wasn't junk. It could barely be classified as an acknowledgment, much less surprise or joy. With a flick of the finger, Raizen sent several hundred back to the dealer as commission. It was extravagant, but that was Raizen's way. It also wasn't his money to begin with. Which was also Raizen's way.

He wore a slate-colored three-piece suit with a vest the color of amber. Beneath it, an embroidered dress shirt of black, a tiny white rose sewn into the collar. On his wrist was a stunning rose-gold Crespling. The strap was crocodile skin and very tasteful. He also wore a large sapphire on his pinky, and his nails were manicured and pristine. If it was four o'clock in the morning, Raizen hadn't gotten the memo. While there were a great many things to critique in the haughty, entitled heir to the Minowara throne, style wasn't one of them.

For an awkward while, Raizen seemed to study Daisuke thoughtfully. After a moment, he stood.

"What is it?" Daisuke asked. It was obvious a quiet game of blackjack wasn't how he was going to end a day that frankly should have ended several hours ago.

"Come with me, kyodai."

Raizen was the only yakuza that still greeted Daisuke as "kyodai." The rest had ceased long ago. They had other names for him now and none of them were pleasant.

Following Raizen's lead, he stubbed his cigarette out in the tiny plastic tray, collected his money from the table, and

48

likewise tipped the dealer. Before departing, however, he bowed to the table in apology for the constant distraction, a gesture that was returned meaningfully by the dealer.

As Raizen led him away, the old man whose seat and money had been borrowed rushed to reclaim his place. When he realized that his earning had been doubled, he shook his fists and flashed a toothless grin.

At least somebody's winning tonight...

They made their way to the other end of the bustling casino and took a guarded staircase up to the fourth floor. Walking in silence, they passed a row of private gambling rooms before stopping at the door to Raizen's office. He unlocked it with a vintage nickel silver key that he slipped back into his coat before pushing the door open.

As Raizen gestured with his head for him to enter, Daisuke couldn't help but pause at the door. Sure, the two of them had a long history, but they hadn't seen one another in months. Relationships among the yakuza change dramatically in that much time. The informant quickly took an inventory of the recent plays that might put him in their crosshairs.

"Please," Raizen said irritably. "If I wanted to harm you, do you think I'd need to do it in private? I could have your brains blown out on the casino floor and not a hand, not a roll of the dice would be missed."

It was true. Unnecessarily colorful, but true.

The office had a panoramic view of Section Seven on one end and a near-total view of the casino floor on the other.

49

In the prelude of day, rooftops juxtaposed like black steps to nowhere before a sun that seemed reluctant to reveal itself entirely. Gulls filled the sky, small like flies in the distance, and beneath them, great ships sat rusting in the purgatory that was the Port of Sun.

The office itself was paneled in expensive cherry-colored wood and stunningly arranged in a classic décor. A great bookshelf as tall as the ceiling; an antique globe of sixteenth-century Mercator design, flanked by smoking-chairs; and a great case of rare and expensive spirits. And at the center of it, there sat a magnificent mahogany desk. Exquisitely detailed, its veneers were carved in likenesses of the Komainu: the male and female guardian lions typically found on t-shirts, shitty tattoos, and occasionally the steps of Buddhist temples.

Raizen motioned to the bar. "Would you mind?"

Daisuke walked over to the bar and selected an unfamiliar scotch that looked expensive but not too expensive. He showed it to Raizen first to get his approval. With the yakuza's sign-off, he poured two tall glasses and dropped an ice cube in each with his bare hands. He crossed the thick carpet in silence and handed one to Raizen. Once more they toasted, this time to Sun City.

They drank, and as the liquid turned Daisuke's esophagus to ash, Raizen motioned for him to sit in the chair opposite his desk.

"I heard you arrested Murakami," Raizen said, plopping down in his high-backed chair, wasting no time.

Shit! I'd completely forgotten about Murakami.

Daisuke kept a straight face. "Murakami was a pedophile."

"Still," Raizen said with a raised hand, "he was Minowara. The agreement was that I would feed you select men, Titans who encroach our territories, and any and all Triads who piss me off. In exchange, you keep me well ahead of any SCPD or Unit One raid on one of my casinos or brothels. And at the end of the day, everyone wins. Unit One pads its stats and the Minowara take only the hits we want to take. I thought the terms were clear, Daisuke. At the time, Daisuke, I feel the terms were clear."

"They were clear. But—"

"You start arresting my people indiscriminately and, well... it's just not a good look."

Not a good look was your typical passive-aggressive Raizen threat.

"I get that," Daisuke replied in a carefully measured tone, "but you've got to realize that there are certain things that — if I'm to keep this badge — I *cannot* ignore. Plus, there's just common fucking decency, Raizen."

Raizen held a hand up once more. The gesture was getting annoying, quickly. "I don't know what's more shocking, that you were once Minowara, or that you're now Unit One. It's actually pretty spectacular. But nevertheless, we've made it work. I would like it to continue to work, so tell me what the heck happened?"

51

Raizen's occasional use of curse-word substitutions had always made Daisuke cringe.

You're a gangster, man. No one's going to come through the door and rap your knuckles with a ruler for swearing.

It was just one of many idiosyncrasies that continually undermined the respect Raizen wanted so desperately from his men.

The yakuza lieutenant shook his head, brows furrowed. "Do you even remember being yakuza?"

Daisuke, once a yakuza with a promising career, tried not to take offense, but felt an undeniable pinch of anger nonetheless.

You may be the son of the great Oyabun Minowara, but as far as I'm concerned, you're still the schoolboy I used to protect from bullies.

"Of course, I remember."

"How does that work?" Raizen asked, swirling his drink.

"What?"

"Being a turncoat."

"Doubling down, huh?" Daisuke stood. It was too early in the morning and he was too tired to let Raizen provoke him. "Thanks for the drink."

"I'm sorry! A joke! It was a joke in poor taste." Raizen motioned for him to sit again, a sleazy grin on his face. "Please, sit down, old friend. Finish your drink."

"I didn't come here to be insulted."

"Please."

He took a seat, staring Raizen in the face as he did so.

Raizen drummed his fingers on the desk for a moment before shrugging. "Murakami was an imbecile and he won't be missed. But, next time? Do me a favor and let me know in advance if you've got a problem that you don't think I can resolve internally, okay? At least give me the opportunity to straighten things out. Otherwise, you make it look like I don't know what's going on. You make me look like I'm not a professional. And I am. I am a professional."

Biting back the urge to sigh at Raizen's banal corporate speak, Daisuke just nodded. "Understood. I'll do that." Eager to leave, he downed his drink. "I should probably consider sleep at some point."

Behind Raizen, the sun had arisen and now engulfed him in a flaming aura that made it all but impossible to see his face. "Daisuke," he said from the shadow, "there is actually something else I wanted to discuss. Something of some import, let's say."

Daisuke, who'd been preparing to stand, removed his hands from the arms of his chair. Trying to make out Raizen's face in shadow, he nodded. "Of course."

Raizen sighed. "My father is very, very concerned."

"Concerned about what?" Daisuke asked, a pit in his stomach. "What's the problem?"

"*Who* is the problem," Raizen corrected. "And I bet you already know the answer. It's *him*, kyodai."

"'Him?'"

"Sugihara."

Enzo Sugihara was as much Daisuke's friend as was Raizen, or at least had been before the now-informant walked away from the yakuza.

"This city has ruined Sugihara," Raizen continued. "He no longer distinguishes between our way and the Western way. His men peddle drugs in our casinos, they do jobs without approval, and, worst of all, they conspire with our competitors."

Daisuke shook his head. "Competitors?"

"Yes," Raizen replied, "the Titans."

Daisuke made a face. "How are the Titans competitors? They're a drug cartel…"

Raizen sighed condescendingly. "Drugs, gambling, sex, immersion… What's the fucking difference? We're all in competition with each other, Yamazaki-san. The Minowara, the Titans, the Hō, fucking computers, fucking television! We're all vying for people's time and money."

Taken aback by Raizen's sudden agitation and frustrated by his inability to see the man's face, Daisuke just shrugged. "I guess I don't get it."

"Time, kyodai. Time! How can we get your money on a shitty bet if you're melting into your couch with a stim mask on?"

"Ok," Daisuke conceded. "I get it now. And Sugihara is working with the Titans? And you're sure of this?"

"Certain."

If Sugihara, a lieutenant of some renown in the Minowara, or anyone in the syndicate for that matter, was working with or *for* another syndicate, Daisuke felt he should have known about it. After all, it was that kind of intel that made him an asset to the Minowara. It was that kind of intel that made yakuza stomaching his presence possible and, by extension, his budding career in the SDC tenable. If Raizen's suspicions were founded, he'd dropped the ball somewhere. Daisuke sat back and ran a hand over his hair. He'd missed something but Raizen, fortunately, didn't appear interested in blame. He decided to deflect.

"Sugihara is one man, Raizen. You're next in line, for fuck's sake. If he's a problem, do something about it!"

He couldn't make out his friend's face, but did notice his shoulders slumped a bit.

You haven't changed one bit, have you? Still looking for someone to fight your battles for you.

Raizen was still a child of privilege; a polite, well-educated, and ambitious child of privilege. Perhaps worse, he was a bureaucrat and utterly terrified of confrontation. As a boy, he would mouth off about his famous yakuza father, drawing the ire of kids with nothing to lose. And when the bullies came, Raizen always needed saving. And that was when he and Sugihara, and even Madison at times, would have to come to the rescue.

Madison.

Daisuke hadn't seen his estranged wife since fleeing Tokyo almost a decade prior, but knew that she, like Sugihara and Raizen, had followed the Minowara to Sun City. In his recent capacity as informant for Unit One, Daisuke knew that running into her was an inevitability. The idea filled him with no small amount of dread. Terror really, if he were being honest with himself.

It was no secret that Raizen's shortcomings placed the Minowara in a precarious position. Oyabun Kazuo Minowara was an old man and had but two living children: Raizen, and his sister, Omoe. The family must pass to Raizen, and it was likely to happen soon. But confidence in Raizen's leadership was a topic of much rumor and hearsay, and not the positive kind.

Try as he might to put himself in Raizen's shoes in that moment and suggest a course of action, Daisuke found that all he could think about now was her.

Is she okay? How much exactly does she hate me?

Without asking for permission, the Unit One informant stood and walked over to the bar. Pain needed elixir, especially the self-inflicted kind.

"Have you tried talking to Sugihara?" he asked with his back turned.

Raizen scoffed. "You really should see him for yourself. It's been a while, I know. If you had, you wouldn't ask me that."

Daisuke made two more drinks in two new glasses. He walked over to the desk, even as day filled the office. He handed one to Raizen and waited for the brooding gangster to clink glasses with him before returning to his chair.

"You know," Raizen continued, "if you were to seek out Sugihara and maybe talk some sense into him, I could maybe talk to Madison, arrange a meeting; something cordial."

Daisuke gritted his teeth as he reclaimed his seat. "Did you just offer to pimp me my own wife?"

"Of course not!" Raizen chuckled nervously. "I mean, I know there's bad blood. Maybe I can... help get her to the table, in the right mindset."

As if! If you think you can control Madison, you've become as clueless as the rumors imply.

"On top of that," Raizen continued, "I could have my people look into what happened with your friend on the 101."

Daisuke ignored the second statement, as there was quite literally no detail the yakuza could glean from what the team was calling the "Diedre Incident" that their own detective Rena Bryant couldn't. As for the first statement, the pitch wasn't entirely ineffective. Daisuke very much wanted to see Madison. And if he could parlay peacefully with her before running into her randomly — and likely at the end of a shotgun

57

— all the better. If nothing else, she deserved an apology, the sincere, forehead-to-floor kind.

"I'll talk to Sugihara."

Raizen raised his glass. "You've always been a good friend, Yamazaki-san."

"Depends on who you ask, I guess. So, tell me, how is she?"

Raizen, whose face was visible once more, frowned. "Madison is not your little 'Maddy' anymore, Daisuke. She's as close to being a real yakuza as any *hakujin-josei* could ever hope to be. And I don't mind telling you, she's probably our most reliable contractor."

"'Contractor,' is that what you call it?"

Raizen nodded, his lips pursed.

Daisuke recalled some of the stories he'd heard about Madison's work. If any of it were true, she was one DNA sample away from headlining in the Queue and from there, a bored Chris away from death or a lifelong stint in Supermax.

"Where does she stay now?" Daisuke asked. "Which patriarch does she work for? Does she have men to get her back at least?"

A sour expression crossed Raizen's face. "'Men?' Who do you think we are? A female *shateigashira*? Imagine a female lieutenant in the Minowara, and a white one to boot! Are you drunk?"

I am, but...

"That shit shouldn't matter anymore."

58

Raizen shook a finger at him. "Now, you sound like *him*!" He sat up stiffly, as though offended; a sharp crease on his forehead reached up to stab at his widow's peak. "Madison is a monster," Raizen told him, smiling mirthlessly, "a glorious monster, and you'd best get that in your head if you want to walk away from a meeting with her. She's content in her life now, Daisuke. You see, the Party Crasher has a very specific role to play these days, and believe it or not, Yama-kun, she is very, very good at it."

The Unit One informant felt sick to his stomach.

Raizen checked his watch and whistled. "In fact, Madison should be wrapping up her work right now."

#Maintenance Channel 14::

[10:16] <gunnywolves> Hello?

[10:17] <kurunaotoko13> I'm here

[10:17] <gunnywolves> how do I know its u?

[10:18] <kurunaotoko13> Your boss is taller than my boss by a feathered hair.

[10:18] <gunnywolves> hahaha Okay

[10:18] <gunnywolves> cool

[10:18] <gunnywolves> and this text shit is safe?

[10:19] <kurunaotoko13> Yes. No one would think to look here.

[10:19] <gunnywolves> Okay 200 gallons of Riot Blood rdy at 450k

[10:21] <kurunaotoko13> 450 is more than what was discussed.

[10:21] <gunnywolves> he set the price not me

[10:21] <gunnywolves> it was harder to get thamn we thought it would be

[10:22] <gunnywolves> checkpoint security in mexico didn't get the bribe or stiffed us

[10:22] <kurunaotoko13> I'll have to run it by S. Let's assume he says "yes" and set a meet.

[10:22] <kurunaotoko13> Text my mobile when you are ready in this format:

[10:23] <kurunaotoko13> date/time: mm-dd/00:00 coordinates: x:00.000**000*** y:00.0*00000***

[10:23] <kurunaotoko13> Delete the "x" and "y" before sending and the asterisks represent

[10:23] <kurunaotoko13> bogus numbers. Put anything in those fields. Make sense?

[10:24] <gunnywolves> yeah I guess

[10:24] <kurunaotoko13> On a side note; one your colleagues met a violent end on television. It gives us pause.

[10:24] <gunnywolves> My homie D. the rules are pretty clear tho. She fucked up.

[10:25] <kurunaotoko13> I'm not sure I follow, but it's neither here nor there I suppose. As long as it doesn't result

[10:25] <kurunaotoko13> in any unwanted attention. Also, no offense, but I sometimes have a difficult time understanding you.

[10:25] <gunnywolves> fuck you

3: The Party Crasher

"My name is Madison Grünewald-Yamazaki. My height is one hundred seventy-seven point eight centimeters. My weight is ten point six stone, or sixty-seven point one kilograms. I am coming into this country for the purposes of pleasure. I have no allegiance to the former DPRK, the Arab Revolutionary Front, or the Sons of Africa. I carry no weapons on my person and harbor no intent to harm myself or other persons of the Pacific State.

"I've read your silly placard. May I have my ID back now?"

- Madison Grünewald-Yamazaki

A two-story restaurant and nightclub, Golden Leaf was a popular nightspot for wealthy young people, particularly those affiliated with Chinese organized crime. Madison sat opposite the building in the cold, the ocean to her back. The chill had her nose running and her temperament set to "irritable." She drew a cigarette from the blue alligator tote at her side and folded her legs to help stave off the cold. The wind had turned the collar of her coat into wings and was tossing her hair in a way that made smoking even more dangerous.

Nevertheless, she sat patiently, her focus sharp, her attention to detail right where it needed to be.

Valet service had ended hours ago and cars were lined in front of the restaurant in a neat but tightly packed row. This would make escape by vehicle damn near impossible. One car in particular held her interest. It was a silver faux-hover sports car, with an armored undercarriage and pipes that jutted from the hood like boar's tusks. It was gaudy and expensive and so, so very gangster. This was her mark's car, just as it had been described to her. Tracking the black society group hadn't been difficult. Like the yakuza, Chinese gangsters in Sun City prided themselves on being distinguishable.

Down to a filter, Madison stubbed out her cigarette and placed the butt in the pocket of her jacket. The tips of her fingers were numbing.

No more waiting, she thought irritably. *The cold is becoming a liability.*

At the same time, entering the club on two hours' worth of surveillance was a hefty gamble. But it was a gamble she had come prepared to make. She blew her nose and prepared to stand. In that moment, another group of men came stumbling out of the restaurant.

Fucking finally, she thought.

Still seated, Madison tugged on the hem of her skirt so that it rode high on her thighs, and exhaled slowly through her nostrils to regulate her breathing and, by proxy, her nerves.

There were four men, and they clustered in the doorway of the restaurant at first. They lit cigarettes and pulled their coats tight against the chill. They were laughing. For a good ten minutes she watched, and it was as they made to disperse that they finally noticed her, as expected.

Holding an unlit cigarette propped against her knee, she watched them sauntering over. As they got close, she planted a modest smile on her lips, tilted her head to one side, and squinted as if drunk.

One man moved at the center of the group and began speaking by first motioning to his car. It was the same gunmetal grey sports car with a horned hood. And just like that, after hours of waiting, Madison's prey trotted into the crosshairs.

You must be Simon Pan.

"Nice car, right?" he said.

"Yes," she replied. "Does it fly?" Hiding her German accent was easy if she let the influence of Japanese over her tongue impact her speech. The result was a curt and crisp take on American English. "Is it a Ferrari?"

He laughed. "That's custom! One of a kind. I could buy three Ferraris for the cost of it!"

Pan wore a suit that had likely been finely pressed hours ago. Now it hung untucked and flapping over his thin frame. He was an attractive man, with angular features and fierce eyebrows. His eyes reminded her of an old friend of her husband's, a guy named Saotome. Saotome, too, was a complete tool.

"It doesn't actually 'fly' fly," he added. "Fucking nothing does."

He was sputtering drunk. Madison did what she could to hide her enthusiasm. The cold yanking at her muscles didn't help.

"What are you doing, sitting here like this in the cold?" Pan asked, leering drunkenly.

Madison sighed and fluttered her lips, as though exasperated. "Just letting the air sober me up for a bit. I just lost my worth at the casino on Eleventh."

Pan's men flanked him like superhero sidekicks. Madison met their gazes in turn and with calculus. The metrics were favorable.

"A light, please?"

One of Pan's men moved in to offer his lighter but was blocked by the boss.

"Quit being so eager to please!" Pan reprimanded his man, shaking his head. Instead, he produced a golden flip lighter from his slacks and smiled. "My men act like dogs sometimes. I'm trying to civilize them."

One of them howled and they all laughed.

"Dogs can be fun sometimes," Madison teased as her cigarette caught the flame.

"Is that so?"

"It is so."

The men looked at one another and chuckled. Pan's eyes narrowed in that moment. He studied her face with the suspicion one would expect of a gangster of his caliber. "You know, you look familiar."

Madison took a drag to buy time. She may have overplayed her hand, but wasn't concerned.

"*Eventualities innumerable*," was something a composer once told her in response to a question about dealing with unforeseen circumstances, with failure. With chaos. The woman's response was now hardcoded into Madison's preparation process.

"I get that sometimes," she replied coolly. "People say I look like that actress, Michelle What's-her-name."

After a moment of scrutiny, Pan snapped his fingers and hit one of his men in the chest. "That's it! Michelle Tamley! She looks like Michelle Tamley."

"Michelle Tamley, but hotter," his man replied.

Pan squatted, arms on his knees, to meet her eye to eye. "Look, why don't we go somewhere, all of us? Let's get out of this cold and have a few more drinks. The night's still young."

"All of you?"

Pan looked to his men. "You said 'dogs can be fun sometimes.'"

Madison laughed with a hand to her mouth. "I did say that." Looking them over, she frowned. "I don't know, though, you look a bit rough."

Pan placed a hand on her knee, and it took a sniper's focus on Madison's part not to flinch. "We're teddy bears."

With a sigh, she smiled and brushed his hand away. It took two attempts. "We've a bit of business to take care of first, do we not?"

Pan scoffed. "Oh, of course! Money? You want money?" He reached into his coat and produced a stack of notes as thick as a novella. "Money's not a thing, baby."

Exhausted and confident in the mark now, Madison gave up the fake accent. "That's a lot of cash. You know, they say all cash now carries trace amounts of feces... and blood."

Pan stood slowly.

"What happened?" Madison asked, her expression feigning disappointment. "You no longer want to touch my leg?"

"What happened to your accent?" Pan replied.

The Party Crasher reached into her purse, smiling and never breaking with his gaze. From it she removed The Madam, a vintage pump-action shotgun, sawed off at the barrel. The feel of it triggered a rush of ecstasy and she couldn't help but smile. Madison dropped it into her lap and took a long drag from her cigarette before picking it up once more and propping it over her shoulder.

"Fake accents are a bear to uphold," she told them. "I don't know how Michelle Tamley does it. Or any actor, for that matter."

The Madam had taken instantly from them that aura of invincibility prevalent most in people just before disaster. That binary state where the impossible is just that, until it isn't.

In that moment, Simon Pan's face became that of a man twice his age. Part of it was the gun, sure, but blended with the simple shock of a drawn firearm was something much more significant. In Pan's face, Madison saw recognition, and even better, resignation. And, while his men turned and ran, Simon Pan just stood there, his expression weary.

"I should have known it was you," he told her. "Sitting in the cold like that. The Minowara send you?"

"Ja."

Pan bit his lip and shook his head, exasperated. "Is Raizen fucking stupid? He was supposed to arrange for a meet first. That's how things are done! Someone steps over the line, you talk first... you negotiate."

Madison shrugged and made an "oh, well" face.

"That's just how things are done! He can have his fucking turf back. I'll have my people off Wilshire tonight, he has my word. Hell, I'll give him Bancroft if he can come to the table. Tell him that!"

Behind him, Pan's men were taking up positions behind the cars in front of the Golden Leaf. They were calling for him, but time was up for Simon Pan. Even Simon Pan knew that.

"You'll start a war!" he screamed.

Madison leveled The Madam. At this range, she would make an awful mess.

68

"Oh, I doubt it. Who were *you* anyway?"

The blast echoed in the quiet of dusk, and Simon Pan was dead before his body hit the ground. The mess was indeed awful and likely ruined her boots.

Madison stood and placed a bloodied boot on the body of Simon Pan.

"Where did my dogs go?" She cocked The Madam. "Here, boys!"

4: Things Are Better in the Cloud

"When you're inside Libra, when you're deep inside, and you've been there a long while, everything becomes... celestial. Things like time, orientation, and even self *become irrelevant. The world becomes an ocean, free from walls, free from fear and consequence, free of superstition. All that matters are facts and the acquisition of facts. And facts, like stars in the night sky, cry out and can't be missed. I hope that makes sense. I don't suspect it does to you, not yet anyway.*

"Oops... I'm bleeding again."

\- Unit One Detective Constable Rena Bryant

[Millennial Tower]

Rena stood at the heart of Section Three, looking down on Sun City's financial district. There was something empowering about the perspective. Below, Capital Street moved in an orange stream like magma, the lives of a million citizens carried on its current. From her vantage, she could see Sun City's lights dwindle to nothing in the south. To the east were the Sierras, a wall of black in the night. And to the west lay the Bay of Sun. Across the moonlit waters was the jagged shore of Section Seven, its shipping container cranes like fingers clawing at the ocean.

Climbing up onto the cornice, Rena stood with her toes clenching the building's edge. Vertigo spun her senses, exhilarating. No matter how many times, the sensation was the same. Fear of falling from such a great height was ingrained in her very being, like a boot sequence, or a root directory.

[555 Capital Center]

With a command, she'd traveled a dozen blocks and now stood on the roof of a second skyscraper. This was the headquarters of the Valhalla Fight League. Sprinting now, she crossed the roof and leaped to the building adjacent. She walked across the skylight, looking down on an office full of workers who toiled, heads buried in their terminals, oblivious to her presence.

"Libra, where am I?"

[645 Capital Street.]

"Occupants?"

[Business: Pong Financial; Business: Eurasian Financial Services; Business…]

"Cease query."

The world she occupied now was Libra: the all-encompassing surveillance network under which most everything in Sun City transpired. Her "form," her presence in the network, was a product of Libra's robust AI coupled with immersive neural rendering. With it, she could call up footage from any number of audio and video sources and traverse a three-dimensional landscape, rendered by their real-time feeds. Where some might use the technology to simply replay events,

71

she used it as it was intended: to recreate a virtual Sun City that moved synchronously with the real world. This network, built over decades, captured nearly every angle of Sun City, from the suburbs of Section Two to the impoverished borough of Section Seven.

Very few people had access to the true Libra user interface, but she did. Partly because her job required it, and partly because she had helped design it. Truth be told, however, they couldn't keep her out if they wanted to. After all, in this state, immersed, she moved about a near-perfect Sun City as spectre and spectator, free of gravity, physics, and time. Her life's blood was now bandwidth, her religion acquisition, and her God Providence, the State-owned satellite whose perspective gave depth and context to the digital Sun City. And like this, she did most of her work. As Technical Detective Constable for Unit One, her job was to take down the worst of the worst, and she loved her job, almost as much as she loved immersion.

Where usually she would savor every moment immersed, spending her time exploring every hidden inch of the megalopolis, today she was all business. And she engaged it with a heavy heart. Her friend and partner was a casualty now, and while the culprit was dead, the motive and truth behind the incident roamed free.

The roof where she found herself standing was blanketed in the light from a billboard. She looked up to find the gigantic face of Unit One Sgt. Chris Calderon staring back at her.

"Oh geez."

The Ministry of Media has been working overtime, she thought.

On the billboard, her other partner wore a crisp black suit and held up a fist. On his wrist was a silver Crespling: an ultra-expensive, legacy timepiece. Above his head were the words, "How our Unit keeps time."

The State Defense Consortium's campaign of productizing Unit One was something she just couldn't jive with. At her most cynical, she could appreciate the brazen greed behind the idea. It was the execution that was lacking. The idea — Premier Macek's brainchild — was to humanize Unit One the same way celebrities and, to an increasing degree, politicians were, by inserting them into the mainstream, by tethering them to popular products. "Cognitive association" was how the brass described it.

It's really just neuro-linguistic programming, she thought with a ping of disgust. *The whole thing would be comical if not for the implications. It's like saying to the people: "You like beer but hate the government? Well, here's an agent holding a whole case of your favorite beer. Now, how do you feel?"*

It wasn't a revolutionary idea. After all, government agencies had been leveraging the media since the first badge was wrought, the first fedora donned. But this was different.

The SDC wasn't using marketing as a means of sending positive or instructional messages, they were using the media to generate positive reception. And the whole misguided endeavor was something she grappled with every time an endorsement deposit hit her account.

Looking down, she watched in real time as Sun City poured into Section Three for a warm and pleasant Sunday evening. She surveyed the area, including City Center and Century Plaza. Bridging sections Three and Six, the superhighway 101 took on the look of an ancient aqueduct as it tiptoed over the heart of Sun City.

That's my destination.

"101, eastbound lane, between Third and Pollue."

She rocketed, electing to enjoy the trip rather than teleport. A command sent her spiraling through the mock-night like a comet to splash down on the superhighway like a fallen angel. Charred concrete and a crumbling freeway barrier wall confirmed she'd arrived at her destination. This was the site of the explosion. Ultima destination.

Geez, the blast must have been something up close...

With a thought, Rena brought the suspect's stolen vehicle flickering into existence. A collection of images captured prior to the wreck's removal was being rendered before her, visually rewinding the clock. Vehicles, moving past in real time, blended with those whose movements had been captured the night before.

74

"Libra, suspend the live feed. Show me yesterday, twenty-one-hundred hours, thirty-three minutes, nine seconds."

She watched as Sgt. Calderon's bike Revenant skidded to a halt. A moment later, she watched as Sgt. Alec Jefferson Moore sauntered up. She stepped aside for him to pass, as though she needed to, and watched the tragedy unfold once more.

She listened as the sergeant engaged the suspect, Diedre Smiley.

" 'Sup? "

"S-son of a bitch... Moore, you goddamn pig!"

"Now, now, you did this to yourself."

AJ's voice had a slightly diminished tone, made distant by the proximity of the highway closed-circuit camera and microphone that had captured it. They went back and forth for some time before the suspect's behavior became erratic.

"Diedre! Stop it! Help is on the way!"

"AAAAAAGGGGGGGGHHHHHHHHHH!"

Rena watched as the giant woman tore her arm free of the wreckage. The report had called out Diedre's mass as something of note. And now, seeing the woman up close, even stuffed in the vehicle's wreckage, the suspect's size baffled Rena.

Was she a competitive bodybuilder? People still do that? Even still, steroids?

In the process of freeing herself, Diedre had created several life-threatening lacerations on her arm. They were the

75

kind of wounds no sober person could inflict on themselves. It reminded her of the story of a biker trapped under an overturned vehicle. The man had been so amped up on adrenaline that he was able to lift the car off of himself.

It had to have been drugs, Rena thought. *Something really, really powerful.*

"Libra, if it hasn't been done, order a toxicology report on Diedre Smiley."

The scene played out.

"Diedre!"

"OH GOD! OH GOOOOOOD!"

Her face less than a foot from where Diedre's had been a night before, Rena watched the woman's eyes roll back into her head. Both arms free from the wrecked vehicle now, she clawed at her head as though possessed.

"What the hell is happening to you?"

She watched as Diedre drew a grenade from her coat.

"Pause."

Rena took a close look at the grenade.

"Let the report show that the explosive device appears to be Army-issued and high-yield incendiary in nature. Can't… can't make out the serial. Looks scratched off. Probably black market. Continue, Libra."

Rena watched the sergeant lunge at the grenade, and was taken aback. It was one of the most selfless acts she'd ever seen and, at the same time, one of the most foolish. She paused Libra and replayed the moments from when AJ's eyes recognized the grenade to his decision to move toward the explosive rather than away.

AJ...

She watched that fateful decision a dozen times or more, studying the sergeant's face.

"You never even thought about it…. Running never even occurred to you."

She sighed.

The explosion rendered Sun City white momentarily before engulfing the area where she stood in flame. When the blast exhausted itself a moment later, Rena crossed several lanes of the 101 to the center divide, where paramedics would find Sgt. Moore. All around her, fire and black smoke sent traffic of hours past careening. She ignored the spectral vehicles and soon found her partner's inert form. He lay curled into a kind of fetal position, his face still. His eyes were closed and his jacket was shredded and blistering beneath flames. His arms, which had come up to shield his face, were mangled and hung from the sockets like expended party favors. The sight turned her stomach.

Rena knelt and moved her hand over his head and across his cheek. She touched his lips.

"Damn, AJ…"

Though her investigation had just begun, the detective found herself drained, crouched over her comrade. The Unit hadn't been told much about the incident, other than what was required to further the investigation. They didn't know it was like this... not yet.

With little to be gleaned from the blast itself, she spent the next hour learning about Diedre from the SCPD databases. Diedre's life played around her in words and images that hung in the air like leaves in the wind, as she called up every report the SDC had on the woman. The deceased Titan drug dealer and murder suspect was an interesting case. Like AJ, Diedre hailed from the Veins, Section Seven's most neglected neighborhood. Her mother had been a school teacher and her father a longshoreman. At the age of sixteen, Diedre's rap sheet started. It was a narrative that touched on all the tragic cliches. First, it was graffiti; vandalism, then possession. A full-fledged assault charge at the age of nineteen. While her record didn't contain signs of "derailment" — external contributing factors like abusive parents — as a cause for the Titan's downward spiral, as far as Rena was concerned, Diedre didn't really need any beyond growing up in the Veins.

Prior to her release three years ago, Diedre had spent four years in Ronart Supermax, quite possibly the worst prison in the first world. Supermax was a subterranean correctional facility that embraced the ideology of "rehabilitation through isolation." Prisoners were kept in a state of constant solitary confinement, their only human interaction being limited contact with guards and a weekly visit from a therapist. It was Hell on Earth. And it was a hell that Diedre Smiley had emerged from, un-suicided.

"So why, Diedre?" Rena asked aloud. "Why kill yourself now?"

[Command not understood.]

"Not talking to you, Libra."

Rena replayed the footage again. AJ was promising — illegally — to spare Diedre from a return trip to Supermax. And Diedre seemed receptive to his words. In fact, she even appeared to be warming to the sergeant a bit.

"Tell me and I'll get your charges dropped. Once they've patched you up, I'll even sneak you out of the city."

"You won't do a day in Supermax. After that, you're on your own. I hear Harbor City is nice this time of year."

"Fuck it... I'm screwed either way."

That's right, Rena remembered, *this is when her neurotrigger went offline. This should be interesting...*

"Libra, broaden query to include network nodes."

The world around her fell into darkness. In the darkness, network addresses appeared. Some moved visibly, as the vessels carrying them moved. A self-driving vehicle moved by, in numbers only, and above, the freeway's traffic cameras appeared as tilted numbers with appended descriptors. Instead of seeing a weatherworn and grey closed-circuit camera, she saw its IP address 10.21.1.755, appended with the descriptor "hwy101_onrmp7_cam2." In the distance, network addresses littered the horizon. She waited, watching the flow of time around Diedre frame by frame like stop-motion animation. She watched the glowing white dot that hung in the air where

Diedre's spine met the base of her skull. This was where her neurotrigger implant was… before the blast.

And in that moment, the glowing node that represented Diedre's neurotrigger interface vanished, and well before the blast occurred.

"What the hell…"

How did Diedre's neurotrigger node vanish from the network?

"Libra. Self-diagnosis for current session consistency. Test the 'handshake.'"

[Self-diagnosis complete. No errors found. Connection: very strong.]

Rena frowned in contemplation. *Was she hacked?*

Hacking someone's neurotrigger was a practice nearly as old as neurotrigger itself. The most common reasons for hijacking someone's neuronet interface were theft of sensitive and most-times profitable information; spoofing a person's neurotrigger address for the purposes of theft in the physical; or disrupting connectivity or signal transmission for the purposes of being a dick. But no hack, regardless of how malicious, was capable of disengaging neurotrigger entirely, unless the network itself went down.

If Diedre were hacked — in real time — I would have seen the connection.

To be sure, she expanded her query to include network communications. This created visual connections between devices that, in Sun City, could be likened to silk-weaving.

Lines innumerable found each other over great distances, blotting out everything until she limited the radius of the query. Like this, among an infinite spider's web of digital device connections, even on the 101, she watched Diedre die several more times. None of the lines that touched Diedre's neurotrigger node lit up with activity.

"Reset query filters."

The black disappeared and the virtual Sun City returned. With her arms folded, she watched the moments leading up to the explosion once more.

I'm missing something. I have to be.

"You're pretty smart for a punk," Diedre said again. *"But you don't get it. He sees and hears everything."*

"Who does? Who sees everything? Who's the boss, Diedre? Who runs the Titans?"

"One man runs the show, Moore. And his name is L—"

Pain, that was the only word that accurately defined what happened next. Sudden, excruciating, maddening pain. Diedre might as well have been burning in that moment. Rena watched, the severity of the torment she was witnessing not lost on her.

This isn't shock she's experiencing, the detective thought. *This is something else...*

"Diedre, no!"

"OUROBOROS!"

The blast altered the perspective of the crash site as it knocked out the nearest traffic cam. The flaming wreck reappeared a moment later, smaller and more from a top-down perspective.

With a thought, Rena halted the feed once more.

Ouroboros...

"Libra, what is Ouroboros?"

She knew of the word's origins, but could use a refresher.

[Ouroboros refers to the ancient Egyptian icon, thought by many to represent cyclicality or the cycle of death and rebirth. Ouroboros has often been depicted as a serpent or snake consuming itself. While some specu—]

"That's enough. Query 'Ouroboros' as a title in technology. Join keywords: 'neurotrigger' and 'hacking' or 'neuralnet hacking.' Declassify content if necessary, applying the credentials of Detective Constable Rena Bryant of the State Defense Consortium's Unit One."

She waited.

[No results with a higher than ninety-five-percent match to the suggested criterium returned. Would you like to modify the terms of your query?]

"Nope."

[Operation Ouroboros: A military campaign launched by the British Navy in 2018 aimed at establishing a blockade between the Persian Gulf and the Gulf of Oman at the Strait of Hormuz. The campaign was—]

"Next."

[Ouroboros in technology: an e-payments company established in 2006 by brothers Frank and Aaron Belong. A merchant processing platform and payment card issuer, Ouroboros was sold—]

"Next."

[Ouroboros in technology: Video Game published in 2001 by—]

"Next."

All right...

Diedre didn't kill herself. There is no definitive proof of this. Everything in her exchange with AJ indicated a woman desperate to live.

"Libra, Ouroboros in media."

[Ouroboros in entertainment: Swedish film released in—]

Suddenly the stream of rendered audio went silent. Rena hung in the air, listening, perplexed. She waited, but the feed did not return.

"Libra! Ouroboros!"

[File not found or you are not authorized to access this content. Please contact your administrator.]

"What? Libra! Ouroboros!"

[File not found or you are not authorized to access this content. Please contact your administrator.]

"I am the goddamned administrator!"

A sound stole into her with a crystalline pitch, a dagger to the senses. Rena screamed and, in an act of sheer muscle memory, put her hands to where her ears would be in an attempt to shield herself from an attack on her very digital being. The sound, if it could even be called that, seemed to wrest from her control of even basic movement. And in that moment, Sun City began to flicker and swim like things on the horizon in summer.

"Libra," she called over the whining tone, "error logs."

[You are not authorized to access these records. Please contact your administrator.]

"Libra! I want logs, including updates to permissions."

[You do not have the appropriate access to view this content. Please contact your administrator.]

Before she could reply, the sound subsided.

Rena, her mind reeling, looked about frantically. "What the fuck is going on?"

"You're outside of your jurisdiction," a voice told her.

She looked for the voice and, at first, found nothing. Then, as the world around her seemed to dwindle in clarity, a figure emerged. It held itself aloft, seemingly on the other side of the city, but at the same time only yards away. Its form was dark and shifting, ethereal.

"Who are you?" she asked.

"You're outside of your jurisdiction," the spectre repeated.

"Bullshit! I am Detective Constable Rena Bryant, Unit One. Identify yourself."

"Who am I? The hubris… I am the center of your universe, Detective; the origin of truth. And, as with the universe, beyond you. Simple, simple. You needn't concern yourself with inevitability, Detective. Your investigation serves no one."

"Who are you?"

"Be banished."

Sun City began to disappear right before her eyes. Sections of the city broke away, leaving behind nothing but void. Buildings, streets, and everything in between flickered and fell away in maddening and, at the same time, quite logical segments. Entire boroughs at a time, the Libra sandbox vanished. Simultaneously, her own physical representation began to peel away, until Rena could no longer see herself. The sensation was terrifying, like being stricken blind.

Despite its staggering mass, it didn't take long for all of Sun City to disappear, which intensified the sensation of falling into something final and unrepairable. With nothing but black where once a megalopolis held, only the figure remained. It waited for her, the only object in a starless night sky, a speck of strewn earth at the ocean's floor.

Oh my God, oh my God…

The figure approached, moving across the void to grow large in Rena's mind's eye. At range, the thing appeared to be a woman, but much of her face was covered in what could best be described as a tattered scarf, and at worst, the decaying tongue of some envious devil. The spectre's hair was black, and swayed as though in water. It was deathly thin, its flesh gray and decayed. Its eyes were glowing orange spirals, terrifying and yet mesmerizing.

"YOU CANNOT BE HERE!"

The sound destroyed her composure, and Rena screamed. Her attempts to disengage from Libra using a series of mental commands that she knew to be immutable fail-safes were met with silence from the neural network. Her control over Libra, over the digital realm in which she had reigned, had been stripped from her. She was no longer even a guest in her own home, but rather the intruder.

The creature, with its spiral eyes, receded into the nothingness and disappeared, leaving the detective alone in the black. Firmly in the grip of panic now, Rena could feel her chest heaving someplace far away. Across what had been the night sky, the words appeared: "GOODBYE DETECTIVE CONSTABLE RENA BRYANT. GOODBYE GOODBYE GOODBYE GOODBYE." The text was massive, spanning the breadth and width of Libra, beyond measure. The words were written in a cruel font, and in the harshest shade of red. Their magnitude was no less than that of Saturn, and the words in this scale carried with them a dread that was maddening.

"No! Come back! Don't leave me here! Not like this!"

Her eyes had sealed shut, likely from her tears drying. Rena used her fingers to pry them open, afraid of what the light might do to her but desperate for it nonetheless. The immersion chair was soaked through with sweat, and her skin was thick with a dried film, sticky to the touch. For what felt like days, she'd been trapped in that digital purgatory with nothing but those horrible, horrible words to keep her company. Once her fingertips left the sensors at the end of each arm on the chair, the back raised, propping her up. Her head lolled forward, unplugging the neural interface inserted into the base of her neck. The detective's hair was matted and clung to her cheeks with perspiration. She sat there for a while, breathing heavily, waiting for her eyes to adjust, and waiting for the trauma to subside.

How long was I under? How long was I trapped?

She brought up her usage history on the chair's display.

Last login: Today July 7, 2050
Session duration: 01:13:22:01

My God...

The thing with orange eyes and tattered scarf had somehow expelled her from Libra's user interface while maintaining its neural connection, a feat that should have been impossible.

"Unless... she... she would have had to overwrite the kill session protocol," she mumbled to herself.

She put a hand to her forehead.

The number of people with the level of access required to append Libra's core logic numbered less than ten and Rena was one of them. The other nine she knew personally.

"She could have killed me."

Rena looked around her apartment in a daze. The furniture, coated in dust, sat pushed against the wall with hasty inconsistency, parted to make room for the immersion chair. Emptied bottles of flavored electrolyte supplements lay strewn about, and a half-eaten pizza sat open, growing mold like peach fuzz. The lights were off and what natural light there was crept in from beneath the drawn curtains.

She slid her legs from the chair but did not stand. She was in her underwear and it was damp, soiled.

"Christ..."

She stood slowly on wobbly legs. Shifting her weight from one foot to another to get the circulation going, she could only shake her head at what her apartment had become. Being trapped in Libra for nearly two days hadn't helped, but her home had been a mess long before that. Really, since she'd obtained her own immersion chair.

The room had a sweet stink of body odor and spoiled food. The smell had been there for a long time, but now she smelled it anew, the way one might upon return from a long trip.

When Rena finally had the strength, she walked to the bathroom and started the shower. The bathroom, too, had not been spared the degradation of neglect. Mildew crept up the linoleum like varicose veins, black and ambitious. Once the steam began to rise, she undressed entirely and stepped over the low ledge. Her legs were pale, and the water, despite barely having time to warm, burned to the touch. She gritted her teeth and began soaping. As she washed, she tried to make sense of what had happened.

She had been logged in to Libra under her personal account, as opposed to the account issued her by the SDC. Operating like this afforded her perks her government account could not, not with the oversight of the Ministry of Communications. Perks like applying personal plugins — snippets of her own code to modify Libra's behavior — without seeking SDC approval. It was in direct violation of Libra Terms of Service and of SDC protocol, but it made her time in Libra more productive and thus made her a more effective detective, which, at the end of the day, was all that mattered. Rena had cloned her administrator's account, which gave her personal account the highest level of permissions possible. That should have made expulsion from the network impossible, as, by design, one administrator could not revoke the privileges of another.

And yet, that's exactly what happened.

Could there be a God-mode? Did someone involved in Libra's design create a backdoor of some kind, from which this mysterious user could circumvent every rule that had been established? If so, who? The team of designers who could claim credit for Libra was a small, tight-knit bunch. And besides her, all of them were still employed at Unicom, the private communications conglomerate which funded the Libra Project. All of them were staunch SDC loyalists and friends, she'd dare say. Perhaps with the exception of John Cholish, the Unicom Network CEO and contributor.

And none of them would risk such lucrative careers aiding an outside hacker, she thought.

Out of pocket for nearly two days, Rena had one priority: get to headquarters and report her findings to Deputy Chief Constable Williams.

5: Unit One

"There was a time when I would have replied with something like 'No comment' or 'If I were privy to such information, blah, blah, blah.' But now, to be honest, I'm past all that. I've been banging my head against the walls of bureaucracy and back-channeling in this organization for so long that I frankly have no fucks left to give. I'm overdrawn on fucks and just got hit with a sixty-five-dollar surcharge. You ask me, 'Is the SDC corrupt?' And I ask you to name one corporation or government agency that isn't. And make no mistake, the SDC is both!"

- SDC Deputy Chief Constable Sean Conrad Williams

"Carla, can you send someone down to the gym? No, don't go yourself, send someone; a dude. I left my loofah in one of the showers." Chief Williams sat back in his chair, quite frustrated, flipping a pen over his knuckles anxiously. Beneath the desk, his leg bounced furiously. "'Which shower?' How the hell should I know? I know it was on the right if that helps. 'What if it's in use?' What kind of despicable creature would use a strange loofah? In a public shower no less, Carla? Oh, the *shower*. 'What if *the shower* is in use?' Well hell, I don't know, tell them to knock politely and ask for the purple loofah sitting on the goddamn soap dispenser. Yes, Carla, purple.

91

Thank you!" He slammed his hand down on the touch sensor to disconnect the call. As he did so, his work returned to be displayed on the desk before him.

Jesus, where was I?

He had no idea what the last three forms he'd signed were; yet there they sat, splayed before him in panels on the desk's interactive surface. At some point in the last two hours, he'd gotten lost in thought. His motor functions had taken over and simply begun searching the infinite forms for 'FIRST NAME,' 'LAST NAME,' and 'SIGNATURE.' It was nothing short of a miracle that he'd been able to sneak a workout in, and now he was out $14.95 in lost loofah for his trouble. Williams looked at the display in disdain.

2050 and we're filling out paperwork like it's 1999. Why can't I just click "select all" and "sign"? Yes, he thought angrily, *I Sean Conrad Williams attest to whatever the fuck is on this document. I Sean Conrad Williams agree that whatever is on this document should or shouldn't happen.*

Television always chose paperwork as the comedic trope when trying to illustrate the humdrum of government work. *And they have no idea just how accurate they are.*

There were equipment requests, transfer requests, vacation requests, requests for public appearances, requests for interviews, and requests for access. And those were just the forms that he'd gotten to today and could remember reading. On top of that, there were the reports. Incident reports, audit reports, inventory reports, and more. Hell, there were reports so laden in technical jargon or legalese he didn't even know how to read them. And, of course, those too required a signature. And no matter how many forms he signed off on, there were always more waiting; a backlog whose "unread" ticker climbed like the odometer on a road trip.

I am Sisyphus, and my stone is bureaucracy.

The phone built into his workstation chimed. The caller ID read *Sun City Chronicle* but the face of the caller was unfamiliar. The man had a round face, and a mustache plucked right out of the seventeenth century. It covered the entirety of his mouth and swept outward like angel's wings.

How the hell did you get this number? Williams asked himself. *And how the hell did that muskrat get onto your lip?*

The chief answered the phone.

"How the hell did you get this number?"

"Mark Nikolaev, Sun City Chronicle. I know you're a busy man, Deputy Chief Constable Williams, so I'll be brief. Was the explosion on the 101 an act of terrorism?"

"Listen, guy, get your pen ready."

"I use a tablet, but sure, I'm ready," the reporter replied.

"You sure?"

"Yes, sir."

Williams took a deep breath. "Well, here goes…"

With a tap on his desk, he hung up.

"Fucking press."

The phone immediately chimed again. Without looking at the display he answered. "What?"

"I think we got disconnected…"

"Ah yes, Mike Nikolips from Teen Beat, right?"

"*Mark Nikolaev* from the Sun City Chronicle."

"Right, what I said. Look, *Mike*, this line is reserved for everything and everyone in life except you. I'll respectfully insist that you forward all inquiries to someone, *anyone* else. Ok now, bye bye."

Williams rapped a heavy knuckle on the desk, and the man with the silly mustache disappeared once more.

"Who has time for this?"

Once more the indicator on his desk flashed and the phone rang. Without looking, he answered. "Listen, motherfuck—"

"Sir?"

"Carla?"

"Everything ok, sir?"

Williams clenched his jaw. "Yes, sorry. I just—"

"I found it."

"Found what?"

"Your loofah."

"Oh, happy day. Gotta go."

Williams hung up and backed away from the contemporary torture rack that was his desk.

As the SDC's Deputy Chief Constable and commander of Unit One, Williams, on a normal day, could justify his salary never leaving his desk, if he were to allow it. And the rampage set off in Section Three by the Titans, now being called the "Diedre Incident" internally, only made things worse.

There's literally not enough time in the day.

Looking at the clock on the wall, he sighed. *And I'm late for yet another briefing.*

Williams picked up his coat and flung it over his shoulder.

His phone chimed, and he was about to ignore it and walk out but glanced first at the caller ID display. The ravaged face now showing from the workstation halted him in his tracks.

Shit, Williams thought. *Precisely what I don't need.*

The Unit One commander held a hand over the menu on his desk for a long while before deciding to answer.

"Deputy Chief Constable Williams' office…"

"Deputy Chief Constable."

"Afternoon, Ace. What can I do for you?"

"That's 'Major,' Chief. Let's not sacrifice decorum for familiarity."

Staring down at the scarred and menacing face of Major Ace Monroe, Williams resisted the urge to sneer. "What can I do for you, Major?"

Monroe's amber, almost golden, eyes were unblinking. "You can start with an update on this weekend's bombing. Has your unit made any progress in the investigation?"

95

The answer that came first to Williams was "That's none of your business," but he held his tongue. "Nothing specific to report yet, but I'll have Detective Constable Bryant pen you an update when we have one. Also, Major, what happened on the 101 was not a 'bombing.' The suspect killed herself with a grenade."

The Major's dour attitude, coupled with his relentless persistence, made dealing with him about as pleasurable as shitting a pinecone. "What else can I help you with, Major?"

"Listen to me carefully, Deputy Chief Constable." The Major's already sandpaper voice now carried with it an insufferable tone of superiority. "An explosion occurred in the public space. Article Thirty-four of the State Defense Act lists unclaimed explosions as terrorism until proven otherwise."

Here we go... The eternal power struggle between Agency Zero and Unit One continues...

"Well," Williams replied patiently, "this explosion doesn't need claiming, Major. The suspect detonated a grenade in her own face and — believe it or not — didn't share her anti-globalist manifesto before doing it. Thanks for the offer of assistance, but we've got this."

"Terrorism comes in all shapes and forms, Chief Constable," the Major replied. His expression was cruel, made more so by what Williams perceived as a smirk.

"Convenient," the chief replied.

The Major's attempt at civility was gone even before it had fully materialized. "Come again?"

If everything is terrorism, Williams wanted to reply, *then old hawks like you are never irrelevant.* But picking a fight with the Major, especially involving SDC policy, was never a good idea. Instead, Williams decided to let the argument slide... at least for now.

Williams knew that the Major was searching for an opportunity to insert Agency Zero into Unit One's investigation. It was a trend that seemed to occur ever more frequently since rumors of Agency Zero's possible disbandment had started circulating the SDC hallways.

"'Duly noted' is what I meant. That said, Major, trust me when I say we are well on our way to uncovering the events around your brother's..."

"My *half*-brother's incident is tangential," the Major snapped. "What is not is my apparent need to remind you that without my explicit recommendation, Chief, you'd still be clawing at a lieutenant colonel's rank in some podunk Army base, struggling to feed those kids of yours."

Williams placed both hands on his desk and brought his face down so that the two of them were as eye-to-eye as technology would allow. "Careful, Major."

The Major's face twitched and his pupils seemed to shrink.

When no apology appeared forthcoming, Williams decided to defuse the situation.

"How could I forget, Ace? You remind me every chance you get. And make no mistake, old friend, my family and I are grateful. Now, as you know, I am up to my elbows in shit because of this incident and have a lot of work to do. And for what it's worth, Sergeant Moore's 'incident,' however 'tangential,' as you put it, may not matter to you, but it matters a great deal to me."

"That wasn't what I meant…"

"I'm glad. And it seems like we're misfiring all over the place on this call, Major. Respectfully, sir, let's reconnect when I have an update for you and emotions aren't so… high."

The Major sat back in his chair, his face shrinking from the screen. "Very well. I'll await your call."

Williams disconnected and moved for the door, his fists clenched, even as the phone chimed again. In the doorway, Unit One Lieutenant Mason Bruce stood, arms folded.

"How long have you been standing there?"

The lieutenant shook his head. "Not long."

"Come to get me for the briefing?"

"Yes, sir. We're ready to begin."

"Thank you, Lieutenant."

"Sir, you'll find pleasure in knowing that Detective Constable Bryant is present as well."

"In the flesh? Well, I'll be damned."

Williams stood before them on the podium, as per the usual. Unit One was a small team, comprised of the sergeants Chris Calderon and Alec Jefferson Moore, Detective Constable Rena Bryant, Deputy Informant Yamazaki Daisuke, and

Lieutenant Mason Bruce. This made Sergeant Moore's absence all the more glaring. The chair he normally occupied sat unused in the midst of them, a sorrowful reminder. Also in the room were several members of the Ministry of Communications and the Ministry of Media. The "press," as they were sarcastically referred to, was just shy of a dozen in number and sat in the back of the room. They waited wide-eyed, tablets ready and fingers poised.

The Ministry of Communications consisted of journalists, columnists, authors, publicists, and bloggers who were strategically selected from the nation's most prestigious publications and network stations. Their jobs were to craft stories that placed and kept the unit and, more importantly, the State Defense Consortium, in a favorable light with the constituency. Nothing they captured from a briefing was permitted into the public light without careful scrutiny and approval by the SDC.

As for the Ministry of Media, it was their job, in all honesty, to look for marketing opportunities. These typically came in the way of brand association through topical parallels and such. Specifically, these people took real events that impacted real lives and spun them into moneymaking opportunities. It was real sleazeball shit as far as Williams was concerned. For example, if the Nichols family of four was gunned down on the corner of Herschel and Whatever streets, and the story — for some reason — drove network news numbers, the Ministry of Media made sure that Niko Cameras

99

and Hurch's Chocolate were positioned to benefit from the phonic association (assuming, of course, they were partners). Maybe it meant more airtime for their commercials, or maybe it meant inclusion in online elastic search algorithms. As in, search for "Herschel Shooting" and get a site with Hurch's Chocolate banners everywhere. Lovely. The chief's disdain for the ministries of media and communications was no secret and often brought briefing attendees great entertainment.

Looking down at the lectern, Williams realized he'd forgotten his bullet points, yet again. It wasn't the first time this week he'd done that. He threw his hands up in frustration, his call with the Major still occupying the more patient aspects of his demeanor. "Well, let's start with the good news, I guess. It looks like Sergeant Moore is going to survive."

The room erupted in cheers, most of it coming from the press, who gave each other high-fives, fist bumps, and other disingenuous forms of congratulation. Williams watched them with visible disgust. "Calm down in the back," he told them. "The sergeant couldn't name half of you if you had name tags on."

On the faces of Unit One, however, he saw genuine relief and happiness, etched against gravitas. It was obvious they were out for a Titan reckoning, as was he.

"What's more," he continued, "the sergeant is expected to make a complete recovery, pending no small amount of MODS work and rehabilitation, mind you. And before any of you with the MOC asks me what the monetary cost of rehabilitation is, don't. I'm not here to talk numbers and I don't care."

"Each of you should make it a point to pay him a visit. Except you!" Williams added quickly, pointing to the members of the press. "Agents only, for now at least. Last thing the poor guy needs is you horseflies buzzing about. You'll see me for any updates on the sergeant's condition outside of these briefings."

"Now, on to business. As i'm sure you know, Dice," he said with a nod to Deputy Informant Daisuke, "a pimp, with suspected ties to the Hō Triad organization out of Hong Kong, was gunned down last night in front of Golden Leaf, a restaurant-nightclub for various Chinese mafia types. The victim's name was Simon Pan. Along with the victim, a handful of armed men, assumed to be his security detail, were murdered as well."

"Simon Pan, huh?" Dice mused, sitting, legs crossed, in his ridiculous white overcoat. "That's sure to stir up a hornet's nest."

"He some kind of bigshot?" Rena asked.

Dice looked at her as though seeing her for the first time and smiled handsomely. "Good to see you, Rena. I feel like it's been a while."

Rena just returned his smile.

Dice, a slender man with high cheekbones and gentle, if not sad, eyes, ran a hand over his sweeping pompadour. "Simon Pan has pretty powerful relations back in Hong Kong, though I wouldn't say he was a particularly heavy hitter. We should expect reprisal."

"Get in front of it, Deputy," Williams said firmly. "Let's get to the killer before the Triad do, and prevent an escalation."

Dice nodded. "Yes, sir."

Someone scoffed. Williams quickly noticed Lieutenant Mason Bruce making a face. "Something to add, Lieutenant?"

It was no secret that the lieutenant did not approve of Deputy Yamazaki's role in Unit One, or of his methods. It was also no secret that the two men hated each other.

Bruce, Unit One's second in command, folded his arms and cocked his head back defiantly. "I guess I'm still befuddled how relying on an ex-felon to catch felons makes sense outside of a poorly written comic book."

Dice turned in his chair to face the lieutenant. "What do you do here, exactly?"

"Gentlemen!"

"You've arrested something like zero people in the two years I've been here. Hell, you don't even—"

"Gentlemen!"

"Who are you to judge me, convict? My role is strategic."

Williams slammed his fist on the lectern and feared for a second that it would fall over. "Lieutenant, Deputy, shut the fuck up! Both of you!"

Both men looked up at him in silence now, though Dice still held his middle finger up and in Bruce's direction.

"Neither of you two are in any position to measure dic— arrest records." Williams looked to Sergeant Calderon, who sat quietly a row behind the others. His bandana was low over his eyes, and his dyed hair sprouted from above it in feathered waves. "Sergeant, how many Class-A cases in the Queue have you closed?"

"All-time or this month?" Chris asked, coolly.

"This month," Williams replied.

"Twelve."

"What day is it?" Williams asked himself, looking at his watch. "Look at that! And it's only the seventh. So, Dice, Mason, kindly table your adolescent bickering and arrest somebody. Arrest each other, for fuck's sake. Just get to work. Moving on…"

Next, Williams nodded to Rena, whose face seemed thinner than he recalled. "Detective Bryant, welcome to the briefing. First time? Should we go around the room and introduce ourselves? I'll go first. I'm the Unit One commander who is always wondering where the fuck his technical detective is." At this, some chuckled. The detective's absenteeism had become somewhat of a running joke.

Rena smiled, but lowered her head, blushing. "Introductions won't be necessary, sir."

"Good, Detective. Have you made any progress on the Diedre Incident?"

"Well, I'm early in my investigation, to be honest, but I don't believe Diedre Smiley killed herself of her own accord."

The sound of tapping filled the room as the press began taking notes.

"What does that even mean? How does a person unwittingly stick a grenade under their chin?"

Detective Bryant was older than the others, and Williams was often grateful for her maturity. She was also one of the most talented young detectives and the most astute specialist he'd ever worked with, the former less impressive an accomplishment than the latter. In his time in the military, Williams had served with many a fine specialist.

The detective, usually fit to the point of intimidation, looked a little under the weather. There were bags under her eyes, and her clothes were disheveled.

"This is purely theory," she continued, "but I think that somehow Diedre's behavior was being remotely influenced. I also believe that AJ was about to learn the identity of the Titan kingpin, just before something drove Smiley to suicide. Furthermore, I believe AJ's theory — his theory about their boss — might not be far off the mark."

Several members of the press raised their hands and opened their mouths to speak. There were strict rules against interrupting a briefing, but every now and again something so titillating came up that they broke this rule. Williams held his own hand up and, like a classroom of preadolescents, the press closed their mouths and lowered their hands.

"There will be time after the briefing," he lied.

Turning his attention back to Rena, who sat with her hands in her lap, he continued. "Until we have actionable intel, let's save conjecture. As far as anyone is concerned the investigation is, as you've said, 'early.'"

Williams pointed to the press. "Why don't you people step out for a few minutes? I want to address my team in private. Get to work on the Moore story, huh? I want to read things like 'City united behind fallen Unit One agent' and 'Stalwart agent fighting to get back on the streets,' that kind of stuff. Get poetic with it."

They filed out of the room, heads down like a row of penguins, tapping away on their tablets.

Williams groaned and wanted to throw something at them.

Manipulating the media shouldn't be this easy.

When they'd gone, Dice locked the door behind them but did not go back to his seat. With the core unit present, Williams stepped out from behind the lectern. Mason, Chris, Dice, and Rena gathered around him in a huddle.

Rena continued in a hushed voice, "Luther Gueye. AJ has it in his head that Luther Gueye, if not the Titan boss himself, represents the money behind the operation."

The Unit One commander looked at her incredulously. "You mean Luther Gueye, the billionaire? The guy that just had a ribbon-cutting at Sun City's first internationally recognized war museum? *His* war museum? That Luther

Gueye? The guy widely accredited for founding East Africa's Resource Reparations Initiative? You know, the reason he's now a Nobel laureate recipient of the fucking Peace Prize? *That* Luther Gueye? Never heard of him, Detective."

"You forget real estate mogul and 'philanthropist,'" Rena added.

"What's a 'lorry-ette?'" Dice asked. Everyone ignored him.

"AJ's a moron," Williams continued. "I love the kid, but he's a moron."

"I second that," Lieutenant Bruce added.

"Luther must be our man, then," Dice replied, looking to Mason. "'Cause you're wrong all the time."

Williams looked at the ex-yakuza and just shook his head. "What about Luther's credentials is lost on you, Deputy? I know your English is bananas to be sure, but surely you understood how asinine the suggestion is. You been drinking, Dice?"

Dice nodded reluctantly.

With a sigh, the commander looked to Rena. "What do *you* believe?"

"As much as you don't want to hear this, Chief, I want to go with AJ on this. AJ's plucked every hard-nosed Titan perp out of the Queue known to stalk the boroughs west of Two and east of Three. In other words, he's worked Section Seven and the Veins — the epicenter of Titan activity — harder than any other official in the State. And despite the

106

perception some have of him, AJ is a shrewd investigator. He wouldn't throw a name like that out there without cause."

"As for Gueye," she continued, "I think he has the money, the autonomy, and the connections to run an operation of this scope. Of Sun City's native billionaires, he fits the probability matrix better than most."

Williams had never met Gueye personally, but knew the man had ties to Premier Macek, SDC Councilwoman West, and a host of other high-profile political figures. He seemed to be a personable guy, Gueye, and was a mainstay on political talk shows. Sun City claimed the man as one of its own and from what Williams had seen, Gueye returned the sentiment.

"What about motive?" he asked. "When you're already wielding that kind of wealth, why take the risk?"

Sergeant Calderon chimed in. "You know it's not about the money for some people, Boss, it's about power. Besides that, name any billionaire not looking for that first trillion."

Williams was silent. He listened as his team traded thoughts on the matter. *A false step here could be devastating to our credibility.*

He took his time, folding his arms, his head down. His men knew to give him silence. Like this, he pondered their next move.

If we're going to move forward with this, no one can know, not until we are one hundred percent certain he's our man.

107

"Gueye is not to be touched, or even approached directly. It's too dangerous. With his clout, he could scuttle our investigation before it even begins," he told them.

Dice shook his head.

"That doesn't mean we can't start laying the groundwork. Start with intelligence, then surveillance. When he sees us for the first time, *if* he sees us, it'll be with a warrant in hand. Rena, I'll leave it to you to delegate tasks. Let's see if Moore's theory holds water."

Rena nodded.

"I shouldn't have to say this, but I will, just so I know we're all on the same page. That name is not to be uttered outside of secure channel communications. No one is to know he is even a suspect until we are certain. Am I clear?"

"Should we adopt a codename for the suspect?" Lt. Bruce offered.

"'Capitalist Pig'," Chris offered.

"Dolphin nipples," Rena countered.

"'I'm Surrounded by Fucking Morons'," Commander Williams said, ending the conversation.

"Love it," Rena replied.

"Meeting adjourned. Get to work."

6: Phantom

"Unit One is more than a branch of the SDC at this point, it's a sigil: a flag on the battlefield. And no matter what the cost, that flag is going to fly, no matter how many times it has to be plucked from the blood and mud.

"A character in a video game I play said that. I just swapped in 'Unit One' and 'SDC.' Cool, though, right? I like the sound of it."

- Unit One Sgt. Alec Jefferson "AJ" Moore

AJ lay with one eye partially open, high as the Horus Bank tower on a cocktail of painkillers. He hadn't the strength to turn off the TV, despite being trapped in an infinite loop of Spanish-language reality television. The time of day wasn't exactly clear to him, but a blue light sneaking in beneath the drawn curtains told him it was either really late or really early. His breath came in whistles through a mouth sealed shut with dried saliva that clung to his teeth like caulk.

His surgery had been a "raging success" according to a man he'd seen only once while hardly conscious. AJ remembered the doctor's name and the pasted-on expression of sympathy, but not much more. Fitzpatrick was the man's name. He could remember that only because his brother Ace's middle name was Fitzryan. The Fitz-sies.

109

The raging success of a surgery had replaced the burnt flesh peeled from his torso, neck, and legs with synthetic tissue and skin. The team of trauma surgeons and specialists had removed the shrapnel and stitched the wounds, all while combating a critical case of cerebral hemorrhaging. AJ's original prosthetic chest plate, shattered, as it were, had been swapped out with a shiny new nanofiber-woven breastplate, courtesy — once more — Deckar Applied Sciences.

Thanks, team.

The good Doctor Fitzpatrick and his surgeons had replaced his fractured ribs with reinforced alternatives and installed two new Type-A prosthetic arms. The best part: they televised the entire surgery for paid viewing on Unicom Network's *Surgery TV* channel.

None of this surprised AJ. He was not just a State Defense Consortium asset, he was also very much their merchandise.

Or am I just being pessimistic?

As a Unit One agent, AJ had made more high-profile arrests and neutralized more targets than any other SDC official, including Sergeant Chris Calderon. His face was plastered throughout Sun City in the form of State-sponsored adverts and marketing partner adverts. He was a celebrity now and the face of the SDC's commitment to a crime-free Sun City. Why else would they spend so much keeping him vertical?

110

Maybe they actually give a shit about the work I did.
And maybe they want me back, doing more good work.

Or maybe I'm drinking the Kool-Aid.

AJ reached with a foreign hand for a paper cup on the bedside tray. He picked up the cup, careful to not crush it, and tilted its contents into his mouth. *Tap water.* He could tell by the copper aftertaste, and that aftertaste was lithium. He groaned and threw the cup to the floor. Despite his misery, it wasn't lost on him that only two decades or so prior, before the rise of neurotrigger, picking anything up with prosthetic appendages would have taken months, if not years, to achieve.

"Nurse!"

The sergeant waited. He could see the shadows of people coming and going beneath the door.

"Nurse! Doctor! Water!"

He looked for the call button that should be hanging on a dongle next to the bed, but found only the empty port where it was once plugged.

"What the hell, man..."

He wanted to scream profanities until someone was forced to quiet him, but reminded himself this wasn't the first time his gig had gotten him laid up in Eden Medical, and it was not likely to be the last. Over the course of his seven-year career in Unit One, he'd been shot (multiple times, multiple times), stabbed, burned, and beaten. He'd taken a sword to the gut, knives to the torso and arms, and even a throwing star to the head.

111

This is different, though…

And maybe it was. Sure, this wasn't the first time he'd suffered severe bodily injury, but it might be the first time he perhaps should not have survived it.

Somewhere along the way…

I forgot I was mortal.

As AJ lay in bed, tethered to an IV rack, humbled, depressed, and scared, he remembered what a Titan woman called "Royal" had once told him. "Everyone gets touched," she'd said by way of threat before escaping arrest for the umpteenth time.

Rachelle Perceval…

He hadn't thought about Royal, one of many nemeses that had come to stand out in his career, in a long time.

What Perceval had meant was that no matter who you were, no matter how strong, how wealthy and connected, you were vulnerable so long as you called Sun City home. And there was truth to it. He knew it now with certainty and wondered just how he had ever come to forget it.

AJ Moore, Unit One sergeant and State-sponsored bounty hunter, had been *touched*. And touched something proper.

Looking down at a pair of prosthetic arms that still stunk of factory oils, he groaned. He could not feel them yet. "Feeling," *true* feeling, or anything close to it, would come through tactile response and neurotransmitter in time, if he was lucky. The brain had to accept the new signals and adapt. Until then, like a parent peering into the room of a deceased child, the mind would continue to look for something that was no longer there, and return to him in its own anguish nothing but phantom pain. By now, his true arms, what might have been left of them, were no longer even evidence and most certainly cremated.

"Nurse! Water!"

Frustrated, he gagged loudly and slammed a metal fist into the side of the bed. The same spiteful nurse that had assumed he understood Spanish-speaking television had likely been the one who'd positioned his bed in some cruel purgatory between upright and flat. He searched for the button to raise the head of the bed, but couldn't find it. It was probably attached to the call button dongle that had gone missing. He gave up and lay there, probably literally dying of thirst, and stared at muted, poorly subtitled melodrama.

It was as AJ's mind and eyes wandered that he finally noticed the figure standing in the corner. It waited just beyond the light, large even at some significant distance. Tall and menacing. In his drug-induced haze, the figure seemed impossibly vague. Dark matter in the shape of a person.

"Who's there?"

Is that you Diedre? Are you here to curse me from beyond the grave? Are you here to finish the job for lying to you? For failing to save you?

No response came, but AJ could hear the shifting of tarpaulin, like the wind against a tent.

"Who's there, goddammit!"

He propped himself up in the bed and tried to move his legs. He reached for something, anything that he might use to fend off an attack, all the while wondering if the drugs and fear had stolen his sanity. He grabbed the tray table stand. "Fuck you, Diedre! I tried, man!"

At this, a man stepped into the light. He wore an olive-colored poncho, torn and sewn many times over, tossed over one shoulder to free a sleeveless left arm. Beneath that, he wore black trousers and a tight-fitting grey-and-orange thermal: the colors of the State Defense Consortium's *other* special unit, Agency Zero. On the visitor's waist was a wicked blade that swung as he approached. His boots were heavy and left dark tracks across the lime-colored linoleum that AJ could only hope were mud. Beneath the man's arm was a box.

"Stay in bed," his brother told him. "And calm down."

"How long have you been standing there?"

"An hour and twenty minutes, give or take."

His brother's voice was gravelly and dry. His words were delivered slowly and precisely, chipped away with no sense of inflection, of self. It was the voice of one who did not speak but rather left words behind for anyone who might be interested. It was a voice as familiar to him as the one in his head. And sometimes it *was* the voice in his head.

"What the hell, Ace! You scared the shit out of me."

"Stop yelling," Ace told him. "You'll draw unwanted attention."

114

"Unwanted by you, maybe. I'm dying of thirst."

"Stop yelling." As his brother spoke, his face twisted and pulled in unnatural ways, as scar tissue tugged at his lips and cheeks. One such tear pulled at the corner of his mouth so that even when his mouth was closed, a canine showed in a kind of permanent sneer. Similar scars littered his sleeveless arm in deep trenches and covered the whole of his body beneath the uniform.

AJ's brother looked down on him with a pair of hazel eyes that might have belonged to a wolf, so devoid of pity did they appear. It was a look that frightened others, but to AJ, it was a look as familiar as any known to him. Before the scars, before being "the Major," before "Iron," before all of that, he was just Ace Fitzryan Monroe. And AJ knew that beneath the large, brooding, and intimidating exterior was a man willing and capable of shouldering terrible burdens in the name of comrade, family, and country.

"Saw the whole debacle on TV," Ace told him. "You should be dead by all accounts." Those cool hazel eyes took inventory of him. "How do you feel?"

"A little like you," he replied.

Ace produced the other arm from beneath his poncho, his right. It was silver and rusted in spots. It creaked as he held it up and flexed it. He smiled and his face looked nightmarish beneath the meager light. "But I still have my left. I'd say you've beaten me."

"'Beaten you?'" AJ scoffed. "What, are we in a race?"

115

"To oblivion, perhaps. But aren't we all?"

AJ wondered what was in the box. His brother wasn't the gifting type.

"How do you really feel?" Ace repeated.

"I feel like I've been blown up and sewn back together. What do you mean, how do I feel? I feel like crap."

Ace put a finger to his own temple and drummed it. "I mean up here."

"You've been through worse," AJ told him, knowing that it was true.

"I'm me, you're you."

You have a point.

"Still got that silly hairdo, eh?" the Major chided.

Instinctively, AJ's hand went to his head. In the poor lighting, he thought he saw Ace's eyes trail the movement of his hand.

"I must look a hot mess. Laid up for a month without so much as a shave. Roots probably all grown out, crappy beard growing…"

"And what difference does any of that make? Does your appearance make you?"

He sighed. *Please tell me you didn't come here to preach, Ace.*

"Of course it doesn't," AJ replied.

Ace paced the small hospital room, appraising nothing in particular before he found Deadbolt propped against the wall.

116

"Hoh!" he exclaimed, shifting the box beneath his arm to his right hand so that he could pick the blade up with his left. He weighed it.

"An impressive stroke to split the car. Despite the outcome, you and 'the bandana' put on quite the show. Not much in the way of government work, but still, quite the show. And that's all that seems to matter these days…

"I suspect that next time you'll get yourself killed," Ace added blandly.

"Um, thanks?"

"Why did you approach the suspect?" he continued. "That was foolish."

"Rena tried to warn me, but I didn't listen. I thought I could knock the grenade away or something."

"Technically speaking, it was her fault, your tech detective." Ace was looking down at him from the corner of his eye, his brows raised.

"Rena? It wasn't her fault."

"Sure it was. She was immersed in Libra. Her job is to act as your eyes and ears, to protect you from threat through counsel."

"Ace," AJ said, more sternly this time, "it wasn't her fault. Diedre pulled a grenade. Nobody could have seen that coming."

"Funny," Ace said, "I thought I'd read she'd thrown a stun grenade earlier in the chase. Shouldn't take a prophet to figure out she was probably carrying more." Ace shrugged but continued to drive his point home. "Your commander is running a loose ship."

Holding Deadbolt out before him, Ace studied it, as dawn stole through the curtains. "This is fine craftsmanship, perhaps the old man's finest," he said, thankfully changing the subject. "And a one of a kind, if I recall."

"Yeah. Te-Mea only made one."

"Have you been to see him?"

"I've been busy, as you can see."

Ace frowned. "The old man gave us a home, shelter from the cold. He got you in school and gave me work. Without his help, I never would have gotten you back from the MFA."

A Ministry of Familial Affairs youth detention center had been AJ's home for the two years following their mother's death. AJ didn't remember much of the time he'd spent there and Ace shared only the tiniest of details.

I was so young that it really has no bearing on my life, AJ told himself, not fully believing it.

Of course, growing up in a State-run orphanage wasn't exactly something he shared freely. In fact, besides Rena, who knew more about his personal life than perhaps anyone in the SDC, no one in the unit knew.

After Ace, still a minor too at the time, managed to free him from the State somehow, a man named Te-Mea Herekiuha generously opened his doors for them.

118

Te-Mea ran a forge in Section Seven, the most famous in the State. And his weapons were hugely sought after, particularly his custom work. With the money his family brought in, he ran charities, particularly in the Veins, which was his home. Te-Mea's kindness was a debt they would never pay back in full, the kind of generosity that literally changed lives.

Ace had worked in the forge, and he'd attended school until they were both old enough to fend for themselves. All in all, they had lived under Te-Mea's roof for more than four years, and in that time the old man demanded nothing of them in payment. Nothing but honest work and decent grades.

"See him. We owe the man a great deal," Ace told him.

"I know." And yet, AJ couldn't help wondering. "Have *you* been to see him?"

"I have not. But I'm me, you're you."

"Ok. Whatever that means..."

Deadbolt wasn't the only gift from their one-time caretaker. The blade on Ace's waist, Soul Crook, was also the creation of Te-Mea, the man known as "Hammer Hands." Ace placed Deadbolt in the corner and looked at him with a curious expression, the box still under his arm.

"I have a confession," the man known by most simply as "The Major" said. "I told myself that I would not blame you if you quit, after this."

"Oh?"

"But the truth is, I would. I would blame you. In fact, I would hate you for quitting."

AJ propped himself up in the bed. "Hate is a strong word."

"That's why I chose it. You see, AJ, I'm going to need you. Events are in motion that cannot be undone." The way Ace said "events" stood out to AJ. His brother kind of hissed the word, as though the word itself angered him. "I'm going to need you, when these things come to pass. I'll need you and perhaps even the rest of Unit One."

"What are you talking about?"

Ace stroked his chin. He shook his head momentarily, as if debating with himself. After some time, he said: "The Eight, AJ. They're real."

"The eight what? I don't understand."

"Of course you don't. Not yet. Not yet, but I will show you." Ace's eyes seemed to glimmer, as though he held some divine secret for which he had no words. After several awkward seconds, he continued. "Men shouldn't be ruled in secret. Secrecy subverts man's right to self-determination, to redemption. And these... *people*..." Ace clenched a metal hand that creaked loudly as the fist grew tighter, smaller. His jaw was clenched, his nostrils flaring. "Do you understand?"

AJ didn't, but he let his head move in some random direction of accordance.

"Do you understand?" Ace asked him more forcefully, moving closer to the bed. He placed a hand on AJ's shoulder.

120

His grip, like his moniker, was iron. "That mankind deserves the right to choose!"

"Yes," AJ replied. "Yes, I understand that mankind deserves the right to choose."

But choose what?

"Good." Still gripping his shoulder, Ace gave it a good squeeze and shake, the way one might appraise cattle. "Hurricanes, wildfires, and earthquakes are the least of our worries, brother. Consolidation of power has given rise to a new race of man, something sinister. Something that seeks to privatize your right to live.

"Does that make sense?" Ace held his arms out, palms up like a tightrope walker. "It's all a balancing act, almost chemical in nature. They can take from us for so long before those who do not sleep, like white blood cells, are forced to react."

AJ nodded, but he didn't understand. He didn't understand any of it. And worse, this tone, the voice coming from his brother was unlike any he'd ever heard. Sadness crept into his chest as he looked up at those searching, wild eyes. Ace wasn't right... and he wasn't making sense. And, as the light of day began to steal shadow from the room, the lines under his brother's eyes and the way his pupils juked made Ace look frenzied. AJ reached for his brother's hand, only to see it yanked away. Ace paced for a while in silence, struggling with something, clearly. As he did so, the contents of the box under his arm shifted, thudding occasionally.

121

"Do you know how many candidates there were for Unit One, viable candidates that you leap-frogged?" Ace asked, his voice less demanding now.

AJ frowned thoughtfully, but ultimately had to shrug. "A lot?"

"Eleven hundred and change."

"Well, in my current condition," AJ replied, "I don't know if I should thank you or throw something at you. It's kind of hard to be grateful for a job that just cost me eighteen percent of my natural mass."

Ace ignored the comment. "I made sure you were chosen because I know what you are capable of. I did that at some great sacrifice to my own career, influence, and access."

"Thanks, I—"

"You don't have the luxury of being a follower anymore. You've endured much and have become too hard for that," Ace continued.

Ace might as well have been talking to himself, about himself. AJ just stared at his hands. He looked up once more when the sound of Ace's booted footsteps started moving towards the door.

"Get better, little brother." Ace offered a mannequin's smile and looked down at the box in his arms. "I almost forgot. I got you something." With a toss, the box hit the bed and bounced. AJ leaned forward — no easy task — and caught the box before it could fall to the floor. He thought for a second he heard a sigh of relief from his brother.

122

Holding the cardboard box, AJ knew the contents already. He'd known the moment he heard the items shift inside and the rustle of wrapping paper. He tore the generic wrapping paper from the box and pulled the lid off. Inside was a pair of shoes. He held one up. "Whoa."

The sneaker was a mock-laces slip-on, matte grey and with a white sole. As he turned it in his hands, the upper, vamp, and tongue shifted to black to match the black metal of his new hands. When he set the shoe down onto the baby-blue bed sheet, the shoes shifted color to match. The toecap of the shoe was white and matched the flat skater's sole. The shoes would go well with anything, but especially khaki or darker shades of denim.

"You picked these?"

"Who else?"

AJ laughed. "When did *you* learn how to dress?"

"A soldier has no need for fashion," Ace told him. "I've always indulged you in the vain hopes that you would grow out of it."

"Well, for someone with no fashion sense, you did good, bro."

Ace simply nodded, his face humorless. And with that, he was gone, a meandering trail of muddy boot prints left in his stead.

AJ sat and admired the shoes for a long while as the day came. He tried to put his brother's senseless rambling to

123

the back of his consciousness but couldn't, even as he admired the first gift his brother had ever given him.

Who knew you had it in you?

Smiling, he laid his head back and let exhaustion take him, the sneaker perched in his lap. Sleep came quickly and, for the first time in as long as he could remember, it felt welcome.

"Wake up, big man!"

His bed rocked like some tiny ship in a squall.

"I'm sleeping!" AJ protested, eyes still closed.

Still, the bed shook. AJ opened his eyes, shielded his face from the light. "I'm sleeping! What kind of hospital is this?"

A massive brown face was looking down on him.

It took AJ a moment to recognize the face. It was hidden now behind several months' worth of untamed silver-and-black beard.

"Jesus, Te-Mea, go easy," AJ told his old friend, one-time caregiver, and role model. "I'm a little banged up."

It had been nearly a week since Ace dropped by, and in that time he'd had many other visitors, some welcome, others not. Chris and Chief Williams came as a duo. They mostly talked work: open cases and what was now being called the Diedre Incident in particular. They shared what little they'd gleaned on what drove Diedre to kill herself, an act that AJ himself actually couldn't remember witnessing. When they left, it was on Hallmark words of encouragement, very perfunctory.

Dice had come a few days later, at an ungodly hour and stinking of whiskey. He stayed longer than any of the others. They played cards and spent a lot of time just watching television and goofing off. Dice's visit had been segmented by cigarette breaks innumerable, until AJ finally authorized the deputy ex-yakuza to pry the window open and smoke inside. In their time together, they were very careful not to talk shop.

The press came in teams, the sessions always prefaced by an hour-long makeup session for which AJ was secretly grateful. They brought a stylist who gave him a new look and much-needed shave. They asked about the incident in pre-scripted, softball questions and took photos of his new arms. At the end of each visit, AJ reviewed the press' work and worked with them to rephrase or omit anything he didn't care for. A blurb that revealed too much about the case, a photo that made him look tired, whatever...

Rena did not come and, though disappointed, AJ was not surprised.

Now, Te-Mea stood in the same place Ace had, with a toothy smile splayed across a spherical head twice the size of most. As he surveyed the room with his massive tattooed arms folded, he grunted sounds of approval. Te-Mea's beard was long with bolts of grey, and touched his chest. He wore oil-stained coveralls, on the chest of which was the logo of the

Iron Horse forge. When the big man smiled, his eyes were little more than slits.

Seeing him made AJ smile uncontrollably.

"Got yourself banged up good, eh?" the blacksmith said.

"Yeah, a little."

"It was on the news!" Te-Mea said excitedly. "The whole thing — you getting all blowed up — was on the news!" As the big man spoke, he jabbed in AJ's direction with a finger the width of a ballpark frank. "The whole block thought you was dead. But I told them, 'No, AJ's tougher than that.' Remember when them boys from Hilltop jumped you and left that shoe print on your dome? That time, yeah, I thought you was dead. But a little explosion like this one? 'That's nothing,' I told them."

"It's good to see you, Te-Mea," AJ said, tears stacked just behind a stubborn frown.

AJ wanted to be strong, but the old man's face was like the sight of rescue to a castaway. It sent an already weakened resolve spiraling. He turned away and wiped his eyes with his bed sheet. "It's been too long…"

"It's okay there, big man. Take your time."

And he did. This was the first time he'd cried since losing his arms and nearly his life, and he was finally in the presence of someone who'd seen him cry many times before. He let it out and, when he was done, felt a thousand times better.

When the tears subsided, Te-Mea lifted the half-sleeve of AJ's gown with a finger and admired the new arm beneath. "DAS Sure-Grip," he said with a whistle. "Factory casing and what looks like DAS dynamic tissue as well." Te-Mea poked his bicep. "Yep, you can tell. Go on, flex it."

AJ reluctantly flexed his arm. Te-Mea grabbed the bicep in his massive hand and squeezed. In the last week or so, his brain had begun to adapt to the signals being sent from the tactile receptors in his arms, providing a kind of distant, numbed version of "feeling" upon touch. He could feel the old man's vice grip, but not the pain that would have accompanied it before.

Te-Mea was visibly excited. "See how the tissue gets harder, the harder I squeeze? Like a rock. That's dynamic tissue density. This arm will stop a bullet!"

"Terrific! Can't wait to get shot."

"You could have used these before you got blown up, no?"

"What kind of paradoxical shit…" AJ sighed. *Never change, Te-Mea. Never change.*

"The SDC spared no expense to get you back on your feet, *tokoua*," the old man continued. "You should be grateful."

Sunlight shone through the window, framed by a sky that was the color of Shallow Ocean. Outside the room, Cedar Medical Center was bustling. Nurses, patients, doctors, and visitors passed in a steady stream, all while the incessant beep of medical equipment played baseline to a symphony of hurried speech.

"Can you walk?"

AJ shook his head but, to be honest, hadn't tried.

Te-Mea reached down with his massive arms.

"Whoa! What are you doing?"

His blankets fell to the floor, as he was hoisted up into the man's arms. "You've got to check this out," Te-Mea told him, as he carried him to the window.

"Why are you carrying me like I'm seven? Put me down."

"Take a look!"

When AJ looked out, he saw a sea of people. "What is that? What are all those people doing?"

Te-Mea laughed heartily. "They're here for you."

"No way."

Te-Mea worked furiously with one hand and finally got the window open. He yelled out to the people below, though they were stories up. "Hey! Hey, y'all!" he bellowed. "Look at what I got here. Mr. 'Skyy Shoes!' Mr. 'Blowed Up!'"

People began to point, and an exclamation rose from the crowd.

AJ could feel the blood rushing to his face. "Te-Mea! Put me down. Put me down, man!"

Te-Mea roared in laughter, his great chest heaving and threatening to catapult AJ out the window. "Isn't that something?"

"Te-Mea! For fuck's sake!"

"Language! You're famous, bro. It's all skinny, drugged-out gen-betas, but what the hell, right? You're still young." The old man made a shocked face and looked at him sincerely. "Wait… you didn't get your pecker blowed off, did you?"

AJ's face was hot, and he didn't have the strength to break free. The embarrassment of being displayed half-naked like the bride of some mad buccaneer was more than he could handle. "Te-Mea, please, please put me down…"

Te-Mea was looking down on the crowd with an expression of admiration. "The cable shows have been showing these artsy-fartsy stories about you. So sad, some of them. I mean, none of them are true but they make you look like a hero. I should have sent them a story about the time you pooped your pants in school because you were too scared to raise your hand in class."

"Te-Mea, please, I'll pay you. Put me down. And, had you seen Mrs. Crutchfield, you'd be scared to raise your hand too."

Te-Mea laughed. "I'm going to set you on your feet, AJ. Are you ready?"

The last time the sergeant had set foot on the ground, it was on the pavement of the 101.

"All right," he said after a moment's hesitation. "Let's try it."

The cold linoleum sent a welcome discomfort up his legs, even as the muscles in his ankles and feet groaned into life. They were stiff and resistant to the weight now cast on them. AJ shifted his weight from one foot to the other. His body was stiff, his muscles weak. Nevertheless, being vertical felt good.

"Wave to them," Te-Mea said.

AJ looked down at the masses. It wasn't all gen-betas and, as he studied the crowd, it wasn't all of a welcoming sort. He saw signs spattered among the masses: signs toting the reversed "5" of the anti-government protest group Fifth Estate. Nevertheless, he threw a hand up. He then kissed his fingers and flashed two fingers in a peace sign. The crowd responded in cheers. He shut the window.

"That's something, isn't it?"

AJ had to admit he was pretty shocked to see a gathering of that magnitude, supportive or otherwise.

"Yes. Yes, it is."

Te-Mea helped him take his first few steps in over a month. As they slowly crossed the room, past the bed, the muscles in his feet popped audibly. Eventually, his joints warmed and loosened and something like strength began to surge through his body. They made several laps around the room, Te-Mea showering him with words of encouragement the whole time. When he'd had enough, Te-Mea released him and he reached the bed on his own strength and climbed on.

The effort, while exhausting, galvanized his spirit. "It's good to see you," he told his one-time guardian.

Te-Mea waved a hand dismissively.

"How's the old neighborhood?" AJ asked, having not set foot on their block in the Veins in years.

"It's bad."

"It's always been bad."

"Not so, AJ. But you're young. You're too young to remember the '20s. I mean, they say it's getting better. They *say* crime is down and what have you, but I say 'no way, man' to that nonsense. Just the other day some poor bloke stood up on the Pollue Street Bridge and blew his brains out."

AJ was aghast. "What the hell for?"

"Dunno, man. Times are bad. People ain't got work. Things keep up this way, I might have to move my shop. I've been looking at real estate in Section Four, over by the mall there."

"You can't move the Iron Horse. That's all the Veins has!"

"I don't want to move. It's my home, *tokoua*. My wife, God bless her, gave me my Mahina there. We made a home there for many years, a happy home. It's where I got to meet and help raise two fine boys, for a time."

The words threatened to draw tears once more. "Thank you, Te-Mea. We can never repay you."

Te-Mea, shaking his head, continued. "I've had to hire security, man, just to keep the thieves out. The old

131

neighborhood is dying. Shops are closing; houses are getting all boarded up. We've got Titans slinging their garbage on every corner and shootings every night. They say it's getting better, but they're lying, AJ."

AJ could only shake his head. "The Pollue Street Bridge," he said, having not said those words in more than fifteen years. "Mahina and I used to catch crawfish down there."

"Yeah, and the two of you would come back all muddy, grinning like some big-time whalers."

They laughed.

"Oh, you're up," a voice said.

A woman and small boy were standing in the doorway. The woman held a bouquet of flowers and wore a lovely yellow dress. Waist-high next to her was a swarthy, stern-faced boy of probably eight years of age.

My God... Mahina?

He hadn't seen his fellow "whaler" in about six years. She'd grown. She was tall, probably close to six feet, and her gorgeous yellow dress with the embroidered lilies fell weightlessly over a lithe frame. Her face was different and yet very much still the same. Her eyes were large, her pupils a perfect brown.

"Hey, Mahina," he greeted her lamely, suddenly at a loss for words.

"Hey, you," she replied with a familiar closed-lipped smile.

She was a year his elder and Te-Mea's only child. Her hair was curly and brown with serpentine locks that fell on either side of her face. A lifetime ago, the boy he used to be had played as best friends with the girl she used to be.

And now we are grown.

Mahina handed him the flowers, a hodgepodge collection of generics. The tag read $17.99 and he would have reimbursed her that very moment if he could without being rude. Instead, he smiled and paused awkwardly, not sure what to do with them before setting them in his lap. "Thank you."

"Of course, silly."

The little boy at Mahina's side looked up at him from the foot of the bed with intensity. His cheeks had smudges on them, and his fingernails were black with dirt. His face was cheeky, his nose small, and something about the child reminded him of one of those infomercials about child soldiers in Venezuela.

"Who's this?"

"This is my friend Bandit."

"What's a 'friend-bandit'?"

Mahina laughed. "His name is Bandit, dummy. And he is my friend."

"Hi!" the boy screamed. "My name is Bandit!"

"Yeah, I caught that. Hi, Bandit."

The boy's clothes were ragged, covered in what looked like axle grease. He wore oversized workman's boots and a beat-up golf glove. Propped on his head was a pair of scuba

133

goggles that he probably thought were sunglasses, and when he smiled several teeth missed the meeting.

"What kind of name is Bandit?"

The boy shrugged and looked away, frowning.

Mahina slapped AJ's shoulder hard. "Play nice! It's Vietnamese." She turned to the boy with a soft expression. "And it's a good name."

"It's a great name," AJ added. *Bandit* is *kind of a badass name*, he thought jealously.

"He wanted to meet you," Mahina told him. "Believe it or not, the boys in the Veins look up to you. Not sure why, but you're a bit of a hometown hero to them." She was smiling and the sun was catching the tiny specks of green in her perpetually smiling brown eyes.

AJ looked to Te-Mea, who was staring out the window at the crowd. "Still taking in strays, old man?"

"Oh, we tried. But this one's made a home out there. He knows them streets better than any of us. Sometimes he comes to visit…" Te-Mea shook his head, looking down at the kid. "But I can't make him stay. He's young but he seems to know what kind of life he wants to lead, and ain't need no instruction.

AJ wanted to speak more on the topic, spout the dangers of Section Seven, of which they were all well aware. But then he imagined the boy's alternative. The Ministry of Familial Affairs was no place for Bandit or any kid like him, just as it had been no place for him.

134

Hell, the MFA has more deaths-in-custody than the Sun City Police Department.

"How's my girl?" Te-Mea asked, changing the subject. "How's... what did you end up calling her again?"

"Deadbolt."

"'Deadbolt?' What kind of name is that?"

"I dunno, just seems to fit. It's like I'm 'closing the door on crime.'"

Mahina coughed into a fist with a huge grin. "Corny!"

AJ gave her a look and she stared back defiantly with wide eyes. He could practically hear her voice from many years ago in his head: *"Watchu gonna do, fool!"*

"She's good," he told Te-Mea. "You built her to last. She's over there if you want to take a look." He thumbed to the corner where his one-of-a-kind machine-sword lay propped against the wall.

Te-Mea walked over and picked the blade up. He held it aloft — much the same way Ace had — and admired his own craftsmanship. "You know, I get a lot of requests from people about this weapon. 'I want the Unit One sword,' they say. 'Make me Sergeant Moore's sword!'"

It was funny that whenever Te-Mea mimicked other peoples' voices, which was often, it was always in a whiny, nasally voice. To AJ, it really said a lot about how the old man viewed people in general.

"Maybe I should take her home with me and make copies," the old man said with a wink.

135

"Sorry, that's registered property of the State now."

Te-Mea looked genuinely concerned for a moment. "They haven't tried to copy it, have they?"

"I won't let them. Perps have tried to get their hands on it, though."

"I bet! I made a wicked little stinger for Ace too. How *is* your brother?"

"He's..." The only word that came to mind was *crazy*. When he failed to continue, Te-Mea recognized his discomfort and gave him a pass by continuing on his own.

"Ace is too serious. Always too serious," he said with a frown. "He's carrying too much weight, I think. I should have done more to talk him out of the military. That kind of life just ain't good for the heart, ain't good for the soul. Besides, they got machines an' shit to do the fighting now. They don't need us poor folk."

You couldn't have talked him out of it.

For as long as he'd been alive, AJ's brother had talked about fighting, war, and soldiering. Even before he joined the military, it was all he could talk about.

"You know, when I built that knife for him, I had second thoughts," Te-Mea continued. "Part of me wanted to hand him a welder instead and make a smithy out of him. But even back then, I swear, all that boy talked about was tanks and fighter jets and guns. I swear, he sounded like he was in love with it or something.

"That blade though, Ace's… that might have been my masterpiece."

AJ threw his hands up. "I thought Deadbolt was your masterpiece."

"Hell, I cooked that thing up taking a crap."

"Dad!" Mahina exclaimed, covering Bandit's ears.

Te-Mea waved a hand at her. "Yeah, sorry, ok? Anyway, do you know if he still has it?"

"He does, and he carries it everywhere he goes. He calls it 'Soul Crook.'"

Te-Mea smiled, his cheeks two tomato-sized balls beneath his eyes. "That's good to hear. That name, though…"

Ace's Soul Crook was less blade and more handheld chainsaw. Tiny rails ran the full length of the blade, silently carrying shards of stainless steel. If left jabbed into a surface, the blade would eventually cut its way free. Like Deadbolt, it was a one-of-a-kind machination of the most gifted private weapons manufacturer in the State, and perhaps anywhere.

"Can I see?" the boy asked, pointing to Deadbolt.

Te-Mea looked to AJ, and he nodded with a slight smile.

Standing the weapon up on one end, Te-Mea let Bandit hold Deadbolt. The weapon, while extended, was a foot taller than the grungy boy, and he beamed as he held it.

"You just made his day," Mahina told him. "Bandit? Do you want me to take a picture?"

137

The boy ignored her and began pulling, trying to unsheathe the blade. Te-Mea took him by the shoulders, his hands the size of the boy's torso.

"Now, now. Let's not fire that thing off in here." He took the weapon away and leaned it back against the wall. Let's go get some chips out of the vending machine and let your hero rest, huh?"

"He's not my hero," Bandit retorted emphatically. "I don't have a hero. I *am* a hero!"

"That's great," Te-Mea said, shaking his head. The old man extended him a hand. "AJ, it was really good to see you. I need to get back to the shop soon. Don't be a stranger, huh?"

Te-Mea led Bandit to the door. Before the blacksmith and the boy left, Bandit told him matter-of-factly, "It was cool when you cut that car in half! I seens it on the telly." He smiled a random-toothed grin and let Te-Mea escort him out.

"It's 'seen' and 'television,'" he could hear Te-Mea say from the hall.

AJ couldn't help but smile. A few more grey hairs and pounds around the waist notwithstanding, Te-Mea looked the same as ever. With Te-Mea and Bandit gone, AJ glanced at Mahina. She was sitting in a chair next to the bed, texting. She met his gaze and slipped the device into her bag. "Well," she said after a moment. "It's been a while."

"It has."

"How come you've stopped visiting?"

Because I hate memories, he wanted to tell her. *Because the old neighborhood reminds me of either the hunger-filled bad days or the good days I'll never see again.* Instead, he shrugged and murmured he hadn't the time.

She stood from the chair and took a seat on the bed, rolling the intravenous pole aside to make way. She put her feet up and scooted next to him until the two of them sat shoulder to shoulder on a bed barely made for one.

When Mahina was six, her mother, Ana, had died giving birth to what would have been a brother. And Te-Mea, in typical Te-Mea fashion, never even considered remarrying. He even remembered the old man once saying emphatically, "I'm *still* married."

Rather, Te-Mea poured his soul into his daughter, his forge, and his community. And his love and dedication showed nowhere as fiercely as in the face of his daughter, who had grown into a magnificent woman.

AJ and Mahina had been as good of friends as Ace would allow. It was Ace who never let him forget they were guests in the Herekiuha house. As such, AJ was never allowed to eat more than would sate the pain in his stomach, and never allowed to ask for anything that wasn't offered. Likewise, he was never allowed to play or study with Mahina outside the gaze of either Te-Mea or Ace himself. At the time it didn't make sense, but as he felt her warmth next to him, he understood clearly what his brother had hoped to prevent.

139

Mahina lifted his arm and placed it over her shoulder, nuzzling into him as though they hadn't been but contacts on social media for the last five years.

"It's heavy," she said.

Blood surged through his face and he could not help but let her fragrance fill his nostrils. It was the scent of maybe raspberry.

"How's school?" he asked, staring at the muted television, frozen.

"School? I'm done with school, AJ. I finished school like six years ago. I have a job now. I'm a graphic designer. Though I'm sure it's not as exciting as being a celeb super-cop."

"'Exciting.' Yeah, I suppose it's pretty exciting learning how to hold a fork again."

"I'm sorry. I didn't mean—"

"I'm just being a sourpuss," he told her.

In truth, his adoption of prosthetics required a fraction of the effort previous generations had had to put forth. And being a MOD prior to losing his arms had made adjusting to the drugs, physical therapy, and overall acclimation far less of a nightmare. It wasn't easy, but it also wasn't as bad as it would have been fifty years ago. He tried to remind himself of that when the self-pity took on too much momentum.

"I'm actually having a pretty smooth recovery."

"I'm really, really glad to hear that. So, you'll go back as soon as you're all better?"

140

I would *blame you*, Ace's voice in his head reminded him. *In fact, I would* hate *you for quitting.*

He sighed and ran a hand over his freshly shorn hair. They'd left a nest of tight curls at the top and tapered the sides down nicely. "I don't know, honestly. I mean, I'm recovering but that doesn't change the fact that I nearly died. And I don't know if it's the meds they have me on or what, but I'm not sleeping like I used to. Weird dreams, sweating. I wake up and forget where I am."

"Talk to the doctors, AJ, but I think that's normal," Mahina replied. "After all, you've just been critically injured. I imagine most people don't recover the way you have, as fast as you have. You should feel blessed."

AJ resisted the urge to respond sarcastically and simply nodded.

After some time, Mahina changed the subject. Her head was resting against his chest now. "You know, it's gotten really bad back home."

"Your dad told me."

"There are dealers on every corner now, literally. And gambling is everywhere. Prostitutes too! You guys should come clean it up."

"I don't think it works that way, Mahina. Unit One isn't the SCPD. We have a mandate: high-profile arrests, high-profile targets. We're like specialists. It's the SCPD's job to stay on top of that kind of thing."

"Well, they're doing a shitty job."

141

"I'll let them know."

"Good," she said, smiling. "Matter of fact, where can I file a formal complaint?"

AJ chuckled. "See that bedpan-looking thing over there? It doesn't look like it, but there's a magic hole at the bottom that sends the contents right to the desk of Police Commissioner Harding. Naturally, I crap in it also."

"Smartass!" She slammed a fist into his gut playfully. "What's that big stick over there for, if not to kick bad guys out of good neighborhoods?" Her face was very close, her scent dizzying.

Before he knew what was happening, her face was pressed into his.

AJ would never have admitted that he'd imagined her kiss, but in this moment, those secret desires and unsent love letters all came rushing back. At once, he was a boy again. Her lips were confident and drew him in until his arms found their own way around her. In that moment, she both robbed him of his wits and gave him the strength to continue. When their lips finally parted, he felt drunk.

Mahina just smiled that perfect, dimpled smile of hers, her eyes laughing. "I've wanted to do that since we were kids, but I saved it for when you really needed it. And so, guess what?"

"What?"

"Time to get back to work, punk."

[12:11] <W8less1> How are you feeling?

[12:11] <SgtMooreU1> Like a drug dealer blew up in my face

[12:11] <W8less1> lol

[12:11] <W8less1> Looks like you haven't lost your sense of humor.

[12:12] <SgtMooreU1> Ace came to visit me

[12:12] <W8less1> And?

[12:12] <SgtMooreU1> He didn't make a whole lot of sense

[12:12] <W8less1> You don't say

[12:12] <SgtMooreU1> I mean it. he was talking about "things brewing" he kept talking about "the eight"

[12:13] <W8less1> The Octumvirate.

[12:13] <SgtMooreU1> the what?

[12:13] <W8less1> Conspiracu theory

[12:13] <W8less1> *conspiracy Some people think the State Defense Consortium is a front for something else; a secret council of Illuminati, Freemasons, lizard overlords or something. It's an old conspiracy, old as Western Civ. Before the SDC, it was the Fed, then the Council on Foreign Relations, then the lodges, the Vatican, etc. The SDC is just next in line to hold the label. Anyway, this will interest you: While investigating the Diedre Incident in Libra, I was confronted by someone.

[12:13] <SgtMooreU1> inside Libra?

143

[12:13] <W8less1> Yes. The woman pulled rank on me too, froze me out.

[12:14] <SgtMooreU1> I don't understand

[12:14] <W8less1> She suspended my account mid-session and left me in a state of limbo. Stuck between booted and logged in.

[12:14] <SgtMooreU1> thats pretty weak

[12:14] <W8less1> It may not sound like much, but it was actually pretty fucking terrifying. The crazy part is I suspect it was Agency Zero.

[12:14] <SgtMooreU1> what?

[12:14] <W8less1> She knew my name. She knew the system. People don't just hack Libra. She was inside!

[12:15] <SgtMooreU1> why?

[12:17] <W8less1> I don't know but the timing was too convenient to ignore. I feel it's related to the Diedre Incident. Do you remember what Diedre screamed before she killed herself?

[12:17] <SgtMooreU1> honestly, the last thing I remember is the wreck and SCPD units flying overhead

[12:17] <W8less1> Well, she said "Ouroboros." I feel like there's more to this case than just a suicide and Ouroboros is the key. In fact it wasn't until I starting trying to find info on Ouroboros that the woman showed up. If we can find Ouroboros, whatever that is, we can find out who or what drove Diedre to kill herself.

[12:19] <SgtMooreU1> saying her death wasn't a suicide seems like a bit of a leap, but let's say you're right. If someone drove Diedre to off herself, it had to be that bastard Luther

[12:20] <W8less1> Talk about "bit of a leap." Oh yeah, about that. I brought up your theory to Williams.

[12:20] <SgtMooreU1> and?

[12:21] <W8less1> He's not convinced. You know who else isn't? Mason. After the briefing he lambasted you. It got pretty bad and I was about to say something but of course your boy beat me to it.

[12:21] <SgtMooreU1> Dice?

[12:21] <W8less1> Who else? I think it's was cute how he sticks up for you. He shut Mason down brutally. You know how he can be.

[12:21] <SgtMooreU1> my man. anyway, Luther is behind this. he runs the titans, I KNOW IT.

[12:21] <W8less1> How do you know this, exactly?

[12:23] <SgtMooreU1> the truth? I remember when Luther first came to Sun City. he started this campaign called the Clean up Section Seven Initiative or some shit. I was in high school at the time and I remember he even came to our school and gave this speech on all the things he did in Africa and how he was going to revive Section Seven. I even remember thinking back then this guy's full of shit. Anyway, his "Initiative" was just buying up public land, parks and stuff. Old warehouses, entire chunks of the red light district. He was going to turn all of this property into community rec centers,

145

tutors, affordable daycare, clinics and stuff. Everybody in the Veins thought this guy was the greatest thing since open bars. Everybody except Te-Mea

[12:29] <W8less1> Your guardian?

[12:32] <SgtMooreU1> Yeah, he told me luther was full of shit and he was right. All that property went to the corporations who're just sitting on the property, leaving it empty. And then the titan's moved in. The rest is history. He's a rich piece of shit and if he ain't the titan boss, he's funding them. I'd bet my… well I ain't got much left to bet but I know I'm right.

[12:34] <W8less1> Being right helps no one. You've got to prove it. His record is spotless. I mean, at face value he's a paragon. I'm looking at the start of my dossier on the guy now. There are photos of him with POTUS, the CEO of Unicom, the CEO of Coastal Power. Huge donations from his foundation. Enormous amounts to finding a cure for chondrosarcoma.

[12:34] <SgtMooreU1> what's that?

[12:34] <W8less1> A type of cancer. I don't know AJ. I think you're wrong on this.

[12:35] <SgtMooreU1> Trust me. you hear things on the street. You start to hear a thing enough times it becomes true. Make sense?

[12:35] <W8less1> Not one bit actually.

[12:36] <SgtMooreU1> well if you hear a name enough times . . . the same name from the same kinds of thugs. It means theirs a higherarchy and people know about it. It means people have been taught who to respect. Name=respect. It's tough to explain

[12:37] <W8less1> Let me first respond by applauding your spelling of "hierarchy"

[12:37] <SgtMooreU1> whatever

[12:38] <W8less1> Well, there's good news. Williams put us on him, sort of. We're not to engage directly. But I personally don't see the harm in checking out some of his properties, and maybe that museum of his. Yeah, maybe start there. I'll talk to Williams, convince him to let Dice check the place out. Maybe send Chris too.

[12:38] <SgtMooreU1> really? That would be awesome Rena. By the way, back to the Libra thing. You're logged into your personal account now. And you probably were then too. you don't suppose that's why you got the boot?

[12:39] <W8less1> I thought of that. Only thing is: the lady addressed me by name, painted my name on the horizon actually. Creepy. Really disturbing shit

[12:39] <SgtMooreU1> Wierd

[12:39] <SgtMooreU1> *Weird

[12:48] <SgtMooreU1> Rena you still on?

[12:56] <SgtMooreU1> guess not :(

[12:56] <W8less1> I'm here

[12:56] <SgtMooreU1> What do you do in Libra at 1 in the morning?

[12:56] <W8less1> Watch you

[12:56] <SgtMooreU1> hahaha creeper!

[12:56] <SgtMooreU1> Srsly tho, doesn't your fiancé ever wonder where you are? You spend more time immersed than you do with him

[12:57] <SgtMooreU1> having second thoughts?

W8less1 has ended the chat session.

7: What the Wolf Sees

[Heavy breathing] "Stay awake! Close your eyes again and I will cut them from your head!" *[Indecipherable]* "— murderer!" "Look at me!" "No…" *[Scraping sounds]* "One man can save you! Only *he* can save you! Go on, repeat—" *[Indecipherable]* "I will show—" *[Indecipherable]* "You *will* learn to beg, or you will crawl forever!" *[Screaming][Metal scraping]*

- Audio Recovered December 3, 2071

Dinner was prefaced with cocktails: two boulevardiers in quick succession. When the meal arrived, it was placed gingerly before the premier by deft hands, and an emptied bread platter was spirited away. His cocktail glasses, too, were removed and replaced with a bottle of Riesling and a pair of spotless Auslesen.

"Looks delicious," Premier Macek said.

The Major wasn't sure if Macek was expecting some kind of confirmation, so he offered none.

People fluttered around His Excellency like sprites, dousing the man with unwarranted praise, even as he moved to stuff his face.

"May I pour your wine, sir?"

"Is everything to your liking, Your Excellency?"

149

"Mr. Premier, sir, if I may but bend your ear for—"

Without responding, Macek covered his glass with a hand and waved away the wine, the waiter, and the others who buzzed around their table. When they were gone, the premier looked up from his meal and frowned. "You won't eat, you won't drink... Some would consider that disrespectful."

The Major ignored the comment and watched as the most powerful man in Sun City went back to carving cubes out of an oversized cut of ribeye. With his hands in his lap, the Major watched as the steak, the aligote, and the mushroom bordelaise were devoured with nary a pause for breath. After that, the premier set to the task of punishing a trio of South African lobster tails, drenched in butter and smoked paprika. Soon after the crustaceans' grisly defilement, the wine, too, evaporated.

It wasn't so much the raw gluttony that bothered the Major, but rather the sound. Smacking lips, guzzling, belching, and the clumsy clank of fork and knife on porcelain. These sounds were maddening.

Chandeliers as large as automobiles spun overhead, misdirecting light in infuriating inconsistencies. Waitresses darted about to the sound of Brahms' *16 Waltzes*, and the smells of roast duck, of buttered artichoke, of garlic and herb–roasted chicken filled the air. The smells of basil and white wine–tossed prawns, of pan-seared scallops, and of beer-braized, mustard-encrusted lamb smothered the Major's senses, unmistakable, and it turned his stomach upside down with hunger.

When Macek was done, he balled his napkin up and plopped it onto the table the way a welder would remove his gloves. The politician then reached into his coat and withdrew a clove cigarette. As he placed it to his lips, the white-gloved hand of a waiter appeared from nowhere to light it. The Major watched in silence as the billows of smoke wafted towards him, filling his nostrils with their slow death. And Macek took lengthy pulls, exhaling from his nose like a shuttle launch, pausing only to pick at his teeth for yet more food. As the premier smoked, the Major regarded him with open disdain. To this, Premier Macek paid no mind.

The restaurant was filled with Sun City's elite. Wealthy businessmen, politicians, State officials, and celebrities sat in intermingling clusters eating, drinking, and celebrating their status. Many of the restaurant's guests stared at their table or made silly faces of exaggerated recognition. They appraised the Major's well-worn trousers, orange thermal, and mangled face as one might a fender-bender. He could feel their disgust but, like the premier's look of boredom and disappointment, these things were inconsequential and powerless to faze him. The Major did not need their approval. Rather, the approval and acceptance of the bourgeois might make him question his path in life, and at a time when he could afford zero doubts.

As the Major sat slovenly amidst the wealthiest Sun City had to offer, he imagined the restaurant blown out like so

151

many shops in Tokyo's Shibuya ward during the Korean invasion.

"Can I take these from you, Your Excellency?"

"Dessert, sir?"

Macek waved dismissively.

The Major watched as the table was cleared quickly. The second hollowed bottle of wine was replaced with another tall glass of bourbon. The black, plasma-like vermouth swirled amongst the ice cubes like blood. The wait staff knew the order with which the premier preferred to imbibe, and not so much as a word need be uttered.

Macek was growing irritable with him; he could see it in the old man's furrowed brows, and the way the man toyed with the giant gemstone on his pinky finger.

Dinner hadn't borne the opportunity for serious discussion. Dinner hadn't borne the opportunity for restraint — or manners, even. Not for the drinks and constant buzzing waiters. The Major, too, was growing anxious, bothered by the noise and light.

"Speak, Major. If I've had a less pleasurable dinner companion, I don't recall."

"You mistake me for a gigolo."

"Ha! Good luck in that line of work." Macek blew a column of smoke his way. "You haven't the looks for it." Making himself laugh seemed to loosen Macek up a bit. "Why don't you eat something? The State is paying for it, obviously."

Obviously, the Major thought. "I had a big lunch in the cafeteria," he lied, "complete with a slice of cake."

Throughout the restaurant, people pretended not to watch him. They pretended not to whisper to one another, not to wince and make faces to one another. They pretended not to gesture and point covertly at his face.

If the body could process the stare of strangers in some kind of photosynthesis, the Major would be gorged — dead, maybe, from a burst stomach.

"Excuse me," a voice chimed in. She was probably in her mid-forties and wore an onyx gown and boa. "I'm *so* sorry to interrupt—"

"Then don't," the Major told her.

The woman blanched and was about to leave when the premier beckoned her to stay. "Ignore my friend here. He's a stick in the mud. What can I do for you, darling?"

The old man's leer at her low-cut gown was appalling.

"I just wanted to thank you personally for vetoing the measure to build that hideous housing complex on the border of Seven and Two. It would have utterly ruined the skyline for one of our rentals."

"You're quite welcome, dear."

That complex would have provided low-income housing to those impacted by your property hoarding, the Major would have told her in another setting. After the wraith of a woman departed, he waited for the premier to finish his cocktail. As Macek drank, more people lined up to kiss the ring. The Major

153

took their sideways glances with the stoicism of a golem and took great pleasure in their inability to meet his gaze.

When the premier's drink was done, he stood and bellowed for his coat. They left the restaurant with no invoice, no wrist scan, and no discussion of cost, and stepped out into a drenched but bustling Section Three. The premier wore a black overcoat that caught the wind and snapped. The Major's own poncho did the same. The air was warm, but the rain came at them sideways on shearing winds.

"This storm will pass us, but there is another, much larger, in the works," Macek said. "They suspect it will maintain the level of category five when it gets here."

The Major noted the lack of concern in the premier's voice.

"Then I suspect we'll raise the Rampart, repelling the storm?"

The car pulled up to the curb, and the driver ran around to physically open a door that was fully automated. The driver held an umbrella over them as they entered, the premier first.

"'Raise the Rampart' he says." Macek's laugh was scornful, as he shifted his weight to get comfortable in the limo. "It costs the State somewhere in the area of eleven million dollars for every minute that wall stands, and nearly as much just to raise it."

The Major shook his head. "Wait. Not raising it will put sections Four and Seven at risk of flood. Lives could be lost. The damage could be beyond repair in places."

"*Old* places…"

Sitting with his hands on his knees, the Major made a fist. "You mean *poor* places. Even still, the long-term cost of repairing these damaged areas will far outweigh the initial losses accrued by protecting them."

"You look to counsel me on spending, Major? Besides, we've already deployed oceanic cooling units in the storm's path, as well as artificial cloud cover. If the typhoon hits us, it'll be little more than a shower by the time it does."

"You're contradicting yourself."

"Please. I was merely making conversation. Do you think I would be so cavalier if I thought the typhoon — which isn't a typhoon yet — posed any real threat?"

The Major did not break gaze with the premier, nor did he reply. Rather, he crossed his arms as the car pulled away from the curb.

The rain drummed against the hull of the limousine, soothing. Behind the stained-glass impressionism of streaking raindrops against a colorful, nighttime Sun City lay the hue of disproportioned uncertainty. The Major sat in silence, opposite the premier, and watched the city move past in a fractured collage. Outside, the red and blue flashing lights of their hover unit escort could be seen.

"Oceanic cooling has yet to yield true results," the Major said after some time. "If the technology works, why do we still have—"

"First, you go the entire meal without speaking," Macek interjected, "then when you do have something to say, it comes in the form of gubernatorial advice." He reached for the minibar and began making himself another drink.

And yet, you're quite drunk already.

In his fumbling, the premier spilled bourbon on his overcoat and batted at it irritably.

My silence isn't accomplishing anything, the Major thought.

"The organized crime rate has nearly doubled since Unit One was founded, and the SCPD has somehow, in that time, become even less effective. The police have allowed the murder rate to triple in parts of the city. A quarter of the police force is in its twenties and less than five percent have served in any branch of the armed services. Community trust in the police is at zero. Both parties could be thought of as belligerents. This campaign to draw fresh recruits is serving only to fill police ranks with delusions of fame and fortune because we've allowed the notion that anyone can be Unit One to spread, largely thanks to the tireless gum-flapping of the Ministry of Media. This places the brunt of true enforcement on the SDC and this most recent incident proves that the measures in place are not working. The Sun City Police Department is ill-managed and Unit One is a joke."

"Which leaves your Agency Zero the only party blameless..." Macek replied. "Convenient."

The Major shook his head. "It's the truth."

156

Macek sipped his drink and scoffed. "Was it not your brother — the sibling that you personally recommended for the unit, no less — that allowed this embarrassing event to take place? I mean, how hard would it have been to simply put a bullet in the woman's skull and move on?"

"Half-brother," the Major corrected, "and any fault to be had should be on the unit's tech detective. The suspect was in the Queue and, while neutralization was well within the Sergeant's right, apprehending the suspect could have aided an ongoing investigation into the Titans."

Macek's eyes narrowed. "An investigation twenty years old."

"Ten years old, roughly," the Major corrected.

"And as long before that on the SCPD's docket, Major."

"Then perhaps it's time Agency Zero took over the investigation."

The premier ignored him. He sat staring out the window and drinking for several minutes before saying, "It's hard to see Sergeant Moore as even your half-brother."

"Why do you say that?"

"You're so different."

"How so?"

"You're… well, *you*, and he is, I don't know, interesting and *fun!*"

The Major wanted to slap the premier sober. "You're drunk."

"Thank you for proving my point," the old man said, smiling.

The comment irked the Major. "Is 'fun' what Sun City needs, Your Excellency?"

"I'll entertain you," Macek replied, sneering. "What would *you* propose, Major? What would you propose that our political scientists, statisticians, and consultants haven't thought of?"

The Major stared at him coolly, careful to not let the man get under his skin. He couldn't help but remember the once-charismatic politician who had been instrumental in creating the State Defense Consortium. But now, the premier had grown fat. He'd become a drunk in the years since his appointment. His cheeks were blotchy, and wobbled when he talked. His beard, which used to be kept at a respectable length, now touched his chest. Even his suit, while sinfully expensive, was untucked and unbuttoned down to his chest. The man had also, at some point, taken up festooning himself. He wore gaudy gems and a legacy timepiece encrusted with diamonds that hung from a chain in the style of previous century tycoons and robber barons.

As the Major spoke, he measured his voice carefully to mask the displeasure he felt at the sight of Sun City's great leader. "Sections Seven and Six are falling into complete anarchy, Your Excellency. It may not appear so on the surface, but between the Fifth Estate, the Huntsmen, the Minowara, and the Titans, there are more criminal elements than lawful

158

citizenry in those districts. At the same time, the clinics are overflowing and child abandonment rates are reaching epidemic levels. Unemployment, too, is at an all-time high, as is illegal immigration. The number of unregistered within city walls has thrown all serviceable statistical analytics for a loop. The black markets are surging, as is shadow surgery. Illegal weapons and MODS — like the suspect on the 101— are becoming more prevalent. The SCPD cannot hope to keep up. In short, Sun City is falling into disarray, and at an exponential rate. And none of this mentions the fact that many territories in Sun City proper are littered with tent cities."

"Slight embellishment," Macek said with a chortle.

"Perhaps from the comforts of uptown it may not appear so, but numbers don't lie. Actually — in this case — nor do the lack of numbers. One in fifteen is homeless in the Veins, Your Excellency. And if it's that bad this side of the Rampart, one can only imagine what's going on in the Outlands."

"You'll have to forgive me if I have my *actual* statistician confirm these claims, Major."

"Please do."

"Again, I hear only criticisms from you. Do you know what sets leaders apart from prol— from the rest?"

Prols was what he wanted to say: a term used by the bourgeoisie to describe the proletariat – the working class. It was a classist slur in Sun City, along with *plebeian.* These were terms the Major had been doused with many times growing up, like everyone else who called Section Seven home.

"Anyone can point out flaws," Macek continued. "Hell, I can list for you, from memory, a thousand things wrong with Sun City. Leaders, however, take it upon themselves to create solutions." He spilled his drink into his lap and cursed loudly. "You've clearly outgrown your current responsibilities, Ace, to have opinions on such matters. Perhaps we should find new work for you."

"During the war," the Major replied, "Section Seven thrived. Men and women worked and raised families. Shops lined the entire length of Market Street: *open* shops. Times were better than they are now, whether you would acknowledge that or not."

"Is that your suggestion, *war*?"

"Of course not. My suggestion is that we bring trade back to Sun City by enacting a few new policies: policies aimed at reversing what I see to be a downward trend."

"'Policies,' you say?" Macek sat up in his seat mockingly. "Well, let me get my pen, Major! I shall write these down."

Once more, the Major ignored the slight. "We begin by penalizing companies that headquarter in Sun City but outsource their workforces for labor and shipping. At the same time, we offer incentives to companies that employ residents of the State. Tax credits, low-interest financing, and bidding advantages on real estate. And for those who refuse to adopt

160

these generous policies and still seek to call the State home, expulsion."

"Expulsion?"

"Precisely that."

"You won't need the threat of expulsion, Major. Enacting policies like that will drive companies away."

"I don't think so. The carrot in this instance is preferable to the stick."

"No corporation of any size has ever been expelled from the State. We've no power over them."

"Absurd!" the Major retorted. "We've *every* power over them!"

The premier's mouth was agape, but the Major continued nonetheless. "We enforce stricter immigration policies and begin deporting illegals immediately. Perhaps, once Sun City's eight sectors are at a respectable quality of life, we'll embrace more liberal ideologies, but right now we do not have the luxury. Next, we enforce registration. Seventy percent of this city's first-time offenders are unregistered and thus untraceable by Libra. Then we—"

"Let me stop you." Macek held up a hand, smirking. "What you sound like, Major, is a fascist."

"Mark my words, Your Excellency, the corporations will have their day at the helm if not reined in soon. They'll pillage Sun City for every scrap of profitability and leave once the wealth and human capital has dried up. And once they're gone, the gangs, the mafia, and the punks will pour into this

161

Emerald City you've built here in Section Three. And your clubhouse friends will have no place to smoke their expensive cigars, or drink their thousand-dollar ports." The Major knew he'd already said too much, but Macek's drunken leer and smirk let loose his tongue. "Or are the corporations already at the helm?"

"Careful, Major." The premier held a finger out lazily. "I've indulged you because, frankly, I find your ravings entertaining, but I will not tolerate this accusatory tone one moment longer. 'The corporations will have their day?' What does that even mean? You sound like that crank who leads the Fifth Estate. The corporations are, as they have ever been, integral to the success and growth of the State. Your suggestions, Major, betray a frighteningly underdeveloped understanding of the complexities of governance. And frankly, Ace, it's a bit disappointing. As for your talk of 'deportation,' 'forced registration' and whatnot, we've tried these things in the past to remarkable failure."

The premier cleared his throat exaggeratedly, preparing his rebuttal. "First of all, we've made great strides despite your cynical opinions. Libra now covers ninety-six percent of Sun City. That's eyes and ears on every corner, Major. Funding for the State Defense Consortium has tripled, largely in part thanks to the companies that you would see deported. Deckar Applied Sciences, for example, has plans to build another campus, this one in Section Four, and the *Musée de Conflit Historique* has opened its doors to international praise, promising to be a

162

source of tourism and revenue for decades, maybe centuries, to come." Macek took a drink and swirled the liquid, the cube of ice clinking proudly. "Think about the jobs created by both of these endeavors. And in December, we host the big fight! Projected to be the single largest sporting event in the State's history. On top of this, the new DAS-sponsored arena, the venue for the fight, is nearing completion and will open its box offices soon. And so grand in scale is the new arena that we believe it will put us in a good position to draw the World Cup in '72." He belched long and loud, clutching his gut. "So, phooey and pa-tooey to your negativity, Major!"

I've just wasted my time and breath, the Major thought.

Looking out, he watched Section Three fall into the distance, a glimmering collection of spires in whose shadow sprawled the low, dark skyline of sections Seven and Two. To the people in Seven, the new arena was nothing but another light on the horizon, another reminder that they were removed from the real Sun City, the Sun City that mattered.

Your words are hollow, the Major thought bitterly. *The advancements you've touted will do nothing for the Veins or the people living there.*

The Major cursed himself for his inability reach the premier. Countless were the number of times he'd played this conversation over in his head. And all of it was for nothing. *I've never been good with politics. I haven't the patience or charisma for it.* It was time to advance the discussion in another direction. "It is my understanding that Councilwoman

163

West intends to place Unit One on security detail for this year's Liberty Day Parade."

"Unit One was her initiative," Macek replied. "She believes that their presence will increase attendance."

Unit One was my *initiative,* he wanted to remind the old man. "Then put them on a float. They can wave like idiots and throw bouquets into the crowd. The unit is for show anyway."

"I'd run that idea by her if I didn't already know what she would say."

"My men grow restless, Your Excellency. Security for the parade has always been a responsibility of Agency Zero. Unit One lacks the manpower, the leadership, and the experience to cover such a massive event."

"As for 'manpower,' the council has approved tripling the size of Unit One. Not to mention, they would have the entire SCPD at their disposal."

"Tripling Unit One's numbers doesn't resolve this issue, Your Excellency. There's no way you'll have even a single agent trained up in time for the parade."

"The council has seen great success in the Unit One initiative," Macek said after some thought, completely deflecting now.

The Major sucked his teeth before he could catch himself. "You must mean 'success' of the monetary kind. Because I look around and see—" He stopped himself, clenching a fist. Retreading that conversation would do no

164

good. "I respectfully ask that Agency Zero remain in charge of security for the parade. For one more year." He paused before adding, "Unit One and the rest of the SCPD can continue to act as auxiliary enforcement if need be. This will show that the Consortium remains committed to the security of the event above all else." He studied Macek's face, looking for any indicator that he was being heard. When he saw nothing but the shimmering eyes of an intoxicated man, he continued with a sigh. "After this year, I will step down as the head of Agency Zero and allow for a younger commander, more in line with the 'new generation' approach the SDC has chosen. My successor will support Unit One as the exclusive face of civil defense in Sun City."

The premier blinked several times. "Are you resigning?"

"As you've said, it might be time for me to do something else with my time. I'll step down, under the condition that Agency Zero remains vanguard one more year. Also, under the condition that Agency Zero be preserved in its current capacity or greater, under the new leadership."

The old man smiled slyly. "You think your job is enough to save the entire battalion?"

"I'm no fool. It's been clear for some time that the SDC looks to sunset Agency Zero. All I ask is that you begin with me and give someone new a chance to lead the unit."

"And you would walk away? Willingly?"

"Under these conditions? Absolutely! What have you to lose? If a new face and perhaps even a new role in the SDC can't boost the Agency's popularity, you can still disband it. You've lost nothing but a year or two in salaries. Salaries that we both know are comical when compared to those of Unit One and other divisions."

"This is true." Macek rubbed his chin. He pondered the offer for a long time before responding. "Your team will manage security this year, and you will retire in a formal address to the city as part of the ceremony. After the parade, we will discuss the next chapter of your career. Specifically, the Consortium has need of an experienced soldier to assist in managing federal influence at the borders. You'll maintain your salary but leave Sun City immediately upon resignation."

"And my men?"

"Too early to tell. Maybe we'll try a new commander or maybe we'll repurpose the unit somehow. Perhaps they'll be absorbed into Unit One — those deemed a good fit by the Ministry of Media."

The Major choked to swallow. *The Ministry of Media deciding who's fit to protect the people of Sun City...* His mouth was dry and he suddenly felt dizzy.

Premier Macek extended a hand. "Are we in agreement, Major?"

Taking the old man's hand, the Major squeezed confirmation into it.

"Good," Macek replied, wiping his hand on his coat. "The illustrious career of "Iron" Ace Monroe will end in 'its current capacity' with all of the pomp it deserves, and I will finally be rid of you nipping at my heels!"

"For a while perhaps," the Major replied, trying very hard to make his voice light. "But someone has to keep you honest and moderately sober."

"Well, you've done a bang-up job this evening."

Outside, the dimly lit streets and curbside garbage, coupled with the labored jostling of the car over potholed streets, told him he was in Section Seven. The limousine pulled up to the curb as rain continued to fall in steady sheets.

"I'll never understand why you come here. Is it gambling?"

The Major shook his head.

"Let me guess, a woman?" Macek laughed heartily at the notion.

"Good evening, Your Excellency." The Major opened the door and stepped out.

"It's a woman, I bet," the old man mumbled drunkenly before remembering something. "Major!"

The Major peered into the car, the rain already cold against the back of his neck.

"Don't let me down," Macek told him sternly.

The Major smiled, the first genuine smile of the evening. As he did so, he could feel the scar tissue on his face pulling in all directions. He knew he looked grotesque, especially in the sputtering streetlight. "Oh, I won't, sir."

The Major walked the streets of the Veins, listening as the rain played Taps on his poncho. He walked for blocks, the low hood shielding him from much of the cold and wind.

From the basin of Section Seven, the towers of Section Three could not be seen but for their glow: a permanent artificial sunrise. He moved past familiar homes and businesses; places he'd once begged for work, ironically boarded up now and black save for squatters' fires and the occasional flicker of a lighter. As he strode through the borough, his presence sent the creatures of the night scurrying. Drug peddlers and addicts cleared at the crunch of his boot steps on broken bottle and vial. Many of them called into the dark, warning others of his approach. The Major committed to the shadows, of which there were plenty, his hand never far from Soul Crook. Like this, he crossed the length of the city's most dangerous district. Along the way, he passed a great mural adorning the sides of a supermarket that had changed ownership so many times it now sat bereft of identity. He paused. In all his years, never had he stopped to inspect the work. It depicted in washed-out colors some kind of civil uprising. In it, the people of (presumably) the Veins were being led by men and women carrying flags of the Fifth Estate. Standing in their way, and depicted as some kind of faceless and tyrannical army in black and orange, was the Major's own

168

Agency Zero. They carried guns and axes, and beneath their oversized boots were bodies whose bullet wounds bled into a sea of crimson paint spelling out the words: "Trust Your Eyes."

Trust my eyes indeed.

Critics of the State Defense Consortium and Agency Zero had long painted both organizations as something undemocratic. But their arguments were invalid and full of holes. After all, what did security have to do with democracy? Just as one cannot worship, share values, or raise a child in a home without walls, democracy is not possible in a state without security. The two things were not intertwined so much as interdependent, with security, of course, taking precedence.

Close to his destination now, the Major reached into his pocket and removed a cylindrical device roughly the size and shape of a pencil. Across the street, an autonomous and newly installed closed-circuit camera watched him. It was one in the innumerable array that made up the Libra surveillance network. He held the device up, its silver matching the silver of his artificial fingertips. He was about to press the button when he remembered an important detail. He transitioned the device to his natural hand and pressed the button. A blue LED flashed three times before turning red and steady. In that moment, his prosthetic arm went limp, just as the red 'recording' indicator on the camera went dark, and the streetlights went black. A smart-ad selling over-the-counter antidepressants vanished, and two blocks away a car stalled and rolled lamely through an intersection.

Satisfied, the Major crossed the street, his right arm swinging at his side uselessly.

The cylindrical device was a prototype tentatively being called an *EMPen* by the small group of people aware of the device's existence. In fact, the device was far more than a simple electromagnetic pulse emitter. It could also send radio and microwave signals, making it a reliable detonator over short distances. The device had been a gift from Premier Macek, procured from someone at Deckar Applied Sciences, likely Elaine Jones-Gutierrez, who had intimate ties to the premier.

Confident that he was no longer being tracked by the surveillance network, the Major entered a narrow alleyway. Once well inside the alcove, he pressed the only other button on the EMPen. Light returned to the neighborhood outside the alley, and he could hear generators beneath the street rumbling back to life.

At the back of the alley, a rusted fire escape, bolted into the brick, served as an emergency exit for a single window. The Major moved to climb the ladder, then realized that something was off. Things in the narrow cleft between the abandoned buildings had shifted. The dumpster, for one, had been moved. Garbage lay strewn about where previously there was none, and… there was a smell. It didn't take him long to source the disruption and the odor. Curled up on the pavement was a body. Rain, in a steady pour from the roof, doused the inert figure.

What have we here?

With a boot, the Major turned the body on its back. The man was young, his eyes closed: sealed shut with yellow excretion from his nasal passage. Protruding from his chest was a knife. The knife was a frame-lock folding knife and very, very cheap. The rain was muffling the corpse's stench, but by morning, that would change. With the same boot, the Major turned the murder victim onto his face and cursed the man for getting killed on his doorstep. *And with a seven-dollar knife, no less...*

He jumped and pulled the fire-escape ladder down, his right arm now squeaking back into functionality. Once up, he pulled the ladder up with him. Two hidden latches unlocked the window, which served as the only way to enter or exit the building: all other entrances were boarded up or walled in brick.

Inside, the track lighting flickered on, and upon recognizing the Major, the ceiling-mounted machine-gun turret disengaged its intruder neutralization protocol. He closed a thick sliding metal door over the window entrance, upon which the door locked itself with three thick bolts, one atop another, that spanned the width of the door. There were no windows in his bunker, and the twelve-hundred-square-foot loft was walled with the same red brick inside as outside. The furniture selection was modest and practical, the most expensive trapping being a six-foot steel-plated gun safe that stood alone in the far corner of the room.

On paper, Major Ace Monroe's home was a condo in Duluth Towers in Section Three, in an affluent neighborhood close to city center. In reality, he visited the condo only to refresh its appearance, dusting, shifting things about, swapping out the contents of the fridge, and otherwise leaving DNA in places where DNA should be. In truth, he had never left Section Seven, never left the Veins. This was and would always be his home.

Beneath the apartment was an out-of-business pawnshop, which he'd also procured the title to, making the purchase through a front real estate firm put together by Agency Zero's tech ops specialist. He left the shop boarded up to keep potential neighbors at bay.

It took a few moments for the effects of the EMPen to fully wear off. When the sensation of control over his right arm returned fully, he pulled the poncho over his head, the rainwater spattering on the hardwood floor. He hung it on a hook that was bolted into the wall and removed his shirt and boots. These he dropped into a pile beneath the poncho, the shirt there to catch the rain.

For his dinner with the premier, he'd worn an artificial epidermis over his prosthetic arm. This he peeled away and left atop the shirt and boots. He hated wearing it. It was a tone shy of his actual complexion, and even the colorblind could spot it

172

as fake. Plus, the fingertips had long torn away, leaving his silver, artificial digits exposed.

Ace crossed the room and opened the safe. The lock was a combination style, old school. Inside were a pair of rifles, one 5.56 NATO in caliber, the other magnetic; a dozen magazines fitted with depleted uranium rounds; three handguns; grenades — concussion, stun, smoke, chaff, and EMP; rope, maglets and zip-ties; knives, a flak jacket, and a recently procured prototype handheld railgun, branded with the Deckar Applied Sciences logo. Also, reduced and hanging at eye level was a partially functional replica of his brother's sword, Deadbolt.

He took his pistol from the holster on his belt and placed it in the safe, on a shelf next to a stack of banded notes. The EMPen he set in its charging cradle. Soul Crook he left where it belonged, at his side. He closed and secured the three-inch-thick safe door and crossed the length of the room to the kitchen. As he walked beneath the bluish light, the torn and re-bound flesh of his torso caught the light in unnatural angles like a disco ball.

In the kitchen, he opened the refrigerator. Inside were Tupperware containers of pre-cooked steak; boneless, skinless chicken breast; and freshwater salmon, all labeled and arranged by preparation date. He took containers of fish and steak and placed them on the counter. Next, he removed a five-gallon pot of cold, pre-steamed brown rice. He stacked the steak and fish high on a black porcelain plate and paired them with two large

173

scoops of rice. He placed the remainders back in the fridge in chronological order and took his plate to the couch.

"Pops!"

[I'm here, sir,] his man replied via neurotrigger.

"We're on for one more year. After this year's parade, though, my career is over."

[And this is to your liking?]

"It's neither here nor there."

The old soldier called Pops grunted, and Ace could imagine his mentor's massive arms folded. *[I take it you didn't call just to tell me that, sir.]*

"Damn right," the Major replied. "I'm going to send you several dossiers. With Hollow Black's help, I want everything on the people therein, and I mean everything."

[Affirmative, sir.]

"And get the core unit together for a briefing tomorrow."

['Core unit,' sir?]

"Hollow Black, Dozer, Legion, yourself and one more... someone reliable. Preferably someone from Tech, someone who knows their way around servers and databases."

[Might I suggest Jennings, sir?]

"No names, Pops, you know that... What's his callsign?"

[Bugger me, Major. I must be getting senile. Of course no names. He's codenamed 'Witch Doctor.' Former Corps.]

"Is this the mask collector?"

174

[That's him. Right strange fellow, but reliable as they come.]

"Have a briefing on the dossiers ready by oh six hundred hours." The Major disconnected from neurotrigger and sat for a moment, eating with his fingers.

"Projector," he said loudly enough for the receiver on the opposite side of the room to hear.

As the projector brought the wall to life, he called for Unicom's local news station. The day's events played out and he watched, grimacing and picking at the cold food with his creaking metal hand.

When he was finished eating, he would go back out into the rain to move the body that lay outside his home. He didn't know, or much care, where he'd dispose of the corpse. And then it occurred to him…. The idea tickled him and, for the first time in a long time, he laughed heartily.

8: The Sixth Way

" 'What do I think of Chris?' Well, when I first met him I thought he was kind of a jerk. The way he never talked just kind of rubbed me the wrong way. I figured it was because I'm just an informant and he's a big-time tracker. But over time I realized that's just who he is. He's not a talker and I can appreciate that. He's a bit too stylish in my opinion, but I guess you have to be, to be a musician these days. Have you heard him play? He's not bad. 'Course he plays under a pseudonym like he's not proud to be Unit One, which is weird to me. But yeah, you ask what I think of him, I think he's a stand-up guy."

- Unit One Deputy Informant Yamazaki "Dice" Daisuke

"Deputy Informant Daisuke? You mean 'Dice?' He drinks on the job, which is unacceptable, even for an informant. I mean, he still carries a gun, you know? He smokes as well, which is also prohibited. Some days he reeks as though he hasn't showered in days. For me, I guess it's just that a lot of people put their necks out there to see this guy turn his life around and he just kind of floats through it all; like he's either unaware or simply doesn't give a damn. On top of that, he's as immature as Moore and when the two are together it's a wonder we get anything done."

"Blobitecture" is what they called it. "Poopitecture" is what he would call it. The five-story complex was seamless on the outside, its walls monochrome and designed (he imagined) to resemble molten metal. The entire structure was built atop and onto the face of a cliff overlooking the Bay of Sun. Shining and amorphous, the structure appeared as silver emerging from the forest to pour into the ocean.

As much as Dice hated artsy style architecture, even he had to admit the *Musée de Conflit Historique* was an impressive structure. And as they cruised along the coast headed for the museum, he couldn't help but let the building draw his eye.

"Oh no, he was quite drunk, I assure you," the voice on the radio said.

"Oh really?" the other show host responded.

"Without a doubt. Go back and watch the interview with Lisa Vega. He slurred the word 'Valhalla.' He couldn't say 'Valhalla.' She had to say it for him."

"Too funny."

"Yes, the heavyweight champion of the world couldn't pronounce the name of the league he fights for."

"And you're sure it wasn't his accent. You know he's not from here."

177

"Yeah, I know. He's some kind of Brazilian-Viking hybrid."

[laughter]

Dice turned the radio up and Chris, riding in the passenger seat, immediately turned the volume back down.

"Vega was looking hot."

"Smoking."

"You know who wasn't there…"

"You and me?"

[laughter]

"Us, of course, but neither was Sergeant Chris Calderon."

At this, Dice took his eyes off the road and looked at the sergeant with wide eyes. "They're talking about you!" The deputy informant raised the radio's volume up and covered the controls with his hand.

"I love those Triumph commercials," the show host continued. *"He's so dreamy."*

"For those of you listening, those are the words of a forty-year-old straight married man with three kids."

"So? The wife doesn't have to know."

[laughter]

"So dreamy," Dice mimicked. "Did you know you were 'so dreamy?'"

Chris sneered and reached for the radio, but Dice was quicker, slapping his hand away. "Why didn't I get an invite?" he asked.

178

"Because no one knows you and even less people like you," Chris replied.

"Ouch."

"*Sgt. Moore wasn't there either,*" the radio personalities continued.

"*Well, we know why. In fact, on behalf of the station, our heartfelt prayers go out to the family of Unit One Sergeant Alec Moore.*"

"*His 'family' was there. At least his brother, anyway.*"

"*Real looker, that one.*"

[laughter]

"*That's wholly inappropriate!*"

"*That's why it's funny!*"

"*That's a war hero you're talking about.*"

"*I know! The* Musée *has a whole exhibit dedicated to his old Marine or Army unit.*"

"*Yes. For those of you who haven't been to the* Musée de Conflit Historique *yet. You have to see it. It is remarkable!*"

Dice took his hands off the wheel and clapped. "Yay, we're going!"

"Please turn the radio off," Chris asked dryly. "Or change the channel? These guys are the fucking worst."

Dice responded by raising the volume further.

"*Mr. Gueye has really built something special. And for those of you interested, there is an exhibit there from now until Liberty Day that—forgive me, but I have to read the message here... 'pays tribute to the Phoenix Battalion, the paramilitary*

179

unit that fought alongside the US Army and Marine Corps in the US invasion of North Korea.' For those of you who don't know who they were — are — they are a group of formerly wounded soldiers from various militaries around the world who underwent these insane surgeries to come back and fight as these kind-of-like super-soldiers, I guess. It's really a remarkable story. Anyway, the exhibit will be there from now until Liberty Day, and is called 'Resilience.' For tickets go to TMCH.com or call the Musée twenty-four hours a day, seven days at 88-233-3398."

"Nice segue. You fell into that ad spot with poise and grace."

"That's why they pay me the modest bucks. Well anyway, the Major looked terrific."

[laughter]

"Well, terrifically dressed. He was in his full uniform. What's it called?"

"What?"

"The full uniform? Military uniform?"

"How should I know? Isn't it just called 'full uniform?'"

"It's called 'full uniform, sir!'"

[laughter]

"We might as well take a break now and go to commercial."

"Yes. You are listening to Dave & Dave's Open-line Hour. Give us a shout at—"

Dice turned off the radio, even as Chris tried to glare a hole into him.

"What? Important information gathering. May end up being pertinent to the mission."

The winding, scenic Highway 4 had a recommended speed of twenty-five miles per hour. Dice pretty much ignored this, along with the "Do Not Pass" and "Watch for Deer" signage. Sixty-five was the speed with which he felt comfortable. "Do you want to go over the plan?" he asked his quiet partner.

"I didn't think we needed to," Chris responded, still glaring. "I'll infiltrate and look for, fuck, I don't know, evidence of malfeasance on the part of Luther Gueye, while you keep the security detail occupied, or did you have an *actual* plan?"

Dice shook his head.

Sergeant Calderon ran a hand through his dyed and feathered hair. "Just keep the guards away from me."

The sergeant's tone was light on manners and heavy on bossiness, two things Dice had never responded well to. Not as a deputy and not as yakuza. "You're a real peach to deal with sometimes, you know that? Between you and Mason, it makes me miss AJ more than ever. I hope he comes back soon, because this unit is in serious need of some personality."

Chris turned away, his eyes rolling first, up into that ever-present bandana that wrapped his skull. The bandana was part of Calderon's "look." The State Ministry of Media was

181

adamant that the SDC wanted visual consistency from them. They'd gotten so stringent lately that even a haircut required a formal request in writing.

Chris didn't look at him, but rapped his knuckles on the window as he stared out. "We're lacking personality, huh?"

"Yeah," Dice continued. "I mean, I don't care that you're socially awkward or whatever, but you don't have to be a dick."

"Socially awkward?"

"Yeah." Dice pulled a cigarette from his breast pocket and jabbed it at him. "Sometimes you go a week and say like two things, and they're always negative."

"That's not true."

"See?"

"That's not a true statement."

"Sure it is. I don't lie. I never lie!" Dice put the lighter to his cigarette and took a long drag. The smoke filled his lungs and felt great against the cool air. "I used to think you were some kind of experimental robot, programmed to depress people or something. But then I thought, 'why would a robot spend so much time on its hair?'"

Chris put a hand to his head. "Ridiculous! I use a conditioner. That's the extent of it."

The sergeant's hair was long and swept high into the air. The ends were dyed various colors and transitioned only at the roots to his natural shade of deep brown. His sideburns, longer than the hair on most peoples' crowns, fell down from beneath his bandana to sweep forward like wings. It was a hairstyle that defied gravity and wouldn't survive a minute if Sun City enacted a prohibition on hairspray.

"Liar!" Dice bellowed. "I bet you have an entire *bar* of conditioners at home. You probably have a live-in beautician. All that" —he searched for just the right word, flittering his fingers in the air— "*fluffery*, and I've never seen you with a woman!"

"I keep my personal and professional lives separate."

"Oh, we know," Dice scoffed. "What's your stage name? 'Crusher,' is it?'"

Chris frowned.

"'Crusher Calderon,' he mocked, taking his hands off the wheel to mimic a dance of some kind. "If you're going to adopt a pseudonym, hotshot, you might want to change the last name too. It's not like you're fooling anyone. Everyone knows who you are!" He pointed at the radio and raised his eyebrows. "'Soooo dreamy.' That's you, dreamy-guy! Getting the old radio dudes all hot under the collar!" Dice took them speeding around another corner on the winding highway and allowed the tires to break traction and the tail of the car to whip out. He wanted a reaction from his introverted partner. "It's not just me, either. I get people asking me all the time if you are some kind of robot."

"Funny."

"No, I'm Japanese. We don't joke about things like this. Not knowing if someone is human or an android is a

183

serious bit of business in Japan. There are entire teams of detectives dedicated to rooting out our would-be android overlords."

Chris shook his head, but a smile was cresting. "How about giving the cigarettes a rest for a while, huh?"

Dice took a long drag, staring Chris in the face as he did so. When he could take in no more smoke, he flicked the cigarette out the window.

"Disgusting habit."

"Yeah, I know, robot. You'll have to help me download some kind of anti-smoking protocol. I know you have one."

They exited the highway, and the car's heads-up display began plotting their course in curt audio snippets.

The town, now host to the *Musée*, was an old community just inside the border of Section Four. White Victorian homes, small dirt driveways, and a farmer's market, nestled in the bosom of an ancient forest. It was the kind of sector that could make one forget they were still within Sun City's limits. They drove on a small two-lane road, following freshly planted signs directing them to the *Musée*. They moved through a quaint but unmistakably poor neighborhood lined with abandoned cars and discarded furniture. And though their cruiser was unmarked, more than a few keen eyes recognized the State-issued vehicle as governmental and went scampering into hiding. As they drove, the forest around them grew denser until, just beyond the tree line, the shimmering smooth sphere of the museum's northern face loomed.

184

"Let me out here," Chris told him, in his typically bossy tone.

Dice pulled the cruiser up to the curb and watched the sergeant climb out. Standing curbside in drizzle, Chris removed his jacket, badge, and gun and set them on the seat. This left him with a short-sleeved white V-neck T-shirt and ballistic vest. The vest would stop most small-arms fire but, more importantly, emitted a surveillance-scrambling signal that would hide him behind a wall of white noise in the eyes of closed-circuit TV cameras. On the sergeant's belt were a black combat knife and a utility pouch that Dice knew contained a flashlight, wire cutters, and first aid kit. From his back pocket, Chris produced a mask that, when pulled over his hair, made his head look extremely large. At this, Dice smiled. "I would take the gun," he told him.

"If AJ is wrong about Luther," Chris replied, his voice muffled by the mask, "I don't want it coming back to the unit."

"Take the gun."

"If I have it, I may use it. If I use it, we're screwed."

"Without it, you may be screwed."

"Do your job and I'll be fine, Deputy. The most important thing is to look for anything that might confirm or dispel AJ's suspicions about Gueye. This is recon, nothing more."

Dice leaned forward so that Chris could see his face. "Calderon, I'd take the gun…"

185

Chris seemed to ponder it for a moment, but ultimately still refused.

With a sigh and a shake of his head, Dice extended a fist. "Be careful."

"You too," Chris replied, slamming a fist into Dice's.

With that, the sergeant took off running into the rain and dark, toward the redwoods and the *Musée* beyond. A prick of genuine concern touched Dice, as he drove the cruiser through an unmanned checkpoint and into the museum's parking lot. He chose a spot far from the entrance, where hopefully the vehicle would go unnoticed. Once parked, he stashed Chris' gun and badge in the glove compartment and balled the sergeant's jacket up to hide the white Unit One delta. Satisfied, he climbed out and removed his overcoat, albeit reluctantly. He dropped the coat into the driver's seat. With a sigh, he rolled his shoulders to get the knots out.

I swear that thing gets heavier and heavier.

Dice's typical role was now reversed. Where he would normally hide his affiliation with Unit One, on pain of death, he would now attempt to leverage it.

Lighting another cigarette, the ex-gangster crossed the lot. Beneath the left arm of his black Unit One jacket was his trusty revolver, loaded with six hollow-point rounds. Of course, if Luther was, in fact, the kingpin of the Titans, and the *Musée de Conflit Historique* his personal weapon stash, six bullets probably wasn't going to cut it.

The main entrance to the *Musée* was the typical triumphal arch, complete with a frieze depicting two ancient armies preparing to engage. The earth leading up to the archway evolved from gravel to well-placed stone slabs the color of steel, whose quartz glimmered in the rain. Once through the arc, he moved along a walkway of stone that split the forest in stark and memorable contrast. Flaming sconces lit the way to the museum and, in the night, the path seemed something out of fantasy. Along the way, Dice passed eternal rivals fifteen feet high to either side. Sculpted from the same stone as the walkway, their meticulously crafted scowls shifted in shadow. He read their brass placards: Alexander the Great meets Darius III, Charles Martel vs Abdul Rahman Al Ghafiqi, Napoleon and Gebhard von Blücher, Robert E. Lee meets Ulysses S. Grant.

Impressive, he thought, *but you forgot Ken vs. Ryu, the Yomiuri Giants vs the Hanshin Tigers, and Godzilla vs King Ghidorah.*

He flicked his cigarette at the booted feet of Grant and approached the ticketing window. There, a burly woman with a mustache looked up from a drawn till that she'd been counting furiously. She was bundled in a parka and scarf and wore a wool-knit cap. Checking her watch, she looked at him, slack-jawed.

"The museum closes in twenty minutes," she said.

"No problem, I'm meeting some friends here and then we're going to dinner."

187

"You're not going to find much to eat in Woodland at this hour and *Le Berger* is reserved for private parties exclusively, until the fifteenth."

"That's fine," Dice replied, applying his most charming smile. "We'll figure something out once I get inside and find them. I want in."

"I still have to charge you entrance."

"That's fine," he replied, readying his wrist for swipe.

"One adult?"

Dice looked around, momentarily perplexed. "Depends on who you ask."

"That'll be two hundred seventy-five dollars, please."

He snatched his wrist away. "Come again?"

"Complete grounds access for one adult is two hundred seventy-five dollars."

Crashing the gate would be one way to make my presence known... "Do you offer a police discount? I'm Unit One. I mean, not *really* police but we share a building with them. I'm kind of a celebrity, like Chris Calderon and AJ Moore. You know *them*, right?"

He held his badge up and turned around to show her the delta on his back.

"Who?"

"Look, I'll give you one-fifty."

"Two hundred seventy-five."

"For thirty minutes?"

"You can come back tomorrow. We have early-bird prices."

Dice thought about it for a second. *A matinee* would *be cheaper. But Chris is already out there in the woods and stuff...* "Listen, darling, there isn't a show on this planet worth two hundred seventy-five US." Actually, he could think of a few but didn't want to get off point.

The lady made a face that was genuine disappointment. "I don't make the prices and I'm new here. I don't want to get into trouble giving you a discount."

Dice sighed dramatically. "I guess I'm stuck. Thanks anyway." He swiped his wrist over the pay-pad at her window, and the register chimed.

Nonchalantly, she slid what looked like a third-century bronze coin over to him in return. "This token will get you inside. Do not lose it."

Dice picked up the coin. It was firm and heavy and felt authentic. With a squint to make out the fine engraving, he studied both sides. Some bearded guy riding an elephant on one side, and a shield-bearing man in a chariot on the other. He rolled it over his knuckles and pocketed it.

"Thank you," he said as she triggered the turnstile.

Past the gate, the pathway took him on a healthy jaunt through the redwoods. He could bypass the walk by way of an arched and elevated Segway but decided the walk was preferable. He smoked another cigarette along the way, cupping it from the rain beneath his fingers. The ocean-swept

189

wind kicked up the rich odor of earth and wood and accentuated the tobacco. He moved along the trail, mindful of puddles, his distressed leather boots finally on appropriate terrain.

Dice wasn't sure exactly how he was going to run interference, but was confident he'd figure something out once inside. If there was one thing he did well, it was drawing attention.

The *Musée de Conflit Historique* was unlike anything he'd ever seen. If asked to describe it, he would use the word "spongy." Smooth walls of mirrored glass reflected the green of the trees and played with his depth perception. Light from the sconces caught the building's curvature and in the rain made it seem larger than it was, like some vessel from another world hidden amongst the trees. Walls seemed to move in contrast to one another, bending in some places and angular to precision in others. The building, a silvery anomaly of massive scale, was "shapes," for lack of a better word.

Massive spotlights adorned the entrance and swung great bolts of white light into the night. Steam rose from their lenses as rain fell and evaporated. Massive banners hung to either side of the oblong entryway, promoting the Liberty Day exhibit of K-Day: the Allied invasion of North Korea. At the same time, triumphant music played from a PA system.

Madison would know what piece this is, Dice thought of the music. Thinking of her suddenly made the clouds overhead denser, the rain colder, and the wind more aggressive.

The snaking queue to enter the museum was empty, and he stepped over black velvet–covered chains to get to the doors. Once through the entryway and into the warmth, he was greeted by a docent and given a map of the museum in exchange for his token, which she dropped into a brass bin. "Is there an exhibit I may help you find, sir?" the young woman asked.

Dice thought for a moment, remembering the radio show with the two flamboyant Daves. "The Phoenix Battalion exhibit."

His host wore a lilac-colored blouse and silver skirt and had iridescent tattoos that curled up her thin arms. Her hair was long and hung over her shoulder in a red braid, and she wore a sleeveless fur coat and hood. She smiled with orange eyes, and her freckles reminded him further of Madison. "It's called the Resilience Exhibit, and if you'd like I would be happy to have someone show you the way."

"I'll be fine," the deputy replied. "I'll just wander around until I find it."

"Be aware, sir, that the museum will be closing soon. Would you like a pair of AR goggles?"

"What goggles?"

The woman smiled pleasantly. "This museum is also an augmented-reality experience. To get the most of it, we would recommend the goggles."

Dice cocked his head back, peering down at her skeptically. "How much?"

"Only—"

"Nope."

The young woman leaned in and whispered. "Good call. It fucking sucks."

Dice gave the woman a conspirator's wink and crossed the threshold.

The museum was still busy, though some rooms were being closed off with gold chains and friendly "come back soon" signs printed in Old English. Dice followed the map to the vernissage that housed the Resilience Exhibit, weaving through tourists with their dizzying, flashing mobiles, and mobs of schoolchildren herded along by vigilant instructors holding signs that simply said "Stop" or "Go." Everywhere, armored mannequins in display cases, hanging weapons, and placards innumerable told epic tales of slaughter.

Dice rode the escalator down into the bowels of the *Musée* and was, for the first time upon arriving, truly impressed. The high curved walls and floors were all of reinforced glass, held in place by great cast-iron arches. Held suspended on wires were a fighter jet he recognized as American from the early 2000s and a massive helicopter he identified as Russian... primarily from the Russian flag on the tail.

Riding the lengthy escalator, he marveled.

Here are two war machines, worth who-knows-how-much, once thought to be the pinnacle of defense. Now look at them, hanging useless, their missile silos cemented over, their

192

cockpits stripped. He doubted either of them had ever even been used.

Stepping off the escalator, his boots clicking on the glass floor. There seemed to be a thousand displays and beyond them, through the crystalline bulkheads, was Sun City, radiant behind the rain and dreamlike. For a moment, he was legitimately awestruck.

There were few things on earth more beautiful than the Shinjuku skyline, whether lit up on a summer night or set against the majesty of Fujisan. There were very few things. Sun City, behind the rain and replicating itself on the waters of the Bay of Sun, however, was one of them.

Looking around, standing among a truly impressive collection of antiquities, the idea of a distraction or, worse, a gunfight just seemed obscene. As Dice pondered his next move, he let the view of Sun City draw him to the windows.

The megalopolis was beautiful. A center of crystalline towers flanked on both sides by cascading light that descended — from behind the rain — into orange.

The map on his disposable museum guide took him across the showroom floor. His destination, the Resilience Exhibit, was marked on his map with a flaming phoenix, the symbol of the paramilitary unit.

Mine is better, Dice thought ironically, thinking of the tattoo that covered much of his torso. It was of a phoenix.

Upon arrival at the exhibit, Dice found himself looking up at the trashcan-sized chain-guns of a bipedal tank. The giant

193

mechanized tank stood nearly twenty-five feet on two armored legs. Its "head" was a dual-barreled rotating turret. The hull of the machine was painted in grey and periwinkle digital camouflage, and on it was the red, white, and blue flag of the former Democratic People's Republic of Korea. The sight of the machine sent a chill through his body.

A battalion of these monsters had stalked the devastated streets of Shibuya, Minato, and Shinjuku, herding Japanese citizens into what would become death camps. This behemoth and the hundreds like them had sent him fleeing his home. They had terrified him into imploring his wife, his friends, and his colleagues to flee as well.

The devastation inflicted on Japan by the DPRK had been nothing short of staggering. In the year and a half their boots touched Japanese soil, Korean soldiers and the fighting to repel them collected millions of lives and stunted the entire infrastructure of a once great global power. And if not for the Allied arrival, the Supreme Leader would have done to Tokyo what his own country of origin did to Nanking, what the Saudis did to Yemen, and what the Bushes did to Iraq.

This particular tank's undercarriage had a blackened hole the size of an exercise ball in it, from which wires still hung.

Someone hadn't been afraid of it.

Dice read about the machine from a holo-ad: its creator, its armament, how many had been produced. Cold paragraphs compared the killing machine's performance to that of Japan's mechanized battalion at the time, highlighting the utter mismatch. The tank was called the "Helon," named after the heron bird.

Photos and videos of Helons herding Japanese to their deaths played heartlessly in a digital montage that he simply could not watch. Behind the tank was a blown-up photo of the Phoenix Battalion. The high-definition image showed the Major, "Iron" Ace Monroe, and six of his men standing amid the rubble of what looked like the Roppongi. On the Major's waist was that blade he carried, and propped over his shoulder was a still-smoking anti-tank launcher. In the photo, the Major's face seemed cool despite the horrible scarring, and there was blood on his trousers. The article next to the photo gave a timeline of the platoon's military record since its formation in 2024. According to the article, the Phoenix Battalion, before disbanding (or becoming Agency Zero, really), fought alongside various countries' militaries in Afghanistan, the Central African Republic, Liberia, Togo, the Philippines, Tokyo, and finally North Korea. Dice didn't know for sure, but it sounded like the ultimate soldier-of-fortune resume.

"Looks like *he* did it, doesn't it?" a voice asked, startling him.

The owner of the voice was tall and thin. She wore a smart-fabric skirt suit that projected the impression of glimmering by passing a graphic wave up from the left thigh of her swallow-tailed skirt to the right shoulder of the short-sleeved blazer. Her hair was up in a playfully woven bun, and her copper-colored eyes were large pools beneath the shade of her winged lashes.

"What do you mean?" Dice asked.

The woman pointed at the gaping hole in the tank's hull with a chestnut hand. "The exhibit suggests that then-Captain Monroe destroyed this tank, does it not? I mean, looking at the picture, one might get that impression, no?"

Standing with her, but invisible to Dice in the shadow of her elegance, was a portly but well-dressed man.

"He didn't destroy the tank?" Dice asked her incredulously. *The Major's a lot of things, but a poseur likely ain't one of them.*

"In truth," the woman continued, "the man to his right with the bandaged jaw fired the shot that disabled this tank. The tank had ambushed them while they were performing house-to-house raids in search of Sodang forces, or so the official military account reads." Her accent was thick and French.

Sodang. The name belonged in eternal infamy. *Right up there with the Khmer Rouge.* Sodang were the North Korean Special Forces, the vicious commanders of DPRK ground forces and the principal architects of the Tokyo death camps. The name had been made famous in the US by the terrorist Changgok, when he bombed Sun City's Liberty Day Parade three years ago.

196

"After the tank was stopped, some say that the Major took the launcher and bludgeoned the surrendered pilot to death with it."

That would explain the bloody trousers, Dice thought. He pretended to study the placard. "I don't see that part listed here."

"Of course, it wouldn't be."

"That's a pretty hefty allegation."

The woman put a hand to her chest, her eyes wide. "*I am not saying these things!* But every weapon has a story, and this was the tale told when the *Musée* acquired this piece."

"War brings the worst out in people," Dice replied, the banality of the comment not lost on him.

The woman turned to him. "Of this, we can agree. Now what brings you to the *Musée de Conflit Historique*, officer?"

"'Officer?'"

She smiled broadly, and it was infectious — gorgeous, in fact. "Anyone could see that hideous white triangle on your back from a mile away. But that is the point, is it not?"

Dice studied the woman's face for a moment before responding. The whole point of the visit was to get attention, but now that he had it, he wasn't quite sure what to do with it. "Hate to put on airs, but I am an *agent*, not an *officer*."

She chuckled. "Is there a difference?"

He returned her smile. "There are a few, of which money is my favorite."

197

"Perhaps you'd explain to me in greater detail sometime? Sun City's dueling law-enforcement factions has always baffled me. There is only one set of laws, is there not?"

He sighed. "I'd love to break it down for you one day, but I'd much rather spend that kind of time *not* breaking that down for you."

She laughed again.

"Are you just arriving?" her companion asked. He was swarthy with striking golden eyes. He wore tight-fitting jeans and a canary smoking jacket that played ideally with his ocular prosthesis. He spoke from beneath a waxed and curled mustache. The kind a villain in an old Western would be proud of.

"I am, just arriving," Dice told the man.

"Oh my," the man said, looking at his watch. "We've but ten minutes before the museum closes."

"'We've?'"

"Ah yes, I am the *Musée*'s curator."

"You're new to the *Musée de Conflit Historique!*" the woman exclaimed excitedly, her transition from English to French flawless.

"First time."

"Well then, I am sure we can accommodate one of Unit One. Especially in light of the Phoenix Battalion's ties to Agency Zero and hence Unit One."

From the moment he'd laid eyes on the pair, Dice had known they were affiliated with the Museum. But looking at

the woman's height, complexion, and obvious wealth, he began
to wonder just how 'affiliated.'"

"Vivianne, that is quite out of the ordinary," the
mustachioed man grumbled.

*'Vivianne.' She looks like a Vivianne. Pretty name for a
pretty woman.*

"Hush," she told the curator. Vivianne extended a
slender hand to him. "And you are?"

"My name is *First Lieutenant* Yamazaki Daisuke, Unit
One," he replied, lying terribly about his rank.

The man bowed slightly. "Arlen Suresh, curator of the
Musée de Conflit Historique. To echo Ms. Vivianne's query,
what brings you, officer?"

Arlen was trying hard to ask in a way that seemed non-
threatening — too hard.

What are you afraid of, big guy? Dice thought. He
decided to stir the pot a bit. "I've come to arrest you, Mr.
Suresh."

The man blanched.

"Money-laundering, racketeering, and ties to organized
crime. How do you plead?"

Suresh looked to Vivianne, whose own face had frozen.

After a few moments of staring into the Suresh's face,
Dice laughed exaggeratedly. "A joke. Just a joke."

"You're a devil!" Vivianne said.

Dice contacted Rena via neurotrigger, careful to feign engagement, even as he initiated the equivalent of an internal phone call.

[Rena.]

[I'm here.]

[The name 'Vivianne.' Doesn't Gueye have a sister?]

[Yes. Vivianne Gueye. Tread carefully.]

"So that we are formally introduced, my name is Vivianne."

"I caught that earlier. What a beautiful name. And that accent... you must be from Section Six."

She laughed, but, as Dice noted, Suresh was no longer amused.

"No, silly man, I am from Togo."

Suresh looked at his watch. "And you are sure you haven't come to arrest me?"

Dice patted the heavy-set man on the shoulder. "I might have a word with you about ticket prices but no, I haven't."

"Well then, sir, I must see about closing. You are welcome to take your time and enjoy the *Musée de Conflit Historique*. I will notify security. Perhaps Vivianne will do us both the favor of acting as your escort." He waved his hand with a flourish and bid Vivianne farewell before walking off, his shoes clicking harmoniously on the glass floor.

"What does bring you, Mr. Daisuke?"

She slipped an arm beneath his with the fluidity of a dancer. So sudden and effortless had she come to touching him that only now did Dice begin to fear the power of grace. Had her thin hand been a knife, he'd be toast.

"I don't know, it's a Sunday night, nothing to do. I just wanted to see what the fuss was about, I guess. My invite to the grand opening must have gotten lost in the mail. Let me guess, you the owner or something?"

"First of all, Mr. Daisuke, today is Friday," she told him with an incredulous look and chuckle. "Secondly, I do apologize. Our marketing team handles special guest invites. The rest is left to auction. Oh, and no, I am not the owner. My brother is."

"Then perhaps I'll go arrest him for these ticket prices. Where's his office?"

"You'd better hush!" She smiled playfully, but there was more to it: an undercurrent of urgency to her reaction that others might have missed. Others would have, but not a gambler, and especially not a yakuza.

"He's working, my brother. If you knew anything about Luther Gueye, you'd understand. My dear brother is a very busy man." She leaned in to his ear and whispered, "*This museum is but the tip of the iceberg.*"

[Did I just hear that right?]

[Yeah, Rena. There's something going on with her. She might be trying to tell me something.]

As they walked, Dice noticed security beginning to follow them. First it was a pair of bruisers in suits. Soon it was a group of five, spread out among the dwindling museum guests, thinly veiled and eyeing him exclusively.

[Security is definitely on to me.]

[Good.]

"And what do you think of the view, Mr. Daisuke."

He didn't have the heart to correct her for using his given name in place of Yamazaki, his surname. Of course, Suresh had called her "Ms. Vivianne." Maybe following an honorific with a person's first name was a rich-people thing.

"It's unlike anything I've ever seen and I'm from Tokyo. She certainly is beautiful."

"'She.'" Vivianne performed her musical little laugh. "You are not the first to refer to the city as 'she.' Why is this?"

"It's something I picked up from the locals, I guess. I guess it just feels appropriate for a city so… *important*."

"And if Sun City is a woman, what kind of woman is she?"

He thought about it for a moment before replying, "A very troubled one."

"Rich and troubled," Vivianne added.

"Rich? Maybe from here. I can tell you how to get to Section Seven if you want. From here, you probably want to go by boat…"

She stopped in her tracks. "How elitist of me! I feel terrible."

"I didn't hear anything elitist," Dice told her. "You're right."

202

Vivianne looked at him, her expression serious, her eyes narrowing. After a few moments of walking nowhere in particular in silence, she said, "Lieutenant Daisuke, you are an interesting human being. I hope that we can be friends."

"Does friendship come with a reimbursement of admittance?"

"It does."

"Have I told you how lovely you look this evening?"

The *Musée* had two main entrances, which had been guarded and streaming with guests exiting, and three service entrances. These were being surveyed by thermal optic cameras and manned by sentry drones. The drones themselves were not run-of-the-mill parking lot attendants, but military grade mini-tanks. Any attempt to sneak by them would have resulted in detection and — depending on the nature of the directives — possibly death. That had left Chris one final option, the sixth entrance.

The sixth way wasn't really even an entrance, not any more. It had been an entrance during the *Musée*'s construction, a port on the underbelly of the bay-facing side of the building, an entry for construction workers. Upon completion of the building, the service ladders, supporting scaffolding, and much of the walkway had been removed, likely to preserve the smooth appearance of the building against the cliff's face.

But man did not come into existence with the invention of the ladder, the Unit One sergeant told himself.

203

Chris' hands were bloodied and he'd torn the nail on his pinky finger away, pretty much at the start of his descent. The pain by now was remote, an afterthought to the rate of his heartbeat. His T-shirt flailed in the cold wind and provided zero warmth. The bulletproof vest felt less like armor now and more like an anchor, pulling him to his death. Very carefully he reached and tugged at an outcropping of stone. It moved ever so slightly, so he selected another. With a hearty pull it did not budge, and he gripped it tightly as he released his other from its handhold and shifted his weight. All the while, his feet worked along the stone face, finding tiny ledges to carry some of the load. When he looked down, the ocean, maybe one hundred feet below, slapped the cliff and broke against a barricade of rocks, only to regroup and crash again.

The mask clung to his face, soaked now and freezing. With his right hand, Chris felt for crevices in the stone, finger pockets, and found none. Beneath the moonless night, he relied on the light from the museum above and from Section Three across the bay. Thunder seemed to shake the stone itself, and when the lightning broke, the shadows all around him scattered and returned, but never quite the same as before. This made his downward climb all the more maddening.

The cliff was a layered, coffee-colored wedge of jagged coast. Its linear grooves were deceivingly devoid of sturdy handholds, and the rain made those that would have been useable slick and obsolete.

Chris took the blade from his belt, a six-inch combat knife with a black blade and pommel. It was a nano-fiber-woven stainless-steel blade with a full tang, very sturdy. With it horizontal to match the layers of rock formation, he found spaces and made use of grooves too thin for his fingertips. Slowly, carefully, he moved laterally across a sheer vertical pitch toward the service walkway at the base of the *Musée.*

Maintain your breathing, Chris told himself. This would help to oxygenate his muscles and, more importantly, keep the panic at bay. It was one of the most important things in life and he applied it to all things — as best he could remember to do so.

His downward climb came to a halt, no suitable outcropping or groove to be found. Chris searched frantically with both feet as he hung from the cliff, gripping the blade in one hand and a stingy lip of stone in the other. He jabbed the blade furiously, looking for a gap, any gap. His hands were moist with sweat and rain, and the strength in his fingers, despite being assisted by Deckar Applied Sciences' Resistance Assist Technology, was failing.

Find a way...

Relying on a groove just barely big enough to hold a centimeter of boot tread, Chris pushed off and leapt: a mortal gambit lost beneath the starless sky. Lightning lit the night and the metal railing of the walkway appeared for an instant and was gone. Time did not freeze because terror, as he was well aware, was pressing and incessant. His left hand missed the

205

balcony, his fingertips just grazing. A millisecond from certain death, Chris let the knife go and grabbed at the iron walkway with his right hand in a desperate clawing motion. Pain stampeded up his arm, but the lieutenant gripped anyway. He imagined his fingers being shorn by the walkway's steel like carrots for a stew, but what were fingers if the whole was lost? Groaning in pain, Chris reached up to secure the platform in both hands and hung there for a moment, adrenaline like mercury in his veins. When his body would allow, he hauled himself up. Only once he'd thrown his legs over the handrails did he permit his heart to beat again.

The Unit One sergeant sat there in the cold for a long time. When his galloping heart began to calm a bit, he took in his surroundings. The rain, pouring from the oblong structure in rivulets thick as tree trunks, framed the city's skyline. Chris soon found himself mesmerized by the view.

There was nothing between him and Sun City but the Bay of Sun. And with every light in Sun City shining against the bay's surface, the sight was doubly radiant. The rain did little to diminish her glow and, if anything, gave it a kind of aura.

Chris was certain that, in that very moment, even as he clutched his fist in pain, no one in the whole world had a better view than him. With a slow exhale, he stood and made his way across the platform.

[Chris.]

"I'm here, Rena."

[Where's 'here?']

"I'm below the museum, ocean-side, and coming up on a maintenance hatch."

[Give me a moment.]

Above, he could hear music, boring classical crap, drifting down from the *Musée*.

[I'm looking at floor plans. I don't get how you're on the walkway. Unless... Holy cow! That would explain the spike in your heart rate, I guess. That must have been some climb. Hmm...]

Rena's tendency to think out loud had always irked him. Chris waited patiently with his hands on his hips, still breathing heavily. He looked at his sliced hand and wiped the blood on his muddy trousers. The walkway stank of chemicals, even in the wind and rain. It was new, like the rest of the structure. Perhaps the paint they used...

From below, the museum looked perfectly spherical and even the grooves, where great panes of glass met, were barely visible. One camera watched the maintenance hatch, and it was closed-circuit and cheap. Right now, anyone watching its feed would be staring at snow. Chris removed the mask and wrang the water from it. He gave his face a few minutes to warm before slipping it back on. From the utility pouch he removed a decoupler. It was a tiny, handheld laser used by police to cut through door hinges.

"I'm going to remove the door, Rena." He waited patiently for her to give him the green light.

207

[The alarm protecting that door is local.]

"So? What does that mean?"

[It means I can't disable it remotely.]

"Are you kidding me?"

Chris looked at the stone cliff and shook his head. He looked down. It was just as risky to dive from this height as it was to attempt a climb back up without the knife. He looked down again. The water crashed against jagged rocks and broke like shattered glass. A jump would be suicide and a hover-unit extraction would blow the case wide open, and not in a good way. "Rena, I really need you to think of something."

After several anxious minutes of silence, Rena returned. *[I think I have an idea. Be ready to move on my word.]*

Chris took the gloves from his back pocket and slipped them on. The rain hit him sideways and thunder beat down on him like artillery. Across the bay, Sun City smiled at him from behind the storm and powered his resolve. "I'm ready when you are."

"So, Vivianne... certainly a personable, stunning beauty such as yourself has better things to do than give impromptu tours on a Friday night."

"Is my tour boring you?"

Dice was dying. History, next to arithmetic, was his least favorite subject in school and perhaps in life. And viewing it through the lens of some rich guy's toy collection

208

was enough to drive him crazy. "Oh, no! I am learning so much cool, actionable, life-changing, inspirational *stuff*."

Vivianne laughed and this time it was Madison's laugh.

[Dice!]

Rena's voice startled him and he produced an audible sound that was something like a hiccup.

[I'm here,] the deputy responded over neurotrigger.

[Listen. I need you to set off the alarm.]

[The fire alarm?]

[Whatever alarm! Chris is stranded. He's in a bad spot and we risk being exposed unless you set off the alarm somehow.]

A solution came quickly to Dice. It wasn't the layered strategy of generals, like those whose busts lined the walls along the corridor they now strode, but it would do.

"Look at this guy," Dice said, pointing to the bust of some militant-looking man with a mustache. "Is this thing heavy?" He placed his hands on either side of the bronze sculpture and tried to lift it.

"What are you doing?"

"Wow, that is heavy!"

"What are you doing?" Vivianne repeated, aghast. "You can't do that!"

He was able to lift the bust just enough to cause the pedestal on which it rested to teeter precariously. As expected, this set off a cacophony of alarms.

"Are you insane?" Vivianne screamed over the blaring.

"What?" Dice replied, looking at her with a mock expression of confusion.

"'Do not touch!'" Vivianne pointed to a neat row of placards that reminded visitors at every exhibit along the hallway not to do the very thing he'd just done.

"I didn't see the sign."

Vivianne shook her head. "Some detective! They're going to kick us *both* out."

The alarms subsided, but Dice could hear the click of dress shoes approaching.

"If so, I'm screwed, but if they kick *you* out, just have your brother kick you back in."

"I'm sorry," she told him. "I didn't mean to snap at you. I'm actually having a great time. Come now, what do you know of Kaloyan the Romanslayer?"

"That he slays Romans?"

"Madam!" a loud, very harsh voice barked.

Security quickly approached them from both ends of the corridor. They were large, the lot of them, and carried the kind of violent expressions not typically found in places like this. Dice took note, his thoughts on his revolver. A large, broad-shouldered man in a black suit approached them first. "Is everything ok, ma'am?" he asked gruffly.

Vivianne looked about with an expression of annoyance. "Everything is fine, Damien."

"Madam, *le Musée* is closed."

"I'm well aware," she told the guard.

All of the security guards wore suits and some had their hands in their coats. Dice took inventory, careful to not look spooked.

"Also, your brother is demanding your presence," the guard named Damien continued.

Vivianne looked to Dice and back to the guard.

Demanding? Dice thought. *Interesting choice of words.*

"You can tell him to wait," she said firmly.

"But, ma'am..."

Vivianne whirled on the guard. "You heard me! I am having a fine time and will not be disturbed by any of you brutes. So, fuck off!"

[Holy...] Dice exclaimed over neurotrigger.

[Dice, everything ok?]

He bit his lip and tried not to smile. *[Yes, I think we're on to something here.]*

9: The Seidai

"My first recital? I was seven, I think, maybe six. The auditorium was packed with about three hundred parents and students. I remember being so terrified walking out onto that stage that I curtsied and thought I wet myself. When I sat down I couldn't remember what I was supposed to play and just started playing. When I was finished I ran off the stage in tears and hid behind a water cooler. When my father caught me behind the stage, he reminded me, in tears, that Twelve Variations on 'Ah vous dirai-je, Maman' was the song I was supposed to play. You know, 'Twinkle Twinkle Little Star?' What I'd played was Debussy's Claire De Lune. After that, I was bound for Tokyo and the Musashino Academia Musicae. You see, 'little Madison from Bad Königshofen' was going to be a child prodigy. I was to be the next big thing. Well, as you can see, things didn't quite turn out that way."

- Madison Grünewald-Yamazaki

The Madam lay tucked in a violet ostrich bucket bag alongside her mobile, a cheap drugstore compact, a billfold, and a raspberry-flavored lip balm. Its pistol grip was covered in silver duct tape that left little bits of residue on her palms. The constant rain in Sun City as of late had forced her to take corrective actions. Likewise, the pump-handle portion of the weapon was now cross-hatched with jagged grooves that were starting to give her weightlifter's calluses.

The Madam, as she referred to her prized shotgun, was not "old school" as some had called her, or "retro." In an era of magnetic weaponry, she was a simple 12 gauge shotgun. The same technology first used more than two and a half centuries ago. The Madam was easy to fire, easy to load, and easy to fire again. She didn't have a ton of moving parts that needed cleaning or required charging, and she didn't take some expensive, hard-to-find ammunition whose purchase was easy to track. But this wasn't to say that The Madam was without style. The Madam was chrome, an eye-catcher even at night, despite the stickers that ran the length of the barrel, her favorite being that of a cartoon penguin holding a Tommy gun.

Her bag hung under her left arm, its heft satisfying. She wore a leather motorcycle jacket and low-cut jeans whose cuffs bunched atop a pair of heavy-duty military boots. In her left boot was a stiletto and in the right a pair of portable bolt cutters capable of cutting through maglets or traditional handcuffs.

She'd been standing for close to an hour, and her feet were starting to ache. Shifting her weight from one foot to the other helped a bit with the discomfort, but she was growing impatient. Seated in front of her was Enzo Sugihara. The yakuza sat hunched over, ravaging a bread basket. To her right was Sugihara's accountant Junichirou: one of the Saga brothers. To her left was one of Sugihara's more ardent supporters, a thug named Hayato Etsuya. Junichirou was an

213

astute and well-spoken bookkeeper and hence utterly useless in a fight. Etsuya, on the other hand, was a vicious prick and thus far more valuable an ally.

Called "The Lobster," Etsuya had angered the Minowara patriarchs enough times that the only fingers remaining on his left hand were the index and thumb. In a move that somewhat defeated the purpose of his punishment, he'd supplemented the missing digits with jeweled prosthetics.

The three of them stood loyally behind Sugihara and opposite Luther's men, who stood in a well-dressed, neat column like dragoons. At the head of them, standing as well, was Gueye's head of security, the Titan enforcer Bleda.

More MOD than man, Bleda's synthetic flesh was heavily seamed from numerous voluntary surgeries. His arms, not covered by any artificial epidermis, were crimson Type-A prosthetics, the same kind wielded by Agency Zero or Unit One. It was very, very expensive stuff. He wore a sleeveless trench coat. Strapped to his back was an assault rifle. The rifle, unlike The Madam, was next-generation and multipurpose. Tattooed on the front of his neck was the Christ. The details of the tattoo were crisp against his dark skin, made so by the use of phosphorescent ink.

They were waiting in *Le Berger*, the class-A dining establishment that occupied the lowest level of the *Musée de Conflit Historique*, for the man himself, Luther Gueye. The restaurant had been empty for some time now, the only souls milling about being the wait staff and cooks. They appeared to

214

have all been trained well, as they were very careful to not make eye contact.

The restaurant itself was gorgeous, one of the finest she'd ever been in. For one, the room was massive, occupying what had to be half of the building's floor, and yet still remained intimate. Like the walls of the museum above them, everything was glass and the layout and lighting had been designed in such a way as to give the place a spherical, snow-globe effect. The floors were glass and lit with subtle LEDs that were carefully placed to not distract from the spectacular view of Sun City. So marvelous was the layout that no matter where you looked, Sun City's glow, her intricate and rolling skyline, was captured in some fixture, some mirror, some decorative bottle, or chandelier crystal. Never in Madison's life had she seen a view so skillfully exploited.

This place must have cost a fortune, she thought.

A loud, nasal sigh stripped her from the view of Sun City, as Sugihara leaned back in his chair and batted the emptied breadbasket away. At this, Bleda glared at Sugihara, and Madison, in turn, glared at Bleda. Oblivious, Sugihara looked at the gaudy watch on his wrist dramatically and groaned.

Enzo Sugihara wasn't your typical yakuza lieutenant. Where the others hid their maliciousness behind a facade of professionalism and sophistication, Sugihara wore his crude disposition like a uniform.

215

At present, the despondent Minowara lieutenant wore a short-sleeved Hawaiian shirt and basketball shorts upon which appeared the logo of a Japanese girls' high-school team. These revealed the intricate tattoos that covered his arms and legs to the ankles and wrists. Winding up and down his body were the black serpent heads of the hydra of Japanese lore, the *Yamata no Orochi*. On his back, though none could see it at present, was Orochi's bane, the lightning lord *Susano-ō*. Sugihara's hair, as usual, was a miniature disaster of feathered mess, dyed blonde in seemingly random patches. He wore a ring on every finger, and his brows, lips, ears, and nose were all pierced with diamond-encrusted platinum. Driven through the bridge of his nose was a black bolt of tungsten.

All of it was chaff. Madison had come to this conclusion many years ago. Sugihara's clothes, tattoos, and jewelry were a smokescreen to cover what beneath was a pasty, frail, and often sickly man of modest stature. But what the boss lacked in physicality, he made up for in cunning and ruthlessness. Sugihara was, without a doubt, as dangerous as the Minowara had to offer, perhaps second only to herself. That said, Madison respected Sugihara and considered him a friend, a friend that she didn't trust one iota.

Just as Sugihara looked primed to vent his frustrations with being made to wait, another cadre of men in suits entered the restaurant. Among them, carried on long-legged strides and a barrage of commands in French, was a man who could be none other than the billionaire Luther Gueye. He approached

216

the table and sent his entourage back into whatever fray from which they'd emerged. Pausing only briefly to offer "Merci" to the folks around the table, he leaned in to Bleda's ear, careful to position his back to them and cover his mouth.

After giving Bleda what appeared to be very explicit instruction, he patted his man on the shoulder and sent him away. On Bleda's parting words to Gueye, the Titan assassin thumbed at Madison. She could read on his lips the words: "Party Crasher."

Warning the boss... I'm honored.

If Luther was at all perturbed, it did not show. He nodded in acknowledgment and even appeared to smile a bit.

As Bleda left *Le Berger* hastily, Luther, a very tall and lean man, pulled a chair out and took a seat opposite Sugihara. As he crossed his legs and unbuttoned his blazer, a waiter set before him what looked to be a tonic water and lime. Luther did not offer them anything, but rather dismissed the waiter and apologized once more for being late.

Madison tried to ascertain Gueye's age, and couldn't. His face was angular, his nose broad. Stark lines ran from beneath his eyes and cheekbones and down his jaw, and yet he did not appear old. His complexion was that of syrup — just shy of a stout beer, in fact — and his teeth were capped and perfectly aligned. He wore a navy blue three-piece suit and a mimi pink shirt that was high-collared and French-cuffed. His cufflinks were sapphires and his watch a gator-banded gold antique that could have cost twelve dollars or twelve million dollars. When he spoke, he produced an ancient-sounding voice that was heavy with French and yet easily understood.

"I'm glad you could make it this evening," he told Sugihara.

Madison wasn't sure what she'd expected in the boss of the Titans, but this certainly was not it. Where the Titans were almost exclusively young men from densely urban places, Luther could have been chairing the State Council or on the board of some law firm. His demeanor, his look, and his mannerisms were that of someone foreign to want or hunger. He had no piercings, no tattoos that could be seen, and no scars. His nails were manicured and the only jewelry he wore was his timeless timepiece and a pin on his lapel that may have been white gold or platinum beneath the subtle lighting. The pin, oddly enough, was a perfect triangle, much like that of the Unit One sigil, and depicted eight owls perched in a neat formation.

As though sensing her appraisal of him, he locked his brown eyes on hers suddenly. As he sipped his lime-and-whatever, he stared, a half-smile frozen on his face. There might have been a time when such a look would cause her to blush. If so, Madison couldn't remember. Rather, as she stood there, vanguard to Sugihara, she just stared back, studying his eyes for the hint of a threat.

"Does Ms. Madison Grünewald, the infamous Party Crasher, enjoy my establishment?"

She hadn't meant to draw his attention, and felt embarrassed for having done so. "Infamous? You flatter me. As for your restaurant, it's magnificent. As is the museum. I find the place inspired." Words were cheap, and so she had no qualms dispersing compliments. Nor did she care if he could ascertain their authenticity or not.

"I'm overjoyed!" Gueye replied, clapping his large hands together. "I've dreamt for so long of building such a place, and now I have."

Bravo, rich man, she thought. *Good for you.*

"You'd best find a new dream, then," she told him plainly. "Without a goal to get you out of bed, you're as good as worm food."

Luther's eyes flashed. "Such a strange saying… But this is true! Whose words are these?"

"Mine. You just watched me speak them…"

Luther winced as though slapped, but chuckled nonetheless. "Your accent is unusual."

"Said the Frenchman. Do excuse me, but English is my third tongue."

"Bravo," Luther replied. "English is my ninth."

"There's a term for that."

"The term is 'polyglot,' I believe."

Madison tossed her hair. "I was going to say 'gloating,' but whatever."

Luther wagged a long finger at her and frowned. "Where did you find this one?" he asked Sugihara. "She's spectacular!"

Sugihara sighed — annoyed, no doubt, to have had to sit through the exchange. "Madison and I go back to high school. Maybe before that, I can't really remember."

"How fascinating. Now look at you, partners in crime."

Sugihara leaned forward, his palm on the table, clearly agitated. "Mr. Gueye. We've been sitting here for more than an hour waiting for you, and frankly" —he flicked a finger at the emptied bread basket— "your bread is not that good."

Luther leaned back in his chair, his brow furrowed. He motioned to Sugihara's mouth and looked as though he was at a loss for words.

"Oh," Sugihara said, covering his mouth like a child with new braces.

This was Luther's first time meeting Sugihara. It was his first time seeing the eclectic style of dress, the tattoos, the piercings, and the devil-may-care mannerisms. It was also his first time seeing Sugihara speak.

Sugihara was a sickly man, but he was a sickly man with wealth. And like most sickly men with wealth, he was a MOD. Sugihara's lungs, spine, and heart were not his own. These were the life-saving surgeries Madison knew of. However, the young yakuza had put his surgeons to use in other ways. One such way was in the form of orthodontic prosthesis. Sugihara's teeth had long been removed and replaced with sharp, shark-like teeth. They lined his bulbous gums in two rows and clicked like the workings of insects when he spoke. So meticulously crafted were they that, unlike a shark, when he bit down, they came together perfectly.

Though Sugihara's back was to her, she could imagine clearly what Luther saw, and what had caused him to recoil.

Luther shook his head, clearly not one for parlor tricks. However, he rebounded like a pro. "I won't pretend to understand what you've done to yourself, but I suppose that's irrelevant to this meeting. Original, I will give you that. Shall we proceed?"

"I thought you'd never ask," Sugihara replied, drumming his fists on the table.

"And yet, it's not polite to leave a lady standing." Gueye motioned to a chair, smiling at Madison. "Please, have a seat. Oh, and do set your bag on the floor. It's clean and you'll have no need for the shotgun inside." With a pinky finger, he pointed to Junichirou. "And you're the money man, are you not?"

Junichirou bowed in acknowledgment.

"Have a seat as well."

Etsuya, the only one of their party left standing, took position directly behind Sugihara, his hands crossed in front of him.

At long last, Luther moved into business. "My man speaks highly of our first transaction."

"The price could have been better," Sugihara replied.

221

"Pricing takes into consideration many things. Risk versus return on investment is one such factor. This was our first transaction, so the risk was high."

Madison watched as Junichirou leaned in to Sugihara's ear, likely asking for permission to speak, such a mouse was he. Sugihara nodded and Junichirou addressed Luther directly.

"Mr. Gueye, in order for Riot Blood to turn us a suitable profit, we would need to see no less than a thirty-three percent decrease in its wholesale cost. As I'm sure an astute businessman such as yourself is aware, we too have assumed risk in this partnership."

"Riot Blood" was the name of a designer cocktail of metabolic steroids. So potent were its effects that results were seen not in cycles or months, but in days. The drug was impossible to detect by contemporary testing procedures, placing Riot Blood in huge demand with professional athletes, insecure middle-aged men and women, and virtually anyone in desperate need of quick muscle. Also, the drug was new and this carried very specific advantages. Particularly, if there were side effects, they weren't yet known and understood by would-be buyers.

Madison had been present for the first transaction between the Titans and Minowara, though neither side knew it. The deal, as Luther said, went off without a hitch. That night had marked the first collaboration between the two largest criminal enterprises in Sun City, though one party was not wholly privy to its own involvement, that party being the Minowara seniority.

"Japanese manners are something I will never tire of." Luther's crystalline smile had returned. "Shitty introductory prices are the unfortunate side effect of a tumultuous market. The police and Unit One continue to harass my people. Between arrests, bail, and the threat of infiltration or reprisal, I've no choice but to ensure that even a moderately risky transaction be taxed accordingly. But that's it." He dusted his hands. "You've proven yourselves professionals and you shall see a stark and immediate drop in the surplus price, effective immediately."

"I want to be explicit in my intention," Luther continued. "My interest is not in short-term capital gain, but rather establishing a long-term bulk distribution network. A network that would rely on the joint efforts of both the Minowara and the Titans."

Junichirou looked about to say something but Sugihara waved him off. "Fair enough," the shark-toothed yakuza interjected, "but perhaps we can talk about other products, products of a more… recreational nature. We don't have a lot of jocks in our casinos. But we do have a lot of people who want to get high as fuck and grab a tit or two. We have fat, rich, old fucks who want to stick their little tiny peckers in tight…"

Luther cut him off, thankfully. "I get it. Coke, stims, heroin, MDMA, DMT, you name it. I could list all of the products at our disposal but frankly, I don't even know them all. We get shipments from South America, Thailand, China, Russia, and Cuba daily. We have every checkpoint and border patrol agent in the State on our payroll. At any given moment, no less than fourteen metric tons of my product is in transit on the 101 alone."

Sugihara rubbed his hands together greedily.

"The point being," Luther continued, "I have access to far more than I can ever hope to move. And I am always in need of trustworthy men and women to move it. This is why we are speaking, Sugihara-san. So tell me what you want and how you plan to move it, and it is yours."

Sugihara looked to Junichirou, who folded his hands on the table and said sheepishly, "We would like to move into heroin, cocaine, sexual stimulants, and... and, um, MDMA next. Yes, these are our initial markets."

Luther's face was stern. His gaze lingered on Junichirou for a long time before shifting to Sugihara and back again.

Junichirou looked confused. "Is something wrong?"

Sugihara licked his lips and, by looking at his face, Madison could tell that he knew what was coming next. And so did she.

The drug deal with the Titans was the first in a campaign of significant gambits on the part of Sugihara and those considered loyal to him. However, colluding with the Titans, the Triad, or anyone other than Minowara yakuza and

224

the families who were considered to be friendly, was strictly prohibited by Boss Minowara. Failure to adhere to this policy was a punishable offense, one for which many a finger and life had been lost. Knowing this and knowing where the conversation was headed, Madison became increasingly interested. Seated now, with her bag at her feet (but well within range), she sat back in her chair with her hands in her lap. She looked at the line of Luther's men, and if any of them were paying attention, you wouldn't know it from their hardened, stoic faces.

"Something bothers me," Luther continued. "Why am I speaking to the enigmatic and sparsely known Sugihara Enzo and not Kazuo Minowara, Oyabun and Chairman of the Minowara? Why *you* and not Raizen Minowara, son of the Chairman and heir apparent?"

Sugihara lowered his head for a moment, his lips curled into a smile that would have been humble if not for his teeth. "Oyabun Minowara, bless his soul, is a very old man," he began, licking his lips. "He is very, very, very old and from a time when things were much simpler. Like a dinosaur, really; a balding, chair-ridden dinosaur with shitty decision-making. But, to answer your question, the boss is not here because he does not know that we are meeting."

Luther swore and turned to look at his men, who stood there with the rigid form of well-trained soldiers. Turning back to the table, he swore once more in French. "And why have you not told him?"

225

"Because he would not approve."

Luther frowned. "Then you should have obeyed your boss. But humor me, as I must ask, why would he not approve?"

The line is cast, Madison thought.

"Like I said, Boss Minowara is an old dinosaur-man; a wretched, piss-smelling coot whose pecker shriveled up into a little grey—"

"Sugihara! Please!" Luther's fist was clenched and next to his ear as if he could catch Sugihara's words before they infected him.

"He's grown stubborn — immovable, really," Sugihara continued. "He sees Sun City as a temporary home. He sees it with his foggy eyes and foggier brain as a vacation spot for the Minowara and nothing more. As soon as tourism returns to Tokyo, he plans to move the family back in its entirety. His rotting, mushy brain thinks that tiny island is enough! He doesn't see the value in establishing long-term relationships while headquartered on foreign soil. That's part of it…"

"Illogical. What's the other part?"

"He despises you."

Luther's eyes narrowed, and for a moment Madison thought she saw something, almost like a light behind his eyes. Luther studied Sugihara's face.

"Look," Sugihara said, holding a hand up. "Boss Minowara is a senile old man. He's so old, so very, very old. And stupid. Probably the stupidest. The good news is that he'll die soon, for sure. Hopefully he'll be the deadest. No one has any business getting that old after all, the fucker. The problem, however, is that his son holds many of his beliefs. It is common knowledge that Minowara intends to forgo a true election and appoint his son as boss of the family. This means that instead of our two families joining forces and getting rich, this old, wrinkled, sea urchin would rather have us fight. That wrinkled, crap—"

"Before you continue," Luther said, his voice low, his head low, and his fist balled, "you should know that Minowara and I have history. We have many mutual acquaintances and many shared interests. I would describe our dealings as professional and at worst rigid, but you — you're saying that he—"

The moment is now, Madison thought.

Sugihara's ploy – essentially to pull Gueye to their side by pitting him against the Minowara Chairman, now hinged entirely on a bond between the two that, until now, no one had known existed. Depending on the nature of that relationship and their "many shared interests," the meeting might now be over. Worse, if Luther Gueye was close enough to Boss Minowara to reject a lieutenant undermining his authority, he was likely close enough to report the occurrence to the man himself. On top of that, there was another layer that had Madison scooting her bag closer to her hand with her foot. If the relationship with Minowara was that important to Gueye, reporting the incident wouldn't be enough. Doing so would put a wedge of distrust between them, and wedges like that always ended in war. Luther would have no choice but to resolve the matter himself, and in a way that Minowara would deem appropriate.

Heads. Heads would need to roll.

She bit her lip to still her thumping heart, and wanted so desperately to smile. The Madam was cocked and well within reach. Luther's men, having stood for so long, were allowing their eyes to wander. She could lay them all low before anyone at the table got to their feet, including Gueye. The thought made her giddy.

"'The Titans are scum. Luther Gueye is an up-jumped despot from a trash heap country not even on the map.'" Sugihara shrugged. "I may be paraphrasing a bit. But this was his message to his son and the other patriarchs. He also went on to say that 'If we had the manpower, we would slaughter every Titan in Sun City and not even bother to claim the spoils.'"

Luther laughed. It began as a chuckle and crescendoed into a roar that had him pounding the table.

Sugihara was not fazed. "As you can see, no deals happen between the Titans and the Minowara without a change in policy."

"The old man really said all that?" Luther's face was incredulous, and yet the vein on his temple pulsed.

"Oyabun Minowara is a fool; a yellowing, flea—"

228

"Why are you here?" Luther interrupted. He was furious now. "Why have you wasted my time?"

"Because apart from the old man and his son, no other Minowara yakuza feels this way." Sugihara turned to Junichirou, who nodded rapidly, terror in his eyes. He turned and looked to the Lobster next, who bowed in agreement. When Luther looked to Madison, she spoke up.

"What *aniki* says is true," she said, using the polite yakuza term for 'elder brother.'

"What good does that do either of us?" Luther asked, holding his hands out. His expression was almost pleading now. "I want to move product. That's it. I want to make money. What's so fucking hard to understand about that? How can Minowara be so short-sighted?

"The lot of you seeing the big picture doesn't help me. It's Minowara *men* I need. Without men to move the product, we've nothing." Luther pushed his chair back and placed his hands on his knees, ready to stand.

Sugihara stood first. "What I am telling you, *friend*, is that I have the men."

Luther did not speak, but rolled his fingers impatiently as though to say, "Keep going."

"The Minowara are starving. Most of us haven't even the money to buy new suits. Many of our men share apartments and many more work regular jobs to survive. This is not what any of us signed up for. Back home, under these conditions, we'd all have gone to work for other patriarch, other families."

229

Luther shook his head in disbelief. "The Minowara brings in billions annually. I *know* this."

"The money from the casinos goes to the Minowara Estate and only breadcrumbs find their way back down."

The Titan kingpin moved his mouth to speak, but did not. Rather, he sighed and seemed to reclaim his composure. After a moment of thought, he said, "What are you proposing?"

Sugihara's teeth were showing now, and he had an intensity in his eyes that Madison hadn't seen in a long time. "Regime change."

There it is again! This time she was certain of it. A light had flashed from behind Luther's left eye. Even now his eye seemed to glow a bit. She looked to Sugihara, but if he noticed it, she couldn't tell.

"And you want my help?"

Sugihara shook his head. "And be forever in your debt? No. Once the Minowara sigil has fallen, a new family will be born of its ashes with me at its head. I, and I alone, will do this. All I ask of you, Mr. Gueye, is that when the dust settles you give us the product we need to make money. I plan to choke my naysayers to death with cash."

Luther probably thinks he's speaking metaphorically. She knew different.

"And how will you pay for this product?"

"Revenue from the casinos."

"This is entirely dependent on the support of bosses who run them, is it not?"

Sugihara did not blink. "I have their support."

"All of them?"

"The ones that matter. The rest will come around once I shoot a three-pointer from half-court with the old man's shit-filled skull."

Madison winced at the thought. She watched Luther drumming his fingers on the table, still very ready to kill if need be. At any point, Luther could give the order for his men to slaughter them. As she studied the Titan's face, she couldn't help but be impressed with Sugihara. Rejecting Luther's assistance outright had shifted the whole tone of the conversation. No longer were they hat-in-hand. And from Luther's perspective, it seemed a bit of a no-brainer. All Luther had to do was… nothing. He could sit back, shut the hell up, and wait for Minowara's head to roll. If they succeeded, his chief competitor in territory was no more. And if the coup failed, he was out nothing.

With a sigh, Luther asked, "How long must I wait?"

Sugihara sat back and folded his thin arms. "Not long."

Madison saw relief in Sugihara's eyes.

"Then I shall wait patiently for the birth of the Minowara 2.0. Please don't make me wait long. I have plans: investments that are time-sensitive."

"'Minowara 2.0?' Hardly. When I'm finished the Minowara name won't even be a memory."

"Oh, and how will I refer to this new enterprise?"

"Do you know what *Seidai* means?"

Luther shook his head.

"It simply means 'prosperous.' This is the family I want to create, a family devoted only to the pursuit of wealth and the power that it grants. You see? It's easy for Minowara to decide from the comforts of his estate that 'drugs are bad' or weapons trafficking is 'not the *gokudō* way.' What I want is a family with a unified vision, a family bound by one creed: 'wealth by any means.'"

Luther raised his glass. "A singular goal is key to success, I can assure you. I will stand by for a time and—"

In that moment, Bleda stormed into the restaurant and made a beeline for their table. As he came close, Luther kept him at bay with a glance. "I would prefer that business not wait while you sort out your affairs, however. One of my men will contact you about two" —Luther held up slender fingers— "*two* new prospects. The first is a continuation of our first transaction but at a dramatically reduced rate. For the second, I will front you as much heroin as you think you can move at a 32/68 cut. Or you can buy wholesale."

Sugihara looked at Junichirou, who nodded slightly before returning Luther a confident, albeit sinister, smile. "We'll take the front. Is this where we shake hands?"

Luther beckoned Bleda to his ear. A moment later he sent him running once more. "My hope was for dinner," he said with a clenched jaw, "but *voleurs maudits*! This goddamn city!"

"What is it?" Sugihara asked.

"I have thieves in my vault."

"Madison." Sugihara looked to her and arched his eyebrows. "Help our friend out?"

Luther smiled. "Yes! Let us see what the Party Crasher is made of. Show her the way," he said to his men. "Deploy the sentries and catch them alive if possible."

Madison didn't appreciate Sugihara loaning out her services like some kind of basset hound, but this time she would make an exception. After all, this was an occasion worthy of celebration. If the Seidai became a reality, she would finally have what she deserved: a legitimate rank and a place in the syndicate. She pulled The Madam from her bag so quickly that Luther's eyes widened and his men sprang for their weapons. She held the gun over her shoulder and stood from her seat. "Lead the way."

10: The Job

"A thermal optic kit would be best but checking one out of Ordnance is going to raise some eyebrows. That said, go in as naked as you feel comfortable but don't be stupid. Get in, see if you can find anything that may tie Gueye to the Titans, and get the hell out. Don't feel like you need to crack safes or anything. We just need enough proof to justify turning the heat up on the man."

"That said, I'm not totally sold on Moore's theory. I just figure the kid deserves a chance after all he's been through."

\- Incoming communication, taken from the log files of Unit One Sgt. Chris Calderon <MIA - presumed KIA>

Chris was never one to mince words. "Holy shit."

The storeroom was massive. Stories-high racks with the space between them to play a rugby match ran the length of the chamber, stocked with meticulously sealed crates of nearly every size. Some crates lay opened, their contents strewn about mid-assembly. Two tanks were parked side by side and behind them a fourth-generation Chinese fighter jet. The racks converged and gave way to narrow walkways and intersecting corridors, walled in antiquities. At the far end of the hall sat what appeared to be an intercontinental ballistic missile.

The floors were lit, but the track lighting cast stark shadows for which he was grateful. He chose one of a trio of paths and moved low and quickly. Footsteps and men speaking could be heard over the sound of classical music.

[Is everything ok?]

"This guy has a missile."

[Is it armed?]

"Too far away to tell. I sincerely hope not."

[Might be worth a look.]

"I'll swing by on the way out. Can you give me my location?"

[Sub-level B. The storage floor. I think Sub-level A is where you want to be. Looks like offices.]

Chris chose a dark corner and crouched in the shadow. He opened the pouch on his belt and removed from it gauze and a stitching kit. His right hand was badly lacerated on the palm and his pinky finger was bleeding where the nail had been torn away. He cursed but was grateful that it wasn't his fret-hand.

Once patched up, he followed green exit signs to the stairwell and climbed to Sub-level A. The floor above was a stylish take on office space. The corridors were lined with ancient frescos, and the offices themselves were walled in tinted smart-glass. Even the cubicles that clogged the center of the floor were hulled in cedar. An ambient soundtrack played, and the lighting was a few notches below casual. The workday was clearly over and the floor appeared thankfully devoid of both employees and guards.

As he infiltrated the *Musée*, he tried to imagine himself as Chris Calderon, employee of the *Musée de Conflit Historique*. He tried to picture working a nine-to-six in plush offices walled in black wood. He tried to imagine wearing his immersion helmet or augmented-reality glasses on the commuter zeppelin on his way in to the office every morning, greeting the same smiling faces the same way day after day, drinking the free coffee and mineral water. He tried to imagine scooting into his cubicle to log in each morning, cigarette breaks, IT requests, team-building exercises, social hours, and one-on-ones with the boss. He tried to imagine being acquiescent to the specifications of a dress code and, of all things, this made him smile most.

"You worked in an office once, right?"

[Lab to be exact, but yeah, close enough.]

"What was it like, Rena?"

[I think I know what you're getting at. Let's just say it wouldn't be for you.]

'Bout what I figured, he thought.

"Rena, do you have any idea which office might be Luther's?"

[I was just scratching my head over that…]

Chris was crouched inside a vacant cubicle. Movement from the corner of his eye caught his attention, and a man wearing an ascot and carrying a portfolio binder moved past, seemingly unaware of his presence. More footsteps approached, keys jingled, and people began engaging in conversations just beyond his audible range. And just like that, the area had come to life. Chris peered over the cubicle wall and could see the black orbs of omnidirectional security cameras. His vest would protect him from those but not the eyes of office workers. "Rena! Quickly!"

[West of your position there's an office. It's almost two hundred square feet larger than the others. Also, the network topology is kind of interesting. That same office has a dedicated network hub and yet no connectivity that I can see. I'm thinking it's probably connected through some kind of proxy router or masked by some illegal service. What if they've got some kind of private shadownet VPN?]

"Or what if they simply never set the hub in that office up?"

[Oh, you're no fun. But that's as good as I've got. You'll want to hurry. It sounds like Dice is running out of excuses to stick around, and he's drawn a boatload of attention flirting with Luther Gueye's sister.] She laughed. *[Dice, that guy... Also, one more thing... The* Musée *has registered with the State two theft-deterrent, non-sentient sentries. These things are military grade: the kind used at highway checkpoints to stop freight trucks and convoys.]*

"You mean mechs?"

[Yes. DAS versa-tanks to be exact; all-terrain anti-infantry drones.]

237

"And we couldn't figure this out before I broke in?"

[I'm doing the best I can, Chris.]

He clenched his jaw, but apologized. Moving quickly, he stayed below the cubicle walls, thankful for the thick carpet that muffled his steps. Beneath the mask, his face was hot, the cloth damp and oppressive.

Every door along the corridor was the same: tinted glass and protected by biometric scanner.

"Am I almost there?"

[Second door up, on your right.]

"Hey!"

Chris turned to find a tall man dressed in black pointing at him. He wore a suit, his hand in his coat grasping what was likely a gun.

No matter how many times Chris found himself in a situation like this, the initial reaction was always the same. His brain, as if booting up, had to process the shock before sending those life-saving signals to his feet, legs, and body. In this tight window of seconds, he watched as the guard withdrew something black from his coat. Then, as though released from a stasis, his legs came to life. He flew at the man, now wholly in control of his body.

His legs were grade-A Deckar Applied Sciences products and part of a top-of-the-line kit. With the response time they afforded him, he was on the man before the pistol could level. With an open palm, he struck the guard in the sternum, driving the breath from his lungs and preventing him from calling out. The second blow was an overhand right to the jaw that rocked the guard unconscious on his feet. Chris caught the man mid-fall and set his body down in a seated position against the wall.

Chris ran for the door of the office in question as the lights went dark and red strobes came to life. He reached for the gun that was not on his waist and swore. "Rena, I'm made."

[....]

"What do I do?"

[I might suggest getting the hell out of there, stat!]

"Well, that's *very* helpful, Rena!"

He went back to the unconscious guard and took his gun. A quick look confirmed his fears. The gun was protected by a biometric trigger lock. It would serve no purpose greater than bludgeon. He tossed it to the ground disgustedly.

He could hear Dice's voice in his head. *"Calderon, I'd take the gun..."*

A new voice joined the neurotrigger channel and in his ear was the moist, muffled speech of a man whose gums were packed tight with chewing tobacco. *[Sergeant Calderon,]* the voice said calmly.

"Sir."

It was Deputy Chief Constable Williams, and he sounded cool as a cucumber. *[You're a very well trained agent of Unit One and an SDC Sergeant with eight years' experience in criminal investigation and gang-busting. And you were selected out of a pool of thousands for your physical prowess and ability to create solutions on the fly. Isn't that so?]*

"Yes, sir. That is so, sir."

It's funny how in moments of panic you become your most subservient, he thought.

[Can't say much for your alter ego and that cat-bashing you call music,] Williams continued, *[but as far as State Defense Consortium work goes, you're the best of the best. Isn't that so?]*

"Yes, sir!"

[And now, you need to calm yourself and create solutions.]

"Roger that, sir."

[Get into that office and don't bother being gentle, you've no time for it.]

With a booted foot, Chris shattered the glass pane of the office, sending shards into the far wall in a glimmering blossom.

[Look for something material; something we can use to tie Gueye to the Titans.]

The commander's voice had renewed his resolve. Chris scanned the desk, searched the drawers, and rifled through cabinets that were empty and nothing more than decoration.

Come on!

He flipped paintings off the wall and knocked the cabinet over, looking for a safe, a false wall, something.

Nothing! There is nothing!

[The computer, Chris!]

The computer was built into the desk and came to life when his palm touched it. As he did so, the OS came to life in 360 degrees of holographic imaging. Rena's voice filled his head excitedly.

[Ok, log in as a guest,] she told him.

Accessing the computer with his own neurotrigger would be the same as planting fingerprints in the shape of his name and address on the desk. Instead he found the sensor to activate manual input. A QWERTY keyboard appeared, hovering just above the desk, each letter represented in three dimensions. Like a man shadowboxing, he began typing. "I'm online."

[Go to this address, it will allow me to remote in and take control. Ready?]

"Yes."

[338.45.2.2.555.098]

He entered the address and waited. After an excruciating minute, the room was lit red with an error that read in bold, black letters, "FORBIDDEN."

"Rena! We've got nothing."

Something sharp struck his neck, and a split second later his body locked up, an excruciating buzzsaw of pain coursing through him. Chris dropped to a knee and snatched the embedded taser prongs from his neck, a move made possible only by the insulating effect of the ceramic in the vest he wore.

The room was a blur, but in the doorway he could make out the silhouette of a person. He charged, struck the man in the chest with his shoulder and forced him into the tinted glass wall of the adjacent office. On impact, the smart-glass came to life, displaying a meeting calendar in bold, colorful icons. But the calendar was visible only for a moment, as their weight shattered the glass, sending them sprawling over pebble-sized cubes that dug into his knees and palms painfully. As the flashing red lights made their struggle appear episodic, Chris punched the guard, with as much force as he could muster, in the groin. The man opened his mouth to scream, and Chris slammed his forehead into the man's nose repeatedly until the struggle ceased.

As he got to his feet, his lucidity began to return. He went back to Luther's alleged office and kicked the chair over in frustration. He rechecked the cabinets and desk drawers, frantic for some evidence, some token to make this fool's endeavor worth it.

"This is all wrong!" he bellowed angrily.

Chris slammed a fist onto the desk, knocking over a framed photo of an elderly black man and a girl. From behind it rolled a silver vial, the size of a crayon. The vial looked medical in nature: the kind easily attached to a syringe for injection. Without a second thought, he snatched the vial and pocketed it.

"I've got something; a vial."

[It's time to get out of there,] Williams told him.

"Roger that."

If I'm fast enough, Chris thought, *I can hit the showroom floor before anyone knows what just happened. Once I'm there, hopefully, there will be people, witnesses. They can't shoot me then. I can force my way out. Straight out the front door. Into the woods. Once I'm there, I'm home free.*

He ran back through the office, past a pair of stunned employees, and followed the exit signs to a stairwell. He ran up the flight of steps only to find the door locked. He slammed a few kicks into the door, but it did not budge.

"Rena! It's locked. Find me another way out."

[I'm on it. One second.]

Chris ran back down to the offices, to find a cadre of security waiting for him. They had to have come from somewhere. He shook his arms out to get the blood flowing, hopping from one foot to the other. He tossed his head from side to side to loosen the joints. Before the guards could coordinate their attack, he pounced.

"There you are."

Dice watched the chair approaching on silent wheels. At the sight of the man in the wheelchair, Vivianne's face lit up.

The man had to be in his eighties, perhaps older. He wore a colorful button-up and a knit cap. Covering his legs was an intricately woven blanket upon which fractal-like runes were embroidered. Beneath that, beneath the gorgeous,

243

handcrafted quilt, was a man of naught more than skin and bones.

The chair moved across the glass floor with a hiss, all the while administering oxygen and liquids to its passenger via a complicated array of medical apparatus. As the elderly man arrived, the men in suits who'd thus far kept their distance closed in on all sides. Some of them no longer bothered to conceal their weapons.

They don't look like Titans, Dice thought, *but they don't look like security guards either…*

He counted no less than fifteen of them, far more than he had bullets for, should it come to that.

Vivianne ignored their presence as she leaned down to embrace the elderly man. "Father."

The man's hair stood out in silver patches behind his ears and nowhere else. His weathered face was gaunt, almost skeletal, and the color of burnt oak. Seemingly ignoring his daughter, he looked up at Dice with his clamshell lips pursed. "Who are you?"

Dice bowed deeply, respectfully. "Detective Yamazaki, Unit One."

"Yamazaki…," the man repeated. "Unit One, eh?" His voice was soft and prefaced by a long inhale like someone preparing to blow out candles.

"Your daughter has been giving me a tour of the *Musée.*"

"Giving tours to strangers, are we?" Vivianne's father looked at her and shook his head slowly, carefully. "She's a doe, this one, gentle and curious. I've been trying to teach her to be cautious."

Dice turned to her, a modest smile on his lips. "Vivianne, is this the 'friend' you're meeting for dinner?"

"This is my father, Elom, my *best* friend."

Her enthusiasm was genuine and rare. She stood next to her father, with a hand on his shoulder that massaged gently and without thought, like muscle memory. "He's ill, but getting better each day."

"Shhh, girl," Elom said before getting caught in a coughing fit that set off LEDs on his chair. With each hack, his body would splash about in the chair like someone being electrocuted. When the coughing finally subsided, a brown droplet of mucus rested on his lip.

"Yes, I am 'ill.' Ill with death. Chondrosarcoma, they call it. Too many years toiling in the sun, I suppose. Or maybe it's as simple as 'too many years.'"

Dice nodded gravely, waiting for several moments before speaking. When it was clear that Elom was finished, he replied. "I imagine they weren't years spent on your laurels, either."

The old man chuckled and held a finger up. "No, sir! That you know is true!"

"I have no doubt." Dice told him with a smile.

Respect for years and experience was a trait he'd learned many years ago. It was a quality shared by the best yakuza.

"You're an odd one," the old man told him, looking up with a scrutinizing pair of weary eyes.

"I've been called worse."

"I'm sure. That hair, the thin mustache… You don't look like Unit One. You look like a gangster." Elom sat up as best he could and, with a gaze that might have been intimidating decades ago, broke him down. "I'm old and don't like to spend a lot of time painting backdrops. Why are you here, Detective Yamazaki?"

The thought of repeating his lie to this man seemed absurd. As he looked about, Dice saw the guards in motion. They were encircling him. Dice smiled. "Tell me about your s—"

[Dice, you need to get out.]

"Evening, Officer," a voice said.

Dice whirled to find the man standing directly behind him. He'd approached in silence and was already well within striking distance. He was short but thick. His complexion was a different shade of brown than the Gueyes' but somehow just as dark. His arms were new MOD tech and definitely looked like class-A equipment. The man's expression was cool, but on his back he carried a large rifle.

"What can I do for you?" the man asked, with as much honey in his voice as could be gleaned from pavement.

246

Dice took a subtle step back, ever so slightly, so as to not spark the fight.

"I'm afraid it's after hours and you're trespassing," the man continued.

"I must have missed the pre-recorded message telling me to go home."

"Strange, because it's been on repeat for the last hour and a half."

"Don't know what to tell you, pal." Dice waved a hand at Vivianne. "Maybe you should talk to this chatterbox over here."

"I think not," the man replied. "Come with me."

"*I* think not."

The man's eyes narrowed.

Dice's hand was in his jacket now, his finger touching the grip of his revolver. One move from the MOD and he would put two in his chest.

"Bleda!" Vivianne moved between them and shoved the man backward with both hands, hard. "This man is my guest."

The man called Bleda winced at the sound of his name. He looked for a second as though he would turn his anger on her, but after a brief stare, his expression softened. "Madam, your brother wishes to speak with you about an urgent matter."

"Does he, now?" Vivianne's hands were on her hips. "Mr. Yamazaki, please excuse our head of security, Mr. Bleda. He takes his role a bit too seriously."

247

[Rena, I can't say I've got evidence but something's definitely not right here. Heavy muscle for a building full of priceless artifacts doesn't shock me, but the style of muscle does. Dig up what you can about a man named Bleda. I suspect we won't like what we find. Regardless, I've run the charade for as long as I can.]

[Then get out.]

"Hey now," Dice said, putting his hands up. "I don't want to cause you fine folks any trouble. Vivianne, thank you for a wonderful evening."

Chris let the blow move his head naturally, hopping slightly on his toes to reduce impact. His counter-punch was not so gracefully received. The guard's head snapped upward and he staggered. Chris capitalized, dashing forward as the man attempted to get his legs beneath him. It was too late. Chris leapt and slammed a knee into his face, ending this particular guard's participation in the brawl.

A bullet struck the cubicle behind Chris. Blows seemed to rain in from all sides. Before a second shot could be fired, he shoved the man closest to him and ducked around the corner. He ran and they followed. There were three guards now. There had been six. He stopped and turned to face them once more, choosing a corridor to make his next stand. Two guards lunged at him with batons. He absorbed the first blow on his forearms, while the second slammed into his spine. One guard moved forward while the other circled. He ducked the next blow and

248

snatched the arm. With it, he yanked the man forward and introduced his chin to a crushing elbow. The baton dropped from the guard's hand and Chris caught it mid-flight, just in time to counter the second guard's strike. The wooden batons clashed with a loud knock.

The feel of the weapon in his hand galvanized him. He twirled it and felled his opponent with rapid, relentless strikes to the torso, arms, and legs. When the guard could defend no more, Chris slammed the baton into his knee and left him writhing.

One left.

The last guard looked up from checking his pistol just in time to narrowly avoid a kick aimed for his head. Chris spun again, letting fly virtually the same kick as before. This time, it struck the man's wrist. The gun went flying. The guard reacted quickly and dove into him, snatching both of his legs in what wrestlers called a "power double." Chris hit the floor on his back, the guard on top of him, already jockeying for position. In the scramble, Chris threw a leg up and over the guard's shoulder, his thigh across his opponent's face. Snatching the man's flailing arm and pinning it to his own sternum, he stretched his back out and dropped the guard onto his back; the arm pinned and hyperextended against his pelvis. The guard screamed and a moment later the arm snapped.

Chris got to his feet, the rush of adrenaline inebriating, and ran for the staircase back to the storeroom.

[Dice is being escorted out. Is your identity blown?]

"I've covered my face. But only a fool would think that Dice was here at the same time by coincidence."

[But they can't prove it. I don't need to remind you that this operation has no legitimacy.] Rena's voice was stern and almost cold. [You can't get caught.]

"I don't plan on it."

[What's your situation?]

"Fought off a few guards. Heading back to the storeroom. The only option is back the way I came."

[Are you hurt?]

"Please."

[That's the Chris I know.]

The storeroom was dark now, the only light coming from the red emergency strobes or flashes of lightning through the glass bulkheads. He sprinted across a metal service walkway in a beeline for the maintenance hatch. His night of rock climbing was not over, apparently, and the thought of making the climb without his knife left an uncomfortable pit in his stomach.

But it's the only way now, and so I'll have to make do.

He was halfway through the warehouse when floodlights came to life with a blinding boom. The shock halted him in his tracks momentarily.

I'm target practice up here. He threw his legs over the railing and leapt down to the floor below. He took cover among the exhibit cases, crates, and metal storage units. He moved low, clutching the baton, head on a swivel.

"Hey-o!" a voice yelled cheerily.

Something struck Chris in the back and the world went dark for a moment.

"How did you get in here?" the voice asked. "You're trespassing."

Chris crawled to his feet, breathless, the world slowly coming back into view. A hand to the small of his back came away with blood and little pellets of buckshot. The vest had taken the brunt of it, but some had gotten through. He looked frantically for the assailant.

"What are you looking for? A painting for your mama, is it?" The voice was taunting, the accent heavy. It was hoarse, but no doubt the voice of a woman.

Chris continued for the hatch, holding the baton out menacingly. Footsteps thudded on the floor behind him, someone running. He turned but found no one.

"We've company, looks like," the voice said. "I think they're here for you."

Terror creeping into his chest, Chris ran.

[Your heart rate is up,] Rena told him.

A loud humming noise filled the chamber, and squeaking sounds like those on a basketball court chirped against the glass floor. The clinking of metal and the sigh of pistons joined the humming sound as two sentries scrambled into view from behind the racks on either side of him. They were roughly seven feet tall and moved on four spider-like legs, each tipped with a spherical wheel. Their hulls were black, the weapons mounted there numerous. The sentries stood blocking his way to the maintenance hatch.

This isn't a fight I can win.

Chris' first instinct was to throw his arms up. In his years in the SDC, never had he been in the sights of a mechanized sentry. The terror of being targeted by something inhuman paralyzed him and a moment's release in his abdomen moistened the front of his trousers.

Just run! Get past them!

He made to run just as another shot rang in his ears. Flechette struck the bulkhead and careened off, some of the metal darts embedding themselves painfully into his arm.

Chris ran towards the shot and away from the mech sentries, the shooter's location still unknown to him. He slipped into a lane between a metal shipping container and a tank, and began moving away through a maze of storage, away from his goal.

My only hope is to lure the mechs away from the hatch and then, somehow, slip past them.

The storeroom had no shortage of cover, for which he was immensely grateful. Unfortunately, it was also all corners, all potential ambushes. Perfect for the woman stalking him.

After a moment of catching his breath, Chris left shelter and ran out into the open in an attempt to draw the mechs away from the service hatch. They locked in on him, their turrets swiveling to meet him. When the ringing of their Gatling gun turrets could be heard, he darted back for cover. In that instant, the shooter stepped out from hiding and fired. The shot struck the cage next to his head and tore a hole in the wire before obliterating the contents of the cage. The metal lashed at his face and tore into his cheek.

The shooter was indeed a woman. She wore a leather jacket and held a chrome shotgun waist high. He ran for her, baton held high, and she stepped up to meet him, loading the shotgun calmly. Chris juked serpentine and caused her shot to go wide. Close now, he swung the baton for the woman's head. The shooter rolled under the attack, spinning, cocked the gun midway, and fired another dose of buckshot point-blank into his chest.

Chris screamed but could not hear his own voice. The blast sent him flying and the world once again dimmed. Dead if not for the vest, he lay immobilized, dazed and shocked, looking up at the floodlights. His breath would not come. When it did, his lungs seemed to flutter like torn kites. Pain unlike any he could recall begged him to give up. To just lay there and die.

[Chris! What's happening!]

The woman approached him casually. She was a strawberry blonde. Her skin was colorless beneath the floodlights. Her eyes were wet emeralds and she was smiling a dimpled half smile. His assailant was beautiful, if a little cold-looking. On her belt were shotgun shells, strategically placed in order: red, green, blue, red, green, blue. Slugs, buckshot, and flechette, he knew. He watched her select a slug from her belt

253

and slide it into the receiver port. Slugs of the old style were large bolts of metal designed to drop virtually anything. And often times those things fell in pieces.

This woman. The hair, the eyes, the shotgun... This was the bogeyman that the gansters in opposition to the Minowara spoke of in depositions: Headless Horseman of the Japanese underworld.

The Party Crasher.

Chris rolled and got to his feet, air creeping into his lungs. Terror powered his movement. He leapt behind a yellow storage container as the slug tore through the metal in a splash of sparks and struck the display case next to him, destroying the case and whatever it had held it. The gap Chris found himself in was thin and he would not be dodging the next shot from inside. He shuffled sideways quickly and found an opening waist high beneath stacked display cases. Crawling into the space was painful, but allowed him to catch his breath. Sitting on the floor, he felt beneath the battered vest. What he felt horrified him. Almost too afraid to look, he peered beneath the vest and found the DAS-branded chest plate beneath what had been his chest showing. His left clavicle sprouted from beneath his fissured skin like a bloody spear. Numbness began to seize his torso and arms. He was thankful, despite understanding the implications.

Holy shit. I'm going to die.

[Are you hurt?] Rena asked.

"I'm hurt."

[Is it bad?]

"It's bad."

[Sergeant!] The DCC's voice was deafening. *[You need to get your shit together and get the hell out of there.]*

"Where's Dice? He needs to be warned."

[He's out already, but he's certain they're following him.]

"I found a vial. Not sure what's in it. It looked out of place. Something's wrong with this place. The Party Crasher is here."

[The what?]

He didn't have the energy to repeat himself. He just sighed. *What a waste, my life. What a waste.*

"I'll see you, Rena."

[I've scrambled hover units! We'll figure the story out once you're safe!]

"We do this for her, Rena. We do this for Sun City. They take away Unit One because of this, and there is no one else. No one knows her like we do, knows her streets. No one knows her people like we do. Agency Zero can't keep her safe like we can. Protecting her, this is the job."

With a neurotrigger, he left the secure channel and selected another: public radio, KMBL Alt Rock in the Evenings. He didn't recognize the song wrapping up, but it didn't sound very good. He breathed deeply and a moment later a bass guitar began strumming in a rhythmic repetition that made him smile. The next song was familiar to him. His heart was a subwoofer as he prepared to step out and meet his assailant. The band was called The Griffins and the song was "Revenge Road." He knew the band, having opened for them a few years back when he was still a solo act.

If you've got to go out, there are worse soundtracks to end on.

"Come out, little man," the shooter crooned.

He crawled out from under the cases. At the far end of the warehouse, Sun City called to him, through large panes of tinted glass. The tanks scurried to flank him, their arachnid steps as unsettling as the miniguns that crowned their turrets. It wouldn't be long now.

His head was throbbing and his hands were completely numb now. Chris had to look down to confirm that he still gripped the baton.

The woman held the shotgun at her side. With her other hand, she pointed. Her words were hard to make out. She was telling him to drop the baton, pointing to the deck where she would like him to drop it. This was it. Chris told her what she could do with the baton.

Behind the raindrops, Sun City looked shattered, a crystalline ornament dropped and discarded on some black surface. A shame he would never walk her streets again, smell her scent, or taste her food. He had a gig and a date with a pretty girl next week.

"Okay, you got me." He held his hands in the air, blood already starting to pool at his feet.

The woman lowered the shotgun to her side and waved at the drones to stand down.

A man stepped into the open. He was tall and dark. His suit was pristine and his face handsome and stern. Chris recognized him immediately.

"Who are you?" Luther Gueye asked.

The rock music in his head made the scene like something out of an action film.

"I'm no one," he replied, pulling the mask down tight over his face.

"What are you after? How did you get in?"

Chris held the baton out, ready for the drones to tear him to pieces.

The man's eyes began to take on a glow.

What the—

A pain like a knife to side of the head turned the room red. Chris put his hands to his head and couldn't help but scream. The man's eyes seemed to grow brighter, their light searing his senses.

"ARRRRGGGGGGGGGGGHHHHHHHHHH!"

He wheeled away, but taking his eyes off the man did nothing to stem the pain. He screamed until he couldn't hear anymore. The music in his head was no more and he wanted to plead for the pain to stop. As he tried to speak, his lips fluttered uselessly and his jaw bit down on his tongue. He tore at the mask on his face and ran, desperate to create distance.

Buckshot tore into his thigh just as a Gatling round blew chunks of his torso away, spinning him. He was lost in a downward spiraling current. All there was to do now was lie down and die, but the pain in his head would not allow it. If he only had his gun, he could put it to his temple and end the suffering.

Then her lights caught him again, from behind the wind and rain. *I can still run!* He ran to her, the city that he loved so much. It took great effort to control his legs, as though learning to walk again, and soon he couldn't tell if he was running or floating. The world was shaking now and his mind was being torn to pieces. He moved his legs as best he could. Sun City was close now, just a breath away. All he had to do was—

Rounds struck the glass, and cracks like spiders' webs split the city's sections until she was no more than a puzzle of lights. A round burst through him and sent a red spray up into his eyes. Chris fell and the glass gave way to night. It was cool, the rain; cleansing. There she was, glimmering like diamonds washed ashore. He reached for her but she did not catch him. Instead, he tumbled into the night amidst stars made of glass, down to the rocks and hungry sea below.

11: The Setting Sun

"A man must be straightforward. If you want a thing, your intention should be made known. This is how the yakuza, the oldest of organizations, have survived for so long. Though we stand in defiance of law, the police, the politicians dare not challenge us. And why would they, when in their hearts they want to be us? When others are browbeaten, we walk with our heads held high. It is because we are true to ourselves and we make our intentions known. That fact is why people trust us and why we will never die."

- First Oyabun of the Minowara-gumi, Kazuo Minowara

In less than two months he would be ninety-two years old. The thought of it hung over him like an executioner's axe.

They say the rolling stone gathers no moss. "They" say a lot of stupid things. For he was earthen now, planted in his chair like the roots of an ancient tree. And none had rolled like he, so far from the tiny farm in Hida. A bouncer, a collections agent, a brothel manager, a lieutenant, and patriarch, and finally *the* boss: Oyabun, chairman of all clans of substance. All bound under his banner. By the time the war with the Koreans came home in the winter of 2040, Kazuo sat at the head of the largest criminal enterprise in all of Japan. Now his name, the name of his house, was something to be feared. Something to be respected.

Six years now in this filthy city, thought Oyabun Kazuo Minowara bitterly.

And yet, what was I to do?

As chairman of the Minowara, he had resisted relocating the family for as long as he could muster. But, where their efforts were once spent on growing and maintaining an intricate network of influence and profit, the post-war had embroiled them in rebuilding efforts that yielded little, if any, revenue. Unwilling to abandon his home entirely, splitting the syndicate was the only viable option. And so Kazuo left Tokyo in the hands of his most trusted lieutenant patriarch, Goh Sakakibara. Goh would maintain their presence in Japan and help stand their country back on its feet, as was the gokudō way. He would take his most trusted, most reliable, and most vicious to the Pacific State, to reinforce an already rooted but weak network of yakuza and establish a second home.

Redundancy.

At first, Sun City had not welcomed him. But with a honeyed word and money, she eventually spread herself for him. His family built, for the second time in less than a century, a massive network of influence. Strong-arm real estate investment, sports books, event-rigging and collection, embezzlement disguised as consultation, and blackmail were the daytime face of the Minowara, the *water*. Gambling, prostitution, extortion, kidnapping, and assassination were the makeup of the nighttime shroud of his empire, the *fire*. Both were necessary to sustain heaven and earth, and likewise his family's prosperity.

However, now he was an old man and his joints hurt. Now, it was difficult to stay awake. A new heart, new lungs, new kidneys, new liver, and new spine kept the inevitable at bay; they kept him somewhat alive, but they did not halt the filthy grip of time.

The Minowara-gumi were thirty thousand strong. And within that, more than five hundred subordinate clans: yakuza families who'd pledged their lives and allegiance. His earnings were north of eleven billion dollars annually. His coffers were overflowing, his family's future secure for generations innumerable.

And yet, all of these accomplishments paled in comparison to his greatest. His influence, connections, and shrewd business acumen had secured him a seat on the Council of Eight.

Yes, Kazuo Minowara, son of a lowly farmer, is now one of the Octumvirate.

In the third act of his life, Kazuo now had unparalleled access to information and resources. Now, after a lifetime of struggle, he had finally been anointed, deemed one of the illuminated. But, like being mortally wounded in the final days of a great war, his final wish had come too late. Because, these days, his mind wandered, his body groaned, and the very act of speaking exhausted him.

Even the things that once gave him joy seemed pointless. He had lost his passion for carnal pleasures many years ago, and even money was something foreign now, meaningless numbers spoken in passing, credits in some database, chits never seen and never touched. All he had now that mattered was his home and his family. His estate was second in acreage only to that of the Premier and adorned a lush hill, high up on the coast, facing the sea. Every morning the sun would rise and the sigil of his family — the great wave against the setting sun — would come to life, aglow.

"Slower," Minowara told his son.

"Forgive me, Father," Raizen replied.

"I am not a cart of horse feed."

"Forgive me, Father."

The chair was automated, but Kazuo's hands had become too shaky to pilot it. And the thought of someone digging around in his brain — the only somewhat reliable piece of him that remained — to install neurotrigger seemed absurd.

The oyabun's chair moved over the plush carpet with a whisper. They were on the highest floor of the Horus Bank building, a restricted floor reserved for those who had taken the blood oath. The hall was long and the walls were hung with great works: marvelous paintings acquired over millennia. Beautiful frescos, painted in the Fourth Pompeiian style, adorned the ceiling, broken only to make way for stunningly ornate archways. From the walls hung timeless works, precious paintings that would rival those in the vaults of the Vatican.

As Kazuo's son wheeled him forward, he studied each painting, the intricacies fresh to him each time. When they reached the halfway point of the long corridor, he halted his son with a raised hand to admire a particular piece, as had become routine.

This one is special…

"What is on the agenda for today, Father?"

The painting was of the Spanish coast. In it, seagulls hung just at the edge of the sky and shoreline. It was painted in stuttering strokes of fallow and mulberry that flirted with the red, orange, and lavender hues of a setting sun. The painting spoke to him in ways that he could not process, let alone share. It told a story: a story of muted accomplishment in the face of inevitability. And at the same time, it spoke of love, loss, and perhaps even renewal. The exhaustion of light, the dread of the unknown and the unfinished, the promise of rest at the end of a long voyage; all of these concepts were present. And they all spoke to him in a way that was beyond intimate. It was as though he'd painted it himself, with a brush carved from the wood of his first home and bristled with the lashes of his first love.

"What is it that draws you to this painting, Father? What do you see?"

"Hush yourself, boy!"

A lifetime of scheming. Pledges of fealty, plotting, betrayal and murder. The worst kind. I see, mirrored there in black amongst the painted stones, my own greed and ambition.

263

He saw his firstborn son, too, dead on the shores of the Korean Peninsula, wrapped in a cloak of foolish patriotism. A lovely daughter, an empire that would live for a thousand years, and a cycle of rebirth. A dragon eating its own tail.

I haven't the words for what I see. He looked up at his son. "You talk too much."

"I'm sorry, Father."

How will Raizen fare as boss of the Minowara?

"Torn to shreds...," he mumbled.

"Did you say something, Father?"

"I was just wondering how your sister ended up with the brains *and* the looks and you can't even push a wheelchair without pissing me off."

The chair paused, and for a moment he thought — hoped really — that his silly boy might retort. But hence, a moment or two and surely enough, the chair began to move once more.

How can I leave my empire to this child?

They soon came to a halt before thick, ornate double doors guarded on either side by soldiers carrying rifles. Their uniforms were black and bore no military sigils, no corporate logos, and no indication of rank. One of the men had a thick mustache, like the ones popular in Japan back in the 1970s, and the other had a statuesque jawline and cleft chin. His pupils were so pale as to almost seem missing.

"State your name," the blue-eyed guard instructed. He held a personal identification device that Minowara knew would scan for voice, retinal, and print verification.

"My name is Kazuo Minowara, Chairman of the Minowara-gumi; the Minowara yakuza."

Most people in Sun City carried chips in their wrists that confirmed identity. But Kazuo Minowara, unlike most people, had had his chip removed on the drive out of Sun City International Airport, just after landing in the Pacific State.

"Your hand, please," the guard said.

Kazuo placed a hand down on the device, unable to lay it flat. His fingers were knotted now, unrecognizable, and dark splotches ran up his arms like leopards' spots.

"Now look into the lens here, please."

He followed the man's finger to a black dot at the top of the device. After scanning his eyes, the device chimed.

"Welcome back, sir," the guard said, bowing deeply at the waist.

Together, the two soldiers pulled the great doors open. A gust of warm air hit Minowara in the face, and the density of the atmosphere in the hall seemed to dissipate, like standing at the entrance to a cavern. Though his son tried to peer inside, there was nothing to see but black. A thick curtain blocked the entrance still.

Behind the curtain, Minowara knew, was the Hall of Maati: the meeting place of the Octumvirate and the forum for which all meaningful decisions in the Pacific were made. In the center of the forum was Spectus, the great archive where these decisions were recorded.

Raizen moved to wheel his father inside, but was halted by the guards.

"Your pardon, young Minowara, but I will see the chairman inside." The mustachioed man gently motioned Raizen aside and took the chair. "Only the enlightened are permitted beyond this point."

"He knows that," Minowara told the guard disgustedly. He glared up at his son. "Get back to work."

Raizen looked as though he would say something, but turned and stormed down the hall, just like the petulant child he was.

"My boy has his mother's impulse and the spine of a hummingbird."

"Of course, sir," the guard replied.

"She was a great beauty, you know, his mother."

"I'm sure she was, sir."

Pulling the curtain aside, the man rolled him into the hall. Unlike his son, the man's pace pushing the chair was slow, respectful, and dignified.

"Session six thousand, one hundred and six has begun, sir. The date is August second, year of the Great Architect 2050. The session has begun, but you may still have time to review the agenda before you are called upon."

"Let us not delay, then."

Inside, the hall was dark and a voice could be heard, amplified by an intricate and immersive sound system. A gentle fragrance of flowers filled the air, and the oxygen being pumped into the room filled him with vigor.

"I understand that you do not require hearing accommodations, sir. Is that still correct?"

"Surprisingly enough, my hearing is as it was fifty years ago."

"*Beati sunt qui illustrantur,*" the guard said reverently.

Blessed are the enlightened.

11.5: Behind the Curtain

"The only true currency is time."

- First Oyabun of the Minowara-gumi, Kazuo Minowara

His private chamber was small and dimly lit behind a translucent wall that acted as a heads-up display. The monitor was presently filled with the stern, angular face of Unicom Network's CEO, John Cholish.

Kazuo touched the console before him, and Cholish's voice filled the chamber. The man had a sticky, wet-lipped style of speaking that never failed to disgust.

Minowara sighed and settled into his chair for what, based on the docket, looked to be a long afternoon.

The session of the Order of the Sun was underway. These hearings were held bi-monthly and served as the only officially recognized venue for matters concerning the Pacific. The Order of the Sun held eight hand-selected members and was one of eight active Grand Councils. Each Grand Council presided over a different region of the developed world.

At present, the active Councils were the orders of the Beacon, Snake, Judge, Mother, Mage, Ferryman, Eye, and lastly the Order of the Sun. The eight orders acted autonomously from one another but all adhered to the Law of

Orders, a binding set of rules numbering in the thousands, that held the active orders to the traditions of the Elders.

The Council of Elders upheld law within the Circle of Orders from the shadows, their eyes and ears the many pages and acolytes that moved between the orders. Acolytes were men and women selected by a given order as a kind of reserve. When tragedy befell one of the Eight, someone would be there, groomed and ready to ascend. The heavy task of managing the world never missed a beat.

Numerology played a significant role in the Octumvirate and, by definition, so did balance. In the event of the death or incapacitation of a Council member, an order would be reduced to the designation of "Council of Less than Eight." When this occurred, any initiatives up for vote were stalled or invalidated entirely. And only an election held by the afflicted order could restore their status and validity.

"Only the illuminated can replenish the Order."

To do this, they would draw from the near-limitless pool of wannabe chosen.

Acolytes — in contrast to their title — were often men and women of extreme wealth and influence. Many times, they were captains of industry, presidents and monarchs, religious figureheads, media icons, generals, and kingpins like Kazuo himself. The voting process to replace a fallen member of the Council was not always transparent, and the vetting process was insanely political. As a result, many elected to the Council floundered in their effectiveness shortly after. This, in turn, created a culture of internal undercutting, one-upmanship, and betrayal that occasionally escalated to murder, at which point the cycle repeated itself.

And in the unlikely event that an order lost more than one member in the time it took to assemble a vote, the order stood to lose its designation permanently, never to be reclaimed. The Order of the Sun would lose all right to the coffer of the Order of the Sun, as well as its archive. Any wealth amassed by the Octumvirate would be absorbed into the greater fraternity. At this time, the remaining members would assume the next order designation, as prescribed by Sumerian text.

The Council of Elders and its orders had been called many names throughout history. Over thousands of years, a great many books had been written by infiltrators of the Order, to varying degrees of accuracy. Likewise, a great many had been written by the Order to muddy the waters of truth. Called the Illuminati in the West, the Assassins in the Old World, and the Dragon Family in the East, they were the hand behind the throne, the men behind the curtain. Mistaken for Freemasons, and believed to be otherworldly, the Order was none of these things and at the same time so much more. The Order was balance. The Order was control. The Order, as he would describe it, was the pilot in the night and at the helm of all things. The Order could never be weeded out or destroyed because the Order was the very institution that would take up against them. The Order was — like the yakuza — immortal.

270

Its members were carefully selected to ensure that sympathy for the Order existed in all facets of civilization. No more could mankind expel the Order than it could eradicate itself.

Kazuo Minowara brought up the agenda in golden text on the monitor alongside Cholish's face and sat back with his hands resting on the padded arms of his chair.

"The rating system will be based on several metrics," Cholish was saying. "Voluntary State contribution record, taxable income, criminal record, and voting history are just some of the factors. We've also created a Citizen Value Quotient: a grade of sorts based on other traits like spending habits and rate of consumption. All of these factors and more will determine the unit's overall score. Scores below X amount will be limited to download speeds of 300 megabits per second or less per thirty-day score review period, and for those with higher scores, the allowances will jump to 660, 900, one point two gigabits, and finally the maximum cap for citizenry, two point five gigabits per second. For the rest of us, bandwidth will remain uncapped. On top of this, users below the pre-specified threshold will only have access to registered and network-approved domains. These domains are all closely monitored and moderated to ensure that all content, hosted or posted, has been screened for message uniformity."

"Scores will not be made public knowledge, of course," a voice asked.

Kazuo recognized it to be that of Sun City's Premier.

271

"Of course not," Cholish responded. "Scores will be encrypted and stored in a secured database, restricted to even the affiliated. This initiative will free up bandwidth for the SDC, the Defense Ministry, and for corporations represented by the Council."

"Sun City will act as the flagship for this program," Cholish continued, "and with the Council's approval, Unicom will expand the program to Eden, Capital City, and lastly to the rest of the State. This proposal I would submit to you for a vote today as Initiative A."

The screen next to the Unicom CEO's face came to life with the words: "Initiative A – Merit-based Bandwidth."

Minowara would vote in favor of the initiative when the time came. Less bandwidth meant fewer people sitting in front of their computers or staring at their mobiles, and more people sitting at his casino tables or looking for entertainment in the flesh.

He removed a small, red notebook from his breast pocket and took a plum-colored pen from its binding. Flipping through to find a blank page, he dated the top and wrote in shaky Kanji "Initiative A – yes." He blew on the page to dry the ink and closed the notebook. Holding on to the pen, he slipped the notebook back into his pocket.

"Next, I would like to congratulate Councilwoman West and Premier Macek on the commercial success of the Unit One Initiative. Their brand sponsors have reported a median increase in sales of roughly nine percent. This stands as further proof of the effectiveness of joint private sector–State advertising. As well, network news viewership has spiked some thirteen percent in the week following the explosion on the 101. Likewise, Skyy Shoes and Paragon Motorcycles have renewed their agreements with the network. In light of this, the business development teams of both companies will be reaching out to the Consortium with offers to renew the contracts of Unit One Sergeants Moore and Calderon as product spokesmen. Other brands have come forward as well, expressing interest in similar sponsorship programs. Moreover, and not to steal Councilwoman Jones-Gutierrez' thunder, but Deckar Applied Sciences will be starting a massive advertising campaign using our network platform, scheduled to begin on the first of September. Potential candidates for celebrity spokespersons will be needed for that as well, and so I would ask of our esteemed Councilwoman West to begin considering candidates within the State Defense Consortium."

Esteemed, Minowara thought cynically. *West is far from esteemed. The woman is vile. And Cholish is an insufferable bootlicker for suggesting otherwise.*

"Considering the commercial success thus far of Unit One's agents, perhaps we can tap Detective…" —he looked off-screen, likely to his own notes— "Bryant or Deputy Informant Yamazaki *Die-soo-kee*. I'm not sure if I'm saying that right, perhaps the venerable Councilman Minowara can correct me."

Minowara leaned forward and held his hand near to the terminal. The light in his chamber turned green. "It's pronounced 'Dai-soo-kay,' or just 'Dice-kay.'"

"Excellent. Deputy Informant Yamazaki Daisuke. It's also worth mentioning, from an advertising perspective, Mr. Daisuke would have a much greater market appeal as a fully instated Unit One agent, rather than a deputy. That is just my thought on the matter."

A voice chimed in. It was Diane West, State Defense Consortium chairwoman. The paper tiger/advertising mechanism that was Unit One was the brainchild of West and Macek.

"Yamazaki Daisuke is an ex-yakuza," she replied in her typically mirthless tone. "Promoting him to improve brand approval seems a bit much."

"What is Unit One if not marketing and psy-ops?" Cholish replied.

West cleared her throat as if to erase his words. "They may have started off as a political and commercial device, but they have shown themselves at times to be quite capable. A recent case in point, the Parkside Strangler. From his appearance in the Queue, it took Sergeant Calderon less than twenty-four hours to locate and neutralize the killer."

And we care because…?

"Unit One can also be credited with dismantling the Russian human-trafficking ring that none of us signed off on, as well as the infiltration and subsequent dismantling of the anti-government militia, Sons of Liberty. Also, yakuza and Triad busts have kept the headlines consistently in the Consortium's favor."

West paused and took a breath.

"In time, I see Unit One possibly replacing Agency Zero, whom we can all agree have the marketability of sawdust. We can speak more on that later. That being said, Councilman Cholish, while Unit One may be gaining some legitimacy, at this time Yamazaki Daisuke's capacity within the SDC is that of a professional informant and nothing more. Should he prove himself more capable, perhaps in time, this will change. His rank and responsibilities are a matter of State, not industry."

Cholish wilted like the worm he was. "Understood, Councilwoman West."

Minowara was flummoxed. The fact that Yamazaki Daisuke, yakuza of modest rank, had somehow weaseled his way into the SDC (and Unit One, no less!) was something he could never quite get his head around. The man was a defector of the clan, true, but no less a gangster. Did they really think that any yakuza worth his salt was capable of reform?

There is something else about the young man, he thought, *something peculiar… Oh yes, he's married to that German assassin. What do they call her? "Party Girl?" What a stupid name. Young people are stupid.*

"In the last session," Cholish continued, "Councilwoman West proposed a 'kill switch' to disable all television and internet traffic during the Liberty Day Parade—"

If I were young again, Minowara mused, *I would have the Triads, the Titans, hell, even the SDC under my thumb. I'd even show these people. I'd be an Elder in no time…*

He awoke with a start.

"—Tuesday, between the hours of 0800 and 1600. Expect a complete outage for all nonessential programming throughout the State. This downtime will be used to migrate signals over to the new relays and upgrade the servers powering Libra and Scorpio in Sun City and Capital City respectively."

"Perhaps we can blame the outage on the Fifth Estate protest group, rather than admitting to scheduled maintenance?" someone suggested.

"Systems upgrade," Cholish corrected.

"Whatever." It was Diane West.

"I like it," Elaine Jones-Gutierrez chimed in.

How long have I been asleep? Minowara put a hand on his face.

"Terrorist act," Premier Macek added. "A ham-handed, softball terrorist attack. It's perfect. It demonstrates their ineptitude and their complete disregard for the people of Sun City."

How long was I out? Minowara wiped his lips and pushed himself up into his seat. *This cursed chair is too comfortable.* Between the personal, soundproofed cell and the oxygen, he was too damn comfortable in general. *Have I been called upon? Surely that windbag Cholish hasn't been talking this whole time.*

"With that," Cholish said, "I thank my honored colleagues and relinquish the remainder of my time."

The next face to appear was that of Jensen Carlisle. Carlisle was a heavyset and thick-necked bison of a man, and president of Horus Bank, the multinational banking institution. His eyes were the color of frozen lemonade. Beneath a thick, black mustache, two thin lips chipped off the words, "I've nothing for this session. From the perspective of the Horus Bank, all affairs are in order." He paused and seemed to reconsider forfeiting his time. "On an interesting side note, for those of you interested, the People's Republic of China has submitted the first of its payments against the principal loan granted them prior to the start of the North Korean conflict. It would appear that Beijing intends to make good on their debt. A bit surprising that they wouldn't ask for an extension, but given time and a review of prepayment fees, I'm sure they'll come around. The Council's share of this initial payment has been transferred to the coffer."

"They'd better pay," Jones-Gutierrez replied. "I could draft the sanctions that would cripple Asian trade on a napkin.

They've left themselves quite open since the war. And perhaps it's time…"

Learning that the Octumvirate had funded both sides of the Third Korean War had been a bit of a shocker for Minowara, at least at first.

Almost as surprising was Carlisle's brevity. When the Horus Bank had a problem, which was often, it was everyone's problem. And bankers were nothing if not obstinate. In the past, Carlisle had turned sessions into days-long marathons over the most minuscule of details. If something like the fiduciary responsibility of a project was not clear in a proposal that might impact the Horus Bank, no matter how fledgling the proposal, everything was brought to a halt. Lawyers, pages mostly agnostic to the agenda, were called in and the details were hammered out right then and there. It was that kind of tenacity that made Carlisle less than pleasurable to deal with. But it was also that kind of tenacity that made him one of the most powerful men in the world. Of the members of the Order of Sun, Minowara respected Carlisle the most.

As Carlisle relinquished the remainder of his time, his face was replaced with that of Elaine Jones-Gutierrez. Jones-Gutierrez was the President of Deckar Applied Sciences and her face, to Minowara, was a welcome sight. A full set of lips, flawless skin, and eyes the color of basil comprised a face that seemed immune to the battering of time, unlike his own.

Kazuo placed his hands on the arms of the chair and blinked rapidly to clear the sleep from his eyes. Representing

DAS, the second largest robotics and augmentation manufacturer in the country, Jones-Gutierrez, or "EJG" as the others called her, was the "Master of MODS." For thirteen years EJG had sat on the council, and today she was one of the most learned and influential people in the Order. In fact, outside of the Hall of Maati, very few knew that the Third Korean War was her idea entirely.

"I have no items to submit for consideration today," she began, "merely requests."

How strange life is, he thought. *To think that I am allied with the woman who orchestrated the war that leveled my home and drove my family across the Pacific...*

She did it to bring us closer. The joke made him chuckle.

"Field-testing has begun on the M-2 'anthro-tank,'" Jones-Gutierrez told them. "We've designated it 'Kodiak.'"

Stupid name, Minowara thought before sleep took him once more.

"—handheld railgun," she was saying, "with a self-charging power core. The shipment was attacked on the 101 just north of Section Four by these highwaymen that continually plague the corridor."

How long had he been asleep this time? Had they called on him? Kazuo looked around his cell. If he could turn the lights on, it might be easier to stay awake. It was ridiculous to meet via video conference while they were all likely in the same hall.

"The perpetrators were bike punks, most likely the Huntsmen. We would like the SDC's assistance in tracking the stolen weapons. If they were to hit the black market it could spawn a host of knock-offs. The profit loss could be astronomical."

West was the first to respond, as was typical when the SDC came up. "A gang that size might warrant deploying Agency Zero."

"Activating Agency Zero should be avoided if possible," Macek replied. "Putting those toys back in the box is never easy. Plus, we don't need them under any measure of scrutiny, especially as we continue to kick around the idea of disbanding them. Let's let Unit One have at the Huntsmen. If anything at all, it should make for interesting television."

Someone grumbled, and it sounded like Luther Gueye.

"Thank you, Your Excellency," Jones-Gutierrez replied. "I was hoping you would see it that way, actually. The marketing team at DAS has drawn up several uniform designs that feature the DAS logo prominently. We were hoping that the unit might wear one of these designs during the campaign against the bike punks, at least for any would-be-televised portions. This would include, of course, interviews, arrests, and subsequent court appearances. We believe this would kick off the new joint DAS-SDC partnership nicely."

"I don't see a problem with that," West replied.

"Excellent. Lastly, and this may affect Unit One as well, we are looking for candidates willing to be outfitted with our latest mech-org direct synthesis kit, designation Type-K. It is a full-body prosthesis and designed to out-perform the Type-A kit in nearly every facet. It is still very much in a prototype state, however, and we are finding it difficult to measure the progression of the design without live test subjects."

"You mean guinea pigs," someone interjected.

"To-may-to, to-mah-to."

West sighed. "The unit is so small, it gives me pause. Every team member, including the deputy informant, is integral to the team's success. What is it with DAS today? You want to dress my unit *and* play cops and robbers with them? Unit One is not a plaything for Deckar Applied Sciences, Mrs. Jones-Gutierrez."

Jones-Gutierrez laughed mischievously. "Sure they are!"

West sighed and even chuckled herself. "Unit One has a slew of potential recruits who have yet to undergo MODS augmentation. I could volunteer one of them, assuming, of course, they even make the cut."

"Brilliant! Thank you, Councilwoman West. As usual, DAS is grateful for your support. That is all. I relinquish the remainder of my time."

Councilman Ruben Liu was next. Ruben was the chairman of Coastal Power. Coastal was the Pacific subsidiary of the multinational utility corporation Global Water &

281

Electric. As though fingering the utility lifeline of the entire Pacific wasn't enough, Liu dominated construction and real estate in the Pacific State. He did all this as a behind-the-scenes financier of the Hō, a massive Chinese criminal enterprise that had its roots in deep in mainland China and now hoped to sink its teeth into Sun City.

Ruben Liu's funding of Chinese gangsters whose interests conflicted with those of his own syndicate made him Minowara's second-to-least favorite Order member, surpassed only by the Titan boss Luther Gueye. Blood Oath or no, Kazuo would love to see both men gone from the Earth. In fact, he fantasized regularly about killing them, even going as far as to lay the groundwork for a strategy. For example, he knew he would have to stagger their murders by no less than four years' time, lest risk casting the Order down to the status of "Less than Seven," which would place the Octumvirate coffer and designation at risk. And then there was the Blood Oath and the hellish punishments for betrayal it warranted…

The physical penalty for going against the will of the Order was straight out of the Dark Ages, literally, while the economic punishment would see his legacy and holdings reduced to ash. In truth, however, Kazuo had never been one for superstition, and never one to quail in the face of warning.

The only oath that bound him truly was the one he'd pledged to his onetime mentor, Daigo. Right before Kazuo blew Daigo's brains all over the deck of his own boat.

"My house, the clan Minowara, will live for a thousand years."

Liu's face was too wide to fit on the wall-sized display, and his lips were like two skinned carcasses draped out across a mottled, earthen terrain. His eyes were small and when he spoke, they smiled at nothing.

Of late, Liu's complaints predominantly centered around construction permits and specifically ways to obtain them for projects in no one's interest but his own. When he wasn't snatching at building rights, his energies were focused on squeezing every last cent out of the already strangled energy grid. As Liu prattled on, Minowara let his head list a bit, his eyes close. Staying awake was such a—

The sun was low in the sky and burning strong. Seagulls rose and fell on warm winds, and the sea swayed below in perfect harmony. He sat and waited patiently from the deck of his home, watching the sun redden until it was like a radish or fresh bullet hole in the sky. When he reached for something to drink, he found it there, cool and perspiring in hands that were not gnarled, and not like the roots of a dying tree.

Sakakibara, his dear old friend, would be there soon and with him Misa and Ryuichi. Ryu and Misa-chan weren't dead, and no longer was he old and failing.

"Otōsan..."

Father...

There he was again, breaking the peace.

"Raizen, you fool."

"Father."

"Ryuichi is the best of me, boy!"

"Father."

Irritably, Kazuo turned to face Raizen, ready to fling his drink at him, but the boy was not alone. Raizen stood there on the wooden deck, with Omoe at his side. They wore white and held hands like they'd done as children. The sight of them momentarily quelled his anger. They were beautiful children. And as they stood there, flames lapped up at them from the deck.

"Omoe, my sweet. There's fire there! Do you not see it at your feet?"

The fire caught the sleeves of Raizen's pristine pearl blazer and danced up the front of his daughter's lovely summer dress.

"Raizen! Omoe!"

Now they were ablaze. Yet there they stood, clasping hands that were melting into a singular charred mess. Kazuo threw his drink at the flames, only to cast sand from the glass. Beneath the whipping tongues of flame, his children were black, and yet still they did not move.

"Father," Omoe called to him in the voice of a twelve-year-old.

The sun was close now, bearing down on them, and as Kazuo shielded his eyes, the celestial body shattered like a

284

bauble. Great shards of blood-colored glass tore into the earth and split the ocean like a stomped puddle. What remained of the sun was black now, a charred and fractured sphere like the eyes of a serpent. It descended on them, filling the sky and scattering the clouds.

Misa was not coming. Ryuichi was not coming. Sakakibara was not coming. No one would survive the end of times. Omoe and Raizen were gone now, reduced to ash that scattered in the hot wind of a punctured and deflating world. Kazuo, now old and very tired, sat back down in his chair and let his grief and the flames of an earthbound star consume him.

The Minowara chairman's own scream pulled him from the dream, and he woke in the dark clutching at the arms of his chair. His heart pounding in his chest, he looked up to find a large face and eyes that were little more than slits smiling down at him. Ruben Liu appeared to be laughing.

"Page!"

There was no response.

"—a series of brownouts across the Pacific State beginning on the eve of November second," Liu continued. "They are to occur sporadically until the surplus is back above eighty percent. I am putting this forward for your consideration as Initiative D."

Minowara's stomach rolled and he was certain he would retch. Looking around the room, he tried to restore his bearings. Reaching forward, he held his hand above a slim red indicator and a voice other than Ruben Liu's filled the room.

"Boss Minowara. What can we do for you?"

"Water," he croaked. "I need water."

The serpent star still loomed in his vision, so real.

"Right away, sir," the voice replied.

As Kazuo waited, with a hand to his chest, he took deep breaths, hoping to still his heart.

Liu's voice returned. "Next, the levels of lithium have been raised in the State reservoirs to eight parts per million to help combat civil unrest. Here, in sections Seven, Four, and Two, this dosage is considerably higher as we come closer to the Liberty Day celebration. The cost for this supplementation has already been deducted from the coffer.

"Lastly, the number of residents in the State who've gone delinquent on their utility payments has doubled since 2045. In response to this, Coastal will be locking sixty-six percent of the delinquents out of their homes, effective December first.

"Delinquents not living in digitally controlled homes will have to be manually evicted. For this, I expect to lean on the police forces of Sun City, Capital City, and Eden. Premier Macek, I assume this will not be an issue to arrange."

"It will not be."

"Excellent. I relinquish what time I have left."

Liu's face disappeared and was replaced by the bullish face of Councilwoman Diane West.

Minowara licked his lips. His heart was still beating feverishly. Never in his life had a dream been more vivid. Even now, the stench of charred flesh filled his nostrils. Light slipped into the room as the door to his cell opened silently. A page, a young man with tattoos on his face and neck, handed him a chilled glass of water and a napkin. The yakuza boss drank greedily, even as the man waited patiently. When the glass was emptied, he gasped.

"Está bien, mi Don?" the page, likely a powerful kingpin in his own right, asked. He folded his hands behind his back — a gesture that looked unnatural for him — and waited patiently for a response.

"I'm fine," Minowara told him. "More water, please."

"As you all know, this year's Liberty Day Parade is rapidly approaching," Diane West began. "With increased activity from the Fifth Estate, the need for enhanced security is greater now than it has been in the years since the Liberty Day bombing. And, as such, I would put forward Initiative E: armored crowd control including, but not limited to, the presence of mechanized units. BTs, specifically."

As much as Minowara despised West, the sound of her voice seemed to help calm him. At least it was of this world. The tattooed man returned with another glass of chilled water, for which Minowara thanked him sincerely. As the tattooed acolyte left the room, Kazuo sat forward in his chair, holding the cold glass in both hands.

Carlisle cleared his throat before speaking. "Refresh my memory, Ms. West: what exactly is a 'BT'?"

"Bipedal tank. These would be outfitted with crowd control devices: sound cannons, microwave, and whatever other non-lethal load-outs are available."

"Won't a military presence only provoke the protesters?"

"Actually, our strategists believe that the majority of citizens outside of Sections Seven and Four are wary of the Fifth Estate and see them as little more than rabble-rousers. Perhaps provoking them on a day of celebration plays into our hand."

"Seems risky to me."

The nightmare was fading now and Kazuo hoped it would soon be nothing more than a chill in the back of his thoughts. He focused on the conversation as a means of further expelling the hellish vision.

"We've no real agenda for this year's parade," Macek added, "beyond the usual perscribed dose of statism. After all, we have to remind the people of how great their lives have become since secession. That said, it's not an entirely vapid effort. I want to use the platform to officially announce the Major's retirement. It will be a good first step in either decommissioning Agency Zero or repurposing the group. Also, if his retirement is announced to the entire world, it will make it that much harder for him to backpedal. And if the Fifth Estate turns the thing into a disaster, it'll only hurt their image and give us further justification for a statewide crackdown. I say deploy the tanks, and let's just see how this thing plays out."

"There is, of course, the minor detail of your own health and well-being," Carlisle chimed in with a chuckle. "Who's to say the Fifth Estate isn't going to target you, or West, or the Major personally?"

"Well," West replied, "the whole of Unit One will be deployed to serve as the Premier's personal guard. As well, the entire plaza will be walled in and the crowds heavily patrolled by SCPD in riot gear. Snipers strategically placed will have the plaza blanketed. I'm personally not concerned."

"Actually," Macek added, "I have decided to deploy Unit One to the checkpoints during the parade to discourage Huntsmen activity and to protect against unlawful entry into the city during the celebration. Agency Zero will, in fact, handle security for the event. For one more year..."

Jones-Gutierrez groaned. She clearly wanted Unit One on the grand stage — wearing their DAS-branded uniforms, no doubt. "Agency Zero played their part like good little soldiers, but now it's time to move on. And as for the Major, he's been a very effective and reliable asset but in the end, he's just that, an asset. These days he's more of a liability to this Council than anything else."

"Agreed," a voice said.

"Let the parade serve to implant his image in the minds of the people one last time before he's martyred," Macek added dryly.

"Martyred?"

Kazuo could not contain his curiosity. "Sounds like we plan to finally do away with Major Monroe. And by what means will "Iron" Ace be dispatched?"

"To be quite honest, I haven't yet decided," Macek said, no small amount of regret in his voice. "Perhaps he'll meet his end at the hands of the Fifth Estate. Maybe gunned down on his front porch one night by 'anti-State extremists.' Maybe suicide… We all know PTSD can be a killer. Regardless, he was a good friend and this talk is unpleasant for me; let's move on."

West continued. "If we're all in agreement that Agency Zero replace Unit One as Councilman Macek's personal attachment, I'm fine bypassing a vote." When no one responded, she continued. "Next I would like to propose a seven PM curfew for the week leading up to the Garcia fight and the week following, the only exception being the day of the event. The goal: to curb reveling and give us the opportunity to upgrade sections of Sun City not currently covered by Libra. The curfew in Sun City is to be accompanied by brownouts that will assist in replenishing the power surplus."

"This is good," Liu chortled.

"I will relinquish the remainder of my time," West said, "but I would like to segue to Mr. Gueye with a question." She

290

paused for effect. "Why have you drawn so much attention to yourself as of late?"

Luther Gueye, industrialist, philanthropist, and kingpin of the State's largest drug cartel, appeared on the screen, large, black, and glaring. He was visibly livid. His eyes were white-hot and his teeth a guillotine as he responded. His French accent required a special focus on Minowara's part to understand. English by itself was still a challenge for him.

"Attention from *your* dogs, Councilwoman West!"

"And would you explain the events that took place on the 101, specifically the explosion that killed one of yours and severely maimed an agent of the SDC, to the council?"

Luther shook his head, his expression cold and mocking. "I believe the council is well aware of the methods I employ, but I'll summarize by reminding you that when my employees speak my name, bad things happen."

Elaine Jones-Gutierrez chuckled. "Glad to see you're making use of Ouroboros."

West plowed over the remark in her typical boorish fashion. "Well, this 'bad thing' has put you on Unit One's radar."

"Oh, I know!" Gueye replied. "The same Deputy Informant Yamazaki Daisuke that Councilman Cholish would see promoted visited the *Musée* — brazenly, might I add — and interrogated my sister." He paused for a moment, his nostrils flaring, a long finger swaying across the screen. "Perhaps, before we go down this road, my esteemed

291

oathsister, I should remind the council of my contribution to coffer this quarter."

Reports sprang onto the screen, framing his face in metrics.

"I have deposited, on behalf of my Titans, six point two billion dollars into the coffer, to do with as the men and women of this Order please. Earnings are up seven percent from first quarter 2049."

"Impressive," Cholish said. Macek, Jones-Gutierrez, and Liu quickly seconded him.

Sitting in the dark, still clutching his water, Minowara was eager to get home and thoroughly uncomfortable. Nevertheless, Gueye's numbers placed a pit in his stomach. The Titans held most of Sun City in a drug-induced state, and if there was one thing bad for gambling, it was drugs. It left men and women who would otherwise fill seats in his casinos penniless and otherwise useless. More than that, Gueye's territory was premium quality, ideal zones for brothels and card houses. Numbers — revenue was power. And Gueye was powerful indeed.

"Now," Gueye continued, pausing for effect, "I move to have Unit One disbanded, effective immediately. And, as for this Deputy Informant Daisuke, I will see to him personally for his disrespect. My men are already tracking his movements."

West scoffed. "Please! You're overreacting."

"Overreacting? Funny enough, I also had an intruder during Mr. Daisuke's visit, a burglar in my storeroom."

"And what did he steal, exactly, that this Council cannot replace ten times over?"

"He or she stole nothing, in fact, largely thanks to my security forces, but the intruder paid for the damages dearly." Gueye's voice took on a snarky tone. "And, on the topic of damages to the *Musée*, I expect the cost to be deducted from next quarter's contribution. Early estimates place the damage, all things considered of course, in the seven-hundred range, give or take."

Voices filled Kazuo's personal chamber.

"Who can cause more damage than a property's worth? What sorcery is that?"

"Hogwash! The larceny is here and now."

Luther's comment had sent the group into a fury. Amidst the chaos, someone was laughing. It was the mocking laugh of the State Defense Consortium's chairwoman. As the voices died, West's obnoxious laughter continued for an exaggerated while. "Disband Unit One?" she replied. "We will do no such thing. Unit One has proven a marvelous success on several fronts. Before the creation of that team, approval for State government and the Consortium was in the toilet. Applications for police jobs were virtually non-existent and I can say without exaggeration that hatred for the government in this state was commonplace. Now, in a few short years, through a master stroke of public relations and marketing, we've flipped those numbers on their heads. Unit One has made the SDC, Libra, and, dare I say, the State itself, 'cool!'

Disband?" She laughed again. "Not likely! And, as for the damages you've allegedly accrued, let's let Order adjusters figure that number out. Yours are clearly operating on the abacus end of the accounting spectrum. Lastly, young Gueye, I would add that you best pray that this second intruder was not from the SDC."

Luther ignored her. "I present Initiative F for the council: the immediate decommissioning of Unit One."

"I hope you've brought more to this session, Mr. Gueye," West taunted.

It was Jensen Carlisle of Horus Bank who responded first. "Councilwoman West, I would ask that you show your oathbrother his due respect. No man *or woman* is above the cohesion of Eight."

"Thank you, Jensen," Gueye replied. "Moving on..."

"Not quite yet," West countered, unfazed by the reprimanding. "This intruder: were they identified?"

"No."

"Then how do you know they weren't Unit One?"

"I suspect they were. Conducting an illegal warrantless search of my property. You'll know for sure when the corpse washes up on Section Four's coast."

"You have overstepped your bounds!"

"I've defended my property, and by extension, the property of this council."

"I understand your position, Luther, but West may have a point," Jones-Gutierrez added. "If you've slain an agent of the SDC, it puts Councilwoman West in a precarious position. She can't appear sympathetic to you in any way, should your relationship with the Titans come to light."

"Is it not her role to control the SDC? Whose strings are loose here?"

"You speak as though every single person in the SDC took the Blood Oath. My influence does not give you carte blanche to kill every person who steps on your toes."

"Can you speak to the details of this investigation?" Luther asked her.

Minowara smirked. *Good question.*

"I will find out the details," West stammered.

Gueye's expression betrayed his satisfaction. His eyes narrowed. "The intruder bore no marking of the SDC. My people, should it come to that, have plausible deniability. Dissolution of the unit will ensure no follow-up investigation. Consider these things, Council."

Minowara had no love for Unit One, Yamazaki Daisuke notwithstanding. Unlike the Sun City Police Department, they were entirely unpredictable. And despite their harmless origins, they seemed at times surprisingly, inconveniently adept. The truth of the matter was simple, however: there was no logical excuse for the disbanding of Unit One. Doing so would draw nothing but negative attention.

Kazuo felt compelled to point out the obvious to his young rival. "And if your dissolution proposal fails?"

"If it fails, I'll be forced to settle matters independently."

"Speak plainly!" West demanded.

"I have, woman!"

The chamber was silent.

The boy has fire, you have to give him that, Minowara thought, toying with the arms of his chair.

West, for once, was speechless, allowing Gueye to move forward quickly. "On to other topics. I would like to make the members of this council aware of Initiative C in your session program."

Kazuo's screen came to life, as specifications appeared alongside Gueye's face. They appeared to provide the details of some kind of chemical compound.

"The drug known as Zeoadrenogen has been procured in tonnage from shadownet distributers in Chosica. With a suggested street price of seven hundred dollars per cubic centimeter, we stand to make a substantial amount in what we consider to be ideal market conditions. The substance goes by the street name of 'Riot Blood.' The compound itself works by feeding the body an artificial adrenaline. In parallel, it produces a sustainable tachypsychia: the adrenaline high known as 'fight or flight.' It also alters the user's perception of time, slowing it down considerably in some cases."

"What's the point of this drug?" Cholish asked.

"Riot Blood requires less than a minute to take effect and the results are wondrous. Users of Riot Blood become, in some studies, up to twelve times as powerful as they are under natural conditions. Users also react faster, considerably so. And the effects of a single dose can last up to thirty-five days."

"I would like a complete study submitted," Jones-Gutierrez said. "This could prove instrumental in several projects underway at Saltland."

"And what are the side effects?" someone else added. "Surely cardiac arrest is a concern."

"The dangers are typical for a drug of this nature," Gueye replied, "Prolonged abuse will likely result in chemical imbalance, muscle deterioration, irregular heart beat, and ultimately dementia and death."

"What about testing?" Macek asked. "How do I know you aren't about to introduce the bubonic plague on Sun City?"

"The product — in lesser states — has been in circulation in South America for several years, primarily introduced to the anti-demonstration forces of Venuzuela and Colombia. Only recently have we been able to accentuate its potency and give it a marketable appeal. I will present case studies at the next session if it pleases the Order."

"It pleases," Macek finished.

"Then it is done, Your Excellency."

Luther's use of Macek's self-granted title in this setting was a slight... a very subtle, very snarky slight. But it was not lost on Minowara, and so likely was not lost on Sun City's Premier.

"With that," Luther said, "I have no more." His face shrank as he sat back, away from the camera.

Macek's blotchy face took over the screen next. His hair was swept back and silver on the sides. He wore a silver ascot and on his breast was a pendant with the seal of the State. "Mr. Gueye, the council has nothing but respect for your commitment and contribution. I know I don't speak alone when I tell you that you are seen as the future of this Order." He paused and pursed his lips in thought. "That being said, as a friend and one bound to you by oath and pact, I would advise that you consider reducing your public profile significantly."

"Hear, hear," someone said.

"You've no need to manage the Titans directly anymore," Macek continued. "This machine you've built can be sustained with minimal effort, perhaps even automated. And that's not to marginalize your impact, but rather to applaud your achievements. There is very little infighting inside your organization and, for the most part, we can predict the behavior of your men with the accuracy of a mathematical equation. For a drug cartel, the Titans create less noise or mayhem than groups a fraction of their size. That is, up until this latest incident..."

It was the typically aloof Carlisle who spoke next. "I, for one, have always wondered why you would maintain such close ties to your organization when you've so much to lose. Surely you've someone you trust that can maintain the day-to-day?"

Luther did not speak, and Minowara could only imagine what he was thinking. What if the Order asked him to step down as the boss of the Minowara? "Never," would be his response, "*Never in a million years!*"

"Like Councilman Minowara stated," Macek continued, "assume your proposition to disband Unit One will fail. Assume that Unit One, no matter how much of a nuisance they are to you, isn't going anywhere, at least anytime soon.

"You see, young Gueye, in my eyes, Unit One represents the counterweight to your very own Titans. They give the people what they need: the belief that we are doing everything in our power to combat organized crime and drugs. If the Titans have a place in the world, then so does Unit One. Does that make sense?"

"Without agreeing," Luther replied, "your words make sense."

"Perhaps Councilwoman West, yourself, and I can have a discussion about how to cull or perhaps better regulate Unit One's interaction with your organization."

"I am willing to have the conversation," Luther said.

"Then you will withdraw Initiative F from consideration?"

"I'll try my luck and leave it in place."

Macek chuckled. "Fair enough."

Minowara sipped his water. *Perhaps it is in everyone's best interest that Gueye is dealt with.* As he was pondering the murder of his oathbrother, a green light in his room signaled his time to speak. From the inner pocket of his blazer, he withdrew his tiny red notebook and, using the golden ribbon bookmark to guide him, began reading.

"I've provided the Council with a list of plots throughout Sun City, Eden, and Capital City upon which I would like to build new brothels and casinos."

"How many?" Macek asked.

"Eleven in Sun City, twenty-seven in total."

Gueye whistled. "That's ambitious. How do you propose to put up twenty-seven illegal dens in three cities without the tribes taking notice?"

"By leveraging this Council's influence, of course. The specifics are in the proposal marked Initiative B. To summarize, we would make the tribes co-sponsors through a sustainable network of back-channel hush money and land grants."

"The locations themselves," Minowara continued, "are ideal and stand to quadruple our gambling take by 2057. Surely the Council can appreciate what that might do for my contribution to the coffer."

"This could justify the expansion of Unit One," West replied.

"Or we could just legalize gambling and prostitution," Gueye responded scornfully.

"Sure," Cholish replied, "and devalue the enterprise while subjecting it to public scrutiny and taxation..."

"Initiative B it is," Macek said, "pending a post-vote approval of the real estate you've in mind…"

"Excellent." Minowara was thrilled by the lack of questions. He was prepared to ask for a six-month moratorium on police raids as a consolation request and was thrilled to keep that card in its deck for future use. He sat back in the chair and allowed himself a smile. "I've nothing more."

The Premier, ever the politician, closed out the session by pouring undue praise on the members, singling each out individually for their contribution the coffer. After his speech, voting began.

As Minowara considered the items and how best to hamper Luther Gueye with his votes, he thought also of how best to have the man removed from existence. Sometimes the best way to do something was the most direct. *What was her name again*, he thought, *Daisuke's assassin wife*?

Ah yes, the "Party Crasher."

#SCPD Anonymous Hotline::

"Nine-one-one, what's your emergency."

"We found a body."

"Okay ma'am, what is your location?"

"I'm not with the body! Are you crazy? We found it the other day, the morning after the storm."

"Where were you when you found the body, ma'am?"

"Crab fishing off the peninsula, over by that new museum. He was just lying there, in the seaweed. I knew he was dead, but they wanted to go see."

"The Musée, ma'am? That museum?"

"Sure, whatever. That hideous, glob-of-snot-looking thing. I wouldn't even be calling you guys but they might find our prints and think we killed him."

"Ma'am, please remain calm and try to explain in as much detail as possible what happened."

"This line is unanimous right?"

"This line is anonymous."

"Okay, fine. So they go check on the guy and decide they wanna take his vest or something. I told them 'no,' but they wasn't listening to me. Then they start talking about prints and DNA and stuff and decide to hide the body somewheres else."

"So your friends moved the body?"

"Yeah. They said if nobody found the body, nobody would come looking for the vest."

"What kind of vest was it?"

"Armored. It looked expensive. That's why they wanted it. Then they started talking about taking 'other parts.'"

"'Other parts?'"

"Yeah, so this guy, the dead guy, was some kind of MOD, we think. So they wanted to see if his parts might be worth something, but I talked them out of it."

"You talked them out of it?"

"Yeah."

"And then what happened?"

"They dumped the body again."

"Where?"

"The Veins. There's a creek by the docks where people supposedly dump bodies. It's all grown over. Everybody knows about it. When you get there, you'll find him in the reeds. You'll find a bunch of folks in the reeds, I bet. They took the vest. I told them not to, but they did."

"Who's 'they?'"

"I ain't telling you that. I ain't no snitch. But since I'm telling you this, maybe we can call it even."

Call ended.

12: Inseparable

"Explain my relationship with Sugihara? Why don't I just explain how I think Libra works? It'll save us both some time and make just as little sense. If I had to sum it up, I'd say, for a long time I thought that 'crazy' meant 'stupid.' And that 'crazy' could be useful. I was wrong on both counts."

- Unit One Deputy Informant Yamazaki "Dice" Daisuke

The Pearl Room was a three-story nightclub in the neighborhood of Dolores Basin. Identifiable for its Victorian row-houses and bustling population of students and young professionals, Dolores Basin resided on the shoreline of the Bay of Sun where northern Section Four met the Southside of Section Five. For a neighborhood where one could expect to find quaint Irish taverns, tiny neighborhood markets, and mom-and-pop shops of every offering, the Pearl Room appeared very much misplaced, as though intended for either the industrial borough of southern Section Four, the shopping district of Section Three, or the red-light district of Section Seven.

Dice's overcoat caught the wind but barely swayed as he approached Pearl's entrance. Beneath the overcoat was his jacket and beneath that, his badge and revolver. He moved like a man condemned: conscious of every step and curious about everything that wasn't his destination. His heart beat with a nervous inconsistency, and the likelihood of what could happen this evening hung over him like a curse.

The line to enter the nightclub wrapped the building in an eclectic mob of scantily dressed young people. He ignored the line and made a beeline for the double-doors. This act, the act of celebrities, was not lost on him and yet was not welcome. On a normal day, this kind of posturing would be fun and worth mocking. This was not the day. This was not the place. He passed the inquisitive eyes and murmurs of would-be patrons and came to stand before the gated entrance, where he was met with the outstretched hand of a Tongan bouncer. The tattooed Polynesian stood well over six feet and wore a suit that looked sewn together from the cloth of two typically-sized others.

"Wait a minute, friend," the Polynesian said with a hand to Dice's chest, "are you on the guest list?"

Dice held up the pinky finger of his right hand, knuckles out in the symbol of the yakuza of the Minowara. The symbol supposedly represented one's willingness to pay the price of insubordination or failure. To Dice, it meant about as much as the half-wave people who know but don't like each other perform.

The bouncer nodded and waved him inside.

[Once you go inside, I can't watch your back,] Rena told him.

"I know. Why don't you focus on finding our boy?"

305

[I've got blue flame under the Port Authority unit searching for Chris. We'll find him.]

"Let me know when you do. The idea that the Titans are dissolving his body in acid doesn't sit well with me."

[Of course it doesn't. We'll find him, you have my word. Just please be careful.]

"Just going to see an old friend, Rena. Nothing to worry about. Sugihara and I go back a long way."

[People change.]

"I'm counting on it."

Crossing the threshold into Pearl was like diving headlong into a pool in the dead of winter. The noise shocked him into temporary paralysis. And the people; the sheer mass of bodies congealed into some kind of frenzied, drunken super-organism, seemed ready to repel him like the foreign body he was. Dice stood there in the entryway and looked out at what had to be the greatest violation of occupancy law in the history of Sun City. The place was packed, wall to wall, with people. With a grim determination, the ex-yakuza Unit One deputy made for the staircase, weaving and shoving his way through the crowds.

Knowing Sugihara, there was zero chance that his old friend would tolerate the lack of personal space demanded on the lowest level of Pearl. If Sugihara was here, in Pearl, he was up top and somewhere comfortable.

The lights were dim, and LEDs sent orbs of every hue dancing across the faces of the people. Music literally shook the place, as did structural feedback: deliberate vibration of the floors and walls, its nuance indecipherable but for a violent baseline. The inner walls of the three-story club were mirrored where they weren't flowing in nauseating holo-ads, only adding to the overwhelming sense of bedlam. Dice focused on the path in front of him, not the beautiful women dancing erotically. He focused on the staircase and not the fireworks explosion of cash currency that doused him in holographic one-dollar bills.

Dice reached the staircase with a fresh cranberry and vodka spilled across the sleeve of what had been a white overcoat upon entrance. Batting at the spill, he greeted another guard with the same gesture that had won him entry. The guard, a heavyset man of indecipherable ancestry, lifted a velvet rope for him to pass. Daisuke mounted the staircase and entered another realm.

On the second floor of Pearl, men in suits and women in pristine, flowing gowns danced and moved about with ease. Behind the bars, men in vests with bowties waited with frozen smiles for drink orders. Drones buzzed about taking photos that were printed in real time and excreted randomly in a wasteful display of excess. Dice paused and exhaled as though free from some stranglehold. Where the bottom floor might have been one of the ancient battles Vivianne Gueye had shown him at the *Musée de Conflit Historique*, this was a palace ball. A littered palace ball…

307

Dice crossed the floor, recognizing several Sun City luminaries along the way, including what appeared to be the massive frame of Valhalla Fight League Heavyweight Champion Omar Garcia.

Garcia, staggering, paced about the floor as though securing territory. No one ventured near the humongous prizefighter, beyond a friendly smile or wave.

The second floor of Pearl was more Daisuke's kind of party than the first but it, too, lacked something, something he knew he'd find one more floor up. He approached the staircase to the third floor and found a familiar face waiting for him. "Kyodai," he said, greeting the man with an outstretched hand.

The man had a round, flat face and thick nose with nostrils that rode up on either side like wheel wells. His lips were purplish and thick, and he was sweating and shiny beneath the strobe lights. Even amidst the fog of cigar smoke, pressed bodies, and cheap cologne, Dice could smell the man's sour. The bouncer's name was Saga Hideki and he was the brother of the Minowara lieutenant and accountant Saga Junichirou. Unlike his brother, Hideki was a brutish imbecile, best known for his perverted tendencies and reckless borrowing.

"You're no brother of mine," Hideki replied, ignoring the attempted handshake. "What do you want, cop?"

"I'm here to see Sugihara."

"You mean *Boss* Sugihara."

"*Boss* Sugihara."

"He's in the champagne room," Hideki said, thumbing up the staircase.

Dice moved to pass Hideki, but was halted by a heavy hand to the chest. Hideki leaned forward on his stool and sneered. "No one said you're going up there."

Dice brushed the hand away, a current of annoyance beginning to stir in his gut. "Get your hands off me, Saga. I'll bash the fuck out of you where you sit!"

There was a moment of silent tension where the two men locked eyes, and for a moment, Dice was certain Hideki would attempt to shove him down the stairs. The moment passed and the elder of the Saga brothers settled back on his stool, glaring.

"You better watch yourself, snitch."

"Always do."

Daisuke's transition from yakuza to professional informant had placed his existence in a state of constant threat, a condition his SDC-appointed psychologist all but promised would lead to an eventual mental breakdown. This was because the information he had access to made him a threat to both the underworld and the State Defense Consortium. However, as both sides knew, it made him a far greater asset than a liability. For the SDC, he provided a link to the hitherto unknown world of the Japanese mafia and a steady stream of high-profile arrests. To the Minowara, he was an attack dog; a force to be unleashed on rivals. The Minowara, Raizen particularly, had learned long ago that getting a competitor locked up was just as efficient as murder, and in many ways preferable. Rivals become assets regularly in the world of gambling and prostitution, especially rivals facing the prospect of jail time.

It's almost funny when you think about it, Dice mused. *Madison and I are but two sides of the same Minowara coin. When they want to make someone go away for a while, they call me. When they want someone to go away forever, they call Maddy.*

As he'd hoped, the third floor had been reserved for, and was full of, Minowara yakuza. In black suits, they sat about in booths, posturing and smoking. They hung from the bars drunkenly like refugees from a dinghy, heads constantly on swivels. In clusters, they laughed and hollered at one another. They clashed bottles of beer and smoked until their brooding forms could barely be made out. There were no less than two hundred of them and when Dice, in his pearl-white overcoat, entered the room, it seemed like all of them stopped and turned to look at him. Like a man before a firing line, he stood there. And under the scrutiny of an army of gangsters, he returned their stare, assessing the room, fearlessness both his mask and shield. Standing there, at the summit of the staircase, he produced a cigarette from his coat and lit it with the bronze flip lighter he kept in the inner lining of his Unit One jacket.

Let your presence be known. Never be afraid.

After all, fear was submission. And submission was suicide.

As Dice stood there, smoking and projecting a nonchalance that was not real, he thought about the first cigarette he'd ever smoked. It had been handed to him, already lit, by the thin, pale hands of a boy named Sugihara Enzo. They were friends once, rambunctious truants and troublemakers.

Eventually, the stares on the third floor of the Pearl Room dwindled and the room resumed its din of revelry. Dice took a long drag and exhaled, masking his relief. Not seeing Sugihara anywhere in the mass, he moved to the bar. As he waited patiently for the bartender, puffing tobacco feverishly, he scrutinized the room the way a soldier on recon surveyed the terrain.

Cocktail waitresses and escorts swam about on stilettos like performers on stilts, their exposed flesh shining beneath the burning strobe lights. Behind the sound of men screaming over one another in Japanese, Korean and largely broken English, a melodic drum-and-bass tune shook the walls.

When the bartender finally made his way to him, the man looked as though he'd just been released from solitary confinement or some yakuza torture room. Serving a room full of gangsters had taken a toll, and the man's nerves were clearly shot. As the bartender asked Dice for his drink order in a kind of frantic, overly polite babble, his eyes darted about nervously, as though a shoe or bottle was heading for his skull at any moment.

The drink was heavy on the ice and short on the scotch but gratis, so Dice couldn't complain. Nevertheless, he placed a

311

twenty and a ten on the bar before putting the glass to his lips. The drink warmed his chest and loosened his nerves a bit, but behind the liquor was an undeniable anxiety that would take bottles of the stuff to fully quell.

The music had switched to a looping, harmonic type of techno he wasn't familiar with. Dubstep, glitchhop, mech-tech, it all sounded the same to him: a bunch of sounds dropped into an aluminum can, shaken and poured out over a glass table.

Sugihara's had been the first familiar face he'd seen after fleeing Tokyo, but even that brief, awkward encounter had been years ago. At the time, the Minowara had yet to establish its foothold in the US, and Sugihara, like most other yakuza, had bigger concerns than admonishing a turncoat.

What did Sugihara make of his defection from the Minowara? Was he friend still, or foe? And was Sugihara really plotting against the clan that had given them both a means of dignified survival?

But Sugihara, for all of the unknowns that could be ascribed to the man, was not the source of the dread Dice felt as he assessed the room. Where he could not know what Sugihara truly felt, he could know (and did know) what Madison Grünewald-Yamazaki felt. Was she here, now? Was she privy to Sugihara's alleged plot? Was she still angry? Did she still carry that godforsaken street-sweeper, the shotgun she called The Madam?

As he took inventory of the third floor of Pearl, he saw Maggie, the waitress from The Lady Nō, sitting on the lap of a

312

man he didn't recognize. The man looked to be twenty years her elder and had a mean scar across his bald pate. Shaking his head, Dice wondered if Maggie's father had any idea of the true cost of his gambling.

Several lieutenants could be spotted in the room, many of them very influential in the syndicate. It was unusual and spoke volumes that so many — at times opposing — clans were in the same room. After all, being Minowara was not some kind of end-all solution to conflict. It didn't guarantee fair play or eliminate conflicting interests. Rather, the Minowara banner lessened the likelihood of yakuza-on-yakuza infighting, giving everyone under the banner an opportunity to focus on what truly mattered, in his eyes anyway: making money. Beneath the Minowara banner, there were hundreds of distinct clans. These clans had their own hierarchies, all following an ages-old schema. But that was where the similarities ended. Clans varied greatly in power, resources, and spheres of influence. There was the perpetually coke-snorting Sadohima clan, with their lawyerly taste for attire. They specialized in flipping commercial real estate, and insurance fraud. He saw the Sakurai-gumi clustered in a corner. They were from Shinjuku: Tokyo's Section Three. They were easily identifiable by the massive gold ring, etched with the kanji symbol for "mistrust," that each of them wore. If you were still unsure you were looking at one of the Sakurai-gumi, you could always bring up sports bookmaking, considering that was their wheelhouse. The largest group in attendance, and quite telling to Dice, was the Bando-ikka. Its boss, Kenya Bando, or Bando Kenya back home, was a comedically vocal critic of Oyabun Minowara, and had been since before the move to the State.

And yet for all Bando's criticisms of Boss Minowara, here he was, still under the banner of Minowara. Bando's clan was too small an organization to challenge for the top spot, but too large and well-managed to crush. At least cleanly. And it was this, Oyabun Minowara's command over so many egos, that was so impressive to Dice. The Minowara-gumi, largest of all yakuza organizations, was a complex, agile, and impressive ecosystem… powered by tradition.

With a drag of cigarette and sip of whiskey, he looked out on a mass of well-dressed men, most of whom would meet ugly, violent ends. It didn't take him much longer to find Sugihara. Behind a group of escorts conspiring, he saw a man sitting behind a circular table in an alcove walled in curtains. The man's head was down, his hair over his face. It was Sugihara's posture that betrayed him first, however. His posture was unmistakable. He wasn't a man sitting, but a man dropped from some great height onto a chair. Only one man could appear so comfortable and at the same time so miserable. In that moment, the man whipped his head back, wiping his nose, and yelled something guttural that got the men around him to hoot and catcall.

Sugihara…

Dice set his watered drink down and moved for the room. His steps seemed foreign. He was trying too hard to walk normally. As he paused and pretended to double-check his pockets for his wallet to reset himself, a mass of men from some unknown origin blazed their way through the crowds in a beeline for the same curtained room.

Among the group, he recognized several people known to be close to Sugihara. As they steamrolled their way through the smaller clans, they made their importance known verbally and physically. Sugihara, though wielding the same influence as clan chairmen like Bando, did not have a clan of his own. Rather, Sugihara and his men existed as part of Minowara-gumi proper.

Among Sugihara's group was the Lobster, followed closely by Saga Junichirou, brother of the bouncer guarding the steps to this floor of Pearl, and two large suits whose faces he recognized but whose names eluded him. At the head of them was a woman. She walked with the conviction of a military commander, and in her wake trailed a length of strawberry blonde.

Dice's heart was pressed by cold hands. His lips moved but he did not speak.

Maddy...

He'd hoped to pull Sugihara aside somewhere and talk privately and candidly about the state of affairs in the Minowara. Not as Minowara informant to Minowara lieutenant, but as an old friend to an old friend… even though the former was closer to the truth.

Dice backpedaled and leaned back onto the bar, deciding to bide his time. He flagged down the bartender and said loudly, exaggeratedly, "Neat, and if I see a shot measure I'm slapping the shit out of you, got it?"

It was tough to make out her face through the colored lights and smoke. Still, Madison looked healthy — hard, even. And the way she walked… like a force, like something out of Agency Zero.

A high school dropout like Sugihara, Raizen, and so many others from Shibuya, this life of gambling, sex, and violence might well have been his calling all along.

But Madison was different… She had talent, a wealth of it, in fact. She had the kind of talent a person could turn into cash without question, and not in the subway-station-performer kind of way.

The bartender slammed his drink down and Dice returned fire with a fifty-dollar bill. At the same time, Madison and her entourage squeezed into the room, where Sugihara sat waiting, and pulled the velvet curtain shut behind them.

Well aware of the potential magnitude of the next hours' events, Dice downed his drink and crossed the room, his gait loose and natural now, his mind walled in a glassy layer of intoxication. Beneath his jacket and coat, Watchman — his trusted revolver — pressed into his side reassuringly.

When Dice reached the curtain that blocked off the private room, which was little more than a huddle of private booths, he closed his eyes and took a deep breath.

Be smart and attentive and you'll live, he told himself. *Look them all in the face, especially Sugihara. Watch hands, control the tone. You're still one of them...*

It'll be good to see her face again.

Taking a handful of the greasy-feeling velvet, he braced for death and yanked the curtain aside. Men who'd been standing guard on the other side were startled into action. They dove on him, seizing him by the shoulders.

The lights were dim and the club's strobe-lights made erratic shadow puppets. In the center of the room were a hardwood floor and brass stripper's pole, presently unoccupied. As the drapes swished shut behind him and their dusty musk filled his nostrils, Dice fought to keep the men holding him from forcing him to the ground.

"Wait! Just wait!"

Something, likely the heel of a dress shoe, struck the back of Dice's leg and forced him to a knee. He reached for Watchman.

"Oi, matte!" "*Hey, wait!*" a voice hollered over the sound of Vietnamese gangster rap. "Wait!"

Sugihara was looking down at him from his booth with a curious expression, his meager eyebrows high on his forehead. "Let him go."

317

Helping Dice up, the guards grunted apologies, one of them going so far as to right the lapel of his overcoat.

The Unit One deputy's adrenaline was surging now and at any point he expected Rena to notice the spike in his heart rate and reach out. Dice did not want that. The last thing he needed was a distraction. "It's good. We're good."

Slowly, his hands held visibly out in front of him, he approached the table. As he did so, Sugihara watched him with a tight-lipped smile and snake's eyes.

Dice's old friend was damn near unrecognizable. Sugihara's thin lips peeled away from shark's teeth in a grin straight out of a horror movie. His face, the bluish-white of a drowning victim, was little more than skin on bone. A bolt was driven through the bridge of his nose, and rings hung from each side of his lower lip. His hair, frosted blonde, might have been a wig on backward for its nonsensical styling.

Sitting to Sugihara's left was Dice's wife.

Madison sat with her hands beneath the table and regarded him with the interest a commuter might grant roadkill. Her eyes were half-lidded and puffy, as though sleep hadn't found her in a long time. Though her demeanor was relaxed and her expression disinterested, Dice noticed the muscles of her jaw flexing.

Resting on Madison's shoulders was Sugihara's arm. His thin fingers moved playfully, twirling locks of her hair.

The table was littered with bottles and thick lines of cocaine that had been fashioned with the flat end of a coaster.

318

The white powder was mixed with another substance, something red and sinister. The ashtray was overflowing with butts that spilled onto the table, only adding to the nauseating clutter. Next to Sugihara's right hand on the table was a chrome semi-automatic pistol with a studded grip and champagne-pink trigger.

"I was wondering when I'd see you again, buddy," Sugihara said, his attempt at English abysmal.

"Kyodai, brother, is that you?" It was a dumb question, but the only thing that came to mind.

"Is this me?" Sugihara replied. "Is this me?" He looked to Madison for confirmation. "Is this me?"

Didn't take long to screw up, Dice thought bitterly, wanting to kick himself.

"I'm sorry. It's just... you've changed so much."

Sugihara propped himself up in the booth, his hand sending a plume of cocaine into the air. "Is this me, Junichirou? I'm starting to worry. What if it's not?"

"Of course it is," a voice responded from somewhere.

"How can you be sure?" Sugihara's eyes were wide. "How can anyone be sure? I mean, what is 'self?'"

"You're you," Madison told him. "Yama-kun's just dumb."

"Who the fuck do you think he is, snitch?" a voice threatened from behind.

Dice turned to find Etsuya standing behind him, hand in his coat.

319

"Apparently, this is me," Sugihara replied finally, licking his lips.

Madison no longer looked bored, but rather quite focused. Beneath the table her hands moved about, no doubt drawing her blasted shotgun. The deputy's heart rate picked up, and Rena was quick to notice.

[What's happening, Dice?]

Just as the tension was certain to dissolve into violence, Sugihara's scowl faded into what might have been a warm smile had he not mangled himself. "Yama-kun, it's been too long."

Sugihara threw a hand in the air and waved it about, his many rings and bracelets rattling like wind chimes. "Someone get Yama-kun a chair. You're staying for a bit, yes? We've got drinks, drugs, and bitches."

Before Dice could respond, a chair was thrust under him and his legs had no choice but to fold onto it.

"You were always a scotch guy, no? Get Yama-kun here a drink. Fuck it," he corrected, "bring the bottle!"

As Sugihara's men scrambled to comply, the yakuza lieutenant leaned in to Madison's ear and whispered something. Madison, in turn, smiled and simply shook her head. The expression on her face, the apathy, stood the hair on Dice's neck on end.

"We all know you don't come around unless it's business?" Sugihara added. "So what business brings you?"

He'd gone over the conversation in his mind a dozen times, each time playing through the various routes the conversation might take. But Madison's presence had thrown everything for a loop. All he could think about was the cold gaze, the drugs, and Sugihara's goddamn fingers in her hair. "I-I wanted to talk to you," he said weakly, all the while looking at Madison.

A pair of arms interrupted him as they slammed a bottle of Jameson and a glass of ice down in front of him.

"Thank you, Urubashi." Sugihara directed his gaze to the bottle. "Pour yourself a glass."

Dice wanted to shake his head and tell the yakuza lieutenant that he was plenty drunk already. He wanted to fling the bottle across the room and pull his wife out of Pearl, but there were several problems with that plan. First of all, the drink wasn't an option. Secondly, flinging a bottle in a room full of yakuza was a great way to get shot to shit. And lastly, Madison wasn't the type to get "pulled" anywhere. Dice twisted the cap off and poured himself a small share.

"Bullshit!" Sugihara said, flicking his fingers at him. "Fucking *pour*, man!" Sugihara was a small, frail man, behind all of the ornamentation. If it came down to it, Dice knew he could break Sugihara in two. But Sugihara didn't hold the rank he held because he was good with his hands. He was a powerful lieutenant because he never put himself in a position to need his hands. He was known to shoot first, and kept a tight circle of killers. And so Dice poured until the glass was half full and capped the bottle. He then pushed the bottle toward the center of the table in a not-so-subtle message that he would concede this time but not be bullied further.

"Cheers," Sugihara declared, raising an empty hand.

"Kanpai," he replied, and put the glass to his lips. As he did so, Sugihara pushed the Jameson bottle back his way. It slid across the table and would have fallen into his lap had he not halted it with his free hand. Finishing the glass in three slow gulps, Dice set the cup down, exhaling heavily. Face flushed and mouth salivating, he bit back bile.

"Another."

"No, enough."

Sugihara regarded him with a cocked head and incredulous expression. He met the yakuza's stare resolutely and slowly shook his head. "I've had enough, brother."

Sugihara leaned back and rapped his fingers on the table. "People say you come and go like you don't have a care in the world. People say you pluck us out at random to sell to the State for cash. People say you're secretly working for the Triad and your whole deal with Raizen and old man Minowara is a ruse to weaken us so the Chinese can take over."

"People say a lot of nonsense, it seems."

Sugihara shrugged. "Is it nonsense? What about Murakami, or Abe, or— what was the name of the doorman at Genma's spot?"

"Akihiro," someone said.

"Akihiro!" Sugihara bent down and inhaled a gigantic mound of coke, not even bothering to wipe his nose. After gagging loudly, he continued. "And that's just the last few months. You send your own people to prison like it's fun for you. Is it fun for you, Yama-kun?"

'Yama-kun' was supposed to make him feel comfortable, like two old friends having a chat, but the tone coming from Sugihara was rich with venom. In this setting, he would have preferred just 'Daisuke,' or even 'Yamazaki-san.'

"Akihiro was back-channeling and selling ass on the side, pocketing money that should have gone to the Minowara-gumi, to pay all of your salaries, mind you. Abe stole twenty grand out of his boss' safe, and Murakami fucked children."

Sugihara looked around. "So you're some kind of hero now? What about me, Yama-kun? You gonna turn me in too?"

"Never," he lied.

"How can I be sure? You're not the Daisuke I used to know."

"You've changed too," Dice told his old friend sincerely.

"Oh, these?" Sugihara replied, grimacing with his shark's teeth. "The doc that cured my anemia knew a guy who could fix my underbite. We may have gone a little overboard. You don't think I need braces, do you?"

The table erupted in laughter.

Dice continued, unfazed. "I'm glad to see you are well, brother, but I wasn't talking about your teeth."

323

Sugihara shook his head and giggled. "'Well?' Glad to see I'm well? What does that mean?" He leaned forward, taking his arm from behind Madison's head and placing it on the table. His other hand came to rest on the pistol. "Was that a threat?"

Dice was quick to respond, very quick. "It most certainly was not."

"Oh, good, because we're friends, you and I. We have a history and stuff."

Sugihara was posturing. This was a gangster thing that yakuza excelled at. Some treated it as an art form, like theatre, only sometimes people got killed in the final act.

I can't let him get a rise out of me.

He was there to uncover the truth of Raizen's claims that Sugihara was plotting against the Chairman, not to pick a fight, and certainly not to get into Sugihara's crosshairs.

"I've been to see Raizen," he said, just loud enough for those closest to the table to hear.

"Have you, now?" Sugihara's hand was still resting on his pistol. "Are you going back to the Minowara now? Are you finished with this Unit One charade?"

"Going back? Don't you mean *coming* back?"

Sugihara chuckled, his teeth clicking like a keyboard. "Ah yes, of course. *Coming* back. Are you coming back to us, Daisuke? Are you done playing cop? Tell me that this is so and I'll order shots. It would be good to work together again! Just like old times."

Madison chuckled. "Shots," she repeated. "I thought you said *shot*." She made a pistol with her fingers, a pistol pointed in Dice's direction.

Sugihara looked to Madison as though realizing her presence for the first time. "Oh, wait! This is a reunion for you two as well, isn't it? How could I forget? Aren't you two like, married or something?"

"Or something," she replied.

Grinning, Sugihara buried his head in her neck and began planting kisses on her face and cheeks.

Sugihara was knowingly crossing the line, skipping giddily over it. Any attempt at suppressing his anger was lost at the sight of Madison pushing the yakuza lieutenant away. Dice slammed a fist into the table. The bottles on it leapt and spilled over, dousing Sugihara's cocaine before pooling onto the hardwood. "Cut the shit!" In that moment the music seemed distant, almost muted entirely.

The yakuza gathered in the small chamber poured out of their booths, just as a woman, naked from the waist up, pranced into the room and onto the hardwood center stage.

The Lobster, who'd been standing behind him, likely pining for just such an outburst, snatched at his collar — but Dice was ready for it. He seized the yakuza bodyguard's wrist and twisted the palm upward with as much force as he could muster. As Etsuya yelped and tried to yank his arm free, Dice shot to his feet and slammed a fist into his nose. The Lobster's knees buckled, and it took very little effort to seize him by the neck with both hands. Yakuza closed in on him from all sides, guns drawn, even as he began to throttle the Lobster.

Choking out Etsuya was certainly not one of the scenarios he'd played out in his head.

Dice's silver revolver caught the strobe lights as he freed it from its holster and slammed the barrel into Etsuya's temple with a thud that sounded in unison to the R&B bassline playing around them.

I'm going to die in front of the woman I love, he thought. *Perhaps at the hands of the woman I love. As good an ending to a strange life as any...*

In a fist, he gripped Etsuya's lapel, even as the man's mutilated hands tried to pry free. Dice held the gun to his head and told them all, quite candidly, that he would spill the Lobster's brains. At this, Minowara yakuza froze in place — all but Sugihara, who took the break in the action as an opportunity to snort more cocaine.

With only moments before total pandemonium broke loose, Dice addressed the shark-toothed yakuza. "What the fuck, kyodai?"

Sugihara looked confused.

"Sugi-kun! What is this shit? I've come to see you as a friend. I have shown you respect. Always!" He ground the barrel of the gun into Etsuya's temple and the man cried out. "I *demand* that you return that respect!"

Madison was smiling, and he could see beneath the table her shotgun's chrome chamber.

Dice's mind raced. He wanted to get the fight as far away from her as possible, but that didn't appear to be an option. Hell, she *was* the fight! This left him one choice and only one choice...

He yanked the Lobster close and whispered in his ear. "If you ever touch me again, I will unload this gun in your face." He released the yakuza and kicked him in the back to create space. He then held the gun in the air for a moment before twirling it deftly and driving it home in the holster beneath his arm. In the same motion, his hand came away with a cigarette.

At any moment, he expected bullets to hit him from all sides. When they didn't, he leaned across the table, putting his face very near to Madison's, a move that gave her hands pause. He stared deep into her core, looking for something, any glimpse of the woman whose cooking was terrible and libido as predictable as the seasons. To his chagrin, if the woman he loved was somewhere behind the cool, green gaze and drug-induced haze, he couldn't find her. "Give me a light, love? For old times' sake?"

After a long time of staring, she dropped her shotgun onto her bag and came up with a lighter. As the end of his cigarette crackled to life, the air in the room seemed less heavy and even the music took on a lighter, tweenie-pop sound.

Dice sat back down, picked up the spilled bottle of whiskey, and poured himself another tall glass. He reached over the table, winking at Sugihara, who sat stone-faced, and snatched the man's champagne flute. He poured the bubbly on the floor and filled the glass with Jameson, all the while expecting the bullet that would end his life.

"You're right, I'm a scotch man," he told the yakuza lieutenant. "But this is whiskey. It's good nonetheless. Next time you want to get me drunk, crack a Speyburn or Balvenie." He offered the flute from across the table, very aware of the finality of his play. Yakuza surrounded him, hands clutching pistols, and someone held back the Lobster, who was filling the room with expletives and waving his own pistol recklessly.

Sugihara snapped out of his trance and took the glass. He looked to Etsuya, who stood disheveled, a thin stream of blood on his lip. "What's wrong with you?"

Etsuya wiped his face with the sleeve of his jacket. "What?"

"We're having a conversation and you have to go and piss Yama-kun off. What's wrong with you?"

Estuya looked about, befuddled.

Sugihara waved dismissively and men began filing back into their booths, all but Etsuya, who stood clutching his bloody nose.

At the center of the room, the naked woman was hanging upside down from the pole with a bored expression on her face.

"Etsuya, you've embarrassed me."

The Lobster went white.

"I would ask for your thumb right here and now, but who would open doors for me? Go sit somewhere and wipe your face. You look silly."

Etsuya licked his lips and stood there in disbelief. His pause was about as severe a display of defiance as Sugihara was wont to tolerate. Just as Sugihara looked as though he would speak, the Lobster bowed deeply and left the room.

Only once the belligerent enforcer was gone did Dice allow himself to breathe. He hid the sigh of relief behind a pull and exhale of tobacco smoke.

As though nothing had happened, Sugihara snorted a line of wet coke, gagged and chuckled. He took a weak pull of whiskey.

"Gah! I still don't know how you can drink this piss."

"It was you who first introduced me to spirits," Dice replied. "Do you remember? You snuck a flask into Mr. Imanari's class and we passed it back and forth until I threw up all over my stupid loafers."

They both laughed, and Madison, who'd been watching intently, rolled her eyes.

"Then you told Imanari-sensei that I had chickenpox and got me dismissed from class. I spent the rest of the day on the roof smoking cigarettes and reading Shounen Jump."

Sugihara frowned. "And I spent the next hour cleaning *botamochi* and well whiskey off the floor."

They both laughed again.

Dice sat back in his chair and couldn't help but stare at Madison. She met his gaze unflinching, with an expressionless face both serene and pitiless.

"I see Etsuya hasn't changed."

"He's never liked you. Partly the cop thing, but mostly I think he just hates your face."

Exhaling smoke from his nose, he couldn't help but smile. "No big loss. You would think a guy down to his last four fingers would have a little more respect, though."

Sugihara's smile faded a bit. The ring pierced into the side of his bottom lip glimmered. "Who are *you* that he should respect?"

And just like that, the warmth that he thought he sensed from Sugihara was gone, as though it had never been there.

"Fair enough. I'm not Minowara, not anymore. But I have earned respect."

"You've also squandered a ton of it. Some might say more than you ever had."

Dice decided not to respond.

After whispering something into Sugihara's ear, Madison slid out of the booth and left the room. She did so without so much as a glance in his direction.

Not a good sign...

He took a pull from his cigarette and watched her leave, wanting to follow. She'd lost weight, and on the back of her arm he saw a mean scar that hadn't been there before.

330

"How is she?" he asked when the curtain had fallen behind her.

"She's the same as she's always been."

He made a face of disbelief and laughed the notion off.

"You're the one who's changed," Sugihara continued. "You laugh but it's no joke. You've abandoned your family, your honor, your wife, even your country. Now you're nothing more than an informant helping to lock up people who are just like you. You're not to be trusted, Daisuke, and I think even you know that."

He had no words. Locked in Sugihara's wicked gaze, the best he could do was take a pull from his cigarette. Down to a stub, all he tasted was filter. This was Sugihara at his most lucid, his most sincere, and yet his words could not have been crueler.

"It's in the way you carry yourself," he continued, "your air of invincibility. You have this sense of entitlement like you can walk between the two worlds without consequence, meddling in affairs that no longer concern you. You flirt with both sides of the law like some kind of... kingmaker, or puppet master. Do you know what I'm saying?" Sugihara's eyes were wide and remarkably clear.

Dice thought it better not to speak, and continued to listen.

"You've no soul, Daisuke. And that's the only reason you're still alive. You fascinate me. You think you're doing good, but really, you're the most corrupt. No one should trust

331

you, because you don't even know who you are or what you want to be." Sugihara waved a hand at him, a disgusted look on his face. "Even now, you skulk about, looking for information that you can sell to the State or Boss Minowara."

"That's not true. Not like that."

"Why are you here, Daisuke? Why has Raizen sent you?"

Dice set the glass down. Sugihara's words were like wounds inflicted in such rapid succession that their pain would not be felt for some time. Unsure of what to say, he opened his mouth and the truth came tumbling out. "He's afraid."

"Afraid of what? What does Raizen have to be afraid of?"

"He's afraid of you."

It was Sugihara's turn to make a face of disbelief.

"Why would the *Saiko-komon* — administrative second in command — and the Chairman's son be afraid of *me*?"

"Don't take me for a fool, Sugihara. I look around and I see a lot of familiar faces. But do you know what faces I don't see?"

Sugihara shrugged.

"I don't see Sato, or Gamakichi, or Inouye. I don't see Kakibara, Ando, Mizoguchi, Maeda, or anyone loyal to First Patriarch Sakakibara or Oyabun Minowara. I see *your* men, men you've known since Shibuya. I see the young clans, the new guys. I see the makings of a coup."

332

"Tch! You wouldn't smell a coup if there was one brewing right under your nose."

Sugihara looked irritated now, and his eyes had somehow become beadier. He took down another line of coke with the aggression of a falcon diving on a hare. When he came up for air, he moaned and swore loudly.

"When are you going to get tired of fighting Raizen's battles for him?" Sugihara wiped his nose this time. "He was always stirring the pot with 'my daddy' this and 'my daddy' that, but when people wanted to test the chin of Chairman's son, it was always you stepping up to take the blows. Have you considered the fact that you might be to blame?"

"To blame for what?"

"To blame for him being so fucking weak!"

The room was silent, despite a lieutenant having just called the heir to the Minowara throne out, audibly, publicly.

"So you admit—"

"I admit nothing!" Sugihara pointed and for a moment just shook a finger at him. "You go tell the *prince* that he has nothing to worry about from me! Also, tell him that if he wants to talk to me, he should come down here himself next time." Sugihara stood and Dice stood quickly to meet him, dropping his burned-out cigarette in his emptied glass. Sugihara came out from the booth, and for a second he thought the much smaller man might strike him. Instead, Sugihara extended an ornamented hand.

Dice looked at the hand incredulously. They'd never —
in twenty plus years — shaken hands.

"It was good to see you, Daisuke."

Sugihara's grip was cold, and his rings bit into Dice's
fingers painfully.

Leaving the third floor of Pearl was like escaping the
losing side of a battlefield, and the feat was not lost on him. He
bounded down the steps, on borrowed time. On the first floor,
he shoved his way to a rear exit and stepped out of the
smothering club and into a rain-pooled alley.

The air was crisp and pleasant despite the hint of trash
and urine it carried.

Raizen was right.

Sugihara's denial had zero authenticity. If not plotting
for the Chairman's seat outright, he was definitely driving a
wedge between the clans of House Minowara. Rolling his
shoulders and still taking in the intoxicating sensation of
escape, he contemplated his next move.

It was then that a sound like cans being crushed startled
him. The sound was followed by the barrel of what had to be
The Madam pressing against the back of his head. Without
hesitation, Dice put his hands in the air. He waited for
instructions or a warning. He waited for a threat… something.
After a few moments, nothing came and terror began to creep
into him.

"Madison, love. I'm going to turn around real slow, okay?"

"Real slow. *Slug* slow."

He turned and faced her. She now wore a stressed-leather motorcycle jacket that creaked as she pressed The Madam's butt to her shoulder. The barrel of the shotgun was in his face, but behind it her eyes were red and trembled in what could be fury or sadness.

Likely both.

"Baby…"

She shook her head, shushing him.

"I've been avoiding you," she said after a few moments of silence.

"I know," he lied.

"But do you know why?"

"Because you hate me. Because I played a stupid, stupid game and left you, in the egotistical hopes that you would come running after me. Because I'm a coward and didn't want to be there when my home was laid to waste. Because I was tired of the direction in which my life was headed. Really, because I'm a fool."

"See? There you go! Talking about yourself when it's not about you. Daisuke, do you know why *I*" —she pounded her chest with The Madam— "why *I* have been avoiding you?"

Her hands were trembling now. This caused the barrel to sway, and he couldn't help but envision the decapitation he would experience should that hair-trigger take a licking. He raised his hands slowly if for no reason than to remind her that his life was hers. "Why?"

"Because I was afraid that I would kill you when I saw you and I didn't want that."

"Well, that's good."

"Now, I'm not so sure."

"That's *not* good."

"Don't even try to be cute, Daisuke! Even now, you talk about 'your life.' It was *our* life, Daisuke. It was *OUR LIFE!*"

She pushed the barrel of the gun into his forehead and drummed it there, painfully, as she spoke. "You broke my heart. You married me, swore your life to me, and tore my heart to pieces before the fucking ring was even paid off. And for that, and that alone, I should scatter your life all over this fucking alleyway!"

Madison...

"Now, let's hear it, Daisuke! Let's hear that forked tongue of yours talk your way out of this."

Her face was turning red, and the vein on her neck bulged. The pain in her expression was unlike anything he'd ever seen, and it made him *want* to die.

"Well, well... Nothing to say for once? No snarky comeback? No long-winded excuse? No one else to blame, Daisuke? I guess we're done here."

She lifted the gun to her cheek, as if she needed to aim from this distance, and for the second time that evening the best he could do was open his mouth and let the truth fall out.

"Leaving you was the single worst mistake I have ever made, and *will* ever make. I'm a coward and a fool and I don't deserve you — *didn't* deserve you, I mean. I can see the pain you're in, love. I can see it clear as day. And it makes me want to die. It makes me wish you'd kill me right now."

And the die is thrown...

"Fuck you, Daisuke!"

"Wait, sto—"

The unmarked SDC cruiser pulled into the lot behind his street-facing apartment on self-drive. A knot the size of a golfball pressed down on his brow just above the left eye. He was no longer seeing double, but his head hurt something fierce. The blood that had been pouring into his eye from his split brow had finally been stanched, kept in check by its own caking and the sleeve of his Unit One jacket.

Madison hadn't scattered his brains, but the butt of her shotgun had certainly scrambled them. The blow had laid him flat, and a brutal followup had officially ushered in nap time. When he came to, some two and a half hours had passed.

[You're lucky to be alive.]

Rena knew of the assault but not the perpetrator.

[Did you get what you were looking for?]

337

"Rena, let's pick this up tomorrow. My head is killing me."

[Sure thing. Take care of yourself, Dice.]

"Hold up! Any word on Chris?"

[Not yet. I promise to keep you posted.]

"All right then, I'll talk to you later."

How did everything get so messed up? With a muddled mind, he tried to plot his next move.

Raizen's fears had been all but substantiated. However, telling Raizen outright would place Sugihara's head on the chopping block. And if it turned out that Madison was part of the plot, which appeared to be the case, her life, too, would be forfeit.

She could have killed me. She wanted to kill me. And she didn't...

If any harm came to Sugihara, Madison would feel the brunt of it. And while Madison sure as hell didn't need him to defend her, she couldn't protect herself from the dagger she didn't know was coming. If he warned Raizen, he would have to warn her as well.

Then what, he thought bitterly, *a race to see who kills whom first?*

He sat smoking as the engine shut itself off, and wondered how he'd allowed the Minowara to so ensnare every facet of his life. He was not free; even now with the delta on his sleeve, he was as much a pawn of Oyabun Minowara as he'd ever been.

If he didn't warn Raizen of Sugihara's obvious ploy, especially now after parlaying in public with him, he was culpable. And even Unit One wouldn't be able to protect him, should the Chairman of the Minowara decide it was his time to die.

A crossroads where all paths lead to death.

And so it was, the life of a yakuza. He was fucked...

...but Madison doesn't have to be.

As Dice stubbed out his cigarette and lit another, a group of men at the other end of the lot caught his attention. They huddled just beyond the glow of streetlight, the red cherries of tobacco, marijuana, or something else lighting up regularly to mark them in the dark like ships.

Raizen needs to know. He's still a friend.

Also, Sun City herself was a factor. Sugihara was not the kind of man you wanted at the head of a criminal empire. In fact, he was precisely the wrong kind of man. He was ambitious to no end and, worst of all, completely unpredictable. He would no doubt seek to expel any competition the minute he took the reins. This would likely mean all-out war with the Titans, the Triad, and God knew who else. Sun City, already a criminal minefield, would descend into complete chaos with Sugihara calling the shots.

He could practically hear Commander Williams' voice in his head. *That can't happen.*

Dice had developed too much of an affinity for the peoples of Sun City to watch that happen.

He would need to warn Raizen soon and at the same time, somehow, get Madison away from the shit-storm likely to ensue.

But how do you get a professional killer, a master architect of shit-storms, to bow out of one?

"What the hell, man?" he asked himself aloud, clutching his head.

A rapid and sharp rapping on the glass next to his head startled him. Dice immediately reached for Watchman. Peering through the window, he saw the face of a man. Behind him and behind the rolling raindrops on the window were other figures. The strange men were no longer smoking at the other end of the lot, and had come for something.

Asking himself aloud, "What the hell?" Dice opened the car door and stepped out. The air was frigid, and daylight was not far away. Even now, the horizon seemed dusted in deepest blue rather than black. As his eyes adjusted to make out the faces of the men standing next to his car, the reality of the situation quickly took root. They stood just a bit too far away to be of no harm, and even the man who'd banged on the window had taken several steps back already.

Sugihara wasted no time, he thought.

But these men didn't look like yakuza. In fact, there wasn't a Japanese among them.

"Look, gentlemen, I've had a long night. Whatever it is you think I can do for you, I assure you I can't."

There were four of them. They were dressed casually, their choice of attire deliberately dark in color, deliberately unrestrictive. One of them wore a horned bucket helmet and a flak jacket. Hanging from one hand and dragging against the pavement was a fireman's axe.

Not Sugihara... This has to be Luther Gueye. These are the Titans.

[Rena!]

"Daisuke Yamazaki, right? Unit One deputy informant?" The man with the axe, clearly the leader, jabbed a finger his way. "That's you, right?" His complexion might have been olive, but beneath the dying light he looked purple. His teeth were scattered and when he spoke, his tongue whipped his words into lisp. In that moment, the streetlights flickered out. At the same time, the glow from the apartment windows behind him went out, as did the headlights of the cruiser. The entire neighborhood went black and, if not for the light from Section Three and the occasional light of a harvest moon behind the clouds of another post-shower, his sight would be gone entirely.

"Rena!" he repeated, audibly and simultaneously via neurotrigger. "HQ!"

"They can't hear you," the man said, his face now masked in shadow. He held up a hand and in it, just barely visible, was a cylindrical silver device. Its metallic surface caught the moon and glimmered. At the top of it was a steady red light.

EMP?

Electromagnetic pulse was hot topic in Unit One training. It was the bane of agents like Chris and Alec: MODS, whose bodies relied on electrical current to function properly. Unbeknownst to these men, he was not a MOD. Nor would he ever be. Dice reached into his coat and withdrew Watchman. *Six shots, four men. The math is in my favor.*

"I should have known you'd come," he told them, "Gueye's not man enough to do his own dirty work, huh? Can't lie, though, your timing is impeccably terrible."

"He's only got the revolver," the leader said, placing a second hand on the axe. The man, his torso bare beneath his tactical vest, was a MOD, and not a cheap one. Dice could see the plates of his armored chest and the tiny screws that held them in place.

Dice bolted, running top speed for the street. About halfway, he tripped over something in the black, likely a parking block, and fell to the pavement. Pain gripped his foot, but he tabled the sensation, rolled and was up running once more. He could hear the crunch of gravel and broken glass as they pursued him, yelling things indecipherable over his own heartbeat. Just as he neared the street, he whirled and fired two shots. The first shot clicked a dud and the second lifted the barrel of the gun and lit the dark momentarily. One man fell forward and did not catch himself. With any luck, he was dead.

Great time to start firing blanks, he thought angrily, cursing his gun.

Dice threw his coat over his head and crouched, covering himself as one would with a fire blanket, just as his remaining pursuers returned fire with pistols. Beneath the overcoat, he could feel the punch of round after round hitting home, threatening to knock him over.

The crack of gunfire against the silence of early morning was sure to startle his neighbors awake… he prayed.

When they were done shooting and Dice heard the familiar sound of pistol slides locking in place, their magazines empty, he stood. Flattened bullets fell and rattled to the pavement. Dice fired two rounds from his waist. In the dark, he couldn't be sure of their accuracy but was pleased to see two more figures collapse.

He ran a hand over the holes in his coat and fingered one to find a still-intact layer of nanofiber-woven mesh. He pointed his gun at the leader, who stood staring with a dumb expression. "Your boss owes me a new coat."

"You've got some aim with that hand cannon, but can you make the last two shots count?"

The man came close, which was good. From this distance, he couldn't miss. He fired.

The axe head had come to shield the man's face just as he depressed the trigger. The round sparked against the steel of the axe and was deflected.

"I knew you'd go for the headshot. Last one…" The Titan licked the axe head.

Dice backpedaled as the Titan spun and swung the axe at him. Not quick enough to fully escape the strike, the blade tore into his coat and again the nanofiber weaving within saved his life. A follow-up stroke aimed to take his head off missed by a hair. Dodging the Titan's attacks left his steps tangled and it was clear this was not the kind of fight he would win. He ran, gripping Watchman tightly.

One shot, one man.

If it weren't for the initial round that had ended up being a dud, he'd have two rounds left in the cylinder. *But*, he thought, *no use crying over spilled milk.*

Dice turned and saw no one. Retreating into an unlit intersection, he could hear chuckling in the night. Chuckling that crescendoed into laughter and the grinding sound of the axe on pavement.

"Why don't you run some more?" the man called to him as he became visible beneath the meager light of the moon. "I get giddy watching you flee for your life. I could do this all night."

"Not me. I'm tired."

"Then I'm doing you a favor. Stay right there and soon you'll have all the rest you could ever want."

"Tempting, truly, but I still have things to do. Not to mention I still have one shot left. I'd hate to waste it."

"You and I both know you've no chance."

The Titan looked like some modern-day berserker, with his horned helmet and axe. As he stepped into the street, he

344

produced the tiny silver device again and held it out. "Pretty neat, huh? It disables power for a half mile in every direction. I'm almost tempted to deactivate it and see if your backup can get here before I've quartered you and left a limb on each street corner."

Dice grimaced. "Do it."

"Nah."

"Smart man." With a sigh, Dice pulled his overcoat off and dropped it to the pavement. The weight of the coat would only hinder his movement. If he hoped to survive in a fight against a MOD, with one bullet no less, he'd need to be quick. As the impending scuffle loomed, he let his rage take the wheel. "You think I'm scared of you?"

The Titan, smiling hideously, shrugged. "What kind of question is that to *axe*?"

Next, Dice removed his Unit One jacket. Beneath that, he wore a long-sleeved dress shirt. He slowly unbuttoned it and let it fall to the pavement as well. The tattoo that covered his body depicted a tiger chasing a phoenix. The tiger's muscular upper body twisted from his back, its claws gripping at his abdomen. The phoenix rose high onto his chest, its wings covering his arms in intricately drawn flames. The image of their courting covered every inch of his body, save for his hands, face, neck, and feet.

The cold against his skin was welcome. It sobered him and seemed to dull the pounding in his head. Standing there, naked from the waist up, Dice beckoned Gueye's henchman forward with the barrel of Watchman. As the neo-Viking moved in, he took careful aim.

His gun was not State-issued, which left him financially on the hook for ammo, and Smith & Wesson ammo for a .38 wasn't cheap. Right now, however, he really regretted buying a box of generics. If the box had one dud, it likely had more. That meant that he might have one shot to take down his attacker… or he might have none.

Just like Chõ-Han… I have a fifty-fifty chance.

He knew that to technically not be true, but why waste time on specifics. Death had been tugging at him all night and it was time to dance.

The man leapt and spun gracefully in the air. The axe swung up and around and aimed to come down and split him like thin boards in a child's karate demonstration. Dice fired directly into what he hoped would be the Titan's face. The hammer pulled back and snapped forward, only to click fruitlessly. The clicking sound struck him to his core, a funeral toll.

He shielded his head in his forearms, knowing it would not be enough, and waited for the pain. A boom filled his ears and something hard struck his arms and face. He screamed and fell back, the pain not yet real. Blood covered his face and chest and blotted his eyes, still warm. Hands that should have been severed came to his face, pawing frantically at the blood. As he fell onto his butt in the street, only the chill of the night and the sticky offal of a bloodbath could be felt.

No pain... Were the wounds so severe? "Christ!"

Lying face down at his feet was the Titan. The axe lay pinned beneath his motionless form.

Gasping, Dice ran his hands over his face and arms, looking for the gash where the axe must have struck him. And yet, still no pain... He was whole, untouched even. He turned his rage onto the gun in his hands, throwing it at the pavement with all of the strength he could muster.

"Goddammit, you ancient piece of shit!"

"Temper, temper," a familiar voice said from the darkness. She stepped into the intersection, her boots grinding gravel into the pavement. As she sauntered up casually, The Madam propped over one shoulder, the peppery smell of ignited gunpowder filled his nostrils.

"You did this?"

He could not tell if Madison was smiling in the dark.

"He would have killed you."

Dice picked his shirt up and used it to wipe the blood from his face. "You underestimate me," he replied with false calm, his heart still galloping.

"You overestimate yourself."

She cocked The Madam, and a shell casing clattered to the street. She scooped it up and pocketed it before chambering another.

"You followed me?"

"Of course I did." She paused to admire the headless corpse at his feet. "Tell me that's not a fucking Titan."

"I can't be certain, but I think so. Why?"

"No reason."

She's lying...

"You followed me... Why?"

In the night, beneath the moon, she looked spectral, like something out of a dream.

"To find out where you lived, in case..."

"In case what, Maddy? I don't do edible arrangements."

She shook her head. "Sometimes I wonder what it would take to sink that flippant attitude forever."

He picked himself up from the street. "An axe to the head for sure. So the joke's on you I guess. But thanks anyway."

She chuckled and for a moment, in the dark, he thought he saw the frost in her gaze lift a bit. But it could have been imagined. He took a step toward her and she took one back, The Madam swinging up from her side. "Not so close," she warned, without an ounce of humor in her voice.

His brush with death had filled him with an undeniable rush and a sensation of invincibility that had yet to wear off. It had also robbed him temporarily of guile and of subtlety. "I've missed you so very much."

"To hell with you."

"Come home with me."

Her mouth smiled, but her green eyes were black under the moon. She turned to leave.

"You'd best not come around the Minowara anymore. I can't protect you." Turning, she added, "I *won't* protect you."

He put a hand on her arm, too tired to give a damn about The Madam. "I'm not letting you walk away from me."

She turned and met his eager expression with an elbow that broke his nose audibly. He hit the pavement for the third time that night.

"Okay, I'm done," Dice moaned. "I'm done with this night..." He patted his bare chest, hoping to find the familiar bulge of his pack of cigarettes, and found nothing. In that moment, a boot struck him in the chest and pressed him down, onto the cold ground. "You win," he pleaded. "Everyone fucking wins! Except me. I give up. I'm just a piece of shit with a broken nose, a broken gun, and a—"

"What do you regret most about leaving me?"

"Everything."

"You might want to be specific here."

The Madam caught the moonlight beautifully and he couldn't help but entertain the thought of sleep eternal.

"The truth?" He sighed, his voice nasally and funny-sounding. "Nothing carries meaning anymore. You were my wife and my best friend. Every good thing that happened to me was ours to share, and now... good things just feel wasted. Sometimes I can't even tell the difference between good and bad because frankly, without you to share the good with, what fucking difference does it make?"

Her hands snatched him by his hair, and when he expected to see The Madam's barrel one last time, her face pressed into his. Her lips worked furiously and her tongue found his and seized control. The cold and the pain and the darkness were, in that moment and irrevocably, vanquished. They kissed there, lying in the street. And for a moment, things were as they had been, as they *should* have been all the while.

When they finally came up for air, he confided, "I'm lying in broken glass."

#Sun City Municipal Surveillance::

Date: Unknown
Time: 22:11:02 – 22:22:14 PDT
Origin: Libra Channel 72-b, Section Seven, 800+block
Suspects/Witnesses: Unspecified

"He has me pulling warrants from the Queue like a recruit. The man is petty and stupid and not fit to command."

[Be patient and when the time is right, you'll be the one giving orders. You'll be Deputy Chief Constable and in charge of Unit One.]

"I don't want to make DCC."

[What do you want?]

"To have real influence, like you."

[You have to start somewhere, build your credentials. Answer me this: who would you rather be, the lord of all beggars, or retainer to the king of an empire?]

"Retainer to the king, of course."

[You must change the way you think. We've no use for followers of any trapping; only kings, only lords, only generals, and only presidents. I've had many jobs and all of them were necessary. Look at them as rungs on a ladder, nothing more.]

"None of your jobs were this dangerous."

[That may be true, but you're tougher than I was at that age.]

"I'm tired. How much longer?"

[Be patient. You've done excellent work. I regularly tell the others of your contribution.]

"You do?"

[Of course! You are my eyes and ears; my spymaster. Now tell me of Williams. What is he planning?]

"Planning? You give the man too much credit. He lets the Unit run around like wild dogs. As you probably know, he sent them to the *Musée* to investigate Luther Gueye on the hunch of Sergeant Moore. Well, Moore is little more than a sewer rat from the Veins and barely an Academy graduate. He's as far from an intellectual as the dichotomy allows. As such, only one man returned from Williams' ill-advised sortie. To put it plainly, Williams is ineffectual and lacks even a rudimentary understanding of protocol, of tactics. His 'hands-off approach' is thinly veiled incompetence."

[What of this man, the missing agent?]

"Don't feign ignorance."

[Tell me what you know.]

"He's missing, that's what I know. He was a MOD, which means that he was not registered to the municipality, but his parts had RFID chips of their own. So for him to go dark completely implies something. Obliteration would be my guess. He's probably at the bottom of the bay. Murdered and buried at sea, unceremoniously. That's what I would have done."

[Interesting.]

"Now tell me what *you* know."

[You're wrong about Williams. He has a laborer's kind of cleverness but you should tread carefully nonetheless. He is by no means stupid. Tell me about Detective Constable Bryant. She intrigues us.]

"She's an addict."

[An addict you say? Do tell!]

"Not drugs. She's addicted to immersion, the same way the previous generation struggled with video game and social media addiction. However, immersion addiction is far more alluring and far more dangerous. I believe it may be taking a physical toll on her."

[And what of Moore? He's out of the hospital, no?]

"Unfortunately. His first day back was yesterday."

[He'll want to pick up on the 101 incident, no doubt. You'll want to scuttle his efforts.]

352

"How do you expect me to do that?"

[Tactfully. Now tell me about the others.]

"Why? There's nothing of value. The yakuza, Daisuke; that piece of… filth. He belongs in prison with the rest of those goons. He brings nothing of value to the unit but mid-level cheeseball arrests. We could obliterate the Minowara in one fell swoop if the SDC wanted to. And these arrests of his come at a price, as I know he is doing favors for them in return.

"The idea of a deputized informant was poorly conceived at inception. We should terminate his contract and lock him up. I've followed him on several occasions and could testify to a whole slew of infractions. Drinking, gambling, probable whoring, all on the taxpayer dime. His very employment is a slight to the SDC. Of all the things I am forced to put up with, that *monkey* is by far the most intolerable."

[And the new recruits? Anyone of interest in their ranks?]

"Well, thanks to Councilwoman West's micro-management, we've only squeezed two through the vetting process."

[Now you're ranting.]

"One shows a bit of promise. Lin, I think his name is. He's a Chinese but if you can look past that, he shows potential."

[That's good, very good in fact. And what of Agency Zero?]

353

"Am I to report on them now? That's *your* man, isn't it?"

[I'm simply asking you to tell me what you know. If the answer is 'nothing,' then say so.]

"I know they've been active, clandestinely. I know they called a briefing two days ago."

[Do you know what was discussed?]

"No, but it was important enough to bring the ghoul in."

[The 'ghoul?']

"Yes, the one with grey skin. She covers her face and has these eyes: augmented eyes that pinwheel. She reeks of..."

[Of what?]

"I don't know, death and alcohol."

[Do us a favor and keep an eye on them. I'd prefer to keep close tabs on the Major while we figure out the best way to retire him.]

"Sure, sure."

[You've done good work, my boy. Be patient a little longer and I will bring you in, I promise.]

"So you've said."

[Your mother was prone to fits of depression. Are you depressed?]

"I am not depressed."

[Remember who you are.]

"Who am I? Am I not Mason Bruce?"

[A silly pseudonym. Would you prefer 'Alan Smithee?']

"You're laughing but I don't understand."

[Nor do you need to, my son.]

13: A Million Stars

"I've never written a song that wasn't inspired by Sun City. One might even say I've never written a song but rather allowed this city to channel her song through me. I know that's kind of esoteric and maybe a little hippie-sounding, but I think it might be true. That's why I have these two identities, you see. On one side, I act as her voice and on the other, her sword."

- Unit One Sergeant Chris "Crusher" Calderon

A dozen little legs carried its bulbous form across his face. It paused for a moment, perhaps sensing flesh, perhaps taking a bite or laying eggs before crawling down his cheek, over his ear and back into the mud and reeds from whence it came. These things, these creatures that dwell in the alleyways, in the vacant lots, and behind the boarded-up doors of Purgatory, visited him frequently. With carrion eyes and beaks that would rend his flesh if not for the faint light of life he held, they came and stayed for a while. With talons, wings, on legs innumerable, they came.

It wouldn't be long now.

The book's closing on this life and here I am without a concrete stance on the afterlife. This is what happens when you make bad choices.

It was cold out. At least he thought it was. Really, he couldn't be sure.

Do the dead feel cold?

It wasn't over quite yet. He still felt something: fear of the unknown. But even that sensation felt distant against the numb of failing organs.

The stars were out, a million of them, like the flashing mobiles of a packed venue. Out there, in the faceless crowd of his mind, ears perked and heads bobbed. And then, more times than not, there was applause. A raucous after-show. Obligatory. Bands that call it a night early and go home to the Ms. don't last long. Drinks spilled on hardwood pockmarked with cigarette burns. Someone always throws up. Somebody always starts a fight. This is rock. This is punk.

"'Lucy Let-me-down' might be the best song you've written," she said from the edge of recollection.

Sis? Is that you, Sis?

Heartfelt appreciation for coming out, or maybe feigned arrogance, depending on the crowd. An autograph, a signed program or two. Maybe not, depending on the crowd. It's all for show. The cameras never stop rolling.

He closed his eyes and cursed his modded exoskeleton for turning what should have been a "wham-bam-thank-you-ma'am" death into a marathon of pain and monotony.

Close your eyes, hombre. You've done enough. The boys will see it from here. Gueye will get his comeuppance. AJ will see to it. You have to trust that.

It was daytime when next he awoke.

Do the dead still move?

He tried to move a finger. It was a bit like dialing an incomplete number; a signal went out but there was no reply.

Sis? Is that you, Sis?

For her birthday, he'd written a song.

I've missed you so much.

It was called "On the Other Side." It was about a young man going off to war. The guitar solo had a cadence inspired by "Taps," and when he played, he'd drum his fingers along the guitar base.

She had cried, but he suspected it was more from exhaustion than his lyrics. The Liberty Day bombing had taken her husband, and despair and cancer had done the rest. 2050 and cancer remained the motherfucker of motherfuckers.

That was the week, Sis… The funeral. The wake. That was the last straw for Mom.

He'd applied for Agency Zero after that. The shortest distance to recompense, but they weren't taking non-military. Unit One, more specifically Williams, had been quick to accept his application.

Pretty shitty brother I was, sure. But at least I could get revenge. Or so I thought. Apparently, I couldn't even do that. She deserved better, they all did.

After the attack and relapse, he'd spent almost every waking hour at her bedside, trying to make up for time lost.

Being dead is an experience best suited for romantics.
The regret... Is that all this is?

The stars were gone now, all but one. Its crown whipped at his face, and a bead of sweat formed on the tip of his nose.

Do the dead sleep?

Day and night had become one. A singular monochromatic experience. Mosquitoes had gathered along the shore to see him off. A fat one, with a trunk of rolled whip, got fatter still on his sweat and blood.

Do the dead die?

The sun was low now, and baking hot. Chris Calderon, Unit One Sergeant. Crusher Calderon, frontman for the band Sin-Tacks, was dying. He was dying in the mud, in the reeds, among the refuse of Section Seven, probably not a stone's throw away from AJ's old stomping ground.

Today's the day! Praise the Lord! Ha! There is no catharsis in death! We've all been lied to. It's nothing like in the movies. When you die, you die sick, alone, full of fear, and full of regret. Anything to the contrary is fiction and not even worth a freestyled rap verse.

A shape blotted out the sun, and it took a very long time for his eyes and mind to adjust. When they finally did, he saw a pair of large, brown eyes — that he couldn't be entirely sure were not his own — framed by a fierce pair of brows.

That's not me.

No, it was a boy, a filthy one. His cheeks were covered in grime, and in his mouth hung a sipping straw, chewed to the point of deformity. Perched on his brow was a pair of scuba goggles.

"Hey."

Do the dead speak?

"You dead?"

Is this real?

"If you's dead, can I have your shoes?"

What kind of question?

Chris moved his lips and they tore from one another like Velcro. When he tried to speak, he produced nothing but a throaty whistle.

The boy jabbed Chris' face with a finger, and the sensation brought tears to his eyes.

"Hey!" the boy said, jabbing repeatedly, each jab sending bolts of pain into his consciousness.

Am I alive?

He tried to ask and coughed up what could only be mud or blood. The action seemed to free something up inside him, and cool air began to fill his lungs. He vomited violently, the contents of his stomach splashing up to pool in his eyes.

"You're not dead so I won't take your belt," the boy told him. "But it's a nice one, better than mine." The boy lifted his filthy sweater and showed him pants held in place by a length of networking cable. "Thirsty?"

The boy held a plastic water bottle over his head, its contents the color of salmon. He tried to shake his head, to tell the boy not to pour the strange liquid into his mouth, but the pain made even the slightest movement impossible.

With more force than a child his size should be able to muster, the boy shoved his head to the side forcefully, sparking a parade of pain that ran roughshod from his fingertips to his toes. He tried to scream but was choked by the pinkish liquid.

Chris gulped until he could no longer work his throat. The boy stopped pouring, as the liquid pooled in his mouth, spilled over, and washed the bile from his face.

The boy capped the plastic bottle and flashed a gap-toothed grin. "Stay here," he instructed needlessly.

Jesus Christ, I'm alive. I can't even die right...

"You owe the boy your life," the big man told him.

Chris nodded from the cot.

Watching the large stranger milling about kept him in a constant state of suspicion. With each passing day, the Unit One sergeant slept less and remembered more. The man, a large machinist named Te-Mea, had removed from his body a length of steel wire, flechette, birdshot, and a two-inch-long shard of stone. From his lungs, he'd pumped enough water and muck to fill an emptied two-liter bottle. This, the big man left sitting next to the cot on which Chris lay recovering, seemingly as a reminder. The machinist had also reinserted his collarbone and bandaged the broken arm to his side.

361

"Do you remember anything new?"

"I remember my name."

"And?"

"Calderon."

"You Filipino?"

"Yeah."

"Thought so. Good for you. Anything else?"

"It's coming to me, but slowly. I remember a long drive through the woods. I remember rock climbing. The rest…"

"'Rock climbing?' You gonna tell me you're on vacation? Lies will get you kicked out faster than you can say 'mugged in Section Seven.'"

After an awkward silence, the big man said, "You're lucky to be alive. Fortunate for you, your lungs are grade-A products and not crappy knock-offs. You see, they've a feature called 'critical partitioning.' It stores fresh oxygen in an ancillary repository, a little backup chamber not accessible to anything but your think-tank. It's like a gas can of oxygen for your brain, for use in the event that you are drowned or otherwise suffocated. I haven't a doubt in my head that this saved your life. You wouldn't even be a vegetable, without it. You'd be dead as fried chicken."

There was something else Chris remembered in that moment… a tall black man with glowing eyes.

Luther Gueye?

An incalculable pain, against which only immediate capitulation could occur. A rending and violent sensation in his head so that, had he a firearm, he would have shot himself without hesitation. Red eyes... Or at least a slight glow *behind* the man's eyes. These things he thought best to keep to himself. These matters did not concern the machinist.

Te-Mea took a seat at a drafting table with his massive back to the bed where Chris lay. The stool groaned loudly under the man's weight. Chris watched him pick up a pencil and begin sharpening its point with a small knife. Then, with a protractor, he quickly and deftly laid out the early markings of some design. As he drew, the augmented-reality surface on which he worked began rendering his work in a slowly rotating three-dimensional hologram. As the early sketch quickly began to take shape, the image floating above the surface in blue began to transform accordingly. "I'm thinking you could apply the same logic to a firearm... Oh, and your lungs are pretty much wrecked now. But you don't need me to tell you that. They'll need replacing — and soonish, you know?"

He was right but there were more pressing things.

Unit One needs to know I'm alive.

Te-Mea kept sketching, talking more to himself than anyone. "—one round o' .22 in the grip. You run out of bullets, you pistol-whip them with the grip and the round fires. One last shot..."

Attempts to reach Rena, or anyone for that matter, over Libra failed. The neurotransmitter in the base of Chris' skull was broken. He tried to prop himself up, and the motion drew the big man's attention.

"You've been in and out of consciousness for three days," Te-Mea said dryly, casting a suspicious look over his shoulder. "But now you look mobile enough to get yourself to a hospital. Guessin' by the nature of your injuries and lack of ID, you're trouble. And since I can't have trouble in my shop, I'll need you to leave sometime today, yeah?"

"I understand, but I'm no criminal."

"Never said you was," Te-Mea told him, "but I found this in your pocket." He produced a small black vial from the breast pocket of his shirt. "Not sure what's in it, but I'm betting it ain't cough syrup."

What is that? Jesus, I remember the Musée. *I definitely broke into the* Musée...

Biting his lip to keep from screaming, he rolled onto his side and carefully slipped one leg from the cot and sat up. "I'm with the State Defense Consortium, Unit One."

Te-Mea set his pencil down firmly and turned around on his stool, his round face incredulous.

"It's true," Chris told him.

"If you're lying, you're leaving. I don't deal in wolf tickets. If you're Unit One, you must know my son, er, my *friend.*"

"Let me guess. Is Sergeant Alec Jefferson Moore your son? AJ?"

Te-Mea placed his hands on his knees and, for the first time, smiled. It was a friendly smile — jolly, one might even say.

"He grew up in the Veins," Chris continued. "He talks about it all the time. He has a brother named Ace who we all know as 'the Major.' This place, is this how you know AJ?"

"Practically raised him, AJ and his brother. His brother less so. He ain't need no raisin' when I met him."

Te-Mea stood and placed his massive hands on his hips. Behind him on the walls hung weapons of all shapes and applications: blades of every logical curvature, and guns of nearly every modern classification. Strewn about on his workbenches and floor were parts unrecognizable. Plates, gears, springs, moldings, fittings, casings, and all the many 'ings of weapon-smithing cluttered the large, low-ceilinged room.

This must be the Iron Horse forge. I would have figured that out if I'd been thinking.

Behind Te-Mea, atop a counter, stood a miniature chrome tiger of intricate detail.

Te-Mea chuckled and shook his head. "They did you over, man! I thought AJ looked worse for wear, but you? I thought you was a goner for sure. I was real close to dropping you on the front steps of Eden Medical, but couldn't risk being seen with… what I thought was a criminal. I got a business to look out for, a little girl."

"It's ok, I understand. Your name is Mea-something, right?"

"Te-Mea."

"'A little girl…'" The voice was shrill and startled Chris. The chrome tiger that had been sitting on the counter came to life and shook its head. Its movement was lifelike as it leapt down from the counter to the floor, its tiny metal claws clicking on the floor. "Big dummy…" With that, the tiger bounded into the next room.

Chris stared, not bothering to hide his amazement. "Wha—"

"It's a prototype," Te-Mea told him flatly.

Chris waited for the big man to continue but it quickly became clear that he had no intention of doing so.

"On television," Te-Mea said, changing the subject, "they hype you guys up as the best of the best; 'young, skilled, next-gen MODS with the tools and the know-how.' Looks to me like you guys just 'know how' to get your asses kicked."

"We've made a few mistakes as of late."

"I'll say."

Shirtless and bandaged enough to mummify, Chris extended his one free hand. "Can you help me up?"

The big man yanked him to his feet mercilessly.

When the rodeo of pain subsided, he asked, "Is that your son, the boy? If I recall, AJ mentioned a daughter…"

"Nah, that's Bandit. He's kind of a scavenger down in the Swamp. He picks through the reeds because people dump there. People dump all kinds of things there, and he has an eye for the useful stuff."

The Swamp was a term for Section Seven's Third Residential District: the thirty-two or so blocks between Market and Villanova. It was the poorest of the poor and, as such, one of the most violent regions in all of Sun City. A popular joke with the detectives of the SCPD was "if you didn't find the body in the Swamp, at least you know it was moved."

How many bodies has Bandit stumbled on? Chris wondered. *Poor kid has probably seen things that no one should have to see.*

"A lot of the things you see in this shop were built from the scraps Bandit finds out there and drags back. I give him money — fair money, mind you — and offer a roof. He'll take the money, but shelter, he won't have it, 'less it storms. He makes a home for himself out there. I try to keep an eye out for him, as does my daughter. But for a boy so young, he's mighty independent and mighty resourceful." Te-Mea sighed and folded his arms. The idea of Bandit being out there didn't sit well with him, that much was obvious to Chris. "I can't *force* him to stay, y'know?"

"I understand. May I have the vial, please?"

"Oh, of course." Te-Mea handed it to him, and Chris quickly pocketed it. "I have to get a hold of the unit. I suspect they think I'm dead."

"I got my shop phone, but for the call you're tryin' to make, I'd ask you to use the pay one up the block. Don't need

367

the State sniffin' around my shop. They might find one or two things in violation of that goddamned Armorer's Act."

Chris nodded. "I wouldn't want to cause you any trouble. You've done so much for me. That being said, can I trouble you for one more favor?"

"Sure thing."

"Can I borrow a shirt?"

"Depends, 'Calderon.' You got a first name?"

Chris of Unit One or Crusher of Sin-Tacks?

Te-Mea didn't look much into punk music.

"My name is Chris."

The hem of the V-neck T-shirt covered his knees as he limped up the littered streets of Section Seven. Pain originating in his lower back caused him to bare his teeth, and he could not feel his hands. Chris limped past a group of men he suspected to be Titans and politely rejected the purchase of something called Riot Blood. Though he was sure they would not recognize him with his torn and muddy jeans, filthy hair, and fresh beard, Chris kept his head down nonetheless. He couldn't win a fight against a toddler in his condition.

Restricted to little more than a pauper's shuffle, it took several minutes to make it up the block. Along the way, he passed doorways clogged with the crooked, sleeping bodies of homeless men, women, and children. He moved past tiny bodegas with bullet-riddled windows, seat-less bus stops encased in glassless frames, and boarded-up shops with realtor adverts so old some of them were on their second or third layer of graffiti. The pavement beneath his feet rose and fell unevenly, and every other parked car appeared abandoned. Some vehicles sat in pools of their own shattered glass like gun-violence victims; others rested on flats or axles. Almost all showed the signs of residency. Overhead, the abrasive advertising cloud of large-scale holo-ads — the kind not permitted in Section Three — looped choppy ads for bail bondsmen and payday loans in an oppressive, low-resolution fog of mind-numbing images.

Pausing for a few moments to catch his breath, Chris leaned against a crooked stop sign and watched an elderly woman naked from the waist down cross the street.

The pay phone Te-Mea had directed him to had been torn from the pavement and lay on the sidewalk in pieces. There was a market at the end of the block, however. They would have a phone. He made his way there on wobbly legs and crossed a parking lot under the scrutiny of recently installed Libra cameras. Overhead an SCPD hover unit passed, its PA system barking orders at someone nearby. He watched the quadcopter swoop low, its gun turrets swiveling until it dipped behind a housing complex and out of sight. A moment later, he heard the low, paper-tearing sound of its miniguns firing.

Firing from a hover unit into civilian territory was acceptable only in the most extreme cases... elsewhere. In Section Seven, the SCPD pulled shit like that all the time.

Chris knew this well from his days as an officer. And he hated it now, as he had hated it then. This was one of the many reasons why he'd left the force. And had Unit One not accepted his application, he would have washed out of government altogether.

Bolted into the brick side of the market was indeed a pay phone. He crossed the parking lot and stepped beneath a yellowing canopy plastered in stickers. He held his wrist to the display. Nothing. The chip in his wrist should have initiated payment. The cracked screen on the phone should have come to life or, at the very least, chimed in some sort of acknowledgment. He looked at his wrist. It was swollen, and the back of his hand was purple.

Unlike Dice, he didn't carry 'cash,' a term now inclusive of payment cards. He used his wrist for all things: payment, entry to his car, starting his bike, entering his home, identifying himself...

No neurotrigger, no chip, I'm basically unregistered. I'm no one.

He left the urine-smelling phone and entered the market. Rows of merchandise were ransacked, the remainder of their contents on the floor. A long queue of people stood with slumped shoulders and faces etched in irritation as an elderly man struggled with the only operational self-service checkout terminal. Chris looked about for a vest, a name tag, any indication of an employee.

Just as he was ready to give up, he found a man crouched in the frozen food aisle stocking ice cream sandwiches from a cardboard box.

"Sir?"

The man did not turn to face him. "You all right?"

"Actually, I was hoping you could lend me your phone. I need to make an emergency call."

"Phone's outside."

"I — my chip isn't working. I really just need to make a quick call."

The man finally looked up at him. He was young, but his eyes held the waning light of one who'd seen things beyond their years. With a tired expression, he repeated: "Look, man, phone's outside."

"I just told you. I don't have any money."

"Join the club. I let you in the office to use the phone and I gotta let every other sorry prole do the same. Sorry, man, you're assed out."

Chris fought the urge to slam his already broken fist through the glass food case.

"My name is Chris Calderon, Unit One sergeant. As you can see, I've recently survived nearly being killed. I NEED to make a call! You NEED to give me your phone!"

"Unit One, huh? Now you *definitely* can't use my phone. Piss off, you fascist pig!"

Chris had grown up in a very different place than this. His house still stood at the end of a cul-de-sac and in it, his mother and father still lived. Like most of the houses in his neighborhood, it was a single-story home. It had a two-car garage and a large front yard, at the center of which stood a lemon tree.

His entire life had been spent there with mother Roxanne, father Efren, and his sister, Jeanine. It was the kind of neighborhood where Halloweens were safe for trick-or-treating and during the holidays neighbors would exchange baked goods. The only drama came in the form of a neighbor's hotrod being too loud or a new parcel drone getting the addresses screwed up.

For him, Section Four *was* Sun City, at least the Sun City he fought to protect. But as he made his way aimlessly through Section Seven, crossing the very heart of the worst part of the city, he began to realize that his Sun City was not the only Sun City. There, too, was this Sun City, a slum in which people with hardly anything just barely eked out a living. A place where distrust was often warranted and bourgeois notions like community had long been dispelled by desperation. This was AJ's Sun City, and being here, "boots on the ground" as it were, was eye-opening. How different of a person would he be if this had been his home? Would he still hold the same priorities? The same fears?

In the distance he heard small-arms gunfire, very different from the hover unit, and yet no less recognizable. It started with a single pop, a handgun of moderate caliber, and soon erupted into a symphony of shots. The unmistakable boom of a shotgun was followed by more handgun fire; what had to be a whole magazine's worth. Chris stood frozen on the curb outside the market, his adrenaline beginning to climb.

Were the shots getting closer?

And while the gun battle raged on from somewhere nearby, people milled about as though completely oblivious. A man loaded groceries into the trunk of his car as a panhandler pestered him for whatever cash he could spare. Children darted across the intersection, chasing one another, and a teenage girl texted from her mobile while waiting for the monorail shuttle. Soon the gunfire died down, and though he waited for it, no sirens followed, no hover units appeared.

They're numb to it...

Fresh out of options, Chris approached the girl at the bus stop and decided to try his luck.

"Is that normal around here?" he asked, trying very hard to muster something like a smile.

The girl looked up from her mobile with an arched brow. She wore an olive-colored bomber jacket and jeans. Her boots were maroon and came up to her knees. Her hair was dyed and fell over one shoulder in an intricately braided bundle. She tapped her temple to deactivate whatever mobile device she'd been listening to. "What?"

"There were gunshots, a lot of them. I was asking if that was normal around here."

She scoffed. "Where're you from?"

"Section Three these days. Grew up in Four, though."

"Don't look like it. You look like you belong right here."

"Rough week."

The girl regarded him and just sort of snorted, disinterested. "Listen for chimes. My da' taught me that."

"Chimes?"

"Yeah, chimes, like when the shells hit the ground. You hear those, you're too close. Time to shake the spot."

"Shell casings... Yeah, I suppose your da' is right. If you hear those, you're definitely too close."

She smiled modestly, revealing three teeth lit from within by LEDs the color of lime.

"Miss, if it's no trouble, may I use your mobile? I just need my friends to know where I am. My chip is broken and I don't have any cash. I'm hurt pretty bad and really need to get to a hospital."

"Damn," she replied, "I didn't need your whole life story and shit." She held her phone out. "Just don't look at my photos or try to run off with it."

"I swear I won't."

"Better not or I'll beat your ass."

14: Declassified

" 'Changgok,' 'Changgok!' I swear the emergence of Changgok might go down as the moment when the wheels in this State finally came all the way off. I mean, I'm not trying to downplay the impact of the Liberty Day bombing or anything but... this fucking guy got all the military types rock hard! What I mean is, would we really have Agency Zero; fully militarized fucking super soldiers *stalking the streets of this city, if not for goddamn Changgok?*

That said, just playing devil's advocate for myself, would I have Libra if not for Changgok?"

- Unit One Detective Constable Rena Bryant

"Major!"

This halted him, but it would be a moment or two before he turned to acknowledge her fully.

"Major?"

Around them, the halls of the SCPD station at Balboa Park were frenzied with officers prepping for the Liberty Day Parade and celebration. Less than a week away, there was still much to do.

A new, sophisticated PA sound system was being erected to deliver the premier's speech to every corner of the city, and this had citizens, merchants, and municipal workers flooding the halls of the Sun City Police Department's Fourteenth Precinct with demands and complaints. Also, there was talk of yet another major storm: a potential super typhoon that — if it stayed its current course — would make landfall in Sun City on the second day of celebration.

Further adding to the confusion, a battalion of ex-Army State Defense Consortium conscripts had been flown in at the behest of the Major. These men and women milled about, armed to the teeth and dressed in the orange and grey colors of Agency Zero. They bounced from briefing to briefing, cussing up a storm, and throwing military terms around like baseball players spat sunflower-seed shells.

"Major, can we speak for a moment?"

"Iron" Ace Monroe looked down at her from a height of six feet and change. His shoulders were broad and his chest barreled. As his eyes widened in recognition, his lips pulled back from his teeth in a modest but ghastly smile.

"What can I do for you, Detective Constable?"

The scars that clutched his face yanked angrily when he spoke, as if threatening to tear his face apart.

How in the hell are AJ and this man related?

"It's been a very long time since we've spoken directly, sir, but—"

"Let's see if my memory serves," he interjected rudely. "Born January 2, 2020, in Austin of the Independent Free State of Texas. Graduated Texas State with a Master's degree in AI Sciences.

"You wrote a thesis on 'Artificial Intelligence and Future Application' that posits wars will one day be entirely unmanned affairs. I chuckled for sure, but not your best work, to be candid. I personally found your work on CRISPR military application to be your magnum opus. Legitimately hilarious!"

"Those were not intended to be satire…"

"You were diagnosed with ADD late in life," he continued, still ignoring her. "You're presently engaged to a Korean — of the *Southern* persuasion. You've been Unit One since the unit's first sortie and came highly recommended by a good friend of mine, the former Army major and current deputy chief constable. Since that time, you've had what I would consider a mediocre tenure. You've shown some promise, particularly with the 'Strangler' case, but other times — *read: recent* — you've been negligent to point of near-criminality.

"But, to your point, we met last September at the 'Ethics in Capitalistic Surveillance' summit in Anchorage, on the third."

"Now, hold on!"

"Have I missed something?"

Rena clenched her fists in outrage. If a person had ever attacked her with such wanton disregard for manners or — at the very least — decorum in such a brutal, vocal, and humiliating fashion in her life, she couldn't recall. *You son of a bitch!* She paused for a second and reset the urge to demonstrate to the Major her own capacity for pedantics. "You seem to know everything but my name!"

"I know your name."

The Major wore a ragged and putrid-smelling poncho. It was torn and patched in several spots and dotted with black marks that were once likely crimson. Beneath that, his uniform was pressed and pristine.

"I repeat: what is it that you want, Detective Constable?"

The Major had a reputation for being a nightmare to interact with but, until now, she just hadn't seen it. Now, it was very clear to her why people did everything in their power to steer clear of the man.

He's a trumpeting asshole.

"Sir, I want to tell you about an incident in which a woman — I believe — of Agency Zero forcefully ejected me from Libra."

The Major's expression seemed to tense up somewhat. His brow descended and his lips pursed.

Telling... He already knows.

"While investigating the explosion that wounded your brother, I was confronted from within Libra."

"What were you doing in Libra?"

"Like I said, investigating the incident."

"Specifically, Detective: *what* were you doing?"

"All due respect, sir, I'm not required to discuss the details of an ongoing investigation with resources outside of the unit, regardless of rank."

"Article 7, section 2a, I believe, of the SDC Detective's Code of Operations. I'm aware of that protocol. Well stated, Detective."

"Are you aware that one of your soldiers impeded my investigation?"

"I am."

"Are you aware that by eliminating access to even basic commands, she — this person robbed me of the ability to log out of Libra?" Despite Rena's best efforts to stay cool, she found herself pointing at the floor angrily as if daring him to cross some imaginary line. "This person left me stranded in a limbo state, an act that could have killed me!"

"And yet," the Major said, shrugging, "here you stand."

"So, you were aware!"

"I was not aware of your stranding, and highly doubt that it was intentional."

Rena's jaw went lax. Her eyes searched his for truth, but came away scarred as if looking into the sun. At the same time, the Major's expression seemed to soften somewhat.

"I can see that this has upset you greatly, Detective. If you feel that you need to file an incident report, I will not stand in your way. After all, Agency Zero and Unit One are on the same team. But if I may ask, Detective, how were you able to access Libra from a personal, unauthorized account?"

I cloned my SDC account and hacked my personal client to emulate my SDC terminal, she could have told him. Instead, she replied, "That's not the point."

The Major regarded her with a skeptic's eye. "What is the point, Detective?"

Police officers, detectives, clerks, and lawyers passed the two on either side in steady streams, as though they were facing off on the 101. Beneath the fluorescent lighting, the air was heavy and humid. Phones rang in a chaotic mesh of overlapping melodies. Suspects were escorted past in zip-ties, in maglets, and in handcuffs older than the station itself. A squadron of hover unit pilots filed past in marine-blue jumpsuits, their helmets butting together comically as they squeezed past.

"I am concerned that your agent may have been deliberately attempting to interfere with my investigation. She cited jurisdiction as cause for her actions, of which your unit has none. But it got me wondering, so I looked her up. Her credentials tie to an empty user profile. The same empty profile has been in use for years and contains no personal information, no proof of clearance, and no date of establishment. As a matter of fact, the only thing the account *does* have is a codename: 'Hollow Black.'"

At this, the Major leaned in close, and she could smell something awful. It was a moldy odor that seemed to permeate from his wretched poncho. The smell caused her to wince, and he noticed.

"I know," he said, feigning sheepishness, "stinks to high heaven. But this is my penance, Detective, my Barrel of Shame."

"Penance for what?"

The Major ignored the question. "Detective Bryant. Hollow Black is an *asset*. Surely you can understand what that term means in this context."

"Enlighten me. Is she a spy or a jackal?"

The Major seemed to contemplate the notion but again did not address her question directly. "According to Article 33 of the State Defense Consortium's Dictum on Counterterrorism, Agency Zero can be activated in response to any incident resulting in moderate- to large-scale damage to persons or property, as resulting from the use of military-grade weaponry. As you are probably aware, even in this war-zone of a city, grenades are still considered military-grade ordnance."

"So Agency Zero is investigating the Diedre Incident?"

"Any incident resulting in the injury of an SDC agent is worthy of our attention."

"Worthy? Perhaps. But activating a paramilitary unit in response to a situation well within Unit One's domain of expertise is—"

What happened next perplexed her. The Major gripped her shoulder with a firm hand and shook it gently. It was the kind of thing people did when they wanted to convey some silent message... or warning. As if to say, 'Words aren't working but I need you to hear me.'

"Hollow Black's work involves the integrity of Libra as a whole, and I assure you that she has no interest in the case you speak of. Her actions are in line with the role she's been given and nothing more. No doubt she saw the illegitimacy of the account you were using and took action accordingly."

"Who is Hollow Black, Major?"

"Detective, I'm quite late for a meeting. Please excuse me."

The Major turned and began walking.

Rena yelled after him. "Major! Sir! What could justify giving an asset that level of access? How could an asset have such a working knowledge of our system? Who and what is Hollow Black?"

Neutrinos don't move as fast. The Major covered several paces' worth of distance in the blink of an eye to appear bearing down on her. His face was close now, his strange eyes blazing. He hissed like a serpent with a thick finger over his lips.

Before she realized it, her hand had come to her pistol and had it halfway out of its holster.

"Detective," he seethed, "my patience is finished. In the interest of departmental cohesion, I've been quite liberal with information, far more so than I needed to be. I've been cordial and accommodating, but it seems you forget your place. Stay in your lane, Detective, and hope against hope that Agency Zero does not impede your investigation — intentionally or otherwise — again. Zero comes before one for a reason!"

The Major waited for a response and, though many came to mind — particularly how zero coming before one was useful thinking only in kindergarten, as zero, being the absence of value, had no sequential relevance, she held her tongue.

"Hollow Black's business is my business, and my business is State business. If you don't like it, file a complaint, Detective. Do that, and I'll slap your whole unit with a gag order. Followed by a nice in-depth inquiry into the warrantless search and seizure that nearly got one of your men killed. Oh, but I won't stop there, Detective. We may want to look into the criminal activities of your deputy informant. After that, maybe we'll shine the spotlight on *you* and the gross negligence you demonstrated that nearly got the sergeant killed on the 101."

The sergeant? "You mean your brother?"

The Major's face twisted into what someone might perceive as a sneer.

Rena was gob-smacked. As her mind spun its gears in neutral to try and formulate a response, the Major winked and was moving down the corridor once more. Before he was halfway down the hall, he turned, eyebrows raised. "Stay in your lane, Detective. Stay in your lane."

Rena's pistol dropped back into its holster, and all she could do was fold her arms and watch the Major disappear around a corner.

"What was that about?"

Rena turned to find AJ standing next to her.

"What was that about?" he repeated.

383

Perhaps unfairly, the sight of AJ and his broad-shouldered similarity to his older brother irritated her a bit.

"What was that about?" he pressed. "What did Ace want?"

"It was nothing."

"Nothing? It's always something with my brother. What did he want?"

AJ's tenacity made him a force to be reckoned with in the field, but right now it was flat-out annoying. "Look, it's nothing!"

The sergeant's shoulders slumped, and the dejected look that crested his face forced an immediate apology out of her. "Sorry, Alec. I didn't mean to snap at you."

He shrugged exaggeratedly, his shiny black arms humming smoothly. "It's all good. Sorry for being nosy. Dice and I are heading over to Eden Medical in a bit to check on Chris."

"I heard he was already up and about. Is that true?"

"Apparently. That's why we're heading over, to make sure he doesn't overdo it trying to get back to work." AJ looked away for a moment with a fist to his mouth, as though remembering something remarkable. "You want to hear something crazy?"

She did. She wanted to hear something crazy. Anything to cleanse the taste in her mouth from her interaction with the Major.

"Mason tells me Chris is likely to make lieutenant because of the steroid he found."

Rena looked around. "Here, come with me."

They found an empty clerk's office and closed the smoked-glass sliding door behind them.

AJ's gossip immediately resumed.

"Can you believe that shit? I've been busting my ass to make L.T. and all I have to show for it are these!"

He held out his prosthetic arms; assessing them was easy, thanks to the Deckar Applied Sciences–branded vest he wore. The arms' metal plating was a shiny, black, faux-carbon-fiber design, and the synthetic muscle fiber was grey and meshed. Blended in with the grey mesh were strands of red, cosmetically woven into the design to give the aesthetic depth. These were the kinds of design intricacies that set DAS apart from the other manufacturers.

My former colleagues haven't missed a beat, she thought. *This is quality.*

She took his arms in her hands and shook them. "They're light!" Turning his hands over, she watched the tiny gears along the wrist work silently. "Excellent range of motion." She turned one hand over nearly 360 degrees. "You see that?"

"Yeah," he said. "It's like being double-jointed. Reminds me of this double-jointed kid in school who used to bend his arm backward all the time. Used to freak me out. I hated that kid."

385

She found herself smiling, her disturbing exchange with the Major becoming something in the rearview. She looked up into AJ's face. His platinum-blond hair had been shaved, and grown in its place was a nest of tiny black curls. His temples were shaved close to the skin, and his hairline was intricately lined, obviously by hand and likely with a straight razor. It was an expensive cut, and so very AJ. The scar on his cheek was still inflamed and thick, but somehow appropriate.

He looked good with his DAS-branded vest and utility trousers, with his expensive haircut and fresh war wound. For the first time that day, she looked down to check herself. She wore a white T-shirt, the same as she'd worn but two days prior. Covering it was her Unit One jacket, unwashed and worn to the point of discoloration. Her jeans were at least a week out from wash, and even her socks were from the day before. She found herself wanting to end the discussion. Also, the small and intimate office they shared was quickly becoming an issue.

She tabled the topic of the Major. Before she ran for a shower and dry-cleaners, she had something to discuss with her partner. "I want to talk briefly about the Diedre Incident."

AJ threw himself onto the clerk's desk.

"What do you remember about that night?"

He exhaled and put a hand to his head. "Well, shit, I remember Revenant. I remember kicking the shit out of Diedre's goons. Still don't remember the explosion, though, and I've watched it several times in the last few days."

"So you don't remember what Diedre screamed just before killing herself?"

"'Fuck the police?'"

"Um, no."

"That's what I would have said. 'Fuck the po-lice!'" He threw up what looked like a made-up gang sign.

"God, you're an idiot. No, AJ. She screamed, 'Ouroboros!'"

"The cookie?"

She laughed. "That's 'Oreo.' She screamed, 'Ouroboros.'"

"Ok, I'll bite, Detective. What's that?"

"Not sure, to be honest. Etymologically speaking, it refers to a gnostic symbol most often depicted by a snake or serpent eating itself. It is thought to represent cyclicality, or the life, death, and rebirth of immortality. However, if taken at face value, it depicts self-cannibalism, or suicide. This got me thinking."

AJ's brows were low, his lips pursed. It was the same face the Major had made, though for different reasons, and it sent a slight chill through her.

"You may not remember, but Diedre appeared just about to reveal the leader of the Titans to you. And, in that very moment, something seized her. Something caused her so much pain that she was instantly compelled to kill herself."

"What are you saying, Rena?"

"I remember, from my days at Deckar Applied Sciences, there being interest in a means of neutralizing a person using neurotrigger."

AJ tilted his head back, his arms folded. "Like a virus?"

"Smarter, more programmatic. The notion was that soldiers compromised in the field were a constant threat. They could be tortured for mission-critical or top-secret information. The idea involved inserting AI logic into a soldier's neurotrigger thought-recognition pathways capable of detecting malicious intent."

AJ seemed to think for a moment. "Okay…"

"Okay" likely meant he didn't get it, but she continued anyway. AJ's brilliance was rarely on-call, and she'd gotten used to that. It tended to manifest itself in other ways, often unexpectedly.

"Think of it this way: you're a soldier and you get captured. They start torturing you for important information and eventually you're going to crack. To stop this, Deckar's clients — particularly the Army — wanted to tap into a soldier's thought process using neurotrigger and stop the soldier before they could spill the beans. Like mental pre-crime."

His eyes lit up. "Ok! That makes sense. Stop them how, though?"

"If I recall, that is where the project went off the rails. No one could agree on an appropriate countermeasure."

"Ok, so…"

"But that was years ago, AJ. You have to realize that ideas like this only get sidelined by ethical questions temporarily. People quit the company, new people come on. People have different ethical standards. The line is blurred and moves frequently. And the woman in charge of product today at DAS has a pretty dodgy ethical track record.

"Anyway," Rena continued, "I wanted to know for sure, so I leaned on a friend."

AJ's eyes narrowed slightly. "You mean your fiance..."

"Yes, I mean Yushin. He did some digging and found requirements for a virus that does precisely what the Army was asking for. It detects a party's intent to violate some pre-defined vocal threshold, and takes action."

"What kind of action?"

"It overcharges the cerebral contacts for neurotrigger, causing so much pain that the subject is rendered incapacitated. At least, that was the goal. In trials, however, it inflicted pain so excruciating, so close to the pain receptors, that test subjects... and I quote: 'demonstrated immediate and inconsolable intent for critical self-harm.'"

"They want to kill themselves."

"Yeah. They *do* kill themselves."

"So, what the fuck, Rena? Deckar Applied Sciences did this?"

"Slow down there, Turbo! This project was scuttled. This shitty idea never went into production."

"How can you be sure?"

"I'm sure, AJ. That's not to say that someone, somehow, didn't replicate the technology."

"Or steal it from Deckar…"

Rena made a skeptical face. "If you had any idea how tight security is at Deckar, you'd know how ridiculous that sounds. People don't steal from DAS."

"It was a rhetorical answer."

She punched him in the chest. He giggled like a child.

"Have you read Chris' report of the infiltration of the *Musée de Conflit Historique*?" she asked.

"Not yet."

"Well, you might want to ask him about it when you see him. He makes mention of a 'sudden and immeasurable pain,' a sensation that he said originated on the left side of his head."

"Where neurotrigger implants are located…"

"Precisely." She pointed to his head. "Do you know how neurotrigger works?"

"Kind of… not at all."

"Thoughts are formed in the frontal lobes." She tapped his forehead. He responded by leaning inward. She stepped back.

"These thoughts are scrubbed by the neurotrigger logic engine for evocable elements; usable commands. Long story short: if you want your new arm to scratch your butt, you have to send the signal to the arm by way of neurotrigger. The logic recognizes the command, and hence you scratch your butt. But if you sent a command to your arm telling it to turn blue, nothing would happen, because that command is invalid. Converting thought to speech takes even longer. But that response time is more than enough time for a well-scripted program to read Diedre's intent to speak a flagged word or phrase, and subsequently trigger preventative measures. Does that make sense?"

"I guess so." AJ's brows were knitted and he frowned dramatically. "Your theory is starting to sound pretty damn plausible. How can we prove it?"

"Short of poking around in Diedre's now-missing skull, I'm not entirely sure. Well, maybe that's not true. We could look for ties between Gueye and Deckar Applied Sciences. I mean, if he is somehow using a prototype virus that they manufactured, chances are it was given to him, not stolen."

"By whom?"

Rena was quiet for a while. The unit had enough pending accusations against powerful people. And the woman she had in mind, the only person who could have taken the prototype, was very, very powerful. "Let me get back to you on that one."

The display on the door to her apartment was lit, and the mailbox icon labeled "Visitors" was dancing. Someone had come by and left a note. She tapped the icon. The note addressed her as "R.B.," a nickname only Yushin used. The message was long, very long. As she skimmed it for trigger

391

words, she imagined him standing there, likely in a sweater and scarf, his umbrella propped against the door, typing on the clunky touchscreen. She could practically hear him sighing audibly at the application's rudimentary operating system. It must have taken him an hour. There were several paragraphs. Words like "anxiety," "frustration," "commitment," and "hurt" struck her like darts.

The program was called "Sorry I Missed You," and wasn't designed for important correspondence but rather the typical "Dude, we're at the bar on 5th" or "Turn your TV down please." In fact, the application only had two options when it came to managing the inbox, and those were *delete* and *forward*.

Standing there at the door to her apartment, so close to comfort, Rena entertained the idea of forwarding the message and *really* reading it. With a sigh, she tabled the decision and placed her palm on the door. It swung open with a hiss, and she stepped into the dark.

Yushin's message had been written with the specificity and attention to detail one might put into a proof of concept. Appropriate, since POCs were but one of his many responsibilities as a biomechanical designer with Deckar Applied Sciences. If the novel he'd thumbed onto her front door had provided an executive summary or back-cover treatment, it would have said something to the effect of "Not seeing you for weeks on end and your inability to commit to the relationship have made moving forward impossible for me."

Never been broken up with by digital post-it before, she thought bitterly.

The apartment was black inside, and there was an immediate uncomfortable, undeniable sensation that things had been moved, or were moving. Rena took off her jacket and called for lights. When nothing happened, she called again. She felt a breeze. Light entered from a living room window and, in the shadow, she could see the window pane swung wide. Moving into the main room, she dropped her jacket on the floor and drew her pistol.

"Lights!"

Yushin was younger than she, and had a very bright future. His work on next-gen mechanized-organic synthesis was… inspired. One day, the barriers between man and machine would be broken down entirely, and his name would be on the list of those responsible. Her parents loved him, as did she. He was a good man, a smart man, the kind of man who would never betray her trust.

"Television!"

Her television was a 3D projection unit, and the lights, swaying beams, lit the center of the room. The motion and colors of some primetime crime drama rebounded off the massive immersion chair in the center of the room. She swept the room with her pistol and advanced slowly, exhaling through her nostrils to steady her pulse.

393

In the living room now, Rena aimed the pistol at the hallway, which remained the only area not within view. It was then that she realized she was being watched from the kitchen.

Yushin knew how busy I was… he knew the importance of my work.

Perched there in the dark, regarding her with red eyes and exposed teeth, was a rat the size of a Chihuahua. It stood on its hind legs, its nose jerking, its large teeth munching. Rena holstered her pistol. She picked up an empty electrolyte bottle, hurled it, and came very close to striking the rat. After it disappeared down the hall, toward her bedroom, she called for the immersion chair. It came to life in an aura of soft blue lights. She could see the cushions were black with grime — her grime. She climbed in.

All he wanted was time. Is that so much to ask?

As she lifted her hair and laid her head back, the sync cable, highly magnetized, snapped into the receiver at the base of her neck. Rena rested her palms on sensor plates that were slick with residue, and closed her eyes.

The rat could be heard moving about somewhere.

Maybe the rat has a friend, like a rat-buddy. Rats… Building management is going to get an earful! Better pick the place up before I call them, though… Pretty sure there's a clause in my lease on cleanliness.

Validation was two steps: first she supplied her SCPD credentials, and next her administrative credentials. This was done through neurotrigger, as was nearly every act in Libra.

Her credentials took a sheer moment longer than usual to return a confirmation, and she noted that. Had Hollow Black added something to the Libra OS? Rena remembered the Major and his snarling threats. The idea of being trapped once more in Libra gave her only a moment's pause. The lure of being immersed and free of time and stupid break-up notes was far greater than her concern.

"Son of a bitch," she murmured.

Libra opened up for her with the majesty of a hidden kingdom. She swung her arms about and let her mind acclimate to the freedom and weightlessness. If her avatar had a face, it would be smiling like the protagonist come home after a harrowing adventure.

The first order of business was operational. Her SDC account needed an upgrade if it would serve the way her hacked personal account had. She began by installing several routines she'd written, and a suite of plugins. Her favorite plugin was a locale emulator: a program designed to convert her typically drab virtual surroundings into environments of her choosing. The plugin was lifted from the DAS product team's cloud account, an account no one had remembered to remove her from since her departure from the company. When the person known as Hollow Black had blacklisted her personal account, Rena had lost all of her plugins, macros, and preferences: the software components that personalized her Libra experience. All of the little functionalities she'd grown accustomed to would need to be replaced. For the inconvenience alone, there would be hell to pay. Hollow Black would pay.

For the task at hand, she would need a place of comfort and isolation. Her favorite locale in the Libra hackers catalog was a lifelike rendering of a secluded beach in Belize. She selected the location and sank into black as the weight of reality was lifted from her. At the same time, her own weight on the world dissolved. For nearly a minute, she hung weightless in the void.

The virtual world came to life first as an endless blue sky that rolled out above like an inverse carpet. Next, clear ocean poured into her world in volume incalculable. Its mass shifted like a freshly poured glass of water, the physics engine playing catch-up. As the great body of water quickly settled into place to assume a natural rolling cadence, the earth sprang to life. First rolling hills in the distance appeared, followed by a treeline canopied in palm. Clouds on the horizon materialized as if in time-lapse. A tiki lounge rose from the sands in the near distance, bustling with fake people; rendered character models that — if you were to scrutinize — performed looping actions indefinitely. Not so different from real people.

Home sweet home.

Rena stepped into the water and took a seat in the sand. The waves, brilliantly rendered and programmed to issue tactile feedback, splashed against her bare thighs and pooled in her navel as she folded her arms behind her head and looked up at the perfect sky. Gulls passed overhead, and the sounds of ocean slowly climbed in volume before capping just slightly over audible realism.

Like this, she rested for a long time. No cooling of evening to drive her inland. No waterlogging to steal the ocean's comfort. No one to disrupt her thought process. No one in need of her time, her attention, her affection...

I wish he could experience this. Then he might understand.

Libra was more than augmented reality, it was transcendence. More than some virtual simulation, it was *induction*, induction into the root of all things; the place where events lay uncorrupted, unmolested, and untainted. Libra was the home of fact... *The Realm of Truth.*

Her fingers driven into the sand, she went to work. To start, she hacked the SDC's criminal investigations library and copied a video recorded only two days prior.

On the video, Chris Calderon sat slumped in a chair. Behind him stood an unknown SDC officer. Facing him was the blockish figure of State Defense Consortium Councilwoman Diane West. Her arms were folded, her demeanor aggressive.

"I literally just told Commander Williams everything I know. I'm beat. I've been in this fucking room for hours."

West cocked her head back. *"All I'm asking for is a quick rehash. Just tell me what you told your commanding officer."*

"There's nothing quick about the story."

"Well then, spare me the break-in. Tell me about the man you saw."

"He was black, I think. He was tall."

"Was it Luther Gueye?"

She watched as her friend and partner lowered his head into his hands. After a few moments of silence, West persisted.

"Was it Luther Gueye, agent?"

"I know you want it to be. Hell, I want it to be. But I can't tell you it was him. Not definitively. I simply can't remember clearly."

"And you looked—"

"I've looked at the fucking photos, Your Honor."

West signaled to the officer guarding the door, and he quickly turned and exited the room. Alone now, West placed her palms on the table.

"Look, Agent Calderon. I know you've been through one hell of an ordeal. But what I need from you is one last try. Just walk me through the end, one more time."

Without looking up from the table, Chris sighed and said, *"The woman with the shotgun had me dead to rights. There were sentries as well, mechs. I was cornered and hurt. Then he shows up. He was tall. He wore a suit. He was black. Other than that, I couldn't be sure. I don't know if it was Luther Gueye, and as much as I want to nail the people responsible, I will not risk fingering someone who is innocent."*

"Fair enough. So tell me about the man. What did he say to you?"

"I can't remember."

"He must have said something."

"I can't remember."

"What do you—"

"His eyes. I remember his eyes."

Chris looked up from the table, his own eyes pleading. *"I remember his eyes. They were glowing. Right before the pain, I think they were glowing."*

"Do you think it had something to do with the pain you felt?"

"I can't be sure."

The video ended. For the sake of thoroughness, she watched it twice more. Though Chris' description of the man was extremely limited, it did match Luther Gueye. Surely, that would be enough to sponsor continuation of the investigation.

Next, she fired off an email to Yushin. This would be their first correspondence since he'd dumped her via digital post-it. The frost of not addressing the message first wasn't lost on her. In it, she asked if DAS' experimental snitch deterrent emitted any visual cues on use, namely glowing eyes on the part of the initiator. She mentioned nothing of his note. She made no inquiries into Yushin's well-being.

Wouldn't blame him if he completely ignored me.

"He sees and hears everything." Those were Diedre's words.

"He sees and hears everything."

While awaiting Yushin's response, she decided to shift her focus.

What's Agency Zero's role in all this? Why are they interested in the Diedre incident? Who is Hollow Black?

A refresher course on Agency Zero was in order. She knew a bit about the paramilitary arm of the SDC, but not enough. She started by querying the SDC databases for information on Agency Zero and quickly found that all non-public records had been encrypted, and recently. A close look at the encryption discouraged her from even attempting a jailbreak of the data. She moved on to the public records and began reading. Words, images, and videos moved across the sky, converting the faux heavenly body to a massive digital display.

As day became night, black text became white against a starry night sky. As the tide came in, she scooted further up the beach, as though it mattered.

There were 234 soldiers listed as active Agency Zero. Every man and woman among them was a formerly wounded soldier from an allied military force. All four branches of the US military apparatus, British SAS, Mossad, Spetsnaz, etc., etc. Each one of these soldiers had been rehabilitated as part of Deckar Applied Sciences' "Investing in the Troops" program.

The program served two purposes that were obvious to her. First and foremost, it reduced military churn and saved money by putting soldiers back in the field whose careers would otherwise be over. While bio-mechanically enhanced soldiers weren't cheap, they were still far cheaper than recruiting and training new talent.

The second perk of DAS' program was calculated and brilliant, if not cold. By waiving their rights as individuals to qualify for admission into the program, these soldiers became DAS' free test subjects. This allowed DAS to advance its bio-weapons programs at a rate far beyond that of their competition.

Twelve of Agency Zero's current roster had begun their new lives of service in the private military unit Phoenix Battalion, under the Major, Ace Monroe.

These would be his closest, his most trusted. The Phoenix Battalion...

The group that would eventually become Agency Zero had enjoyed a brief stint of international fame following the invasion of Pyongyang. An invasion they'd spearheaded. It was this fame that carried "Iron" Ace Monroe into the limelight as the face of the State Defense Consortium.

It occurred to her that she didn't know much about the group prior to the Third Korean War. She dug deeper.

The Phoenix Battalion's first official mission had come at the behest and funding of the United Nations. The mission sent them into the midst of a civil war in the West African country of Liberia. On the side of the UN-backed president, the paramilitary battalion took the fight to the army of the would-be usurper. The conflict lasted all of five months, the end result seeing the rebel army dispersed, its leader captured and eventually tried in the international courts on a laundry list of human rights violations.

After the disposition of the Liberian warlord, the Phoenix Battalion were set loose on Togo. Their new objective was the Ligue des Géants: a drug cartel and anti-government rebel faction. This marked the beginning of Ace Monroe's career with the Phoenix Battalion.

Monroe's dossier opened with a recommendation authored by an Army lieutenant colonel named Daniel Santos. The recommendation — if one could even call it that — read less like a character endorsement and more like handling instructions. It read:

To whom it may concern,

Staff Sergeant Monroe, prior to the unfortunate demise of his career at the hands of those shitless rebels, was the finest, most reliable man in my unit. We spared no munition reserves repaying the pound of flesh lost. I don't know the whole ends and outs of this DAS shit but if you can get my man back on his feet, you can have him. Just know two things:

1) ain't no returns
2) his "off" switch don't work so good

P.S. Do right by my boy, he's been through a lot on behalf of these forty-seven States.

If not for the official government seals, the document could have been scrawled on loose-leaf for the amount of professionalism and reflection put into it.

"Ain't no returns." That could have a few meanings…

Between the years of 2024 and 2026, the campaign to uproot the League of Giants had taken a heavy toll. The well-armed cartel had proven to be a worthy adversary for the young company.

It was at this time that the volume of content on the Phoenix Battalion skyrocketed. And unsurprisingly, much of it was negative. Open conflict between the Phoenix Battalion and the League during this period had resulted in a civilian death toll that the world could no longer ignore. In the fall of 2026, the Phoenix Battalion was recalled at the behest of the Togolese government. For them, according to one famous media correspondent, it was cheaper in both cash and human lives to barter with the Ligue des Géants than it was to let the war between to two entities continue. In the end, the campaign was a resounding defeat for the UN and the Phoenix Battalion.

That's funny, she thought. *No one talks about Togo as having been a loss. It's always brought up as a selling point on behalf of interventionism.* And yet, here it hung before her in plain text: the order of withdrawal issued to the Phoenix Battalion, penned by the President of Togo and cosigned by the then UN Security Council president.

After Togo, the Phoenix Battalion was sent to Iran. From Iran, it was Pakistan. And, as she retraced the company's assignments, she tracked their registry. New recruits came on board and many were killed in action. Their ranks would swell to just shy of 300 and sometimes plummet until they were barely a platoon. Rena studied the churn of soldiers, looking for Hollow Black and yet, as the tale began to dovetail into the most significant and recent of their battles, still, she found nothing.

Shortly after the Phoenix Battalion landed in the South Pacific, the war with the Democratic People's Republic of Korea broke out. On September 18, 2033, North Korea, backed openly by the People's Republic of China and privately by the Russian Federation, made good on its century-long threat and launched two ICBMs at its arch nemesis, the New Empire of Japan.

Shortly after the start of what would balloon into the Third Korean War, the Phoenix Battalion, no longer under the guise of a "peace-keeping" force but rather a "peace-making" force, were unleashed on the Asian Pacific. This time around, the company was under the leadership of a new commander, the now-Major Ace Monroe.

A jump from staff sergeant to major? Under standard military procedure, such an advancement was unheard of, even under field promotion standards. Apparently, someone in the Phoenix Battalion organization thought very highly of Ace Monroe. It didn't take a genius to piece the situation together.

After all, Arthur "Pops" Quinn ran the battalion when Monroe came on board. And now Quinn, despite being seventy-two years old, enjoyed a cushy SDC salary as an active lieutenant in Agency Zero.

Old guy hands off the reins, skipping a few dozen legitimate candidates in the process... Fast-forward a few years and the same old guy gets to stick around way *past his prime under the protection of his boy. Cute.*

In the Pacific, the Phoenix Battalion was thrown at any conflict the Allies didn't want to expend enlisted on. And it was then that the Phoenix Battalion's record began to stink like the Major's poncho. Accusations of murder, rape, torture, and mass execution filled embassy inboxes from countries throughout the Pacific. Headlines in languages she didn't read scrolled across the sky, crowning images of destruction and carnage. Injunctions innumerable called out specific members of the company and painted a very different picture of the Phoenix Battalion than that commonly accepted today.

As she poured through hundreds of articles, Rena could barely contain her disgust. *None* of these stories, these tales of pillage and conquest, had made it into the mainstream political discourse in any meaningful capacity. Had they, there was no way the people of the Pacific State would cosign on Agency Zero.

By the end of the Third Korean War, the Phoenix Battalion and the United Nations were villainous in the eyes of the Asian Allied media.

And still, knowing all of this, the State accepted this company of resurrected war masters from the bloodied hands of the UN with open arms, nay, billions in gratitude.

Lying there, in a purgatory of her own creation, Rena collected her thoughts. *How could the SDC keep these people in their employ? And to what end? What threat could possibly justify maintaining a battalion of hardened killers?*

Surely it wasn't the threat of terrorism. After all, the Liberty Day bombing had *happened*, and the Phoenix Battalion and its like had been powerless to stop it. After a long period of reflection, she picked up the gory history of the Phoenix Battalion and continued.

The unit's roster was a constantly fluctuating meat grinder during the Asian Pacific campaign. Men and women died or were injured beyond repair and replaced. She studied their ranks, looking for the emaciated person with the parasol eyes, the woman — she presumed — with the grey flesh and ragged scarf. The one called Hollow Black.

As the Allied forces fought to drive the DPRK out of Tokyo, the Phoenix Battalion were sent to the front lines. Unfettered by the lumbering machinations of the US war machine, they struck for the head of the Korean army, hunting down the officers of the North Korean Special Forces unit *Sodang.*

In the final days of the war, the Phoenix Battalion had spearheaded the force sacking Pyongyang. It was during that time that the battalion took on one Charlie Cox. Obviously a pseudonym, Charlie Cox became a mainstay in the company (now barely a platoon). The name followed them on flight manifests and in lodging ledgers. Wherever the Phoenix Battalion went, Charlie Cox went. And yet, no soldier by that name or any variation appeared on their official roster.

They picked up Charlie Cox in Pyongyang. Charlie Cox is Hollow Black.

Sure, they were generous assumptions, but you had to start somewhere.

Rena pulled current travel and boarding records and — without fail — found Charlie Cox every time. If they were trying to hide Charlie Cox, they were doing a lousy job of it. *So, why no dossier? Why no military records?*

"Military contractor maybe? Consultant? Libra, sweetheart, give me everything on persons 'Charlie Cox,' focusing on military from rank down and excluding the deceased... Hell, don't exclude the deceased. Fuck, this is going to give me Facebook."

"Charlie Cox: field marshal in the Australian army between the years of 1978-1994. Died July—"

"Next! Wait, Charlie Cox as female."

"Catherine 'Charlie' Cox: warrant officer in the Canadian Royal Air Force between the years of 1989-2001. Died March 17, 2001, in Kandahar, Afghanistan. Charly Cox, first name spelled C,H,A,R,L,Y; E-1 private in the United States Marine Corps between the years of 2017-2017.

Dishonorably discharged for drug possession and dereliction of duty."

"Ok…?"

"Currently being detained for indecent exposure and public intoxication by Miami PD. Ms Cox' recent arrests include attempted arson, assault with intent to do bodily harm, fabrication of legally binding documents, th—"

"What documents?"

"Writ of Legal Custody, Florida Proof of Ownership, Florida Proof of Registration, Florida Permit to Carry a Concealed Firearm, Flor—"

"Stop! Jesus, Charly's got some problems."

This definitely is not the person we want.

"Libra, compile an offline report. Name equals: Charlie Cox with 'I, E' first name spelling, sex equals: female, mortality status equals: dead *if* military record spans greater than four years and registered date of death equals: less than fifty years from today. Also, exclude: ranks private and below with international considerations applied. You can send it to my inbox when it's com—"

"Report complete. Zero matches found."

"So 'Charlie Cox' is definitely a pseudonym."

They picked up Charlie Cox during the war in North Korea. If she were part of the Allied forces, why hide it? Unless of course, she was DPRK…

Holy shit! Would the Major be ballsy enough to conscript an enemy combatant?

408

"Well, shit… Libra, let's try this another way. Give me female officers of the People's Army; Korean Sodang Special Forces and the like. Give me political officials with an emphasis on… hacking or technical subterfuge. And don't limit the query to anything other than exposure to virtual and augmented reality theory or technology. If no women are found sh—"

"Report complete. One match found."

Rena sat up in the virtual world and slapped the water with her hands. "I GOT YOU, MOTHERFU—"

15: Into the Dragon's Lair

"Mama, Papa, Please read this message in its entirety and I promise I won't write you again. I understand that police have contacted you. I can only imagine what lies they've told you. I pray that you'll believe me when I tell you that I am not the woman they are seeking. My life is a simple one. I work for a piano tuner in Shinjuku. I can only suspect that they have mistaken me because of some poor associations I may have made in the past and, I assure you that criminality has never been my way.

Mama, I miss you. I miss our walks. I miss your crumble more. I hope that you are keeping papa away from the bottle and on his bicycle.

Papa, I love you. I know that I have not become what you had in mind for me. I know what sacrifices you made to send me to Musashino and I am forever grateful. I only hope that you can find it in your heart to forgive me for letting you down."

- Email intended for account holders Gunter & Elle Grünewald. Intercepted by INTERPOL on May 2, 2038

The shrill cry of her mobile startled her awake. Throwing the covers off irritably, she sat up. A hand went instinctively to her face. Her eyes and cheeks were puffy, her brain one size too large for her skull.

"What fucking time is it?"

It was impossible to tell with the blinds shut. Her apartment was pitch black.

As the phone continued to ring, a voice mumbled a complaint from beside her. She peered beneath the covers and saw bed-matted hair, once styled in an obnoxious pompadour.

You...

The events of the night before began to surface.

She dropped the covers over his head and slid her feet from the bed. The urge to punch the mound beneath the covers was undeniable. "Go back to sleep."

The room stank of gin and sex. She stood and moved through the darkness, naked but for a cheap and small wedding ring. The constant ringing of her mobile led her to a mound of clothes in the corner, and her jacket. She fished the phone from the breast pocket and put it to her head without checking the display for time or caller ID.

"Yeah?"

"Madison," the voice said.

A terrible pulley hoisted her heart into her esophagus. *Fool!* she thought. She looked at the display, too late, and saw the name "Raizen" displayed.

"I'm outside. It's time to go. My father wants to see you." His voice was cool.

"Raizen, hey. Give me—"

The line disconnected with a clap. Madison stood there, staring at the phone, just as a ray of light split the window blinds and caught her eye.

"What was that about?" Daisuke groaned from under the duvet.

She ignored the question. This whole thing was probably his fault. "You should have left me alone."

"What?"

"Never mind. Go back to bed."

She picked up her bag. It was heavy with The Madam. She pulled the shotgun out and checked the chamber. She was short one slug and, after a moment, she remembered killing the Titan with the silly Viking hat. Removing a shell from a near-overflowing dresser drawer, she replenished the round in accordance with her system. Red, blue, green, yellow, repeat. Slug, flechette, buckshot, birdshot, reload. That was the rhythm. Slugs were for the torso, flechette for the legs, buckshot for limbs — any, really — and birdshot for the face. From a distance, birdshot would disfigure and incapacitate but not likely kill. She'd tapered many a situation with birdshot.

At the sound of the gun cocking, her husband was on his feet, naked, bruised, and ridiculous-looking.

"Do you remember the night you gave me this?" she asked him.

"Gave you what?"

"The gun, stupid. You came home stinking drunk. You said, 'I'm getting my own club, baby. So this is for the apartment, in case someone comes looking for trouble.'"

The look of remorse on his face pissed her off.

"At the time, I said I didn't want it. But really, I was just angry. I was angry that despite being as much Raizen's friend as you, despite being just as reliable as you, not once did it cross anyone's mind that I was Minowara material just as much as you."

"Baby," he started.

She leveled the gun at him. "I'm still talking."

Daisuke raised his hands for a moment. "Sorry…"

"That was about three months after the wedding; the wedding where your aunt said two words to me and your cousin hugged me like I had Ebola. There were a lot of suits, Daisuke, a lot of empty, yakuza suits. And not a lot of friends."

Daisuke slowly took a seat on the bed, his hands on his knees, his face down.

"I mean, what the fuck makes *you* special?" Despite not wanting to be angry with him, she found the sight of him incensing. "I know more about what it means to be yakuza than any of you! I mean, what is the problem, Daisuke? Is it my face? Is it what's between my legs?" She pointed the gun at him again. "Now, you can talk! Let's hear it, Daisuke. What makes you so special? What makes Sugihara so special? What makes a fucking moron like Etsuya so special?"

As Daisuke seemed to genuinely ponder the question, she dressed, not very concerned about how the articles of clothing she selected paired.

"I don't know," Daisuke said finally.

She chambered a round in The Madam.

"Is it because you're Japanese and I am not?"

Daisuke shook his head slowly.

"Of course that's not it. Koreans have been yakuza since before the Minowara, as have Chinese, Taiwanese..."

"Madison, what's going on? What can I do to help?"

She ignored the question and walked over to the closet. In the closet she fished around before finding a small, serrated knife with a stainless-steel pommel. She slipped it into the waistline pocket of a smart-fabric skirt, whose color-matching technology was currently being thrown off by the room's darkness.

"Hey, talk to me," said Daisuke, still sitting on the bed lamely. His face was almost entirely purple, and she secretly applauded his durability.

"I'm not stupid, and I *am* more yakuza than any of you. Sugihara doesn't care that I'm a woman. Sugihara's vision will put the tired old way to bed once and for all."

"Maddy, love. Tell me you're not really buying into Sugihara's bullshit..."

"I've got to go."

"Go where?"

She almost wanted to tell him. She wanted to tell him that Raizen and his father probably knew that she had sided with Sugihara. She wanted to tell him that she was off to pay the piper, likely with her life.

Daisuke sensed her hesitation. "Where are you going?" He stood and moved to block the door.

"I have to go to work."

It was a look she hadn't seen on his face in a long while: a look of desperation. "No love. You don't."

"You look so pathetic," she said viciously, as she slammed her closet door closed. "So fucking pathetic! Also, *dear husband*, you stink!"

"You're mad, I get that. Who was that on the phone?"

"Yama-kun." She placed a hand on his chest and pushed him aside with minimal effort. "You don't get to tell me what to do anymore. You've forfeited any say over what I do."

"I've never— You make it sound so bad…"

"Maybe it was. Maybe it *is*."

Daisuke lowered his head and placed his hands on his hips. "What about last night?"

"Please."

"I love you," he croaked.

"I don't doubt that you believe that."

He backed away from the door and she opened it. Light flooded the room, and wind sent cigarette butts skittering across the hardwood. She looked at her tiny little apartment, perhaps for the last time, and felt nothing.

"When will you be back?"

Daisuke, you fool.

She took his hand and, despite the anger she still felt, squeezed it.

"Maddy, love, please don't go."

She kissed his hand and held it to her cheek for a moment. Those thin fingers and dented knuckles. This new Daisuke wasn't the man he once was. Unit One had given him purpose, and it fascinated her, but...

It's all too late.

She couldn't take back what was done any more than he could. Betrayal had drawn borders between them where previously there were none, and mistrust had gouged great chasms across which even love dared not venture.

If last night was anything to her, it had been an experiment, an experiment to see if going back to the way things were was a possibility. The experiment was over. The results were negative.

She contorted her face in a smile that must have looked so fake. "I'll only be gone for a short while. Stay and wait for me if you want."

As the car took them to Chairman Minowara's estate, Raizen sat staring out of the window, brooding. One of his men, a bruiser named Maeda, sat opposite them in the back of the limo. Her bag and The Madam lay beneath the heel of Maeda's cap-toe Oxford Ferragamos. As they rode in silence, he stared at her unblinking, his fists clenched.

The driver merged onto the 101, headed for the coast. The drive from Section Four to the Minowara estate was roughly forty-five minutes. They were well past halfway, and Raizen hadn't said two words. Her palms sweaty, she kept one hand within reach of the small blade in her skirt. Her mouth was dry, and she would kill for a glass of water.

"What does the boss want?" she ventured, trying hard to sound normal.

Raizen did not speak, but rather played with the ring on his index finger.

She sat back and did not speak again. The buildings of Sun City moved by like a forest line, multi-colored lights stretching between the buildings like vines in preparation for the parade. Entire sections were being walled off to create new, larger avenues for parade traffic. Above, huge cranes, like sewing arms, worked on City Center, preparing the grand stage for the parade assembly. She wondered if she would be around for this year's celebration. She wasn't even sure if she cared. For people like her, the Liberty Day Parade was little more than an excuse to get drunk and high and walk the streets of Sun City armed.

As much as she didn't want to, she began playing out the scenario she was being ushered into in her mind.

Once the car arrives at the estate, several men will drag me out of the vehicle. There will be a lot of them because that will be — in their minds — my last chance for a fight. They won't know about the knife.

They'll likely take me to the west wing of the compound where the indoor basketball court, pool, and bowling alley are. They'll find some room with modest, easy-to-replace wallpaper. The kind with cheap, easy-to-clean linoleum floors. Or, maybe, they'll take me to a room already prepped, lined with a tarp. They'll spend an hour, maybe two, beating the shit out of me. For this, the Oyabun himself will want no part. They may or may not, at this point, grill me about Sugihara's plans...

It really depended on who was running the interrogation.

You always want to soften the victim up before the first line of questioning. If I'm to be raped, it'll happen in this phase. No one's gonna want what's left after the "softening-up" phase.

She swallowed and fought back the urge to shake her head.

After that, they'll present me to the Chairman, what's left anyway... They'll make me kneel before the old man, prostrate myself. They'll coax me to beg. That's how the muscle gets confirmation from the boss that they did their jobs; that I'm softened up. Only then, once I've pleaded sufficiently for my life, will the actual *questioning begin.*

418

"What does Sugihara want?" they'll ask. "Why does he think he can take on the Minowara?" "Where is Sugihara?" "What were you and Luther Gueye planning?" "Where is Luther Gueye?" "Who else is in on the plot?" "Are you all fucking stupid for thinking this could work?" Blah, blah, blah...

This was likely their plan. This was how others were handled. She'd been on the giving end of the softening-up phase enough times to know.

But this is not what's going to happen. Not to me! she promised herself.

Once the car stops and the door opens, I strike. As soon as the hands reach in for me, Raizen's dead. I'll stab the traitor in the neck twice before diving on Maeda. If I'm lucky... very, very lucky, I might get into my bag. From there, I'll take my odds. I'll take those odds all day.

Guns blazing... They'll remember the Party Crasher, goddamnit!

Even as she told herself this was how it would go down, the tiny blonde hairs on her arms stood at attention. How many others had gone to their deaths saying the same things? How many had been beaten, defiled, and discarded in the ocean for the old man's pleasure?

Her plan seemed to erode with every freeway exit they passed. Soon, her mind went from strategizing to blaming.

Everything is Daisuke's fault.

I followed him and got a taste of the underworld. He, of all people, should have known that I couldn't go back once tasting the power, the freedom.

What did I even see in him?

She banged a fist on her knee. The move got Raizen's attention momentarily. But after a brief glare, he went back to staring out the window.

Be honest with yourself... What did you see in Daisuke? He's funny, but that's about it.

She frowned as she watched the city give way to a rural stretch of highway.

She could technically stand her ground here and now...

The driver's no idiot. The speedometer hasn't dipped below ninety-five mph once. Kill him and I kill myself.

A burning sensation pressed from behind her eyes as the highway rose and climbed into the hills. The estate was not far now.

Daisuke, the fool, and the coward, is sitting in my shitty little apartment, waiting patiently like some puppy for me to come home. He'll probably do something pathetic like clean the place or stock the fridge. How long will he wait? A day? Two days? Will Unit One search for me?

She knew the answer to all of those questions. The answer made her want to cry.

By the time the limo pulled up to the gate of the Minowara estate, she was numb. Pretending to stretch first, she let her hand fall next to the waistline pocket and the modest knife there.

The gate to the mansion was massive and took several seconds to swing wide. As it did so, she steadied her breath, wiped her hands on her skirt, and readied herself. The taste in her mouth was foul; it was adrenaline.

The car moved up the long driveway to the main entrance, and she was shocked to see but two men waiting, the same two that typically stood guarding the main entrance. Raizen exited the vehicle first and waited for her. She thought about playing stupid and reaching for her bag, but decided that the odds weren't worth a backhand from Maeda. She stepped out and Maeda followed, leaving the bag and The Madam inside.

Men in black suits milled about the compound, some carrying sub-machine guns openly. Maeda motioned to the main entrance.

"Go! Don't wait! Go!"

She crossed the threshold and entered the mansion with Raizen walking just slightly behind her.

He's finally grown up, she thought bitterly. *He plans to oversee the torture himself.*

The foyer was floored in marble that could cover the space of most homes. Spiraled staircases, wrought beautifully in iron, framed a sun-lit sitting area that looked like something out of a seventeenth-century romance. This was by no means her first time on the estate grounds. Typically, however, she

421

was met out front by some lackey, like a pizza delivery person. Sometimes, she wouldn't even need to exit the vehicle, as Raizen, ever his father's errand boy, would go inside alone and come back with instructions.

Under different circumstances, she might be honored setting foot in the chairman's home.

Under different circumstances.

Taking in the gorgeous décor, she couldn't help but hear Habanera.

As Raizen ushered her deeper into the compound, they passed a sunken living room with a thirty-foot ceiling, an ocean-facing bar, and a massive kitchen. Etched into the marble floors were reworks of Muromachi-era paintings: landscapes, mostly. She admired these as she walked, not wanting to meet the gaze of her soon-to-be torturers.

From the floor above, men looked down on her like some doomed gladiatrix, off to meet the lions. Next to her, a miserable expression on his face, Raizen couldn't even meet her gaze.

We were friends once, Raizen. Inseparable. Hell — you shifty bastard — you've pledged your love for me no less than a dozen times.

The group arrived at a crossroads. To the right was the west wing, where people went to die, and to the left, the main living area and master suite. When Raizen and his guards continued to the left, she couldn't help but feel a sense of pride. Had she somehow — through her years of loyal service —

422

earned a quick death? Would she get to face the man against whom she conspired, face to face? If so, this was no small honor amongst the yakuza.

You did the best you could. You made one hell of an assassin. And if it weren't for that legendary spectre, the "Killer With a Thousand Faces," you'd go down as Sun City's finest.

Behind them, more men joined the death march, pouring out of rooms at the sight of Raizen Minowara, future heir to the clan. In her mind, Georges Bizet's Habanera gave way to some Mozart piece. Though she could hear every instrument with clarity, she couldn't place the piece. It was something epic, something final, from the Requiem, maybe...

Ah yes, Rex Tremendae.

She couldn't hold the tune as they neared the end of her journey. At the sight of the sitting area, which she knew to be their destination, her mind quickly became a jumble of unfinished works; an orchestra of pots and pans.

I'm going to die. I'm going to die and it's your fault, Daisuke.

But is it really his fault? Be honest with yourself!

Was it not Daisuke that begged me to flee Tokyo before the war? Was it not Daisuke that sent countless letters, begging me to come to America? Begging me to leave the Minowara...

The corridor bled into the main living area. Walled in glass and carpeted in pure white, it was a gorgeous, panoramic view of the Pacific. At the bar sat several men in suits. In the

lounge area sat several more. Another man switched off the
television when they entered, and stood at attention.

This is it, end of the line.

At the center of the room sat Oyabun of the Minorwara-
gumi, Kazuo Minowara. His high-backed throne sat facing the
sea. Next to it was a so-so painting on an easel. It was a
landscape of the coast and done in the kind of broad strokes
that contemporary artists favored. The kind that she attributed
to lack of precision and talent. How much coast did the old
man need?

The group dropped her off at the foot of Lord
Minowara's chair. Maeda and the rest of the muscle bowed
deeply. Raizen, less so. They all backed away several steps,
lest there be any confusion as to who was on the old man's
shit-list. She stood before the chairman, arms at her side, head
lowered.

A window was open, and a cool, ocean-scented wind
swept her hair up and into her face. She inhaled deeply and was
thankful for as pleasant a final breath as one could hope for.
She tucked her hair behind an ear and smiled the way a person
might smile stepping out of their car after rear-ending
someone.

Boss Minowara wore a magnificent grey suit and
crimson dress boots. He sat in a gorgeous chair crafted by the
same designer that had created Raizen's precious desk. The
arms of the chair were carved in the shape of dragons, and his
gnarled and bejeweled fingers toyed with their beards as he

regarded her. Expression of any kind had long been extinct on his ancient face. It was only in his eyes that the spark of *anything* still shone, and, at this moment, they projected on her a kind of anti-light. No hate, no malice, no resentment behind the fog of glaucoma. No *nothing*.

A life of bad choices had led her to this moment, and her heart was steady. They hadn't frisked her. They hadn't found the knife in her skirt. Before they hauled her off, she would spring on the chairman. She could get to his throat before the first shot was fired. This would be her gift to Sugihara for offering to bring her into his new world as an equal. Oyabun Minowara's life at the expense of her own.

Sugihara will grant me the rank of waka-gashira posthumously, she thought, *as the catalyst; the flame that ignited the Seidai inferno.*

It was fantasy, but it warmed her nonetheless.

Minowara sat forward, an effort that took more than a second. His fogged-over eyes squinted to view her. "Party Crasher. That's what they call you, is it not?"

"Yes, Minowara-dono."

She wanted suddenly and maddeningly to say goodbye to Daisuke. Certain she could close the door on him and meet the end alone, now, in the maw of the dragon, her resolve was wavering.

At least a text message, something to set him free.

The thought of him sitting in her apartment as they beat her, shot her, and dumped her body to sea was a little more

425

than she could handle. A simple word would suffice. *"Goodbye?" "Sorry?"* What was most appropriate? *No*, she thought, *"forgiveness" is the word, if any. He'll understand that. We both have much to be sorry for.*

Her mobile sat in her bag next to The Madam, which sat outside in the limo. There would be no goodbye. She'd had her chance less than an hour ago, and let her anger get in the way. They'd said their last goodbye, in that passionless kiss in the doorway of her shitty apartment.

Raizen, standing at her side, pushed her forward with a gentle hand in the small of her back.

With summer winding down, Bad Königshofen would be laden with tourists. The meadows would be as green as the word could conjure. And right now, it would be close to 7:00 in the evening. Her father would be preparing dinner. Her mother would be sitting in her chair on the back porch, writing or reading. The air outside would smell of petunias. The sun would be low, just above the hills behind their home. Shadows would creep down the hills like rivulets of ink, and the only sound would be that of their neighbor's children playing.

Fool, she thought, *the neighbor's brats are grown now.*

"Of everyone, I brought *you* in first," Minowara said with a raised finger. "How does that make you feel?" His mouth gummed in anticipation of her answer, the massive ring on his finger scraping against the wooden arm of his chair, deafening. The red velvet chair-backing framed his pale face, and he could have been Dracula.

First? Of all the conspirators, I'm first to the gallows? Even Sugihara, for all his machinations, would be granted at least a few hours' clemency? Nice. Just-fucking-wonderful.

"I am honored," she replied, bowing once more. This time she bowed the way Japanese schoolgirls do: with her hands in her lap. And when she rose, there her hands remained, close to the waistband of her skirt, and the blade hidden there. She looked at the floor respectfully and did not meet the old man's gaze again. She would see him plenty in the next few moments, and hopefully from the inside out.

"I pictured you differently," Chairman Minowara continued. "I knew you were a woman. We've worked with female assassins many times, but never a gaijin and never a woman with your penchant for brutality." He coughed. It was a terrible cough, and she could hear things rattling about in his body. It was the kind of cough Sugihara would have loved to hear, and the kind that surely caused more than a few uneasy glances among the yakuza gathered.

"You've killed a few men for us, have you not?"

"Six, if you count explicit targets. Of course, there's always collateral damage. All in all, who knows?"

The chairman nodded thoughtfully, his ring scraping the chair agitatedly. "Sakakibara called me a fool for using a woman — a white woman, at that — for such sensitive matters. But it was my son who convinced us. He sees you as a friend, trusted you as a friend. How does that make you feel?"

"Honored."

427

There was a long silence. In it, she heard the crackle of cigarette drags from around the room, followed by exaggerated exhales. She heard people talking in other rooms. She heard gulls crooning outside. She even thought she could hear the hands of Raizen's ultra-expensive watch ticking away the moments of her life.

Her hand was positioned on her waist, the hilt of her meager little blade hard beneath the cotton of her skirt. *Here we go... Just don't get knocked out. Don't let them subdue you. Even if you have to stick yourself, don't get captured!*

Minowara raised his hand in the air and waved at his men. "Leave us!"

She looked up.

Boss Minowara waved with both hands, the rings on his fingers clinking. "Everyone out!"

Madison stared once more at her feet as the room emptied of all yakuza except for Raizen and the boss himself. She kept her gaze on the floor to hide her astonishment. She kept her gaze on the floor to hide the wicked grin bubbling.

Are you stupid? With your men gone, I could kill you and your son, steal the 1911 pistol most certainly under his right arm, and make a mess of half the men in this mansion.

The doors slammed shut, and it was quiet momentarily. She took those precious moments to lay the groundwork for her escape.

428

The patio may have a walkway that will take me around the building. But if it doesn't and I get caught on the patio… Guess I'm walking the plank.

"Look at me." Minowara's voice shattered her train of thought.

With a mask of a face, she met the old man's gaze boldly.

"Do you know who Luther Gueye is?" the chairman asked.

"I know who Luther Gueye is."

"I want you to kill Luther Gueye."

Without hesitating, she replied, "I want to kill Luther Gueye."

"Then, we have a contract."

She struggled to keep a straight face, pretending to have an itch. Her hand moved away from the blade on her waist to wipe her nose with the sleeve of her jacket. She stood up straight and stared into Minowara's over-ripened face with confidence. "Luther Gueye isn't the typical contract. A billionaire philanthropist?" She feigned ignorance and was impressed with how authentic she sounded.

"Know this: Luther Gueye is not what he seems. He is the boss of the Titans!"

She cocked her head back and made a mock expression of shock and disgust. "Gueye… really?" She looked at the ceiling, as though formulating new notions at this revelation.

"Understanding how difficult it will be for you to get close to him," Minowara continued, "we will triple your usual fee."

She bowed deeply at the waist, mania taking her from within like ecstasy. "It is done, Minowara-dono."

She turned, eager to leave the building with her soul still attached.

"Don't you want to know why?"

The question spun her around. "Why, what?"

"Why I want Luther Gueye dead."

Because he plots to usurp your men to bolster his drug distribution network. Because he is a willing enabler for the man who would see you and your progeny scattered. Because he is younger, richer, and has a brighter future than you. That is why.

Poker face...

"It is not my place to ask questions, Minowara-dono."

Oyabun Minowara smiled, the corners of his purplish lips pulling up until browning teeth were exposed.

16: Vertigo

"Assuming a candidate survives the ridiculous screening process, the Unit expansion program consists of three steps. Step 1: Find some asshole from the SCPD who thinks they have the chops to be Unit One. Step 2: Throw him into the Unit with a negotiable cybernetic augmentation agreement that almost everyone opts out of. Step 3: Provide little-to-no relevant skills training. Steps 4a-4d/e: Watch them quit, get fired, commit suicide, or get raped and/or murdered by one of the many factions in Sun City for wearing the wrong jacket with the wrong qualifications.

Get past all that and it's a cakewalk."

\- Unit One Sergeant Alec Jefferson "AJ" Moore

"Goddamn, Dice! Your face looks like it just gave birth."

His partner's face was grotesquely discolored, and he really wanted to laugh. The bridge of Dice's nose had been split and was covered with a blood-crusted Band-Aid. Both eyes were showing shades of purple beneath the lower lid and on the right side of the brow as well. His left eye was all but shut entirely.

At a glance, a person might think Dice had lost a long, possibly drawn-out fight, but AJ knew better at a glance.

Someone had hit Dice cleanly and really, really hard with one or two solid shots. And it must have been a doozie, delivered horizontally, to dust up both eyes like that.

Putting on his detective's hat, AJ assessed the bruising.

Looks like Dice ducked right into a head kick. Or, he was hit with something like a bat, or maybe an elbow. A good forearm to the face would certainly have done the trick.

They were on the far end of a car park facing the eastern side of Eden Medical Center, Sun City's largest hospital. Their cruiser was set to autopilot and seemed hell-bent on taking the slowest possible route to the hospital's western entrance.

With time to burn, he let his curiosity get the best of him.

"What the hell happened to you?"

"Cheap shot," Dice replied. "Never saw it coming."

"That sucks, man. You really need to watch your back out there."

Dice looked at him with an incredulous expression.

With most people, AJ wouldn't bring something like this up for fear of hitting a sensitive nerve, but his relationship with Dice was different. After all, Dice had seen him take a few lickings as well.

"We're on the opposite side of where we need to be," Dice said, changing the subject immediately. He took the wheel, which disengaged the vehicle's auto-pilot. "Not sure why we're taking the scenic route."

AJ was tempted to let the beating drop, but the topic was simply too juicy. "So, who whooped your ass, Dice?"

"No one whooped my ass," the yakuza scoffed. "I wasn't paying attention and someone hit my face."

"On purpose?"

"Yes."

"And did you return fire?"

"Like, shoot them?"

"No, like hit their face back!"

"No, that wouldn't have been appropriate."

AJ looked at his partner, waiting for his face to crack a smirk, but none came. "Wait, someone 'hit your face,' and you didn't hit back because 'it wouldn't have been appropriate?' I'm pretty sure that's the very definition of an ass-whoopin'."

"Yeah well, it doesn't even hurt... that much. I've had worse." Dice took a drag from his cigarette and squinted at him. "How bad does it look?"

"I would probably stay off of dating apps for — like — ever."

Dice laughed, which signaled it was okay for him to laugh too.

"You look like you owe eleven Samoans money. You look like you got beat with a pillowcase full of doorknobs. You look like—"

"Okay, AJ. Okay. That's enough."

It was difficult to know just when it was that Dice had become his best friend, but it was an undeniable fact.

433

Dice was a bold and genuine character, the kind of guy who would have your back no matter the odds. He was candid in all things, and not because he was a moralist (though he did display moralist tendencies from time to time), but because he was simply too lazy to lie. What you saw with Daisuke Yamazaki was exactly what you got. He was as consistent as a machine in the things that mattered, and as inconstant as the wind in the shit that didn't. And yet, all these traits were subject to an ethical code best described as "enigmatic."

Dice pulled the car into a parking spot designated for emergency vehicles, just outside the western entrance of the hospital. They exited the cruiser and made their way inside. As they walked, a question occurred to AJ. "You *do* know how to fight, right?"

Dice made a disgusted face.

"I only ask because, in thinking about it, I don't know if I've ever seen you square up with someone. I know I've seen Chris throw down, I've seen Rena floor someone, and I saw Williams damn near decapitate a guy with that kick of his. But you? I just can't seem to recall...

"I mean, I've fought quite a few yakuza and most of them can't fight for shit," AJ continued. "They shoot with decent enough accuracy but typically suck in close-quarters combat. To be fair, it's not just yaks. It's the same with the Huntsmen, the Titans, and the Triad too. Thugs can shoot a gun and typically don't hesitate. That's what makes them

434

dangerous. But for the most part, unless they've done a stint or two in prison, thugs have *no hands*."

"You're saying I am a 'thug'?" Dice looked genuinely hurt but probably wasn't.

"Not at all. I'm just asking, seriously. You're a deputy now, but I think you want to be an agent. *I* want you to be an agent. But not if it means I have to attend your funeral."

It was the truth. The thought of Dice in some of the scenarios he'd been in since becoming Unit One kind of scared him. And maybe he was underestimating the ex-yakuza, but the question deserved asking.

And better from me than Deputy Chief Constable Williams.

Dice reached out and patted his shoulder as they walked. "Thank you. I know that what you're saying comes from the heart."

"The SDC has offered to MOD you," AJ persisted. "I mean, that's like a million-plus dollars of free augmentation: the *good* kind. All grade-A, DAS shit. For a deputy, that's unheard of. Why haven't you agreed?"

Dice smiled and took another long drag. He exhaled and picked his nose for a while before answering. "MODS are good," he said thoughtfully. "Agents with robot shit inside of them are good because there are bad guys with robot shit inside of them."

"Yeah?"

"But robot doesn't mean better than human."

"What do you mean?"

"How do I say this?"

The deputy informant looked up at the sky as they walked, and took his time formulating his thoughts. When he was ready, he said, "If I were like you, meaning more durable. If I could run like you do and had your agility. If I had a sword that only a MOD could wield, I would have a different... let's say *confidence* than what I actually have. Which is good! But it's different. But, because I am not more confident, I see things differently. Things like threats. I am more suspicious because I am in greater danger than someone like you. I'm going to see things that you aren't. You're going to ignore a lot of things that I see as warning signs."

Dice looked at him, with his thin brows arched high on his head. He cocked his head back and smiled.

"You see? All this slows me down. Having to worry about being shot constantly forces me to put more thought into the way I engage people. Fear forces me to respect even a nobody. And that is why I am alive when most other candidates aren't. Does that make sense?"

"Surprisingly," AJ replied, "it does. It makes total sense."

"It's all about perspective, AJ. And we need to see *everything*, from all angles. We need to see what the little guys are up to just as much as we need to see what the cyber robot fucks are up to."

"'Cyber robot fuck?'"

436

"Yeah, the CRFs."

By the time their laughter subsided, they were well inside Eden Medical Center. They stopped briefly at the information desk to confirm Chris' room number before heading for the acute assessment unit.

It was there, in the hospital admissions area, that two people, dressed in a very familiar garb, accosted them. A man and a woman of similar age wore black jackets and trousers. The jackets were high-collared and adorned on the sleeves with the white delta of Unit One.

A small organization; Unit One was a tight-knit bunch, which meant one thing...

"Fucking initiates."

Dice looked at him quizzically.

"Recruits."

The recruits approached and stood at attention, the way the soldiers of Agency Zero did. The woman was tall, perhaps over six feet, and stared back at them with black eyes and a stern brow. Her partner was a thin Asian man — likely of Chinese or Hmong descent in AJ's estimation — with blue hair and a blank expression.

The woman spoke first. Her voice was deep and her words carefully articulated. "Corporal — formerly Sergeant First Class — Adriana Gonzales," she said, motioning to herself. "This is Corporal Kevin Lin."

Her bit about "formerly..." was pretty common with newbies. When joining the State Defense Consortium, initiates

437

were forced to relinquish whatever rank they held in their previous department, branch, or agency. This helped to dispel the sense of entitlement veterans had coming into the SDC. It also leveled the playing field. At least that's how Ace had explained it to him.

"We've recently been called up," Gonzales continued, "and we were instructed by Deputy Chief Constable Williams to seek you out for instruction."

AJ leaned in to Dice's ear. "He pawned them off on us."

Dice shook his head.

"Let me guess," AJ said, addressing Gonzales, "were his words something to the effect of: 'Get the fuck out of here, I'm busy! Go find Moore and Yamazaki?'"

The blue-haired man snickered and looked to Gonzales, whose expression all but confirmed his suspicions.

"Actually, that's pretty close," she replied with a clenched jaw.

"Sure it is."

AJ did not want to entertain the idea of a pair of initiates hanging on their coattails. So, after a moment's consideration, he did what he felt was right. "You guys should quit."

"Come again?" Gonzales stuck her chest out in indignation.

"Seriously," AJ replied, "you don't want to end up in a place like this. Look around you."

"I see a hospital, Sergeant. What are you implying?"

"Nothing," AJ said with a shrug. "Just that I've seen at least six bright-eyed initiates just like you two fragged and I don't feel like getting to know two more future headstones."

"Hey, hey." Dice put a hand on his shoulder and stepped in front of him. "Don't listen to him. He's just insecure."

"Hoh! Is that so? Well then, Dice, why don't you instruct our eager recruits?"

"Happy to." Dice looked about. "I could go for a burrito…"

The initiates looked at one another. The man identified as Corporal Lin smiled and nodded as though he, too, could go for a burrito. Gonzales, on the other hand, looked ready to add to the bruise count on Dice's face. "'Burrito,' huh? That some racial shit? You got something to say?"

Dice's jaw dropped and he looked to AJ for guidance.

"No, Corporal — that's so funny — Gonzales, no…" AJ paused and laughed. "He wasn't, phew… He wasn't trying to make it racial, but if you want to file a complaint or two, I totally won't stop you.

"Look," AJ said, kind of wanting to defuse the situation, "we're going up for a bit to see a friend."

"Sergeant Calderon?" Gonzales asked.

"Yes, Sergeant Calderon. And we'd rather go up alone. I'm sure you guys can understand."

Corporal Gonzales smiled. "That's all you had to say, Sergeant Moore. Corporal Lin and I will sit tight down here or go get some lunch."

Dice's face lit up.

"Not burritos," she added. "The deputy informant can get his own fucking burrito." She closed her eyes for a moment, and it was clear she was new to neurotrigger. After a moment she said, "I've sent you both our communication keys. Let us know when you're done and we'll meet you."

Corporal Gonzales has potential, AJ thought. *Game tight...*

"All right," Dice said. "That'll work. Thank you, Ariana."

"Adriana," she corrected, "but please call me Corporal Gonzales."

Dice reached out and patted her shoulder condescendingly. "Thank you, Adriana Corporal Gonzales."

Gonzales looked as though she wanted to reply, but just bit her lip. Instead, she performed a crisp about-face and stormed off. The blue-haired man stood, watching her leave.

Not sure what to make of Corporal Lin but also not caring, AJ nudged Dice and they continued on their way, headed for the elevator.

Eden Medical was a beehive of activity, as were most hospitals, but Eden — a state-of-the-art care center — handled its steady traffic more intelligently than most facilities. Pre-check-in and non-critical care were administered through

440

intuitive augmented-reality kiosks with tiny queues if any at all. Doctors did not need to locate patients, as patients were carried to in-person appointments on seated segways that lined the walls, carrying people in rows that, in places, were three individuals high.

In the organized confusion, no one paid them any mind: a fairly uncommon expectation for uniformed Unit One, but a welcome one nonetheless.

As they waited for the elevator, AJ turned to Dice and shook his head. "Fucking recruits."

They boarded the elevator, only to find the blue-haired recruit standing in the elevator, facing them.

"What the fuck, man?"

Corporal Lin smiled with his mouth. His eyes, meanwhile, looked clear — almost blank, as though he'd just awoken from a very fulfilling nap.

"Didn't get the bit about staying behind, huh?"

Corporal Lin's fake smile dipped a bit as he looked to Dice.

Rather than argue with the corporal, they silently agreed to just ignore the man. They exited the elevator on the seventh floor and made their way to the nurses' station.

"We're looking for Sergeant Chris Calderon," AJ told the nurse.

The nurse seated at the station pointed with an overly manicured finger to a room at the end of the corridor. "His room is there, 16A. He's probably not in, however. He never is.

441

Security found him on the roof last time. You might want to try there."

Dice looked at AJ, and he could only shrug.

"What kind of place are you running here?" Dice asked the nurse. "Patients just hanging out on the roof?"

The nurse set her pen down. "Try the roof. You can get there from the thirty-eighth floor, at the end of the east-wing corridor. You can check there, or not. Whatever makes you happy."

They started with the room, Corporal Lin in tow.

The bed was empty and freshly made. A vase of flowers sat on the counter. It was the same generic assortment AJ had received during his stay in the same hospital not long ago. It was from the SDC and came with an unsigned, preprinted card that most likely read: *"Your sacrifice is not in vain. Get well soon. From your family in the State Defense Consortium."*

"Dice, let's go check the roof. Corporal... *Lin*, was it? Why don't you hang out here in case Sergeant Calderon shows up?"

From the roof, they could see far beyond Section Three. If not for the orange haze blanketing the city, they might even see the ocean. The wind was moderate but, up forty stories, carried with it a needling cold. For a while, they stood and looked out over Sun City, the familiar sound of an acoustic guitar playing nearby.

442

When they were done appreciating the view, they found Calderon sitting in a lounge chair next to one of the hospital's helipad stairways. Next to him was an empty chair of the same poolside design, and next to that a bucket of sand filled with cigarette butts.

"Employee lounge," Chris told them without looking up. "The whole thing's in violation of heliport/helipad safety regulation; at least, that's what I tell them when they try to kick me out."

Chris sat finger-picking his guitar, and next to him on the gravel was a six-pack of Mexican beer.

Without hesitating, Dice plopped into the chair alongside him and snatched up the first of the six-pack.

"That's not mine," Chris told him.

"So? You've crashed some poor guy's lounge and *now* you give a shit?"

"It's been sitting there for at least two weeks and God knows how long before that."

"So? Beer ages."

"Everything ages," Chris replied patiently. "But not everything ages well."

Dice twisted the cap off and looked at the sun-faded label. It was barely discernible. With a devil-may-care expression, he put the beer to his lips and took two long sips.

AJ watched intently. After some swishing of the liquid in his mouth, Dice shrugged and offered one.

"Fuck it."

AJ caught the beer, the bottle clinking against his metal fingers.

"Who's this?" Chris asked, looking behind them.

AJ sighed audibly. *You've got to be kidding me.*

Not only had the young corporal ignored their request to fuck off for a second time, but now he just stood there with that same silly expression.

"This is Corporal Lin," AJ said. "A new recruit."

"And Corporal Lin was just leaving," added Dice, making the same scooting gesture parents gave children to get them out of the kitchen.

Lin's smile faded more noticeably this time, and he saluted before turning and walking away.

When he was perceivably out of earshot, Dice motioned to Chris and shook his head. "This guy is so fucking strange. Even stranger than you!"

Chris did not respond, and began playing his guitar once more. As his hands moved deftly over the strings, he stared out over the city with a melancholy expression on his face.

AJ opened the beer carefully and sniffed it first.

At least it smells like beer.

He put it to lips and let just a splash touch his tongue. It was flat as Dice's chest, but otherwise drinkable. He said as much, hoping for at least a smirk from Sergeant Calderon. If Chris heard the joke, he certainly didn't think it was funny.

Their wounded partner wore a blue hospital gown and black sweatpants. The gown was open to the navel and spread wide as he sat in his chair. On his feet were a pair of cheap hospital slippers. With the gown open, the work Eden had performed on him was plain to see. Thick, black stitches ran from his left shoulder to the center of his right pectoral. Large abrasions of black, purple, and yellow covered his abdomen, chest, and arms, contorting the designs of his extensive tattooing. Chris' damage looked significant, but nowhere near what AJ had gone through.

At least you still have your limbs…

"What happened at the *Musée*?" Dice asked, breaking the silence.

Chris looked at Dice with an annoyed expression and stopped playing. "Read my report."

"Come on, man."

"What happened to your face?" Chris asked.

Dice brought a hand to his face.

"You look like you French-kissed a battering ram."

Dice threw his hands up. "Okay, fuck it. Makeup. I'll wear makeup! What the hell happened at the *Musée*, Chris?"

Chris sighed, which they all knew to be his form of apology. "It's all a bit fuzzy, to be honest."

Dice took a sip of his beer and leaned back in the chair. "I've got time. Waiting on a burrito."

After a perplexed glance at Dice, Chris strummed his guitar, as if to open the tale. "Well, it wasn't a shit-show straight out of the gate. The climb down was tough, but I made it relatively unscathed. After that, Rena was able to trigger the alarm somehow just as I took the door off of its hinges."

"I might have helped a bit there," Dice added, smiling wryly.

Chris paused to see if Dice would add some color. When Dice didn't, he continued.

"Inside, I had to make my way through the warehouse and up into the offices. If I recall, that bit was smooth. Rena helped me find what I suppose was Gueye's office, and that was where I found the vial."

"Has anyone told you about it yet?"

"Williams didn't say much, only that it was 'something.' I guess *something* is better than *nothing*."

Chris reached over to Dice. "Give me that."

Dice handed him the beer, and he took several gulps. Swishing it around first, he polished it off and chucked the bottle over the building's edge. They all waited in silence, and then hooted when they heard the bottle burst somewhere far below. Dice opened another and handed it to Chris.

"Tastes like piss," Chris said.

"You've tasted piss?"

Chris just looked to Dice with a tired expression and continued. "Truth be told, that's what I was afraid of most, once recovery began."

"Tasting piss?"

"Christ, Dice!"

"No, that all of it was for nothing. *That* was my fear."

"After the vial, then what happened?" AJ asked, trying to get Chris' story back on track.

"That's where it starts to get hard, man." Chris put a hand to his head. "I mean, I had days and nights of crazy hallucinations and dreams. For a long time, I thought I was dead."

"Just try and recall."

"Well, I remember fighting. I fought guards, a bunch of them. I tried to get back to the entrance to the storeroom, the spot of the breach. In the storeroom… yeah, it was there I think things went bad."

AJ listened intently. An investigation of Luther Gueye was something he'd been pushing for since first donning the Unit One jacket. Luther Gueye was corrupt and he knew it. Proving it, though… that was the rub. And the key to it all was sitting right in front of him.

Chris strummed his guitar and looked out over the city for a while before speaking again. "There was a woman."

"A woman?"

Dice sipped his beer.

"Yes." Chris looked down at his chest. There were clustered, circular wounds beginning just below his neck and ending at the top of his stomach. "There were guards, there were Gueye's unmanned sentries, and there was a woman, a professional. She had a shotgun, an old-style pump-action. She was white, German I think, as in, *from* Germany. She fit the

447

profile of the Party Crasher. I went through her case file while I was laid up. I'd bet it was her."

Dice cleared his throat, and AJ thought his expression looked odd.

"But she's yakuza," AJ said. "At least, she works for the Minowara. Are you sure it was her?"

"I mean *certain*? I can't say it was her definitively. I wouldn't testify to it. I mean, like I said, it's all a bit fuzzy. There's a chance I dreamt it, but I don't think so. She was blonde, with freckles, and attractive. She wore a leather jacket and, like I said, carried a shotgun."

Chris stared at Dice, who just shrugged.

"C'mon, Dice! Surely you've crossed paths with her before in your time with the Minowara?"

Dice's eyebrows arched high onto his head, and he frowned. After some thought, he slowly shook his head. "I've heard of her, yes. But I've never actually seen her. Some people think she's a myth to scare Minowara opposition, like the 'Killer With a Thousand Faces.'"

That's strange, AJ thought, *Dice's playing dumb.* He made a mental note to broach the subject with his friend in private.

"Really?" Chris asked, pressing Dice. "You've *never* met her?"

"What the fuck did I just say!"

"You have a problem, Dice?" Chris looked ready to stand up from his chair.

AJ, confused by Dice's outburst, was ready to step in between the two.

"I'm sorry," Dice replied, looking away. "I just have a headache from this." He pointed to the blackest of his bruised eyes.

"Like I said," Chris continued, "I can't be sure. I fell however many stories and hit the rocks. I could fall from that height a thousand times more and not survive one. I don't know how I'm alive right now. So, to be honest, I barely trust the here-and-now, much less my memory."

Dice stood up. "We shouldn't keep you from your rest." He extended a fist that Chris punched with his own, without a moment's hesitation.

It was a sight that AJ never got tired of. *Like brothers...*

"How long are you expecting to be out?"

The sergeant shrugged. The chords of his guitar covered the roof with harmonious melody once more. "Maybe I'm done."

"What?"

"Maybe I'm done, AJ."

Dice groaned exasperatedly. "You're just tired. You need sleep. Take your time and come back strong. No need to think about these things right now."

"But I am," Chris replied. "I can't stop thinking about these things." He moved the beer to his lips but stopped himself. Instead, he tossed it. "I'm being pulled in too many directions."

"By whom?" AJ asked him.

"I don't know, by my desires? I love this." He held his guitar up. "I've got a good thing going with the band. I've got dreams of doing it big, you know? A part of me thinks I should do music full-time."

Dice scoffed. "You'd get bored."

"I don't think so."

"I think so."

"Bored is better than dead."

AJ looked down at his partner and in that moment, Chris looked small to him. He looked weak and tired, and that angered him. It angered him because that wasn't who he was. *You're just tired*, he wanted to tell him. "Get the fuck out of here!" he said instead.

"You know why I'm alive, AJ?" Chris said, his expression angry.

"Why?"

"A little boy found me. A little boy named Bandit."

Bandit? Mahina's little friend?

"This little boy spends his days sifting through the garbage, in the reeds along the shoreline, AJ. You see, while the SDC and SCPD were following up on that anonymous tip, and searching the other side of the peninsula, I was laying there, fucking birdfood until this boy found me. And Bandit spends his days collecting trash, trash he can sell to the man who took me in and nursed me back to health."

"Te-Mea..."

Chris smiled mirthlessly, nodding his head. "Te-Mea loves you, AJ. And from what he tells me, his daughter loves you too. And though I couldn't say for sure, I suspect even your brother loves you."

Chris rattling off the names of the people closest to him to make an argument irritated him immensely. "Where are you going with this?"

"I've got people who love me too. And I'm not sure I'm ready to throw my life away for this thankless city anymore."

"'Thankless?' If we let the press run the story of what happened to you, the people of this city would be right down there, right now, showing their support. Just like they did for me!"

"Please, AJ." Chris sneered. "Tell me you're not this naive. You think those people, those *fans*, give a fuck about any of us? I mean, really? They don't love you! They love the idea of you. The idea that there are superheroes out there protecting them against all the things that would hurt them. We're playthings to them: wind-up toys that crash into people they see as the enemy. Not even soldiers, just paper tigers. We're a farce, AJ. Half the things we do on a daily basis were illegal twenty years ago. Hell, most of the shit we do is either not helpful or flat-out criminal. Be honest with yourself!"

Chris threw his legs from the chair. "I've spent a lot of time thinking about this. Now you think about it. Let's say it *was* Luther Gueye at the *Musée*. Try to see things from his perspective. A man broke into his museum wearing a mask and beat up a handful of his guards before stealing something. Did he not have every right to defend himself and his property?"

"Get the fuck out of here, Chris! Are you serious right now? If it *was* Luther, then he tried to kill you! And if it *was* the Party Crasher, that puts a person suspected of ties to organized crime with someone else suspected of ties to organized crime."

Chris put his head in his hands. "I don't know, man. It just seems like we're in the wind sometimes. Kites without strings, in the fucking wind…"

"We do what we are told."

"And you're fine with that?"

"If it helps people, fuck yeah! And you can't tell me we don't help people."

"We could do so much more."

"Then write a fucking song about it, bring your ass back to work, and let's fix this shit!"

Chris made a face and threw his hair back. "Fix what, AJ? The SDC? Please… you're smarter than this."

"If you want to quit, quit! But I'll tell you honestly, it's not you. The music shit is a hobby, man. None of this is really *you*."

"What would you know?"

"You're right! I've only saved your life a dozen times. What the hell would I know?"

Chris scoffed. "I've saved your life dozens of times. *Dozens*, AJ!"

"Well, guess I'm out of luck going forward, huh? So much for me and those people who love me. That about right, Chris?"

Chris looked exhausted. "Thanks for coming to see me."

"Dice, how do you say 'asshole' in Japanese?"

Dice moved his lips dramatically. "*Asu-horo.*"

"Thanks, guys," Chris repeated while waving, his back now turned to them.

As they left the roof, both of them in silence, Corporal Lin came running up. "I can see my house from here!"

"That's great," Dice told him. "You should go there."

Peering back at his friend and rival, AJ could see Chris sitting with his chin on his hands, looking out over Section Four. His guitar lay several yards away on the ground, as if thrown.

17: I Look For You

"I had a blankie when I was a kid. It was a little, raggedy, blue blankie. I sucked my thumb when I held it. For years. No one ever stopped me from sucking my thumb, so I did it until my teeth made an indent. I was probably six or seven when I finally stopped. Even now, the skin's a different color. Look! Well, shit, nevermind... that thumb's gone."

"I don't know why I was so attached to this blanket or where it even came from, but it never left my face. Of course, Ace — I mean 'the Major' — hated the thing. So, one day he ripped the thing out of my hand and tore it into little pieces. When he was done, he dragged me across the street and made me watch him bury the pieces in a vacant lot. He told me, 'If you don't stop sucking your thumb, I'm going to break it off and bury it next to this baby's rag!'

Sure, I cried at the time, but in hindsight, that was probably the nicest thing anyone has ever done for me."

- Unit One Sergeant Alec Jefferson "AJ" Moore

He banged on the door with a closed fist until a neighbor popped her head out of a window. AJ apologized and showed her the white delta on the arm of his jacket. That seemed to placate the woman, as she retracted her head back into her ultra-expensive condo like a tortoise.

All signs pointed to Rena being home. The app on her door listed an occupancy count of '1' and her car was in the garage. From the walkway, he could see the curtains flailing from her living room window.

"Rena!" He waited a little bit before calling once more. "Hey, Rena!"

Attempts to reach both her personal and SDC neurotrigger accounts had been met with 'unavailable' messages. While going dark wasn't exactly a rare occurrence for Rena Bryant, there was something about her appearance earlier that day that didn't sit well with him. The detective had looked disheveled, out of sorts, and frankly, exhausted.

Rena wasn't a large person by any stretch of the word. Her frame stood at a modest five foot six. And the rigorous close-quarters combat training required of all Unit One agents had given her a muscular and almost stocky physique. But today, seeing her in person for the first time in more than a month, she'd appeared bent, her posture unnatural, as though pain somewhere was altering the way she moved. On top of that, it was obvious that she hadn't showered in some time.

Where he'd grown up, drug addicts were a dime a dozen. Stim addicts, pill-poppers, dust-heads, wolfers, stackers, herbalists, needlers, and nose-boarders. They were as distinct in appearance and habit as megafauna. And the Rena he saw this morning… the version he met today of the otherwise upbeat, enthusiastic and brilliant Detective Constable Rena

Bryant shared with those lost souls in the Veins the same kind of haunted detachment.

The idea of Detective Constable Bryant, the woman they called "H.Q." for her operational influence and logistical mastery, popping pills and dozing off on her couch was stomach-turning.

If a narc like Dice got popped with coke in his system, nobody would blink an eye. But if the principal detective navigating the SDC's billion-dollar immersion network got busted on anything north of marijuana or over-the-counter antidepressants, well, that would likely be the end of that person's career.

Mounted to the window of Rena's apartment was a small prefab balcony barely wide enough to hold the long-dead potted plant that sat there. From the walkway, the leap would be about nine feet, the drop thirty or so.

Below, the street was busy with evening traffic, as commuters fought one another to start their weekends early. Storefronts were bustling and street vendors called out their wares in rhythmic repetition.

AJ threw his legs over the railing and stood looking down from the third story of Rena's apartment building at the street below. With his modded legs and spine, he would probably survive the fall... probably. Regardless, the SDC probably wouldn't take kindly to their "product" heading back to the shop on account of what some might mistake for peer-on-peer voyeurism.

Whatever.

He leapt from the railing to the tiny balcony. His new arms snatched the metal bars and used the momentum to swing up and onto the small ledge. Paint and drywall fell away as the balcony began tearing away from the building with a loud grinding sound.

He slid the window open and climbed inside before the ledge could give way entirely. Once safely in the living room of Rena's apartment, he assessed the damage. The ornamental balcony hung loosely from the wall of the building, almost certain to fall with the next moderate breeze.

"Well done, asshole," he told himself.

The inside of Rena's apartment was dark but for the beam of sunlight that framed his shadow from behind. It didn't take long for him realize that something was amiss.

After a few moments of listening carefully in silence, he drew his pistol.

In the Academy they had taught him to listen carefully, to survey patiently, to speak only when necessary, and to recognize odors. Rena's apartment smelled. It reeked of body odor, rot, and *death.*

Rena...

Slowly, quietly, he pulled the curtains aside and let the light in, his pistol aimed from the hip.

What in the holy hell ...?

AJ was speechless. Holstering his pistol, he carefully stepped through trash that covered his shoes. Looking down, he saw to-go boxes and emptied water bottles lying mingled with articles of clothing. He saw crumpled fast-food bags whose odors betrayed half-eaten contents. Balls of tissue pock-marked with the tell-tale signs of blood. The trash was everywhere. So much so, that barely a swath of carpet could be seen beneath it. His heart sank.

AJ made his way to the immersion chair at the center of the room, where the glow of the chair's ambient blue lights played off the still face of his partner.

He checked her pulse. After a worrisome moment, he detected the faint thud of blood flowing. Kicking through the trash, ruining his shoes, he snatched the quilt from the couch to cover her. As he did so, dust filled the light of day in a blizzard.

The chair upon which she lay was black with filth. Sections of the cushions upon which her arms lay were worn and cracked, their stuffing sticking out like cauliflower florets.

As he studied her face, he couldn't help but swear profusely. The sight of someone he… cared about living in these conditions filled him with both sadness and rage, even as the smell of the room forced him to cover his mouth and nose.

Where the hell was Yushin? How could he let this happen? If only I'd known, I would have… I would have done something.

Rena's eyes were closed and her lips moved slightly as if she were talking.

"Rena."

She did not respond.

He tapped lightly on her forehead. "Rena."

Her lips continued to mouth words indecipherable but her body did not stir, nor did her eyes open.

Unsure of what to do in that moment, he decided to check out the apartment. He went into the kitchen first and found it overflowing with dirty dishes, some of which sat on the linoleum floor. He opened her fridge to find a horror show of spoiled food.

"Jesus Christ, Rena…"

Slamming the door shut, he left the kitchen and went into the bedroom. The walk-in closet was stripped barren, with nothing but hangers remaining. Every article of clothing she owned lay strewn about, making it impossible to move without stepping on something.

Next, he checked the bathroom. In doing so, he was not surprised to find makeup and toiletries piled up in the sink, and a shower not fit for a labor camp. He peered into the toilet.

"Oh, thank God!" he said, pumping his fists. "At least she flushes."

While on one of Unit One's many wild goose chases to catch the Killer With a Thousand Faces, he and Mason had once raided the home of a suspect, only to find what Mason referred to at the time as "a hoarder's Heaven and everyone else's Hell." The suspect, a Bosnian immigrant, had kept *everything*.

Fingernails, he recalled, *hair in sandwich bags, jars of bio-waste, emptied food containers... If it belonged in the trash, the fucking guy kept it, labeled it, and stored it.*

That place was the undisputed innermost chamber of Sensory Hell. And while Rena's place wasn't really in the same league as that guy's, the fact that it had conjured the memory was saddening.

AJ left the bathroom and returned to her side in the living area. He clutched her shoulders to find them slick with perspiration that he thankfully could not truly feel. "Rena!"

Movement around his feet caught his attention. "Reacting" more than moving, just as his ergonomics coach had drilled, he let his augmented body do the work. He crouched and snatched up a rat the size of a raven.

Holding the creature aloft as it hissed and clawed at his metal-plated arm, he bit back the urge to scream. "Rena, are you kidding me? Rats? You have fucking rats?"

The rodent's eyes blazed pink as it squirmed furiously, fruitlessly, to free itself from his augmented grip.

Rodents... Is there anything in the world more disgusting than rodents?

He took a deep breath and lifted his arms over his head. Looking both ways first, checking the bases, he shook off the invisible catcher's sign before nodding in agreement.

Fastball, low and inside.

He kicked a leg and threw what would have been a slow fastball way off the plate. The rat squealed and caught the drapes before tumbling out the window, taking the curtains with it. A moment later, he heard a man scream from below and allowed himself a moment's chuckle.

AJ had been to Rena's apartment a few times over the years.

More so before she started dating that Deckar Applied Sciences nerd.

The place, as it was today, was unrecognizable.

This is no way for someone to live. Especially not someone so...

Her chest rose and fell with a whisper, as though sleeping, even as her fingers worked the sensor pads furiously. A thin trail of spittle fell from the left side of her mouth to pool on the filthy headrest.

AJ leaned in close to her ear. "Rena, wake up. Please."

After a long time of waiting and trying to wake her, he left through the front door, frustrated, and angry with himself.

When he returned a few hours later, she lay in the same position as she had before, beneath the dusty blanket. Her fingers darted across the sensor pads manically, like a pianist, really, and every now and then she mumbled incoherently or suffered some kind of spasm.

"Lights!" AJ yelled, hoping that the sound of his voice might wake her. Bluish light filled the kitchen and main living area.

With the kitchen counter strewn in old takeout and emptied bottles of electrolytes, he opened the bag he carried and poured its contents out onto the couch. Cleaners: spray and wipe, disinfectant, deodorizers, detergent, window cleaner, dish soap, and body soap. He had brushes, sponges, and scouring pads, scented candles and a very large box of industrial-sized garbage bags.

He took the mobile from his jacket and opened the music app. Already on "Top 40," his channel of choice, he turned the volume to maximum and set it on the counter next to a molded-over carton of what might once have been fried rice.

"Hope you like hip-hop as much as you like germs, Rena."

He began with the bedroom. As he collected the mounds of dirty clothing, he cursed her for not having a washer in the unit, or better, property-paid dry cleaning, like in his building. Fortunately, the community washroom was on the same floor and only two doors down. After starting what would be at least a dozen cycles of laundry, he set about the other rooms. Outside, the sun was in its final frames, casting a gorgeous orange into the place and driving away much of the gloom.

The bathroom was easiest. He began by returning the toiletries to their proper place behind a massive, LED-lit smart mirror. Once that was done, he tossed powder cleanser liberally in every direction and waited for it to settle, covering his nose and mouth with a black metal forearm. Once the toxic dust had settled, he turned on the shower and attacked the grime with a heavy-duty metallic scrub brush. In impressive time, he made short work of the mildew and mold that had usurped the tiles. He scrubbed the sink and the toilet — a task much less daunting with prosthetic arms — and used a towel to dry the walls and floor. When he was done, he tossed the towel onto a pile of items still needing a wash, and advanced to the kitchen.

"Bathroom's good to go," he told her. "Feel free to wake up and chip in at any time."

As dryer cycles finished, he piled the clean clothes on her bed but did not fold them for fear of looking like some kind of underwear-sniffing weirdo. He vacuumed the bedroom and bombed it with air freshener, leaving the windows wide to set free the catacomb-like stagnation.

On to the kitchen...

The kitchen was a true test of his loyalty. It was there that he bore witness to the entire evolutionary cycle of growth and decay.

"This is some bullshit, Rena. No wonder you have rats."

Stuffing tissue in his nostrils, he clenched his jaw and dove in. Before long, he'd filled six large garbage bags with rotten food, pizza boxes, emptied water and juice containers, expired condiments, over-frozen foods, and a pot of what might have been a soup or a pot roast, he couldn't be sure. After literally running those bags out to the dumpster, he returned for the dishes.

As a child, he'd hated doing dishes more than anything. It wasn't about the food or the germs or the waterlogged fingertips. It was the monotony. As he scrubbed and scraped at food that had been partnered with plate longer than some marriages, he tried to hum with the music or talk to himself to stay engaged. He knew that if he took a break there was no way he would finish, so he kept on, even pretending at times that Ace was behind him, yelling commands.

"Faster, Sergeant!" "What the fuck is wrong with you, Sergeant! You'd better change that water out before I skull-fuck you!" There were less effective ways to power through an arduous task.

After about an hour, he hung the final glass on the overflowing dish rack to dry and stopped to catch his breath. Looking around, the place looked almost normal, except of course for the giant immersion chair that rose up from a sea of garbage like a wizard's tower over a haunted forest. The device was covered in soft blue lights, but otherwise looked like something you'd find in a dentist's office.

How the hell did you even get that thing in here?

Pulling bag after bag from the huge box of garbage bags, he filled them quickly and piled them by the front door. Once the last bit of refuse had been bagged, he made another set of trips to the dumpster, picking up the last of the dried clothes on the way back.

After another breather, he vacuumed the carpet in the main room before mopping the linoleum of the kitchen and

464

bathroom. As that dried, he wiped down the counters and dusted the furniture, the easy-to-reach stuff. It was in doing this that he found what must have been the rat's nest: a browning patch of carpet behind a large cherrywood bookshelf. With the vacuum nozzle, he removed the animal's detritus, then sprayed the carpet with disinfectant.

Lastly, he opened all of the windows in the main room to let the cool evening breeze flow through.

Plopping down on the couch, he took a moment to actually admire her apartment.

Gorgeous paintings and tasteful minimalist furniture paired well under subtly changing mood lighting. All of the amenities were stainless steel and the countertops black marble. The ceiling was high, very high. So much so, that considering her apparent comfort with rodent infestation, he was surprised there were no bats.

Wow, this is actually a really nice place.

And residing in any part of Section Three wasn't cheap, much less downtown. He knew this all too well, having spent the last two years only a 101 exit away.

He checked the time via neurotrigger. It was 10:45 PM. Not exactly the kind of Friday night he'd had in mind.

What kind of Friday night did I have in mind? Drinks at Portal? Darts? Can you even play darts with these arms?

He hadn't tried yet, and the thought kind of terrified him.

All things considered, I'm probably not missing much.

465

Some Fridays, even Saturdays, it wasn't uncommon for him to pull a perp or two out of the Queue to occupy his evenings. After all, it was a hell of a lot better than sitting at home alone, browsing dating apps.

"All right, Sleeping Beauty," he said, getting up with a sigh, "enough is enough." He came to stand once more over Rena and the filthy chair that stole her living area like a zit.

For three years she had been in his ear: the wise voice of warning, counsel, and reason. From Libra she had guided him, protected him, praised him, and when necessary, chastised him. Now, he stood looking down on what he believed to be the cost of that vigilance.

"Who knows what Libra is doing to your brain? And here you are, dead to the world, and for what? It's time to wake up, Rena. We need you. I need you."

Her body was drawn out and dehydrated, her muscles overly defined. The lines under her eyes were dark, in contrast with her fair skin. Her hair was thick with perspiration, and she looked feverish. He brushed the hair from her eyes and spoke her name softly. When yet again she did not respond, he spoke her name loudly. She might have appeared sleeping if not for her rapidly working hands. Her head was to one side and her lips pursed. He followed her neckline to her shoulders with his eyes.

You're beautiful. And I look like a total perv right now…

Gripping her head in his hands, he shook her gently. "Rena!"

Out of options, he found the chair's power cord. He took it into his hands and traced it to the wall outlet. Gripping the plug, he wondered briefly about the consequences of unplugging the chair while she was still immersed. He tried to remember their Libra training.

"*Not a big deal,*" he seemed to recall Williams saying. "*It's like turning a TV off. They look around and go 'what the hell' for a moment, but that's it.*"

Before she awoke, he felt obligated to tell her, "When I joined Unit One, it was you that helped me first. You took me under your arm. If it weren't for you, I would have washed out for sure. I owe you, Rena. I'm doing this for you."

Looking at his dear partner and friend with pure appreciation, he secured his grip on the plug. "Here goes…"

"That won't be necessary," a voice said, stopping him in his tracks. "Besides, the chair runs on a generator. The cord recharges the generator."

He dropped the cord.

Rena was looking at him with wide eyes, her head to the side.

"I guess we'll get to what you're doing in my house in a moment…"

Rena sat up slowly, her muscles creaking audibly. She looked at the blanket he'd placed on her with a moment's confusion. Clutching the cloth, she threw her legs from the

467

chair and stood gingerly. Looking around, she gave him a quizzical expression. She pointed to the kitchen and looked as though she would say something, but didn't.

Covering herself, she walked quickly to the bedroom. After a few moments, she emerged in a T-shirt and sweats, a clean T-shirt and clean sweats.

"What time is it?" she asked.

"Basically midnight."

"I can't fucking believe you."

Oh fuck, he thought. *What have I done?* "Look, I just… you had rats, Rena! Rats!"

Rena went into the kitchen and opened the fridge to find nothing. She picked up his phone and silenced the rap medley that was playing.

"It was all moldy," he said defensively. "Literally everything. I didn't even know relish could rot. I mean, it's already fucking *pickled*, right?"

She turned on the faucet and took two long gulps straight from the tap.

You've done it now. You've way overstepped your bounds…

She placed her hands on her hips and looked around. "This must have taken you… Christ. You must think I'm…"

"Look," he said, feeling very uncomfortable. "I'm just going to go. I just saw a rat and did what comes naturally…"

"You saw a rat from outside?"

He motioned to the window. "The balcony. The curtains. There was a rat…"

"Forget it," Rena said, her voice cracking. She tilted her head back and gasped before turning away.

Standing there, unsure of what to do, he just watched her shoulders rise and fall, her hands work furiously to wipe away tears.

AJ took those moments to scoot subtly towards the door.

"Look," she said her voice still wavering. "There's something I need to tell you, AJ."

She crossed the kitchen quickly and came to stand before him, close enough that he could smell her. The smell was visceral and intoxicating, if a bit sour.

Looking up at him, her large eyes glimmered.

Before she could speak, he blurted, "I'm sorry! I overstepped my bounds. I just didn't know what to do. Seeing you like this… it… it broke my fucking heart. Rena, I…"

She was quick and her lips found his cheek and just the tiniest bit of his mouth. Before he realized it, his hand came to his face.

"AJ, I'm so sorry," she said.

"What? What do you have to be sorry for?"

The strange look on her face quickly killed the yearning left by her kiss.

She took his hand in hers and seemed to search for the words.

"Rena, it's okay. Rena, I—"

"Hollow Black is DPRK and your brother is a fucking traitor."

AJ snatched his hand away.

"Wha— what did you say?"

18: Future War

"In the face of what I saw that day, it's hard to imagine a world not engulfed in flames. Mankind was not meant for this world and Deckar Applied Sciences will be the proof of it."

- Luther Gueye

Thirty-five miles south of Sun City's southernmost borough Section Six, nestled in the green, suburban valley of San Palomino, lay the sprawling complex of Deckar Applied Sciences. A private defense contractor primarily focused on robotics research and ergonomics, Deckar Applied Sciences could also claim credit for notable advancements in defense, counterterrorism, nuclear non-proliferation, alternative energy, and genetic engineering.

Since the company's founding in 1997, Deckar Applied Sciences, known by most as simply "DAS," had struggled to surpass its older, more globally recognized competitors. That all changed with Mechanized/Organic Direct Synthesis, or MODS, technology. The prosthesis kits made famous by the paramilitary company Phoenix Battalion — later to become Agency Zero — and more recently Unit One had since catapulted the multinational tech behemoth into the role of an industry leader, and its brand into a household name. This was especially evident in Sun City, where the defense contractor boasted employing a fluctuating eleven percent of the megalopolis' citizenry.

The DAS complex, shaped like a triangle, consisted of over three hundred unique laboratories and administrative offices and occupied a site of one point five square miles, a measurement that did not include its ten thousand–acre experimental test site and adjoining airfield. The facility, which sat at the base of Mt. Guillory, was dug out of the once-rich valley to reside below sea level. This allowed a span of the 101 supercorridor to pass over, splitting the delta-shaped site in two, almost right down the middle. This, in turn, also provided occupants of the taller offices and laboratories a provocative view of the massive highway and the horrendous commute that awaited them five days a week.

On the thirteenth floor of the Mechanized Weaponry/High Explosives Application facility, the largest of all buildings on campus, a shamelessly lavish gala was underway. Deckar executives, political figures, generals, celebrities, and carefully selected members of the media mingled drunkenly to a soundtrack of contemporary pop.

With his back to the bulkhead, Luther Gueye sat watching, engulfed in a burnt tobacco cloud of his own creation. Among the crowd, he identified his fellow Octumvirate council members John Cholish, the Unicom Network CEO, and Ruben Liu, Coastal Power's chairman. Cholish was drunk and could be heard from virtually any distance in the great hall, and Liu couldn't be missed for his garish cadre of strumpet escorts.

Luther wore a three-piece, slim-fit Valentino suit that had been acquired back when brand meant something to him. It was paired eloquently with a rambling plaid bowtie and matching antique opal cufflinks. It was one of his favorite suits. While the color and fabric were second to none, the cut was what set the suit apart.

Tailors make all the difference, even amongst the finest clothiers.

The Valentino had been cut by a man named Van Ngô, arguably the best fitter in the game. The suit conformed to his body with the perfection of nothingness and offered a range of motion and level of comfort his other suits just couldn't.

On the lapel of his blazer was a pin on which eight owls sat in a perfect triangular formation: the symbol of the Octumvirate.

As Luther sat, reflecting on his own appearance, he couldn't hold back the sensation of loathing he felt watching his peers.

Look at them… falling over themselves in self-congratulation.

As he went to ash his cigarillo on the floor, a robot about the size of a two-year-old child rolled up and extended an ashtray on a thin metal arm. He tapped the thin Dutch cigar over the tray and watched the autonomous helper speed off on a single wheel.

And for what? After all, their accomplishments paled in comparison to his own.

On the surface, everything in his life was going precisely as planned. Business was good. Drug sales were way up in preparation for the Liberty Day Parade, as dealers throughout Sun City stockpiled. On the legal front, the Gueye Foundation, the philanthropic face of the *other* Luther Gueye, had been nominated for the prestigious Shuttles Award for its efforts in the Liberian reclamation effort. At the same time, the *Musée de Conflit Historique* continued to ride a wave of social and commercial success. So much so that his curator, Arlen Suresh, now director and president of Gueye Historical Holdings, was already needling him for a grant to expand the museum grounds.

Things were progressing. Things were good. And yet...

He caught himself sneering and feigned a cough before straightening his expression.

Pigs... all of them.

As he smoked, he ignored the incessant tremors of his mobile.

What are these victories if there is no one to admire my success? Father no longer warms to me, and Vivianne has become openly, blatantly disrespectful. And after everything I have done for them...

With a sigh, Luther watched Omar Garcia, the Valhalla Fight League's reigning heavyweight champion, stagger by. Behind the mega-famous prizefighter trailed a procession of hangers-on, like some ancient prophet or pharaoh. As he watched Garcia pass, he couldn't help but marvel at the man's physical makeup. The white-haired martial artist's back was the shape of a blown kite and his arms were wider than most men's torsos.

What a gorilla. What would he *look like on Riot Blood?*

Luther spat a flake of tobacco at the last member of Garcia's entourage, just as a figure plopped down on the couch next to him. The sudden depression of the bench cushion jostled him, causing ash to fall from his cigarillo onto his pant leg.

"Idiot! I sat in the middle of the couch for a reason," Luther declared, batting at the ash irritably.

Meanwhile, the intruder nestled into the couch the way cats do: overly animated and with little regard for personal space.

Premier William F. Macek, one of the most powerful figures in the Pacific, leered up at him and growled drunkenly from behind a greying mane. "Good day, my good man."

His Excellency wore a maroon suit of velvet with a black shirt and cummerbund. It was precisely the kind of cigar room loungewear that Luther despised. On Macek's breast was a black rose, symbolic of who-cared-what. His hair was slicked back neatly, his beard combed and flowing. Long streaks of silver ran from his cheeks to where his beard stopped on an exposed chest. He wore a monstrous ring on each thumb: one platinum and engraved with ornate floral designs, and the other

475

tungsten and dotted with black diamonds. In his hand was a crystal tumbler more than half full with the familiar brown of rye whiskey.

"Quoi de neuf, Bill."

"We need to talk, Master Gueye."

"Are we not speaking?"

Macek squinted. "Don't be smarmy, my boy, I bring you a gift."

Macek's "gifts" were never dull affairs. It was the only thing the old man did right. "Do tell."

The old man leaned in closely, his demeanor that of a gossip. "Buy heavy in LL Cartier Construction, ticker LLCC. Buy heavily, my good man, as in metric tonnage *heavy*."

"Heavy like the scent of whiskey and whore's lips emanating from you?"

Macek guffawed. "Precisely!"

"I'll message my broker straight away," Luther replied, already reaching into his coat pocket for his mobile.

"Looks like 'the big one' is going to make landfall," Macek continued, "on the second day of the parade. Category Five, they say, the largest to ever come ashore this far north. Climatologists say that this represents a tipping point for climate change and that the global ramifications could be dire indeed."

"When have they not said that? Doomsayers, are they not?"

476

"Indeed. They *are* wrong, however, on one point. The consequences may be dire, but only for some. Sections Four and Seven will see the worst of it, Seven taking the brunt due to its sea level and proximity to shore. Not to mention the whole place is built on landfill. Cartier will have the restoration contract exclusively. Estimations in the double-digit billions."

"That will cripple the State budget, will it not?"

"Budget smudget," Macek replied, waving a hand dismissively. "We've been trying to get the proles off that land for decades. It would appear God has seen fit to intervene on our behalf. With Section Seven in ruins, we'll appropriate the land and auction it off to the highest bidder. These fine folks," he continued, waving a hand at gathered crowd, "are looking for new facilities closer to City Center, if I'm not mistaken, as are others. Truthfully, had I known, I would have delayed construction on the arena and placed it right where the Veins run today. What a sight that would have been! Visible from right across the bay, the grandest of arenas!"

You're drunk on power and whiskey, Luther thought. *But tell me more, fool.* "What about the *Musée*?"

"High enough on land and it will have its 'back' to the storm, so to speak. The State will cover the damages, of course. You won't lose a dime even if the whole thing falls into the ocean."

"Watch your tongue, old man! 'Tis my life's work, that place."

"Hardly, I'd say," Macek replied, smiling genuinely.

477

As Macek continued to fill his ear with empty compliments, Luther texted one of his aides, who would, in turn, forward the message to his broker in code:

Looks like rain
Looks like we may have to cancel
Can you call me when you get a chance?
Call my mobile

Hope this finds you on the up and up

Several shell companies he owned would make the purchases in bite-sized chunks. Others would monitor the prices closely and sell in similar bite-sized chunks when they deemed Cartier's share price to have apexed. The profit would be held offshore in dozens of overseas accounts. It wasn't entirely foolproof, and a Ministry of Revenue agent with the will and interest could piece the transaction together if they tried. But one thing he'd learned since coming to the Pacific State was that no one was looking… because no one was being paid adequately to look.

He extended a hand to Macek, who shook it and patted him on the back.

"Now on to more serious matters," the old man continued.

First the gift, then the demand. Like a djinn, this old codger, just like a djinn.

"The Counci—"

In that moment, the lights went dim. An exclamation traveled the width of the hall as the walls, which had been projecting an image of solid white, fell away to reveal their translucence. The overcast skies and infinite green of Palomino Valley filled the room. The 101 ran adjacent, clogged in traffic. And below that, all could see the beaten brown of the DAS experimental testing grounds.

A woman's voice filled the chamber, eloquent and melodic.

"Ladies and gentlemen, esteemed friends and colleagues!"

Though Luther had yet to place her location in the banquet hall, he recognized the flawless tempo of Elaine Jones-Gutierrez, his fellow "owl."

"I want to thank you all for taking time out of your busy lives to join Deckar Applied Sciences on this momentous occasion."

Ah, there you are, witch…

Jones-Gutierrez stood atop a podium as a squadron of drones trained their colorful spotlights on her. They circled silently on tiny rotors, moving in mesmerizing unison, even as the podium rose and spun slowly, as though Jones-Gutierrez was the latest model BMW at a car show. She was dazzling in a crystalline gown and shawl of pale blue. Her neck and wrists shimmered in diamonds and, despite being well into her forties, the woman could have put any television fragrance model to shame.

"This is not your typical product-release party," she continued, "and all of you have been chosen participants for very specific reasons, reasons unique to each of you." As she spoke, she motioned to select individuals. "For your efforts in this project," she said, motioning with a hand to a nobody who went red instantly, "for your financial commitment," she said to the banker with the teenaged girl on his arm, "for your role in the State, for your social status, for your influence, or," she smiled brightly, winking at the hulking prizefighter, "simply because we like you."

The crowd laughed, charmed by her. And though his mood would pick her apart, Luther could not deny that Jones-Gutierrez was magical.

"For many of you, this is not your first Deckar gala. Some of you were here last November when we unveiled utility fog. And some of you were in this same hall, way back when we announced the Type-A MOD kit for the first time. Whether this is your first DAS product launch or not" —she paused, the platform upon which she stood rotating slowly that the hundreds gathered could see her face— "forget what you know! Forget what you think you know about the future of warfare!"

There wasn't a secret of any scope Deckar Applied Sciences could hide from the Octumvirate with Jones-Gutierrez on the council. And this, surely their biggest accomplishment in more than a decade, was no different. Nevertheless, seeing their latest monstrosity rendered on screen in the Hall of Maati was one thing, but to see it up close… Luther couldn't help but hope for spectacle.

He turned to Premier Macek. "Shall we?"

Macek nodded, and he helped the old man to his feet. Together, they made their way to the window under the scrutiny of many. Several stories below was a massive staging area, the kind one could perform a military procession on… or fight a battle. A runway of concrete, flanked on both sides by earthen bunkers, pockmarked and charred in places.

Everyone in the hall moved to the windows, shouldering one another for a view. Macek's personal vanguard, three Agency Zero soldiers in suits, established a kind of human barrier around them, ensuring that their privacy was not encroached upon.

Below, sirens sounded, and after a few moments, a pair of bipedal tanks emerged from out of view. At the sight of these massive machines, the crowd began to cheer. Jones-Gutierrez, grinning ear to ear, chastised the crowd playfully, explaining that these tanks were not the objects of interest.

Luther recognized the tanks immediately, having purchased one salvaged from the Third Korean War. They were the bipedal tanks built by China and used by the former Democratic People's Republic of Korea in the invasion of Japan. Designated "Hwangsae-ho" by the DPRK and known as the 'BT Type 55' in the US, they stood at a little over nine

481

meters. They moved on tall, bird-like legs, propped up by three "toes." The term used to describe the design in the manual he'd procured along with the purchase was "digitigrade," which he assumed meant something to the effect of "walking on your fingers."

The two tanks moved toward the center of the demonstration area, their steps sending plumes of dirt and debris into the air behind them. Once in position, next to one another, they trained their turrets collectively on the closed hangar to the north.

"For decades," Jones-Gutierrez continued, "the Western World has allowed Chinese and Russian contractors to dominate the face of mechanized warfare, focusing our efforts instead on air and sea superiority, as well as technologies centered on things like personnel safety and combat effectiveness. Well, today, we close the loop on the Pacific State's full-spectrum dominance once more and we remind the world of the power of Western ingenuity. Today, I give you the next generation of mechanized infantry support, DAS' newest main battle tank, designated M-A MBT, and codenamed 'Kodiak'!"

The hangar doors slowly opened on the opposite end of the field. Luther waited patiently, half-expecting the same slow, lumbering strides that carried the Hwangsae-ho units. What emerged from the hangar — after a frustrating period of sixty seconds — loosened the hinges on his jaw and sent a chill up his spine.

Despite the machine's size, equal if not greater than the BT Type 55's, its movement was unbelievable. It burst from the hangar, into the shadow of the 101, sending the hall into an uproar. While the Chinese Type 55s, awesome in their own right, moved on crane-like legs, the Kodiak moved on armored legs that bent and bounded like a human's. Swinging on its sides were arms, likewise human in their mechanics. As the massive tank moved, it picked up speed until it was "running" across the field like some great golem come to life.

This can't be real...

Macek's hand was gripping his shoulder, hard.

The sheer mass of the machine seemed to make the fluidity of its motion impossible to the senses. And yet, there it was, running towards them, with the size and momentum to tear the building in half.

It crossed the field of more than four hundred yards in a matter of seconds and came sliding to a halt in a tidal wave of earth.

The hall — those who weren't scrambling for the exits in terror — was silent. People stood petrified, mesmerized in the face of a machine that could have been plucked from the grandest of celluloid fiction.

Macek was no longer clawing at him, but stood wringing his hands. "My God, man... My God."

In that moment, the war machine dubbed "Kodiak" spread its legs and squatted.

"Hold!" Jones-Gutierrez commanded from the podium.

Macek was raving now. "This changes everything, Luther. Everything!"

The Korean units stood, waiting patiently for their demise, their turrets pointed impotently at the technological marvel that had already made them irrelevant.

Jones-Gutierrez, not immune to the gravity of the moment, made a wide-eyed, feverish expression. "Behold the world's first anthropomorphized mechanized combat unit!" She held a fist out, the vein in her neck throbbing. "At twenty-nine feet in height and weighing in at just under two hundred thirty-nine tons, meet the *new* heavyweight champ of fighting machines!"

She paused, pointed, and winked once more at Omar Garcia, who yelled something back in Portuguese and flexed, spilling champagne on his tracksuit.

Luther's mind raced. Macek, for all his drunken blabbering, was right. This *did* change everything! *Nothing has ever existed on the battlefield so intimidating. At the sheer sight of this thing, entire battalions will halt and break ranks. If I'd had this years ago… All of Africa would be mine. This is how you elicit pacifism. This is how you conquer peoples!*

"Designed with composability in mind," Jones-Gutierrez continued, "the Kodiak has an almost infinite list of variant configurations. Minigun mounts for anti-infantry, missile silos for anti-aircraft, 406-millimeter cannons for anti-tank scenarios, or microwave emitters for crowd control. You name it and it can be mounted, thanks to Deckar Applied

484

Sciences' world-renowned focus on extensible design. Imagine! Exploration, excavation, demolition. Nothing is out of the the question for the Kodiak."

People were cheering, grinning like morons and flooding back to the windows.

"But what is it people really want?" She paused, though she had no intention of sharing the microphone. "A *deterrent*! The fabled 'end to all wars!' The Kodiak can and will give developing nations, countries situated on contested territories, and peace-keeping forces just that. But don't take *my* word for it." She smiled broadly once more, showing off what Luther knew to be a half-million dollars' worth of orthodontics. "Kodiak! Let 'em have it!"

Luther tore his eyes from his peer's comely smile just in time to see what must have been a hundred missiles taking flight. They erupted from the Kodiak's back in three rhythmic cloudbursts. They filled the air, their vapor trails briefly taking on a heart shape as they arced in the direction of the Type 55 units. Involuntarily, Luther moved away from the window. More voluntarily, he dragged Macek back a few paces with him.

As the missiles struck their targets in waves, the concussions shook the hall and rattled the chandeliers. The more skittish onlookers headed for the door once more.

"*Bon seigneur dans le ciel*!" Luther heard himself scream.

The explosions tore into the Chinese mechs, sending shrapnel spinning into the air or skittering across the earth in a terrifying show of destruction. Fire and black smoke covered the field and momentarily blotted out the whole affair. When the warm afternoon breeze finally pushed aside the pillars of smoke, the Kodiak stood to its full height, at the center of it, defiantly... *peerlessly.*

Thunderous applause filled the chamber, and Luther, too, found himself clapping. After all, it would be blasphemous to pretend that the world hadn't just changed irrevocably.

Being one of the 'enlightened' had many perks. There was nothing he could not purchase or otherwise acquire. His influence spanned the globe, and his family would enjoy being a dynasty for generations upon generations. All this, and yet it was these moments that charmed Luther most.

I've just witnessed this generation's Trinity test.

He backed away from the window in a convoluted daze of shock and ecstasy.

Most people will never know such a thing even exists... until it is on their doorstep.

Elaine Jones-Gutierrez disembarked the podium to greet a crowd who bathed her in acclaim.

"Jolly good show!" the Premier catcalled.

"Indeed," Luther admitted. "Bloody good."

Looking up at him, Macek motioned to the bar. "Come with me."

He walked with the ruler of Sun City to one of several bars. Their stools were filling rapidly now that the show was over. As he leaned against the bar counter, another autonomous robot rolled up to extend an ashtray, reminding him that he was even holding the cigarillo. Luther stubbed it out.

"Gentleman," the bartender greeted. "And Your Excellency…"

Macek downed the drink already in his hand and ordered a bourbon, neat.

"And for you, Mr. Gueye?"

Hearing his name, spoken verbally, openly, snapped Luther out of his daze. It doused him in ice water and drove a knife into his ear.

"Mr. Gueye?" he mimicked, no small measure of venom in his voice.

This bartender… this churl believes he knows everyone in sight. "I'll have a Manhattan, bartender-man, drink-waif."

The bartender, a young man in a white sport coat and bowtie nodded slowly, a confused expression on his face, and turned to leave. It was then that Luther reached over the counter and snatched his arm. The man, a look of shock now overwriting his previously befuddled expression, opened his mouth but did not speak. Luther reeled him in, his grip unrelenting.

"Refrain from using my name for the rest of your miserable fucking life, drink-slut, cocktail-prep. Do you understand?"

487

The man's eyes were wide, and Luther could see a familiar, mortal fear in them. It stirred him, quickened him. It also enraged him and made him want to drive his fist through the man's skull. Instead, he released the bartender slowly, his hand still raised to let the man know that violence was still very much on the table.

The bartender choked on his first attempt at speaking and instead made a kind of wounded animal sound. He then sputtered an insufficiently constructed apology and hurried away.

"Well, that's a bit harsh, innit?" Macek said with a chuckle.

"When you were younger and soberer, you would have done the same." Luther leaned on the bar with an elbow and looked Macek in the face intently, the tingle of raw rage still flowing through him. "What have I got, if not my name? Am I to let any roach that would run it through the mud do so? Why is this? He is not my peer! He is not even my employee. He's done nothing to earn my acknowledgment. Who is he, Bill? Who the fuck is he!"

Macek's smile diminished but Luther was not done.

"Hear me out, Bill. I have many names, and all of them carry the weight of my efforts, my *successes*! Who is this man to wield my standard? What has he accomplished? He wears a coat and pours drinks. He will toil away, unable to save, unable to build. He will marry an ugly woman *or man* and have children who will, like him, one day vanish from this earth having left the impact of dust. Less than grains of sand!"

"I get it…"

No, you don't. "Bacteria."

"I *totally* understand," Macek continued. "It's like a tribal pride thing, a code-of-the-streets thing."

The urge to snap the Premier's neck right then and there was enough to stir Luther in his slacks. "I don't need you to understand, Bill. Our friend the germ understands."

Macek nodded as though to process the statement, before saying, "Your esteemed colleagues and I have come to the conclusion that it would be best if you left Sun City."

Though he knew it was coming, the words struck him like a slap. Luther leaned back and rotated his neck, appraising the vaulted ceiling, the chandeliers. "So, the council met without me?"

"Unofficially, of course."

"Official, unofficial. You know as well as I that these terms are meaningless. The Council met without me. And were other matters discussed, or was this purely a meeting to collude against me?"

"Come on, Luther! What have we been doing this whole time? Of course, members of the Council communicate outside of Maati. This is the way things are done, *have* been done" —Macek paused as a group meandered past, heading for the exit— "for centuries."

Luther weighed the benefit of arguing with the old drunk and concluded that the time that would be wasted was far more valuable than what he stood to gain.

In truth it doesn't matter, he told himself. *Even if I had forced a vote on the issue, I would have lost.*

The bartender returned meekly and placed the drinks down before bowing like the Japanese do and walking away.

What can I do if they've already decided? Luther picked up his drink and scrutinized it for insects, dirt, or any other malicious additions. *Those fucking Unit One pricks are the cause of this. Sniffing around where they don't belong. How had they even caught wind? It had to have been Diedre. That steroid-junkie freak of a woman!*

Despite all my efforts! Even with Ouroboros! There really is *no accounting for stupid. That maggot spoke my name, likely just before her last breath...*

He'd taken a liking to Sun City. For all her bloated avenues and Babel-like spires, no finer testament to his achievements could be found. He ruled the drug trade in Sun City and, with that, the narcotics supply lines from the State to São Paulo. He controlled the checkpoints along the 101 and, by extension, the very lifeblood of Pacific State trade. He had wealth beyond measure and no wife to appease, no children to fret over. He could go anywhere in the world and do anything, except, of course, remain in Sun City...

Macek took a sip of his drink, his lips pursed. He waited patiently.

490

The old fool's expecting rage. Why would I give him the pleasure? I lost this fight weeks ago. I lost the moment Deputy Informant Yamazaki Daisuke walked into the Musée. *Or really, the moment Diedre went off the fucking rails.*

Luther raised his glass to the Premier. "To Sun City."

"To Sun City," the old man returned. He took a sip and smiled. "You never cease to amaze me, young man. Let's go rub elbows."

They took a long parade around the hall. They greeted State Defense Consortium policy-makers, shook hands with various titans of industry — many of them fawning pages behind the velvet curtains of Maati, fruitlessly campaigning for seats on the Council of Eight that they would never have. All of it served only to drive home the bitterness Luther felt.

As if reading his mind, Macek whispered in his ear. "The world is your oyster now, Luther. It is important that you realize that you aren't *losing* anything. You'll retain your chair, your vote, and all of the privilege of which you've grown accustomed. You'll just do so remotely."

"It's not the same. This city is as much mine as it is yours."

Macek scoffed. "Come now…"

He glared and the old man straightened up, puffing his chest out. "Look, once things die down a bit and West reins in her dogs, who knows? Maybe you come back. The point is, Luther, you are far too valuable to the Council to risk an investigation, or worse, drawing the attention of the folks outside of the State Defense Consortium."

What folks? No one is beyond the controlling hand of one Council of Eight or another. The old man is blowing smoke.

Macek was talking to him over neurotrigger now. [*What you've accomplished and with so little assistance: it's stunning, really. You built an empire out of sand in Togo. You architected the most intricate narcotics networks this country has ever known. And now, you sit alongside the true rulers of the free world, a king of kings.*]

They came to stand once more looking down on the testing grounds. They watched as crews worked to remove the wreckage of what were once state-of-the-art war machines.

"Folks outside of the SDC" or no, the Council was not completely in the wrong and he knew it. He was as exposed and as vulnerable as he could ever remember being. All he could hope for was that Diane West would do her job and curtail Unit One's investigation. Given enough time and distance, maybe... just maybe he could walk the streets of Sun City once more.

He sipped his drink.

Still, killing Yamazaki Daisuke and perhaps the whole of Unit One makes just as much sense as going into exile. The respect the Council is giving West's stupid pet project is very, very irksome.

Yamazaki... He should be dead by now...

The thought made him feel better.

"It's funny," Macek continued, his words slurred, "you and the Major are not unalike."

Luther gave the old man a sneer and replied over neurotrigger. *[The Major. That deformed wreck of a man is little more than your foxhound. Anytime the Council needs wetwork, you go to the Major and his "Agents in Orange." The man's a butcher, nothing more. Monroe and I have nothing in common.]*

"How are the Major and I similar in any way?" he asked the old-fashioned way, still conscious of the people around him.

"You're both incredibly driven."

"Then I share that trait with half the world."

"Don't compare yourself to the rest of the world, Luther. Like the Major, you have the kind of ambition that makes you dangerous."

[Is that a threat? You plan to have the Major killed! Are you trying to tell me something, Bill?]

[Don't be ridiculous! I meant it as a compliment. But don't think the cock-measuring between you and Oyabun Minowara has gone unnoticed.]

The Premier was glaring back at him defiantly from behind two wild, silvery eyebrows.

Luther was seething now, his vision going dark.

[That old yakuza fuck had a hand in this?]

[Of course not! But don't think that the potential for an all-out war between your gangs didn't factor into the decision.]

"Then why me, Bill!" Luther blurted aloud before redirecting his rage to the secure channel of communication. *[Why not send that ghoul back to Japan and leave me? My contribution far outweighs anything the Minowara could ever hope to achieve.]*

Macek's chuckle was metallic-sounding over neurotrigger. *[Why? Why would we, when we can have you both? And besides... think about it, Luther. He probably wouldn't survive the trip. His days are numbered, and when he's gone we'll take steps to aid you in absorbing the Minowara into your organization.]*

[What?]

Luther studied Macek's face. *Does he know?* he wondered. *Does the bastard know that the plan is already in the works? Just how cunning are you, old man?*

Truth be told, whether Macek knew of his plot with Sugihara or not was irrelevant now. Macek had just offered on a silver platter the Council's acquiescence to a takeover. The Minowara would be his, and not only with the Council's consent, but with their help.

What does this mean for my alliance with Sugihara? Do I even need to play games with him anymore? Should I just wait for the whole thing to be handed to me?

No! At the very least, I'll want a figurehead in the Minowara; my puppet at the helm. Someone with the appearance of power…

Suddenly Luther wanted to leave. He had work to do.

[Look, William, I appreciate what I think you are trying to do, but don't waste my time. Minowara's yakuza are of no interest to me and the only similarity between the Major — a man that I liken to your personal Shih Tzu — and myself is the hue of our skin. And frankly, even that isn't very close.]

Macek reared back as though struck, and made a sour face.

[That being said, I respect you, Bill. I respect what you have accomplished. And I have made my decision. I will leave Sun City. I will attend all sessions remotely, as does Carlisle, and my esteemed council members will see no decline in my contributions.]

"Then who will—"

[I'll leave the Musée *in the hands of my curator and promote a lieutenant to run the Titans… superficially. Behind the scenes, everything, every decision, will continue to flow through me. I will maintain my seat on the board of the Gueye Foundation, of course.]* He forced a smile. *[Lest people get suspicious.]*

Luther finished his drink and looked about for a place to leave the glass. No robot came to service him, so he dropped it on the floor. "I'm tired of this fucking place anyway."

It was then that Jones-Gutierrez sailed over to them on a sea of adulators. With a hushed word, she sent them away. She first greeted Macek with a quick embrace and peck on the cheek before extending a slender hand Luther's way.

Luther had seen villages razed for stones smaller than the diamond on her wedding finger.

As he took her hand, their index fingers intertwined in the greeting of the Octumvirate. It was a disturbingly intimate gesture, and one that he found ostentatious and completely unnecessary. Jones-Gutierrez leaned in and planted a kiss on his cheek. She held it there for a few seconds longer than was appropriate. He knew why. He'd always known what she wanted.

"Have you made a decision?" she asked.

"It sounds as though my decision has been made for me."

"There is truth in that." She leaned in close and placed her cheek against his once more. "This is not goodbye, Master Gueye. Thrones are markers for assassins. Do not limit yourself to this place. The world is yours."

"That appears to be the theme of the evening."

Likely sensing his irritability, Jones-Gutierrez changed topics. "I am dying to know what you thought of my Kodiak."

"I'm speechless," he told her sincerely, though dryly.

"Utterly magnificent!" Macek added. "And I must say that your demonstration got me thinking."

She was already smiling, and slowly nodding her head.

496

"What if the Kodiak made its public debut at the Liberty Day Parade?"

Elaine Jones-Gutierrez sighed audibly, dramatically. "You are becoming so very, very predictable, William! Contract discussions don't begin with the State until spring of 2060 and we've no plans in place to handle that kind of press."

Luther watched them pretend to engage under legitimate circumstances and rules. He watched with disgust as they downgraded the nature of their conversations and influence the way geniuses used colloquialisms to fit in.

"Rubbish!" Macek replied, "We both know that a contract with the SDC is but a foregone conclusion. Once the Consortium sees the Kodiak firsthand they'll be falling over themselves to get the agreements in order. Why not give them a sneak peek? Boost sales! Get the people talking!"

Jones-Gutierrez covered her mouth and laughed. "You're drunk. Besides, it isn't the SDC you are concerned about, but rather the Fifth Estate."

"I confess. I *do* want to see those Marxist ingrates soil themselves. Picture it, my dear…"

The old man put his arm around her, and Luther couldn't help but think of how stupid it was for the three of them to be seen together unnecessarily.

"…me standing at the podium, Agency Zero behind me, and behind them, the Kodiak. The Fifth Estate will eat their protest signs before scurrying back to the hovels from which

497

they crept." Macek took her hands in his. "Do this for me and I will be *very* grateful. The *State* will be very grateful."

Jones-Gutierrez' smile was warming, rehearsed, and utterly fabricated. "I will give it some consideration."

Bored with the exchange, Luther was glad when his mobile rumbled in his pocket once more. He checked the screen to find a message from Bleda. His aide-de-camp was waiting with a car, and his timing, as usual, could not be better.

The Octumvirate was no gentlemen's club, no lounge for crumbling old white men. The Eight was not a designation so much as a responsibility. Crafting a new world order required commitment, and politicking was only one half of what it meant to be enlightened. The other half, the important half, was delivering. Expulsion from Sun City did not absolve him of his promises. It did not absolve him of the Blood Oath. And if the Council demanded that he reestablish his base, then he would do so, willingly.

But it doesn't mean that I have to entertain these fools and their ceaseless, exhausting conspiring.

Luther bid Macek farewell with what felt like a mechanical hug. As for Jones-Gutierrez, he parted ways with an insincere promise to visit her private villa before he left. On his way out, he stopped by the bar and flagged the bartender over. This time the man came forward with his head bowed, his eyes averted.

"Look at me," Luther told the man. "What's your name?"

"Come on," the bartender muttered, "I said I was sorry."

"Tell me your goddamn name!"

"Frank. My name's Frank."

"I'm leaving this country, *Frank*, and will not be returning for a very long time, if at all."

The man's eyes were wide, but behind them, Luther thought he saw relief. His need to stamp out that relief was instantly maddening.

He leaned in so as to not be misheard. "But before I go, my men will know who you are. It may be hours, days, months, or even years but, when you are at your most vulnerable, when peace finds its way into your heart, the dagger will follow!"

Luther reached into his coat and withdrew a bill from his wallet. Without bothering to observe the denomination, he set it on the counter and pushed it forward with a finger.

"*That* is the price for speaking my name."

Bleda met him in the back of a self-driving Rolls Royce limousine. He wore a loose-fitting plaid shirt and khakis. On his feet were workman's boots, on the tread of which appeared to be blood. As Luther settled into the seat, he regarded his old friend quizzically. "Been busy?"

"Always."

Luther was grateful for the black-tinted windows. He was grateful to be out of the conference hall and away from so many foreign eyes. As the car pulled away from the curb, Bleda began updating him on Titan affairs.

"The shipment from Peru arrived this morning without incident."

"The first shipment unmolested in some time. It seems that paying off the Huntsmen was a good call."

It had been Bleda's idea to barter with the road pirates rather than take a fight to them.

"Since the last shipment, their leader has reached out. He wants a meet."

"Who is their leader?"

"A man named John Shaw. He goes by the nickname 'Trash Head.'"

"Well, thank Mr. Shaw for the professionalism displayed in not touching my merchandise, and express our interest in a continued relationship. We will match the amount paid, once every quarter, and in exchange, they are not to touch any of our trucks. Violation of this agreement will not only dissolve our partnership but be treated as an act of aggression."

Bleda nodded thoughtfully. "And a meet?"

"There will be no meeting. Not now. Not ever. He can work with you." Luther frowned. "The temerity of these fucking people!"

Bleda winced and ran a finger over his cheek. "Is everything okay, Boss?"

"I'll explain later. We have much to do and not a lot of time with which to do it. How are sales? Are inventories depleted?"

"Bursting at the seams, inventories…"

"What! Even with the parade coming up?"

Bleda's gaze did not waver. It was a trait Luther respected tremendously in the assassin.

"We're selling like crazy," Bleda told him, "but we're still sitting on a lot of product."

"Christ!"

"We need bodies, Boss."

"This is why I need the" —Luther slammed a fist into the door— "fucking yakuza! Shit!"

"About that…"

Bleda paused as they merged onto Highway 82, one of the many smaller freeways that would carry them around the Deckar campus and ultimately to the 101.

"I've been wondering, Boss. If we need men, the Veins are overflowing with unemployed, many of which are ex-cons, illegals, and unregistered. The yakuza are not the only bodies."

"If only it were that simple, Bleda. To entertain the notion: what would you suggest? Do we begin with an open house? Hand out flyers, maybe? 'Excuse me, sir, would you like to sell drugs? There's no 401k or equity but you can keep thirty percent of what you sell. Oh, and if you short payments or ingest it all, we'll fucking kill you.'"

Bleda almost looked ashamed.

"I get where you are coming from, old friend, but it takes time and trust to grow a syndicate. And, to be honest, perhaps this is my fault for not planning ahead. What we need now are *experienced* men.

"And it's not just the men, Bleda, it's the property, the territory, and the know-how. The yakuza have all of these. They are lifelong gangsters. They've built an entire culture around evading and dealing with the law. They have the casinos to sell out of, the property to store, and the discipline to bring it all together."

Bleda frowned thoughtfully and leaned back. "I see. And this is why you are the boss. I don't envy you."

"These are my problems to figure out. What of the cop?"

"I sent some men after him."

"Good! And?"

"Not 'good,' I'm afraid. He's a dead-shot with that shitty old revolver. Nonetheless, Borsuk had him dead to rights. Axe poised to split his noggin."

"What happened?"

"He was saved by an interloper."

"*J'en ai ral le cul!* Son of a bitch! Who? Who intervened?"

Bleda hesitated.

"Speak, man!"

"Ze German…" Bleda licked his lips. "Sugihara's assassin."

"What in the hell is going on?" Luther knew he was making a dumb face but couldn't help it. Nothing about the hatching relationship he had with Sugihara made sense. "I don't get it. I just don't fucking get it. Whose side are they on? They approached *us*, did they not! In a thousand years, I wouldn't have considered partnering with the yaks. It was them that started this and now… I just don't understand."

"Nor do I, Boss. I followed agent Yamazaki to the club. I know he met with Sugihara. My *eyes* confirmed it. He left after an hour and was confronted in the alley by the Party Crasher."

"And she didn't blow his fucking brains out?"

"Quite the contrary. They parted ways, after she broke his nose, mind you, and he headed home. I followed him, had the troops waiting for him at his home. They ambushed him, just as instructed, four of them. Borsuk was just about to split his melon with an axe when she showed up. She shot Borsuk dead. Apparently, she'd followed him from the club as well."

"Were you seen? Did she make you?"

Bleda made a disgusted face. "Of course not, Boss. '*I am where holiness looks and lurks. I am shadow.*'"

"That's great, Bleda, really fucking great. I love poetry, or whatever, but I still don't understand the connection." He spat on the floor of the limo. "Goddamn, this city! It's like one giant game and everybody's playing."

"After she saved him, they left together, back to her place."

503

"What? Yamazaki and the Party Crasher left together? I'm riveted, Bleda! Fucking compelled by this serpentine tale of intrigue. What the hell happened then?"

"Sex, I would imagine."

Striking Bleda was not a good idea, so Luther took the fist that had materialized at the end of his arm and placed it to his temple.

Are they all in on it together? If the Party Crasher is with Unit One, then what does that make Sugihara? At best he's exposed, at worst...

Luther's head hurt. He reached into his coat and withdrew his mobile. There was a text confirming a stock purchase of LLCC. He brushed it aside irritably with a thumb and dialed a number from memory. The phone rang for nearly a minute before a voice answered in Japanese.

"Nan da? What the fuck do you want?"

"I will see Sugihara, NOW!"

Luther hung up irritably and slipped the mobile back into his coat. "Before I forget," he said, leaning back, "DAS hired a bartender named Frank. He's probably an employee of whatever catering service they used. I want you to slit his throat... slowly. Take your time. Follow him and make it obvious that he's being tailed. Make it a project, if you will. And when the time comes, preferably months from now... I want him facing you when you do it. I want him to know it's from me."

504

Bleda's expression betrayed nothing, just as it should. Just as it always did when the man was tasked with murder.

Sugihara's casino, called "True Blue," was on the west side of Section Two in a district known as Havenscourt. Havenscourt held mostly industrial complexes and ultra-low-income housing. If one were to pass through Section Two and continue east, they would eventually watch suburbs give way to rural farmland. Section Two was a quiet and dilapidated piece of Sun City, its most notable asset a cold-fusion power plant that operated on the southern bank of the Sun River delta. True Blue, a rather nondescript, single-story building, could be found dividing a collision repair shop and a boarded-up laundromat, in the shadow of the Havenscourt station of the Sun City municipal monorail.

By the time their car pulled up to the address, the sun had dipped below the skyline. A roiling cloud canopy had been set alight in shades of lavender, orange, and red. It might have been beautiful if not for the rusting and forsaken foreground that was Havenscourt.

Luther left the vehicle, with Bleda at his side, and approached the brown double doors of the casino. At the entrance, a short, flat-nosed Japanese man met them. He wore a cheap and ill-fitting suit that, beneath the setting sun, may have been slate, green, blue, or black. The man halted them and grunted something in Japanese while making the universal sign of the gun with his hand.

"I am not armed," Luther told the man, before turning to his confidant.

Bleda calmly drew a pistol from his belt and handed it to the man. Satisfied, the doorman waved them inside. They pushed upon the double doors and stepped into the smoky hall, at which time Bleda took another pistol from his ankle and tucked it into his belt.

The casino floor was bustling. Slot machines rang without pause, as men and women poured their meager livelihoods down insatiable chrome chutes. Others stood or sat around tables, throwing dice, flipping dominoes, or turning cards. Security guards, unmistakable in their size and demeanor, eyed the floor from elevated positions at the room's four corners.

It was Luther's first time personally setting foot in a Minowara gambling den, and he was surprised at just how busy the place was, despite the lack of interactive machines, digital games, and augmented-reality attractions.

And this casino is far from City Center, he thought. *If they can do these kinds of numbers way out here…*

As they crossed the casino floor, not really sure where they were headed, men, predominantly Japanese and clearly yakuza, talked in muffled voices and eyed them suspiciously.

At the back of the room was another door, flanked on both sides by two large men in suits. Before they could ask for Sugihara's whereabouts, the men greeted them.

"Welcome to True Blue," one man said, his English exceptional. "Right this way. The boss is eager to see you."

Is he, now?

Luther placed a hand on the door and told his man, "This is far enough, Bleda. Feel free to take the car and go. I'll be in touch."

"I'd prefer to wait here."

"I might be a while."

"Then I will be here a while."

"Very well."

The Titan kingpin pushed open the flimsy wooden door and entered a musty corridor. It took a few moments to place the smell, but once Luther did, there could be no doubt of its origin. Sour and coppery, it was the unmistakable stench of blood. Paired, as typical, was the smell of shit. He made his way down the hallway, past a shrine to some unknown serpentine deity, and came to stand before a bead curtain.

Beyond the curtain he could hear thudding, coupled with grunting, panting, and pleading. It was the sound of a beating being administered, and the violence was close. It filled his nostrils and, though familiar, still made his skin crawl.

Perhaps I let Bleda go prematurely... Luther entertained the thought of turning back for his enforcer when a voice summoned him.

"Come on in," the heavily accented voice crooned.

With a hand, Luther parted the oily beads and stepped through. What he saw turned his stomach.

507

Sugihara sat on a tattered and flayed leather couch, naked but for a pair of welder's mitts. Next to him were two young women, also naked. One woman was shooting what looked like heroin into the vein of the other. On the floor at their feet was a small boy in denim overalls.

Luther appraised them with unmasked disgust, even as the pleading and beating drew his attention to the center of the room. There, handcuffed to an iron rack, was the captive. Beating on the man with police batons were two men in yellow surgeon's gowns. Blood and human offal pooled on the floor, just inches from the feet of the small boy.

Sugihara acknowledged Luther but otherwise seemed preoccupied with the torture. Dangling from the yakuza's pierced lips was a cigarette.

"What should we do next?" Sugihara asked the boy, mussing his hair.

The boy, leaning against Sugihara's bare leg, put a finger to his chin thoughtfully. "What if we cut off his lips and put them on his face like a baboon?"

"What?" Sugihara asked, an annoyed expression on his face. "That doesn't make any sense."

The boy cupped his hands to each side of his face like blinders on a horse. "Like this!"

"Oh, you mean an orangutan!" Sugihara tilted his head back and laughed lengthily, cruelly. The yakuza ran his hands over his own torso as if aroused. This drew Luther's attention to the yakuza's thin, sickly frame. The would-be usurper's body was covered in an intricate tattooed depiction of an eight-headed snake, the same serpent enshrined in the corridor.

The man shackled to the rack moaned something from behind a shattered jaw. One of the surgeons drove a baton into his ribs to silence him. The victim, his face already an unrecognizable mess of blackening blood, just whimpered and shook his head furiously.

"He's got little lips, though," Sugihara told the boy. "It won't work. Besides, this one already looks like a monkey."

"So?" the boy replied defiantly.

Sugihara waved a hand to the torturers, who stood breathing hard from exertion, hands on hips. "You heard him! Lips off! Staple them to the sides of his head like an orangutan. If you need more meat, add fingers, or his cock… but that probably won't give you much. There's a staple gun in the cabinet and don't spare the staples. They're $2.99 a box." He chuckled to himself. "Or two for five dollars…"

This sent the fettered man into an uproar. He twisted and pulled at the rack that bound him until streams of blood ran from his wrists and ankles. This tickled Sugihara, and he leaned forward to watch the man's suffering with immense pleasure in his eyes.

Luther was no stranger to torture, though admittedly, it was usually a task he delegated to others. In the instances where he *had* been compelled to do the deed himself, he'd taken no pleasure in it.

"Did I catch you at a bad time?"

"How rude of me." Sugihara stood and motioned to the couch. "Have a seat. Can I get you anything? Would you like some heroin, some coke? Or water? I think we have water too."

Luther made no move toward the filthy couch. "Who is he?" he asked, thumbing at the man on the rack, even as the men killing him worked diligently with a blade and an industrial stapler.

"Who is he?" Sugihara shrugged. "Just some orangutan now."

The boy at his feet watched the butchery, mesmerized.

"No, seriously," Sugihara continued, "he's nobody. Raizen Minowara's driver, one of them anyway. We had some questions about the young Minowara's schedule. Questions he didn't feel obligated to answer."

"I'd say he's ready now. And I'm not sure how he's going to tell you anything with no lips."

Sugihara shrugged once more. "Whatever. It's too late for that." He leaned forward and grinned with his shark's teeth at the now utterly deformed man. "You should have fucking talked, neh?"

After prodding his men to inflict further damage on Minowara's chauffeur, and taking in a hefty pinch of cocaine, Sugihara perked up, as if recognizing him for the first time. "So what brings you, Mr. Gueye? You sure you don't want some heroin? It's *your* product, after all, excellent stuff. I've got a 'prick' around here somewhere. You don't have to get all 'bassist' wasted. You can have just a little taste if it suits you."

This is the difference between us…

"It does not suit me," Luther replied irritably. "Business suits me."

Sugihara nodded and waved his hand regally. "Then, on to business…"

Luther locked eyes with the pale yakuza. "My man believes you were visited by a Unit One officer recently, at one of your clubs, a man named Daisuke Yamazaki."

"Yamazaki Daisuke, you mean," Sugihara corrected. "Yama-kun is my old friend."

Sugihara's nonchalance was infuriating.

"Your 'friend' showed up at my museum, questioning my sister. Before that day — our first meeting, mind you — I'd never seen or heard of a Yamazaki-fucking-Daisuke. And you say this man is your friend?"

"He was at the museum?"

"Yes. And, on the night in question, the night where he visited you at your club, I sent men after your 'friend.' Specifically, I sent men to cut your 'friend's' head off."

Sugihara's brows furrowed.

"And do you know what happened then? The tale is rife with intrigue, Sugihara. A mystery that I am simply *dying* to get to the bottom of."

Sugihara held a hand up to halt his men from the torture. "Look—"

"And before my men could send him to the hell where pigs go," Luther continued, cutting him off, "your assassin, this

511

'Party Crasher,' intervenes, killing *my* men and saving your 'friend!'"

"Oh, my…" Sugihara tilted his head back and moaned. "That is a real shame."

Luther's fists clenched behind his back. The urge to break the much smaller man in half seized him like apoplexy. Before he could speak, Sugihara shoved the boy aside with his foot and got to his feet. The room went silent. Even the victim had passed out and hung limply from his restraints. The only sound to be heard was the steady drip of his blood onto the bare concrete floor.

"Listen to me very carefully, Sugihara," Luther said through clenched teeth. "I don't know what kind of game you're playing, but you've cost me a great deal, more than you could ever hope to repay."

Sugihara ran a hand through his wind-blown hair and exhaled, letting his lips flap in exasperation. "They were together?"

"That's what I just said."

"Fucking lovebirds, those two. That is a *real* shame."

"You came to *me*," Luther said, pointing, "I didn't come to you. You promised me trained men, professionals. In exchange, I offered to make you rich, to make your men rich, rich beyond your imagination. And this is what I get? Fucking games?"

"Look, Yamazaki Daisuke used to be one of us," Sugihara explained. "It's common knowledge, he's an ex-yakuza turned informant. He keeps Raizen in the loop on affairs, and Raizen, in turn, snitches out people he sees as a threat. Usually, he only hassles small fries. He sells out competitors, Titans who encroach on Minowara territory — no offense — or low-ranking Minowara who've fucked up too many times. 'Quid pro quo,' I think they call it. These kinds of partnerships between yakuza and police are commonplace in Japan."

"We're not in Japan, Sugihara, and he isn't police. He's fucking Unit One!"

"Well, when we take care of Raizen, their little partnership will be over." Sugihara pretended to dust his hands off. "Easy-peasy."

"'Easy-peasy?' I don't know what your fucking problem is, Sugihara, but I would suggest that you begin to take my words more seriously."

At this, the two torturers grunted something in Japanese. One of them began bouncing the baton on his shoulder, his chin in the air.

Sugihara, too, cocked his head back defiantly.

Luther then realized that he had found the proverbial "line in the sand" and crossed it.

"Are you *yelling* at me?" Sugihara asked softly.

Luther stared into Sugihara's eyes. What he saw there was a coolness bordering on boredom. But it wasn't a coolness foreign to Luther. He'd seen many a cool expression turn to pleading, and then agony, before turning to lifelessness.

Nevertheless, he did see that the yakuza lieutenant also wasn't going to back down. Though his own anger and frustration compelled him to push, the tactician in him decided to walk the aggression back a bit.

"I'm going to ask you plainly, Sugihara. Whose side are you on?"

"Yours," the yakuza replied without hesitation. "The side of business. Always. But I don't *do* yelling. It hurts my ears and makes me want to do bad things to people." He motioned with his head to the man on the rack, his expression indifferent. "I don't even like opera."

In a much calmer voice, Luther continued. "If we are going to do business together, I need to know that you are wholly invested."

"Trust me to take care of the situation. Let me demonstrate to you what it means to cross my Seidai."

"And the Party Crasher?"

Sugihara dug a pinky finger into his ear as though he couldn't hear the question. "I said I'd take care of it."

I need your men for now, but when I no longer need them, I'm going to teach you some manners, Luther swore to himself.

Satisfied, he decided to change the subject. "What's with the boy? You some kind of pederast?"

"Pederast?" Sugihara looked around the room for help and got none. "I don't know this word. The boy? This is Pedro. Pedro's mom is out there playing Pai Gow. All day, every day it's Pai Gow, Pai Gow. She sends Pedro back here because the stupid cow thinks this is a daycare. The silly, fat whore never bothered to come see for herself. So, I take care of Pedro, free of charge. I teach him things."

Sugihara turned to the boy, a sympathetic expression hideous on his face when paired with his sharpened teeth. The boy sat at the feet of one of Sugihara's wenches, a freckled woman whose head lolled as the heroin stole her lucidity. Pedro was maybe seven years old.

"Pedro is going to know all about life when he grows up," Sugihara promised. His pronunciation of 'Pedro' contained an extra syllable.

Pedro is going to be a monster, Luther thought. *Pedro is going to be someone's serious problem one day*. In that moment, it was as though he were smelling the ghoulish den again for the first time. He looked at the bead curtain exit.

"But before I go, one last thing… I'm leaving Sun City, perhaps for good. But this means nothing to our arrangement. I will still be in charge, but someone else will be communicating with you directly. Remember the name: 'Clark.' Once you have settled things with Oyabun Minowara and his progeny, Clark will approach you. You are *not* to approach us before then. And, as for this affair with the Unit One informant and the Party Crasher, I trust you'll bring that to a close, and *quickly*."

"I'll be sorry to see you go," Sugihara replied with an artificial sad expression, ignoring his remark about the Party

515

Crasher. "We were just starting to get along, I think." He turned to the couch. "Maggie, Morie, come here." He slapped his thigh, as if summoning dogs.

The girls stood and walked over. One still held the heroin needle.

"My friend is going away," he told them. "Send him off."

"That won't be necessary." Luther turned and was about to leave when the darker of the two women snatched his hand. She poured herself onto him, likely ruining his suit with a sheen of perspiration and who knew what else. She began planting kisses on his lips and neck. The other woman began working his belt.

Sugihara stood watching, his sinister eyes smiling. "That's a beautiful pin on your lapel…"

Luther opened his mouth to reply but was silenced by the messy kiss of the woman with freckles.

"Very beautiful," Sugihara repeated absently, turning away.

Luther tried again to respond when the other of the two girls yanked his pants down. At the thought of his Valentino slacks touching the filthy floor of Sugihara's den, he snapped. Luther snatched the freckled woman by the throat, his massive hand encompassing her thin neck effortlessly.

"Do you have any idea who I am?"

With his other hand, he slapped the needle from her hand. He did not interrupt the other woman, who seemed completely unperturbed as she planted kisses on his stomach.

"How dare you put your filthy hands on me!"

The woman clumsily fumbling with his underwear stopped at this, looking up at him with wide eyes.

"No one told you to stop," he hissed.

Luther's jacket hit the floor and his shirt soon after. Ruined. He drew the freckled woman in by her throat, staring into her face. Behind the fog of heroin in her gaze was an unmistakable layer of terror. It aroused him.

Their advances were passionless, robotic, but they were comely women, even beautiful. Luther controlled them, put them where he wanted them. He hadn't made time for sex in weeks, it occurred to him. Too many concerns, too many moving parts to account for to allow for such a frivolous waste of time and energy.

But to hell with it! I'm leaving Sun City, after all.

He allowed their hands, their lips. He closed his eyes and accepted the gift.

"Hey!" Sugihara yelled, immediately getting their attention. "Take it into the other room." He was back on the couch, leering at the dead man on the rack. "There's a child present."

19: Iron

"Whenever someone mentions Section One as part of Sun City, I cringe and get that spicy 'I might cry' sensation in my nose. Section One is Sun City the way that dude sleeping on your couch the next day after a house party is family."

- Unit One Sgt. Alec Jefferson "AJ" Moore

Of the Sun City's seven boroughs, Section One was the largest. The center of the mostly rural municipality could be found ninety-four miles northeast of City Center, the commonly recognized heart of Sun City proper.

Recognizable for its predominantly flat terrain, factories, farms, and really... little else of interest, Section One had the lowest crime rate of any of Sun City's boroughs. And, of the crimes that did occur, a large portion of them were the doing of the Huntsmen: a notorious motorcycle gang that took advantage of the area's long, arrow-straight highways to do what they did best, which was to waylay, harass, and pirate transport units heading into Sun City from Capital City to the north. These crimes were sporadic, as the Huntsman were nomadic in nature. And these crimes rarely ended in casualties.

For this reason, the lowly, rarely discussed Thirty-first Precinct of the Sun City Police Department, which resided in Section One, was repurposed. It went from being a hub for the highway patrol exclusively to the home of the State Defense Consortium's rapid reaction force, Agency Zero.

The location of Agency Zero's headquarters suited most parties involved. For the State Defense Consortium, having the large, militarized force out of plain sight helped placate dissidents of the Consortium. And for the officers of Agency Zero, not being under the constant scrutiny of the ministries of media and communications, as was the case with Unit One, suited them just fine. For Unit One Sergeant AJ Moore, however...

"This place suuuucks..." he groaned aloud as he climbed out of his coupe. A pair of SCPD highway patrolmen who'd been strolling past turned their heads at the comment.

Though he'd been to the Thirty-first at least a dozen times, it never ceased to depress AJ. A low-to-absent skyline, nondescript; quiet suburban neighborhoods, mobile home parks, and shopping malls; it was precisely the kind of place newcomers to the more urban sections of Sun City fled from. And to make matters worse, Section One typically ran ten to twenty-five degrees hotter than Section Seven on any given day. For AJ, who took pride in wrinkle-free clothing and armpits without sweat marks, Section One and himself were simply, intrinsically, and irrevocably at odds. In fact, the only positive in all of Section One, as far as he was concerned, was the non-existent speed limit which made escaping the district easier.

Though his vocal criticisms of Section One offended some, they were entirely merited in his eyes. After all, Section One offered nothing of interest. No monorail to get you from pub to pub on a Saturday night, no Friday night fireworks, no heavily crowded City Center with its shops, clubs, and restaurants. No smart-ads, no scantily dressed women, no block parties...

Just heat, brown buildings, and long stretches of highway where getting jacked by the Huntsmen was likely to be the most interesting thing to happen to a person.

AJ entered the Thirty-first and registered with the clerk. The clerk, a white-haired, elderly police officer past her recommended retirement age by the number of years he'd been alive, scanned his wrist and set him loose without so much as a glance up from her desk.

The Thirty-first was a small complex compared to the Fourteenth where Unit One was headquartered. It had a helipad, a detention center, and a barracks for the soldiers of Agency Zero, but it lacked many of the amenities he'd grown accustomed to. It did not have a spa and rehabilitation center, an officer's lounge, or an indoor bowling alley. It didn't have seg-ways to take you from department to department. It didn't have a media center for the paparazzi, or the green rooms that typically adjoined. Hell, it didn't even have a food court.

No shortage of pity in his heart for the soldiers of Agency Zero and the cops stationed here, he crossed the complex on foot in search of a familiar face, most preferably that of his brother. As he met the gazes of myriad cops and officers, he prayed silently that no one would recognize him, despite the white delta on his chest. He prayed that he would not get sucked into a banal conversation about search and seizure, acceptable use of force, MODS technology, or worst of all... the process for submitting an application to Unit One.

As he moved through the Thirty-first Precinct's corridors largely ignored, he credited his recent change in professional wardrobe.

AJ wore the new Deckar Applied Sciences–sponsored Unit One uniform prototype. It consisted of a vest and trousers combo that looked a little more militant than he would typically go for, personally, but the colors suited him. The vest was black mesh with a red inner lining. On the back, the Unit One pinnacle was grey — rather than the common white of the standard jacket — and had the scaled look of carbon fiber. The trousers were black and loose-fitting and went well with Timberland boots, of which he wore a black pair with tan tread.

As he strode past the requisitions office in a beeline for the office of his half-brother, the Major Ace Monroe, something roughly the size of a human head struck his shoulder and spun him in place, like a top.

The fuck?

AJ reached for Deadbolt out of instinct, even as a large, smiling face descended on him like the sun.

"Look at these fancy, shmancy twigs!"

AJ's assailant stood at seven feet and was half as wide. He had a silver beard and mustache that waved like a wedding gown when he spoke. The man's cheeks were red bulbs and his eyes emeralds. The giant wore a uniform of blood orange and ashen grey and on his gigantic chest was the falcon sigil of Agency Zero.

The blow that drew AJ's attention had not been soft, not by a long shot. "Jesus, Pops! You nearly knocked my arm out of its socket."

"That fragile a thing, are ye? Well, fook me if the Major's lil bro ain't gone soft on us."

Pops was old, real old, like "pushing seventy tombstones in a wheelbarrow old," as AJ would have — and had — said. But Pops was also a testament to bioengineering. His body was layered in muscle, the kind most often wielded by competitive bodybuilders. The soldier's limbs were mostly MODS technology of the DAS, first-rate quality, and what wasn't artificial was pumped pink with designer testosterone and nanomachines.

Like every member of Agency Zero, Pops carried a "cutter," in his case two. The term "cutter" referred to any reinforced weapon capable of slicing through nanofiber weave, and it was the Major Ace Monroe's mandate that any soldier in the agency equip themselves with at least one. The Major's logic was simple: some MODS couldn't be put down with bullets. It was also tradition for soldiers of Agency Zero to name their cutters. As such, Pops carried two swords on his belt: both very large, single-atom–tipped blades capable of cutting through even the sturdiest synthetic limbs. The one whose hilt could be found to his right was "Gog," the left "Magog," and combined, their body count rivaled that of anyone in the Consortium, save perhaps the Major.

With a fist the size of a head of cabbage, Pops punched AJ in the chest with enough force to knock him off balance. "So this is the kind of gear they give you fookin' benchwarmers?" He pointed to his mid-generation prosthetic leg. "While we grunts get the pig shit scraps!"

AJ held his arms out for the old man to see. "Well, Pops, maybe if you guys made an arrest once in a while, they could justify the spending!"

Pops chortled. "That's rich!" The old man went to punch him again, but this time AJ slipped the blow effortlessly. Pops smiled broadly at this.

"To be fair," AJ taunted, still bouncing on his toes, "I'm sure they'd hook you up with a new leg to replace that pirate's peg if you caught Changgok or something."

"'Caught Changgok,' he says. Ain't that a twisted tit! Sure, we'll catch that terrorist piece of shit Changgok! Just got a couple of things on our plate to square away first."

AJ arched an eyebrow. "And those being?"

"Well, winning the war on terror, snuffing out anarchism, and crushing communism, of course."

AJ folded his arms. "Well, what the fuck are you standing around for, soldier? Hop to!"

Pops roared, his face not unlike one jolly purveyor of holiday cheer and merchandise.

"Is my brother around?"

"He's somewheres, I would imagine," Pops replied, with a shrug of his pauldron-like shoulders.

The movement drew AJ's eye to the large duffel bag the old soldier carried.

"What's in the bag?" he asked.

"Pea-shooters."

"For the range?"

Pops stroked his beard and changed the subject. "The Major isn't in his office. He's downstairs, adjacent the armory. Since you're not provisioned, you'll need a keycard." He reached into his pocket and produced a card on a lanyard. The old man handed it over and patted him on the shoulder before turning to leave. "Just leave it on a shelf down there. I'll get to it later. It's good to see you, boyo. You take care now."

The armory was two floors down. To get to it, AJ had to be buzzed into the detention center. Once inside, he underwent a mandatory screening. The officer, a woman in her early forties, recognized him immediately.

"So it's true!"

"What's that?"

"The Major is your brother."

"Yes, that's true."

As the Agency Zero officer returned his pistol to its holster and handed it back, she leaned in and whispered, "Your brother is kind of a dick."

AJ took his time pondering. After a few moments, he came to the conclusion: *Yup, that's the truest statement ever spoken.*

AJ extended a fist that the soldier met with her own. The woman, a brawny, red-headed sergeant, shrugged. "I'm just saying. He'd be cute if he wasn't scowling all the time. Maybe you should tell him so."

Cute?

The sergeant smiled politely and continued on. No one had ever called his brother cute before. He'd heard every adjective under the sun describing his brother, and most were prefaced with the words "that fucking" or appended with the words "son of a bitch."

Ace walked and talked like a man on a battlefield... *always.* He had no time for things like manners or patience, behaviors he considered to be luxuries. The near-universal perception of Ace was that he was an insufferable stickler, a callous bureaucrat who put the State Defense Consortium's Protocols Manual over all else.

AJ could confirm all suspicions about the Major first hand. He *was* a "stickler." He *was* a "bureaucrat." He was also an *asshole.* But beyond that, he was Ace...

He crossed the width of the building, through a corridor of holding cells walled in looping political holo-ads, and interrogation rooms small enough to yield unprompted confessions, before taking the elevator to the second sub level. Along the way, he passed many a new face. The Liberty Day Parade hiring storm was well under way. This annual, knee-jerk practice of the State flooded the SCPD's ranks with "cops" who wouldn't be "cops" come January: people hired to bolster the perceived size of the city's police force.

Of the soldiers currently enjoying Agency Zero rank and status, he recognized only two. One was the South African, Blake Turner. His codename was Dozer, and he and Ace shared a lengthy military campaign history. Blake was an ex-soldier-of-fortune and a present-unapologetic-asshole. The other, a former Phoenix Battalion lieutenant of some renown in the SDC, had been speaking to Blake when AJ approached. She turned to face him, pivoting on legs that could have belonged to a rugby forward. Her codename was Legion — allegedly because of her ability to turn back whole armies single-handedly — but her real name was Rose. Rose was a brown-skinned woman with dyed hair and a prosthetic neck and spinal column. While her looks were certainly remarkable, what AJ remembered most about Legion were the pair of magnetic submachine guns that she wore on her hips at all times. As he passed them, both stopped speaking and watched him. Neither greeted him. Blake, his metallic jaw moving slowly, mumbled something, and the two of them chuckled.

Assholes.

It wasn't uncommon. Interactions between Unit One and Agency Zero were always frosty. And it was for good reason, in AJ's opinion.

With terrorism at an all-time low and organized crime at an all-time high, he thought, *we get all the work, while they're stuck on the sidelines playing touch-butt.*

His rapport with the police wasn't much different. Most of the SCPD — the ones that weren't trying to make Unit One, anyway — outright hated Unit One. Additionally, the recent dismantling of a white nationalist gang operating from within the SCPD at the hands of Unit One hadn't helped their relationship.

Pops' keycard worked, and the door slid open silently. The precinct sub level was probably not going to serve well for conversation, as deafening firearm reports from the gun range echoed through the narrow halls.

AJ entered the dimly lit room and, as the door shut behind him, was relieved to find the gunshots significantly muffled. He found himself standing in a server room. The floor was carpeted in thick cables intertwined efficiently like mesh. The walls were glass and behind them servers taller than Pops reported their efforts in a dizzying display of red and white flashes. As AJ stood at the entryway, Ace's gravelly voice could be heard over the hum of cooling units.

"They must be planning something."

Another voice replied from what sounded like a speakerphone or audible neurotrigger.

[Large weapons cache suggestive... something more than a rally. Insurgency...]

AJ listened with a smirk, not at all feeling guilty for his voyeurism.

"That's fine," Ace continued. "We'll give them the same taste as the rednecks. This year's parade *will* not be interrupted."

[Small team... current clandestine protocols will suffice for a single squad.]

He could hear Ace grunt. "Good. With regards to the parade, how are we looking from a logistical perspective? Are the barricades in place?"

[They are.]

"Bring up a map of the route."

AJ leaned against the shelves with his hands in his pockets. *Geez, he's bossy... Must suck bad working for him.*

"I want fireteams stationed *here* and *here*. I want a squad *here* and another *here*."

[Advisable positioning.]

After several minutes of event planning, AJ got bored. He moved into the room, careful to keep his steps muffled, feeling mischievous.

Can I actually get the jump on "Iron" Ace Monroe? he wondered, a part of him already knowing the answer.

"What about my tanks?"

[B.T.'s shipped from Eden to arrive in time. Their presence... appropriate deterrence.]

"And what about the other matter?"

[Penetration taking longer than expected... Antiquated protocols; War-era encryptions... Designed to keep out the Chinese. Longer to bypass. In time, the wall will obey...]

"Are you confident you'll meet our deadline? *She's* expected to arrive on day two of the celebration. Before all else, we must be ready for *her*."

[Assassin, Major.]

AJ moved into the open, and what he saw stunned him. Just as he opened his mouth to speak, his brother, whose back had been to him, whirled. In the blink of an eye the Major's knife, the serrated blade Soul Crook, was at his throat.

[Nay,] the robotic-sounding voice corrected, speaking to itself, *[the Major's kin.]*

Ace held his shoulder with a crushing grip and kept the knife to his throat, even as recognition revealed itself in his eyes.

"Jesus, Ace! It's me!"

This close to his face, AJ could make out Te-Mea's signature along the blade of Soul Crook, even as Ace slowly retracted it. Only once the mech-knife had been lowered and the grip relaxed did AJ allow himself to breathe.

"Why are you here?" his brother asked coldly.

AJ ignored the question, his heart rate still more treble than bass. Instead, he moved past his brother to take in the thing that caught his eye. The *thing* behind the Major.

In the center of the room was a tank, not unlike the ones that introduced children to sharks and sea anemone. It was large, illuminated, and filled with a syrupy blue substance. In that liquid, wired to the system whose flickering lights illuminated the base of the tank, was a woman. The woman's flesh was grey and her physique deprived, starved. If not for the steady swell and depression of her atrophic stomach and the glow of her orange, spiraling eyes, AJ would have thought her a corpse truly.

In an attempt to defuse the situation with eloquence, AJ decided to be candid. "What the hell is that?"

The woman in the tank turned away and a voice, projected from the system itself, filled the room. *[Sergeant Moore, Unit One. Should not be here…]*

"What is that, Ace? *Who* is that!"

His brother moved to block his vision with his massive body, and forced him back the way he had come.

"An agent," Ace told him. "How much did you hear?"

AJ honestly couldn't remember anything beyond talk of a wall. He told his older brother as much and allowed himself to be ushered out.

The sandwich was terrible, so AJ set it aside and went after the cookie that came along with it in the shrink-wrapped package. It wasn't much better, but at least it had sugar.

Ace did not eat.

The brothers sat on an old wooden bench, facing the Thirty-first Precinct's main lot. Sitting shoulder to shoulder, they watched cars race by on the 101, beneath a milky white sky, checkered by lazy streaks of jet contrail. Behind the raised span of the mega-highway, Section Three's financial district could be seen through the man-made haze. Chief among the high-rises was the spire of the Horus Bank building, discernible for its constant crimson warning light.

"What's with the DAS logo?" Ace asked him, looking at his vest.

AJ thought about it for a moment. "Free advertising, I guess. Probably part of some co-branding."

"You wear it and you don't know why."

AJ sighed audibly. *Here we go…* "I'm following orders, Ace. It's just a vest."

"Wrong." Ace spat and jammed a finger into his gums for some unknown reason, as if feeling for something. "Wrong! It's a repurposing of SDC resources to benefit a third party. It's a brazen display of corporate influence in the Consortium."

AJ shoved the cookie into his mouth in its entirety and replied with full cheeks. "Or, it's just a vest, Ace."

As he chewed, AJ noticed that his brother had a week's worth of beard, which was unusual. The Major typically kept a meticulously clean shave. Grey hairs gathered to one side of his mouth like drool. Behind that, Ace's eyes were thick-looking, red, and swollen. For the first time in AJ's life, his big brother looked old to him.

"I notice you're not wearing the shoes I got you," Ace said after a moment of silence.

"They don't go with the pants," AJ told him plainly, honestly. "Not everyone is comfortable wearing the same smelly shit every day like you."

Ace's gaze was cold at first. But then his expression softened in a way that AJ knew only he would recognize. It was a very, very subtle disarming of the expression that said, "I acknowledge you, brother," and it filled his heart.

"I'm glad you got rid of that stupid hairdo," Ace grumbled. "Maybe now people will start to take you seriously." He sat forward, his eye on the horizon.

Ace wore the trademark orange-and-grey uniform of Agency Zero. On his arm was a stylized golden oak leaf. His boots were heavy and worn. His uniform stank of perspiration. Ace placed his creaking artificial arm on his knee and prepared to stand. "Good to see you."

"Wait!" AJ said, "There *is* something I wanted to talk to you about."

"Of course there is," Ace responded, now standing in a shadow cast by the tallest tower in Sun City. "You want to talk about the detective constable."

"Yes, how did you know?"

Ace did not look at him, but rather at the Horus Bank tower that stood behind the raised 101 superhighway. "My words to her might have been a little harsh. Extend to her my apology. Inform her that Agency Zero plans to assist in her investigation as best we can."

AJ knew his brother's words were hollow. He had many a broken promise to call on for confirmation.

"I know you dote on her," his brother continued, "despite the fact that she's spoken for. You lust for her despite the fact that she exhibits symptoms of Immersion Addiction Disorder and Acute Net Compulsion."

"How did you—?"

Ace spat once more, spittle catching on his young salt-and-pepper beard. "Because it's my job to know. I know everything that happens within the Consortium. But worry not… I'll stay out of the constable's way."

The Major turned to him, his expression very serious. "She's Unit One's problem after all, and yours. Not mine. But from us, you've no concern."

Ace had never liked Rena. AJ suspected that her intellect threatened his brother, as did her confidence. But he couldn't be sure. He formulated the only response that made sense. "Thank you."

Even though he was clearly preparing to leave, Ace asked, "What does the deputy chief constable have you working on these days?"

"Retrieving some stolen DAS hardware from the Huntsmen biker gang."

AJ picked chocolate out of a molar, and considered another cookie.

"Hoh!"

"What?"

Ace was smiling hideously. "Whose idea was this?"

"Orders from high up."

"The councilwoman?"

"Probably."

"No 'probably' about it," Ace replied. "She says 'jump' and the DCC says 'how high.'"

AJ extended a hand to his brother. Ace took it in his own metallic hand. The contrast between the shiny, black metal of his own and the rusting chrome of his brother's was not lost on either of them.

Ace stared at the horizon in silence for a long time before saying something. When he spoke, his words were drowned out by an oil tanker barreling past on the 101. Without repeating himself, Ace departed, back towards the Thirty-first and likely the dead-looking woman in the water.

"What did you say?" AJ yelled.

He was sure that Ace could hear him, but his brother did not stop.

20: Burning Highway

"What makes Unit One so fun to cover is the overwhelming likeliness of failure. And that's not me just being a cynic, which I am!" [laughter] *"But seriously, never in my thirty-five years of reporting have I followed an individual or a group so vastly in over their heads. And to be clear, it's not their fault. That's the tragedy of it. They're tasked with an impossible responsibility and ill-qualified to handle it. But that's because — you ready for it? They weren't created to win! We have to be honest with ourselves, at least in that. Their purpose is to humanize the undemocratic machine that is the Consortium, nothing more. They're a construct, a farce, and yet the SDC throws them at problems that are very big and very real."*

- Mark Nikolaev of the Sun City Chronicle in an interview with the Unicom News Network

Unit One Lieutenant Mason Bruce climbed into the hover unit and strapped himself in. It was a previous-generation manned quadcopter. This meant the large aerial transport had four rotors, each attached to the disc-shaped fuselage by independent, movable booms. Because of the uniquely shaped fuselage, passengers sat in a semicircle behind the pilot, facing away. This was an annoyance to Mason, as he

535

had to yell his orders to the pilot over his shoulder, straining his neck to do so.

"Lieutenant Mason Bruce, Unit One!" he screamed to the pilot. "You'll do exactly as I say until the sortie is finished, is that clear?"

He found it was important to establish authority early on when dealing with the Sun City Police Department.

"Now, get this junker off the ground!"

The pilot gave him a thumbs-up but did not turn or make eye contact, which he hated.

They took altitude quickly, and in seconds the helipad was little more than the size of a coaster. The falling sensation hit Mason hard, and he closed his eyes to avoid being sick.

"Listen up, Unit One," he began once his nerves settled. "Our mission is this—"

[Mason] a voice interjected, *[Deputy Chief Constable Williams will be giving the sortie briefing.]*

Goddamn Bryant...

They were high now, very high, and Section Three was disappearing rapidly as the hover unit followed the 101 away from the clustered high-rises of City Center.

As lieutenant, Mason was the highest-ranking agent in Unit One after Williams. And it had been his understanding that Williams, as per the usual, would be sitting this one out.

Apparently, he thought bitterly, *I was wrong.*

He turned and tried to see the pilot but couldn't. "Lower! Way lower!"

536

The hover unit dipped, and again the falling sensation hit him. This time a chunk of half-digested sandwich climbed back up his esophagus to rest on his tongue in a pool of bile. The pilot brought them to within dozens of feet of cars moving along the 101. Freeway signs whipped past with slapping sounds.

At this speed, we'll be onsite in minutes. The lieutenant's heart rate rose accordingly.

[Unit One, this is Deputy Chief Constable Williams with your final sortie briefing.]

Mason rolled his eyes, preparing to be annoyed by the sound of the commander's voice.

[As you know, the Huntsmen have plagued the corridors for decades. But until recently, their attacks have mostly targeted the defenseless. However, under this Trash Head fella, the bike punks have grown more brazen, attacking larger transports and even rival gangs. This time, however, the Huntsmen have hijacked a Deckar Applied Sciences shipment bound for Ontario, officially earning the ire of everyone's favorite defense contractor.]

[As you know,] Williams continued, *[the Huntsmen have been tough for us to wrangle in for a few reasons. For one, they typically don't travel in packs greater than a dozen or so. Secondly, they lack a home base, that we know of, anyway. They're known to pitch camp along highways, hole up in flea motels, mobile communities, and abandoned warehouses like the one we're headed to.]*

537

[I'm highlighting all of this for a reason, Unit One. Though they like to travel small, we've reports of a massive detachment of Huntsmen operating in the Veins, along with unsubstantiated reports of some kind of heavy machinery operating in the area of operation. We believe this machinery may have been used to carry off the DAS shipment.]

[If the reports are true, they may mean to sell off the stolen ordnance before divvying up the profit and going their separate ways. This means our window is narrow. We cannot allow this cargo to hit the black market, and once these assholes disperse, our chances of nailing their leader go from terrible to fuck-all.]

[Our mission priorities are as follows: first, secure the ordnance; second, identify and neutralize their leader. The present leader of the Huntsmen is a man named John Shaw, but you all probably know him as Trash Head. If Trash Head rears his ugly... well, head, I want him in maglets or a body bag.]

[But use your heads, agents. We do not want a fight with the Huntsmen spilling out into the Veins, and definitely not onto the 101. Consider that your third priority. Mason is coordinating the strike and will give you the details. Mason?]

Finally, my turn.

"Listen up, Unit One, our targets have taken temporary residence in what appears to be a dilapidated paper mill. We will not be on this mission alone. The SCPD will be in position around the complex and establishing—"

[Mason?] It was Moore.

538

"What?"

[You're cutting out, man. We can't hear you.]

Mason was using a standard audio-to-neurotrigger connection. He covered his mouth, a means of shielding the transmitters in his jaw from external noise. "The SCPD will be in position around the complex," he continued, agitated by the muffled sound with which he now spoke, "and are establishing roadblocks and checkpoints designed—"

[Still can't hear you. That stuff about SCPD being positioned around the complex? And the stuff about roadblocks and checkpoints, we didn't hear any of that.]

They're chuckling, Moore and Yamazaki. The lieutenant gripped his knees. *Probably Calderon and Bryant as well. They're laughing at me.* He slammed a fist into the seat adjacent. *Son of a bitch! You goddamned son of a bitch! Everything you do is to belittle me, to chip away at my authority. You low-born bastard!*

"Sergeant Moore, you—"

[Lighten up, Mason. Just a joke. Go ahead, we're listening.]

"We're about to engage the enemy, and you choose this moment to joke around like adolescents on a playground. And two of you are only now back after near-fatal injuries. If death can't teach you to begin taking your work seriously, Sergeant Moore, what will?"

[Jesus Mason, take it easy.]

It was Deputy Informant Daisuke now. Mason could practically *hear* the smile on his face.

[It was a fucking joke.]

"Joke on your own time, with your own life." Mason exhaled through his nostrils slowly, just like his yoga instructor had taught him, before continuing, "I've instructed the SCPD to set up roadblocks on Kerney, Alameda, and Thirteenth Street with checkpoints on Market, Eleventh Street, and Industrial. The 101 on-ramps for Eleventh and Kerney are blocked off. I suspect that once you breach the compound, they are going to try and flee for these 101 on-ramps, especially once they realize the 101 has been blocked off. These roadblocks will funnel them down Market—"

[Directly into the Veins?]

"That's right, Moore. Do you have a problem with that?"

[You're damn right I do! It'll be midday. The streets will be full of people and you want to send a gang of bike punks up Market? Weren't you listening to Williams just now? We're 'not to pursue.']

"That is correct, *we* are not to pursue. And that is why the Sun City Police Department has given us sixty officers, a dozen cruisers, and a half-dozen hover units in support. Market Street is ideal for this strategy — in the unlikely event that they escape the compound, mind you. The narrow avenues will make turning around difficult."

[And what about the pedestrians?]

540

"The sound of the motorcycles should prove ample warning."

[And what about the psychos riding them? Williams, are you hearing this shit?]

"Listen to me very carefully, *Sergeant*. This plan has gone through several iterations and has received approval from the SDC as well as the SCPD."

Williams chimed in. *[Well, hold on now. We don't need to route them through the Veins. Rena, get on the horn with the police commanding officer. I want Market blocked off as well.]*

"Commander! This plan—"

Williams cut him off, ignoring his protests. *[Bryant, I want the 101 on-ramps manned but not barricaded. If the Huntsmen run, and some of them are* sure *to do so — they are on motorcycles, after all — I don't want them on pedestrian streets.]*

They're all in collusion against me... Mason watched the complex come into view and yelled to the pilot to assume a surveillance pattern. *They're all colluding against me. All of them.*

[This is big for us, Unit One,] Williams continued. *[Our image is in desperate need of a low-carb diet and a new wardrobe. Get it done!]*

The SDC mobile command center was a generations-old acquisition from the Sun City Police SWAT team and was mounted on a Peterbilt 18-wheeler chassis similar to those still

541

used to haul beer. It rumbled along the 101, wholly incapable of keeping up with even the most modest commuter sedan. Nevertheless, it currently occupied the superhighway's two fast lanes, leaving behind it a long line of angry commuters.

"Low-carb diet, huh?"

Deputy Chief Constable Williams gave her a thumbs-up. "Keep it light, Rena. I'm just trying to keep it light."

His gums were packed with tobacco, a sign she'd come to recognize over the years. It meant the commander was anxious. She took her seat at the communications console, as the walls of the old command center rattled noisily around her. The console was small, the counter space dotted with rings of ancient coffee stains and burns where people had stubbed out cigarettes. She picked up the Peeping Tom and slipped it onto her head. "This is garbage," she told her commander honestly.

"We make do with what we've got," he replied. "You ask me, I'd say we've gotten spoiled. Many a task force has made do with less. Much less."

The Peeping Tom was a cheap excuse for a mobile immersion device, similar in its design to the VR helmets popular in the twenty-teens. It would allow her to traverse a digitally rendered Sun City like her immersion chair, albeit manually — as in, through tactile input rather than neurotrigger. On top of that, it was slower by orders of magnitude.

As she powered the device up, the pitch-black cast upon her by the clunky helmet came to life. And Sun City, like a forest growing in super-fast-forward, sprang up around her. She sighed in disappointment, leaning back in the squeaky, uncomfortable chair.

"This thing is as heavy as a football helmet."

"Quit pretending you know what a football helmet feels like."

The commander was right. She had no idea what a football helmet felt like. But nonetheless, the Peeping Tom's weight was causing her head to bob violently. "Whoever used this piece of crap last left the workspace cluttered with old case files — unencrypted text files, mind you! And they left shitty applications running in the background! *Aaand* the headset smells like cheap hair gel."

"At least it looks good on you," Williams replied.

The headset was almost perfectly round, like a child's drawing of an astronaut helmet. "Funny, but all kidding aside, sir, I don't have my presets, my macros, or my plugins. The hell with Sun City, I might as well be looking at Gotham City without those. It's going to take me twenty minutes just to figure out where the hell I am!"

And, as if to taunt her, the Peeping Tom had dropped her squarely in the center of Sun City rather than finding her current location with geo-tracking.

"I'm going to throw this fucking thing in the trash."

"You'll do no such thing," Williams said through a mouth full of tobacco, "unless your badge and gun follow."

She wanted her immersion chair. She *needed* her chair.

543

"If you're prepping me for some kind of colossal fuck-up on your part, Detective Constable," Williams continued, "*not* duly noted. You're going to focus, un-fuck yourself and get all-the-way ready to be useful to this operation! Are we clear?"

"We're clear, sir."

Once she'd cleaned up her preferences in the Peeping Tom, she attempted to locate the area of operation. After an excruciating amount of time tracing the 101 from a virtual height of ten thousand feet, she found their command center, just north of the Section Six line. Large and white, it was tough to miss. It looked like a lower-case 'i' in a font not unlike Hollow Black's vicious warning to her. And this diesel-powered 'i' took up a quarter of the 101's northbound lane, forcing vehicles to bow around it like water around the prow of a ship. She tagged their mobile command center so she could jump back to it quickly, and began scanning their projected route, looking for the target site. A minute later she found the complex. "I see it. I'm eyes on the target."

"What do we got, Detective?"

"Not a whole lot. I see a few people milling about the premises. No guards. No guns."

"Good."

She zoomed out and scanned the roadblocks, the checkpoints. "SCPD is in position. They're making themselves pretty obvious, though. We should probably go green before they spook the Huntsmen. I think it's time. Wait, they still haven't unblocked the 101 on-ramp…"

She heard Williams spit, presumably into a cup, but probably onto the floor. "If the boys are ready, give them the green light, then light a fire under the SCPD. Let's do this!"

The Unit One Strike Team was typically a two-man affair comprised of the most heavily modded and combat-ready agents on the team. This duo included the newly promoted *Lieutenant* Chris Calderon and himself. On rare occasions like today, Williams would throw Dice into the mix. Despite not being a MOD, or a salaried field officer even, Williams trusted the ex-yakuza to handle himself. As did AJ.

The three-man strike team waited for the go-ahead in a lot adjacent the abandoned paper mill. Separating them from the complex was an auto salvage that had been quietly evacuated some hours ago. From their vantage point, they could see groups of bikers coming and going from the complex in small but thunderously loud groups.

The mill itself was condemned, or whatever was one step past condemnation. It was originally three stories, but three-quarters of the third floor had collapsed onto the second. The outer walls of the mill buckled inward as though the building itself was inhaling, and seemed propped up on nothing. The hollowed-out curtainwalls leaned inward at precarious angles that defied what AJ thought he knew about gravity. The mill's smokestack, which must have once stood

545

two hundred or more feet, lay broken next to the building in severed concrete rings like calamari.

AJ studied the mill through a slide-out rangefinder mounted to the back of the fingerless glove he wore. He patiently familiarized himself with the layout and was surprised at how few Huntsmen there appeared to be. One might assume they were inside but, considering the condition of the mill, it simply didn't seem plausible.

That place is a rat motel if I've ever seen one.

He banged the rangefinder back into concealment by slapping it against his thigh and leapt down from the second floor of the salvage yard's tow truck depot. More excited than anxious, he swung his arms to loosen up the joints and checked for Deadbolt on his waist.

There were about thirty SCPD officers in SWAT gear, gathered in clusters around an armored personnel carrier. Next to the APC was a large, red, commercial tractor truck. The truck, retrofitted with a six-foot-tall grille guard to act as a battering ram, looked like something out of post-apocalyptic fiction. Sitting in its cab smoking was Dice. Dice had been dour all morning. His face had healed but for a thick purple band under his left eye.

Next to the rig, perched on the sleek black motorcycle Revenant, was Chris. He wore black armored gauntlets and kneepads over his new DAS-branded uniform. The gear was not SDC-issued, and was unlike anything AJ had seen before. And yet... the craftsmanship seemed very familiar. Chris' head bopped and it was clear that he was listening to music over the SDC coms network. Approaching him from behind, he swatted the bandana-wearing agent's shoulder.

Chris glared at him, but that was nothing unusual.

"Where did you get those?"

Chris muted his music with a tap behind the ear. "Come again?"

AJ rapped his knuckles against the metallic kneepad Chris wore. "These! What are they and where'd you get them?"

Chris smiled subtly. "Te-Mea Herekiuha."

"Oh yeah?"

AJ was not surprised that Chris had taken a liking to the gunsmith. After all, Te-Mea was one of the nicest people in Sun City. But he was a little surprised that Chris had been to see him again. He was a little surprised and perhaps a little bothered...

Chris had a strange expression on his face.

Since his return, he'd been a different man. Chris had killed all the bullshit about quitting the unit and even seemed to have a renewed interest in Unit One. AJ chalked it up to his promotion and salary bump.

Chris leaned in and whispered, "What's your relationship with Mahina?"

AJ studied his partner's face carefully. There was a gleam in the bandana'd prima donna's eyes, and he didn't like it. Not one bit.

"Why the fuck do you ask?"

Chris jabbed his nose in the air. "No reason. I mean, I met her... obviously. I went to the Iron Horse, after I got out of the hospital, to thank him for saving my life. Well, to relay the message to Bandit, really..."

The cadence with which Chris spoke was unusual, as was the look on his face. And inexplicably, both the cadence and the look made AJ want to test out his new fist on the lieutenant's face.

"That's when Te-Mea gave me these." Chris held up his gauntlets. "It's like he was expecting me. That's also when I met Mahina..."

AJ stared at the lieutenant with squinted eyes and chose his words carefully. "You're not even her type. You're no one's type!"

Chris frowned but otherwise ignored the insult. "And what's her type?"

"Heads up!" someone yelled.

Rumbling that shook the ground approached and crescendoed as a fleet of more bikes fell in on the paper mill. Two riders dismounted and began pulling open the gates of the dilapidated factory.

"What the hell are we waiting for, Rena!" AJ was immensely agitated, and the Huntsmen had nothing to do with it.

It was Mason who answered. *[Specifically, Sergeant Moore, we're waiting for the Sun City News Network and the BBC.]*

"The fucking press?"

[I know the inner workings of the Consortium don't appeal to you, Sergeant Moore, the 'politics,' as you have called it, but Unit One doesn't exist if the brand doesn't exist.]

"Fuck brand."

The word 'brand' got tossed around a lot in the SDC, but nowhere else did it carry the weight as when referencing Unit One. Brand: that constant reminder that every action had some monetary impact. Brand, as far as AJ was concerned, served only as a reminder that, at the end of the day, it was all about dollar signs. Remembering his brother's disgust upon seeing the DAS-branded vest, it suddenly felt cheap, the logo nothing but a plastic name tag.

In Ace's eyes, brand was why Unit One had the money, but why Unit One would never have the respect.

Ace is wrong though. Unit One will *have the respect if I have anything to say about it.*

[Looks like the buzzards are here,] Williams said over neurotrigger, referring to the media helicopters and hover units.

[That's your cue, team. And remember: goods first, Trash Head second.]

"And civilian safety a distant third... Yeah, got it. In the pipe. Five-by-five."

AJ climbed up onto the driver's-side running board of the monstrous red truck, as Dice started the engine. The growl and subsequent roar as the diesel came to life sent a chill up his spine, and he couldn't help but catcall.

"Never driven one of these," Dice said after a long drag and exhale. "Always wanted to. Even more, always wanted to crash one into something."

"Well, today's your lucky day!"

Dice smiled, the truck's massive engine jostling him in his seat.

"All right, men," AJ yelled down to the officers of the Sun City Police Department. "You guys are to back us up so long as it makes sense to do so. Corporal Gonzales is the boss, as far as you guys are concerned." He nodded to the Unit One recruit, who stood leaning against a patrol car, her arms folded. She took the SCPD officers' measure and gave him a thumb's up with her red prosthetic right hand. "You are not to endanger yourselves," AJ continued. "If you get an opportunity to safely nab yourselves a Huntsman or two, don't hesitate. Otherwise, keep them pinned in and off their bikes." Satisfied, AJ banged on the truck door.

Dice floored it and the truck burst through the double doors of the garage, nearly tearing him from the running board. AJ held on, laughing.

The Huntsmen have no idea what's about to hit them! I'm going to nab Trash Head and drag his ass out for all the world to see. And then Mahina, Rena, and Ace will know exactly what I'm capable of.

The truck tore through the salvage yard, sending gravel and a hurricane of dust and dirt into the air behind it. The rusted hulls of long-dead vehicles became little more than autumn underbrush as the truck picked up speed.

AJ took Deadbolt from his belt and triggered its extension. The pole snapped to its full four-foot length. He held the multipurpose weapon close to his body, as the truck smashed through the chain-link fence of the salvage yard and bounced from the curb and into the street violently.

They had the attention of the bikers in the yard now, but it was too late. AJ gripped the driver's-side assist handle as the truck roared up the paper mill's entryway and exploded through the gate, sending the bikers who'd just arrived scattering from their vehicles.

Dice showed no signs of slowing, but rather laughed maniacally as a recently evacuated motorcycle exploded against the reinforced grill of the truck. He drove headlong for the wall of the mill.

This was AJ's cue to make his own evacuation. He leapt from the truck just before it struck the building's southernmost stone face in a thunderous boom. He rolled deftly to his feet and ran to engage a pair of stunned Huntsmen.

The police APC, which had been tailing Dice closely, skidded to a halt in a cloud of dust and gravel, Unit One and police already pouring out. Gonzales led the officers efficiently, yelling commands and brandishing a large rifle.

With a finger poised over the trigger to eject the blade within Deadbolt, AJ flew at the Huntsmen. In that moment, the southern wall of the mill gave way, the red diesel truck having punctured the building like a balloon. The wall collapsed in epic, terrifying phases and all the men in the yard could do was shield themselves from the debris and wait for the destruction to cease.

As the wall settled in a tall mound of concrete, glass, and rebar, the bikers, now straddling their bikes, looked to one another briefly and throttled their engines.

"Don't do it!" AJ warned.

The first sped into the street, where she was met by Chris on Revenant. AJ lunged at the second as the bike sped by, and triggered Deadbolt. The red-hot blade struck the rear wheel and sent the biker tumbling to the dirt. Quickly sheathing the blade in a flourish of twirling motions, he pounced on the fallen bike punk. A knee to the spine to pin the man in the dust and a tight pair of magnetic bracelets forced his capitulation.

AJ left the man in the care of the corporal and looked to the mill. Where the paper mill wall had been now stood what looked like the outer hull of a battleship. And that was torn open and bent in massive triangular tears, punctured inward by the tactical entry vehicle.

"What in the holy hell? Rena, you need to have a look at this..."

Chris' quarry rode a "squid-bike," a three-wheeled, reverse trike. The two front wheels were roughly three feet tall and angled inward from the top down. The design was fast and could maintain a straight course hands-free — which was the point — but squid-bikes had a terribly impractical turn radius. It was because of this that Revenant had no trouble catching and keeping up with the fleeing motorcycle punk.

The biker, a woman wearing a pickelhaube and smart-fabric vest, made a beeline for the 101 on-ramp, diving headlong into traffic.

Swerving to avoid oncoming vehicles, Chris accelerated. It didn't take Revenant long at all to pull within striking range. Glancing at him over her shoulder, the biker reached into her saddlebag and withdrew what could only be a grenade, and probably a stolen Deckar Applied Sciences grenade at that.

Chris leaned and banked Revenant to such an extreme angle that his metal-shod knee struck the pavement, spouting a stream of sparks. The grenade bounced off the ground before exploding, and the concussion blast lifted him and the bike from the street momentarily. As the bike touched back down, he released the handlebars and let the bike's stabilizers work their magic. A second later he throttled, the bike righting itself smoothly.

Revenant's engine was glorious, familiar music. Attack! A low pitch grew melodiously. Attack again, as the gears parted the engine's growl like the staccato of a snare drum.

In an expectedly wide turn, the Huntsman swung up the 101 off-ramp, which — with the SCPD barricade removed — was open for business but would take the not-very-maneuverable trike directly into oncoming traffic. Chris went to follow, but was met by a barrage of incoming traffic. Throwing the bike sideways, he slid across three lanes before coming to a halt in a fog of tire smoke. The road pirate wasn't so lucky. In a petty attempt to evade an oncoming truck, the trike struck a canary-yellow bollard and folded, throwing the rider. Her body flipped over the hood of the pickup, striking the windshield. The truck driver skidded to a halt in a panic, leaving nothing but the Huntsman's German-style pickelhaube jammed into the truck's hood by its spike.

After a brief look at the woman, Chris felt no need to remain. She wouldn't be going anywhere.

AJ was right, he thought. *If Mason had his way, I'd probably be chasing that woman up a crowded sidewalk right now. And the grenade… We'd likely be dealing with casualties.*

Chris revved Revenant with authority and throttled her back towards the paper mill.

Dice was gob-smacked, a term he wasn't even familiar with. He sat in the rumbling truck cab with a cigarette burning

554

wasted in his lap. The inside of the "paper mill" looked more like the inside of a submarine. The walls were steel, the floors steel, covered in grip-lock tiles, the kind used to keep dumb fucks from slipping in department store doorways when it snowed. Overhead were metallic walkways, interconnected and accessible via gangways and accommodation ladders. Where there should have been empty chemical vats and rusting dryers, there were active hydraulic pumps and control rooms alive with blinking lights and display panels.

At the center of all this sat the Huntsmen: a large cadre of them. A dozen raggedy couches formed a giant semicircle in the center of the machine. Scattered haphazardly around and traceable by a vine deck of extension cables were drink coolers, a fridge, a self-standing stripper's pole, and a hologram television. Playing for the group of slack-jawed bikers was what appeared to be hardcore porn.

Dice brushed the cigarette out of his lap and dabbed at the hole in his jeans, unsure of what to do next.

"Rena."

[Dice, what is it?]

"I don't know."

[I don't understand.]

"Neither do I."

[I mean, what are you talking about?]

"Yes."

[Dice, snap out of it! You're inside. What do you see? Is there something inside?]

555

"There is stuff inside, for sure."

[What's inside?]

"For starters, Rena, there's a Fisher-Price 'My First Stripper Pole,' and about two dozen bike punks watching smut."

She laughed.

"Oh, I'm not done, Rena. I'm not in an abandoned factory. They've done something to the place. There's more…"

A bullet struck the windshield. A second knocked the wiper up to twelve o'clock.

[Is that gunfire?]

"It is."

[Well, get to work, agent!]

"I don't know…," he replied. "To be honest, I'm just kind of taking it all in."

The holographic television lit the room with three-dimensional scenes of someone doing just that.

AJ threw the door of Dice's red truck open to find a pistol in his face. "What the hell are you doing? Let's go!"

Most of the bikers hadn't even gotten up from the filthy couches yet, but a couple had drawn their guns and were taking shots at them. One man still had his hands in the fridge. Another, who'd been engaged in the act of coitus with another biker on a Formica patio table, was frozen, mid-pump, pants around ankles.

"Hold your fire!" a voice roared.

The gunfire ceased, allowing AJ to pop his head out from behind the truck door. When it became evident that the Huntsmen would honor the ceasefire, AJ approached the group, holding his own pistol aloft. "Seriously guys, what the fuck is going on in here?"

A couple of Huntsmen began getting to their feet slowly. Some backed away, others advanced.

"I mean, is this what the Huntsmen call a good time?" AJ asked, somewhat sincerely, "Sitting around, dicks in hand, staring at one another in a circle?"

The bikers looked to one another. The couple that'd been having sex stared at him blankly, no intent to start dressing evident.

It was then that Corporal Gonzales, at the head of a cadre of SCPD, poured into the chamber through the punctured steel wall, guns drawn.

AJ smiled as the officers spread out, guns drawn. "You are all under—"

"I'm not one to play the 'harassment' card," a voice bellowed, "but this is an inordinate amount of attention for a bunch of motorcycle enthusiasts and lowly highwaymen!"

The crisp yet booming voice that showered them from above belonged to what could only be the leader of the Huntsmen. Crazily tall and gaunt, the man leaned on the metallic balustrade casually, shirtlessly. As he talked, he waved around a cigar the size of a gear shift. At the same time, he punctuated his speech by shoving the thing into his mouth and grinding on it with large, LED-white teeth. His torso was a war zone in which neither body hair nor tattoo had yet to seize total control, and yet clear territories were drawn in veins that crisscrossed inexplicably. Half his face was covered with a salt-and-pepper beard, and what wasn't carpeted was pierced.

Trash Head...

Chris is outside somewhere, probably up to his ears in Huntsmen, and Dice couldn't give a shit about the Queue, AJ thought, practically rubbing his hands together. *You're all mine, Trash Head. You and the bounty on your cluttered head are all mine...*

"What brings Unit One to our humble abode?"

Hundreds of acts of road piracy... Not to mention the kidnappings, extortion, and vehicular homicides. People like Trash Head were why Unit One existed. And yet, in all this time, the closest anyone had come to an arrest on the leader of the Huntsmen was still-warm tire marks.

AJ shifted his grip on Deadbolt ever so slightly, positioning his finger next to the trigger that would eject the blade. He wanted to smile. He wanted to goad Trash Head into a fight, and for a moment he no longer cared what the collateral damage of all-out brawl meant.

"Agent Moore!" the giant biker announced triumphantly. He ran a finger over the chrome spikes that jutted from his brow, and gnawed on his cigar. "What a pleasure!"

Movement borrowed his attention, and AJ turned to find Dice standing at his side.

AJ pointed a finger at Trash Head. "Tell you what, *Slim*, just point us to the DAS shipment you hijacked, and I might let you finish that cigar before the maglets come out."

Trash Head looked at his men and grinned charismatically. "Looks like someone didn't get the memo."

"Know what?" AJ pulled another magnetic bracelet from his belt and threw it up onto the walkway. It landed right at the thin man's feet, and he couldn't be prouder of the throw. "Forget your cigar. Go ahead and put those on."

Trash Head kicked the maglets aside. "No, thank you! I've jewelry aplenty."

"Well, you're not leaving me a whole lot—"

"Funny thing," Trash Head replied, cutting him off, "your people came and shot this place to hell three days ago. You think you're the star of the show, don't you, Moore? When really, you're stuck in a shitty reboot."

"What are you talking about?"

"Your buddies took all the fun stuff, well, most of it anyway." He raised his long arms and spread them. "If you want the rest, well, you're too late. We sold it to the yaks last night. The only reason we're still here is 'cuz we couldn't get this fucking rig started."

Rig? What rig? AJ wanted to ask, but Dice chimed in before he could.

"Which family? You said 'the yaks.' To which family did you sell the weapons?"

559

AJ noticed that Dice was carrying something new: a new gun. Unlike his classic revolver, this gun was sleek and modern-looking, most likely magnetic.

"Which family?" Trash Head replied. "How the fuck should I know! No offense, but I can't tell one suit-wearing, Chinese pimp from another."

"'Our people' shot this place up? What are you talking about?"

"Jeez with the fucking questions!"

More SCPD units poured into the room through the tear in the hull. AJ held up a fist to alert the newcomers to the tentative ceasefire. When the new players had settled in, guns aimed in every direction, he addressed Trash Head once more. "You're lying!"

Trash Head, unfazed by the new guns pointed his direction, waved a hand dismissively. "Sure! I'm lying! You fuckers have your own version of history, everybody knows that. But, if you think we're gonna go quiet, especially after the massacre you put on, you're mistaken."

"Don't move!"

Trash Head flicked his cigar down (and would have caught AJ in the chest had he not side-stepped) and charged back up the walkway to a chorus of "freeze," his workman's boots squeaking on the grating. As if an afterthought, he paused and turned, mid-way up the gangway. "Huntsmen, LET'S RIDE!"

Voices drowned one another out in a cacophony of unintelligible panic, and then gunshots sounded.

AJ watched with a hawk's attention as Trash Head took a seat at a console on the upper deck and slipped what appeared to be a remote monitoring device onto his head. "You're not going anywhere!"

"Sure I am," Trash Head replied scornfully. "Hell, so are you. We're *all* going for a ride!" His hands worked the console, and suddenly the room was filled with classic rock. At the same time, the earth began to tremble. "Buckle your seat belts, ladies. Or don't! Who am I to preach safety?" He roared laughter, an authentic, genuinely amused, psychotic laughter.

The Huntsmen raced for their bikes, whistling and cat-calling, even as the cops — some of them, anyway — aimed their weapons flaccidly at everything moving. Even as porn still played out before them, the actors like nude giants. Even as the growling of choppers and the whine of street bikes filled the air.

AJ fired his pistol at Trash Head and missed by a mile, largely thanks to the sudden jolt of the floor, and pandemonium ensued.

"Something's not right. Heat signatures everywhere!"

The paper mill was red with heat in Rena's thermal view.

"What do you mean?"

The building itself had come to life. Not only were there heat signatures, but seismic readings as well.

"Rena! Speak to me, and not in that techno-jibber-jabber. What's happening?"

She was struggling to find words, even though she could feel Williams' hand on her shoulder, shaking her.

The paper mill was engulfed in debris, collapsing outward in every direction. Before long, massive plumes of powdered brick obscured her bird's-eye view entirely.

Now the chief was in her ear, directly. "Rena! What is happening?"

"The building, sir! The signature was off. It has been this whole time, but this crappy hardware… This is why I need my chair! I thought maybe I was looking at generators behind some kind of thermo-masking, but no… the building itself is—"

"Is *what*, Detective?"

"See for yourself." She sent her feed to the monitor in the command center.

The brick walls of the paper mill lay strewn and the entire complex was shrouded in a white mist of debris.

"My God," was all he said, followed by a hefty spit. "Are they dead?"

Clouds of grey dust blotted out the perimeter of flashing red and blue lights until nothing was visible but white.

Rena pulled off the headset to find Williams gripping the console.

The cloud of debris, pulled from the site reluctantly by wind from the bay, gave way to something black. Something massive and black.

Rena threw the Peeping Tom back on. "Do you see it now?"

"Rena."

"Sir?"

"Rena."

"Sir?"

"What am I looking at?"

Revenant came to a halt of its own accord with such urgency that Chris was forced to stand, his boots gripping desperately at the bike's foot pegs. Too late to reverse; the cloud of debris engulfed him. He covered his nose and mouth and squinted through the searing burn of ground brick in his eyes. In moments, his jacket, gloves, and person proper were covered in fine silt. In his mouth was the taste of chalk.

The earth trembled as another of the mill's walls folded in on itself. Brick was ejected from the wall of dust and tore away whole sections of the surrounding fence. As SCPD officers raced to escape, debris that had been thrown outward by the force of the collapse struck them, wounding at least one that he could see. Another was being carried to safety over the shoulders of Corporal Gonzales. Chris watched her escape the wreckage, carrying a man much larger than her, with impressive speed.

The lieutenant reversed Revenant without so much as a glance over his shoulder. Once he was out of the debris cloud, he watched, awestruck, as a black shape appeared from wafting clouds of white.

The thing was half as tall as the building from which it emerged and was almost perfectly square and black. Its walls looked to be of smooth, reinforced steel, lined only where the massive plates met. Its base was a row of continuous tracks, like those of a tank, only more of them and much, much larger. It roared to life and great black ejections of exhaust sprang from its roof and rear to blur the sun.

"Rena..."

Williams snapped Rena out of her trance with a flick to the earlobe, as knocking on her immersion helmet hadn't worked. Just as she said something, another voice filled his head via the SDC private network.

[Deputy Chief Constable Williams!]

Her voice was shrill and somewhat avian, an amalgamation of indignation and authority. It was SDC Councilwoman Diane West.

"Good day, Madam West."

['Good day' indeed! The whole world is watching what appears to be the unsanctioned demolition of...] Her voice trailed off.

On the monitor, Williams watched the black shape emerge from behind the fog of soot and debris. Massive and squared, it appeared to be some kind of retrofitted excavator, the kind used to move or level mountains.

[Williams, what on Earth is that?]

"Madam West, let me get back to you." He disconnected. "Rena, I could really go for an update on the situation."

"Well, sir, I wouldn't have believed it… if I weren't looking at it. And I still don't believe it."

Rena raised her hands and just let them fall.

"Apparently, the stories are true."

"Stories? What stories, Detective?"

"Well, rumors, to be precise: urban legends. Tales shared in chatrooms and forums, in conspiracy threads on Shadownet. You know, places where you'd find" —she made quotations with her fingers— "'details' on urban myths like the Thin Man or the Killer with a Thousand Faces. But these stories speak of a mysterious black box."

"You can't be serious, and why are you talking like that?"

"A black dreadnought of the highways, said to travel the 101 in the wee hours, crushing anything foolish enough to be in its path."

Rena's sense of humor, if you could call it that, always surfaces at the worst times…

Williams peered over her shoulder to stare at the exposed portion of her face. He was looking for a smile, a smirk, some indication that his tech detective had chosen yet another beautifully inappropriate time to be funny. And yet she was not smiling.

"You're serious?"

"People call it Pandora, the black frigate of the 101."

Williams put a hand to his temple. The vein on the side of his head was throbbing. "This is the dumbest—"

"We're witnessing firsthand the world's first verified URO."

"Don't, Detective. Just don't…"

"An *unidentified*—"

"Don't say it, Rena. I'll fire you."

"—*rolling object.*"

The jolt knocked Dice onto his back. As he got to his knees, he pointed his service weapon at the motorcycle speeding towards him. Its rider held a spiked mace covered in blood from the police officer whose face it'd just claimed.

Control your breathing.

He took aim and fired, but the shot sailed wide.

This better work…

Dice dropped to his chest and could feel the wind from the mace just missing his skull. He rolled onto his back just in time to watch the rider's back explode in a pink plume, as the self-guiding bullet performed an aerial one-eighty to strike him.

"Oh, hell yeah!"

Gone were the old revolver and the aftermarket rounds that had nearly got him killed in his dust-up with the Titans. This new gun was state-of-the-art: an electromagnetic coil gun, complete with a target acquisition module and self-guiding bullets. Because all guns should have a name, he'd named it Bloodhound. Unlike Watchman, this semi-automatic held thirty-five ferromagnetic rounds and could collapse down to an easy-to-conceal three inches by two inches.

The Huntsmen had opened the loading bays and were fleeing the complex in disorderly waves. With the bay doors open, he could see the partially collapsed paper mill, and it was clear that the building was moving. The floors lifted and fell like the deck of a ship at sea, and this sent furniture tumbling, only adding to the mayhem. The bikers who'd been able to mount their bikes rode out through the bay doors to disappear in the dirt churned up by whatever it was they were in. Meanwhile, AJ had engaged the Huntsmen still on foot and was trying to work his way up to their leader. A mass of men had swarmed on him with knives, bats, and chains, and all his partner could do was keep them at bay, whipping Deadbolt's heated blade like a whip.

I guess that leaves Trash Head to me, the ex-yakuza thought, not all that disappointed.

He advanced towards the gangway, and Rena's voice exploded into his ear.

[Dice!]

"Jesus, what?"

567

[You need to stop that thing. You're heading for the 101!]

"This building is heading for the freeway?"

[It's not a building. It's an unidentified—]

He could hear a voice beyond hers growl something.

[It's some kind of modified dozer,] she corrected.

"That would explain the décor."

[Can you stop it?]

Trash Head was hunched over his terminal, guffawing, pulling at levers, turning knobs and otherwise piloting.

"Yeah, I just need to put a bullet in the driver." He pointed Bloodhound at the massive back of Trash Head. The LCD display on the slide of the gun indicated a lock on the target. "Hate to shoot a guy in the back, but…"

He pulled the trigger. The gun made a hissing sound. A burnt smell filled the air. He looked at the display once more. It read, "Error 3002" in bold, red text. "Please see the manual for details."

Dice filled a room already brimming with the sounds of motorcycle engines, gunfire, and the meat-packing sounds of fisticuffs with just what it lacked: a long string of Japanese curses. When he was finished, he threw the gun at the floor. As it hit the deck, it fired a round that whizzed past his face and struck something that erupted in steam.

At the sight of this, a pair of Huntsmen who'd been encircling the whirling dervish that was AJ Moore broke away to take on easier prey.

568

Mason watched from high up in the SCPD hover unit as the massive machine flattened the perimeter fence and left the lot. It moved through the repo yard, crushing everything in its path. Gone instantly were cars, trucks, and even the salvage yard office where they'd stationed not an hour prior. Never in his life had he seen such immediate and total destruction.

A rolling nebula of earth and rubble followed the machine, climbing hundreds of feet into the air. Civilians ran from their cars as the behemoth moved into the street in a devastating beeline for the 101.

"If that thing gets onto the 101 we're looking at total, unbridled devastation. A monumental loss of life."

No one responded.

Even now, the 101's several lanes were becoming thick and sluggish with midday commuter traffic.

The Huntsmen's rolling land carrier ripped chunks of pavement free, firing them like projectiles in its wake. At the same time, bikers continued to spring from its hull and into the street. The cars on the highway off-ramp had no chance. One vehicle disappeared beneath the monstrous machine and another exploded on impact, sending flame and black smoke to also disappear under its hungry treads. The machine began to climb onto the freeway, now unabated.

"It's too heavy," Mason said, more to himself than the pilot. "There's no way it will make the climb."

Behind the black box, and weaving through throngs of Huntsmen, was a motorcycle, also black, that he recognized as Calderon's. The sergeant was pursuing Pandora and behind him, having ejected from the machine like insects from a hive, were a thick swarm of bike punks in hot pursuit.

The on-ramp, a huge concrete structure four lanes in width, buckled. A tremendous boom resounded even over the sound of copter rotors. It was the sound of concrete snapping. The on-ramp began to sag under the tremendous weight of the excavator. As it gave way, a pillar, reinforced concrete the breadth and width of a school bus, stood upright and began to crumble.

If the off-ramp collapses, the machine will slam into the buttress that supports the 101. It will be messy and the damage costly, but it should halt the thing.

A pillar broke away and the ramp listed precariously, but still Pandora climbed.

"Collapse, goddamn it!"

When the ramp finally broke away from the elevated highway to hit the street and break up like a smashed plate, it was too late. Pandora was on the 101. Its treads came down flat on the asphalt of the mega-highway and churned the pavement like butter as it fought to pick up speed.

A squadron of Huntsmen made it up onto the 101 as well, while the rest, unable to flee into the Veins, fled in wide circles from SCPD cars and hover units in pursuit.

The last to escape the collapsing off-ramp was the black bike Revenant. The police cars behind the lieutenant were not so lucky, disappearing into dust, their red and blue lights extinguishing one by one as they fell.

This is a disaster! Mason thought. *This makes the circus at the* Musée de Conflit Historique *look like... like nothing. If we don't stop this thing*, Mason fumed, *it's over. This whole charade is over!*

I cannot be associated with this kind of failure...

Mason craned to see the pilot. "Get in front of that thing. Do it now!"

The hover unit lifted up quickly, nauseatingly, weaving through a swarm of other police hover units and commercial media choppers. From their height, Pandora looked no larger than a Lego. As he scanned up the ten-lane-wide super-corridor, the dots that were cars began to cluster closer and closer. On the horizon, perhaps a dozen or so miles ahead, the cars came to a halt, gridlocked.

Mason had no love for Unit One. Mason had no love for Sun City. But the idea of watching hundreds of people crushed beneath...

"Faster!" he yelled at the pilot. "Get in front of that thing or I'll have your pilot's license."

In the rearview, the collapse of the four-lane on-ramp looked like a great chasm opening in the earth. As his heart rate soared in the range of mania, Chris raced to catch the rampaging machine.

Revenant was low now, and broaching ninety miles per hour. The machine that Rena was calling Pandora was moving at an alarming velocity, much faster than anything its size had a right to move. The sheer scale and motion of the thing turned his stomach as he raced to catch it. Behind him, Huntsmen on lesser bikes tried in vain to catch up. The other Huntsmen now flanked Pandora en masse, protecting it like fighter jets protected bombers.

They rode bikes of all shapes and sizes. Choppers with large chrome exhaust pipes that jutted behind and spat black exhaust. Nimble little street bikes that whined bitterly and darted about like gnats. Trikes and four-wheelers. But the worst of them were the "junkers," custom bikes made from the parts of other conveyances. Some of these junkers consisted of two or more bikes welded together. Between the two refactored bike frames, platforms had been erected, and on these platforms were typically gun turrets and sometimes flamethrowers. Men and women, themselves armed to the teeth, aimed these weapons. Others threw axes, knives, bricks, Molotov cocktails, and grenades.

The 101 had quickly become a war zone: a war zone moving at breakneck speed.

Huntsmen kept Chris at a distance effectively with their projectiles. Bottles exploded on the highway in front of him, and he could do nothing but ride through and cover up. Bricks bounded at high speeds past his exposed head. Grenades exploded, sending concussion waves about, wobbling Revenant precariously. Commuters caught in the high-speed fracas pulled into the service lane or swerved inexplicably, only adding to the chaos.

From the loading bays of Pandora, more Huntsmen ejected, their motorcycles producing thick clouds of burnt rubber as they struck the highway and swerved desperately to right themselves. Sticking the landing appeared to have fifty-fifty odds, as many of them lost control and tumbled to violent deaths. The bikers that landed safely joined the rest to form a rolling squadron around the one-time earth mover. Before long, there were dozens of modern-day Hussars protecting Pandora.

"AJ, Dice! What's your status? Are we anywhere close to stopping this thing?"

Chris waited but there was no response.

I just need a way inside, Chris thought. *I can take out whoever's inside and stop this thing.*

A swarm of Huntsmen now stood between him and Pandora.

I have to engage them...

With one hand on Revenant's throttle, he drew his pistol with the other. He fired into the group and struck one biker in the thigh. Rearing back in pain, the biker dropped his Molotov cocktail, swerved and struck another motorcycle, upending it. Both bikes and their riders tumbled by in a wreck of parts and people. He trained his pistol on a junker whose

573

mounted machine-gun had been chewing up the pavement around him. Just as he fired, a brick struck Revenant and snapped the right rear-view mirror free. The mirror, held in place by a wire, swung up and smashed him in the face. The blow was sudden, as was the loss of sight and of orientation. He let go of the bike's handlebars instinctively. The machine's stabilizers were, in that moment, more reliable than the rider. When his vision returned a moment later, he snatched the dangling mirror free and tossed it aside. Blood, warm even against the cold of the rushing wind, was pulled back across his face to pool in his ear. With no small prick of hubris, he decelerated out of the machine-gun's range.

"Rena, I can't stop this thing alone. We need backup!"

"Where do you pigs wanna go? Somewhere fun? Should we take this party all the way to Eden?"

Dice gave the bike punk the finger. Trash Head's response was more insane laughter.

Two attackers writhed at his feet, one the victim of a genitalia punt, the other, a good old-fashioned eye gouge.

[Dice!]

It was Rena again.

"What is it?"

[Chris needs backup. Are you in a position to help?]

The police had taken up positions of cover and were engaged in a heated firefight with the Huntsmen. AJ, too, had his hands quite full in the all-out melee. Corporal Gonzales, who had boldly and wisely ordered the SCPD officers on-site to withdraw, had led their retreat as soon as the "building" took on the behavior of a vehicle.

"Looks like there's no one else."

He made a pistol with his fingers and aimed at Trash Head. "You're lucky!"

With his head down, covering up with his trusty bulletproof overcoat, Dice ran back to the truck and climbed into the cab. Driving the truck through one of the open docking bays was an option but, from the look of things outside, they were positioned in such a way that the truck would drop onto the highway horizontally. Doing so would be suicide.

The only thing to do is back up.

In the rear view, through the torn steel, he could see motorcycles weaving in and out of the debris being churned up by the moving paper mill.

This is going to be messy...

He put a cigarette to his lips and lit it.

Madison, baby. Kiss those beautiful lips of yours for me.

"The 101 is gridlocked. Pandora is going to pulverize them!"

"The hell it is! Not on our watch." Williams paced with his arms folded. "Mason! Get the fuck down there and start diverting traffic. I don't care what you have to do, but get the path of this thing cleared. Do it now!"

Williams moved up the command center corridor to the cabin. The truck's driver was one of the new recruits, a Chinese man named Lin.

"Can you catch that fucking thing, Corporal?"

The blue-haired man turned to him with a blank expression. "Probably?"

"Wait? Was that a fucking question? 'Probably' is not going to cut it, Corporal. Catch that fucking thing and do it now!"

Pandora was at least a quarter of a mile ahead. Smoke and debris pockmarked the freeway, forcing the corporal to swerve the massive command center to avoid it. The sky, meanwhile, buzzed with choppers, hover units, and drones. The smell of destruction filled the command center.

This was supposed to be a simple search and seizure. Now, what do we have? A goddamn road war.

If Mason was right, they were heading straight for midday traffic. Trapped on the elevated highway, commuters would have no escape. The death toll would be catastrophic.

Williams left the cabin with a warning to the corporal. "Catch Pandora or start getting your resume out there. Just know, Corporal, that companies don't hire people with blue hair without sterling recommendations."

He stormed back down the corridor, his shoulders touching both sides. "Ulcers!"

"Sir?" Rena turned toward him despite being blind behind the massive helmet.

576

"Ulcers, Rena. You're giving me ulcers. You're giving me ulcers, and cancer, and irritable bowel syndrome, and AIDS, and SARS, and fucking swine flu. ALL OF YOU! Rena, you're damn smart. I know you're damn smart. I beg you, I fucking *besiege* you to think of something."

"You mean *beseech*, sir."

"Jokes huh, Detective? Lin! Get us in front of that thing."

"It will crush us, sir," the corporal hollered back.

"So be it! The detective has jokes!"

"Take us down... I guess."

Mason watched the mayhem grow in scale as the hover unit dipped and weaved back through the murder of network choppers.

"I mean *way down*, and faster! We need to move ahead of all this and divert traffic."

The pilot turned to look at him, and for a moment they stared at one another over their respective shoulders. "I don't know how you expect to do that."

"Just get us down there quickly and prepare the armament subsystems, officer."

The pilot smiled and shook his head. "I think you mean 'ready doors for gunner support,' fucking bureaucrat..."

The doors on either side of the fuselage slid open, filling the hover unit with a cold wind that sent everything not tightly fastened flailing about. The door gun dropped down from the roof at the same time that his seat slid forward to meet it. Holding the spade grip with clammy hands, Mason looked out over the 101. The highway swarmed with motorcycles. Explosions dotted the highway, sending pillars of smoke into the air like trees. The pilot weaved through these, but he could still smell it.

The guns that rose up from the deck of the quadcopter were called 'Banshees' and had a rate of fire of 117 rounds per second. Mason knew this because he'd read the DAS user's manual for the YXG-06 Hover Unit, just as he'd read — at least once — the manual of every device he was likely to come into contact with as an SDC official.

Mason trained the barrel on the swarming, speeding horde of bikers, careful to make note of the black frame of Revenant.

"Short bursts," he said aloud to himself, quoting the manual. "'To avoid compromising the control dynamics of the mounted vessel, fire should be limited to short bursts.'"

Unlike the rest of Unit One, Mason had yet to kill a man. Mason singled out a three-wheeled motorcycle whose gun was threatening to tear Lieutenant Calderon apart.

He paused... and not out of fear.

I should let them kill him... Let's see him undermine my authority from the grave.

"You waiting for something special, gunner?" the pilot called. "You're weapons-free, Lieutenant."

"Mind the flight of this thing!"

578

A Molotov cocktail struck the ground in front of Revenant and, for a brief instant, the entire bike was engulfed in flame. At the same time, he could hear Calderon's frantic cries for backup over neurotrigger.

[Mason!]

"What is it, Detective Bryant?"

[What's your status and position?]

"I have orders from Chief Williams to divert traffic." Mason took his hands away from the mounted gun, his expression stone.

"Get in front of them," he told the pilot. "I'll not tell you again. I want civilian traffic diverted. And turn on the sirens! Use the PA, microwave, or the sound cannon to alert drivers if you have to."

The pilot did not respond, but the hover unit sped up and moved past Lieutenant Calderon and the flaming war that looked likely to overtake him.

A bead of sweat had collected on Mason's brow. With a finger, he collected it and placed it on his tongue.

Good luck, Lieutenant. *Perhaps next time you'll pick your allies more wisely.*

Chris had been driven away from Pandora and could no longer ignore the Huntsmen riders that harried him. He fired his pistol at them until the magazine was emptied. Ejecting the cartridge, he took his hands from the handlebars and quickly punched another magazine into the base of the pistol. It was the last.

'High-speed combat' or HSC was a contingency Unit One had been trained for. Highway piracy was a harsh fact of life, with highwaymen responsible for billions in lost, stolen, or destroyed goods along the super-corridors annually. HSC training consisted of courses on evasive maneuvering, combination and parallel tailing, vehicle boarding, high-stress marksmanship, vehicular close-quarters combat, and of course vehicular evacuation. The last had been Chris' least favorite of the mandatory drills.

The Huntsmen, like the security guards of the *Musée de Conflit Historique*, were not trained adequately, in Chris' opinion. As a bike swung to meet him, the passenger — sitting reverse in a sidecar — fired a flare that struck him in the chest and threatened to knock him off the bike. The flare seared his jacket and burned a hole in the bike's heads-up display.

He returned fire and struck the rider on the side of the head. The bike swerved towards the middle divide, the passenger helpless in its sidecar. They struck the divide and disappeared behind him in what must have been an ugly way to go.

No sooner had he taken his attention from the first attacker than another slammed into him from the opposite side. The blow sent Revenant into a series of stomach-wrenching, serpentine, oversteering corrections that drew black S's into the highway for a quarter of a mile. The Huntsman attacker, helmeted and wielding a chainsaw, swerved in again and drove its hungry teeth into Revenant's fairing, nearly gutting her.

"Where the fuck is backup, Rena?"

The Unit One lieutenant snatched the wrist of his attacker before he could bring the chainsaw up and into striking range.

All right, Te-Mea, let's see what these gauntlets can do!

Taking his free hand off the bike once more, he flicked a switch at the base of his wrist and backhanded the side of the Huntsman's helmet. The impact set off the four 9mm cartridges positioned on the knuckles of the gauntlet. The rider's helmet exploded inward, and the Huntsman immediately went limp. With a boot, Chris sent the bike tumbling away.

Matching their speed from above was a police hover unit. The weapons bay doors were open and he could see a man sitting in the gunner's seat.

"Hey!" he screamed, waving at the man behind the turret. "What the fuck are you waiting for!"

Taking his eyes off of the road had been a mistake, as an explosion blinded him and flame took him from all sides. At this speed, the fire dissipated quickly. Training his pistol once more, this time on a group of street bikes, Chris prepared to open fire.

In that moment, through the fog kicked up in Pandora's wake, he saw something emerge from the rolling superstructure. Red and large, it dropped from the machine's rear as though defecated, to plow into the Huntsmen.

The red truck struck the highway, leaving the Huntsman chasing Pandora no time to evade. They collided in a swirling snow globe of motorcycle parts.

AJ was "flowing" now. The "flow" state was what every martial artist sought in the midst of combat. It could be best described as oneness with one's body and mind; a state in which nothing comes between what you know and what you can do. In that state, timing was less of a conscious thought and more of a natural, effortless occurrence.

He pivoted and lunged, driving Deadbolt's blade into the chest of an attacker. Yanking the blade out required minimal effort as the heated obsidian blade seared everything it touched. Bending his knees, he leaned back to avoid a hatchet that would have parted his skull, and spun to bring his blade to bear on the biker. The slash caught the Huntsman in the underarm and sent the offending appendage flipping into the air.

Dice was gone now, having hopped back into the truck, but it didn't matter. He was more than enough for a bunch of drunken stim addicts. He spun Deadbolt over his head, behind his back, and brought the blade down in an arc that tore the flooring into sizzling bits. He then reversed the stroke and sent molten rubber and steel up into the faces of his attackers.

"The panther evades the net and responds!"

He stepped over a body and drew his pistol. He fired twice into the legs of a man and holstered it once more, even as his other hand swung Deadbolt over his head like a lasso.

"Ha! Bet you didn't see that coming. Behold! The dragon dances!"

AJ leapt and spun, whipping the heated blade under his own feet like a jumprope and took the legs out from under a biker wielding a cutlass.

They're starting to back off. There were about twelve in the beginning, and now... He counted four.

His arms were performing marvelously, their response time near-perfect. Their strength made wielding Deadbolt something like ribbon twirling. At this rate, he could cut through their entire gang. Nevertheless, he took the temporary pause in the action to address them.

"First and foremost, one of you shot me in my brand-new arm, and I don't appreciate it. Secondly, we're getting into *grand inquiry* territory with the amount of dead you's piling up, so I'll do you a favor." He pulled the remaining maglets from his belt, thirteen or so, and scattered them onto the deck as though feeding pigeons. "Cuff yourselves now and I won't filet you."

"Any man or woman who takes that offer will answer to me!" Trash Head bellowed from above.

AJ sheathed Deadbolt but left the device extended. When sheathed it acted as an effective metal staff.

The remaining bikers advanced and were met emphatically with blunt violence. As much fun as a good old-fashioned brawl was, AJ knew they were running up against the clock. He pressed the remaining bike punks mercilessly, using the sheathed Deadbolt's blunt ends to batter the Huntsmen into submission. In short time, they were left unfit to continue.

With no one left to challenge him, and the firefight between the police who hadn't met Gonzales' call to retreat and the Huntsmen dying down, he turned his attention to Trash Head.

"No more lackeys, beanpole!"

"Always more," Trash Head replied. "Always more..."

"It's you and me!"

Trash Head stood from his terminal with a broad, almost handsome smile. "Well, and *them*."

AJ followed the Huntsmen leader's gaze along the walkway to find the couple who'd been having sex doing so once more. They waved. AJ could only shake his head. "You people..."

The diesel tractor fell onto the highway and sent Dice rebounding from the cabin walls like a pachinko ball. The big rig struck what he presumed were bikes, and sent metal flying in every direction. Clenching the cigarette in his teeth, he slammed the gas pedal to the floor. The truck, still tumbling over bikers and bike parts, roared and he felt compelled to pull the horn.

As bikes passed, he could see Chris riding Revenant, gun drawn and firing. He gave his partner an emphatic thumbs-up but didn't get a response. He honked the horn twice more… Still nothing.

Well, he does *have his hands full,* he thought, a little embittered.

"We're not going to make it…"

The feeling in Rena's gut was a rabid mix of adrenaline and raw terror. She watched Pandora speeding along the 101 leaving nothing but waste behind. In less than five miles, it would plow into seven packed lanes of vehicles. The casualties would be…

Williams hit something and, from beneath the helmet, she could hear that thing break. "Unacceptable," he growled. "This is un-fucking-acceptable!"

"Well, I don't know what you want me to do…"

"I want you to do what you swore to do when you took the oath, Detective. I want you to save those people!"

"I don't know!"

The chief was silent for a while. In the quiet she could hear horns honking, engines whining, and explosions. Even the air smelled of fire and fuel.

"Rena," he said, his tone softening somewhat. "Of every agent in the SDC, I trust you the most. Do you know why?"

"No, sir."

"Because you're by far the brightest, and you have the most potential. But you know what?"

"What, sir?"

"I don't think you're inherently intelligent."

"Um, okay, sir."

"I think your intelligence comes as a result of your unwillingness to fold. I think you're smart because you want to win. And I think you want to win because deep down you know you're *supposed* to win. You've put in the time and made the sacrifice to be what you are, which is better than the opposition!"

Chief...

"That's what I see. But what the fuck do I know, right?" Williams spit. "Sounds to me like you're folding now."

I'm not folding!

She began working through the problem as she would any other.

Define the problem. Well, that's easy. The problem is: there's a retrofitted earthmover running roughshod on the 101, headed directly into traffic.

What's the solution? Well, the solution is simple: stop Pandora.

And how do you stop a three-story tank, moving at full speed?

From the inside. Kill the driver.

"AJ!"

AJ's response was near instantaneous. In it, he sounded winded. *[I'm a little busy...]*

"Pandora is about to smash into a wall of traffic and kill hundreds."

[How much time do I have?]

"Three minutes. Tops!"

Was that an honest estimate? As she scanned up the 101, past Pandora and the high-speed war raging around it, traffic became more and more dense, gradually. *Pandora isn't going to strike a wall, it's going to kill soon, and over the course of the next few minutes, accelerate its murder rate, like an avalanche.*

How else would you stop a three-story tank, if not from within?

Destroy the road.

Destroying the 101 in the machine's path could save lives, but it would definitely cost lives as well. Civilians caught in the rolling war had largely been ignored, and (so far) none had been caught and crushed by the expropriated excavator. Collapsing the freeway, assuming they had the firepower to even do so, would risk the lives of all non-belligerents and almost assuredly kill AJ, Chris, and Dice.

[Detective!]

587

"Mason! What's up?"

[Do you see the Mercedes?]

She did. It sat in the middle lane, directly in Pandora's path. The black machine was gaining on the coupe.

[I've done everything in my power to warn the driver, but ram them to the side of the road. The immigrant *is just staring at* me *as though* I *have a problem!]*

You do, she thought. *You're a prick.*

She quickly brought up the Mercedes' specifications via its remote frequency identification CPU. It was a 2046 Mercedes Ambassador: a large luxury sedan with self-driving capabilities.

Driver's probably asleep, she thought. *Wait, why didn't I think of it sooner?*

The RFI CPU was how traffic cops and checkpoints slowed down vehicles going too fast. It could be used to move a car out of the way or even to the shoulder.

This is the answer!

"Commander, I think I have an idea..."

In seconds, she was viewing the list of eligible commands for the Mercedes' CPU. As expected, the CPU specifications were not proprietary — not unique to the Mercedes.

I've got you, baby!

"I can't stop Pandora," she said excitedly, "but I *can* stop the cars in front of it, or more accurately, move them out of harm's way."

She took control of the Mercedes, appropriating its own self-driving logic, and steered it into the highway's service lane. As Pandora rolled past harmlessly, she deactivated the car's ignition to ensure the driver didn't rejoin the bedlam.

[Well done, Detective Bryant!]

Receiving praise from Mason was a strange, nauseating feeling.

"I can see you're on to something," Williams said, pride in his voice. "Don't let me distract you, Detective Constable."

She could hear Williams march off, likely back to the cab to harass Corporal Lin.

One vehicle out of harm's way... Let's get the rest.

As AJ mounted the walkway, Trash Head advanced towards him quickly. For such a tall man, he moved with surprising fluidity and grace. Without a weapon, however, Trash Head was in waters deeper than he knew.

In the moments before what looked to be end of the Huntsmen, AJ thought of something the man had said.

"You said our people attacked and took the stolen DAS weapons."

"Agency Zero," Trash Head replied.

"How do you know?"

"I know what Agency Zero looks like. They're the only morons in Sun City wearing orange head-to-toe like Supermax inmates."

589

"Go on…"

"It wasn't my first rodeo with those fucks. The big old guy, that hot number with the orange hair, and the idiot with the Honda bumper on his face. They've been on our radar longer than we've been on theirs. And of course, the leader, *'Iron' Ace*," he sneered derisively, "the sorry bastard that looks like a bear got to him."

"You're lying."

"What I got to gain by lying? If I'm lying, I'm dying. Tell you what, though, no offense, but they're a hell of a lot better at their jobs than you are at yours." He laughed.

AJ drew Deadbolt slowly and pointed the blade tip in Trash Head's face. "Enough with the lies. Stop this thing now!"

"Go fuck yourself, Moore! The only way the mothership stops is over my dead body."

"I gave you a chance!"

He dashed at Trash Head and leapt. Spinning in the air, he brought the red-hot blade down in a slash that split the walkway bars and dug into the metal floor, narrowly missing Trash Head. He was well in range now, and the follow-up attack would be the finisher. AJ spun again, bending at the knees to avoid a haymaker from the biker. As he swung the blade up, he found Trash Head simply not there.

Impossible—

Not only had Trash Head slipped well outside of the attack, but now he was aiming a weapon of his own.

The shot struck AJ in the abdomen and, remarkably enough, felt little more than a prick.

What the hell?

AJ tried to bring his hand to his chest but found that he could not move. He tried to take a step forward but felt as though he might faint instead. Deadbolt dropped limply from his hands, as his arms fell lifelessly to his sides.

My spine! Did he hit my spine?

Air left him and he fell forward, unable to catch himself. Behind the drumming of his heart in his ears and a cascading sense of terror, he could hear Trash Head's laughter.

"So quick to spray the place up, they missed this bad boy."

Looking up from the floor, he could see Trash Head holding a gun out for him to see.

"'Micro-pulse Destabilizer' is what the manual said. 'Localized electronics interference.' See, that's geek-speak for 'shuts down robo-shit.' And that means your fancy little arms and whatever else you got implanted are useless."

EMP! That's why my arms don't work. My arms and...

With barely any air to speak, he struggled to be heard over the roaring engine of the machine they were in. "Shaw! Listen to me," he wheezed. "Please... you have to stop this thing or a lot of people are going to die."

"People die all the time, Moore. Someone's dying while we stand – some of us – talking about dying. It's as inevitable as the sun rising and as vital to the nature of things."

591

AJ scissor-kicked his legs and rotated his hips, using the momentum to roll onto his back. He sat up on nothing but abdominal strength. "I don't need arms to beat you..."

"Shit, look at that." The biker chuckled. "That's damn inspirational!" The thin but powerful man seized him by the neck and lifted him into the air effortlessly.

The biker's grip was mangling. AJ could feel Trash Head working his thumb to crush his windpipe. Air, already at a premium, was slipping away.

"Worrying about death is as silly as worrying about being born," Shaw told him, grinning. "You're powerless to stop it. What's a death today versus a death tomorrow, or ten years from now? Now you're quibbling over schedule when time is irrelevant beyond this dumpster planet. I'll laugh when we find out the whole circus is connected and no one ever really gets out."

Darkness pressed on AJ's vision from all sides.

"Innocents, Shaw... children. Innocent people..."

Trash Head's expression was pitiless, made more so by the cigar that bobbed in his mouth when he smiled. "'People,' he says... Commuters aren't people, Moore, they're *cattle*. And cattle get butchered and ground into burger. At least these cows can die knowing they were eaten!"

Rena had the knack of it now and was moving cars, trucks, SUVs, eighteen-wheelers, twenty-eight-wheelers — two, sometimes three at a time.

This whole thing reminds me of something...

There was a popular game in the retro game application marketplace that she'd fallen in love with for a time. It was a simple game. Its objective: as symmetrical shapes dropped into a play area of limited capacity, a player had to maximize the use of space by fitting the blocks together as neatly as possible. Success would remove blocks from the play area, scoring points in the process, allowing for the continuation of the game. Failure meant the end. It was a simple game at first, but one that grew in difficulty the longer you played. Blocks would drop with ever-increasing frequency and at greater speeds until eventually the player was forced to succumb.

This is just a higher-stakes version.

The blocks were cars, and the rapidly shrinking capacity was the space between Pandora and traffic. The points she accumulated now came in human lives.

She kept her own score.

Seventy... I've moved seventy vehicles and counting.

Like the old game, however, time was running out and inevitability was rapidly approaching.

"Mason! Red Chevrolet, late 2000s. This one doesn't have a self-driving module. Mason! Mason, do you copy? Get him!"

She watched the hover unit as it raced ahead of Pandora. It did not make a move for the red convertible. Sweat had soaked her hair and was now pouring from beneath the Peeping Tom to pool in her shoulder blades. She worked now

593

with the grim realization that every life she saved might be the last.

Her stomach turned. Pandora was moments away from becoming Sun City's greatest tragedy. And Unit One's greatest failure.

The truck swung wildly from lane to lane, warding off the wave of bike punks.

"How are we looking, Rena?"

[Not good. AJ has gone radio silent…]

Dice had taken out a dozen of the Huntsmen since backing out of the moving complex. It hadn't been difficult, really. Most of the bikers weren't even looking when he slammed into them. And frankly, it was a bit like bowling. He'd hit one and that one would hit others until they were all just garbage on the freeway. It would have been fun under other circumstances.

In the truck's rearview, he could see Chris and Revenant swerving to dodge the wreckage his truck sent.

Fuck it… It's time to end this.

Dice accelerated, the truck howling monstrously as it picked up speed. The bikers, likely as tired of him as he was of them, did not pursue.

Will this thing be big enough?

Getting around the giant black tank was not unlike driving through a blizzard, as ground cement struck the truck in a deafening hailstorm.

594

Why haven't you taken out their leader, AJ? Are you dead?

The idea of doing what he was about to do with AJ alive and inside was almost more than he could muster. But in the end, AJ had signed up for this, as they all had. The people stuck on the 101 had not. His friend would understand, as would he if the roles were reversed.

AJ's thighs were now locked around the giant bike punk's neck, squeezing with as much force as he could muster. The bike punk had released his neck and now clawed at his legs in desperation.

"I won't let go!" he growled into the purpling face of Trash Head. "I'll… choke you to death you son of a—"

When pounding on his legs with his fists failed, the giant resorted to slamming him into the railing of the walkway, an act that forced Trash Head to lift and slam his entire weight repeatedly. While striking the metal balustrade with his back was painful, he could feel the biker's strength waning. Trash Head's eyes were blood red, as the oxygen his brain wasn't getting turned his head into a radish.

"GIVE UP!"

Trash Head's arms dropped to his side, his eyes rolled up into his head and his back arched. The big man fell back, struck the railing and broke it free. AJ released the big man, but without the use of his arms could not catch himself. He and Trash Head tumbled from the walkway down to the deck. The

595

fall lasted what seemed minutes and the best he could do was bend his legs for the impact. He landed squarely on the filthy cushions of a couch with an almost pleasant bounce. Trash Head did not. His massive frame struck the deck with a rapid, wince-inducing series of crunches, not unlike a bag of recyclables hitting the ground.

With no time to waste, AJ sprang from the couch and ran back up the walkway, his useless arms swinging wildly — comically, even.

"Rena! I'm at the controls!"

[There's no time!]

"I get it! Just tell me what to do!"

[What do you see?]

"A bunch of buttons and dials and shit. Um, a big screen. I — uh, wait! There are two big levers, one to each side of the chair."

[We can't stop it in time, AJ! The levers must steer the thing. Pull back on one of them!]

Attempts to move his arms did nothing.

No choice.

He bit down on the lever closest to him with his teeth and threw it backward with all of his strength.

Dice parked the truck sideways, covering the two center lanes, directly in the path of Pandora. He was the only thing now that stood between the tank and a wall of commuters,

596

many of whom had exited their vehicles and stood watching the spectacle.

This won't be enough, but it's all I can do.

He reached for the handle to exit the cab and machine-gun fire peppered the truck, shattering windows and covering him in glass. Taking cover on the floor of the cabin, he tried to place where the shots were coming from. Pandora would be on him any moment.

[Dice! Get the hell out of there!]

Dice sat up in the cabin to find the giant, square behemoth blotting out the sky. He tried to suppress the fear, but couldn't. He screamed, but couldn't even hear himself over the terrible roar of highway becoming mulch.

Ground highway and crushed car parts splashed into Dice's red truck, flipping it onto its head. Likewise, the Huntsmen who'd been swarming on Dice were buried in the debris. Pandora, as though controlled by God, turned on a dime. The left-most treads had reversed suddenly and were now tearing up the highway in the opposite direction. The earth mover, in turn, took a hard left and smashed through the center divide before crossing the opposite lane harmlessly to fall from the 101 superhighway.

Rena watched the terrible machine tumble and knock over a large electronic billboard in an amazing display of sparks before crashing to the street below in a nuclear

597

explosion of powdered concrete. All she could do was hope that AJ was alive inside.

As the cloud of debris rose above the 101 a thousand feet tall, she stripped the helmet from her head and threw it to the floor of the mobile command center.

"We did it!"

She tried to call to Williams, but vomited on her console instead.

21: One Too Many

"I watch you. I bet you didn't know that. I bet you didn't know that. I watch you all, Unit One, but you intrigue me most. I wonder what you'd be capable of without that sword of yours. I wonder if you would break and fold into a ball or fight me with your fists. These questions I ask myself regularly, 'Hero of the 101.'

I wonder if your tech detective will decode this and send you to me or if I will have to call unannounced. I hope for your sake it's the former. For my own selfish sake, I hope it's the latter."

- <Log_entry_u1_78766>Voice message #13,097 of SDC Mailcenter: co Unit One Sergeant Alec Jefferson Moore. Origin: VOIP via unregistered IP. User_note11034JX: "Incident not reported. Recipient not informed per Article 7a of the Consortium's Dictum on Inter-departmental Communications, specifically "threats should be assessed by both the Ministry of Operations and the Ministry of Internal Affairs and formally reviewed prior to disturbance of the agent of implication." Agent's supervisor will be notified, pending positive assessment of the threat by the appropriate parties.</Log_entry_u1_78766>

The Unit One sergeant climbed out of the car to find himself immediately surrounded. The flashes against the dark of night blinded him, forcing him to cover his eyes with his forearm.

"Sergeant Moore!"

"Sergeant Moore!"

As cameras stole about a million shitty photos, he covered his eyes and locked his face into what a Ministry of Media publicist had once called the "Hunter Surveying the Terrain" expression. He squinted his eyes, locked his jaw, and stared off into the middle distance. Apparently, statistically speaking, it was the expression least likely to produce internet memes.

Like this, he ignored questions for what seemed like a minute before his driver and two members of the Ministry of Media security force began driving the press back. Shielded by a small platoon of security now, they made their way to the front of the building. At the entrance, venue security opened the door for him. Once inside, he would have no opportunity to address the press, and so in the doorway, he turned to give them a minute, as he was explicitly instructed to do.

"One question," he said, raising a black, carbon-fibered finger.

"You gotta throw the unaffiliated press a bone. Otherwise, they're just gonna scribble some fiction that the Ministry'll have to redact or gag later, assuming those morons catch it," Williams had told him.

One reporter, a short and portly man with an epic mustache, shoved his way to the front of the group with such aggression that for a moment it looked as though a brawl might ensue. The man pointed a boom mic in his direction and cleared his throat lengthily. Above him hovered a trio of camera drones, each with their own tiny lens and light.

"Mark Nikolaev of the Sun City Chronicle!" the cylindrical man proclaimed.

AJ leaned his head in, his lips pursed (indicating attentiveness) and looked up, as though the heavens would yield all of the answers.

"Sergeant Moore, many see the events of last week as a turning point in the public perception of Unit One. In fact, one might say the State Defense Consortium as a whole. Others though, might suggest that your team's very involvement in the raid escalated what might have been a simple police matter. How would you respond to those people?"

Landmines, right out of the gate, he thought.

There were several approved tactics he'd learned from the Ministry of Media that he could employ here. *Indignation, feigned ignorance*, and *confusion* were a few.

Confusion was his favorite. Confusion peppered with indignation.

"That's a strange question," AJ replied. "Assuming that I understand you correctly, I would start by explaining to 'those people' that there are no 'simple police matters.' After that, I would probably have to respond with a few questions of

601

my own. Like, 'Would the SCPD appreciate being tasked with the recovery of commercial goods?' Or, 'Would the SCPD be equipped to fight what your colleagues are calling the 'greatest highway chase in this country's history?' And lastly, 'Would the SCPD, the under-manned, under-funded—

None of this is true...

—police force, already tasked with keeping the peace in the largest city in the Pacific State, have the resources and the know-how to achieve all of that without a single civilian casualty?'"

Nailed it. Take that!

"That was pretty much the answer I expected, Sergeant Moore," the reporter responded, his mustache seemingly laughing of its own accord. "Thank you."

Wait, what? What the fuck does that mean?

The reporter continued. "So, what would you say to reports of an undisclosed Agency Zero intervention days prior to the Unit One raid?"

"Well, I would—" He pretended to hear a voice over his right shoulder. "Really? Ok, coming! Look, good talk. I've gotta go. Thank you for the kind words. We really try our best and when you guys shower us with praise like this it just... well, it just makes it all worthwhile."

AJ waved to the sea of flashing lights, even as the reporter barked another question at him. Dipping behind one of MOM's agents, he slipped inside. Once the door was closed behind him, he exhaled and took a moment to go over his responses. After some time, he nodded to himself.

I'm good. I think I'm good.

Who the fuck was that guy?

Inside, he found the place packed. A world-famous music venue and bar, the Brick House resided in a tragically gentrified suburb of Section Two, not very far, as the crow flies, from the Veins. Inside the stuffed building were all of the State Defense Consortium's chief players. He saw members of the Consortium elite and their entourages, a few dozen orange-clad Agency Zero, the chief of the Sun City Police Department and his cadre, and the heads of both the Ministry of Media and the Ministry of Communications. He also saw a few celebrity notables. He saw a Mexican pop star whose name he couldn't remember, as well as the turtle-like back of what could only be the Valhalla heavyweight champion, Omar Garcia. And that was on his first scan of the first floor of the place.

"Unit One's at the bar upstairs," a MOM officer told him. "The upper deck is reserved for the guests of honor."

Finally. The red-carpet treatment we deserve. "Long time coming, huh?"

The Ministry of Media officer just smirked. "Have a great evening, sir."

AJ extended a fist, and the agent crashed his fist into it. Upon striking his metal fist the agent looked down, startled. Before the man could rein in his expression, AJ thought he caught a tinge of disgust... or pity.

603

"I turned my back and Dice was long gone. I saw the truck reverse out of the place and I swear to God, this guy" — he slapped the back of his hand against Dice's chest— "was smiling!"

Dice shrugged. "I was very happy. I've always wanted to drive a big rig. I was honking the hell out of that horn. It's too bad what happened to that truck." He looked legitimately sad. "We could have been friends."

The Brick House had been reserved by the SDC to celebrate what was being considered a big win for the Consortium. The capture of Trash Head, the most notorious highwayman in recent history, and (alleged) reclamation of stolen Deckar Applied Sciences ordnance had been achieved in spectacular, albeit destructive, fashion. 'Alleged' because the official Ministry of Communications message was that all stolen goods had been recovered when in reality only a very small portion had. However, according to Williams, DAS seemed more than satisfied with the result, so much so that they were footing the bill on the event.

From where the team sat, Unit One could look down at the whole of the venue and its packed main floor. Officials, most of which had nothing to do with the Crisis on the 101, crammed in front of the stage, drunk and dancing poorly to Top 40.

"Yeah, but why not stick around and help me take out Trash Head, buddy?" AJ continued, his expression that of

604

mock derision. "Rather than leaving me alone with a guy that's nine feet tall."

Dice wiggled a finger around in his ear and scrutinized what he found nonchalantly. "I'm not much of a punchy-punchy, kicky-kicky guy. I shoot people. I was going to shoot him, but my gun didn't work."

"You might have done better than me anyway. He shot me in the stomach with something that killed my arms and knocked out my lung."

"What do you mean?" Rena asked, sitting forward at the table.

"Wait," Dice interjected. "Listen to *my* story. My brand-new super space gun—"

"Wait!" Rena held a hand in Dice's face while looking to AJ. She urged him on. "Tell me about the gun Shaw shot you with."

Not much to tell, AJ thought, trying to conjure up a description. "I don't know. It was nondescript. It wasn't chrome, it wasn't large, it was just a plain *gun* shape, really."

"And your arms went limp?"

"Dead. I couldn't move them." AJ wobbled his arms around like octopus tentacles. This made Rena laugh, which made him very happy. "And my lung, the new one, went out. It was like breathing through a straw."

Chris, too, now perked up at this. "Did you mention this in your report?"

"Of course I did! It was like Trash Head flipped an invisible power switch. Hell, if I'd had two artificial lungs or an artificial heart, I'd be dead."

"It's gotta be some kind of EMP." Chris looked to Rena, his expression genuinely concerned. "If something like that were to hit the streets… we'd be in a lot of trouble."

Corporal Gonzales looked at her hand. It was new-looking and metallic red. She flexed it thoughtfully.

"You handled yourself well, Corporal," Chris said, leaning into her.

The corporal smiled and thanked him.

"*You* would be in a lot of trouble," Dice said, wagging a finger at the two of them. "That's why it's better to be all-natural. Like me!" He waved his hands over his torso. "Like grass-fed beef."

AJ looked at Dice and extended both hands in an attempt to sincerely drive his point home. "Please, try not to ever refer to yourself as 'beef,' 'beefy,' or any variation of 'beefdom,' ever, *ever* again."

Dice pretended he didn't understand AJ's English.

They sat and talked some more about the day now widely being called the "Crisis on the 101," and drank copiously. Before long, AJ's lids became heavy, his thoughts scattered and unfiltered. As he let his gaze wander from Rena's profile to the venue and its occupants, he tried to imagine Ace moving through the crowd, drink in hand, mingling… The thought was absurd.

No fucking way. He wouldn't touch this place with a rocket launcher. But Ace wasn't the only notable absence. "Where's Williams?"

"He'll be here," Rena replied. "No way he'll miss this. In a lot of ways, you know, this is a *big* 'fuck you' to our detractors."

"You mean Agency Zero?"

"And others…"

"Funny," Dice added, "they don't seem very anti-Unit One right now."

It's true, AJ thought. *Look at them.*

Unmistakable in their garish orange uniforms, Agency Zero represented at least a quarter of the room's occupancy, and nearly all of them were partying like *they* had just saved the people on the 101.

Looking down at the throng of people crammed onto the floor below turned his stomach. AJ looked away and fought back the urge to gag.

"It's a wonder you weren't killed," Rena said. "When I saw Pandora go over the side, I… I worried."

Her scent. She smelled of something sweet, something intoxicating. AJ let it envelop him, but was careful not to leer or lean inward.

"What *did* happen inside of that thing? And I don't mean this as an insult," Chris prefaced, "but what took you so long?"

He thinks he could have stopped Trash Head faster...
AJ found himself immensely and massively annoyed.

"Well look, *Lieutenant*. The place was full of bikers, and the cops started a fucking firefight. At the same time, there's a giant by the name of Trash Head with an EMP gun. Oh, and let me not forget to mention the people fucking!"

I'm not making sense...

"People fucking?"

"Yeah. Full-on 'I know you, you know me' *fucking*. And Trash Head is no joke. He almost killed me. I'd say he put up more of a fight than... than almost anybody I can remember."

Chris made a grave expression. "I believe you."

"Yeah," AJ continued, ranting now, "and as soon as I pulled the lever on that thing 'Pandora' or whatever... *omnishambles*. Everything went to Hell. Bikes, couches, *people*, and who knows what else, went flying in every direction. The whole *building* or whatever turned upside down!" His words were slurring horribly, but any attempt to enunciate properly made him sound British. AJ was drunk.

And then there were those damn levers... he thought.

"Get this!" AJ stood — which took a bit of effort — beer in hand. "So here I am, with no arms, mind you, trying to figure out these levers. And I *know* we're running out of time. I ended up doing one of *these*." He bent over and made an exaggerated biting motion. He then mimicked yanking the lever back with his teeth and in the process splashed beer onto the shoulder of Rena's crimson leather jacket.

"Oh, fuck me!"

Chris started chuckling, and soon he and Dice were roaring laughter.

Gonzales shook her head and made an expression that said: *You're lucky that wasn't my jacket.*

"Shit, Rena, I'm *so* sorry."

Dammit! I'm drunk.

He reached for the napkin dispenser at the center of the table.

"It's fine," she told him, a hand extended to keep him at bay, "forget it."

God, you look magnificent…

Rena wiped the shoulder of her jacket and frowned. "If this is ruined, I want cash! No excuses, AJ, no bullshit. Straight cash."

"Not a problem," AJ replied, "With the bonus I got for Trash—"

"La la la la! Nobody wants to talk money," Chris yelled, plugging his ears.

Dice nodded in agreement. "No stupid money talk. Let's do shots."

"On me," a voice interjected.

They turned to find Lieutenant Mason Bruce standing there.

"A round of whiskey shots for these four!" Mason yelled to the bartender.

"What kind of whiskey? We've got dozens." the bartender shot back.

"Whatever the well whiskey is," Mason responded almost angrily.

Well, I'll be damned, AJ thought. *Mason actually showed up.*

If Unit One had a black sheep, it was Lieutenant Mason Bruce. When he wasn't lording his rank over the unit, he was often attempting to micromanage them or otherwise subvert Williams' directives. It had earned him many nicknames among them. Chris' nickname for Bruce was 'Do Not Answer,' because he made it a point to never respond when Bruce called or pinged him over neurotrigger. 'Commander in Cheese' was Rena's nickname for him because she claimed (and this was yet-to-be-substantiated) that Lieutenant Bruce packed cheese sandwiches for lunch rather than eating the gratis lunch from the precinct food court. AJ's nickname for Mason was far simpler to divine and rolled off the tongue effortlessly: 'Poo-tenant.'

The bartender, a distracted-looking man with a name tag that read "Frank," acknowledged unenthusiastically and began pouring.

"Well whiskey, huh?" Chris chided, looking a little drunk himself. "Slow down, now, big spender."

Mason made a sour face. "Well, if you don't want them…"

"He's just tickling your undercarriage a bit," Rena told him. "Relax."

"Don't worry," Mason replied dryly, "I won't be sticking around. I felt obligated to provide an update. That's the only reason I'm here."

Over the sound of the music, Mason was practically screaming.

"John Shaw, 'Trash Head,' who's been at Cedar Medical since the incident, appears likely to recover from his injuries," he told them. "As I'm sure you all know, this is fantastic news. I am confident that, once faced with the list of charges the SDC and SCPD are prepared to indict him with, he will be compelled to divulge the names and locations of his Huntsmen officers, his black-market buyers, and perhaps more."

"You can't be serious, Mason," AJ replied. "Do you really think a guy like Trash Head is going to turn State's evidence?" He looked to Dice, who returned his smirk. Mason's naiveté was funny.

The bartender delivered the shots in person, coming out from behind the bar to line them up at the table. The morose-looking man bowed awkwardly and walked away, the weight of the universe clearly on his shoulders.

"There's a chance," Mason replied indignantly. "But anyway, on behalf of the SDC, I just wanted to say, 'Damn

611

fine work, agents!'" He picked up a shot and held it out to them.

Dice, not bothering to toast, drank first. Rena downed her shot next, and Chris followed.

AJ looked down at the shot with dread. *I've had enough, I think...*

"Come on, AJ," Dice spurred.

Aww man, am I going to blow chunks if I drink this?

"Come on, AJ, do it."

This is not good... This is how people die...

He picked up the shot from the table and studied the brown liquid.

Cheap whiskey, too?

He threw the shot down and, like a liquid boomerang, it immediately fought to resurface in his esophagus.

Meanwhile, Dice stood and offered a hand to Mason. "You're a good man," he said, almost authentically.

Mason smiled with a closed mouth and patted Dice on the shoulder. At the same time, he pulled his hand away and wiped it against his blazer. "Thank you, Deputy *Informant.*"

Did Mason just wipe his hand... Or am I drunk? He did emphasize 'informant...' I think we all caught that. What a dick. AJ's thoughts were scrambled, but he'd succeeded in keeping the whiskey shot down. *Whatever. It's so cool having everybody here like this...*

AJ suddenly found himself filled with emotions and opinions, all of them right.

The only people not *here are Williams and Ace...* A few seconds later: *We should do a chant.*

"Unit-One! Unit-One! Unit-One!"

After screaming 'Unit One' over deafening motor-rock, AJ stopped to find his colleagues staring at him. Rena looked at him with arched brows, while Chris and Dice rolled their eyes before re-engaging in their own conversation.

That was lame. I shouldn't have done that.

The room was moving now, rotating around him both directions at once, paradoxically. AJ took a deep breath. At the same time, the bass from the band playing below only served to further distort his perception. He gripped the table as if he could stop or at least *steer* the spinning room.

Chris stood up. "It's time."

Rena immediately began catcalling. Her screams at such close range were piercing.

"Where the fuck are you going?" AJ asked.

Dice laughed. "He's going to show us all how to put on a show."

"You're performing?"

"My band is, yes."

"No shit?"

AJ had heard his partner's songs on the radio, and on a few occasions met a few of Chris' rocker friends, but he'd never actually seen him perform. Even drunk, the idea was less than appealing.

Where the hell is Ace? he thought suddenly, his mind in free fall. *He can't be here for my big day? He's never around—*

A hand took him by the forearm. It was Rena.

"Let's get some air, champ."

'Champ?' She never calls me 'champ.' That's what you call drunk people. Wait. I'm the drunk guy. Have I been acting a fool? Oh my God! Did I fall? I didn't throw up, did I?

He looked down at his shirt. He wore a black, short-sleeved button-up by a local designer named Rocco Sphinx. The shirt had a high collar, and buttons that were black opals. Embedded in the shirt's inner lining were LEDs that emitted lavender light. The effect was like a subtle aura. His jeans were loose-fitting and factory-distressed. His shoes, black high-top retros with white tread, complemented the outfit flawlessly. On his belt hung a platinum chain with his badge, and around his neck was a diamond-encrusted dog-tag with the Unit One logo.

"I look good," he muttered. *You're not even that drunk, man*, he lied to himself. *Just keep it together.*

At Rena's prompt, he stood up and almost fell forward. He righted the ship, but not before drawing a glimmered smirk from Dice.

"Let's just go for a walk outside, AJ."

He let Rena lead him down the stairs. Once at the bottom, he was immediately greeted by Corporal Lin, the blue-haired Unit One recruit. Lin, surprisingly enough, seemed less concerned about making his way upstairs to be with the rest of

614

Unit One and more so genuinely happy to see them. He greeted Rena with a firm handshake and smiling eyes.

"Good to see you, Detective Constable."

"You as well, Corporal Lin."

Lin then turned to him and extended a fist.

Does he know that I don't like handshakes? Bashing his fist into Lin's, he patted the recruit on the shoulder. *I should give him words of encouragement...*

"Most new recruits die like right away. You should *not* do that, Corporal. Don't — you're listening, right — die. *Don't* die! And especially not right away. That shit would just be embarrassing."

"Ok," Rena said, squeezing AJ's bicep. "Let's get you away from people. Have a good evening, Corporal Lin."

Lin, with a kind smile, thanked her before walking away.

Fighting through the crowd only added to his nausea.

"Unit One, guys! This is them," someone yelled.

"Detective Bryant! Way to go!"

"Attaboy, Moore!"

After an excruciatingly troublesome time, they made it through the crowd and to the patio area in the rear of the venue. The whole time, despite the noise and chaos, AJ found himself acutely aware of Rena's grip on his arm. Even through a network of tactile-to-synapse translation, her hand on his arm carried *weight*, emotional weight.

She never touches me. She's touching me...

Outside, the air was chilly and the stars hidden. Reporters stalked in the dark with their night vision cameras, held at bay by a squadron of venue security and Ministry of Media muscle.

The patio was modest but comfortable. It had lounge chairs and a tiny, manned bar, accompanied by an outdoor fireplace. The few people currently there, likely due to the live acts going on, added to the charm.

Rena released his arm and he moved to lean against the red brick wall. A deep breath helped to clear his mind, or so he thought.

Cigarette smoke also filled the patio area, held in place by a canopy. The smell of cigarettes had always disgusted him.

Rena came to stand beside him, also leaning against the brick, a half-smile on her face.

I know that look... I've fucked up. She's going to rattle off SDC regulation, just like Ace. I got too drunk. "Have I made a fool of myself?" he asked sheepishly.

"No, AJ. Not even close."

"I didn't throw up?"

"No. You did not throw up. But you looked like you might, so I thought it best we get some air."

"I'm fine," he replied, waving a hand. "It's just noisy in there."

"Well, it's about to get noisier. I don't know if you caught it, but Chris is taking the stage soon."

"Oh, that's cool. You gonna go watch him?"

"Aren't you?"

The idea, the notion of supporting his partner's *other* occupation didn't appeal to him in the least.

Chris is Unit One, he thought bitterly. *He should focus on being Unit One.* "Nah, I think I'll chill here for a bit."

She seemed to contemplate that in silence. She smiled and it was lovely.

Her hair was down and had been highlighted with streaks of magenta. Beneath her leather jacket she wore a grey V-neck tee and copper-colored jeans. She looked terrific.

Thinking about her apartment and the abysmal state in which he'd seen it had him contemplating her personal life. *Is she back now? Back to normal?* He drunkenly considered asking her directly.

Her expression was almost apologetic as she moved a step closer. "I wanted to thank you."

"For what?"

"For not telling anyone."

"Telling anyone what?"

"About the mess of my apartment, of… me. About *my* mess."

In the blue light cast by the logo of the Brick House, she looked regal. She projected the blue back to the world, that which her brown eyes had not overwritten. Her makeup was subtle and yet effective, and her skin seemed cast in porcelain. He extended an arm for her, no conscious thought required to do so. As she moved within range he could not help but

617

compare the twisting gears, oiled joints, and black carbon fiber of his own arms to her natural flawlessness. The contrast, in this moment, was terrifying. He opened his mouth and nothing sensible came out.

Rena... I should tell you...

He was lost; removed psychologically, intellectually, and emotionally from anything that wasn't Detective Constable Rena Bryant and her red leather jacket. As his fingers came to touch her waist, tactile sensors flooded his mind with signals, all of them warnings. All of them to be ignored.

"AJ..."

He straightened his back against the brick and tried to lure her closer.

God, I wish I was sober. Am I crossing the line?

"I'm fixing things with Yushin," she said.

His hand left her side for his own as though holstering a pistol.

"I just wanted you to know."

Oh my God... What have I done?

His mind raced for a way out, the behemoth that was soul-crushing rejection bearing down on him. "Okay? What does that have to do with me?"

She pursed her lips and made a skeptical expression.

Fool! You stupid, drunk fool.

She blushed. Even in the dark, he could see it. "Ok, well, I just thought that... Well, never mind I guess." She laughed nervously. "It's just that... well, you and Yushin kind of know each other, I guess. I just thought you should know so that when you see him it won't be weird."

I need good words, he thought in a panic. *What would Dice say in this situation? What would Ace say? What would I say if I could think straight?* "I didn't want to date you anyway. I mean, we're not even the same age."

Never in his life had he lied so egregiously.

Just kill yourself...

Her expression was incredulous, her smile more of a knowing smirk now.

"Hey!" she said. "Chris is on. We should go back inside. How are you feeling?"

Like shit. "I'm fine. Yeah, let's go watch Chris—" — *play his guitar and be fucking cooler than me. Dammit! I'm an idiot. Why did I say that? What did I think was going to happen? She's not into me and I'm stupid. And drunk. Stupid drunk! Stupid! Stupid!*

On the way inside she walked ahead of him. No more holding of the arm.

Lights flashed from the black beyond the patio, and he could picture the little man with the mustache fighting to get a clean photo of him getting rejected by his work crush.

He raised a middle finger in the direction of the camera flashes and went back inside.

As long as I don't puke I'm fine.

The entirety of the venue, once word got out that Unit One's own would be performing, had massed in front of the stage. On it, Lieutenant Chris Calderon, now acting under the stage-name "Crusher Calderon," stood shirtless. He held a rusted metal guitar with a chain shoulder-strap, and leaned in to the microphone.

"Thank you for coming out! I know you all know me as Lieutenant Chris Calderon of Unit One, but as some of you know, that's only one half of this coin. If you would all be so kind, I would like to show you the other side of that coin. I've been making music in some form or fashion since I was old enough to bang on shit. And to be able to perform in front of my team and my colleagues in the SDC is a treat. With that, hold on to your butts, you motherfuckers! We are Sin Tacks! ARE YOU READY TO FUCKING ROCK, SDC?"

AJ looked up at his partner, his rival, on stage.

I've never heard Chris talk like that... Is this how he really is? Fucking potty mouth...

So caught up in Sin Tacks and the loud and energetic show they were putting on, he'd at some point lost Rena. Now, he stood among the mob gathered before the stage, surrounded and yet very alone. Occasionally someone he didn't know would come up and congratulate him. He did not speak to these people. He simply nodded and smiled weakly. Anything more in this state was dangerous.

Rena doesn't love me. Hell, she probably doesn't even like me.

That's nonsense, he responded to himself a few moments later.

But is it? She's getting back together with a guy so dull she'd rather be unconscious in a VR world than spend time with him. And yet he's still preferable to you... What does that say?

What does that say?

He stood, surrounded by colleagues on what was the biggest day of his professional life, and might as well have been stranded in the Sahara.

What, are you going to pout now? It was Ace's voice in his head... at least his own drunken version of his brother's gritty speech.

I'm healthy, I have money, and I'm — at the very least — moderately attractive. And, I'm undeniably the best dresser in the SDC.

It didn't take long for ego repair to turn into salt distribution...

Yushin is a nerd and not the cool kind. I'm AJ-fucking-Moore!

The crowd was cheering now.

He looked around, perplexed. *What happened to the music?*

Jostled around by the crowd, lost in his own head, he no longer had his bearings.

Wait a minute... Chris was just on stage, wasn't he?

"AJ."

Someone gripped his wrist. There was a woman standing next to him now. Her shoulder was touching his. She was looking up at him. A beautiful, brown face, framed in curls.

"Mahina?"

"Congratulations, AJ!"

"For what?"

"For being the 'Hero of the 101,' silly. Your face is on every channel in Sun City right now. They keep replaying the scene of you climbing from the wreckage of that... *thing.*"

She's talking. I know that much. But why... how is Mahina here? I'm still at Brick House, aren't I?

Mahina was clearly excited. Her lips were moving quickly now and words were flying at him like Huntsmen bullets.

She's talking, that's for sure. He craned his head forward to try and make sense of her words, and lurched into her.

"You feeling ok?" She had her hands on his shoulders now, steadying him on his feet.

Sometimes when he was really drunk, his left eye would go lazy on him. Conscious of this and not wanting to let the eye wander on Mahina, he made a concerted effort to control his pupils.

"Why are you looking at me like that?" she asked.

She wore a teal skirt and knee-high boots the color of amber, an ornate bronze cross on her neck, and a leather

622

bracelet embedded with micro-projectors that sent holograms of daisies slowly rotating around her wrist. Daisies had always been Mahina's favorite.

Mahina? Whoa, what is she doing here?

"Mahina? W-who invited you?"

"I did."

Chris, at some point, had changed his whole "look." He was no longer topless, tattoos oiled-looking beneath the stage lights. His hair was high and swept forward in feathered spears. His face was still shiny with sweat, and his signature bandana was wrapped around his neck. Though clothed now, his shirt was still open, exposing his chest and abdomen.

"You were *just* on stage," AJ told him.

Chris laughed. "Are you drunk?"

"You were *just* on stage."

"Yeah, I was, for four songs. You were standing right here the whole time."

AJ's stomach churned. He reached for a bar or a railing or something, and did not find one. He staggered and slipped a little, but caught himself. It felt like everyone was staring at him now. And, as he surveyed the crowd, it *looked* like everyone was staring at him. He focused on the faces he knew, careful to keep his eyes wide, lest the left one attempt to wander.

How did I get this drunk?

Images of brown liquor filled his mind's eye, and he could feel his face scrunch up. It was then that Chris, now standing very close to Mahina, placed a hand on the small of her back.

"Whatthefuggeryoudoing?"

"Are you okay, AJ?" a voice asked.

"He looks green," another voice said.

He cupped his hands to try and stem the tide, but all it did was disperse the mess outward, like sprinklers. An explosion of beer, whiskey, and portobello and arugula salad sprayed against his hands and outward onto the people surrounding him.

Oh no. Jesus, no. Buddha, no. What have I done?

His stomach felt lassoed; as though someone was tugging on it. People were yelling but their words made no sense. People were flailing but their movements only served to spin the room faster.

Just need to get outside…

He took a step forward but slipped. He tried to catch himself but the spinning room had gotten the best of him. He knew early that this would not be a graceful fall, so he closed his eyes and folded his arms across his chest like a vampire in its casket.

I'm finished. Life is over.

He hit the deck and no, it was not graceful.

#SDC Investigations Secured Channel 43::

[03:11] <W8less1> You there?

[03:16] <Rora_Dice!> hello rena

[03:16] <W8less1> Simon Pan's murderer, I know who she is

[03:18] <Rora_Dice!> everyone knows about the Party Crasher

[03:18] <W8less1> I know who she is, to *you*

[03:26] <Rora_Dice!> what are you doing rena?

[03:26] <W8less1> Specifically? Looking at an Affidavit of
Competence to Marry for one Madison Grünewald,
legitimizing union with one Yamazaki Daisuke. There are
parents' names listed for both sides if you don't believe me.
You were pretty young

[03:26] <Rora_Dice!> rena. what do you want?

[03:26] <W8less1> I just want — NEED — to understand
what you're thinking. How did you think we wouldn't find
out?

[03:26] <W8less1> You need to meet me. In person. You need
to make me understand this, Dice.

Rora_Dice! has ended the chat session.

22: Sand Castle

"They're no different than the Gestapo or the Khmer Rouge. The only reason you see them differently today is that they have something those others didn't: a go-to-market strategy."

- Thiago Garcia

"Do you know what the *zeitgeist* is?"

Thiago paced, looking everyone at the head of the crowd in the eye.

"Sexy Totalitarianism!"

There were many familiar faces in the crowd, and this speech was in no way new material. The folks applauding at this knew exactly where he was headed. And the extra attention he paid to these loyal men and women paid dividends in applause.

"That's right, Sexy Totalitarianism. It looks good, it tastes great, and it's music to your ears… at first."

He pointed specifically to a man in the crowd who stood, pinned against the barricade, holding a sign of shoe polish–painted cardboard that read, "S.D.C. = State Disinformation Corporation." It was partially true, like most everything.

"Do you know what that means?"

"Tell me," the man replied.

"It means: I'll blanket your neighborhood in closed-circuit television cameras. It means: I get to slap a meter on your front door, on your water faucet, and on your car, and if you're late on a bill, or accused of a crime, *any* crime, I get to lock you out and kill your right to vote. It means do as I say or I'll sic my paramilitary hit squad on you. Obey me, or I'll send my sideshow of sword-wielding super cops after you. And who knows what will happen then! Maybe I'll detonate a bomb and blame it on you. Maybe I'll destroy your block with a fucking tank and blame it on motorcycle punks. I mean, who knows?" He shrugged dramatically for emphasis. "Maybe I'll conjure up the spectre of a super-assassin of a thousand-plus murders to cover up what we all know to be extra-judicial kidnappings and assassinations. After all, I'm the State Defense Consortium and I can do whatever I want!"

The crowd began booing.

"But wait! It's okay because Sexy Totalitarianism looks good. It gives you pop stars on holo-ads, movie actors on billboards and athletes on the television telling you a hundred times a day that these things are here to protect you, to make you safe. You see, you and I are all a bunch of idiots in their eyes. 'You need Libra to protect you from the Russians and the Chinese!' they say. 'You need Agency Zero to protect you from the terrorists. And you need Unit One to protect you from the cartels and the mafia. Trust us,' these bourgeois liars tell us!

"Meanwhile, the State drugs your water supply and clones your food!"

The cloning thing was not true, to his knowledge, but it worked so he rolled with it.

"It fills the sky with hover units to x-ray scan your home in the dead of night. 'This is for your safety!'" he screamed in a mocking voice. "That's what they say!

"They fill the bay with their industrial waste and send your jobs to Brazil, to Peru, and to Argentina. Meanwhile, they build factories over our dilapidated blocks, only to fill them with foreign workers."

Thiago had the crowd wound tightly now. Beneath the afternoon sun, he could feel their anger churning, propelling him like a full sail and fair winds. He used the microphone to channel their anger, to reshape it and project it back to them.

"But it's all good," he continued, "because the face of your oppression is young and sexy. Your oppressors wear Skyy shoes, ride expensive motorcycles, and make cameos in your favorite movies. They party and live like celebrities at night, only to brutally police our streets by day. Our oppressors are the new samurai caste, the new knights! Sounds cool, right?

Well, my brothers and sisters, what does that make *you*?"

"Serfs!" someone screamed.

"Serfs, peasants, peons, and proles! We have become less than the working class in their eyes. We are less than human to them. Hell, they will cut you down with impunity."

He laughed. "'With impunity?' They get bonuses! They've *gamified* oppression!

"They *pose* as you! They wear regular clothes and talk like you. But are they really like you? Can you swap body parts out when you get bored? Will you live twice as long as the average person, thanks to a million dollars' worth of nano-machine injections? I don't think so!

"So why do you kowtow to the ruling class? Why do you look up to the military State? Could it be Stockholm Syndrome?" He shrugged. "I don't know…" He *did* know. At least he thought he did.

"Sexy Totalitarianism means doing away with a trial by peers, just so long as the execution is *televised* and performed by a punk with a flaming ninja sword."

"Sexy Totalitarianism means more police in places like Section Seven, but *never* on the corners where the Titans peddle their poison or where the *yaks* keep their whorehouses and casinos. Of course, they don't police *there*, because *that's* big business. That's *sexy*! Drugs are *sexy*! Prostitution is *sexy*!

"Sexy Totalitarianism means tanks on the streets and half-human androids with big guns and swords protecting the ruling class… from *you*.

"Let me repeat that: 'protecting the ruling class from *you*.' From you! Isn't that rich? They're scared of you!"

Many in the crowd began to applaud and cheer. It was that time.

"It wasn't *you* that pushed for secession and repealed *habeas corpus* and *posse comitatus*. I mean, after all, it wasn't *you* that murdered two-hundred and sixty of your own citizens and blamed it on a mythical figure."

The crowd erupted.

"Oh yeah, I said it! LDB, the Liberty Day Bombing, was *their* doing. LDB was *their* doing! Not some renegade North Korean general. Not some internationally recognized but universally invisible super-terrorist. Changgok doesn't fucking exist. Look it up! Don't let me tell you! Look it up! *The SDC* set those bombs. They set those bombs and blamed it on a man that no one can prove *ever* even existed. *They* did that, not *you*, and yet they're afraid of *you*!"

More people were arriving, even though his speech was nearly finished. As he stood atop a rusting shipping container in an abandoned part of the now-defunct Port of Sun, he looked out on his people, his *followers*. They were gathered in one of the few areas known to not be covered by Libra.

"Isn't that about the craziest damn thing you've ever heard of?"

He ran a hand through his hair and shook his head before chuckling. "Yeah, it's fucking crazy, right!"

He was fairly certain that this claim was accurate. *Moderate-to-fairly certain.*

What difference does it make really? he thought. *The SDC is corrupt and that's undeniable.*

Nevertheless, this was the part of the speech where he would typically dial the rhetoric down a bit and adopt a more moderate, inclusive tone. It was time for the sales pitch…

The goal, after all, was to *galvanize* the people, not *radicalize*. He wasn't a cult leader…

"There are a lot of people here, man, a *lot* of people! That's good. That means people are waking up. The message is being heard!" He rubbed his chin. "You know, maybe they're right to be afraid of you!"

People began cheering once more, as they were *supposed* to.

"Some of you must be wondering how I know all this, yeah?"

Thiago wore smart-denim jeans and a shirt that depicted Premier William Macek's face superimposed over the uniformed torso of Josef Stalin. The caption below the image read, "*I do my dirt on the low-low.*"

He paused for dramatic effect, at which time he engaged in banter off-mic with the people in the front row. It was also an opportunity for him to catch his breath. There was very little shade where they were, and he was sweating profusely.

After a long, dramatic sigh, he brought the mic to his lips once more. "I know this because I was once one of them."

An exclamation rose from the newbies in the crowd, a crowd now numbering in the hundreds.

This always gets them, he thought. *It's always the same.*

He held his arms out and banged the mic against his chest. "Take a look at the face of evil. Thiago Garcia was one of the elite!"

When the crowd's surprise died down, and after no shortage of physical theatre, he continued. "Anyone know who my brother is?"

"Omar!" the crowd returned.

"That's right, Omar Garcia! That's right! The Valhalla Heavyweight Champion of the World, Unified Fight League Heavyweight Champion of the World, and Honor Asia League Heavyweight Champion of the World, Omar Garcia, is my big brother."

He adopted a fighter's stance, careful to do everything wrong. "What? You don't see the resemblance?" He flexed for them, knowing his tattooed arms hadn't lifted a dumbbell in more than a decade.

The crowd laughed, as usual, as they were supposed to.

"Truth is, I was a millionaire-by-association when I was fourteen! By my nineteenth birthday, I'd been to every country worth visiting, owned and totaled two million-dollar cars, and been to the Academy Awards three times."

The sun was baking them now, and many in the audience were using their signs as cover.

"I don't think you guys realize what true fame is. I mean, Beastly G is famous, Catarina Mina is famous, and that jackass pundit on *Inside Sun City* is famous, right? Wrong!

632

These people are rich and popular, not wealthy and famous. In the grand scheme of things, none of these people are shit!"

He paused to catch his breath, pacing feverishly. This was when he was *supposed* to appear agitated.

Repeating the same stuff over and over has to be the most taxing thing a person can do, he thought, careful to keep his boredom in check... visually.

"I probably don't need to explain to you just how famous my brother is, considering half of you are wearing the Ozone brand right now. For the one or two of you who don't know, the Omar Garcia brand, the Ozone brand, is a multi-billion-dollar business with multiple, competing clothing lines, athletic and entertainment promotions, a record label, and a fitness supplement line. My brother's popularity is such that his last fight sold a whopping three million pay-per-view buys. At $130 a pop, that's a record take, second only to the 'Landing at Normandy Interactive Experience.'

"The Garcia Estate owns a fleet of private jets. These jets take him to his homes in Rio, Caracas, Las Vegas, Tokyo, New York, and London. Last year, for the fourth consecutive year, mind you, my brother was named the wealthiest athlete in the world. The runner-up was Leonis Martin... You know, the footballer whose face has been plastered on every billboard in Sun City since work on the new stadium began? Martin's net wealth came in at just under one-tenth of the combined Garcia estate. And Martin just bought one of the Greek islands for himself!

"Get the picture yet?"

He paused for a long time to let the crowd process the numbers. This was the point in the speech when the realization of just how much capital he had access to drew in the stragglers. The crowd stood wide-eyed, the idea of infinite wealth swimming in their minds like the remnants of a fantastic daydream.

I'm no anti-establishment scrub, no anarchist, no socialist, no secessionist, and no technophobe. I am the real deal because I am elite, he could tell them. *Where others failed in halting the Octumvirate agenda, I will succeed! Because I can think like them…*

"My brother has a saying; a timeless token among fighters really. It goes: 'If you want to *be* the man you have to *beat* the man.' Well, that's true, but it also works in reverse. I believe that if you want to *beat* the man, sometimes you have to *be* the man!

"I know these people because — of course — they approached my brother. At first, and probably because my brother was so young, they started with my father. Gifts, prestigious visits, invites to lavish parties, etcetera, etcetera… But when they realized that Omar is who he is because he doesn't listen to our father, they tried our mother. And when they realized that she had no interest in that lifestyle, they finally, reluctantly, approached my brother directly.

"You see, when you break that wall, that monetary barrier that separates the *thems* from the *us*, you don't have to seek out the elite. By that point, they already know who you are. In fact, by then, they already know everything about you. They know your strengths, your weaknesses, your fears, and most importantly... your desires!

"They hit us with the golden sink. Parties, gifts, business partnerships, insider tips on investments... Whenever we got in trouble, that trouble vanished without so much as a phone call. I mean, they made my brother, and me by extension, invincible.

"And they didn't just send the celebrities or the athletes to woo us. Oh, no! Those people are pawns for the Octumvirate. When they have a real need for you, they send senators, moguls, and presidents. They send the Gods of Industry. They send the rooks, the bishops, and the knights. When they realized they wanted Omar, they sent the president of Argentina to call on us.

"Imagine that; the President of Argentina pining to speak with *your* big brother because he punches and kicks people exceptionally well. The whole thing is insane.

"They look just like you and me, the men behind the curtains, but they know each other under different names. The Order of the Snake, Order of the Pharaoh, Order of the North Star. That's what they go by... Order of the Minaret, Order of the Spider, Order of the Assassin."

I have them. He looked down at them from his elevated platform and did his best to contain a sneer. It was becoming too easy. In the early days, there were debates. Oh, how he missed the debates…

"Their power lies in secrecy. They meet in secret chambers in some of the most remote places on Earth or beneath the waves in submersibles — fucking submarines! They meet on deserted islands and in areas illegitimately quarantined. We've proof of this! Armed guards with explicit orders to 'shoot on sight' guard their meetings because they know that if the truth of what they discuss ever got out, they wouldn't be able to hold back the tide.

"When they finally got their hooks into my brother Omar, it was 'promote the now-defunct Space Elevator project!' The dead, asinine project that our grandchildren's grandchildren will still be paying for. That half-finished eyesore on the horizon that looks like a middle finger to us all. After that, they wanted him to be an ambassador for the Libra spy network, to appear in adverts, to speak out against opponents… Basically, his job was to align his brand with whatever they needed him to. And, in exchange, they would groom him for a life in politics after fighting. *That* was the plan!"

The crowd was silent. As the sun began to take his back, he could see their expressions through manual visors, beneath signs acting as umbrellas. He wound up for the punchline.

"What they didn't take into account, though — is that my brother is dumber than a solar-powered flashlight."

636

The people gathered before him burst into laughter. He absorbed it, welcomed it. He let it crescendo uninterrupted. And when the laughter and applause finally died down a bit, he chuckled along with them, as though he hadn't said that joke a hundred times.

"I mean, they must have known. The man gets punched in the face and choked unconscious for a living! For 'elites,' I swear these people are dumb as shit sometimes."

This is the part they love most... Ridicule the Octumvirate. Demote them and promote the people.

"I imagine they thought my dear brother was 'a work in progress,' or something correctable." He shook his head emphatically. "Nope! I'm here to tell you, unequivocally, that my brother, Omar Garcia, is a brick. Always has been and always will be, a molded, fired, brick."

They were roaring laughter now, but this part of the speech was not easy for Thiago. Omar was not a bright man, this was fact, but he was a good man, and if he knew that he was a punchline, reused for the purposes of influence, he would be heartbroken.

"I love him," he told the crowd honestly. "I love my brother, but it's true! He has the body of a bear and a heart to match, but goddammit" —he started mock-laughing— "what made these people think that they could confide in him is beyond me. Day one, he told me *everything*! He told me how they only gather in groups of eight, at the highest levels, and how they have a headquarters at the top of the Horus Tower, right here in Sun City.

"He also told me that, ironically, everything they do is done by vote.

"Let's pause on this for a second. Isn't that funny? They afford themselves democracy but deny us ours."

"The appointment of the Premier; now, was that done by vote?"

"NO!"

"Was the establishment of Libra a bill or even a Council resolution?"

"NO!"

"Of course it wasn't!"

Thiago sat down on the edge of the container, playing up the role of the exhausted messenger. He kicked his feet playfully and dangled the microphone from his fingers as though he wasn't sure if he wanted to continue.

Rehearsed. Every motion had been rehearsed meticulously, obsessively.

"Everything I've told you is true, everything! Now what you decide to do with the information is up to you. You can go back to your homes in the Veins, in Bayshore, in Hunter's Peninsula." With each district, he pointed at a segment of the crowd, guaranteed to strike home with at least a few people.

"You can go back to the Bricks, to Old Chinatown, to the Swamp, and pretend we never had this discussion. Frankly, I wouldn't blame you. You can feed your children sludge water from the tap and slip back down onto the couch for more televised execution — or porn... I mean, like I said: the flavor of Sexy Totalitarianism is good. Who am I to judge you if you want to keep sipping?"

He propped himself up on an arm, still kicking his legs like a child seated at the edge of a dock.

"Or" —he held a finger in the air, as though struck by genius, and pointed to them— "you can show up on at the Liberty Day parade in City Center, along with a million of *your* brothers and sisters, and together *we* can let the Eight know that we've had enough."

He jumped to his feet, appearing shocked awake by the notion.

"Yes, you can come out and help us remind them that *we* are Sun City!"

Spattering applause... tough crowd. Good thing I'm not finished.

"Right now, they're celebrating the chaos that they started on the 101; the destruction unleashed on this city's poorest district. At the same time, they're setting up checkpoints, installing even more cameras, and conscripting private police. They're activating Agency Zero. They're sending Unit One to the parade, *our* parade! And the SCPD will be out in full riot gear, ready to greet you. This is fact! Because, after all, this is a celebration, is it not? A celebration of FREEDOM! A celebration of LIBERTY! And a celebration of the souls lost on that horrible day when..." He whirled,

639

clenching the microphone in both fists. "THEY KILLED YOUR BROTHERS AND SISTERS!"

As the crowd cheered and then broke into chants of "THIAGO, THIAGO," he scanned the masses for her. When his gaze finally met hers beneath the afternoon sun, he felt replenished. Only then did the effort seem worth it. He stomped his feet and roared into the microphone until the crowd threatened rampage.

Thiago and a small detachment of Fifth Estate "revolutionaries" rode back to their headquarters in a nondescript van older than he was. Older even than the movement itself. In the cargo compartment, he sat opposite *her*, the only person at the rally whose attendance had been vital. He stared at her until she finally lowered her hood and returned his smile.

"That was amazing," she told him in a thick French accent.

"You're too kind," he replied, feigning humility.

"The way they respond to you and the way you speak to them… it's mesmerizing. It must scare you to have such responsibility."

"Scare me? Why would it?"

"They trust your every word. What if you are wrong?"

Thiago smiled and reached for her hands. His tattooed arms were mere bones, pale in contrast to her dark and slender hands.

"The fact that you understand this is what makes you so special, Vivianne."

He took her hands in his and caressed the back of them with his thumbs. As they sat staring face to face, the van swept up onto the freeway and out of Section Seven. He could feel the ancient vehicle change gears, as the driver merged into the fast lane and accelerated.

"So you were wealthy at a young age?"

"A playboy jet-setter, I was."

"And what changed you? Why do this now?"

Should I tell her? What if she…

He had weighed the pros and cons of being forthright with her some time ago.

"Archer's Disease. I have Archer's Disease."

He released her hands, in case she wanted to pull away from him. Her large eyes seemed to tremble for a moment before falling. She did not take her hands away, but rather placed them on his knees. She looked at the floor and shook her head slowly. "I'm so sorry."

He'd come to terms with his condition long ago, but her reaction nonetheless rocked him.

"One in a thousand wannabe MODS acquire Archer's Disease," he said. "Guess I'm just that lucky."

"I've read a little about it but I just… it sounds so awful I just couldn't imagine," she told him, her voice barely a whisper.

The effects of Archer's Disease, also known as *Cytocidal Calculia*, could best be described as 'random cellular cannibalism.'

Selfishly and somewhat mercilessly he prodded her. "What have you read?"

Vivianne sat up and moved about uncomfortably. "I don't know... that's it's fatal. That it's..."

That it pits the body against itself. That I'll die slowly, miserably, organs failing with nothing but suicide as an alternative to living decay.

Thiago smiled mirthlessly. "I've accepted my fate."

Vivianne swallowed. "And how, may I ask? How did you acquire Archer's?"

"Well, drugs and alcohol destroyed my kidneys to start," he told her, cocking his head back and biting his lip. "And the plan was to swap them out for a synthetic pair. Like most rich people these days, I thought I could shuck my responsibilities and start the process of self-destruction anew. It was during the procedure that I contracted Archer's."

"That's terrible."

"Is it? Or is it justice?"

She looked up from the floor, her eyes very sad. "No, Thiago, not justice. Never say that again."

The look on her face was sincere and it made him feel like shit for being so artificially cavalier. "I'm sorry."

"But there are treatments now... I thought there were treatments."

"Treatments?" He didn't mean to scoff. "One could hardly call the only option a 'treatment.' The only 'cure' for Type II Archer's is vitals transfer."

Vivianne clenched his knees powerfully. "Then you must take this treatment!"

He shook his head. "Imagine, Vivianne, waking up with no legs, no body, and no face, but that which they give you, assuming you even survive the procedure. Even then, more than half the patients that survive go insane from depersonalization. I don't know if living, at the cost of a new body, a new *me*, is really worth it."

"It would still be *you*."

Thiago made an incredulous face, smirking. "Would it?"

Vivianne looked as though she might reply, but didn't.

"I don't really want to get into a philosophical debate on the nature of self, but, as far I am concerned, 'thanks but no thanks.' And it doesn't help that the procedure is disgustingly expensive, even for someone like me. If I were to invest in that, it wouldn't leave me with the resources to fund the Fifth Estate movement."

"So, what then?"

"I have a nanoparticle treatment that sustains me, well," —he lifted his shirt to reveal large black splotches of decaying flesh— "as best it can."

Vivianne sat back and folded her arms. Like this, she looked at him in silence. For some time, they traveled this way.

643

After a while, arms still folded, she asked, "But what good are you to them dead?"

"Truth be told, love, I'm not much good to them alive."

"What could you possibly mean? You are their leader. This is *your* movement! They will march on the parade and bring the whole affair to a halt. The Premier and all of the State will be forced to listen to your demands, *OUR* demands. And once the rest of the city hears you speak, even more people will rally to your banner!"

"But then what, Vivianne? Yes, let's say we grow our movement to outnumber the fascists. We grow to outnumber the anarchists too, but so what? Are we to assume power?" He made a face. "Vivianne, I am not fit to govern. I don't know the first thing about politics, let alone maintaining order in a city of millions! We don't need a shadow government, but we do need *some* kind of government. Even I know that.

"I've gotten the Fifth Estate this far, but to be quite honest, I do not know where to go from here." Leaning forward, he pointed. "And that is why I need you, Vivianne. That is why you are here.

"You're young, wealthy, and highly intelligent, Vivianne, but so am I. What you have that I don't are connections. And, most importantly, time."

"I don't understand."

"You are like me, Vivianne, born into a life of excess."

Vivianne reeled back at this, her eyes wide. "Our wealth is very different, *very* different."

"It's not your fault that your brother is what he is."

Her expression was pained, just as it had been when she'd first confessed the origin of her family's ill-gotten fortune. "I wish I believed that."

"But you can make good use of your unique situation. You have access to resources, to people who may be ready for a populist revolution. People sympathetic."

She laughed scornfully. "You will not find sympathy for your situation, or any situation, in the Titans!"

"I'm not suggesting you look there. Thanks to the *Musée* and your brother's philanthropic endeavors, you have access to politicians and business leaders."

"Coming from you, Thiago, this is quite funny and odd. You just spent an hour railing against politicians and business leaders. Now you would use me to gain their support?"

"Vivianne, that's rhetoric. It's necessary to inspire people. I'm not so feeble-minded to think that *all* politicians are corrupt."

She shook her head. "So, it's all an act?"

"Hardly! All I am saying is that there are still honest people in the world, even in the State," he said. "I'm simply asking is that you leverage your connections to help find others like yourself."

"Suckers with money?"

Vivianne...

He locked his gaze on her.

"Vivianne, my time is short. And for you, this is your opportunity for redemption. An opportunity to give back to this city what your brother has taken from it."

Hunter's Peninsula, for nearly half a century, was known for two things: first and foremost, upon its landfilled surface sat the concrete superstructure of Sun City's professional football team, the Cobras; secondly, Hunter's Peninsula was the last stop for Sun City's municipal monorail.

Today the stadium, built by Coastal Power only later to be sold to Skyy Athletic Apparel, sat abandoned, unused and unclaimed. And the monorail station, which had once been a massive bus depot to boot, was home only to the Fifth Estate.

The van pulled into the gated lot of the Fifth Estate complex, the sound of gravel beneath the tires a familiar and welcome sensation for Thiago.

"Home sweet home."

She moved to get a better view through the van's rear windows. "It's lovely."

"You're a terrible liar, Vivianne."

Once the van had come to a halt, two of his men raced to open the doors for them. Thiago climbed out first. As usual, the air was crisp and cold but made it so very easy to breathe. A breeze sent litter tumbling across the yard in a light vale of dust. He turned and offered his arm to Vivianne, who stepped down from the van gracefully.

Decommissioned buses and subway cars were lined in rows as far as the eye could see. At the center of it all was the old transit hub, a three-story brick building with massive bay doors and rails that entered in one side and exited the other. If one were to follow those rails, they would touch every section of Sun City in a wide orbit before arriving back at this point. Flanking the building were the pillars that once held the monorail. The rail itself had long since been dismantled, leaving the pillars to stand there like horned sentries, petrified and sun-beaten.

High on the face of the red brick building hung a banner that read, "Fifth E5tate." Beneath the banner was a quote from writer James Baldwin, that read, "To act is to be committed and to be committed is to be in danger."

"That banner is pretty brazen. Not afraid of reprisal?" Vivianne asked.

"We're not hiding. I own this yard and everything in it, legally bought and paid for. The land title is public record. The SDC is well aware. They know where to find us, always have."

"Is that safe?"

"If they were to attack us without cause, they would only legitimize our movement. We should be so lucky. This is what I choose to believe. That's not to say there won't be a time when becoming an underground movement makes sense, but now is not the time. We organize demonstrations, sit-ins, protests, and other peaceful acts of public defiance. We model ourselves today on the peaceful protests of Dr. Martin Luther

King. This approach time and again has proven to draw the greatest pan-demographic support. And more than anything, we need numbers."

As they made their way across the yard to the building, he took Vivianne's hand. "You're a marvelous woman, Vivianne. An angel come down to help us."

"Please."

"I mean it!"

"I'm no fool, Thiago Garcia. I'm no fool." Her smile was warm, but her eyes were piercing and sober. "You want to use me, but it's ok. I believe in your movement and I will help you."

"It's not just the movement…" He squeezed her hand as they crossed the gravel lot for the building.

She sighed and rolled her eyes before changing the subject. "Why not headquarter in Section Seven or Section Four where the people you want to help most reside? Why way out here?"

"A couple of reasons, really. For one, establishing our base in either of those districts might appear antagonistic to the SDC. Second, we're outside of Libra's range, which could prove useful should we need to… I don't know, mobilize. As for the third reason, simple economics. Real estate prices out here are much more favorable and, as you'll see in a moment, real estate is something the movement needs."

At the door to the Fifth Estate headquarters, he paused. "Ready?"

648

She laughed in her melodious way. "Sure, I guess."

He pushed the door open, watching her face as they stepped inside.

Inside, the building was buzzing with people. Fifth Estate activists moved about at a frantic pace, carrying papers, laptops, and tablets. Phones rang incessantly and people exited conference rooms in herds only to pile into others. Printers ran indefinitely, printing flyers, banners, and eco-friendly, washable graffiti decals. People spoke in hurried, hushed tones to one another. Behind the action, music played in the background. It sounded like some kind of hip-hop but, behind the din, one couldn't be sure.

He marveled in her awe. Vivianne's brown eyes were so wide that he could probably plant a kiss on the white of them. "Describe what you see in a word."

She looked at him with half-smile. "Clerical."

Precisely! Just as we have to be to beat the SDC.

Thiago stood in the doorway a moment and admired his own handiwork. Founding the Fifth Estate had been every bit like starting a business. But unlike most start-ups, he had seen success early and had yet to falter. He had his mother's business acumen and his father's charisma to thank. And maybe a little of his brother's bull-headedness…

"Four years ago, the Fifth Estate was nothing more than an idea. Now, we are the most relevant anti-Consortium movement in the State, with new chapters sprouting up almost daily."

A man whom he didn't recognize walked by and greeted them. "Good afternoon, Mr. Garcia, sir."

"Call me Thiago."

She was impressed. He could see it on her face. "When I was a boy, I knew that one day I would lead men."

"Is that so? And what are these people actually doing, 'leader'?"

"I have no idea."

They laughed and she fell into him playfully. The touch of her body against his sent bolts of excitement through him.

"All kidding aside, they're maintaining our blog sites and online forums, managing our outreach programs, namely our food bank, drug rehabilitation program, and homeless shelters. They are crunching the numbers of our targeted advertising algorithms and fine-tuning our social media messaging. They're forming relationships and partnerships with the independent media outlets. They're on the Shadownet, coordinating the upcoming LDP demonstration. And they are doing more, I'm sure. We are very busy, as you can see."

She turned to him and spoke so that only he could hear. "This stuff about the 'Octumvirate,' the 'Eight' as you say. That's the only part I can't really get behind. Are you sure you aren't losing people with that bit of rhetoric? It's a bit nutty-sounding, you know? The 'men behind the curtain' and all that."

He leaned in to her. "I know it does. And I bet we do turn some people off when we talk about it, but Vivianne, the

650

Eight are real. And they are a real threat. In fact, more than the SDC, the Octumvirate are the threat. The Eight must be unmasked."

She exhaled dramatically and shrugged. "Sounds like you've put a lot of thought into it."

"They're real."

"Perhaps you can reframe the discussion," she said. "Humanize them in your speeches rather than hoist them up as this shadowy menace. People are more likely to take on a fight against a foe they can visualize."

"*This* is why we need you, Vivianne. That beautiful mind of yours!"

"It *is* truly remarkable what you've accomplished," she replied. "These things, these movements — when you see them on TV at least, they are always so… disorganized. There's usually some guy with dreadlocks and a bullhorn. And everyone looks nutrient-deprived. And everyone's smoking weed."

He laughed. "Sweeping generalization, but I get your point."

"But this… this is something else entirely." She was looking up at the tall, vaulted ceiling and the people racing around on the second and third floors. "This is an enterprise!"

"Thank you, Vivianne, and please, keep critiquing my approach. There are better ways to do this, and I know it. It's only once we begin to believe we've figured it all out that the door opens for failure. I value your opinion, perhaps over that of anyone else."

She looked at him and rolled her eyes again. "And how many members do you have?"

"The numbers lie, Vivianne. It's very difficult to know for sure. We might have seven thousand full-time activists, but one event could change that in an instant. It's best not to think of the Fifth Estate as a group of people but rather a realization. The Fifth Estate is an *idea* that resides in all oppressed peoples. It only requires an event to awaken that realization within them. And it begins with fear. But, through education, that fear can be tempered into courage as the realization becomes obvious."

"And what exactly is 'the realization?'"

"That it is on the people — all of us — to change the world. The world is a machine that runs on lives and produces nothing but that meaningless token we call revenue. And, regardless of who's to blame, the machine is not going to correct itself. Human beings built the machine. Human beings must fix it."

Vivianne's expression was incredulous. It was a look Thiago found particularly attractive on her. One eyebrow would lift high onto her head and the other would sit low and mimic a tilde.

"Too sales-pitchy?"

"Yes, and very, very corny."

They laughed again, now standing very close to one another as though sharing a secret.

"Vivianne, these people, this Council of Eight, have been doing things their way for hundreds, maybe thousands of years. And, in all that time, you might think their tactics would have evolved. Oddly enough, they haven't. They use the same ploys today they used one thousand years ago. First, it was fear of starvation, then fear of damnation. Today, it's fear of terrorism! Regardless, it is always fear. Fear is what they know, it's all they know.

"Well, I am not afraid," he told her. "I have nothing left to fear."

Vivianne was very serious, stern even. "Thiago, you can't believe you're the first to stand up aginst 'the system?'"

"Of course not! But *how* we are fighting back is different. We will be the first technically proficient, internet-savvy, data-driven resistance. If it worked to build the system, it will work to dismantle it. That's why we've employed AI and machine-learning algorithms to measure our message online and in speeches. We're rapidly applying the same methods used by advertisers to formulate the counter-message. However, since our message was crafted using modern methods and practices, we can circumvent the timely, costly, and failure-ridden ploys of yesteryear. Our message, the Fifth Estate's message of 'Empathetic Populism and Social Accountability' is bespoke. It's lean, mean, and backed by data-driven decision-making."

Vivianne shook her head and smiled. "You are a crazy person, Thiago Garcia. But I must admit, the way you talk... it's effective. And this place... You're serious."

"When I first saw this place, I said to myself, 'This is perfect.'"

The central space was three stories of vaulted ceiling, having once been able to hold several buses side by side. The offices lined the circular room on three floors, the upper made accessible by ornate metal staircases and a fire escape–like walkway. The brass railings were held in place by iron balusters twisted into intricate gothic designs. The offices themselves were walled in glass, a look that complemented the beige brick walls and cast-iron archways. The archways themselves held the ceiling together in a dome of thick, yellow-tinted glass.

The building reminded Thiago of New York City, and in particular the architecture popular at the turn of the nineteenth century.

"This building was once someone's pride, an achievement of no small measure. Now, it's a thing of compromise; a makeshift headquarters I purchased for a fraction of what it probably cost to build. The whole thing is steeped in irony. A municipal transit hub repurposed to deliver truth to an enslaved people. Leftovers, indicative of a corporatocracy's myopic wastefulness weaponized. It's perfect in every way... just like you, Vivianne."

Another staffer unfamiliar to him, this one wearing a Fifth Estate T-shirt, approached with an armful of documents, but he waved her off. "Another time please."

The woman looked dejected but nodded. A moment later she was gone, vanished in the crowd of activists, carried away on hemp slip-ons.

Vivianne looked as though she wanted to shrug off his comment as more flattery, but stopped herself. After a moment, she said with a smile, "I thank you for the compliment."

The rally had taken a lot out of Thiago — in particular, the heat. His arms were sunburnt, and dehydration had him licking his lips more than he should.

Right now, I want nothing but a cold glass of water and to take you to my office and test your resolve, he thought, looking at her. *On two fronts...*

He opened his mouth to suggest as much, but she spoke first.

"I'm sorry," she said, with a hand to her face, "I can't pretend any longer. What *is* that smell? Do you smell it?"

The smell she spoke of now haunted their headquarters. It had appeared a couple of days ago and only seemed to be getting worse with time. It was a frustrating combination of rank and sweet, like rotting garbage if somehow masked only slightly with the smell of berries. It was more acute in the offices on the second and third floors and, for some reason, on this day, was particularly powerful.

655

"A clogged sewage pipe or something," he told her. "We're not sure. It is embarrassing, I'll admit."

"Think nothing of it, but fix it!" She laughed. "It's unbearable."

"Vivianne, please come with me to my office so we can continue our conversation in private. We've much to discuss still, and frankly, I am exhausted. How does a sit-down chat over beers sound?" He smiled. "I have air freshener in my office. It doesn't stink nearly as bad in there, I promise."

She smiled. "Okay but—"

A sound like coins hitting a glass table top sounded above the drone of printers and the ring of phones. People stopped mid-step to listen, their necks craning like antelope at the scent of a predator. The sound resumed again, this time in rapid succession and from multiple locations; vicious rapping sounds that overlapped, deafening.

Thiago moved for the staircase but in that instant, a movement above caught his eye. He looked up to see the domed glass ceiling exploding inward. A hailstorm of shattered glass rained down. The iron crossbar hung loose for a heart-stopping moment before coming free. Thiago shielded his eyes and put his back against the wall as the skylight came down in an almost musical crescendo of chimes. The iron crossbar struck a desk and sent wooden splinters spinning into the air. The person who'd been sitting there disappeared beneath the iron, only to reappear in the form of a rapidly spreading pool of blood.

Vivianne stood next to him, her back wisely to the wall as well.

"Are you ok?" he asked, ashamed that he had momentarily forgotten about her.

As she opened her mouth to reply, a form struck the concrete floor and burst like an over-ripened melon, sending blood and offal sliding across the deck to pour over Vivianne's black leather flats. She screamed, and so did he.

The ceiling was gone now and the building reduced to merely a vertical tunnel through which one could see only an apathetic grey sky and small shards of still-falling glass like raindrops.

"What the fuck is happening?"

Thiago walked over to the body. The deceased was young; his skin, once dark, apparently, was now purplish and loose on his skull. Lying next to his busted torso was a cheap folding knife. The blade on the knife was rusted.

More gunshots sounded, sending everyone in the room scattering. In the chaos, he lost Vivianne. Windows burst in on the first floor, and bullets struck the stone walls, sending powdered brick outward in little plumes.

We're under attack!

"Vivianne!"

Men and women were bolting the doors, some already flipping desks to barricade the windows. It was then that one of the massive wooden garage doors was torn open. A great impact exposed sunlight, as shards of cherry oak flew inward.

657

Another tremendous blow tore the doors open in the opposite direction.

Terror welled up in him, and the sensation of being trapped and helpless made him want to hide somewhere.

One terrible slash after another sent people fleeing to the opposite side of the room. Before long, the double-doors fell to the ground in splinters. Gunfire poured into the room, forming an aura of death around a man whose mass took up nearly the whole of the breached entryway. He was the largest man Thiago had ever seen, larger even than his brother Omar. The man stepped into the room casually, as though the gunfire pouring in around him was mere wind. Thiago recognized his uniform immediately.

Oh no... They've come, they've actually—

The man held two broadswords the width of a lesser person at each side. His face was hidden behind a thick, white beard and, if not for his immense and muscular frame, he could almost pass for a garden gnome. The lower half of his left leg was some kind of contraption; a metal spike piston that blasted holes into the concrete floor as he crossed the threshold. With one good eye, the giant surveyed the room. The man's uniform was orange and grey, and on his head, was a bandana of olive drab that must have been the size of a grown man's T-shirt.

I've got to get upstairs...

Thiago bolted for the staircase. At the same time, people ran in as many directions as there were bullets filling the air. Some ran for the emergency exits, others for the stairs, like him, and some for the windows. Others still took up weapons and returned fire.

Oh, Jesus, he thought, *don't shoot back!*

The orange of the big man's uniform had told Thiago everything he needed to know about the situation — that escape or surrender were the only options.

Make it to the office, wait out the firefight, surrender...

Another movement from above caused him to stop and find the wall once more. Two people had leapt into the room from above, from where there had once been a ceiling. They jumped from fifty or so feet to the floor as nonchalantly as a child might leap from the couch, landing in the center of the room gracefully, mechanically. They both wore the orange uniform of Agency Zero.

The first was a woman with hair the same shade of orange as her uniform. She surveyed the chaotic scene for a moment with her hands on her hips before producing a pair of sub-machine guns from her waist. She opened fire with a look of glee, gunning down the fleeing. She sent out waves of death in sweeping, almost dance-like motions.

The other soldier to drop into the chamber appeared to be a man wearing a mask. Wicker protruded from it in some tribal design that Thiago did not recognize. The eyes of the mask were black tubes behind which only the tiniest of pupils could be seen. From beneath the mask a sound, similar to stones rattling in a can, momentarily drowned out the sounds of gunfire. In his hands, the man held two grenades. The first he threw behind him, where it exploded in a blinding light. The second was lobbed underhand... directly in Thiago's direction.

Thiago covered himself as best he could with his thin frame, as the masked man made an exploding gesture with his hands and produced a clicking sound in the cadence of laughter.

Certain he was going to die, Thiago screamed. But as the world went white, the sound, too, went out.

Moments became minutes, and before long the snow-white blindness became a watercolor landscape of rapidly moving objects. His hearing returned as well, nudged along by gunfire and people screaming in terror. When it became clear that he was, in fact, not dead, Thiago moved for the stairs once more, gun smoke filling his nostrils.

Amidst the fog of exploded concussion and flash-bang grenades, he saw the massive bearded man swing his great sword like an axe and split the friendly-looking staffer he hadn't made time for in two.

Holding on to the railing with a trembling hand, Thiago began climbing the staircase. The whine in his ears soon settled, and once more he could hear the crack of gunfire fully, terribly. He looked for Vivianne from his now-elevated position, but could not find her.

I hope you made it out.

One stair at a time, he climbed with his head down. He climbed over the body of someone who also had tried to make it upstairs. At the top of the first flight, he found a man waiting for him. He raised his hands quickly, instinctively.

"Thiago Garcia?" the soldier asked.

The man's jaw was missing. In its place was a black metal contraption similar to the blade on a bulldozer. When the soldier talked, it moved up and down but not in unison with the word being produced. Behind that, the man's accent was thick, Australian or South African. Thiago could never tell the difference.

His office was just behind the man, and in it, his own firearm. If the massacre below were any indication, surrender did not appear to be an option. Below, the female soldier's murder spree was dying down, her fatal dance nearing its conclusion.

It's now or never!

Thiago moved to pass the man, running hard.

The safe that held his pistol was hidden in the floor beneath his desk. In his right pocket was a key ring. The safe key was tubular and would be easy to pluck out from the rest. He needed only moments. With a gun, he might be able to hole up, buy time, and maybe negotiate a surrender of some kind.

The uniformed man with the metal jaw was large and heavily armored, while Thiago was lean and light.

I'm quicker!

Thiago juked as he neared the man, hoping to slip by in the space between the soldier and the wall. He was proven

661

wrong... quickly. A shoulder-check not unlike the defensive technique employed in ice hockey struck him in the side and sent him careening into the wall. Unable catch himself in time, Thiago hit the brick with his face and fell to the walkway floor. Thiago rolled to his side, not sure what to do, pain already threatening to blind him once more. Looming over him was the soldier. His eyes were the color of ice, his hair matted and sawdust-colored.

"I asked you a question," the man told him through an inanimate face both grotesque and at the same time spellbinding.

In moments like these, Thiago couldn't help but think of Omar, just as little brothers typically did when facing a bully. If screaming would bring his brother, he would scream long and hard.

The soldier's powerful grip hoisted him from the floor by his belt.

"No!"

The leader of the Fifth Estate attempted to grab the railing, but was too late. The man threw him down the stairs the way one might hurl a sandbag. Thiago's efforts to break the fall were rejected soundly by physics, inertia, and gravity. As he tumbled down, all he could do was close his eyes and let the typhoon of impacts run its course. When the violence against his body subsided, Thiago found himself lying face down.

Oh, God... I can't breathe.

An effort to pick himself up only resulted in more pain. A quick and terrifying self-assessment revealed a bone jutting from his forearm, and his fingers bent in ways he might once have thought unfathomable.

The thing about Archer's disease and a body dying from within was that sometimes, having dead pain receptors worked in your favor. Still lying on his belly, he used one hand to try and fix the other. Straightening the broken digits as best he could, he rolled onto his back to find the man with the metal jaw descending the steps. In his hand was a curved skinning knife.

Thiago tried to get to his feet, propping himself up on the elbow of his less-broken arm. The pain, though somewhat muted, was nonetheless excruciating. He got a leg under him and stood momentarily, only to keel and fall over once more.

Something's not right. Broken hip, maybe.

This scenario — an attack by Agency Zero — was one he'd imagined many times. But never had he envisioned an assault so brutal, a massacre so *wanton*. It was as though all of his amplified rhetoric about their subversion of the law and violence was *true...*

He scooted away from the soldier on his butt with a hand extended. The time for pleading was upon him. "Please, man. Please, please..."

Many a dark fantasy he'd had about a militant Fifth Estate engaging with Agency Zero or Unit One 'on even terms.' The raw, unfiltered truth was nothing like those musings. One couldn't even call what Agency Zero had done to them a 'siege.' It wasn't a siege, or even a massacre, really… because those things took time. Agency Zero, in a matter of minutes, had *deleted* his movement. In one bloody keystroke, they had stricken years of planning, organizing, and preparation from the world.

They might as well have dropped a nuke on us, Thiago thought, even as his own death descended the staircase.

"You having second thoughts, mate?" Death asked.

"Please…"

"It's always like this with people, y'know?" the metal-faced man mused, "They poke the bear. All day. And then, when the bear wakes up… it's always like this. I'm starting to think people are the problem."

The soldier flipped the knife into the air and caught it effortlessly without looking. Beneath the light of day, the blade seemed to glow. The soldier was down the steps now, and standing over him.

"Don't worry," he said, his metal jaw moving rapidly, excessively, "I'm only going to take a little trophy from ya. You won't even miss it."

The soldier crouched and snatched him by the hair. The blade of the knife touched his upper lip, as the soldier positioned it under his nose.

"No! NOOOO!"

"Dozer!" a voice yelled.

The woman with the orange hair and dark skin approached, her gun leveled at the man with the knife, her comrade.

"I told you not to point that fucking rat-cannon at me, Legion!" the man Thiago now knew to be 'Dozer' roared.

"Then start following orders," the woman demanded, her gun still leveled. "The Major's instructions were explicit!"

The woman, a butcher in her own right, turned her disgusted look to him. "Are you Thiago Garcia?"

In far too much pain to lie, he nodded.

The woman placed her weapon against her hip, where it snapped magnetized into place, and raised a fist to the man with the metal jaw. "Dozer, you fucking idiot! He looks like the loser in a rodeo-clown contest. He's no good to us dead! What don't you understand about that?"

"This'n ain't dead," Dozer replied. "If I wanted him dead, he'd be dead!"

The big man with the white beard and metal leg — the one who'd cut down the staffer — wiped one of his blades across the back of another murdered volunteer and slung it back into the scabbard on his belt. He did the same with the second blade, slowly and methodically. Once his blades were clean and sheathed, he murmured something indecipherable and graced himself with the sign of the cross. As he lumbered over to them, his pike-leg shook the very earth. This man, too, looked down at Thiago. "Is this our man?"

Legion nodded.

"Dozer," the big man said, addressing metal-jaw but pointing down at Thiago, "*you* get to explain to the Major why this one looks like half-eaten shepherd's pie."

Another voice chimed in. Now that the gunfire had subsided, Thiago could hear it clearly. It was deep, gritty, and very, very confident. "Explain to me what?"

Remaining conscious was a battle now, and the pain was such that Thiago could do little more than clutch himself and rock in place on his side.

The man in the mask, who'd been stalking the great room, likely looking for survivors, stopped and stood at attention at the sound of the voice.

"At ease," the voice said. "We've done enough killing for today. This roach ain't getting up."

The masked man saluted the newest entry to the bloody site. The last man to stride into Fifth Estate headquarters wore a tattered olive poncho and, beneath that, an orange thermal and black trousers. His face was a horrid collection of scars, and in his hand was a foot-long blade dripping with freshly drawn blood. The man walked like a hunter in the wild, surveying the room with a cool, analytical expression.

We meet at last, Thiago thought bitterly. *Major...*

"Iron" Ace Monroe had been the arch-nemesis in Thiago's speeches for years. After all, the Major represented the brutal hand of the corporate regime, the heartless black knight. But now — and one could not discount the power of fear here — part of Thiago felt guilty for some of the things he'd said about the Major. You know, never actually having met the man in person and whatnot.

Now, as the Major stepped over the bodies of the deceased with not so much as a glance down, Thiago knew that his rhetoric had not even scratched the surface. Agency Zero, this whole time, had been the worst-case scenario. Not the SCPD, and not Unit One.

If only I'd realized it sooner.

"What happened to him?" the Major asked.

Dozer slipped his knife into its holster on his chest quickly, *very* quickly. "You see, sir, this'n 'ere tried to get up to the offices, no doubt intent on barricading himself in or mounting a counter-offensive."

The Major regarded his man with a cool expression. "That so? And you felt so threatened for your person, for your physical well-being, that you conveniently ground him to man-dust?"

Dozer shrugged, and the Major's eyes narrowed menacingly.

From the deck, the Major looked immense to Thiago. His arm, as scarred as his face, was fortified with muscle. As he dressed down Dozer, his finger caressed the hilt of the blade now holstered on his hip. Like this, he regarded his man for several awkward moments. If the Major wasn't considering fragging his man, he certainly could have fooled everyone. Even the big man with the swords and beard took a cautionary step back.

"This is becoming a thing with you," the Major growled after a few menacing moments of silence.

"Major!"

More soldiers entered. Among the group, being restrained forcefully, was a very angry, struggling Vivianne Gueye.

"We found this one hiding under the buses."

Oh, thank God! Thiago thought. *You're alive! You must think I'm the worst kind of coward...*

Seeing him lying at the soldiers' feet, she began kicking her legs, swearing in French.

"Release her," the Major instructed with a hand up.

The soldier released Vivianne, pushing her forward and almost sending her tripping over a corpse. The Major stepped to meet her.

"Well, what do you know?" the woman with the orange hair crooned. "You do recognize her, don't you?"

"Of course I do," the Major replied. He went to touch Vivianne's face with a gloved hand. "You're even more beautiful than I'd heard."

Vivianne's reaction was surprisingly quick, slapping the Major's hand aside. "Don't touch me, murderer!"

Thiago tried to sit up once more, his body trembling at the effort. "Vivianne..."

"Murderer?" the Major replied.

With a speed unlike anything Thiago had ever seen, even from his brother, he watched as the Major seized

Vivianne. He snatched her up the way someone might a live lobster. The Major contorted her mercilessly, pinning her arm across her own throat and locking it into place behind her head with his own metal arm. With his other hand, he snatched a handful of her hair at the crown.

The sight sickened and infuriated Thiago. He shuffled on the floor, cursing his own helplessness.

"You there," the Major said to the soldiers who'd captured her. "If you found this one, there must be more. Find them!"

"And when we do, sir?"

"Well, I've no need for 'more,' and I especially have no need for witnesses. Sweep a klick in every direction and leave no hovel unturned. I want a blanket sweep. And make sure you deploy scramblers. I don't want to see this operation on social media! We clear?"

The soldiers saluted crisply and were gone.

From the ground, Thiago could tell the soldiers of Agency Zero were enjoying every minute of this. The woman with the orange hair smiled prettily, even as the blood of the people she gunned down continued to pool in spots on the white concrete floor of the Fifth Estate headquarters like discarded Japanese flags.

At the same time, Dozer busied himself with "souvenirs" from the fallen.

Thiago's heart was heavy with fear for Vivianne's safety. He watched helplessly as the Major walked her forward

— her arms bent precariously — to the cold corpse who lay burst on the floor. With a chilling disdain and cruelty, the Major stuck her face before the corpse the way misinformed people potty-trained puppies.

"*This* is murder," the Major growled into her ear. "We found this corpse on the premises. This… innocent young man! We found this young man stabbed to death. Someone stabbed him to death and left him to rot!"

"You found him here?" The moment the words left Thiago's lips, he knew he'd made a mistake. The woman with the orange hair drove a boot into his chest with as much force as she could probably muster. Probably.

"Shut it!"

Thiago held a hand up as she reeled her leg back menacingly.

The Major was seething now. He looked ready to snap poor Vivianne in two. "But *you* know all about murder already, don't you?" he hissed.

Vivianne, unable to turn her head, spoke through gritted teeth. "What are you talking about?"

"Don't play dumb with me! I know who you are. Your family is singularly responsible for an infinite pile of corpses! The poisons you litter our streets with, the lives snatched, the homes crushed under the weight of addiction…" The Major flexed the fingers of the hand gripping her hair and leaned in to her. He took in a long, loud inhale of her neck. "Chanel? What's a bottle of that go for in corpses? How many kids lose their mommies and daddies to heroin, stims, or poppers so you can smell like Euro-piss? And we've yet to tally the atrocities committed by your brother's *Ligue des Géants* in Togo. Hell, we're still unearthing mass grave sites."

"Look, I don't know—"

The Major cut her off with a loud shush. "I could tear your arm off and beat you to death with it, woman. Don't you dare lie to me!"

Please don't speak, Vivianne, Thiago would tell her if Legion's boot wasn't positioned to kick him again.

Clutching at the bone that jutted from his arm, Thiago watched breathlessly. The pain he felt was something like a drug at this point; something unreal.

"I don't expect you to understand the misery you've inflicted on this world," the Major continued. "Your kind are incapable. No better than sharks, really."

"And what of you?" She craned her head to meet his eyes, even though it clearly caused excruciating pain to do so. "You killed these people! Innocents!"

"Please," the Major scoffed. "There are no equivalencies. You might as well compare the blaze to the fireman. We are in sync with the way of the world, where you profit on creating distortion and mischief. The world cannot have birth without bloodshed, nor shade without sun. But when my battalion's work is done, peace ensues, *always*!

"You, on the other hand, eat at peace. You erode it from within, like cancer. You grow fat on it until it is no more.

671

Where there is joy, you bring misery. Where there is life, you bring death." He released her slowly, his head still near her ear. "Do not conflate the killer with the blade."

Vivianne stood there, arms at her side, her head down. From Thiago's vantage point at their feet, the exchange made him feel worthless, utterly and irrevocably so.

The Major, flanked by the motley crew that made up Agency Zero, pointed to the door. With his free hand, he drew the foot-long blade from his belt. He held it to his side, poised to strike. "Get out of my sight, or I will show the world what truly drives you!"

Vivianne's contorted face was soaked with tears now, making her shiny. Her shoulders heaved as she sobbed. She looked at the door with longing and shook her head. "You'll cut me down from behind, won't you?"

"Unlike your brother, I'm no coward," the Major replied. "Go! But know this: you're my herald now, and your message is simple. You're going to tell your brother that I am coming for him and there is *nothing* he can do to stop me. If he runs, I will cut a swath to him, starting with your father and you!"

The Major was screaming now, the rage on his face, coupled with the scarring, making him into some kind of werewolf.

"If he takes his own life — as would be most prudent — I take your father's and yours in turn! There is nothing he can do but wait for me. You will tell him to wait for me! Do you understand my words?"

Vivianne nodded in rapid succession.

The Major was not finished.

"THERE IS NO PENANCE FOR WHAT YOU'VE DONE TO MY HOME! NO FORGIVENESS! WHAT HAPPENS NEXT FOR THE SCUM THAT INFESTS SECTION SEVEN IS WHAT HAPPENED HERE! THE TITANS AND YOUR MAGGOT FAMILY ARE FINISHED!" He poked the blade in her direction. "GO NOW! GO BEFORE I GUT YOU AND STRING YOUR INSIDES AROUND LIKE CHRISTMAS LIGHTS! RUN TO YOUR COWARD BROTHER AND TELL HIM THAT THE SUN IS SETTING ON ALL HE KNOWS!"

She stood there, her beautiful eyes wide and shattered.

"Go, Vivianne," Thiago told her softly. "Please go."

"I'm so sorry, Thiago."

She began walking for the door, watching the Major and his blade over her shoulder. The farther she got, the faster she walked. Until she was out the door and out of sight.

"One exiting the building," the giant with the white beard said, likely into their coms system. "She's to exit the AO unmolested but 'cat-eyes blind.'"

When she was gone, the Major seemed to calm a bit, though it was tough to know for sure. "Follow her, Legion. You know the prey. You know how they move. Be discreet."

Legion smirked and quickly bolted through the door.

With that bit of business done, the Major turned to the ancient-looking giant with the white beard and spike piston leg. "Pops, take the others and help canvas the area. I want some alone time with our boy here — what's left of him, anyway."

The giant grunted and motioned for the others to follow him out. Agency Zero, but for their leader, exited a building still fresh with death. As Thiago watched them leave, their moods cavalier, it was clear to him that the Fifth Estate never really had a chance.

Everything we built was meaningless. We built a sandcastle, and Agency Zero just stomped it into oblivion.

"Looks like we're alone now," the Major said, crouching to meet him eye-to-eye. As he did so, his shredded poncho pooled around him like the roots of some dying tree. "You in a bit o' pain, huh?"

Playing tough with the Major, alone, was suicide of the worst kind, and so Thiago adopted candor. "I am."

The Major pursed his lips and nodded. "Sorry to see. That was not part of the plan."

'Not part of the plan!'

"And what about the rest?" Thiago asked, the Major's nonchalance emboldening him. What about—" He looked at the bodies strewn about, the pools of blood everywhere. Tears took him and his voice became difficult to conjure.

"Heavy-handed, to be sure. But if it saves us an upheaval at the state level, I'd butcher your people nine times over."

674

"You're a monster."

"Fact."

"What do you want from me?"

"A lot." The Major nodded his head matter-of-factly. "What burns me up, is that you ain't even a citizen." His eyes rolled up into his head, recalling – or researching over neurotrigger. "São Paulo, Brazil, born February 13, 2020. Mommy and daddy are healthy back home. You've got a sister working on her PhD in physics, a brother who's a celebrity prizefighter, hell, *the* celebrity prizefighter." The Major licked his lips. "2020: same year my kid brother was born. Know what else happened that year?" The Major, his gnarled face grimacing, smashed his fists together.

The scariest thing to Thiago about the Major wasn't the scars that crisscrossed his face like a city map. It wasn't the deprecated metal arm that squeaked like the robot in a children's cartoon every time he moved. It wasn't even the rotten poncho with the aged and plum-colored stains that just had to be blood. It was his eyes. They were the eyes of a predator. The eyes of a wolf.

"I don't know."

"Your little sweetheart that just ran out of here? Her brother formed a group in Togo called the Ligue des Géants in that same year. Not sure if you caught that bit. You heard of them?"

I've heard of them, he thought but did not say. *I remember the documentary about them that won at Cannes.*

675

"Bet you didn't know that the Gueyes put that little operation together with the help of the Chinese. With Chinese funding and some genetically enhanced seeds, the Ligue des Géants turned the cocoa and cotton fields in Togo into poppy fields almost overnight.

"Did you know that?"

Thiago nodded.

"And to keep the villagers working for nothing, they'd send their men into the homes to drag out the girls, some just babies. They'd rape some, chop some up, and put a few to the torch. The rest they'd send home with a pretty clear message. 'Show up for work, men!'

"Your lady friend's family put that together, the brother mostly, but the old man, too, probably had a hand in it. Shitty company you keep, especially for an uh, what the fuck are you? A revolutionary?" The Major's laugh was scornful and quite brutal. "So, tell me now. Did you know *that*?"

He's testing me.

"No. I did not know that. I knew… I knew about the Titans. I did not know about Togo."

The Major's eyes narrowed. The hazel orbs therein darted, studying him, parsing the data. A decision would be rendered and Thiago's life hung on that result.

"São Paulo has a staggering economic disparity," the Major continued, "has for centuries, and you've got those stacked shit-holes, those shanties. What do you call those things?"

676

"Favelas," Thiago replied softly.

"Yeah, 'favelas.' So how come you spew that 'we the people' shit here and not back in your own country?"

"The truth?"

The Major chuckled, and it was quite genuine. "You can't afford to lie. Trust me."

"Because I love Sun City. I love the people, the diversity, the opportunity, and the heart."

The Major looked around the room at the devastation his men had caused. Making a 'not bad' expression, he arched his brows. "Well, I'd say the Fifth Estate was done in Sun City. What do you think?"

That's where you're wrong, Thiago thought. *With Vivianne free to spread the message, my death is precisely what we need.*

"I think you're right." Not sure if it was the pain or the anger at having his life's work smashed like a piñata that gave him the courage to speak, Thiago added, "And now, what about me?"

"Lucky for you," the Major said, smiling, "I need you."

"For what?"

"A contingency plan." The Major extended his artificial hand and ran the dank metal over Thiago's face. "And for that, I'm gonna need your pretty mug."

23: Scattered Toys

"What? Stand over the body, fists shaking? Grimacing as I fight back tears? Ha ha ha, no. My first time wasn't like that at all. After getting over the sheer sight of it, I spent the day imagining all of the reasons that man deserved to die. And it wasn't hard because most men deserve to die."

- Madison Grünewald-Yamazaki

Alla Breve, the finale of Rachmaninoff's Piano Concerto Number 3. In college, it was unequivocally her favorite piece of music. Now, serving as the ringtone on her mobile, it was usually the sound of Sugihara wanting to check her whereabouts, or of Raizen calling to offer more dog's work. Lately, however, she had a new caller. As she reached into her jacket to retrieve the device, annoyance appeared on Sugihara's paper-pale face.

Terrible timing, as usual, Daisuke.

Without even looking at the phone, she silenced it and dropped it back into her coat.

"Who was that?" Sugihara was studying her, his reptilian eyes scrutinizing her every facial twitch.

She shrugged. "Didn't look."

"Why not?"

"I already know who it is and I don't have time for him."

Sugihara sneered. "New boyfriend?"

"Something like that."

"Does Daisuke know?"

"Why would he?"

"You two haven't been seeing each other?"

They sat in the back of a black BMW 5-series. The driver, an ex–mixed martial artist named Saotome, pretended to not hear their conversation. As did the man riding shotgun, an enforcer goon named Kunimoto. Though they both sat stone-faced, she knew they were listening. If not, they weren't doing their jobs.

Careful... she thought. *Be very careful.*

"He's reached out, sure," she replied, her expression cool and confident.

Sugihara sighed and asked her, looking at his own knees. "Have you been spending time with him, Madison?"

"No."

Sugihara's mouth smiled, but his eyes were laser focused. "He's your husband," he continued, his voice taunting. "If you guys are talking, I'd understand."

Liar.

Sugihara was many, many things, but understanding was not one of them. Madison had seen first-hand just how "understanding" Sugihara could be when he suspected betrayal.

"I haven't seen Daisuke since the club."

Sugihara, still not looking at her, nodded. After what seemed like some serious thought, he added, "It's probably for the best, then..."

With that, Sugihara's line of questioning ceased and Madison was afforded the opportunity to prepare herself mentally for the task at hand. She ran herself through an extensive and detailed series of hypothetical scenarios. She also tried to recall every turn, every corner and every piece of furniture she'd seen in Minowara's mansion. She rehearsed in silence what she would say to the guards if spoken to, and to Minowara himself.

After a long time, riding in silence, she stopped planning. Over-planning, after all, was very real and — in her line of work — potentially fatal. At some point, you just had to trust yourself.

She studied the horizon from the back seat of the luxury sedan. The sky along the coast was like something out of a Roman mosaic. The clouds folded in on one another like porridge being poured slowly. Silver crowns atop black and dark-grey canopies heralded the approach of Typhoon Yvonne. She studied the rolling clouds and imagined — with no small amount of longing — the end of the world.

When they finally arrived at the Minowara estate, Madison pushed the door open, her adrenaline already beginning to soar. As she began to exit the vehicle, Sugihara grabbed her arm.

"Be careful, Madison."

"I will."

It was an interesting expression Sugihara wore, one new to her. His eyes were wide and his thin lips pursed. He looked less like someone concerned and more like someone making a "concerned" face.

Seemingly as an afterthought, Sugihara reached into the ridiculous pink vest he wore and produced something small. He extended his hand to her. In his palm was a silver, maybe platinum, pin of some kind. It was in the shape of an elongated triangle and crafted to feature a collection of owls. The owls were an eerie affair, their bulbous eyes hollowed-out and empty.

"What is this?"

"It was Luther's. Give it to the old man. He'll know what it means."

Madison stepped out of the vehicle and onto the granite driveway. The driver wasted no time and sped away even before the door could shut entirely. For a while, she stood there, watching the storm bearing down on Sun City; light rain and wind cooled her face and whipped her hair around playfully.

This is nice. The literal calm before the storm.

Before long, she could hear the hoofed sound of dress shoes on the cobblestone, as yakuza descended from the mansion down to the main gate to meet her. Before they came into sight, she swung the bag containing The Madam over her shoulder.

The guards recognized her right away, as any Minowara stateside would.

"What do you want?" one asked in pristine English.

Before Madison could respond, the other man silenced the first with a gesture and called for the gate.

As she stood waiting patiently for the gate to swing wide, a breeze kicked up her skirt and caressed her thighs. The shifting of her clothing reminded her of the pistol tucked in her belt and the knife in her boot.

When the gate parted enough for her to slip through, she did so. Madison made her way up the driveway in a beeline for the main entrance. At the doors to the estate, the men escorting her departed, leaving her with another pair of nondescript yakuza who stood sentry.

This is where they'll frisk me.

As she came to a halt before the archway, she pulled The Madam from her satchel and held it out for them to see. "I've news to report on the job I was given."

The head guard's name was Tadamasa. A shrewd and lifelong yakuza, Tadamasa, like many others, had become disgruntled as of late, and vocal with his displeasure on a wide range of issues. He was most explicit on the topic of pay, specifically how little of it he received.

"What news?" he asked irritably.

"Luther Gueye is dead. I was really hoping to tell the boss this in person."

Tadamasa's eyes widened.

"Now, I wonder if I'll get paid what was promised, you know?" she added.

Tadamasa waved the others off and opened the door for her. When only she was in earshot, he leaned in. "Oyabun Minowara is a miserly son of a bitch! We're barely getting by out here. If he pays you what he owes you, I'll double it. That's how certain I am he'll weasel his way out of paying you!"

"I'll take that bet. I may be a stupid white woman, but I'm very serious when it comes to money."

"That you are!" Tadamasa replied, laughing.

"Wait, a 'stupid white woman' or 'very serious'?"

Tadamasa waved a hand before his face, still laughing. "Both!"

She laughed with him as he opened the door for her. Slipping The Madam back into her bag quickly, she patted Tadamasa on the shoulder. "Hang in there, kyodai."

"'Kyodai,' she says! Like hell," he added in Japanese as he pulled the door shut behind her.

We're inside.

With The Madam at her side, this venture into the Minowara compound had a very different feel. No longer were the men perched on the Victorian balustrade menacing. No longer were the rooms and their torturous secondary uses a concern.

She strolled casually over the Muromachi-era paintings, past the living room and kitchen, down the plum-carpeted corridor to the main living area and lounge, unaccompanied.

683

And all it had taken to enter the premises armed was a little small talk.

On the day when you needed vigilant guards most...

She had a plan. She had a script. She knew what she would say in almost any logical scenario. And yet, admittedly, she had a bone to pick with the old man. She had questions not from or on behalf of Sugihara and his Sedai, but personal questions that deserved answers. Questions about loyalty, respect, and fairness.

She exited the corridor and stepped down onto the plush white carpet of the main living area. The old man was not alone, far from it in fact. He sat at the center of the room facing his son Raizen, who knelt. Behind him stood six men, their backs turned, watching the ominous clouds on the horizon. Another two sat at the bar, eyeing her as she entered the room.

Oyabun Minowara was growling something to his son when he noticed her standing there. She'd hoped to find the boss in the company of only two or three of his most trusted aides. Tadamasa's carelessness made sense now. The Oyabun was already heavily guarded. Raizen turned and, by the colorless look on his face, she wondered if he knew everything. He looked anchored with exhaustion. Raizen stood slowly.

I hoped you wouldn't be here, old friend, she thought.

"Well, well," Minowara said from his high-backed chair. "Can't imagine why you would be here."

She approached, her palms sweaty. When she was within arm's length of the chair, she extended a hand, palm up. Resting in the center was the owl pin. With a shaking, mottled hand, Minowara took from her the trinket. He held it aloft, the light glimmering from it. "Do you know what a flock of owls is called?" he asked, a toothless, ghoulish grin on his face.

"Not a 'flock.' I presume."

"A *parliament*. It's fitting, really. Highly self-sufficient creatures, apex predators, and rarely seen together. But when they come together, the world changes."

"How interesting," she lied.

"*This* parliament," he continued, pocketing the pin, "is now short one, it would seem."

His laugh was heinous, a cackling and wretched cacophony of malice and vitriol. It was almost otherworldly in its cruelty.

What are you?

"Why are you the first to tell me?" he asked. "No one knows?"

"It's going to take some time to find the body. But he had a rather large body, so it's sure to surface at some point."

Minowara clenched his fists and contorted his body in a most obscene gesture. "Rest in hell, you black son of a bitch!"

Seeing his joy, the men around him began to applaud and catcall as well. Raizen, too, joined in.

"This is *excellent* news! Father, with the Titans leaderless, we can seize their corners—"

685

"Shut up, fool!" Minowara yelled, glaring at his son. "I did this, not you!"

Technically... no one did it, she thought, *but if anyone here should take credit it should be... forget it.*

Minowara was not done barking commands at the poor, browbeaten Raizen. "Your sister is in town, and I want you to make this trip very special for her! You've instructions, do you not? Why are you still here?"

Raizen became red-faced. He looked at her with eyes of bottled fury and shame. Like a good boy, however, he turned to his father and bowed deeply before heading out. As he passed, he leaned in to her ear. "Call me as soon as you are done here. We've *much* to discuss!" With a handsome half-smile, young Minowara was gone.

'Done here.' She could have laughed. Nevertheless, she was glad that the boss was sending Raizen away.

Interesting... Omoe Minowara is in town. I wonder if this has anything to do with Sugihara's timing? If that's the case, it means Raizen...

Her musing was cut short as Minowara called one of his men over, gesturing to him the way people summon dogs. "Pay her! Pay her, and see her out!"

The man bowed and signaled for her to follow him with a grunt.

"The Council will *have* to grant me his network," the old man mumbled to himself, giddily. "No one else can manage it. I am the logical choice. I will take it all! And without so much as a shot fired!"

Madison did not move, but rather stared down at the old man.

The guard beckoned her again, this time barking in Japanese for her to follow.

My work isn't finished.

"Oyabun Minowara."

The old man shook his head and looked at her, startled as though acknowledging her presence for the first time. "What do you want, woman! Take your money and get the fuck out of here!"

The words were like a slap in the face. The Madam tugged on her shoulder, begging to be released. "A moment of your time, Minowara-dono. Please!"

His face twisted in disgust, and he looked past her at the man who should be seeing her out. "Absolutely not. Now, go! Honda! Get this wretched woman out of my home."

A rage that seemed to begin at her toes and end in flames behind her eyes consumed Madison, parting her lips and stealing her tongue. "For seven years I have served the Minowara, *selflessly*. For seven years I have slain your enemies most brutally and most efficiently, protecting the Minowara from police, from politicians, from rivals, and even from innocents. Now, you *will* listen to me!"

Minowara sat back on his throne and looked up at her in disbelief. The men at the bar stood up; she could hear their

687

shuffling. She could also make out their movements in her periphery.

"I have served loyally," she continued. "Have I not?"

Minowara gripped the arms of his chair, glaring up at her. "You've done only what you were paid to do."

"Keep your money. It has never been about the money!"

Minowara chuckled and looked towards his guards with a mock-confused expression. "Not about money! What in life is not about money? Then what has it been about, you stupid woman? Why am I even talking to you? You there! Get this madwoman out of here!"

"Love," she told him.

The word halted Boss Minowara. The hand that had been waving frantically for guards fell down into his lap. The old man was legitimately stupefied. "Love?"

"I've only wanted one thing, Oyabun Minowara: to be a part of your family." She knelt, setting her bag, with The Madam inside, down beside her. "I will start at the bottom. I will work my way up the ranks. Give me a chance and I will prove to you that—"

"Shut up!" he screamed before descending into a fit of rattling coughs. When he was done hacking, he propped his arms on the chair, trying to stand. "Stop this nonsense! Get her out of here! I'll not ask again." He waved his men forward. "If you don't want money, fine! Get her out of my sight and give her nothing."

Madison's rage was gone now. All that remained was a cold sense of loneliness and the apathy that came with it.

All this time and effort. To get so close... Only to have this dying, old...

"To think I would make you Minowara?" Minowara continued. "You stupid whore!"

Green was buckshot, and sat first up in the chamber of The Madam. She didn't bother standing before firing the first shot. The blast tore her bag in two and sent one of Minowara's men pinwheeling backward, his insides already pouring out. She tore the gun from her bag in a blizzard of incidentals and cocked it, even as her compact, eyeliner, and Q-tips tumbled to the floor. She fired flechette into the faces of the two men who stood by the bar, dumbstruck. One gripped his face, screaming, and ran for the door; the other, the closer of the two, was nearly decapitated and died instantly.

You old, near-sighted fool!

A shot was fired in her direction and missed, striking the boss' chair. Shards of expensive wood flipped into the air like confetti. She shot back, firing a slug that took the arm from another of Minowara's men. Wailing, the old man struck her harmlessly. She snatched him up the way she would a toddler. Using the old man as a shield, she fired, cocked one-handed, and fired again from behind the great chair. When the chamber was empty, she quickly reloaded, pinning the Oyabun of the Minowara to his chair with a knee. The cartridges were as familiar in her hands as poker chips were in Daisuke's.

689

The room provided shoddy cover for his men, and in moments the last of them lay face down, his back torn asunder as though he'd erupted from within.

Minowara was a sputtering mess.

"You bitch! You're dead! I'll see you cut to pieces. Your body won't be fit for fishes. I'll see you ground down until not a yellow hair remains. You whore! You—"

The barrel of The Madam was very hot. She stamped it on him and seared a thick red circle on his forehead. His scream filled the chamber, and she couldn't help but laugh.

I've never branded someone before.

She took her time loading The Madam once more, selecting a red cartridge first this time, a slug.

"You know, you aren't exactly helping your cause right now."

Oyabun Minowara sat clutching his forehead in agony, and at the moment he looked very small, very old, and very fragile.

"For years I've received jobs from you, through intermediaries or through Raizen. In all that time, never once have you thanked me for my efforts, directly or indirectly. And my efforts have kept you and your progeny out of prison many, many times. And so, I'm curious, *Boss*, are you just being aloof? Is it arrogance? Or is it something else? Does the great and mighty Boss Minowara even know who I am? Am I so small to you as to not even matter?"

More men will be coming soon.

"What's my name, you pathetic old leech? Say my name."

"I know who you are, you wench! You're the Party Crasher! I know who you are! I know you have a family as well. I'll find them and—"

"Now, now. Threats at this stage serve only to exasperate the gruesome details of your demise."

Minowara sneered. His eyes were wide and defiant. "I have lived a long and prosperous life. There is nothing that you can do to unmake what I have accomplished. I am an old man, I've no illusions. What I have built is something a *worm* like you could never hope to accomplish. The Minowara will live on long after I am gone!"

I wouldn't be so sure.

She thumbed at her chest proudly, jabbing him in the shoulder violently with The Madam's barrel as she spoke. "Ich bin Madison Grünewald von Bad Königshofen!"

The slug evaporated everything above the shoulder and blew out the window. Minowara's body pooled in the chair before spilling over to collapse at her feet. In that moment, a merciless wind filled the room and set the curtains to flailing. Outside, Yvonne claimed the horizon, her outermost rain band a churning, maddening executioner's wall.

The Madam fell to her side and, for a while, all she could do was look down at the mess she'd made.

Like a frustrated child knocking toys about.

691

Bodies lay in bits about the room, their contents the inexplicable lashings of an abstractionist's brush. The ramifications of slaying the most prevalent yakuza boss in the State would reach far beyond any protection Sugihara's new Seidai could provide. And Sugihara knew that just as well as she. She'd been played, used. She'd allowed herself to be played, used.

How is this my life? Am I cancer? Am I unfit for the world? Why won't anyone accept me?

"Fool!" She slammed a boot into the old man's corpse. "I would have made an excellent yakuza!"

A shot sounded, and a handful of padding from the old man's chair flew into her face. She spun and fired in time to catch the assailant in the chest with a burst of buckshot before his next shot could be fired. She could hear the shouting voices of what sounded like an army.

I've done my part, Sugihara. The rest is on you. Hopefully, you'll teach your men that the Sedai was born from my efforts. Let them at least know my name. Even as she entertained the thought, she knew how ridiculous it sounded.

Men began pouring into the room from both entrances. She decided to head back the way she'd come, and blazed her way in a merciless barrage of shotgun fire. Men drew weapons on her but died, as these types of gun battles were not decided by aim but rather hesitation, and she had none. In truth, that was her secret. With The Madam, all she had to do was fire. If the shot connected, which most times it did, great, if it didn't, the boom always startled her opposition out of their shoes, at best freezing them in place and at the least throwing their aim off. While they struggled to act in the eye of her barrel, she was free. She fired efficiently, choosing the most opportune times to pull the trigger. She fired between people, letting the spread of buckshot hit targets in pairs. She fired from the hip and always at center mass. When the last shot had been fired, The Madam smoked, practically sighing in ecstasy.

If murder were sex, The Madam could grind a man into the bed until they were little more than a quivering, exhausted sack of expletives.

She left the main room, stepping over a mound of corpses, and began to jog for the entrance. A hallway was no place for a gunfight, and so her jog became a headlong sprint. At the end of the hall, she paused, holding herself up against the wall. She checked the chamber to find it halfway spent, and loaded three more shells, no longer discriminating between shot types. She stuck her head out momentarily and could see suits taking up positions around the foyer. Shots were fired from the other end of the corridor. Rounds shattered windows and tore a painting from the wall. She returned fire down the now-empty hallway. A moment later a hand and pistol fired blindly at her once more. These shots struck the ceiling and carpet harmlessly. Nevertheless, the corridor was shoddy cover and it was just a matter of time before they had her pinned and trapped totally. She took a deep breath and darted across the marble for the entryway. Gunshots echoed and rounds struck the marble to make almost musical twanging sounds.

You are going to die. Accept this as fact and die messily. Savagely!

She couldn't be sure how many there were — a dozen, maybe more. The yakuza dress code, however, played to her favor, as their black suits could be spotted easily against the pearl-white walls.

Something tugged at her jacket from behind, most likely a bullet. She threw herself down to slide across the marble on her side. She saw muzzle flashes like cameras and fired at anything moving. A figure fell. She cocked and fired again at the person. Getting back to her feet now, the entrance loomed like a single ray of sunlight in the destruction that would be Typhoon Yvonne. The double doors were open wide.

Holding The Madam to her side like a bayonet, she ran as fast as she'd ever run in her life. No longer could she hear the crack of small-arms fire. In her ears now were the dueling banjos of the heartbeat in her chest and yakuza shoes against the marble. Something struck her calf, yanking her leg out in front of her. As she twisted her body to break her fall, something struck her in the face. The flash of white in her eyes was accompanied by the crunch of bone on bone. Her head struck the marble and for a second she slid like a child in the snow.

Flat on the marble, the pain in her leg excruciating, she waited for the bullet that would end it. A man was yelling something in Japanese that she hadn't the energy to process, and a dress shoe crashed into her midsection.

She swung her hands blindly in search of The Madam, even as foreign hands lifted her from the marble. Helpless, she was hoisted into the air with what seemed like a minimal effort. With a rapidly swelling eye and a brain full of bees, she peered into the furious face of one of Boss Minowara's most trusted men, Johjima. It was the seasoned grunt's fist that had leveled her.

The bullet that hit my leg was probably his too. Impressive...

Johjima positioned her over one shoulder, as though to carry her off. But as her wits returned, injected with nature's all-natural performance enhancers, fear and adrenaline, she recalled that Johjima was a judoka: a practitioner in the Japanese art of throwing people. He wasn't carrying her anywhere, but rather preparing for a spectacular slam into the marble that would almost certainly kill her.

Madison reached into her boot and withdrew the modest serrated knife hidden there. Perched on his shoulder with not a moment to spare, she thrust the blade into Johjima's jugular just as he bucked his hips to fling her over his shoulder. She gripped the blade tightly, even as it popped buttons from his dress shirt and tore the lapel from his blazer. As the entirety of her body flipped over his shoulder, and with her blade driven to the hilt in his chest, the result was the ghastly unzipping of Johjima's torso. Madison struck the marble on her back and was immediately doused in the yakuza's blood. The warm sensation of his death, mixed with the crushing impact of the floor, sent her into a frenzy. Remembering the pistol on her waist, she drew it. The black blurs of yakuza in her sight were fired upon until they were felled or retreated. She emptied the remainder of the magazine into Johjima's face.

Scrambling on hands and knees now, she reached The Madam and rolled onto her back, firing back the way she'd come to catch a pursuer in the pelvis. She cocked and fired at another, all the while scooting on her back for the front door. A third man fell, followed by a fourth. She cocked and fired. A fifth fell. She cocked and... nothing. The cartridge rolling depleted across the chipped and blood-pooled marble had been her last.

She aimed The Madam at anyone dumb enough to stick their head out until she was in the doorway. If men were alive, they were in hiding. As if on autopilot, she watched the world descend as she got to her feet and limped across the courtyard, taking cover briefly behind Minowara's ornate fountain. She watched, deaf to it all, as the gate grew larger, as the black BMW came into view and as the only man between her and freedom, Tadamasa, stared at her slack-jawed.

"I talked to the old man about your pay," she told him, ridiculously out of breath, ridiculously in pain, and ridiculously covered in the blood of his colleagues.

Tadamasa's pistol was aimed at her chest, and at this range there wasn't a fight to be had. Behind him, Sugihara's driver had exited the vehicle and was aiming at Tadamasa's back. But, with the gate closed, it was all for naught. She hadn't the strength to climb it before the rest of Minowara's men could get to them.

Tadamasa's eyes were wide, his pistol steady. "And? What did the miserly old fuck say?"

Still aiming the harmless and empty shotgun, she replied, "He said, 'tell Tadamasa that he can have whatever he can carry from the vault.'"

Tadamasa's smile was mirthless. He dropped his gun to the ground and turned his back. "Make it look good, woman. Don't hold back."

The wind and rain had picked up, but she felt none of it. "Open!"

As the gate began to swing, she charged in and slammed the butt of the shotgun into the back of Tadamasa's head with enough force to split his scalp and knock him unconscious.

"Thank you, Tadamasa-san," she said to his folding form.

She limped hurriedly down the cobblestone driveway to find the car door open for her. She fell into the car. Manic and breathless, she could only lie curled at the foot of the back seat as the car sped off.

"Things went well, I see," a voice said.

Sugihara.

It was a long time before she took her seat, and even longer before she truly came to terms with being alive. It was then, speeding along the 101 beneath a dark and heavy sky, that she finally allowed herself to cry.

24: You Should've Had My Back

"You're not just asking me to denounce my wife and the woman I love, you're asking me to denounce my best friend. And for what? An old tyrant that no one will miss, and some dead gangsters? Please."

- Unit One Deputy Informant Yamazaki "Dice" Daisuke

"She's not answering."

[This might be a message,] Rena replied coolly. Dice could practically hear her shrug.

He gripped the steering wheel irritably, his knuckles turning white. "A message from whom, Rena? You of all people shouldn't be spouting nonsense about fate."

[I... I just want what's best for you, as a friend.]

"Then keep your word and help me find my wife!"

Dice could hear her sigh. Over Libra, a sigh sounded a lot like a plane flying too low.

Doing laps around a seven-block radius of the Veins, he was hoping to put himself within a short drive of whatever Minowara gambling den Madison might be in.

His plan was simple: flee Sun City. With Boss Minowara murdered, likely by one of Sugihara's men or perhaps Sugihara himself, anyone associated with the would-be usurper was a dead man, or *dead woman*. The streets would be a war zone soon, and not even the Party Crasher would be safe.

They would leave for Eden together. There, Sugihara wouldn't try to reach them, nor would Sakakibara. Eden was the turf of several rival gangs; gangs an organization freshly down one Oyabun wouldn't dare encroach upon.

Sakakibara, the old friend of Boss Minowara, was now the most senior chairman of the syndicate and de facto heir to the throne. He would most certainly name Raizen the new head of the family, but not until vengeance on the traitor Sugihara had been wrought. Yakuza vengeance was a bloody, bloody affair, and something he and Madison had best not stick around for.

[Dice. To help you, I've had to violate the Libra terms of use on several counts. I've hacked the Unified Cellular Network. Your woman has gone to great lengths to avoid even accessory registration.]

"Well, what have you got?"

[Someone in possession of the mobile whose number you gave me is moving along Highway Nine, towards Section Four. Looks like a black BMW. The car certainly looks like your typical yakuza transport.]

Dice breathed a sigh of relief. "First of all, that's racist. Secondly, thank you, thank you, thank you!"

Hitting a corner close enough to scrape the wheel against the curb, he sped the car towards the 101.

[Dice.]

"Yes, Rena."

[I don't know how to say this.]

"Then don't."

[I'm going to try anyway.]

He took a cigarette from the pack sitting in the passenger seat.

[I know you feel like you are tied to them. I know you think you have a responsibility, to them and to your wife. I would even go as far as to say, I know you think you are that way. What I mean is, I know you still think you are like them.]

"Rena, please."

[Listen to me. You've come so far and we are all so very proud of you. You've proven yourself to be more worthy of a Unit One jacket than anyone. You shouldn't let these people drag you down. You're better than that and your future is bright. Now is the time to cut ties.]

"There's no future without Maddy."

[Daisuke, she gunned a man down in cold blood. And you and I know it wasn't her first.]

"Rena, please! Simon Pan was a pimp and likely a murderer himself."

[And what about Chris?]

"Chris is alive."

[Barely, and would he be if she'd had her way?]

After a long pause, Rena continued, a new tone in her voice. It was a stern, cautionary tone. He hated it.

701

[I feel obligated to remind you, Deputy Lieutenant, that the oath of the State does not permit a relinquishing of responsibilities, even for deputies. You can't quit, not legally, not without being processed out. If you run, they — we — will hunt you until your dying day.]

For some reason, the cigarette would not light, and he cast it aside irritably. He pawed for another and found the box empty. He remembered her face, framed in the wispy white of a wedding gown purchased with extortion money, and began chuckling. It was a mad, mirthless chuckle.

[Dice. We love you, all of us. You're family! Do the right thing. Find Grünewald and bring her in. She'll be safe with the SDC.]

"In prison," he finished.

Rena was silent.

"Fuck!"

A weight under his eyes caused him to frown and, as he swung onto the 101, he couldn't help but groan. He thanked Rena curtly in Japanese and disconnected.

His mobile rang just as he disconnected from the Libra channel. He picked it up and greeted the caller gruffly, hoping sincerely to hear Madison's voice.

"Yama-kun?"

The voice was barely audible.

"Maddy?"

"Yama-kun, it has been too long."

702

The voice was feminine and could have been delivered by a sprite, so fragile it sounded. He could hear sadness, a wellspring of it. He pressed the mobile to his ear with great force and listened intently.

"Yama-kun, do you recognize my voice?"

He did, and it dredged up an Atlantis of suppressed or forgotten emotions.

"It's been a long time, Omoe," he greeted her in their native tongue.

They say that when you die you get to relive moments in your life. If that were true, Dice's memories could be found in specific categories, romantic relations, of course, having their own partition. In that slim manila folder labeled "love," the dossiers of only two women would exist. The bulk of that folder would belong to none other than his wife: the German assassin he sought at present. The rest of that folder, however, while not as thick with vivid images, was pristine. And it would detail his time spent with the daughter of the now-former boss of the Minowara yakuza, the beautiful Omoe.

"My father is murdered, Yama-kun."

He could hear her sniffling.

"My father is murdered, Yama-kun, most brutally."

The highway shimmered in a fresh coat of rainfall, and beaded droplets, caught in the red taillights of the cars he overtook, ran across the windshield like tiny fireballs, apocalyptic and beautiful. It gave the impression of rapid, intergalactic travel, though nothing could be further from the

703

truth. They were here. They were on Earth. And there was nothing grand or new about their journey.

"Yama-kun, can I see you?"

He had no choice but to consider it a trap.

Sakakibara was as cunning and vicious as they came, even in his old age, and using Omoe as a lure was well within the boundaries of acceptable stratagem. After all, he had to assume that at least some would find him implicit. In the interest of prudence, the old man would squeeze him for everything he knew about Sugihara's plot, no matter how little, and have him killed in the end, just to be safe. If he and Sakakibara were to coexist, his only hope would be to somehow convince the man of his innocence *before* falling into their hands. Anything else was certain death.

He chose his words carefully, very carefully.

"My team will be investigating, but information is still sparse. For what it's worth, I plan to do everything in my power to help."

Per the detective's playbook, he revealed nothing about what he knew or did not know about the incident. A perfect, receptive blank slate.

Omoe responded but in that moment his mobile chimed, drowning her words out.

It was a call. From Madison. He answered.

"Madison!"

On the other end he could hear nothing but the muffled sounds of cloth against the receiver. The call disconnected but a few moments later the phone chimed. Looking at the screen, he had one new notification. Dice pressed the "Messages" icon.

It was also from Madison.

"yu shouldh ave hadmy bvack"

He stared at the message, it's meaning unclear.

German?

Dice's unwillingness to even attempt to learn her native language had always been a point of contention between them. As he drove, he tried to imagine what the message could mean but soon it became impossible to focus on anything but the hypnotic influx of Botts' dots and highway lane markings.

It didn't matter what the message meant, after all. He would ask her soon... face to face.

Dice raced along the 101 for nearly thirty minutes before he realized that a black motorcycle with a missing side view mirror was following him. He lowered the window and stuck a middle finger out. Both the rider and his swarthy, un-helmeted passenger returned the gesture with their own. Their black jackets flailed in the wind and rain, and Dice couldn't help but feel grateful that somebody had his back.

25: Diminuendo

"My name is Madison Grünewald. I am from Bad Königshofen, Deutschland. My favorite pianist is Martha Argerich, and I want to attend the Musashino Academia Musicae because I want to one day play as well as Mrs. Argerich. Also, I am excited to learn about Japanese culture. Domo arigatou gozaimasu!"

- Applicant: Madison Grünewald

Age: 16 years

Date: April 2, 2028

Application Status: Approved

She'd been shot twice in her mad dash to escape the Minowara estate. One bullet had torn the upper part of her left ear away. A second round, of significant caliber, had struck just above the boot on her right leg and had left for an exit wound a flap of flesh about the size of a maple leaf. This, she had wrapped in a bandana that did little to mitigate blood loss. With the adrenaline gone now, the pain was excruciating.

A hospital was not an option, and so she would have to wait for a yakuza physician.

Who knows how long that'll be, she thought despairingly, *and who knows which side of the coup they've fallen on? If I lose this leg...*

For now, she would have to hold her tongue and deal with it as best she could. Sugihara had given her a bottle of Jack Daniels from the trunk of the car, and she clutched it to her chest in a tight grip.

She climbed out of the car somewhere in the industrial part of Section Four. As she exited the vehicle, Sugihara loyalists greeted her. Both Saga brothers, Senjuro and Junichirou, were on hand, as was the Lobster Etsuya. Several senior yakuza she wouldn't have expected to see were there as well, along with about fifty others. These were mostly lieutenants, but she spotted at least two patriarchs. All in all, she estimated about half of the Minowara leadership.

Sugihara exited the vehicle with his hands in the air, howling like a wolf. He hugged himself and bowed like a rock star at the end of a concert. He wore a black T-shirt and Scottish kilt. Covering his head of dyed and feathered hair was a crocodile-leather bush hat, the strap of which he chewed in his mouth as he greeted the mass of Minowara defectors.

"Welcome, everyone! Welcome," he greeted in Japanese. "We'll get the party started soon. We're only waiting for the guest of honor."

Madison propped herself up against the car to take the pressure off her calf, and wiped at the blood on her face with a handkerchief soaked in whiskey.

A light and refreshing rain began to fall. She stared upward at a starless sky. The light of Sun City reflected against the clouds and gave the appearance of exposed brain matter.

I can't believe I made it.

She thought about Minowara's body, crumpled at her feet.

You stupid old man! I could have helped you stamp out this rebellion, but you just couldn't get past your prejudices. She spat on the pavement and watched the drizzle mingle with it. Blood loss was making her lightheaded.

The newly minted Sedai defectors were gathered between two large factories very near to the coast. The patriotic music heralding the Liberty Day parade could be heard. According to Sugihara, the parade would not be postponed, but rather moved up one day in light of Typhoon Yvonne. The State hoped to power through the event and use the storm as an excuse to clear the streets of revelers early. The parade music was being broadcast via a PA system that seemed to cover the whole city. The looping, triumphal piece was utter shit not fit for a child's recorder and would play until nine PM, only to begin again at eight AM the following morning.

The headlights of a car appeared at the edge of the compound, its halogens highlighting the tiny droplets of water that swirled in the air. At the sight of the vehicle, Sugihara jauntily skipped to meet it. The men gathered there followed, and she limped to do the same.

A silver Cadillac pulled up and the driver, a man she recognized as Urabashi, an elder yakuza on the side of Sugihara, exited from the driver's seat. He walked around the car and opened the passenger-side door.

"What the fuck is wrong with you?" a voice demanded. "You stupid mule! You had *one* job!"

Raizen Minowara stepped out of the vehicle and snatched Urabashi by the collar, oblivious to his surroundings. "I told you to take me to my father's! Does this look like—" His words caught in his throat as he noticed the mass of suits watching, waiting just beyond the light of the car. He released Urabashi. It was then that Sugihara, grinning ear-to-ear like the Cheshire cat, emerged from the crowd to greet him.

Madison watched with a grim fascination. So mesmerized had she been that she hadn't noticed the accountant Junichirou come to stand beside her. Somewhat surprisingly, he extended an arm to help her stand and offered a gentle, almost sympathetic smile.

In contrast to Junichirou, there was a vicious energy in the group at the sight of Raizen Minowara. Men paced like hyenas surrounding a wounded lion.

"Sugihara!" Raizen yelled, shaking a fist. "What the hell is this! What's going on?"

Raizen, as usual, was dressed impeccably. He wore a slate-grey suit with a crimson dress shirt and ivory tie. His shoes were wingtips and spotless. He'd changed outfits entirely from when she had seen him at the estate only hours before.

Sugihara approached and extended a hand, which Raizen accepted impatiently.

"What's going on? I can't reach anyone at the estate."

Still gripping his hand, Sugihara smiled, his shark's teeth glimmering. "Have you tried séance?"

"What?"

The men in the crowd who understood his words guffawed. Sugihara turned to Urabashi, the driver. "Where's the daughter, where's Omoe Minowara?"

"She wasn't at the hotel. We're still looking for her."

Sugihara released Raizen — who stood slack-jawed — and removed his ridiculous hat slowly. "Find her, find her, find her, FIND HER! FIND HER, YOU FUCK! DO IT NOW!"

Raizen raised a hand limply, visibly stunned, as Urubashi raced to climb back into the car.

"Sugi—" Raizen croaked. "What have you done? What is this? Where is my father?"

Madison nudged Junichirou, and he helped her hop forward on her good leg.

Sugihara turned to face her, still talking to Raizen. "Your father could be a bit bull-*headed*," he proclaimed. "I guess what I'm trying to say is, many of us weren't happy with the direction the family was *head*-ed. I mean, it takes a lot to be the *head* of a criminal enterprise!"

His joke was cruel and really only intended for her. No one else knew yet that The Madam had taken the old man's head off.

"Enough," she said, not sure if he could even hear her over the grumbling of the crowd.

Sugihara cackled. "His efforts, at least, were *head* and shoulders above the rest!"

"Enough!"

The men who'd been chuckling went silent. Propping herself up on Junichirou's shoulder, she came to stand before predator *and* prey. "Enough, Sugihara."

Raizen shook his head as though dazed. "Maddy, Maddy, what is he saying?"

She looked him in his face. "Your father is dead."

His knees buckled, and Raizen fell. Unable to catch him, she could only watch as he hit the filthy, oil-streaked pavement on hands and knees. "Maddy, what are you saying?"

Raizen. This is pathetic. Don't let them see you like this...

"Maddy, Maddy—"

She felt a rage building up in her at the sight of her old friend being broken so easily. "Don't call me that!" she yelled. "We aren't children anymore!"

Raizen looked up at her with tear-filled eyes. It was then that he seemed to notice the blood covering her jacket and skirt. The blood that covered her leg and pooled in her boot. "Was it you?" His lips quivered, his eyes searched. "Maddy, did you kill my father?"

Instead of the heir apparent to the largest yakuza family in the State, she saw only the boy who would loan her money to play pachinko. The generous but boastful boy who would buy them all shaved ice rather than suffer to eat it alone. She

711

saw the boy who always wore the nicest clothes, the boy whose first car was a luxury sedan. She saw the boy who always talked of one day being king.

"We were friends, Maddy," he blubbered. "Yama-kun, Sugi-kun, Maddy-chan and Rai-Rai, remember?" His head was down, and he swatted at the gravel aimlessly. "Father..."

Get up you fool! Where is your pride?

"Stand up!" she yelled. "Not like this, Raizen. Stand up! Don't you see what's happening? Stand up, you fool!"

Raizen's head was down, his brow nearly touching the pavement. "But Maddy, we were friends..."

She moved to get him, but it was Sugihara who extended a hand first.

A lump in her throat, she watched as Raizen took Sugihara's hand and was hoisted to his feet.

"It's not as bad as it sounds," Sugihara told him with a patronizing frown. "At least it was quick. Not everybody gets a quick death..."

Raizen snapped out of his grief-imposed paralysis and reached into his coat, but Sugihara was faster. He snatched the heir to the Minowara throne by the collar and bit down on his throat. Raizen screamed, and a geyser of blood arched into the crowd, dowsing men. His eyes as wide as silver dollars, Raizen fought to break Sugihara's grip. When he finally managed to tear free of the much smaller man, his esophagus came free as well.

Madison choked back bile as Raizen's dying gaze fell on her. His mouth opened and closed, even as it filled with blood. His lips were flicking, trying to make an "M" sound.

Even now he's calling for me...

She watched as Raizen fell on his face in the rain and filth. He convulsed on the damp pavement, his wingtips kicking wildly as he tried in vain to delay the departure of his life. Like this, Raizen Minowara died. It was a slow death, and when it finally ended, no one, not even Sugihara, seemed pleased. The sight was made even more absurd by the patriotic soundtrack blaring throughout the city.

Sugihara was the first to break the silence. He signaled to someone in the group, and was handed a canister. Tipping the canister over, he doused Raizen's back, thighs, and head in kerosene.

"Tonight, we celebrate the sacrifice of the Minowara clan! For it is upon their ashes" —he pulled a Zippo from his kilt and flicked it alight— "that the *Seidai* is born!" Sugihara's expression was sad. "Good-bye, brother."

The crowd erupted in cheers at the sight of Raizen's flaming corpse.

If pressed to put words to how she felt in that moment, Madison knew she would be incapable. In her quest for recognition, she had brought this new era into existence. And, as she looked down on the crackling grey suit of a man who'd shown her nothing but admiration and kindness, she felt sick with herself. Sick with the world.

713

Raizen. Goddamnit. You didn't deserve this…

Thankfully, in the wind and rain, men soon became restless and the savage bonfire quickly lost its macabre appeal. Sugihara, frowning, soon gave the order to disperse. "We'll meet at the club at ten o'clock. Tonight, we celebrate! YOSHA!"

As the crowd departed, Sugihara came over to her and placed a hand on her shoulder. She did her best to mask her grief, but she knew it wasn't enough.

"How are you?"

"I'm fine, just a little banged up. I've lost a lot of blood."

Sugihara smiled with his mouth closed. It was the smile he used when he was trying to be nice but looked nothing short of vile covered in blood. "Okay. Let's get you cleaned up," he said, walking towards the car. "You've done a great thing for the Seidai, *Maddy*."

He placed the stupid hat back on his head and turned to face her.

Sugihara never calls me "Maddy." He hates that nickname. It's "Madison" or nothing at all.

She reached for the pistol on her belt, but found nothing. It was then she remembered leaving it on the marble floor of Minowara's foyer.

"On second thought…"

The gun was in his hands quickly, the barrel aimed at her chest.

714

"Where are we going to find a good doctor at this hour, *Maddy*? Besides," he drawled, "I have a party to go to."

The muzzle flashed twice.

Junichiro — whose arm she'd been leaning on — yelped and released her.

Madison tried to reach for his throat, but her arms were unresponsive. Everything went sideways, and for some reason she thought of the Titanic. Something hit her hard in the back. The mud and rainwater splashing up and into her eyes told her that "something" had been the ground.

Stunned, Madison found herself looking up at Sugihara, unable to speak.

"Fuck…" Sugihara said, making an expression like he was frustrated with himself. "I didn't want this. In Hell, blame Yama-kun, not me." He looked as though he might say more, but spun on his heels and began to walk away.

She tried to yell after him, to promise the most brutal of reprisals, but her mouth was already full of blood.

The pain in her chest began to numb quickly and this — she knew — was not a good thing. With shaking hands, she managed to fish her mobile from her jacket.

Daisuke…

She found his contact and called but couldn't bring the phone to her ear. She hung up and selected "Message" with a finger that felt made of wood.

What do I say?

715

It was cold and the clouds seemed to churn faster. Madison watched rain flitter through the mangy yellow streetlight towards her like a million shooting stars, searching for the words that would be her last.

What do I say?

"You were right?"

No! Fuck you, Daisuke!

She gripped the mobile in a fist that was shaking so violently she thumped herself in the torso.

Madison tried to lift her head up, but it was pointless. The pain in her leg was gone now, replaced by something far more terrifying.

I shouldn't blame you for this. You warned me. And yet... we could've done it together.

She tried to thumb in a message but it was becoming very hard to breathe.

No. This isn't what I want to say.

Holding the phone to her chest, she searched frantically for the words, the terror of leaving in silence greater even than the unknown bearing down on her.

She fantasized drunkenly about the vengeance she would enact on Sugihara.

When she looked at the screen once more it was covered in blood. She wiped the screen with the back of her hand but it didn't help. She keyed in a message, unable to read the text, and pressed the "Send" key.

716

Can't even read my own dying words, she thought bitterly.

She tried to swear, but her lips just sputtered fruitlessly, splashing her own blood up into her face like a fountain. This made her laugh, but it was short-lived. Likewise, her rage petered out quickly and left the door wide open for terror.

I'm not ready to die.

Terror came but, reliant on faculties lost to the dying, flailed at her with the same efficacy as Boss Minowara. Madison, lost in a blizzard of rapidly decoupling fears, dogmas, and ambitions, focused instead on the galaxy of raindrops. They moved in a magnificent ballet, one never touching another. An infinite ensemble, really, never ending, never predictable, never dying.

Chapter 26: Estranged

"Hey, baby. Sorry I didn't write sooner. The correspondence officer is a fucking hippo-faced mall cop and restricted my access to the computer lab because he's a hippo-faced mall cop. Anyway, things are good now that Kempachi's out. With him gone I don't think his people will continue to give me trouble. Hell, I might be able to finish this stretch in peace.

I miss you and I hope you are doing well. I talked to Raizen and he said you were asking about work. Is this true? I thought we talked about this. There haven't been yakuza on'na in my lifetime. And to think they'd take a Westerner is absurd. I hope Raizen is exaggerating. Please just sit tight, love. I'll be home soon."

- Message from inmate #1776 - Daisuke Yamazaki to mgrunewald@{redacted}.com

Fuchū Prison, Fuchū Tokyo

Ministry of Justice

[What do you see?]

"You've no coverage?"

[No. You're in a part of Section Four with pretty spotty coverage.]

"I don't see anything, but the smell…"

[The smell?]

"Rena, please keep this channel clear for mission-critical communications."

[What? AJ, you—]

AJ disconnected from the secure channel and peered over Chris' shoulder as the bike pulled alongside Dice's rapidly decelerating cruiser. The car came to a halt and the motorcycle skidded to a halt a split second later. AJ climbed off, careful to avoid searing his jeans on the bike's muffler.

The rain was blowing sideways, and yet he smelled smoke in the air.

Chris dismounted Revenant just as Dice's car door flew open with a heel. The deputy informant burst out of the car sprinting, his long, white overcoat trailing behind him.

Without a word, Chris and AJ drew their firearms and ran after.

They followed their partner to a staggering halt in a clearing between two large warehouses. The area reeked of something foul, something that stood AJ's hair on end. Through the alleyway, formed by the three-story commercial buildings, he could see the light of Section Three reflecting off the turbulent waters of the bay.

The ground was strewn in cigarettes, hundreds, some still smoldering. In the center of the clearing, a blackened mound lay, steaming in the rain.

AJ knew instantly what that mound had been.

Dice staggered into the clearing drunkenly. AJ watched as he went to a knee over the recently burnt corpse.

He looked at Chris. "That explains the smell."

Chris did not respond verbally, but holstered his weapon.

As they approached, AJ noticed that there were, in fact, two casualties. The first lay facedown and was smoldering. The person's legs were bent at terrible angles, angles indicative of a struggle and of a drawn-out, miserable demise. The second victim, a woman, lay on her back but a few yards away. Her eyes were closed, her face white as wave crests, and she lay surrounded by a shimmering black substance that he knew was blood.

After what looked like a prayer, Dice moved away from the burned figure. He quickly saw the woman, and what happened next confused AJ greatly.

Dice let out a moan that could be heard over the rhythmic slashing sounds of rain, over the patriotic melody of Sun City's Liberty Day Network, and even over the low drone and accompanying whoop of rapidly approaching hover units and their sirens.

The deputy informant collapsed onto his knees next to the woman and scooped her up into his lap.

AJ could hold his tongue no longer. "Dice, what the hell is this? What's going on?"

His partner and friend ignored him and, in the strangest gesture, straightened the dead woman's skirt, bringing it back down over her exposed thighs. Though he appeared to be sobbing, he held her head gently and placed an ear to her chest.

"There are bodies," Chris was saying, most likely to Rena.

AJ approached slowly.

He knew her…

Dice's face was contorted, his eyes scrunched up, almost invisible in the knot of his brow. "Dice, man. Talk to me! What's going on?"

"I recognize one," Chris continued. "It's the Party Crasher. The other, I couldn't say. Looks like he was wearing a suit. Nice shoes, probably yakuza. He's burnt through and through, execution-style."

Dice took the woman's pulse and listened for a heartbeat; his movements had become frantic.

AJ moved closer, his hands outstretched. "Talk to me, buddy."

Dice, whose head had been pressed against the woman's chest, looked up with eyes that might have belonged to an owl.

"Get a medic, AJ! Get a medic! Do it now!"

AJ wanted confirmation from Chris, but he appeared to be engaged in dialogue with Rena via Libra. Dice held the woman in his lap, rocking her gently, even as the rain pitter-pattered off the leather of his overcoat.

"Dice, man. That's the Party Crasher, the assassin that tried to kill Chris. What the fuck are you doing?"

721

His friend looked up, his teeth exposed, his nose wrinkled like tin foil. His movement was almost imperceptible, so fast it was. In his hand now was a chrome revolver, very similar to the one he'd discarded a week ago. Dice held it in a shaking grasp, his face, too, a quivering mess. "AJ, get a medic," he said with a snarling lip. "Get a medic, or I swear to God..."

AJ leaned against the brick and watched as the mechanized ambulance scooped up the woman. Her motionless body slid down the silvery chute into the body of the vehicle.

The rain came down now in lashing, windblown sheets, and the alleyway had become a howling vortex. Over its whine, he called out to Dice. Either his partner didn't hear or didn't acknowledge. Instead, Deputy Informant Daisuke Yamazaki climbed into the ambulance without so much as a glance. As it sped off — no doubt headed for Cedar Medical — AJ could only watch, befuddled.

They were friends, he thought. *Dice and the Party Crasher were definitely friends. I guess it makes sense, considering all the time he spends with the Minowara.*

Sun City Police Department detectives were next to arrive. They quickly established a parameter, deploying video drones and stationing officers. AJ watched them work, with no small amount of admiration for their efficiency.

He must have known... He knew that she attacked Chris, and kept it from us.

One senior detective approached him, requesting to proceed with the investigation, as was protocol. After appearing to give it some thought, AJ gave them clearance. The investigation would now proceed as a municipal homicide rather than that of State pertinence, which, despite the unit's apparent personal ties, was appropriate.

If it stays with the State Defense Consortium, she'll never see justice. After all, she tried to take out one of our own. Investigating the murder of the Party Crasher will fall dead fucking last on our list of priorities, right after arresting the city's last skyrail defecator.

It's the least I can do... for a comrade.

AJ watched the detectives collect what were believed to be the murderer's shell casings, collect cigarette butts and take photos of a gas canister, scan the burn victim and x-ray them. Likewise, AJ watched as the coroner's unit removed the body with its spatula-like arm, and would forever remember the tearing sound the corpse made leaving the pavement.

Apparently, silk turns into a fine powder when burnt, a powder that takes on an oily, inky quality in water. He knew this now because when the coroners picked the dead man up from the pavement, his blackened corpse was naked but for a belt and shoes.

What a fucked-up way to go out, he thought.

Chris, who'd been wrapping up his own forensic analysis, approached with his head low. "You want a ride back?"

AJ found himself reluctant to leave the scene, though unsure why.

"No thanks. I'll take the cruiser back."

"You ok?"

The question kind of surprised him. *None of this is about me*, he almost said.

"I'm fine. Why do you ask?"

"I know you and Dice are close."

"I feel for him. I don't fully understand what's happening, but I feel for him."

Chris crossed his arms. "Yeah, I guess I do too."

"But that doesn't change the fact," AJ felt he needed to add, "that she tried to kill you."

His partner seemed to contemplate this. After a long pause, Chris extended a fist. AJ slammed his fist into it, and Chris was on his way. After the lieutenant had gone, he went back to watching the police work.

After decoupling the personal aspects, it was quite clear that something big had just occurred. Something bigger than Dice. Something bigger than the Party Crasher. Something bigger than Unit One, even.

Boss Minowara gunned down. The Party Crasher gunned down. All in one night...

Somebody's making a move.

AJ's mind immediately went to Luther Gueye.

The Titans and the Minowara had held a truce for years, with only minor skirmishes occurring from time to time.

But now the yakuza boss was dead. For better or for worse, the landscape had changed.

AJ walked over to where the woman's body had been. There was a phone on the ground. He knelt and looked at it. The display was covered in blood.

If they were friends, this phone could spell the end of Dice's career.

He looked around. Confident no one was looking, he picked up the phone.

"Did you find something, sir?" a voice asked.

Startled, AJ turned to find an older detective watching him from the shadows.

"A phone, but it's my partner's. Looks like he dropped it checking for vitals."

The detective studied him for a moment. AJ was careful to keep his expression blank, the phone in his grip. He was ready to crush it if need be. After all, that was what it meant to have your partner's back.

The detective scoffed but after a moment added: "Carry on, then, sir."

27: Abdication

"I accept the Nobel Prize for Peace at a time when my home, the proud nation of Togo, finds itself in the maw of another civil war. Even now, men and woman fight to know peace from the oppression of rapacious and apathetic drug lords. I accept this award on behalf of them, the people.

While the Gueye Initiative has saved tens of thousands of lives by giving homes to those displaced by the conflict, it can do more. And so, I accept this award not as a mark of accomplishment, but rather as a charge; an entitlement as heavy in responsibility as it is in recognition. I accept this only on the self-imposed terms that I will continue to work for the people of Togo, the peoples of Africa, and the nations of this world."

- The Nobel Peace Prize Acceptance Speech of Dr. Luther Gueye

"Why have you not packed, Vivianne?"

She sat in the window seat of the living room with her feet up. She was staring at her phone, a stupid expression on her face.

Bellhops moved about, loading luggage to take down to the cars waiting. At this very moment, Luther's jet was being fueled at Sun City International. He was hoping to be airborne within the hour. Before the rapidly worsening weather grounded all flights.

"Vivianne!"

She looked up at him wearily.

"Pack your things, woman! Why are you just sitting there?"

Looking around frantically, Luther could not find his pin. The sigil of the Octumvirate held great meaning to him.

"Have you seen my pin, the platinum one?"

"I'm not afraid of the Major," she said blandly.

Her comment caught him off guard and took a moment to process.

"The Major? What? Nor should you be. He's a paper tiger. Is that what's bothering you?"

"No, brother. It's you."

She was staring at him, eyes wide.

"Are you trying to pick a fight? I don't have time for this, Vivianne. Pack your things. Do it now!"

Tossing her phone aside, his sister stood and walked toward him with her fists clenched.

Luther dropped the tote bag he'd been carrying.

"This is all your doing!" she screamed. "It's *you* they want! *You're* the one! I should have told them where to find you!"

The accusatory tone, the finger she pointed at him. Luther's mood soured quickly.

"You don't know what you're saying."

727

"Oh, but I do!" She was speaking French now, a transition she made often when she was angry. "You're a monster. And because of you, a good man is—"

She cocked a fist as though she would throw it.

"Enough, woman! Who cares? I can only presume you're talking about Thiago Garcia. Your friend was a joke. Do you know what *my* friends call him? '*Meh Guevara.*' Not 'Che Guevara' but '*Meh*' because no one with a brain thought his little movement was going *anywhere!*"

Vivianne's eyes were huge now and she was biting her lip.

"What? Didn't think I knew about your tryst with that sickly little man? That cripple? Grow up, Vivianne! I know everything."

I really don't have time for this, he thought, *but if I can put this Fifth Estate nonsense to bed, I'll make time.*

"Do you think I trust you, Vivianne?" he continued. "Are you stupid? I watched the footage of you with that Unit One detective. I saw how you batted your eyelashes. I saw how you giggled. I saw how you swung your hips. I am ten steps ahead of you today, just as I was on the day of your birth. And as I will be ten steps ahead of you on the day of your death."

"One can only hope." Her teeth were bared, her eyes blazing ferociously. "I pray for the day you die!"

Luther leaned in close. "Vivianne, I will outlive you. I will outlive Father. Just as I will outlive most people on this planet. All that is left to the unknown is the span of time between our deaths." He waved his hand between them. "If you continue on your present course, it will be long; the span, Vivianne, very long indeed."

She lashed out and struck his shoulder. She had been aiming for his face. Luther snatched her thin wrist, tempted to crush it in his hands, and yanked her in to him.

"Listen to me very carefully, little sister. *Pack your things.* And when you are done packing the garbage I've purchased for you, you will assist in getting Father ready for travel. You will do these things now, Vivianne. You will do these things now or so help me God... Do it now. NOW!"

She stopped struggling and he released her, only to be struck across the face.

"We are not going!"

My face!

Luther punched her with the intent to knock her unconscious, aiming for her temple. Instead, the blow caught her turning, and he could feel the depression of her eye in its socket as his knuckles collided. She crumpled to the carpet.

"How dare you strike me, cow! Where was your indignation at my work when you were emptying out the Prada store? Where was this disgust when I bought your condo in the Heights? Tell me, Vivianne! Where was it when I was paying for father's infinite series of treatments, surgeries, and that godforsaken money-pit chair he's bound to? Tell me, Vivianne! Tell me!"

729

Vivianne did not lose consciousness. Instead, she grabbed at the hem of his slacks, groaning. He raised a foot, prepared to drive it into her skull.

"Blood or no, you will learn to respect me!"

"STOP!"

The voice was unmistakable. Even behind the groan and grind, the hiss and whistle of rage, it was unmistakable. And, as it had done countless times before, it halted Luther.

"Stop this instant, fool!"

Father sat in the entryway to the piano room. His eyes were wide, his teeth bared, just as Vivianne's had been.

He straightened his suit, still standing over his sister, who lay curled in a sobbing ball at his feet.

"Father," he said calmly, "I will not tolerate disrespect. Not from her, not from anyone."

From his chair, Father beckoned. His hand, thinner even than Vivianne's, reached up from his lap, a simple gesture that required great effort as of late. "Come here, Son. Come here, you cursed fool."

Bellhops who'd been taking their luggage down to the car had stopped, and stood stunned, watching the commotion. Luther threw his hands in the air. "What the fuck are you people looking at? Get to work. We have a flight to catch!"

Elom Gueye waited, hand extended. Begrudgingly, Luther complied. Stepping over his sister, he resisted the powerful urge to grind his heel into her face.

"Luther, listen to me," his father said, taking his hand.

"Father, we've no time."

Acute disappointment spread across his father's weather-worn brow.

"Why are you looking at me like that?"

"Son, I've been complacent," his father said, clutching his hand firmly, "and I take full responsibility for what you have become."

"What I've become?"

"I had many opportunities to address your course. I saw where you were headed, and yet I did nothing. If a parent would take pride in their child's successes, as I have, then they must take responsibility for their failures."

"Tell me, Father, what have I 'become?'"

"Son, I do not wish to fight. I want only for you to listen. Now is the time to listen."

His father's grip was as hard as he knew the man could muster. And, as his father held his hand, Luther could feel his father's body trembling.

"What do you think of me, Son?"

Luther did not have to think.

"I love you. You are my father."

"What do you think of your sister?"

"I— well…"

"That you would strike her and leave her there, your sister."

Vivianne was on her knees now, clutching her face and sobbing.

"Father, she needs to learn to respect me."

"And who are you?"

"Father, I don't have time for this."

His father's yellow eyes were shaky but locked on to him. "You will *make* time. This needs to be said. No matter what your friends and their technologies would have you believe, my time is near. I know it. I can feel it."

"Father—"

Father pulled him close until his ear was next to his father's lips. Dehydration and medication made his breath foul, and when he spoke his lips peeled apart and resealed, not unlike the flap of a kite in the wind.

His father locked eyes with him and in them, Luther saw a spark commonly attributed to men much younger. It looked like rage.

"I should have killed you many years ago."

Luther pulled himself away instinctively.

"In the beginning, it was love that allowed me to ignore the signs. Then, as you grew older and stronger, it was fear. But now, I am finally free of both."

"What are you saying, Father?"

"Imagining that you might one day amount to more than slaughter, corruption, theft, and murder is *my* crime. Ignoring the obvious fact. Failing to accept what you are, what I helped to create, is my crime."

Father, not you too…

Luther's eyes were smelts, his face a fresh brand or brush fire.

"Please stop talking."

His father tilted his head back, as though searching the heavens. "My son created the Ligue des Géants and benefits from their rape and murder even now. My son created the Gueye Foundation, a corrupt organization that collects billions in donations only to sprinkle millions — breadcrumbs in comparison — onto the very people impacted by his Ligue des Géants! Tyrant and savior. Arson and firefighter. And, as if this weren't enough to clearly mark you as the son of Satan himself, you begin your reign of terror anew in Sun City, a city already beset by corruption. Titans!" He spat on the floor. "A legion of worms! An army of leeches!"

His father took his hand away as though grasping it had been a penance of its own.

"I've lied to you for so long, Luther," he continued, "I do not love you. I have not loved you since you were a child. And I will never love you again, for you are not something that should be loved. You should be despised. You should be hounded and driven from this world as the mistake you are."

Luther tried to speak and failed several times before choking on the words. "You're delirious. You cannot mean these things."

His father attempted to advance on him, but his chair hit the threshold and sputtered, a wheel whining briefly on the carpet.

"Son, please go. Please go. Leave us. For a butcher, it would be a great deed for you to leave your poor sister and I be.

"Go, Son. Do *one* good thing in your adult life and leave us."

Luther folded his arms. "You'll die."

His father's smile was broad and genuine. "Then that will be my punishment for bringing you into this world."

Luther and Bleda waited on the tarmac in a torrential downpour. Holding an umbrella for him, despite the absurd difference in height, Bleda took the time to update him on affairs, most notably, the massacre of Minowara and his son. In doing so, Bleda had to yell to be heard over the wind, rain, and warming jet engines.

"All in all, thirteen were slain, including Boss Minowara."

Luther took a hard pull on a damp cigarillo and could not help but chuckle. "Decapitated, you say?"

"Yes. The old man was unrecognizable, I hear."

It was welcome news, ripe with implications and promise, and yet Luther found himself still heavy with the wounds his father's words had inflicted.

"I should have killed you many years ago."

"If my sources are accurate," Bleda continued, "the German breached the complex *alone*. Perhaps we both underestimated her."

734

"I'm almost tempted to give the Party Crasher clemency as a reward."

"Come again, Boss?"

"I said, I'm almost tempted to forgive her."

"You're too late."

"Oh?"

"Sugihara made good on his word and put two bullets in her chest. She's dead."

Well, I'll be damned. You kept good on your word, even after she did your work for you. Sugihara, you're a vicious little man.

"Do me a favor, Bleda. Once I'm abroad, I want you to close the loop on this whole nasty affair."

"You mean the Unit One agent?"

"Deputy Informant Yamazaki Daisuke's lease on life is expired."

"Consider it done."

Bleda had been his personal aide for two and a half years and in that time, he would like to think, they'd developed a friendship.

I'm going to miss you, Bleda. An efficient assassin and a vigilant retainer. More so, a reliable confidant and friend.

"Where will you go?" Bleda asked.

He exhaled and shrugged. The wind was strong and his overcoat flapped noisily in the wind. "I'll decide once I'm up in the air and outside of Libra's range. Ideas that important should only be formulated outside of the neural network." He looked up at the miserable sky. Typhoon Yvonne had come with the sunrise. Beyond the Bay of Sun, she appeared as an impenetrable wall of grey and black, or as the dust churned up by some great military on the march.

"I'm going to miss the parade," Luther announced, legitimately disappointed.

"Do you care?"

"It's funny, Bleda. I've missed every parade. Always traveling. Always! Say what you will about the State Defense Consortium, they know how to throw a party."

"I believe it's started. Maybe you can catch a glance from the air."

"Maybe I will. And that reminds me! Remember that *today* is the most important day of the year in terms of revenue. Ensure that my replacement checks in with the lieutenants frequently and keeps inventory moving. We're throwing Clark in the deep end, you know?"

"Clark?"

"Oh. That's right, I never told you… I've chosen Clark to be my face in Sun City. He'll be here any moment."

"Clark? As in, Clark from Eden?"

Luther studied Bleda's typically expressionless face and saw what he thought was a shadow of concern.

When the truck finally entered the tarmac, the wind had become such that an umbrella was a fruitless endeavor. The two of them stood, bundling themselves against the weather.

Though Luther tried to remain patient, Clark's tardiness, coupled with the limited window for his departure, had his nerves on edge.

The truck pulled up to them, a dull, drumming bass preceding its arrival. It was a massive SUV with yellow-tinted windows and an aftermarket lift-kit that added another four feet to the cabin's height. The passenger-side door of the truck came down to become steps that a man descended clumsily.

At first, Luther couldn't be sure if it was Clark. The man's head was down, and he seemed heftier than the man he knew. This man, whoever he was, walked around the truck at a leisurely pace. He wore a baseball cap pulled low, a mechanic's jumpsuit, and workman's boots. As he approached, he removed his cap. It was indeed Clark, just a fifty-pound or so heavier version.

"Boss!"

"You're late."

Clark looked at his wrist, though he wore no timepiece. Luther extended a hand that Clark took firmly.

The man known simply by his first name had come under Luther's employ by way of acquisition, specifically, when his Titans absorbed a small cartel based out of Capital City.

What were they called again? After a moment, it came to him. *Ah yes, "Murderers' Row."*

Of the former members of Murderers' Row, Clark had, by far, shown the most potential. Given a very modest territory

737

on the north side of Sun City's Section Four, Clark had quadrupled the sales of the previous corner boss in a matter of months. Employing a combination of highly aggressive sales techniques and an iron-fist policy with employee shrinkage, Clark whipped the Titans of Four into shape. So effective was he as a leader that it only made sense to expand his influence to include all of Section Four. After a year, Section Four had become the highest-grossing district in all of Sun City.

But if I recall, Luther thought, *the number of Titans killed as punishment for short-changing the take tripled as well.*

You can't make an omelet without breaking some eggs...

Recognizing talent was a talent. Luther firmly believed this. And deciding that Clark's talents were still underutilized, even as the head of all Section Four, he sent his man to Eden, Sun City's sister city to the south, with two assignments. The first was to manage the backchannel relationships the Titans shared with the Customs Ministry and the Border Division, ensuring that their shipments from South America remained unimpeded as they made their way into the Pacific State. The second was to establish a base in Eden.

The first of these tasks Clark handled with the tact and skillfulness of diplomat. This was illustrated by the fact that in the decade since sending Clark south, the police bribery costs had only increased by 115 percent, give or take.

738

But if that weren't enough, Clark had — in that time — not only established a decent distribution network in Eden but also "chained" that network to Eden's neighbor Harbor City. The addition of the two cities made a sizable contribution to their business' overall profitability. And, in the process, Clark also made himself a very rich man.

Stated plainly, Clark was an extraordinary human being. But, like many extraordinary men, he came with a few quirks.

"It's raining…" Clark yelled over the wind, a hand on his head.

His skin was white and freckled, his hair blond and shaved close at the temples. He glowered up at the clouds with pink eyes.

"It's been a long time, old friend!"

The albino man nodded but did not respond. This was typical. Clark had only two modes: bored and upset.

You haven't changed one bit.

"What's wrong?" Luther asked him, amused.

"Long drive."

"Worth it, I'm sure. This is a big day for you."

Clark shrugged, pursing his lips.

"I haven't much time, Clark. Do you have any questions for me?"

"Where do I stay?"

"What?" Luther looked to Bleda, who just shook his head, clearly as confused as he was by the question.

It was then that Luther remembered. Clark and Bleda had never gotten along well. And anyone who knew both men would not be surprised in the least by this. Bleda was a consummate professional and it carried through in everything, particularly his vocabulary. Clark, on the other hand, was abrasive always and not afraid to escalate a non-situation into something much, much more. And Clark's vocabulary, though effective for his line of work, was very limited and buoyed with expletives.

You two had better play well together while I'm gone, Luther thought.

Clark sighed and repeated the question more slowly. "Where. Do. I. Stay?"

"Where will you stay? Buy a fucking house, Clark. Buy two houses! Consider yourself more or less in charge of the entire operation in the Pacific State once I board this plane. Is there something about this that remains unclear? For Christ's sake, Clark, get it together. We spoke extendedly on the matter only two nights ago!"

Clark scrunched his face up. He turned to the truck and motioned for the driver to lower the window. The tinted window lowered to reveal a heavyset woman buried under a laundry bag's worth of curls. "Kind of thought you were fucking playing," Clark said to them with a smirk before addressing the driver.

"Yeah?" she replied rudely with a mouth full of chewing gum.

"I'm in charge now!" Clark yelled at the driver, thumbing at his chest.

"You've been in charge!" she replied.

"Nah, bitch! I'm in charge of everything now!"

"That's good, baby! Can I put the window up now? The rain's getting inside."

"Get Royal on the line. I want her up here with me."

Clark motioned irritably for her to raise the window, before turning back to them. The rain had soaked his head and was pouring down his brow in rivulets. He smiled to reveal a mouth of perfectly maintained teeth, bracketed on either side by deep and tall dimples. It was a handsome smile.

"Once I'm airborne," Luther continued patiently, "I will be sending Bleda info about my destination and how to reach me. Otherwise, wait for me to contact you directly. Other than that, the rules have not changed. Use my name and Ouroboros will end you. Betray me, and well, you know how that goes…"

"Please, Boss. How long have we been at this?"

Luther felt a bit petty for the threat, but it *had* to be said. After all, he was leaving Sun City, his most prized possession, in the hands of a man he hadn't seen in years.

"I want things run as they are in Eden, and as they are in Harbor City. You'll find the work here much simpler, as you'll have an army of loyal lieutenants trained by Bleda and I personally. And you don't need to worry about our operation in Capital City. I've decided to leave that under the care of

741

someone else for now as a kind of diversification; a means of minimizing risk, should things here go to shit."

"Sounds good, Boss. Have a safe flight, now. Ta-ta!"

"I'm not finished!" Luther put a finger in the smaller man's face to let him know he was serious. "You'll want to call the lieutenants together and give them an opportunity to meet you. Do it soon. They've been informed of the situation, but you'll want to make it real for them. I don't expect anyone to try you, considering I'll merely be remote and not really out of the picture. But should someone try to test you, I—"

"Come on, Boss! Who the fuck are you talking to? Don't try to *son* me!"

Luther flicked his dampened cigarillo to the ground. He'd forgotten just how crude Clark was. He'd forgotten just how infuriating his flippant attitude could be. But...

Time is short. I need to be airborne.

Clark seemed more focused on the cigarillo he'd tossed than his words or the aggressive stance Bleda had adopted in response. "You got another one of those?" he asked with arched eyebrows.

"Are you fucking kidding me?"

Again, Luther couldn't help but look to Bleda, who hadn't blinked. His laser stare paused only to flash bewilderment at the statement.

Luther sighed.

Fucking soft skills are a lost art form.

"Sure."

He reached into his coat and pulled out the pack. He extended it to Clark, who unabashedly grabbed several. He slipped them into the pocket of his overalls, not even putting one to his lips.

If this maniac wasn't about to take the helm of his life's work, Luther would have laughed, or maybe slapped him senseless.

A millionaire many times over who still acted like a man recently paroled.

"Fuck it, I don't pay you to be professional, even respectful. I pay for results. Get me results, Clark!

"Now, are you sure you don't have any questions?"

Clark shook his head and turned to the truck once more. "Let's go! I've got smokes. We need to buy a house, 'cuz it's raining!"

They watched as Clark stomped around the truck and climbed inside, rocking the whole vehicle with his girth. Once the truck had left the airfield, Luther turned to his most trusted advisor. Grabbing Bleda by the elbow, he put an arm around the assassin. "Keep a vigilant eye on my kingdom and you'll want for nothing."

Bleda's expression was sincere, almost melancholy. "Call me to you, if need be. I'll fly to you, under any circumstances, wherever you are."

Luther felt Bleda's words deeply.

"Clark's an odd one," Luther said, "but under that mess lies the mind of a kingpin. Support him as you have supported me."

"I trust your judgment." Bleda furrowed his brow thoughtfully. "Would you like me to post men to your sister, your father?"

Luther thought about it for a moment. Malice wanted him to order Bleda to harass and torment them. Resentment wanted him to order Bleda to tourniquet their access to the estate. And sorrow wanted him to order Bleda to…

Others have gotten worse for less.

"No," he told Bleda, "leave them be."

Bleda nodded and the expression on his face — the half-smile — betrayed what looked like pride.

"Will you visit home?"

"No, I don't think so. I think first I'll check out the parade, and then see where the wind takes me. I suspect to move frequently."

Bleda seemed lost on the horizon. "Foul weather to be caught unanchored."

Luther nodded solemnly. He embraced his friend one more time and started up the gangway. About halfway up, he remembered.

"Almost forgot!" he yelled. "Our friend the bartender, forget about it!"

Bleda had closed the umbrella and drawn his hood. From beneath the shadow, his eyes glimmered. "He made one of my tails. Couldn't take any chances. I did what I had to do!"

Unsure about how this made him feel, Luther simply shrugged in response. "Take care of yourself, Bleda!"

Once inside the jet, he ordered the pilots to take off, and assumed his seat.

"Where are we headed, sir?" the co-pilot asked.

"Let's start with *up*. After that, give me the best possible view of the parade. I'll give you further instructions from there."

The pilot tipped his cap and entered the cockpit, closing the door behind him. The flight attendant approached with a tray, upon which an assortment of flight aids rested. Luther leaned forward and took a long line of cocaine. After that, he popped two antidepressants and two muscle relaxers that he downed with a shot of mescal.

Turbulence was a foregone conclusion and, though Luther would never admit it, turbulence terrified him.

Through the window, he could see the Horus Tower. The base of it appeared bluish-white in the glow of City Center while the tower's peak disappeared in a sea of red, lost in a canopy of molten cloud cover. The sight filled him with an inexplicable dread, like some great sword being forged, a sword that he could run from but never truly escape.

28: Liberty Day

"Let the setting sun shine on the golden coast,
O' beautiful Pacific host.
The best of a nation, the first to stand,
brought together on shores of sand.
From Eden to Sun City and Wayward Pine,
And so devote your body and mind,
To supporting this State and kind.
For nowhere else will you find,
Liberty and independence so perfectly entwined."

- Anthem of the Pacific State

[Dice has gone dark.]

"Damn."

[It's probably for the best. The SCPD and INTERPOL are launching a joint investigation into any involvement he may have had in his wife's murders.]

"That's ridiculous! Didn't you say he was already stateside when she killed her first victim?"

[Still speculation, really. Honestly, I doubt they'll find anything. I trust Dice. However, considering they can detain him for the duration of the investigation if they want to, he's

better off someplace else. At least until the investigation is complete.]

"He wouldn't kill someone, not like that. Not like her."

[I feel the same way, but there's a lot we don't know about Daisuke.]

"I didn't know about her," AJ replied, "that's for sure. I feel like such an ass for that night. I had no clue what she was to him."

[He doesn't fault you, AJ. He went to great lengths to hide his wife from us. There's no way you could have known. We can see now that he hid her for obvious reasons. The question the SCPD is posing is, 'Did he know and actively work to conceal her crimes?' I personally think the answer is 'no,' but things have to legally run their course.]

"Anyway, Sergeant Moore out."

[Stop it! Just stop already!]

"Stop what?"

[You're being childish.]

"How am I being childish?"

['Sergeant Moore out?' Since when do you talk to me like that? You've been acting strange ever since the party.]

"You mean ever since I threw up all over my childhood friend — who for some fucking reason is dating my partner — in front of like a hundred people?"

[More like three hundred people. And there was the way you fell. That deserves discussion, too, but you know what I'm talking about...]

747

"Rena, I really should be focusing on my duties right now."

That couldn't be further from the truth. AJ was stationed along the 101 along with a dozen uniformed SCPD officers, manning one of the city's many checkpoints.

The parade had begun in earnest and, according to the media, the turnout was already approaching record numbers. They were still more than an hour from noon. But he was nowhere near the event, much to his chagrin.

The city on the verge of possibly the greatest party ever held and here I am, stuck manning a shitty highway checkpoint with a bunch of nosy cops.

"Where's Chris?"

[Surveillance atop the Coastal Power building.]

"What? That's right in City Center! Are you fucking kidding me? *He's* downtown, under the lights, while I'm stuck miles from anything even remotely resembling a boob? I mean *beer.*"

[Well, if it's any consolation — and for you, it probably will be — he's probably eating a ridiculous dose of radiation from those lamps. Word is, a few of the officers on that duty requested dosimeters and were reassigned for their trouble. Besides, talk to your brother. He designated the assignments.]

AJ had heard that the buildings of City Center had been retrofitted with microwave lamps: massive heat emitters designed to evaporate what would otherwise be a torrential downpour.

"This is garbage! And, on a side note, what the hell's up with Rampart?"

[What do you mean?]

"Rena, a typhoon's going to make landfall at daybreak. Why not raise the wall and let Yvonne pass overhead?"

[Well, if I had to guess, I say it's the money. Raising that thing is a massive drain on resources.]

"So is repairing the Veins if Yvonne floods Section Seven!"

[The Premier must know something we don't. No way he'd let a whole section of the city get demolished.]

"I suppose…"

[How are things on the 101?]

"Boring as hell. The only vehicles on the road are trucks, unmanned mostly. And, I'm surrounded by idiot cops gawking at my arms."

"Sir."

AJ looked up from his terminal to find a young officer standing over him. "I mean…"

"We've halted a convoy en route to City Center."

"A convoy?"

"It looks military. Please, come see."

Deadbolt sat propped against the desk. He snatched it up and hurried outside. "Finally, something to do. Anyway, Rena, *Sergeant Moore, out!*"

The checkpoint building was a small, two-story office flanked on two sides by inspection stations, each positioned at one of the ten lanes. As he stepped out into the wind-blown rain, it wasn't hard to find the convoy. It occupied the two centermost lanes, and at the head of it was a massive tractor-trailer, standing twice the height of a commuter bus. The lead transport's cargo was hidden by an olive tarp but was clearly heavy machinery.

Beyond the 101, the microwave projectors of City Center had turned the sky into something nightmarish. Clouds blown over the center of Section Three did not simply disappear. As they were superheated into nonexistence, they gave off flailing bursts of lightning. The sky had become like that over a volcano, with flashes highlighting the details of the city's tallest buildings in burning clarity before descending back into the muted grey of heavy cloud cover.

AJ walked to the transport's cab, shielding himself from the rain with a metal hand. The officer who'd summoned him followed, as did a small cadre of other police.

The Unit One sergeant jumped up onto the sideboard and peered into the cab through the driver's-side window.

"What's the cargo?"

The driver, a soldier, wore a black basic-dress uniform and black cap.

"BDs, sir," the soldier replied. "BDs on the order of the Major. BDs already late to their post, sir."

"Bipedal tanks?"

"Yes, sir."

750

"ID, soldier! What branch you with? Why the black uni's?"

The soldier extended his hand. AJ touched his wrist to the soldier's, and his credentials read aloud over the neurotrigger network.

Specialist Dan Osburn, United States Army. Age: thirty-two, Height: five foot eleven inches, Weight: 211 lbs...

"You under orders, Specialist Osburn?"

"Wouldn't be here if I wasn't."

"Whose orders?"

"The Major's. Believe I said that out of the gate."

The Army was full of majors, but in the Pacific State, "the Major" meant one man and one man alone: his brother.

"Sit tight for a second, soldier."

AJ hopped down from the cab and pinged his brother over Libra. The connection took several seconds longer than usual.

This is odd, he thought. *Ace may be the man in the SDC, but he has no influence over the Army.*

"Ace."

[I think you mean 'Major,'] his brother replied, his neurotrigger-rendered voice as dry as his actual voice.

"Jesus. Ok, *Major*. We're holding a convoy at Station Thirteen. You know, Station Thirteen, on the 101; the freeway, out in the middle of nowhere where you stationed me? It's an Army convoy, carrying tanks."

[Let it through immediately!]

751

"Geez, relax!"

[Next time, Sergeant, *read your goddamn assignment! In it, I explicitly mention the arrival of a battalion of peacekeeping units!]*

Geez, he's really pissed!

"My apologies, Major."

[Your apologies are shit. Don't fuck with my schedule!]

"Okay, Ace. You made your point."

He waved to the station agent. "Let 'em through!"

Once the convoy had passed, AJ stormed back into the station and tore his jacket off irritably. No one could get under his skin so instantly and effectively as the man who'd raised him.

"God, why do you have to be such a dick!"

He sat at the console and put his feet up on the desk. With a vocal command, he switched from the progression of military trucks to Channel Eleven.

Unicom always has the best parade coverage.

The parade had already begun. Downtown streets were packed wall-to-wall with people, and a long line of floats – many purely mixed reality exhibitions that bended reality in extraordinarily entertaining ways– had begun the first of five laps around the core of Section Three. It looked as though all of Sun City had come out.

"There must be a million people," he thought aloud.

No wonder Ace is so high-strung.

752

While the parade rumbled triumphantly up Market Street, the footage of the world outside of City Center looked like something out of a video game. A wall of clouds, the first lashes of Typhoon Yvonne, covered the horizon at sea. At the same time, the storm clouds above the city were being evaporated in the glow of the Premier's lamps, but not before dying in spectacular bursts of lightning.

AJ watched the progression for nearly an hour as it made its way to Century Plaza, the site of the Liberty Day attack that had killed so many, only three years prior.

The plaza itself was an epic sight to behold. The sheer number of people amassed there could wholly populate a lesser city. As the footage came closer to the crowds, he could see signs bobbing and people in masks.

Looks like the Fifth Estate came out in force.

Word on the street was the leader of the Fifth Estate, the rich kid-brother of fighter Omar Garcia, had gone missing, allegedly abducted. Apparently, the Fifth Estate believed that State Defense Consortium was responsible for their charismatic leader's disappearance.

Unlikely, he thought. *If the SDC snatched up its most vocal critic, Unit One would know about it. Hell, we probably would have done the snatching.*

As AJ sat, arms folded behind his head, he watched the procession closely, looking for his brother.

When the cameras panned and captured the lead float, he spotted Ace. He sat in an elevated row of chairs just left of the Premier. The column, already on its last lap apparently, came to a halt in front of the steps of Sun City's Capital Building in an intricately choreographed sequence. Event staff descended the steps in a hurried wave and quickly, effortlessly, converted the float to a stage.

AJ groaned as the Premier stood and ascended the podium. "Here comes the speech."

"He's such a blowhard," the police officer standing next to him added.

"Yeah, but the speech is the last part before the party begins."

The police officer looked at him quizzically. "Haven't you heard? Ain't gonna be an afterparty. They're shutting it down after the speech, on account of the storm."

"What? You can't have a Liberty Day Parade without parties!"

The cop shrugged. "Yeah, it's bullshit. They should have postponed the whole thing. I think they saw this as an opportunity to shove the ceremony down our throats without having to deal with the post-parade cleanup."

"Motherfuckers."

"Well, here comes the Motherfucker in Chief."

AJ turned back to the screen. Premier Macek, resplendent in a suit and cape, mounted a cherrywood podium draped in the State flag. As he did so, the city erupted in cheers. It was a sound that could be heard through the very walls of the station and much of it was digital, pre-recorded, and amplified.

"Poor suckers are cheering because they think they're about to be partying."

Premier Macek's uniform, strangely enough, had a kind of military flare, replete with medals and a golden saber hanging from his belt. His cape danced in the wind, as did his silver beard.

Behind Premier Macek sat Ace, and behind him, Pops. Ace wore a dress uniform but above that, the same tattered poncho he'd carried throughout his career. He sat stiff and looked upon the crowd with what appeared to be a half smile. He looked calm, almost content. It was a strange expression, one that AJ couldn't recall ever seeing his brother make. The sight of it inexplicably filled him with discomfort.

The Premier waited for the crowd to settle down before beginning. As he waited, he held his hands up, like a toddler wanting to be picked up.

"He's so full of himself."

After several moments, the cheering and chanting died down.

Macek lowered his arms and turned his palms outward. "Brothers, sisters, sons and daughters of the State, it is with great pride and privilege that I greet you today, on this most momentous occasion."

On the thirteenth floor of the Coastal Power Building, Lieutenant Chris Calderon and a cadre of SCPD officers surveyed the crowd, searching for signs of trouble. Several sniper stations equipped with long-range viewfinders allowed them to see every one of the million citizens gathered below.

Above, the microwave lamps seared the rain away but also turned their floor (still four from the uppermost) into a sauna. Wiping sweat from his brow with a finger, Chris looked down at the crowd with a hand in his pocket.

Despite the weather and the threat of Typhoon Yvonne, everyone came out, he thought. *Remarkable... if not stupid.*

There was no doubt that the Liberty Day Parade was special for the people of Sun City. It was *their* day, a day to commemorate the State's secession. It also served now as a defiant homage to the lives lost when Changgok attacked Sun City.

The parade served yet another purpose: a venue for civil unrest. A place where people could gather to voice their displeasure with Libra, the police, the SDC, and the Premier. Chief among the belligerents was the Fifth Estate. It was upon this group that the police and the SDC focused the bulk of their attention.

X-ray and thermal optics found weapons scattered among their numbers — small arms, mostly, and not worth disrupting the ceremony. At least not without an immediate sign of threat.

Premier Macek had taken the podium in a ghastly uniform of pseudo-militaristic design. Behind him sat the Major, accompanied by the massive, elderly Agency Zero agent called Pops. They wore the orange and grey of Agency Zero, and the Major had donned his State dress uniform, which he wore beneath that wretched poncho he so favored.

Police — many in crowd-control armor and with riot shields in hand — lined the street on both sides of the parade path. Though out in full force, they looked grossly outnumbered against what looked like the whole of Sun City.

As the crowd settled in for the Premier's speech, a tradition in and of itself, Chris trained his attention on the main stage.

"Brothers, sisters, sons and daughters of the State," Macek began, "it is with great pride and privilege that I greet you today, on this most momentous occasion! Today marks the third anniversary of a most cowardly act: the single worst attack ever committed against the stalwart peoples of Sun City. And yet, we stand here, shoulder to shoulder, bound by our courage, resilience, and unwavering resolve in the face of adversity. We stand in defiance of terror, both from man and from nature, and in camaraderie as children of the State!"

"Equating terrorism with a natural disaster?" Chris muttered. "Really?"

The response from the crowd was mostly positive. Mostly. Jeering could also be heard. Below, members of the

Fifth Estate, distinguishable by their masks and signs, fought to get closer to the stage.

"Today, we also gather in celebration; a celebration of freedom, of social responsibility, and of liberty. This year marks a turning point in the destiny of our great city. Our borders have grown, our industry is booming, and our people are some of the wealthiest and happiest in the world."

"Did he really just say that?" someone behind Chris said. He turned to find a group of Sun City Police marksmen watching the speech on a portable holo unit.

Fool! Why would the Premier start talking about money when a large percentage of the city's residents are unemployed? Sure, the people from Sections Three and Four are wealthy, but everyone else, the other five sections of Sun City? Not so much. "Is this jackass looking to start a riot?"

Chris had never been a fan of Sun City's first Premier. His powers were vague and seemed to evolve conveniently when it benefitted him or the State Defense Consortium. As for the man himself, his interactions were few and always from a distance. That said, the man seemed... decandent.

From his vantage point, Chris watched as the "wealth and happiness" bit turned a large portion of the crowd against the Premier almost as soon as the words left his lips. The Fifth Estate, having successfully forced their way to the front of the stage, were chanting now, trying to drown out Macek.

"I know, I know, it doesn't seem that way sometimes," the Premier continued, back-pedaling, "but the numbers do not lie!"

"Rena, maybe somebody should take His Excellency's microphone away before things get ugly."

[I know, right?]

"As I look out upon the beautiful and diverse *free* peoples of this great State, it saddens me to see that some of you have come not in the spirit of brotherhood and unity, but with disruption and anarchy in your hearts. To you, I would say: put down your signs! Lay low your ambitions, if not for good, just long enough to be in peace and celebration with your neighbors."

Many non-protestors cheered at this, mostly the folks pining for the party, Chris figured.

"As you know, a storm approaches! And though my colleagues and advisers pleaded with me to end the celebration after this speech, I am insisting that we celebrate regardless of Typhoon Yvonne. I *insist* that we celebrate our time together until the very last minute!"

"Rena, can you confirm?"

[Technically, we have until approximately four AM. That's when Yvonne is predicted to make landfall.]

Chris put a hand to his temple. "You've got to be kidding me! He's willing to postpone the evacuation to win a few popularity points?"

"Tonight, thanks to Yvonne," Macek continued, his arms extended outward, "we will be cramming two days' worth of revelry into one single electric night."

At this, Sun City erupted. Even the police in the room began catcalling and embracing each other.

"That time should be spent getting these people back into their homes," Chris said, acutely disturbed by what he was seeing.

[Chris, I agree with you one hundred percent. But technically, if the celebration ends at nine on the dot, that still leaves us plenty of time. I'll confirm...]

"Rena, listen to yourself! When have we *ever* been able to clear the streets on time?"

[I guess that would explain the Major's tanks. I don't care how drunk a person gets. When a thirty-foot bipedal tank aims its guns at them and starts firing sound cannons, they're going to get their ass indoors.]

Chris could only shake his head and spit. "You've got to be kidding me, Rena. Who's running this circus?"

"Tonight, several of Sun City's biggest celebrities will perform and share their stories." Macek continued. "Some of these include singer, songwriter, and actress, Olivia Setty. Also, hip-hop artist, actor, and fashion mogul, 'Beastly G.' And last but definitely not least, Valhalla Fight League CEO Arianna Firestone will introduce the fighters of next month's Mixed Martial Arts super card!"

Sun City's collective voice drowned out the whine of the storm and the chants of the Fifth Estate.

Macek gripped the lectern with both hands. "But, before the party begins, I would like to take a few moments to honor one of Sun City's true sons."

At this, the Major stood from his seat behind the lectern. He turned and leaned in to the ear of Pops, whispering something. He then patted the massive man on the shoulder, almost reassuringly, before moving to stand next to the Premier.

Macek extended a hand to the Major, which the Major accepted stiffly before climbing up to the podium. From behind him, the Premier continued.

"This man has spent his life in defense of our country, later our State, and our city. His wisdom and expertise helped to build the State Defense Consortium, all to ensure that attacks like the one we suffered in '47 never happen again."

"After seven years of service in the SDC and twenty-two years of service in the Armed Forces, the Major has decided it is time to spend more time with his family. And, after a lifetime of service, no one could deny this soldier, this *warrior* the rest he so rightly deserves!"

Chris scoffed. The idea of the Major stepping down to spend time with AJ seemed absurd to the point of satire.

"And so, it is with great sadness and yet great admiration that we bid farewell to the man many of you know simply as 'Iron' Ace, our very own Major Ace Monroe!"

761

The response from the masses was awkwardly muted. Ace stood before them silently, his face emotionless.

It was time to let the Major speak, but Macek continued, forcing the Major to stand atop the podium in silence, like a slave on the auction block or a condemned man before the scaffolding. The sight was cruel, and angered Chris.

Macek continued. "My friend Ace will be retiring, along with the other brave veterans of Agency Zero."

"What the hell?" Chris looked around, but the magnitude of the announcement seemed lost on the officers of the SCPD. "Rena, they're dissolving Agency Zero?"

[First time I'm hearing it, too, Chris. I don't know what's going on. Why is the Major just standing there? Is the Premier gonna fucking let him speak or what?]

The implications of this announcement were enormous, especially for Unit One. Agency Zero held a very specific and yet wide-reaching role in the State Defense Consortium. Technically, they were a counter-terrorism rapid-reaction force but, thanks to the Major, they played a huge role in SDC policy making, particularly around affairs of State security. If the Premier's words were true, this would bring an end to the silent tug-of-war that the two departments had been engaged in since... well, pretty much since Unit One's inception.

"Pay attention, officers!" Chris yelled to the police around him, genuinely annoyed that for all their self-congratulation they'd missed one of the most significant and impactful political moves in Sun City's history. "This is big news! There's sure to be crowd reaction!"

He buried his eye into the scope, desperate to make out the Major's mannerisms as he gave what would likely be his last address to Sun City.

"Let's please give a warm round of applause for Agency Zero and all that they have done for Sun City!" Macek continued. At this, much of the crowd applauded. It was perfunctory, however, and died quickly.

Chris focused on the stage, watching as the Major got the signal from Macek that *finally* he would be allowed the courtesy of a statement.

The Major's torn face, beneath the light from above the stage, gave him the look of something poorly crafted, an unfinished work chiseled into imperfect stone with inadequate tools.

The Major folded his hands behind his back, his chest out and his head high. He cleared his throat and looked out onto the people of Sun City with an expression that was almost serene. Like this, he looked out at the crowd in silence for a long time.

The Fifth Estate was first to seize the moment. They began chanting and pumping fists into the air.

It was impossible to know what they were saying from the top of the Coastal Power Building and, as if reading his mind, Rena chimed in: *[Release Garcia, Release Garcia. They're talking about their leader. Apparently, he's gone*

763

missing. Some are chanting 'fascist,' and others 'murderer.'
Not pretty.]

Chris was mesmerized. The Major seemed completely and utterly immune to their chants.

Finally, the Major raised a gloved hand into the air and, at the sight of the massive man in uniform, his tattered poncho flailing in the wind, even the Fifth Estate soon went silent. Chris watched as the Major's hand became a fist. It was then that movement on the other side of City Center caught his eye. He swung the scope in time to catch the action occurring on the opposite side of the plaza. He watched, his mouth opening in silence, as a bipedal tank, the same used in the Korean War, stepped over the police partition and into the crowd.

"What is this!"

An exclamation from the people gathered drew his gaze elsewhere. At the opposite end of City Center, two more tanks were emerging from closed-off streets. Like massive metal birds, they stepped forward, their gun turrets sweeping over the crowd, sending a shockwave of panic through the masses.

"Rena! What the hell? Those pilots need to stop pointing their fucking guns at the crowd. They're going to cause a stampede!"

Rena was silent for few moments, before saying flatly, *[Unmanned.]*

Unsure of what to make of the situation, Chris returned his gaze to the main stage. The Major, upon sight of the tanks, wrapped a gloved hand around the microphone and leaned in awkwardly, stiffly, to address the crowd.

"Citizens! Citizens! Be silent! I know that I am not popular among you, but you *will* lend me your ears!"

The Major pulled the State flag from the lectern and cast it aside. He then reached beneath the lectern and produced what appeared to be a document of some kind. He waved it in the air. "This is the speech that was prepared for me by the Ministry of Communication, or, as we refer to them behind closed doors, the Ministry of Propaganda."

He tore the page to bits and threw them out over the crowd. Behind him, the big man Pops had forced the Premier — visibly upset — into a chair.

"The stage!" Chris screamed at the officers around him. "Watch the stage! The big man! Watch the big man! Protect the Premier at all costs!"

He ran over to a sniper post and shoved the officer posted there aside. Tearing off his bandana, he quickly made adjustments to the rifle's sights, zeroing in on the Major.

"Not everything the old man just told you was a lie," the Major continued. "Sun City is indeed at a turning point. We have come to a crossroads and where we go from here will determine our place in history. We have to decide — as one — if we are willing to come to terms with uncomfortable but undeniable truths; truths that will challenge everything that we have come to believe."

Premier Macek tried to get to his feet but was immediately shoved back into his chair by the massive hand of Pops. This time, Chris noticed, Pops seemed to yell a warning at the Premier. At the same time, all along the perimeter of the plaza, police were breaking rank, some moving among the crowd to get a better view of the stage, others slipping out past the partitions to disappear down walled-off streets. Many of them were running.

Chris checked the chamber of the rifle and focused on the Major. He released the safety and took several deep breaths. Calmly, he said: "Rena, sitrep please?"

[I don't know! Stand down for now. I'm trying to reach Williams.]

"I was born in Sun City; in the Veins," the Major continued, "as was my brother. We grew up homeless, the victims of Sun City's post-war complacency and corruption. When I was close enough to the enlisting age, I joined the Army. This, you already know. It was in fighting for the people of Liberia that I lost my arm. It was at this time that I believed my life of service to be over. This, too, you already know. However, I was saved, saved by the man you see behind me." He turned and pointed at Pops, who nodded sternly in response.

"Given a second chance, I spent the next ten years fighting in Togo, the Philippines, Japan, China, and in North Korea." With each country he rattled off, he held a finger in the air. "This, too, you already know. I picked up a lot of scars along the way, but not one unearned or unaccompanied by a

lesson. I became this *thing* you see before you! Admittedly —
and I will not make excuses — somewhere along the way, I
lost *myself*!"

The Major stepped down from the podium. "'Beware
that, when fighting monsters, you yourself do not become a
monster... for when you gaze long into the abyss, the abyss
gazes also into you.' This famous quote, I can tell you, is fact.
Long have I stared into the abyss!"

"Any idea what he's talking about, Rena?"

[No clue.]

"Might want to reach out to AJ."

[Already talking to him.]

"Men who appear like us but do not share our
compassion and desire to exist in relative harmony have built
for themselves a machine of infinite war, through which churns
the blood and bone of men and women who hold patriotism
and unity in their hearts, and from which flows only death,
disease, despair, and hardship. This machine is what fills their
bellies, an infinite well from which they drink. It is evil
disguised as wealth, greed disguised as merit.

"I allowed myself to become a weapon of oppression, a
weapon of evil. A cog in this machine. I watched my brothers
and sisters die on distant battlefields for wars unrecognized by
society only to see their families denied the privileges and
promises made by the institutions sending them into the fray.
Today" —the Major paused— "I will strike back at that
wickedness!"

Major Monroe turned to face Premier Macek and beckoned. In response, Pops lifted Macek from his seat by the front of his suit and shoved him forward roughly, to the shock of everyone. As the breath left Sun City at the sight of their figurehead being manhandled, Pops gripped Macek by the shoulder, holding him out like a trophy to be examined.

Men, officers of the SCPD, rushed the stage, only to be frozen in their steps by the shrill warning cries of the tanks, that now numbered seven and had also been advancing on the main stage.

[Chris! Are you watching this?]

It was AJ, and he could hear the panic in his partner's voice.

"I see it. Where are you?"

[Checkpoint Thirty-two, 101 north of Sutter. Basically, on the other side of the fucking city!]

"Then get your ass to Century Plaza, quick!"

"Three years ago, this city was attacked," the Major continued. "Many of you still believe the culprit to be Changgok, an alleged DPRK general-turned-terrorist. I am here to tell you emphatically, this is a lie!

"The attack three years ago set into motion a campaign against freedom, a war against you: the people of Sun City! The true culprits, some of whom are among us today, call themselves 'enlightened.' They meet in secret and conspire to keep you in blind submission. They operate in disinformation, marketing it to you as truth, whole and unbiased. This is a lie!

768

Their weapons are their crooked souls; their mantles, secrecy; and their mission, domination. This is the truth!"

This is the same rhetoric that the Fifth Estate espouses, Chris thought, a cold chill running up his arms. *What the hell is happening?*

"The Major's compromised, Rena. I have a shot! We should end this before it escalates!"

[Hold your fire, Chris! Hold your goddamn fire! Those tanks are unmanned and we don't know what their prerogatives are. You kill the Major and they could massacre the city.]

His finger hovered next to the trigger and he did not reengage the rifle's safety. "Standing by. Still in position."

"In our fear of an assumed terrorist threat, we have allowed an ancient evil to burrow deep into the marrow of this city. To claim governance!" The Major's voice carried through the speakers and PA system like some great chasm opening up to let fly its demonic denizens.

"This evil rests unopposed upon its throne and I needn't tell you that the 'throne' of this great State is Sun City and the evil king is none other than America's first *and last* Premier!"

In focusing on the Major, Chris had completely missed the man perched on the lighting truss above the stage. He wore the orange of Agency Zero and held in his hands a length of thick, black cord.

The Major twirled a finger in the air and the man on the truss threw down the cord with the accuracy of a wrangler, to snag Premier Macek by the neck. With a "Yee-haw!" that was picked up by the Major's microphone, the man leapt down to the stage. In doing so, he yanked Macek up into the air violently. After holding the Premier in the air on sheer strength for a few moments, he bound his end of the cord to a support beam, lynching the most powerful man in Sun City. The soldier, a black metal contraption covering the bottom half of his face, dusted his hands and appeared to be laughing.

The crowd, those not gobsmacked entirely, ran to exit the plaza. The result — from Chris' vantage — appeared that of a stomped anthill. Thousands of people plowed into each other, trying to move away from the main stage, only to be driven back and scattered by the tanks.

"William Macek," Major Monroe continued, now bellowing into the microphone to be heard over the mayhem, "for the crime of treason and in accordance with Article Sixteen of the State Defense Consortium's Dictum on Judicial Facilitation, I sentence you to death!"

The Major had formally declared coup d'etat against the Premier, and by extension the SDC. Chris had no intention of sitting back and watching. Breathing out slowly, he aimed the rifle at the cord that bound the flailing Premier, and fired. The shot sailed wide. He fired once more, only to watch the bullet strike the deck of the float. Chris soon learned that, with the wind and Macek's desperate flailing, it was an impossible shot.

In response, the Major took cover behind the lectern. He was pointing in their general direction.

Chris yanked the rifle bolt and chambered another round. This time he took aim at the Major himself. Just then, something thudded against his head. The sudden pressure against his temple came with a warning: "We have explicit orders to stand down, Lieutenant Calderon. Take one more shot and I'll blow your brains out."

Chris released the rifle with an exaggerated show of hands and turned slowly to find an SCPD officer aiming a pistol at his face.

"Careful now," he warned the officer, raising his hands slowly. "Let's not make a mistake we're both going to regret."

Behind the officer, the other men and women of the Sun City Police Department had also drawn their guns and were aiming at him. All of them had looks of great confusion, uncertainty, and concern etched on their faces.

"Look, don't make a mistake here," Chris repeated. "The Major has just declared war on the SDC and is *killing* the premier…"

"Lieutenant Calderon," the officer said with a very measured tone, "right now, the Major is the ranking officer. At least until we hear otherwise from Commissioner Harding or someone higher."

Chris raised his hands and backed away from the rifle station slowly. "Then get Harding on the line. Fucking *stat*! The premier doesn't have time for us to play phone tag."

771

"We're already hailing the appropriate parties. In the meantime, sir, please hand over your service weapon."

Chris' shoulders slumped. He shook his head. "You guys are making a huge mistake."

Lieutenant Mason Bruce watched Premier Macek twisting and kicking in the air from a television in the lounge of the Imperator Hotel. When the Premier's lashing finally stopped and the leader of Sun City hung lifeless, body swaying in the wind of pre-Typhoon Yvonne, he sat frozen, mouth agape, tears already forming.

"For those who have come with your children, I sincerely apologize. However, in time, their young hearts will grow to understand the magnitude of the deed, as well as the importance of the deed. After all, the premier's death is my gift to them!"

With a shove from his mechanized arm, the Major sent the lectern flying from the stage to strike the pavement and shatter. Wood shards slid across the ground to stop at the feet of a wall of terrified citizens.

"Effective immediately, we are a city at war. And, in accordance with Articles 2a and 11c of the Consortium's Dictum on Transfer of Authority, I — as self-appointed Grand Magistrate of the State — am declaring a state of martial law."

Trying to both listen to the Major's words and address the situation on the thirteenth floor of the Coastal Power

772

building, Chris held his hands out and spoke clearly and distinctly to the police officers attempting to detain him. "Listen, listen! Officers of the Sun City Police Department, we are on the same side. Unit One and the SCPD are on the same side!"

"Hand over your firearm, Lieutenant!"

He pointed at that officer in a sign of warning with one hand while placing his other on his firearm. "Don't try it."

[Rena, Chief Constable Williams, sir, please tell me what to do,] he implored over neurotrigger. *[The situation at Coastal Power is deteriorating quickly. The police here have sided with the Major but I have a shot. I can put him down.]*

[Stand down,] Williams replied, his voice stern but remarkably measured. *[Macek's dead. There's nothing we can do at this point. We need to regroup. Defuse the situation where you are and find a way out of there. That's an order, Lieutenant!]*

The Major's words drew the officers' attention back to the holo unit. As their attention left him, Chris quickly took note of all of the floor's exits. He began formulating an escape plan, should it come to that.

"This war, unlike our campaign against the myth that is Changgok, is very real and will take place on these very streets! Effective immediately, the following parties and individuals are considered traitors to the State and will turn themselves over to Agency Zero for judgment in accordance with Article 37f of the Warrant Protocols.

773

"The members of the secret Council of Eight have been identified and deemed enemies of Sun City. They must turn themselves over or risk..." —he paused and seemed to choose his words— "*indiscriminate slaughter!*"

The people of Sun City, trapped in the epicenter of their own great city, stood in awe, waiting with bated breath, no doubt, to find out if they would hang next. The Major recited the names and crimes of his targets, seemingly from memory.

"Elaine Jones-Gutierrez, Chairwoman of Deckar Applied Sciences! Your crimes include illegal arms trading; dissemination of classified intelligence for the purposes of profit; insider trading; violations of the Santa Ana Accords, including the manufacturing of unsanctioned munitions and illegal biological experimentation; and collusion with a known enemy of the State. Know that you cannot hide from me!

"John Cholish, Unicom Network CEO! Your crimes include unsanctioned propaganda, dissemination of private and confidential information, insider trading, illegal price-gouging, fraud, bribery, election engineering, and collusion with a known enemy of the State. Know that no matter your resources, the breadth and width of the world is only so much. I will find you!

"Jensen Carlisle, Horus Bank Chairman!" He pointed to the tallest tower in the city. "Your crimes include economic terrorism, as defined by Roark's Guide on Financial Malfeasance; insider trading, bribery, extortion, embezzlement; attempted murder, murder, intent to commit murder; and

774

collusion with a known enemy of the State. Know that around every corner my blade awaits!"

The Major took a massive deep breath, his voice, already gravelly, now monstrous.

"Ruben Liu, Coastal Power chairman! Industrial sabotage, insider trading, collusion with a known criminal enterprise, extortion, murder, intent to commit murder, dissemination of confidential intelligence to a known enemy of the State, and collusion with a known enemy of the State. Know that China cannot hide you. Even now, the noose tightens!

"Luther Gueye, 'philanthropist!' But in reality, an expatriate warlord and drug kingpin whose crimes include insider trading, murder, attempted murder, conspiracy to commit murder, mass murder, terrorism, distribution of a controlled substance, racketeering, election engineering, and collusion with a known enemy of the State. Say hello to your father for me, when you meet him in Hell!

"Diane West, State Defense Consortium councilwoman!"

Every name that came out of his mouth was a haymaker, but this one almost knocked everyone flat. The cops who were pointing guns at Chris paused and cocked their heads at the sound of Diane West's name.

"—propaganda, treason, political sabotage, insider trading, and collusion with a known enemy of the State. Your betrayal cuts deepest! I will carve every word of the Oath of Office into your gelatinous spine!"

"Posthumously, Oyabun of the Minowara-gumi Yakuza, Kazuo Minowara! Your crimes included fraud, theft, murder, conspiracy to commit murder, murder, racketeering, prostitution, unsanctioned gambling, false imprisonment, human trafficking, exploitation of a minor, distribution of a controlled substance, and collusion with a known enemy of the State. Know that no one mourns your death. May Hell torment you in ways innumerable and for all time!" The Major spat.

"And lastly," —he waved a hand at the Premier, whose corpse swung wildly above— "William F. Macek: political saboteur, traitor, extortionist, assassination financier, money-launderer, insider trader, and would-be murderer of the people of Section Seven; *my* people!" He spat again. "Die forever, pig!"

The Major paused, breathing heavily. Chris watched, as did the officers of the SCPD, with eyes wide.

"Effective immediately, no one is permitted to enter or leave Sun City until such time as the aforementioned persons have been arrested. Furthermore, officers of the SCPD, soldiers of Agency Zero, and other agents of the SDC, including Unit One, must report for reassignment no later than 0900 hours, three days from today. Make straight your familial affairs and report for duty. Failure to do so will be treated as an act of aggression!"

The Major looked as if he would drop the microphone to the deck, but after a moment he put the mic to his lips once more. "I am doing what must be done!"

AJ watched the scene in horror, frozen somewhere between standing and sitting, his hand flat against the terminal. He'd been trying since the noose tightened around Macek's neck to connect with his brother over neurotrigger.

"Rena, I still can't get Ace. Can you connect me to him, by force if need be?"

On the monitor, it appeared that something had caught his brother's eye. From the stage, Ace looked into the sky and pointed. Just then, Rena forced a connection and suddenly he could hear his brother's voice.

[Black, is she ready?]

"Ace! What are you doing!"

[Shoot it down!]

"Ace! What the hell is going on? For God's sake, stop this!"

[Is that you, little brother?]

"Ace, you have to stop this! Stop now before it's too late!"

['Too late?' Grow up, fool! You no longer have the luxury of ignorance.]

On the terminal, the crowd churned chaotic once more and the drone cameras scanned the area nauseatingly before zooming in on something massive in the distance. It entered the plaza from behind the Horus Bank building, and AJ couldn't ignore the impression of one of those "lost footage" monster movies. It was a mech unlike any he'd ever seen. Larger than the bipedal tanks and with arms that swayed as it stepped haphazardly through the crowd, it had to be at least two stories in height.

"People of Sun City!" Ace bellowed. "If you would question my resolve, behold!"

He pointed from the podium, and the cameras swung upward to follow his signal. A plane, a smaller aircraft that may have been a private jet of some kind, was flying low over City Center.

"I repeat!" Ace roared into the microphone. "*No one leaves Sun City!*"

Like the sound of a spitball leaving a straw, only magnified by ten thousand times and repeated over and over, a barrage of missiles burst from the shoulders of the mech and raced into the sky on silver vapor trails.

The plane seemed immobile when contrasted against the missiles racing towards it.

"What have you done, Ace?"

[Weren't you listening? What needs to be done!]

The first explosion tore a wing away, but before the plane could even pitch, a second, third and fourth explosion tore the fuselage into pieces. These pieces, too, were struck with missiles, and in moments the plane was gone, not so much as a smoking chunk of debris left to fall. The blossom of flame was caught instantly and smeared away by the wind.

AJ slammed a fist into the monitor, leaving a spider's web of broken glass. As if in response, alarms sounded throughout the city. They blared in bursts of three and repeated in short intervals. This sound could mean only one thing...

He darted past the officers that had gathered behind him, staring, as he was, in macabre fascination at the monitor. He burst through the station doors and into the rain.

Sure enough, he did indeed recognize the sirens. Already, she'd risen beyond the low, dimly lit skyline of Section Seven. Giant aircraft warning lights crowned her every mile and these flashing red lights, too, rose slowly into the night like warning flares. As the wall around Sun City climbed, the swirling curtain of Yvonne, once terrible on the horizon, begin to disappear.

AJ stood and watched Rampart climb to its full height of just over 900 feet, a process that took a little over twenty-two minutes. The great wall, designed to protect the State's greatest city from military invasion and bombardment by sea, effectively shut the door on the storm. But even as he breathed a sigh of relief for the people of Section Seven, whose lives would have been turned upside down by the storm, a new and equally terrible realization crept into him.

He's trapped us all inside.

A howling, deafening sound filled the city as the typhoon's winds were pushed up into the air. The introduction

779

of Rampart sent the first waves of Yvonne spiraling into the atmosphere and turned the night sky into something like a portal. Deep grey and black clouds, some burning orange with the light of Section Three, twirled upward, tens of thousands of feet. It gave AJ the nauseating impression of falling into a great chasm, a black abyss from which Sun City might never emerge.

29: Wolf Court

"The last time a 'belligerent' seized territory in the United States was June 1942, when the Japanese seized the Aleutian islands of Attu and Kioka. At the time, the population of those islands is estimated at fifty-five people or so, combined.

Sure, we're no longer part of the United States but I took what could have been the capital of the United States; a city of thirty million. And in days, no less! Let the historians tell that!"

  - Ace Monroe

#SDC Investigations Secured Channel [masked]::

[21:31] <DCCWilliams> Is everyone present?

[21:31] <W8less1> Bryant here.

[21:31] <LtCalderonU1> Chris here.

[21:31] <LtBruceU1> Lieutenant Bruce is present.

[21:32] <DCCWilliams> is AJ here?

[21:32] <SgtMooreU1> yeah

[21:32] <DCCWilliams> how are you holding up, Sergeant?

[21:33] <DCCWilliams> You'll feel better once you're back out there.

[21:33] <W8less1> Hey AJ

[21:34] <SgtMooreU1> will i?

[21:34] <DCCWilliams> Any word from Dice?

[21:34] <W8less1> He's not responding.

[21:35] <DCCWilliams> Keep trying

[21:35] <LtCalderonU1> In less than ten hours we are going to become enemies of the State if we don't report to Agency Zero. What's the plan?

[21:35] <DCCWilliams> Assume that reporting to the Major is suicide. I've no reason to believe that Monroe trusts any one of us. Until we know where we stand with the Major and with the SDC, we stay underground.

[21:36] < LtBruceU1> With the SDC? What do you mean?

[21:36] < W8less1> Agency Zero has been in direct contact with senior members of the Consortium and the United States Army, particularly with a General Maecht.

[21:36] < LtBruceU1> are you suggesting that the SDC may be complacent in the coup?

[21:37] < W8less1> This General Maecht could be involved. It might explain the tanks.

[21:37] <DCCWilliams> Let's not jump to conclusions. Get Dice in here. It's time to get you underground and I think he's just man to help

[21:37] < W8less1> Isn't he still under investigation?

[21:38] <DCCWilliams> We can lock him up later if we need to. Right now, I trust Dice more than anyone in the SDC, present company accepted

[21:38] <LtCalderonU1> I may have a suggestion on where we can hide, sir

[21:38] < W8less1> One second. You said "you" with regard to going underground, implying WE'RE going into hiding. What about you?

[21:38] <DCCWilliams> I can't go into hiding and risk putting my family or you in danger. I'll report in on your behalf. Maybe I can talk some sense into the Major.

[21:38] <SgtMooreU1> You'll die

[21:38] <DCCWilliams> excuse me?

[21:38] <SgtMooreU1> You'll die.

[21:39] <DCCWilliams> Don't underestimate me, Sergeant. Besides, I don't see another way. If things go as planned, I'll have Unit One officially disbanded. That will take you off of the Major's radar. Then, we can figure out what to do.

[21:40] < W8less1> What about the SCPD? What about Commissioner Harding?

[21:40] <DCCWilliams> Harding has a white flag where his spine should be. Also, the SCPD appears to be falling in line, with Harding leading the way. I've no reason to believe they'll stand up to Agency Zero. As far as coups go, Ace really put some thought into this one. He's got Sun City by the ornaments.

[21:41] < W8less1> What a disaster.

Rora_Dice! has entered the room.

[21:41] <Rora_Dice!> I knew your brother was bat-shit, AJ but wow!

[21:41] <DCCWilliams> Dice! I'm glad you're here.

[21:42] <SgtMooreU1> I'm sorry about that night. I didn't know she was, you know...

[21:42] <Rora_Dice!> Forget it

[21:42] <DCCWilliams> I know you're processing a lot right now Deputy Constable but we could really use your help on this one

[21:42] <Rora_Dice!> what do you need?

[21:42] <DCCWilliams> As sad as it sounds, I'm not exactly sure yet. Just stay accessible.

[21:56] <Rora_Dice!> I might be able to get us some backup, but it'll cost

[21:56] <DCCWilliams> Cost what?

[21:56] <Rora_Dice!> In the short term, probably nothing. In the long term, a lot I think

[21:56] <DCCWilliams> I'm worried about today. Make it happen.

Rora_Dice! has left the room.

Williams parked along the street, an impossible feat on a typical Monday in Century Plaza. On this day, however, the storm-battered streets were empty. He pulled up to the curb just a block from the Horus Bank building. Typhoon Yvonne had passed with minimal structural damage, thanks to Rampart, but her winds had made quite the mess. The streets were littered with debris with not a collector in sight, and storefront windows were shattered without a looter in sight. Holo-ads whose projectors had been blown off kilter played looping images at nonsensical angles, some skipping in seizure-inducing flashes. And the emergency ticker at the base of them all had not been turned off. "Warning" could be seen scrolling on walls and even across the ground in white text against a red banner.

Turning off the engine, Williams drew and checked his pistol. Loaded and ready, he slipped it back into the holster under his arm and exited the vehicle. Not bothering to lock the car, he crossed the empty street, stepping over tree branches, a toppled streetlight and a shredded and waterlogged marquee to do so.

Major Monroe, now self-proclaimed Grand Magistrate of Sun City, had moved Agency Zero out of the Thirty-first Precinct and was now holed up in the Horus Bank building. Initially, Williams found the move a bit puzzling. Why move your battalion out of easily defensible and strategically distributed positions around the city and into a centralized position with little more to offer of military favor than one hell of a view? The answer to Williams was simple: Horus Tower was the prize and perhaps had been the whole time.

Crossing a vacant City Center in the middle of the day was an eerie sensation. Where thousands of people would pass one another on their way to and from work, only rainwater coughed up by an overburdened drainage system passed, met only with the sound of a prerecorded warning to the masses that stated in the Major's own sandpaper voice:

"Attention: Sun City remains under martial law until further notice. City Center, from Eleventh to McGeary Street and Clark Street to Thirty-second has been deemed restricted. Anyone caught in City Center without authorization risks being detained or fired upon."

The message repeated every minute.

Commander Williams made a beeline for the Horus building. The building itself had been walled off by tall metal partitions, the kind used for short-term forward operating bases. They were easy to stand up and could stop small arms fire. As he stepped into the shadow of Sun City's tallest building, armed Agency Zero sentries came into view. They were positioned at the four corners of the building and watched him from gaps in the barricade. Some manned heavy machine guns and eyed him suspiciously as he approached. Others paced the bank grounds, carrying military-grade assault rifles and wearing combat exoskeletons. Among their ranks, he saw a disturbing amount of blue-uniformed police officers and black-clad SWAT.

In the days since the coup, an interesting shift had occurred. Where, in the beginning, most police and SCPD officers had gone AWOL, likely waiting for outside assistance, most had since fallen in line. As the majority tilted in favor of the coup, the race to Major Monroe's side sped up exponentially.

The police and the SDC move as one, no matter the move, even if it's wrong.

The Unit One commander rounded the tower, headed for the main entrance. As he did so, a long line of people, wrapped along the opposite side of the building, came into view.

"What the hell is all this?"

Simply by their grooming, he could tell they were police.

Ahh, the holdouts.

These were the cops that had held out until the last minute of the Major's deadline. Many of them looked disheveled, unrested, and visibly troubled. He felt their pain. These were the men and women who tried to resist, but could not put their families in harm's way, should the Major hold true to his promise of branding them "enemies of the State."

As he bypassed the queue and made directly for the front doors of the bank, two of the Major's loyalists, a cop and a soldier, charged him, weapons drawn.

"Down! Down on the ground!"

Williams held his hands aloft and stood motionless as they drew down on him.

"Deputy Chief Constable Williams reporting for duty!" he screamed loud enough for the plaza to hear.

"And what makes you special? Get in line!"

At this, the cop looked anxiously at the soldier. "The DCC, sir. We should let him pass."

The soldier, on the other hand, seemed hell-bent on escalating the situation. He aimed the barrel of his rifle recklessly at Williams' chest. "You heard me! Get in line!"

"I'm not getting in line! Do I need to repeat my rank to you," —he looked at the man's badge— "Petty Officer?"

The soldier's face flushed.

"Stand down," a new voice demanded. It was gruff and heavily accented.

Another man in an orange uniform stepped out from behind one of the machine guns and walked over. His hair was slicked back and receding. The bottom of his face was held in place by a black metal plate. As he spoke the plate rose and fell, but nowhere near in unison with his words. His eyes were bloodshot and manic-looking.

"Deputy Chief Constable Williams... the Grand Magistrate has been expecting you."

Dozer. This is the man that hung the Premier.

The man with the metal jaw waved him forward. "I'll escort you inside. Are you armed?"

"You'd better believe it."

Dozer's eyes narrowed and it could have been a smile, but with most of his mouth replaced he couldn't be sure. "Produce your weapons slowly."

Williams removed his pistol from the holster and handed it — grip first — to the cop who now stood to Dozer's left. Just as the officer snatched the weapon, a loud boom in the distance caused him to flinch.

"What—"

Before he could get the words out, another loud boom sounded, only closer. The terrible banging got louder and louder, jackhammer salvos against the pavement until the earth itself shook. The hair on Williams' arms stood up, and the unmistakable urge to flee crept through him.

"What is that sound?"

Dozer nodded his head, his eyes aimed across the plaza. Just then, the massive red mech from the parade rounded the corner. It made its way across the plaza on lengthy steps that left cracks in the pavement. As it passed them, the people gathered — on both sides of the barricade — watched with expressions of awe and terror, some cowering visibly.

Jesus. That's why your quarantine of Century Plaza has been so effective. Where the hell did you even get that thing, Ace?

In all his years, never had Williams seen a war machine so menacing, and yet so mesmerizing. It moved with the grace of a person, its parts whirring and humming quietly, and yet it stood taller than most homes. Moisture, perhaps from the morning dew, caused its armored hull to glisten, highlighting the arsenal it carried. On its back was a huge missile carriage, the same missile carriage that had shot down the private jet days prior.

"Proper gear there, eh?" the jawless man said.

"Yeah, frightening shit. Manned or autonomous?"

Dozer's eyes smiled unmistakably this time. "Wouldn't you like to know. Let's go."

The lobby of the Horus Bank building was chaos. The floor had been turned into an officer processing center. Manning the process were high-ranking SDC officials and Agency Zero soldiers of varying ranks. Orders were barked verbally and cops were sent running — sometimes literally — from the building to comply.

"What is this?"

"What does it look like?" Dozer replied.

"Reassignment."

"That's right. Shufflin' beats, mostly. Can't have cops and civvies palling around under martial law. That's why we're sending them to new districts, to keep 'em on their toes."

I see. The last thing Monroe wants is police siding with the people. So he's sending cops to areas they're unfamiliar with, upsetting any rapport that may have been established. Strange, he must know that's only a short-term solution...

As Dozer led him deeper into the building, he spoke with an air of self-accomplishment. "Before nightfall, the entire SCPD and SDC will have been reassigned."

"And what are their orders?"

"Keep the 'proles' in their holes, what else? We have a curfew to enforce."

"And the fugitives?"

Dozer looked at him with incredulous eyes.

"'Fugitives?'"

"The Major's list of traitors."

Dozer laughed. "Billionaires suck at hide-and-seek! All that money becomes an anchor when the real shit pops off."

"You seem pretty proud of yourself, soldier," Williams said, growing tired of Dozer's devil-may-care demeanor.

"Why wouldn't I be? We took this city like panties off a Chechnyan stripper. At least the fucking commies in Pyongyang put up a fight."

"They knew they were in a fight."

Dozer stopped and glared into Willaims' face.

"You don't impress me, Blake. Never have. You're a fucking punk. You cheap-shotted this city and now want to prance around like some sort of warlord?" Williams leaned into Dozer's face. "Go fuck yourself, Blake."

Dozer laughed. "Yeah... the Major was right about you."

In the few moments of silence that followed, Williams knew that Blake wanted him to ask for elaboration. But the truth of the matter was that he simply didn't care. He continued walking and Blake resumed the depressing escort.

791

On the other side of the building, Williams was led through a pair of massive double doors. The placard at the entrance read "Magnolia Conference Hall."

Dozer opened the door for him with a warning. "Try anything, anything at all, and I'll gladly put two in your skull."

Williams entered the conference hall to find it filled with Agency Zero and SCPD, all of them yelling. They faced a stage upon which a great desk had been placed. The floors were littered with emptied bottles, clearly confiscated goods, emptied containers of drugs, and trash. Men and women in uniform were throwing these things at the stage and catcalling. A few even discharged their firearms into the ceiling.

Seated at the desk was the Major. He sat forward with his hands cupped as the object of the crowd's disdain was ushered onto the stage. Four people, heads down and covered in filth, were being brought before the recently self-proclaimed Grand Magistrate of Sun City. Their hands were unbound, which Williams knew was a bad sign. It was indicative of the kind of treatment that would make escape or resistance on the part of the captive seem such an impossibility that binds were unnecessary. It was a message. Just the kind of message Major Ace Monroe was wont to send.

Commander Williams proceeded toward the stage via the center aisle and, as he did so, many in the crowd stopped what they were doing. Men and women behaving no better than marauders righted themselves at the sight of him. He stared them all in the face, taking account of identification where he could.

When this is all done, he thought irritably, *all of you are going to prison.*

By the time he came to stand before the stage, much of the catcalling and tormenting of the prisoners had ceased. It was as though the parent had walked in on the children behaving badly.

"Why not just seize the Superior Court building?" Williams yelled, silencing the last few rabble-rousers.

"Strategically inconvenient. I'm surprised to see you," the Major said with a gruesome smile. "I was afraid you'd do something stupid."

"Give me time, the day's still young."

The Major pointed with a creaking hand. "I hope not, for your sake. And you'll address me as 'Grand Magistrate,' going forward."

"Grand Magistrate, huh? That's quite the promotion, I suppose. Didn't know you had a law degree. Or any degree, for that matter."

"Desperate times call for desperate measures."

"Convenient."

"Hardly." The Major raised his voice so that the hundred or so gathered could hear. "I want nothing more than a quick end to this. I've no interest in policy-making or jurisprudence. All I want, all *we* want, is *true* justice!"

At this, the chamber cheered.

Ace waited for the soldiers and cops to quiet once more before continuing. "Stand witness, Deputy Chief Constable! Witness justice as it used to be. Before the robber barons and politicians defanged it to save their own corrupt skins!"

The Major summoned the captives forward impatiently. Legion, apparently acting as bailiff, shoved the captives forward. Williams knew Legion to be one of the Major's inner circle. He could not recall her real name, only that it stood in contrast to her demeanor and attitude.

The captives moved as the injured, starved, and sleep-deprived would. They shuffled on uneven steps, all of them clutching themselves as though cold. The first two captives were both male and wore black, unmarked uniforms.

Private security, Williams thought. *Probably from right here in the bank.*

The first of the uniformed men had a thick mustache, the kind only cops and outdoor enthusiasts who wanted others to know they were outdoor enthusiasts wore. The other man had perhaps the squarest jaw Williams had ever seen, and almond-shaped eyes. The other two captives were business-types, one male, the other female. It was difficult to identify them, as they both stared at the floor, not daring to look up. Legion lined them up, soldier, soldier, man, woman. Addressing the Major, she poked the first man in the chest with two fingers. "Francis Berryessa, this one. His ID says he works for the bank but Black ran a check on him and he's never been employed, either for Horus or for the *actual* security firm

Horus has contracted out. My guess: he's a private military contractor."

"That's not true," the man replied, his head up now, his eyes defiant.

Without a moment's hesitation, Legion backhanded him with a closed fist, almost knocking him off his feet. The blow sounded throughout the chamber and sent cheers through the crowd. The captive standing next to the man caught him from falling and held him until he regained his footing. As Francis stood upright once more, blood poured from his nose unabated. After a moment, he picked his head up once more and locked his eyes on Legion. At this show of strength, many in the crowd whistled and called for Legion to hit him again.

"Speak again and I will cut your lying tongue out, *Francis*," she warned, a gloved finger in the soldier's face.

Williams watched the exchange and was sickened.

Mark my words, Legion, when this is all done, I will see you in maglets.

She continued on to the next man. "Chester Nguyen, same wetworks outfit."

Before announcing the man in the suit, Legion turned to the Major and smiled. It would have been a pretty smile if it weren't powered by malice. "And now, on to the main course!" She brushed the shoulders of the next man's suit mockingly and picked his head up by the chin so that the Major could see him clearly. "Jensen Carlisle, Chairman of Horus Bank."

The hall erupted. Men and women jeered in unison, firing their guns into the ceiling, which created a kind of artificial snow of plaster. Some threw things at the stage, and more still laughed evilly, congratulating themselves as though they were doing something great, as though they were not shitting on their oath and responsibility as law enforcement.

Williams had seen enough. "SHUT THE FUCK UP!" he roared, his blood boiling. "SHUT THE FUCK UP RIGHT NOW, YOU PIECES OF SHIT!"

Monroe stood from his seat, propping himself up on the desk with his fists. His eyes glimmered beneath the cold white light in the hall, and his lips peeled back from his teeth in a wicked grimace. A few flecks of plaster landed on his stretched and callused muzzle.

Williams expected a response from Ace, but instead the Major made an expression as though impressed, proud even. Without a word, he turned his wicked attention to his captives.

Legion, visibly enjoying herself, continued to the woman. "And, last but not least, Elaine Jones-Gutierrez: chairwoman of Deckar Applied Sciences."

Williams, a head or more taller than anyone in blue, looked around the room, daring someone, anyone, to catcall. There were no takers.

The Major waved a metal finger at the soldiers. "We'll start with these two."

The Unit One commander wanted to interject but knew it would only worsen the situation. He was powerless, a witness to a terrible tragedy whose devastation had yet to truly occur. The whine of tires. A car wreck inevitable.

"I'm going to ask you a series of questions!" the Major yelled, loud enough for the hall to hear. "If the answers given are spoken honestly, you'll be escorted out of Sun City under the protection of the SDC, never to return, upon penalty of death. However, if your words fail to provide adequate proof of your innocence, or are not forthright and candid, you will die here, now, in this very hall." He paused, his eyebrows arched. "Am I understood?"

"Listen, *Grand Magistrate*," Williams began, "you can't do—"

"SILENCE!"

Everyone jumped at the sound of the Major's voice, allies included.

"YOU WILL NOT INTERRUPT ME AGAIN!"

Once more, the Major turned to the captured soldiers. "Have you ever uttered or heard the words, '*beati sunt qui illustrantur?*'" He motioned to the man whose face Legion had bloodied. "You first."

"No, sir!" the man replied, his eyes wide, his chest out.

That's a poker face if I've ever seen one, Williams thought. *You might just make it out of this, soldier.*

"He's lying!"

It was the second soldier. He pointed a shaking, accusatory hand at his comrade. "I've said the words, many times, in fact! He has too! We're instructed to greet them with that exact phrase."

The first soldier, Berryessa his name was, looked to his partner with an expression of utter exhaustion.

"Legion," the Major said with a wave of his hand.

"ACE, WAIT!"

Legion drew one of the two submachine guns on her belt, spun it gunslinger style and put the barrel to the soldier's head. She blew him a kiss and pulled the trigger, sending the contents of his skull cascading down the back of his head.

The sight of the soldier's body collapsing sent the three remaining detainees into a pleading, sobbing frenzy. Legion gleefully and violently silenced them with blows from the butt of her gun. All the while, a bloodlust filled the room once more, a bloodlust that the chief's status, stature, or statements could not quell.

Ace turned his attention to the second soldier, the one who'd just signed his partner's death certificate. "I don't know what outfit you're from, soldier, but when you get back, I hope they frag your ass for snitching out your brother." He motioned to Legion. "Have this trash escorted out of my city."

Legion grabbed the sobbing, black-clad soldier of unknown origin and shoved him toward a pair of Agency Zero officers, who quickly dragged him from the hall.

Once a modicum of order had returned, the Major flicked a finger at the man in the suit, the man identified as one of the most powerful bankers in the world, the man the Fifth

Estate painted as a soulless oligarch, Jensen Carlisle. "Bring him forward."

Carlisle walked to the front of the desk of his own volition. He came to stand before his murderous accuser with his hands at his side. His suit was exquisite and his posture, despite being in his sixties, looked like that of an athlete. He raised his head slowly, deliberately, to meet the Major's gaze. "Grand Magistrate Monroe."

"What are the access keys for Spectus?"

What is Spectus? Williams wondered.

To Williams' great surprise, Carlisle tilted his head back to look down his nose at the Major. "What do you hope to accomplish?"

Monroe moved from behind the desk quickly, the rustle of his poncho like the march of invading forces. "What are the access keys for Spectus?" His voice had not changed and yet, just by repeating himself, the Major had silenced the hall.

"You misguided fool. Even if you could unlock its secrets, the truths held there would serve only to flummox your simple mind. Imagine, *Grand Magistrate*, what could a child do at an air traffic control station, but cause turmoil and death?"

The Major drew the blade from his belt slowly. Nearly a foot in length, the sound of it leaving its scabbard sent a chill through Williams' spine.

At this, Carlisle turned to Jones-Gutierrez. "Remember your oath. Our world is all worlds, and death is a construct."

"So," Ace asked menacingly, "you admit your guilt?"

Carlisle scoffed. "You would threaten me with death? That, too, is a sign of your ignorance. What is death to the immortals?"

"Immortal, you say?"

Ace drove his blade into Carlisle's stomach. Carlisle, even as the blade known as Soul Crook spilled his blood onto the stage, fought to push the Major away.

"If you are truly immortal," Ace hissed, "why struggle?"

The Major drove the blade deeper and used it to hoist the banker into the air, even as the banker's body sputtered and was torn asunder.

"Immortality… is there anything more gluttonous?"

Carlisle's kicking and punching died quickly. When the man once known as Jensen Carlisle was most evidently deceased, the Major, with an insane show of strength, sent his body flying from the stage into the third row of the crowd. As exclamation filled the chamber and quickly descended into an Iron Age kind of barbaric celebration, men and women picked up the parts of a man like they were playthings; blood, once revered and feared, became material for decoration and war paint. Monroe stood above them like the last or first belligerent in some Earth-ending conflict, breathing heavily, drenched in another's blood, his teeth bared.

Still holding his knife, the Major pointed to the Deckar Applied Sciences executive.

Williams, though his mind was reeling, found his voice once more. After all, it was not his first war. It was not his first atrocity.

"Ace!"

From the stage, the Major looked down on him.

"I'm not going to watch you kill her…"

"My patience is gone," Ace warned.

"These people might be afraid of you, Ace. Your brother might be afraid of you. But I ain't afraid of you, motherfucker."

Some of Carlisle's blood was parting the Major's already furrowed brow. "You never were that smart."

"I'm not going to watch you kill this woman," Williams told him, the stakes evident and real.

The Major licked his lips.

The chief was prepared for Ace to leap from the stage. The plan was already in place. He would catch the Major midair and drive him into the stage with all of his might. If he was lucky he would crush the Major's spine. Sure, he'd be a dead man after that, and likely in a disgusting hail of gunfire, but at least the pack leader would be out of the picture.

A voice interjected. Later, Williams would come to believe that it had probably saved both his life and the Major's.

"Grand Magistrate Monroe, you can holster your weapon," Jones-Gutierrez, the last of the captives, said matter-of-factly. "I will give you everything you need to access

Spectus and, in return, gratefully accept escort out of Sun City."

Ace winked at Williams and wiped Soul Crook on his poncho. He slipped the blade back into its sheath. "You'll also tell me where to find the kingpin, the propagandist, the energy tycoon, and the SDC traitor."

Jones-Gutierrez, not missing a beat, responded immediately. "Cholish, Liu, and West have disappeared, likely into the protective arms of your dissenters."

To Williams' horror, she thumbed at him from the stage. "Unit One might be able to help you in that regard."

Goddamnit!

"As for the rest... Kazuo Minowara was murdered the day before yesterday, as you must know, and Luther Gueye left Sun City for an undisclosed destination. His sister and father, however, may yet know of his whereabouts. I can tell you where to find them."

The Major made an impressed expression. "No loyalty amongst thieves, huh?"

He nodded to Legion and she seized the Deckar Applied Sciences executive.

"Get the kingpin's family's whereabouts from her, and the Spectus access codes. After that, get her out of my city."

"Sir!" It was the brutish soldier called Dozer. He was ascending the stairs to the stage. "Surely you're not going to let this bitch off that easy." Dozer came to stand before the Major. "Think about it. The defective parts, the men we lost to 'upgrades.' Fuck! Samuelson fought back the Sodang with half a fucking leg and I went into Korea with no fucking hearing or sense of smell." Dozer was almost pleading now. "Think about it, Major, all the times our leave or R&R got denied because of their fucking disclaimers. Major! They fucking toyed with us, kept us in a constant state of extreme fuckery.

"And what do you think she's going to do the minute she's over the Rampart? She's going to send every military force under the sun at us."

"We'll be long gone by then," Ace replied.

"Of all the game... This'un, Major, this'un has me salivating." Dozer's palms were up and his legs bent. "Please, Major. Gimme this'un."

"I get it."

Ace seemed to ponder Dozer's words for a moment before shrugging. "When you've finished with her, she is to be released, *alive*.

"After all, I'm a man of my word."

Dozer clapped his hands giddily. "Give'r 'ere!"

"You can't!" Jones-Gutierrez erupted, already attempting to free herself from Legion. "Hurt me and I'll give you nothing!"

The Major scoffed. "You misunderstand. We don't need you to talk willingly, we only needed confirmation that you had the information we need. There are a thousand different ways to extract info. And I'll make sure that — speak or not — you experience at least ten of them."

Jones-Gutierrez spat at the Major's feet. "What *are* you?"

"What am I? What are you? You'll tell us what we want to know and after that, you'll feel pain unlike any you've ever felt before. And perhaps, in that time, you'll come to realize that being the enemy of peace carries with it consequences." He smiled, genuinely. "Who knows, you might even see God. Some people do."

Jones-Gutierrez tried to scream, but Legion clasped a gloved hand over her mouth. She shoved the woman into Dozer's greedy arms.

Williams kicked the front of the stage with a boot. "*Major* Monroe!"

"You will address me as *Grand Magistrate* Monroe!"

"Fuck you!"

Ace hopped down from the stage and charged towards him before his lofty plan of counterattack even occurred to him. "Where is my brother, Deputy Chief Constable? And where is the rest of Unit One?"

"They've gone underground."

"Was that your call?"

"It was."

Ace came to stand before him, his poncho flowing around him like an evil aura. "Well, that was ill-advised."

"Was it? After witnessing your take on 'justice,' I'm feeling like it was precisely the right call."

For a long time, he held the Major's gaze. Monroe's eyes were sunken in his face, and the scars that laced his head seemed to take on a purple quality. He looked like Death.

I won't back down to you, Williams thought.

The Major cleared his throat into a gloved fist. "My orders were clear."

"Crystal."

"Yet you ignored them all the same."

"I won't send my people to the executioner's block."

"So you came in their stead? Admirable."

"Did I?"

"Aye," the Major replied, "you most certainly did."

Deputy Chief Constable Williams turned to the crowd. "Men and women of the SCPD and SDC! You stand in violation of your oath as officers and as agents. This man" — he put a finger in the Major's face, lest there be any confusion— "has usurped the Premier's office and is using you. His agenda is personal and his targets 'fugitives' only under his gross misinterpretation of the law! I implore you—"

The blow struck the back of his head and was intended to floor him. It did not. He turned to find Legion smiling prettily, if viciously, at him.

"Say the word," she hissed. "Say the word, Grand Magistrate, and I'll shut this guy up for g—"

Williams hit her as hard as he could with a right hook: his best punch. The result was what he figured it would be. The Central American mercenary's body crumpled, much as the soldier on the stage's had. Only, sadly, Legion would recover eventually. Guns were drawn throughout the hall and Williams was certain the bullet that would spare him the remainder of this circus would soon take flight. Instead, he watched as his old friend Ace smiled.

"Still got one hell of a right hook."

"Ace, you're wrong on this one."

"No!" Ace leaned in and spoke so that only he could hear. "We're close now, close to the truth. At the summit of this unholy building sits the meeting chamber of the Octumvirate. Do you understand?" The Major's breath was staggering: a combination of dehydration and whiskey. "Within that chamber, encrypted, lie their protocols, their transactions, records of their members, and their plans. We *will* break their encryption, and when we do, everything that I have done will be vindicated."

"There's only one vindication for murder."

"I know."

"Grand Magistrate Monroe. *Brother*. I can't get behind this. Unit One can't get behind this. Think about your brother! Do you have any idea what this is doing to him?"

Monroe seemed to ponder the notion for all of two seconds before warning, "You have two hours to round up Unit One and report to me, here. Two hours! After that, if we see a white delta, we shoot to kill. Am I clear?"

At their feet, Legion was starting to stir.

"You would do that, Ace? Kill your brother?"

806

"Don't test my resolve, Deputy Chief Constable. You have no idea what I'm capable of. You have two hours. Not a millisecond more."

30: Friends in Strange Places

"Conservative pundits like to point to the fact that during the 'Iron Insurgency', Sun City's crime rate plummeted — as justification for a firmer stance on crime. What would you say to that, Commander Williams?"

[Audible sigh]

"I've heard the same shit from Liberals and my response is this: Some people position themselves very carefully to benefit from chaos and are willing to do almost anything to mask the fact that they don't really care about crime or the well-being of others, but really just empowering themselves. I would also add that those people can eat all the world's shit and die in individual, personalized volcanos."

- SDC Deputy Chief Constable Sean Conrad Williams

The doors of the Brick House bar and concert venue were now barricaded from within. The windows too, high up on the wall, had been covered just to be safe. The strobe lights hung motionless and black, and the floodlights were on, revealing in the light of day just how abused the place was.

In the center of the scuffed dance floor sat Rena's personal immersion chair, moved from her apartment to the venue under the cover of night, and at no small amount of peril. Next to the chair sat a cluster of tables, upon which was

808

projected a holo-map of Century Plaza. Standing around the map were the members of Williams' unit. They were visibly tired, their eyelids heavy and their stomachs empty. Still, the sight of them so focused made him proud, and he told them so often.

A little longer and this will be over, for better or for worse.

At the bar sat State Defense Consortium Councilwoman Diane West and chairman of Coastal Power Ruben Liu. Standing with Unit One and also looking at the map was the CEO of Unicom Network, a dry, beady-eyed man by the name of John Cholish.

Cholish wore a V-neck sweater, skinny jeans and boat shoes. His arms were folded and he listened in silence as they discussed the plan of attack.

Addressing his men only, Williams swept a hand at Moore, Calderon, and Bruce. "It's vital that you guys don't emerge from the crowd until you get the signal. The doors of the bank are manned by machine gun, and if you jump early, you'll be mowed down."

"How do we know there will even be a crowd," Lieutenant Bruce responded.

'*We don't know,*' was the honest answer, but Williams kept a straight face. "They'll be there. Trust our boy and trust Rena."

The plan was less than perfect, but it was all they had. After more than a week under martial law, it was clear that no help from the outside was coming.

This fight is Sun City's and Sun City's alone. At least, that was the conclusion he'd personally come to.

"Any questions?"

The blue-haired rookie, Corporal Kevin Lin, raised a gloved hand. "I think I understand, but I would like to go over my role once more." His fellow new hire, the stone-faced Corporal Adriana Gonzales, nodded in agreement.

Williams nodded enthusiastically at the young recruits. "Good! If *any* of you have questions, speak up. There are no stupid questions, now that Daisuke isn't here. We're only going to get one shot at this. And I don't need to tell you that failure means death, and not just ours. Wholesale death for everyone."

When no one else spoke up, he slowly and meticulously explained the rookie's role to him again, tracing his finger over the map and garnering confirmation from the blue-haired man every step of the way. When he was done, he looked them all in the eyes, one by one, even Cholish, whose involvement was non-existent.

"The most important piece in all of this is getting to the Major. If the attack succeeds but the Major escapes, we lose. He'll just show his face elsewhere, and his movement continues. We have one shot, just one. The Major must be neutralized! With extreme fucking prejudice!"

AJ, who'd been staring at his feet, turned at this and left the group.

Williams watched the sergeant walk away, very aware of what the young man must be going through.

He's not the same, your brother, he wanted to tell him. *I've seen him murder with my own eyes.*

When he was gone, it was Cholish who spoke. "Can he be trusted?"

"Don't question my men," he told the billionaire. "What we are doing, we do for Sun City, not for you. Hell, your friend Carlisle, before the Major turned him into a piñata, pretty much admitted to some secret society shit. So, if there's anyone here I don't trust, it's the three of you." He nodded over to the bar where Liu and West sat staring, just out of earshot. "For all I know, the Major could be right about you."

"Then why help us?"

"Because right is right, murder is murder, and we still believe in the rule of law." He grabbed the businessman's shoulder and physically turned him to face the group. "Now, if I'm not mistaken, I believe Detective Constable Bryant has a way for you to contribute."

Rena, who'd been distracted throughout the briefing with God-knew-what, turned at the mention of her name. Her mouth was agape, her expression worrisome.

"What is it, Detective?"

"They've identified the plane; the one the Major shot down during the parade."

AJ, who had taken a position sitting on the steps, away from the group, looked up.

"Four crew members, including the two pilots," she continued, "and one passenger."

Rena's flair for the dramatic never ceased to annoy Williams. "Well, Detective?"

"Luther Gueye."

At this, Cholish looked to West and Liu, who were still seated at the bar, shock on their faces. The network magnate went over to them, a move Williams found somewhat odd. The group began conversing with themselves hurriedly in hushed tones.

"I can't believe it," Chris said. "After all that…"

Rena just shook her head, and Williams knew what they were thinking.

No satisfaction in it ending like this. After all that work, after the losses, the injuries, to see Gueye escape justice like this…

It's fucked up.

AJ slammed a fist into the stairs, bashing a hole in one.

"There's nothing we can do about it now," Williams yelled, "except focus on the task at hand!"

Rena seconded the statement. At the sound of her voice, AJ seemed to re-engage. Chris put his hands in his pockets and cocked his head attentively. Mason folded his arms and arched his eyebrows.

"Hey, Cholish!" Williams yelled, interrupting the visibly heated debate occurring at the bar. "We're not done here yet!"

Rena went over to the Unicom CEO and seized him by the arm. She escorted him over to her immersion chair.

"Have a seat, sir," she told him.

"What for?"

"You wanted to contribute? Well, this is how."

As he climbed up onto the chair, Rena explained. "An Agency Zero soldier who goes by the call sign 'Hollow Black' has locked my government account out of Libra and I can't go after them from my personal account because technically it's against the law for me to have one. Also, it's likely she's booby-trapped it by now. I go in, it's likely I'm never coming out."

"Well, what do you want from me?"

Rena motioned for him to assume a proper seated position in the chair. "Glad you asked. I need you to tell me everything you know about your product's 'God' mode."

Cholish studied her face, his expression stone. After a few moments, he asked, "Have you accessed proprietary code?"

Rena smiled politely. "If we're talking about the authorization protocol, sure it's 'proprietary' now, but it wasn't even a thing when I was writing code for it. Like getting a tattoo of my own drawing, it's not hard to see where someone clown-shoed their way through my solid programming. You had changes made to the the authorization layer."

Cholish's expression was cold. "Deckar was foolish for letting you go..."

"Additionally," she continued, "Hollow Black locked me out when I had what I thought at the time was the highest clearance. Couple this with the fact that Hollow Black didn't appear in Sun City until 2038. That's three years after Libra's beta rolled out. That tells me that someone granted her access, someone who didn't need to try and breach the encryption around Libra's codebase. Someone who knew there was another level in the permissions hierarchy."

Williams watched as the vein on the side of Cholish's head pulsed.

"And you're suggesting that I have that access? That I granted it to this Hollow Black?"

Rena held a hand up. "I'm not making accusations here, not yet. We've bigger fish to fry. But, as CEO of the nation's largest internet-access provider, and one of the principal minds behind Libra, you'd be a fucking idiot if you didn't have that kind of access."

Cholish made a face that was neither smile nor frown. It was the expression one made when they smelled something strong for the first time.

Williams felt obligated to chime in, to put the CEO at ease. "Look, we don't care about how the access got away, not now anyway. Maybe you were hacked, maybe you're not telling us something. Either way, that's not what this is about."

Cholish nodded slowly, though his expression was still dubious.

Rena placed a hand on his head and gently pushed his head down onto the headrest. "Once you've logged in, Mr. Cholish, I'm going to suspend your session using a remote-access plugin I've designed. This will keep you logged in, even after you disconnect from the neuro-actuator. Then you're done, and free to join your friends at the bar. At that point, I'll take over. Is that clear?"

"You hacked Libra," Cholish said flatly.

"Hack is such a strong word. I've *optimized* it. And you're welcome."

[Williams, this is unbelievable.]

"What is it?"

[Everything! Hidden access points, credentials, logs, secret cloud databases that have been under our very noses this whole time. I mean, I thought I knew Libra. Apparently, I've barely scratched the surface. They're not just tracking people's movement, but so much more. Things like pace, account balance, interactions with others... they've even found a way to track mass, as in when you were carrying something and set it down. There is an entire predictive overlay that I never knew was here and it's gobbling up data like a black hole. In a year, they're going to know not just where you've

been but where you're going, with a disgusting level of accuracy. This is some next-level shit. It's awesome!]

"Stay on task, Rena. Can you seize the network feeds or what? That's what you're in there for."

[You'd better believe it. Which one do you want?]

"Let's start with all of them."

Seizing control of the major networks took all of six minutes, and hijacking their feed and directing it to the modest set they'd built on the stage of the Brick House, another four minutes.

From Libra, Rena watched as the Deputy Chief Constable stepped into view of the cameras they'd set up. He straightened his Unit One jacket and cleared his throat harshly.

"How do I look?" he asked.

[We'll want to zoom out a bit. I forgot just how large you are.]

"Large and in charge," the chief replied.

She watched as his massive bald head and torso came into view. *[That's much better.]*

"So, we're good?"

[There's a booger in your left nostril.]

"This is no time for humor, Detective."

[This is also no time to look like a homeless person, Chief.]

Williams drove a finger into his nostrils, swirled it around violently, and rubbed the extract on the rear of his slacks. "How about now?"

816

[Better. Gross, but better.]

"Okay, let's do this! Let me know when we're live."

[We've been live this whole time.]

"Shit, Rena!"

[Now that was a joke.]

"Well played."

[We go live in three, two, and one...]

The Deputy Chief Constable flowed right into the script, not missing a beat.

"People of Sun City, my name is Deputy Chief Constable Sean C. Williams, Commander of Unit One; the only law enforcement agency in Sun City still acting in accordance with State law!

"To state it plainly, you have been lied to. At this moment, a man who positions himself as your protector has taken hold of City Center, establishing for himself a command center within the walls of the Horus Bank tower. From this stronghold, he plots to keep you hostage until he has completed a purge of any and all who stand in violation of *his* law." The DCC pointed into the camera as though pointing at the Major himself. "The man who has granted himself the title of 'Grand Magistrate;' the *Major* Ace Monroe is the enemy of peace and nothing more than a would-be dictator! But, make no mistake," he continued, "there will be no dictatorship, no terror, and no junta in Sun City so long as Unit One draws breath.."

['Draws breath?' You wrote that?]

"For fuck's sake, Rena!"

817

[That went out.]

The Deputy Chief Constable sighed. "Today, the Major has, at his back, the whole of Agency Zero, as well as many, too many, supporters in the State Defense Consortium and the Sun City Police Department. It is *you* men and women that I address now, the agents and officers of Sun City!"

Rena zoomed the camera in for effect, dulling the color contrast until Williams' face was just shy of black and white. *I should have been a director.*

"To the officers of the Sun City Police Department and to the agents of the State Defense Consortium, I remind you of the oath you've taken." He quoted: "'From this day until my last, I swear to uphold the laws of the State and defend its citizenry from all enemies, foreign and domestic.' Well, that last line should hold special significance. If that is not enough to spur you into upholding your word, I would warn you that, while the self-titled 'Grand Magistrate' may claim to represent the SDC, he is in fact in violation of several articles of the same act he quotes as justification. For example, Article 5f of the State Defense Act clearly states: '*In the event of severed, unintelligible, or illegal communications between municipal forces and the Council of the State Defense Consortium, the status quo, as defined by the most recent and/or applicable Report on State Affairs, is to be maintained. If this has been made impossible, the closest reasonable status should be pursued as directive until such time as clear and legal communications are reestablished.*'"

818

"I know that sounds like a lot of lawyer talk, so I'll translate for those of you who, like me, don't talk turkey. What that article is saying is that some jackass can't just appoint himself King of Sun City and start rewriting the Constitution. So fall in line, officers! It's not too late to be on the right side of history when this thing is over!"

"And, to the people of Sun City, the citizens currently being held hostage, I would say to you, stay in your homes. Protect your families and your neighbors. DO NOT take to the streets. This is our fight, and *our* fight alone!"

She left the feed open for dramatic effect before fading to black slowly.

"How was it?"

[A little campy, but effective, I think. Did you just attempt reverse-psychology on a macro scale?]

"Of course not."

[Some people are definitely going to read that as a thinly veiled call to action.]

"Not sure what else I can do besides tell people to stay inside. If people read something else out of that, chances are they were going to do whatever they wanted to anyway. And let's hope those folks show up."

[I don't like the idea of civilians in harm's way.]

"Of course you don't. Neither do I, but they're already in harm's way. We all are."

31: The Padded Paw

"My father, a pacifist of the purest order, was a strong proponent for constitutional reform in Togo. It was one of his passions and a topic that he was never afraid to engage in debate about. It was that passion that I drew from when I established the Gueye Foundation. So, in many ways, my father created the foundation."

"How would you describe your father on a personal level?"

"A dedicated family man, first and foremost. Patient and extremely fair. In fact, if one had to find fault in the man, it would be his patience. As a child, it allowed me to get away with a lot!"

[Laughter from the studio audience]

- Luther Gueye March 2, 2072

"Good Morning Pacific State" Episode: 3,245c

The clouds had broken, dispersed in clustered arrays that looked orchestrated and deliberate. Sunlight, like the legs of a great and yet holy spider lit up sections of Sun City as though highlighting opportunities. Warmth filled the room and seemed to find its way effortlessly into his bones. He directed his chair eagerly towards the window, that the heat might relieve the buzzing he felt in the tips of his fingers.

The signs were not lost on him.

Elom Gueye was hungry, but his daughter had stormed out long ago and he hadn't the energy to fend for himself. As he moved into the light, he looked out onto the city. From the top floor of the Ritz Carlton, Sun City looked blue, the rooftops pooled in rain reflecting back a still-mottled but otherwise gorgeous blue sky.

In his hand, he held a yellowing photo. In the washed-out image, there stood a father and his son. The father wore jeans the color of moss and a well-worn vest of yellow. The boy wore a pair of lime-green board shorts and was standing barefoot in crimson dust.

Elom had many photos of his son, but this was his favorite. This was the only photo that didn't conjure unpleasant memories. He remembered the day it was taken, vividly. A three-hour bus ride from a beach in Lomé and they were both grinning like idiots, like men privy to some secret.

He would have been six... maybe seven.

In his son's hands was a pink bucket of sand that he'd carried home dutifully. They would later border the garden in front of their home with the sand, much to his wife's displeasure and to his boy's delight.

A fear crawled its way into his stomach and chest. His wife's tongue would flay him in the afterlife. Surely, she'd seen the man their son had become.

How can I face her?

The birds, sent into hiding by the storm, had returned. He watched a pigeon peck at the stone head of a gargoyle across the street, absently.

Luther's sins are my sins and my sins alone. I will tell her that.

He thought he heard footsteps in the corridor.

And she will curse me for eternity...

A loud bang caused him to jump in his chair. It was followed immediately by the sound of wood splintering and objects hitting the floor.

"Vivianne!"

Behind the door to the study, he could hear the sound of hurried boots, of men commanding each other.

"You needn't break the door!" he yelled to the best of his ability.

Hushed voices, men breathing in measured cadence, and he knew that guns had entered his home.

The handle on the double doors of his room turned slowly before the doors were thrown open with such force that one slammed into the wall and the other into an accent table, breaking it. Men and women in orange uniforms flooded into the room, guns drawn.

Elom Gueye, eighty-three years old, watched in silence as they quickly took inventory of the room, checking in closets, behind curtains, and under furniture. Only when they were confident that he was alone were their guns holstered. And only then did the last man enter the room.

In Togo, particularly during the war, he'd seen many maimed individuals. Some were wounded in fighting and some by ritual. Others by disease, and more still by hunger. But never in all his years had Elom seen a man — a living man — carry such signs of physical devastation.

The presence of these people and what it meant was not a surprise. After all, the signs were not lost on him. But, upon seeing this man... Now, and perhaps for the first time truly since his diagnosis, did Elom Gueye admit fear into his heart.

The man was tall, not as tall as his boy, but thicker in mass. His shoulders were rigidly angled and wide, his neck like something found on cattle. He wore a ghastly tarp poncho and beneath that a mechanical arm, seemingly ancient in design. Thick scars parted the man's face like borders on a map, twisting and pulling in ways that made looking at him sustainedly almost impossible.

These traits alone made the man fearsome indeed, but, for Elom Gueye, it was the soldier's eyes that brought terror. They were brown; like his own, deeply set; like his own, and yet nothing like his own. They seemed to feed on light rather than reflect it and, worse, they appeared utterly devoid of humanity.

Like looking into the eyes of an almost *lifelike drawing.*

"Do you know who I am?" the man asked him in a voice that might have come from Hell.

I know, all right. You're the one the news spoke of,
before the looped propaganda seized television. You're the
man who some say single-handedly seized Sun City. You're the
warlord of the Pacific State, the self-styled 'Grand Magistrate
of Sun City.'

I know who you are, young man, Elom would tell him,
had terror not seized his lips. *You are my end.*

"Who am I?"

Behind the man, soldiers continued to search the suite,
poring through his belongings recklessly in the process.

"You're the man they call 'Iron' Ace Monroe," he
replied meekly. "You're the usurper."

"Usurper?"

"Or so the television says," he added quickly, "well,
said before... things changed."

Monroe seemed to ponder this for a moment, his dead
eyes looking off into the distance. After a moment, he shook
his head as though driving a thought away. "Well, I know who
you are. And for so very long I've watched as you spread the
same destruction you profited from in Togo to my home, to my
city."

The scarred man, the usurper, was standing over his
chair now, a position that made Elom extremely
uncomfortable. When he moved the chair back slightly,
Monroe advanced slightly.

"Until now," he continued, "I've had to wait. Because,
while you're no small prize, I've bigger game on my list."

"I know of your 'list.' Everyone in the city knows of your list now."

"That so?" Monroe's smile was atrocious. "Your son had lists too. Activists, blue helmets, politicians, religious figureheads, and humanitarians, mostly. The people who stood in the way of his drug trade, of *your* drug trade. It was us, the men tracking him, that found the mass graves, you see. We were always one step behind the massacre, and that used to drive me mad! Bodies stacked high like kindling. Enough to build a bridge from here to Timbuktu..."

The words came from such a place of unfiltered truth, and yet, with such unbridled hatred that it hurt Elom physically. "Please," he said, holding a hand up.

"Am I lying?"

"You are not."

"Where is your daughter?"

"Gone. Driven from here by my son."

"'Driven from here' is not a place. *Where* is she?"

"She's not the one you want."

"Oh really? What do I want?"

"You want my son."

The Grand Magistrate's laugh was cruel. "Your son is dead."

The words were like a bolt to the chest. Elom gripped the arms of his chair, certain that he would die in that moment.

"Just found out this morning, actually," the Grand Magistrate said, smiling. "Want to know the funny thing about that? He was on that plane we shot down at the parade." He bent at the waist and put his twisted face close to Elom's. "I had *no* idea he was on board when I ordered its destruction!"

With his metallic arm, the usurper shook the chair as though to shake him awake. The motion, in turn, sent pain spiraling through him.

"Please stop."

"I had no idea! Can you believe that? Tell me, old man, what does that tell you?"

My son is dead. Luther is dead.

"Come on now, what does that tell you!"

"I… don't know."

"It tells me that what I am doing is *supposed* to happen! Of all the planes in the sky, I shoot down the one that has your good-for-nothing, maggot-of-a-human-being son on it. It really has me thinking…"

"Please, sir. Please stop."

"What if God exists?" The Grand Magistrate of Sun City paused, wide-eyed. "If only sometimes?"

"I don't understand."

"What if — and hear me out here — the need for your son's death invoked the presence or even the *creation* of God? Just like how white blood cells form when too many red blood cells die. Have you considered that?"

"I have not."

The soldier whose face could fuel any nightmare, whose heavily muscled frame still somehow never implied

826

athleticism so much as predatory necessity, and whose poncho reeked of murder, penetrated his years and experience as if brushing aside children and locked his gaze on Elom's very soul.

"I am the white blood cell," he said.

The light was gone now and darkness had crept into the room, the sun likely blotted out temporarily by one of those puffs of white Elom had found so beautiful only moments earlier. He wondered if he would see the light again.

After a long silence, the shuffle of one of his men prompted the Grand Magistrate to speak. He made a disappointed face. "You don't know what to say. Of course you don't. Your kind never does."

Decades of fending off cancer had done remarkably little to prepare Elom for this end. He was frozen by fear now, knowing that this man would never let his soul find that of his precious wife, Halewat. And, as the Grand Magistrate moved his poncho aside to place his hand on the hilt of a blade on his belt, Elom yelped involuntarily.

Though the Grand Magistrate's expression softened perceivably, he still drew from his belt a blade that seemed infinite in length. The sound of it being drawn turned Elom's stomach and filled his mouth with a copper taste.

"Everything that has happened is my fault!" he blurted. "My fault and Luther's fault! Please show my daughter mercy! She's innocent!"

The Grand Magistrate showed him the blade. "If you place your ear next to it, you can hear it. My Soul Crook sings for you."

"I am so truly sorry!"

"That's because," the Major continued, "though it looks like a blade, it is in fact a machine. It works constantly, like the families you forced into the fields. It never sleeps, like the father of a daughter abducted by your cartel. And, it'll cut through anything."

"I caused this. It was me."

Ace did not respond; rather, he positioned the tip of the blade over Elom's heart.

No longer capable of speech, Elom extended his hand, the same way he would to beckon his son. At this, the self-styled Grand Magistrate's eyes widened. After a long moment, beneath the now deafening whir of a thousand spinning shards of steel, the Grand Magistrate took his hand in an iron grip that could have crushed it easily but didn't.

Elom Gueye mouthed the words "thank you" and gripped the the scarred soldier's hand in return, only there finding the courage not to scream as the howling blade took everything.

32: Lords of the Pacific

"I'm looking for a gift. It's not for a child, but rather a man that dresses like a child. You know the type? You look like the type. What shoes would you buy, if you had money?"

- Agency Zero Major "Iron" Ace Monroe

Breaching the Octumvirate's inner sanctum had taken longer than expected. The doors to the forum known as the Hall of Maati were nearly two feet thick and reinforced. But with a little persistence and a lot of semtex, the breach had been successful.

Once inside, a cool sense of vindication began to take hold in the Major. It was obvious that the uppermost floor of the Horus Bank tower was more than just that. He could see it in the wide-eyed faces of his men as they swept the hall.

The circular chamber held eight private rooms, each equipped with expensive, cutting-edge virtual conferencing equipment. The walls were painted in grand frescos, the pillars sculpted in the ostentatious style usually reserved for fine art museums and casinos. The hall, though pumped nearly to the point of bursting with oxygen, held a faint odor behind that almost minty smell. It was an odor unmistakable to the Major, an odor he himself carried with him everywhere. The Hall of Maati smelled of blood.

As he took inventory of the weapons they would need to hold the tower, the Major witnessed officers milling about, many of them un-tasked. Others patrolled the building in small, heavily armed units, soldiers paired with soldiers and police with police. He hadn't time to formulate a middle command structure that made sense, and so the bulk of his force managed itself. It wasn't the tightest use of resources, and was sure to crumble under even moderate pressure, but it would do in the short term.

At the center of the chamber, ripped halfway out of the floor, was the massive, steel-encased brain of the Octumvirate: the server Spectus.

Just connecting to Spectus had taken the better part of two days. Physical access points on the truck-sized server were plentiful, but each was locked behind iron hatches several inches thick. And all access points had been painstakingly booby-trapped to fry the contents of the database, should anyone attempt to plug in directly — all but one, apparently. Getting access to the device alone was like navigating a minefield. And that still left the matter of encryption.

Sitting on the floor, legs akimbo, was the second lieutenant, call sign "Witch Doctor." From the Agency Zero soldier's laptop ran a thick, shielded cable that plugged directly into the single valid access point.

As the Major came to stand over the young soldier, the man did not acknowledge him, but this was not a surprise. Witch Doctor and Hollow Black were engaged over neurotrigger, as they had been since seizing the Horus Bank tower. Witch Doctor, the most technically proficient besides Black amongst his inner circle, had been delegated the arduous task of acting as Hollow Black's eyes and hands. Regardless, he nudged the soldier with a boot.

"Where are we?"

"Close now, Grand Magistrate," the swarthy soldier replied. "The DAS Chairwoman got us past the lion's share of security protocols. Now, all that is left is decrypting the data and migrating it to our own data warehouse. Black is handling the migration, but it's tricky. They went as far as to trip-mine select data elements to self-delete upon recognition of brute force queries."

"I understand brute force, Lieutenant," the Major replied, "but that's about it, so spare me the jargon and tell me the solution."

The young soldier looked up with an exhausted expression. "Black figured out how bypass the subroutines."

"How? And keep it simple."

"The subroutines, the 'traps,' are set at unit level in the database, and understandably. "'Unit in this context representing data elements or files. Hollow Black wrote a script that will extract the information in random sequences, breaking objects apart into metadata and separating files from their folders, while simultaneously recording their schemas, paths, and hierarchies. All of this occurring at the cellular level. 'Cellular' in database-speak, obviously…"

"I'm not that stupid."

The second lieutenant coughed awkwardly. "Of course, Grand Magistrate. Well, as data elements are extracted, they are tagged. These tags include the schema details and paths and form a kind of codex, the instructions her system will use to reassemble the data. To do this, she's borrowing Libra's processing power."

"Brilliant."

"Imagine attempting to steal a vase through a small hole and breaking it first, only to—"

"I get it. How long?"

"At this rate? Four, maybe five more hours. Maybe."

"And how long on the back end? How long to reassemble?"

"Tough to say, but we don't need to stick around for that part."

The Major grimaced. "Keep at it. No breaks. Pee in your pants if you have to. We're running out of time."

"Roger that, sir."

Once Spectus is hacked and its records extracted, the operation is finished. A journey started so long ago will finally be over.

His mission had begun nearly a decade ago when his friend and brother-in-arms US Army General Rudolph Maecht had insisted that he meet with a captured North Korean information specialist in secret, even as the fires of war still burned around Pyongyang.

Oh Jin-ah.

Before she became Hollow Black, her name was Oh Jin-ah. During her interrogation, Oh, remarkably candid for a prisoner of war, revealed more than just the locations of the DPRK's remaining leadership. She also — eagerly, in fact — shared information about her role with the Sodang, North Korea's special forces, and her secret mission before the invasion. Oh, as it turned out, was the chief engineer of North Korea's surveillance network: the same network whose framework would go on to inspire Sun City's own Libra. And Oh, a young and apparently highly skilled information specialist, had for some time been embedded in China's central intelligence network. And it was while spying on China, then the DPRK's ally, that she uncovered China's own classified investigation. The People's Republic had for decades been trying to uncover the truth about a group known as the Council of Eight. Described as "a constantly cycling cabal of industrialists, never to number greater than eight," the Octumvirate, as they called themselves, allegedly held control over the Pacific, including its commerce, its laws, its media, and by extension its people... according to Information Specialist Oh.

At the time I thought you were just trying to save yourself, he recalled.

According to the young specialist, the People's Republic of China had learned of the Council inadvertently while interrogating a downed US Navy pilot during the early

833

years of the Cold War. The pilot, under China's harshest interrogation program, not only told the Chinese everything they could ever want to know about America's forces in the Pacific but went on to share his own family's sordid details. According to Oh, the pilot revealed himself to be the son of a billionaire energy tycoon. He then went on to name his own father as a "member of a secret council older than the United States."

Oh Jin-ah would go on to tell him that before his death the pilot also told China of a great archive. This archive, later to become a database, according to Oh, housed damning records: records that would shed light on the true motives behind every major conflict in the Pacific, going as far back as the "Bakumatsu:" the Tokugawa Shogunate in Japan, ergo the 1800s. This database of transactions, contracts, and secret dealings was called "Spectus." And the captured pilot, whose tongue would spark the butterfly effect still swirling more than one hundred years later, was named Colonel Leon Macek.

In truth, as intriguing as her story had been, it wasn't until the name "Macek" fell from her lips that any semblance of truth began to surface. William F. Macek, the US senator who would capitalize on deteriorating faith in the Executive branch to champion "Cal-exit," the secession of what was once California from the Union, had been a vocal proponent on US intervention in North Korea.

Though turning the captured North Korean captain over to the CIA was standard operating procedure, there was

834

something to the woman's tale. For one, it was too specific, too rich in detail, and delivered with too little regard for believability to be a lie. Ace would not turn her over. After all, there was a reason General Maecht had insisted on a private meeting between the two.

So, rather than turning Oh over to the CIA, Monroe found other uses for the talented information specialist. He embedded Oh Jin-ah with the Phoenix Battalion as a faux–soldier of fortune from an "unspecified Asian country." She was prohibited from speaking, allowed only to communicate through auto-translated neurotrigger, until such time that her English became passable. Over time, together, they crafted an origin story for the DPRK defector and before long, the enemy Information Specialist Oh Jin-ah became the Technical Specialist Hollow Black, formerly of the Phoenix Battalion and now a commissioned soldier of Agency Zero.

When the war ended, the Pacific State elected its first-ever Premier. William F. Macek, the architect of the Pacific State, was the obvious choice. Bill Macek was the grandson of Colonel Leon Macek, the captured Navy pilot of Hollow Black's tale.

The need to unpack the truth of Hollow Black's mission drove the Major to attach himself to Macek.

Befriending the amiable William Macek didn't take long. It turned out that the two benefitted from a relationship. Macek and the State Defense Consortium would give his men a home away from the battlefield and a purpose as Sun City's antiterrorism rapid reaction force Agency Zero, and he would give Macek the fangs he needed to truly control Sun City.

For a time, they accomplished some truly great things together, busting several terrorist cells and creating Unit One. But, in that time, the Major never forgot his mission. Similarly, Macek never forgot *his* true calling. In the late spring of 2047, Macek, for whom the Major had then become a military advisor, gave the Major orders of a different kind...

"Major!"

Legion was running toward him, crossing the marble floors of the Hall of Maati at double-time.

"I mean *Grand Magistrate*," she corrected, as she slowed to a walk, "you need to see this."

The Major followed her out of the Hall of Maati and down the art-strewn corridor to a window on the other side of the building, facing Century Plaza. Along the way, Blake and Pops caught up with them, equally flustered. When Monroe peered down onto Century Plaza below, he was aghast.

"Leave your best men to guard the chamber, and head to the lobby. Why are we only now seeing this? Who's in charge down there?"

Through Libra, he contacted Hollow Black. "Black!"

[Major...]

"Where's the Kodiak?"

[Where do you want it to be?]

He thought for a second. "Heading down now. Have it waiting for me at the south entrance!"

836

The Major's heart rate soared. He expected a response, but not like this and not so soon. He slammed a metal fist into the wall.

"It's too soon!"

33: About the Killing

"I don't want to talk about him. I agreed to do the show, and we can talk about anything else. I'm not talking about him."

- Unit One Sgt. Alec Jefferson "AJ" Moore

The streets of Sun City quaked as the people marched on Century Plaza. The citizenry, coming in all form of classification, including those who spat on classification itself, flooded the streets. They stood shoulder to shoulder, hardened and fearless in their solidarity. Though a measly turnout when compared to the Liberty Day Parade, the number of those willing to step into harm's way in defense of Sun City was staggering. A true insurgency of the people, they were as varied physically as were the neighborhoods they marched to protect.

AJ, with Chris and Mason at his side, moved several yards ahead of a mass of people that stretched far beyond visibility. The sensation of their voices and of their very movement and energy seemed to move his feet for him. He was certain that if he were to simply stand, their voices and collective outrage would carry him forward. As they moved into the shadow of the Horus Bank building, fanning out to fill the plaza, the people comprising the Anti-Major Insurgency of

Sun City were met with a much smaller but heavily armed group of men in suits. Of the group of predominantly Asian men, one man in particular stood out. His meticulously coiffed pompadour swept back from his head, only a single strand blown out of place by the cool breeze. He wore a long, white overcoat and beneath that, the familiar black jacket of Unit One.

AJ and the rest of Unit One advanced to meet him, even as the people of Sun City halted at the sight of so many armed yakuza.

"Oi," Dice said behind a wobbling cigarette and smile. He extended a hand.

Just seeing Dice's face did a lot to raise AJ's spirits, more than he would ever admit verbally. Ace's coup, the *thing* between Rena and himself, and Dice's departure had left him feeling very alone. "Hey, Dice. Your face is healing up pretty good."

Dice snorted. "Fuck you."

AJ laughed. "I was being serious."

His friend and partner threw his arms wide, tossing his overcoat outward in a flourish as he did so. "I brought some friends."

Behind him was a battalion of yakuza. A virtual wall of black suits, AJ could only rely on the variety of body types and hairstyles to tell them apart. Short and stocky guys with big rings and thick knuckles. Tall and lanky guys with lazy expressions and exposed chests. He saw perfectly coiffed pomps similar to Dice's, feathered and intentionally mussed mops, and many shiny, meticulously razored pates. Some wore sunglasses, some had piercings, and many had tattoos on their faces and necks. The only thing universal among them were the black suits, cigarettes, and brandished weapons.

"The Minowara?"

"The *real* Minowara," Dice corrected, "what's left of them?"

"How did you…"

"Minowara's daughter loaned them out to us, in exchange for assistance combatting their coup."

"You mean Sugihara?"

Dice nodded, his expression stern. "Shall we do this?"

"Just waiting on one more group."

Several minutes later, at the north end of the plaza, another large mass poured into the streets. They streamed toward the yakuza and the unaffiliated in waves, the sight awe-inspiring. Thousands of people. Many wore bandanas on their faces, some ski masks, others simply caps pulled low. They wore sweatpants and hoodies, T-shirts, frayed jeans, and tennis shoes. Some carried sticks, others guns, and many more bats and crowbars. Gone now were their protest signs and spray cans. This new army crossed the plaza to meet them on a sea of chants.

"FREE THIAGO GARCIA! FREE THIAGO GARCIA! FREE THIAGO GARCIA!"

"The Fifth Estate?"

"They were the first to reach out to us after Chief Williams' PSA."

The armies bled together to become an ocean of people ready to fight, and from the last army to join, a tall woman in a hooded sweatshirt and jeans emerged to greet them. As her long stride carried her forward confidently, Dice began laughing.

"Something funny?" the woman asked as she joined their huddle.

"Just never thought I'd see you again. Especially not at the head of the Fifth Estate." Dice extended a hand and they shook. "AJ, meet Vivianne Gueye."

"Gueye?"

"Please don't let the name bother you," she replied. "I am *nothing* like my brother."

AJ extended a hand to her. "A lot of that going on right now." He was about to elaborate when an exclamation rose from the crowd. They turned to the Horus building to find the lobby emptying itself of forces. Hundreds of armed police and Agency Zero agents poured out of the building to take up defensive positions.

"Jesus!" Vivianne exclaimed.

"They're protecting the building."

At that moment, the ground began shuddering once more. Bipedal tanks, pulled from their checkpoints around the city, began closing in on the plaza. Another, largest of them all and painted red, came sprinting. Their PA warning systems

841

deafened the crowd. The red mech took a position in front of the tower's main entrance and aimed guns innumerable at the civilian army.

The sight of such an arsenal sent a shockwave through the crowd and indeed, many turned and fled. Many more however, stood their ground. Not a single yakuza took to heel.

AJ turned to face the combined armies of The People. "Everybody, listen up! You've done a great deed. You got us as close as we need to be. Now, it's time to head back and leave the rest to us!"

We can't ask these people to march on that!

With a grim resolve, AJ began walking towards the Horus building. Almost immediately, the red mech began blasting its prerecorded warning, ordering them to disperse.

The sun shone on the shiny black Gatling guns mounted on the mech's shoulders, and he knew that should the mech open fire, death would be instant. Shrinking, retreating in the face of his brother's tyranny, however, was not an option.

AJ drew Deadbolt from his belt slowly.

Is this it, brother? Are you going to kill me?

The sergeant heard a loud sigh and turned to find his partners walking alongside him. Behind Dice was a reluctant but nevertheless obstinate wedge of advancing yakuza.

"I guess we're doing this…"

"Fuck it," someone said.

At the sight of them, the giant red mech charged down the steps of the Horus Bank tower, folding the handrail with its

842

legs like a crazy straw. Its movement, so lifelike, turned AJ's stomach in terror. He clenched his jaw and refused to balk, though his steps faltered momentarily.

"Brother! You've come!" the machine bellowed.

AJ triggered Deadbolt's extension, a sensation that bolstered his courage, and placed it on his shoulder casually. After all, he didn't have to *look* terrified.

"Ace? You in that thing?"

"You will address me as Grand Magistrate!"

"Why don't you climb out of that fake-ass Transformer and face me like a man, Ace?"

The mech seemed to glare at him in response, its soulless "face" looking down at him from thirty feet.

"Little brother, you are going to get a lot of people killed needlessly. Assist in sending these people home at once. Once that's done, you will report to me, along with the rest of Unit One, for reassignment. This game has gone on long enough!"

"There you go again, talking to me like I'm twelve. Fuck you, Ace!"

He spat on the mech and slammed the butt of Deadbolt into the pavement with a very satisfying bang that sent an exclamation through both the civilian crowd and Ace's forces. AJ would have grinned triumphantly at his own badassery if a light trickle of urine wasn't presently warming his crotch.

Thank God I decided on black jeans...

"Your posturing serves only to demonstrate how unfit for the uniform you truly are. Are you prepared to have the lives of all of these people on your head?"

"Are you?"

"Yes, and more! *Many* more!"

"Then you're a monster!"

"You have no idea!" The mech widened its stance, and missile pods slid silently up from the shoulders on either side. At the same time, the mech trained the guns on its arms at the crowd. Gatlings, they began to spin in preparation to fire.

"Ace! Look at me! Aim that shit at me! You've preached your whole life about the virtue of the humble people of the Veins. You've gone on forever about your dedication to protecting them. Was it all a lie? Is this your idea of protection?"

The Gatling guns slowed and came to a halt. "What I am doing, I do for the people. Give me time and I will show you. All will be made clear!"

"And how many people will be executed in that time?"

"As many as it takes for truth!"

[AJ, you might want to take a few steps back.] It took a moment for Rena's voice to penetrate the boom of his heart in his ears.

"Listen to me, brother," the mech pleaded in its megaton-decibel volume. "We can talk through this. You and I!"

The sincerity in his brother's voice gave him pause, but so did the visceral scene of the Premier's limp form swinging wildly in the wind. AJ pretended to ponder his brother's words as a roaring sound grew louder. When the sound began to drown out Ace's condescending instructions, AJ turned and sprinted back towards the crowd. As he did so, the sound, like a million blenders running in unison, became deafening.

Across the plaza, from behind the Horus building, a massive black shape emerged. It turned the corner with an ear-piercing whine and churned a storm of ground concrete that poured over storefronts in waves. The stories-tall black box on treads barreled at high speed straight for the base of the Horus building.

No longer a perfect square — more pear-shaped, thanks to its tumble from the 101 — Pandora still had plenty of life left. The retrofitted earthmover sent Agency Zero and SCPD officers scrambling.

The bipedal tanks trained their turrets and fired booming shots that tore huge chunks out of the rolling complex. The tanks themselves, however, were not spry enough to avoid being crushed violently by Pandora in a mesmerizing display of destruction.

[Up yours, you fascist piece of bat dung!] an unrecognized voice yelled into Unit One's neurotrigger channel.

"Who the fuck is that?" Dice asked.

Pandora hit the stairs and was airborne, with parts of bipedal tanks dangling from it like the ribbon from a winning sprinter.

"The rookie!" AJ hit Dice in the chest hard. "That's the rookie!"

"Corporal-fucking-Lin?"

"Yeah," he said, laughing maniacally, "the oddball!"

The red mech, despite having an opportunity to evade, moved into Pandora's path, granting the soldiers and police gathered at the base of the building an opportunity to flee.

The two massive machines collided and were driven into the lobby of the tower. The impact sent machine parts the size of cars spinning high into the air, where they embedded themselves into the walls of the building or came crashing down in bedlam-inducing shockwaves.

As Agency Zero struggled to gain some sense of cohesion, Dice ordered the Minowara to charge with a war cry that would have made any of the great shōgun proud. The yakuza charged, the tip of their spear a heavy torrent of small-arms fire.

[This is it, Unit One!]

It was Chief Williams.

[This one's for real! You've always wanted to be taken seriously, and this is your chance. Get in there and take the Major out! Oh, and uh… someone should check and see if the rookie survived.]

In the chaos, AJ couldn't see Dice and Chris following him, but he knew they were. He mounted the now crumbling steps of the tower to find the red mech lying inert and smoking. The "torso" was caved in and crushed beneath one of Pandora's now independent treads. And both of those occupied what used to be a cafe. The menacing red mech's limbs were gone, including most of its menacing arsenal. Parts lay everywhere, and fire threatened to finish that which hadn't been obliterated. The cockpit, however, once where a human's throat would be, was open, its one-time pilot nowhere to be found.

AJ's relief at not finding his brother's corpse among the wreckage was short-lived, as the tower's lobby filled quickly with fresh faces. Orange fatigues and black uniforms rushed to meet them with guns drawn.

It had been a simple affair to locate her nemesis while, at the same time, directing Chief Williams' *vox resistebat.* In reality, The Unicom Network CEO's access might not have even been necessary. Apparently, the woman calling herself Hollow Black wasn't the mobile type. A sweep of Hollow Black's session logs revealed that not only was she a home-body, but she hadn't moved since their first encounter. The former DPRK information specialist immersed herself from one place and one place alone: the Agency Zero headquarters in Section Four's Thirty-first Precinct. And, from the look of it, she'd been online for a long time. A very, very long time.

The Thirty-first Precinct might as well have been haunted. The compartmented complex was empty, with not an officer in sight. Computers were left running, doors and vehicles unlocked. The entire police force of Section Four had gone missing. The sensation was eerie, like those videos of post-meltdown Pripyat or Fukushima. Likely, Rena figured, there were two reasons. One: the officers onboard with what people would one day call the "Iron Insurrection" were in City Center defending the Horus Bank building. And two: the officers not onboard were terrified of returning to work, lest they be rounded up by Agency Zero to face God-knew-what as punishment.

And so, the Thirty-first Precinct of Section Four sat unmanned, unguarded, and completely vulnerable.

Rena navigated the precinct with her gun drawn nonetheless. It had been a long time since she'd felt the exhilaration of fieldwork. In the foyer, she stopped to review the directory.

This is kind of exciting, she thought. *Real, analog agent work.*

AJ had spoken of a room adjacent the gun range of the first sub-level. After confirming the existence of such a place, she crossed over to the building at the north side of the complex, which, according to the directory, housed said training range.

Along the way, she saw what looked like signs of a fight. Scattered shell casings, scuff marks of shoe sole on the

848

marble deck, and even the congealed and blackening modern art of blood splatter.

Looks like somebody fought back.

Through a pair of pearl-white double doors, she found the stairwell to the Thirty-first Precinct's basement. The floor was dimly lit, with several track lights out. Shards of glass on the floor and bullet holes in walls and ceiling explained clearly why. Another set of double doors, and now she could hear her own breathing.

The corridor beyond was a crime scene, and a recent one. She passed the sickeningly contorted corpse of a police officer. The apparently one-sided gunfight had left a gory mural around the corpse, and a perfunctory examination all but confirmed the homicide.

It was impossible to know which side of the coup the dead man had chosen, but it didn't matter. Both sides had failed the moment blood was spilled.

Unfortunately, the investigation into the officer's murder would have to wait a while longer. Reporting him to the SCPD would alert Agency Zero to her presence. Instead, she sent a series of comprehensive, if hurried, videos and photos directly to Chief Williams before moving on.

Rena found the door opposite the gun range entrance, just as AJ had described. The sliding glass door was locked by keycard. Positioning her body intelligently in case of ricochet, she fired her pistol twice into the base of the door. With a kick, the glass exploded inward and tumbled to the floor in a series of cringe-inducing crashes. Taking cover, she braced for gunfire. When no shouting or shots rang, she peeked inside.

"Unit One! If you're inside, hands high and announce yourself!" After a moment: "I'm coming in! Announce yourself or risk being shot."

The room was dark, but she could make out a faint blue light coming from within.

Here we go...

Exhaling slowly, she turned the corner and entered.

Industrial shelving as high as the ceiling created a kind of mini maze for the server room. Racks strewn with computer and telecom knick-knacks looked ready to collapse under the weight of the gear they held. Above, a cool blue light played off the ceiling in the telltale wavy display of illuminated water.

A pool in the server room? Counter-productive...

She entered the room's main area gun barrel first, no longer bothering to announce herself.

"What in the bloody hell..."

At the sight of the massive immersion tank, she couldn't help but smile. Her smile soon faded when she saw the corpse floating within.

"Hello, Hollow Black."

Far less terrifying than their first encounter, her Agency Zero counterpart floated, submerged in the bluish liquid, neurotrigger relays connected not just to the base of her neck, but all along her spine. A breathing apparatus covered Hollow Black's mouth and ran from the tank to an oxygen concentrator outside. Her skin was grey, and necrosis had taken root in great patches along her bare, skeletal torso. Her eyes, partially hidden behind a mat of swaying black hair, were lidded and dark. They did not stir, even as Rena rapped the butt of her pistol on the glass.

Hollow Black was deceased, and had been for a long time, by the look of it.

Rena couldn't ignore the disappointment she felt. A part of her had greatly desired to meet Hollow Black face to face. Now, it was highly unlikely she would ever meet another soul so versed in Libra as herself. Sure, John Cholish had been involved in the early stages of Libra's development, but really, he was just the money man. He couldn't hack his way through a turnstile.

She watched the lifeless corpse that, under not-too-outrageous circumstances, could easily have been her. Hollow Black hung in the water like a wraith. Her exposed ribcage, ghastly cheekbones, and knobby knees… signs of extreme malnutrition. Her horrible grey complexion and the tattered and filthy scarf that did little to hide the repulsive thin lips and exposed teeth. Hollow Black.

So this is the cost… If so, I won't. I can't make this kind of sacrifice.

While the Major was seizing the territorial expanse upon which Sun City rested, Hollow Black had seized everything else; everything of substance. While women and men with guns were turning Century Plaza into a fortress,

Hollow Black had done God-only-knew-what with the data, the evidence.

It all makes sense now...

The Major's first action, after the public execution of Premier Macek, had been to send forces to take the Ministry of Information building in Section One. At the time, Rena had assumed the Major's goal was to manipulate the message going out over the networks and to protect against counter-propaganda. The real reason was quite clear to her now.

Taking the Ministry of Information was about removing the authoritative body over Libra. With no one monitoring usage, behavior, and traffic, a person could easily leverage Libra to seize other facets of the SDC network. And from there, who knew? With an asset like Libra at a person's disposal, it would really only come down to skill and imagination. And from her one interaction with Hollow Black, she knew both of those to be significant.

But now she was dead. When had she died? Was her work finished?

I wonder, Rena thought, *was Sun City even the goal? Or was the true agenda something more?*

"Only one way to find out."

She holstered her pistol.

Immersion was in many ways a state of trance. A user wasn't plugged in and suddenly rendered unconscious. Rather, the REM-like state of synchronicity required a zen-like concentration to initiate. Once synchronicity was fully

852

achieved, staying connected was fairly simple, assuming one could minimize or entirely eliminate external disruptions. Because of this, immersion chairs were typically padded with gelatinous cushions that lined the back, head, and wrist-rests. The idea was to minimize physical pressure, as discomfort could weaken the sync, or in some cases cause desynchronization.

With an isolation tank like Hollow Black's (and the appropriate feeding apparatus and waste disposal equipment) a person could — at least in theory — remain immersed indefinitely. Or, as was the case with the withered and greying form submerged before her, until the body finally rotted away from acute waterlogging and atrophy.

Her sacrifice... admirable if nothing else. But when had she died? And did the Major have a hand in it? Had she fulfilled her mission and been discarded?

"Shit. Did he poison her tank?"

As if it could tell her anything, Rena sniffed the fluid of the tank. It smelled like chlorine. She put a pinky finger into the liquid and left it there for several minutes. Finding no discoloration or sensation in her digit to be worried about, she grabbed Hollow Black by the hair and used a handful of it to pull her body towards the tank edge. The corpse struck the wall of the tank with a dull thud.

Rena scooped her rival's body up by the armpits and made to lift her from the tank. She was aghast. It was like lifting a three-year-old. The sensation turned her stomach, and for a moment she was certain she'd vomit.

She fireman-carried the body down. As she did so, the interface cables along Hollow Black's spine disconnected audibly, almost in unison with each rung of the ladder she descended. She lay the deceased Agency Zero soldier on the concrete floor gingerly. And, though she handled the woman with the care of a porcelain doll, Rena's hands still left visible contusions on the body.

"Rest in peace, soldier."

With a heavy sigh, Rena connected to the unit over neurotrigger.

"Williams, I've found Hollow Black."

[Is the target secured?]

"The target is dead, sir. Dead for a while, it seems."

[I don't understand. If she's dead, who activated Rampart? And who was controlling the Kodiak at the parade?]

"I don't know, but the likeness of the body here and the figure I met in Libra are too close to be a coincidence. This is definitely her. I'm as confused as you."

[Well, shit. I guess collect any evidence you can and get the hell out of there.]

"It may not be a total loss, sir."

[Explain, Detective.]

Rena placed a palm on the tank. "We may have the keys."

[The keys?]

854

"Why, the keys to the kingdom, sir."

She disconnected and kicked off her shoes. Removing her holster, she hid it and the pistol within high up on one of the racks. As an afterthought, she left the room and checked the corridor once more. It was empty.

Climbing up onto the ladder, she took hold of the primary cortex interface cable that had been plugged into the base of Hollow Black's neck and the breathing apparatus.

She lowered herself into the pool. The liquid was warm and had the consistency of hand sanitizer. With a hand on the edge of the tank, she inserted the interface into the port in her neck and slipped the respirator over her head to cover her nose and mouth. The smell was maddening. Closing her eyes, she released her grip on the tank and descended into the muck.

The sudden arrival of Pandora and the utter pandemonium it had caused gave the yakuza and the Fifth Estate ample time to rush the building. Behind a hail of gunfire and a veritable carpet-bombing of Molotov cocktails, the SCPD officers guarding the base of the tower splintered. Many officers threw their hands in the air, only to rejoin the fight on the side of the people of Sun City moments later. Others found themselves unable to fire upon unarmed citizens and were rounded up by yakuza, who had no such qualms. The holdouts, mostly Agency Zero soldiers, turned and began retreating for the lobby of the Horus building, pursued only by the most brazen yakuza, as their returned fire came in the short,

855

controlled bursts of professional soldiery. The tanks not crushed by Pandora began blaring their PA crowd dispersement warnings to deaf ears, as the citizens that hadn't fled the plaza had already taken up skirmishers' roles in the fight and were beating the Major's forces back with bricks, bottles, rocks, and fists.

In the lobby, AJ, Chris, Mason, and Dice, along with a small cadre of conscripted Minowara yakuza, quickly found themselves engaged with the highly organized and highly skilled forces of Agency Zero.

Most of the men and women surrounding AJ's brother day-to-day could be described fairly as "unapproachable." They were terse at best and, more times than not, flat-out belligerent. The exception to the rule, for AJ, was Pops. For as long as he'd been in the SDC, Pops had treated him as the hair-to-tousle little brother of the Major. He'd always been kind and polite, even when there wasn't a need. A seven-foot-plus behemoth, Pops was easily the most physically impressive senior citizen he'd ever met. Hell, the only thing Pops had on him more than years were muscles. And it was Pops now who stood blocking the elevators in the lobby, swords drawn.

"Fall back, young Moore!" he yelled, as his fellow Agency Zero soldiers continued to pour into the lobby. "I can't let you any further!"

Pops held aloft his ridiculously large broadswords, Gog and Magog. Crouched in front of him, guns aimed, was the orange-haired soldier called Legion.

856

It had always irked AJ that Unit One couldn't adopt cool nicknames. He had a great one picked out already, too.

"Dollar-sign…"

Around them, the yakuza, spurred on by hoarse commands from Dice, were giving Agency Zero a respectable firefight.

"Pops, I just want to talk to Ace — I mean, *the Grand Magistrate*." AJ approached carefully, Deadbolt sheathed but held openly.

The giant soldier shook his head slowly, turning his own swords in his hands for AJ to see. "Grand Magistrate Monroe has given an order, young Moore. You are to be kept from the premises, forcefully if necessary. Now's the time to walk away. I don't want this, and you *definitely* don't want this."

"Ace is wrong, Pops. He's stepped way over the line, and you know it. If we don't stand up to him, we're no better than the crooked cops flocking to his cause, or anyone else for that matter. We can't just take the law into our own hands."

"It's not my job to question the politics."

AJ spat. "Then whose is it?"

"Alec, turn your people around before it's too late. We're soldiers and we've fought with the Maj— Grand Magistrate a long time."

AJ pointed. "You see that? You know this is bullshit. He's no Grand Magistrate! You can still do the right thing, Pops. Join us!"

More Agency Zero agents, many carrying assault rifles, poured into the lobby from the stairs and from the elevators behind Pops. They began taking up positions, using the reception desk, the pillars, and corridors for cover.

"Hold your fire!" Pops hollered. "Hold your fire!"

Legion sucked her teeth. "You talk too much, old man." With her guns trained on AJ, she gestured. "So you're the little brother. I've seen you around, but I don't see the resemblance."

"Different daddies. Mine was much better looking. Put down your guns, Legion."

"Go fuck yourself."

"And I was just about to compliment you on your hair."

"Forget it, AJ," Dice said, his gun aimed at Legion.

A loud snapping resounded above the gunfire, and outside a massive explosion sent concrete and bodies into the air.

"Holy shit! What was that?"

"Who's firing on civilians?" Pops roared.

"Who do you think?" Legion shook her head and pointed upward. "*He's* the one you should be concerned about."

"How much you want to bet that's one of DAS' missing railguns?" Chris added. "We've no time. I'm heading for the stairs."

Chris took off running, and Legion immediately aimed to fire at him. With the press of a button, AJ fired Deadbolt. With a lashing, upward motion, he cut deep into the marble

858

floor and sent the heated debris flying into Legion's face. She fired at the same time, but missed Chris by a wide margin. Before she could recover, AJ darted in. As he ran, Dice sprinted in front of him, his bulletproof white overcoat held up over his face to absorb the rounds from Legion's sub-machine guns. As the two got close, Dice slid across the marble on his knees and returned fire with his revolver. Running hard behind his partner, AJ used Dice as a springboard. Planting a shoe in the ex-yakuza's back, he leapt high into the air. With a forward flip, he brought Deadbolt's blade down on Pops, who met the blow with both swords.

The great blades Gog and Magog shattered under the heated obsidian blade. The downward blow slashed into the old soldier's left shoulder, and cut cleanly at an angle to end just under the big man's right pectoral. Pops' uniform fell away in sheets, seared on the ends and smoking.

The cut was severe, fatal even for the giant. AJ waited for the old man to fall, as gunfire struck the marble around them. With a great moan, Pops slashed with his broken swords. Not expecting the counter and not quick enough to bring Deadbolt up in defense, AJ was defenseless. Pops' blades struck him in the side like a bat, and for a split second things went dark. AJ hit the marble floor on his side and slid for what must have been yards. When he did not bleed out, and could get to his feet, he realized what the old man had done for him.

He hit me with the flat ends ...

In the meantime, Dice had thrown his jacket over Legion's head and was beating her with the butt of his revolver. "You're lucky I don't shoot clowns!" he screamed, as she struggled to free herself.

At the same time, yakuza had taken up position around the lobby and were driving Agency Zero back with some degree of success. Moments later, heralded by pools of exploded Molotovs, the Fifth Estate began pouring into the building as well.

With the gunfire beginning to subside, and smoke driving people out of the lobby, AJ scrambled over to Pops, who lay on his back staring at the ceiling. A terrible pool of blood framed his massive body like an aura. AJ knelt beside the old man and placed a hand on his chest. The wound was wide and partially cauterized. Bone, organs and the complex mechanisms that kept the eighty-year-old man in fighting condition were exposed. Pops would die, and soon.

"Legion!" the old man yelled from behind polar tufts of beard. "Legion!"

At that moment, Legion finally managed to free herself from Dice with a stiff boot to the groin that sent the ex-yakuza to his knees first, and then his side. Before AJ could drop Deadbolt and draw his own pistol, Legion already had the barrel of her gun to the side of Dice's head.

"Rose!" Pops bellowed, blood now dripping from his beard. "Rose Montenegro!"

Cursing Dice in what sounded like Spanish, Legion lowered her weapon and came to stand over Pops.

"Enough, Rose. Enough…"

The orange-haired soldier holstered her weapon and removed a field surgeon's kit from the pack on her belt. Acting quickly, she began spraying sealant into the gaping wound. "No names, Pops. You know that."

"Enough, Rose. Listen to me." With a massive hand, he seized her arm. "You were the first to speak out, Rose. You were the first." Pops' lips quivered as he spoke, and the rosiness in his cheeks was becoming harder to make out beneath the cold lighting.

Legion's jaw was clenched, but her eyes shimmered. "You're fragged, Pops. That doesn't change the mission."

"This isn't the raid on the Fifth Estate," he gurgled, blood already pooling in his mouth. "And Blake, right now he's killing civilians, not anarchists, Rose. *Civilians!* And if the Major gets what he's looking for, many more will die."

Legion stopped struggling and dropped the clotting gel. Standing wearily, she wiped a tear away with an orange sleeve. "No fucking names, Pops. You know that."

"Names…" Pops wheezed. "You know why he won't use our names. You know why."

After a deep breath, Legion pointed at Dice, who was getting to his feet, still clutching his genitalia. "Come on, you. We're going to stop Dozer."

861

"What if I don't want to go with you?" Dice replied. "You're mean."

"Move it!"

At the sight of Pops fallen and Legion charging for the stairs, the last few living Agency Zero soldiers in the lobby lowered their weapons and began screaming for dialogue.

AJ, still kneeling at Pops' side, looked down at him helplessly. "I'm so sorry, Pops."

"Shut up and listen, Alec."

Pops' massive hands were tracing circles on the marble. His eyes searched and were full of fear. It was a sight AJ knew he would never forget.

"You're not so different from him, you know?"

"I know, Pops."

"He loves you. I know this."

Tears welled up and before he realized it, AJ was crying. "This is *because* of him!"

"Bullshit!" the soldier barked. "We choose to fight. We *choose* to kill."

"Pops, please."

"We dress it up in duty. We tell ourselves it's for the 'greater good.' It's just killing, Alec. It's always just killing. But you two don't have to kill each other."

"Pops, Ace is responsible for this. He has to pay."

"I had a brother once," he continued, his eyes closed now, "a very long time ago. His name was Logan."

"That's a good name, Pops."

862

"Aye. He was a bit like Ace; headstrong."

Pops' grip on him lessened, and soon, AJ found himself holding the old man's hand up.

"I couldn't… I couldn't save him. Maybe now…"

AJ waited for the veteran of countless wars to finish his thought, but it was done, Pops had passed.

Maybe now… What? AJ thought bitterly. *What happens now, Pops?*

The answer was simple. There was only one thing left.

Ace has to pay.

With Hollow Black's access, seizing the tanks was simple. Rena hijacked their command protocols and put them in defense of the citizens who'd remained in the plaza. When the last of the coup soldiers and cops had gone into hiding or surrendered, she set her attention to opening Sun City up to the world once more. Soon, sirens blared around the city as the great wall, Rampart, began to lower.

They exited the stairwell on the fifth floor and found the place decimated. Walls had been leveled and massive holes threatened the building's very integrity. The air was thick with ash and, through the roaring wind, they could hear what sounded like the woot of a hyena.

Legion took off on her own, guns drawn, her head low and her footsteps silent. Dice watched her moving quickly and efficiently, darting from cover to cover. She soon disappeared into a blown-out office space. He spotted Chris and Mason soon after. They were hiding behind adjacent pillars, peeking into another office at the end of the hall.

Dice began making his way towards them, stepping over the remnants of an office. Slabs of concrete, shattered desks, broken glass, and the cotton-candy-like plumes of ventilation. He kept his head way low, as the shooter could be anywhere. Suddenly, the air left the room. A twang, like that of a god's guitar, sounded and then everything turned upside down. Dice landed on his shoulders and was pinned immediately after by some heavy piece of rubble, even as a force seemed to suck the very consciousness from him. At the same time, carpet, glass, wood, and brick were churned into the air as though a bullet train had passed through. When the debris settled, Dice could hear the hyena's laughter.

Pulling himself out from under the wreckage, he could see the soldier with the metal jaw clearly now. He was laughing and working to reload a rifle as tall as he was. Both Chris and Mason were gone, as were the pillars they'd been hiding behind.

Dice stifled the fear building up in him by focusing on his breathing. He hadn't been spotted yet, or at least the Agency Zero soldier didn't seem to acknowledge his presence.

"Stand down, Blake!" a voice suddenly screamed. It was the orange-haired woman, Legion. She'd taken up position behind a collapsed concrete pillar whose importance should have given everyone pause.

"What the hell are you using my fucking name for, *Rose?*"

"The Grand Magistrate gave explicit orders that civilians were *not* to be harmed!"

"Oh, come off it! The man's delusional!"

"You're firing on civilians!"

"'Civilians!" Dozer finished loading the rifle and was hoisting it up once more. "All I see are armed combatants. Come, take a look!"

Though the gun wasn't pointed in his direction, Dice dropped to the deck.

The concrete pillar where Legion had taken position disappeared as though a giant vacuum nozzle had sucked it away. An explosion not unlike the initial moments of a volcanic eruption filled the floor with thick, blinding soot. Legion was nowhere to be seen in the aftermath.

Dozer's laugh was pure maliciousness. He dropped the butt of the huge rifle to the deck and began working the bolt-action port, whistling as he loaded another graphite round.

Dice leveled his revolver. Exhaling slowly, he pulled the trigger.

The shot spun the soldier but did not drop him. His cover blown, Dice quickly found himself looking down the barrel of the railgun.

Daisuke Yamazaki knew more than fifty swear-words in English, German, Japanese, Chinese, and Korean and yet, in that moment, none came to him.

"Say goodnight!"

Chris rounded the office corner from seemingly nowhere, hair ever-spectacular, as Dozer prefaced the kill-shot with meaningless dialogue. The Agency Zero soldier saw the Unit One agent in time, but holding the giant gun would prove to be his undoing, as he wheeled to face his opponent too late. Chris struck the railgun with a gauntleted fist. The punch ignited with a boom, splintering the gun in two and sending Dozer back on his heels.

Dice came out from his hiding spot, prepared to race to Chris' aid, but it wouldn't be necessary. A lazy slash with a blade from Dozer set Chris up nicely. The Unit One lieutenant slipped the attack effortlessly and snatched the soldier's head in his hands. As Dozer moved to stab, Chris leapt and slammed a metal-plated knee into his face. Like the gauntlet, the knee plate, too, "fired." Dozer's head disappeared in a pinkish cloud and his metal jaw was sent spiraling into the air in a chewed-bubblegum ball of warped iron.

34: "Liberator"

"It's too much."

"Speak freely."

"It's all too much. And to take these kinds of measures..."

"Think about it. Can we afford not to? Imagine... All the wars, all the death. To be told forever that war is human

866

nature and not simply the nature of a vicious few, as we've
always known. Have we not?"

"But like this? You can't ask me to do this... I can't."
"You can. You may be the only one who can."
[Duration of silence: 00:12:04:]
"Sir, if I do this... Sir, if I do this I'll have to come for
you too. On principle."
"I know, and I am prepared to make that sacrifice if
you are."

- Partially decrypted communication intercepted May 3, 2047. Participants unknown.

"Legion, Pops, Dozer, respond!"

A box of cartridges lay at his feet. He kicked it and sent its .45 ACP contents skittering across the marble. Witch Doctor looked up at him, concern etched on his face.

"Focus on your work."

"Yes, sir."

A few soldiers stood about, the small attachment he'd kept to secure the Hall of Maati. The rest had gone to try and fend off the Unit One–led uprising. Ace pointed to a small group of them.

"You lot! Find out what's going on down there. I want a status report and I want it yesterday! Find my men! Hop to!"

The men stormed out of the hall, their boots squeaking like shoes on a basketball court.

They're coming, the Major thought, pacing. *I've run out of time.*

Soul Crook hung heavy on his waist, thirsty as always. Failing to counter the blade's heft on the other side was his pistol. He removed it from its holster and checked the magazine. He knew it was full, but somehow the act itself had meaning.

"Witch Doctor, talk to me. How close are you?"

"All data has been sharded and a cipher drawn. The server stands by for data migration."

"How long, goddamnit!"

"Sir, forty-five minutes or so, sir!"

"Black!"

He waited, but his tech specialist did not respond.

"Do you read me, Black?"

[Sir.]

The voice was faint.

[Legion, sir.]

"I need an update, Legion! What's your position?"

[I'm on five, sir. Dozer, that piece of... he opened fire on us.]

"What's your status?"

[Banged up but alive, sir. That fucker tried to kill me. Dozer tried to kill me. He killed the other soldiers who were with him on five. They must have tried to stop him first.

Bulldog, Warmonger, and... and hell, sir, I can't remember the other guy's name.]

"What's Dozer's status?"

[Dead, sir. I'm not sure what happened, but I suspect Unit One killed him. Also... Arthur is dead.]

Arthur...

"No names, goddammit!" Ace put his metal hand to his face. *Fuck... Curse it all.*

After a deep breath, he apologized. "Pops... How?"

[Your brother, sir. Your brother cut him down.]

"I... I see."

[Sir, I'm headed your way.]

"No."

[Sir?]

"You've done enough, Legion. Someone needs to initiate our contingency plan."

[But sir, they will be coming in force.]

"I only need a little more time."

[I understand, sir. And sir?]

"Legion."

[It has been a pleasure and an honor to serve under you.]

"Duly noted."

He disconnected and drew Soul Crook from its sheath. He pointed it at Witch Doctor, who had sat stinking in the same spot since early that morning. "No matter what comes through those curtains, you stay at it. The data is all that matters now. Not my life and not yours! Do you hear?"

"I understand, sir."

"Do you understand!"

"Sir, I understand, sir!"

The Major braced himself and took position opposite the entrance to the forum. He could hear the doors beyond the hall of Maati open and close. Footsteps in the hall, maybe a dozen. Voices. They were upon him.

"Sir?"

"Yes, Witch Doctor."

"Might I suggest using these?"

The Major turned, and the first lieutenant had donned a mask of some kind. It was a mess of baseball skins sewn together. The eyes were camera lenses that twisted and extended to focus with a hum. Witch Doctor tossed him a heavy rucksack. In it were grenades of various tactical application, discernible to the Major by their shapes. Cylindrical: gas; spherical: explosive; oblong: concussion.

"If you can lure them to the roof, sir, that may give me enough time."

"Keep at it, soldier."

The curtain was pulled aside and a familiar face appeared at the top of the steps. Ace scooped up the bag of grenades and threw the strap over one shoulder. Next, he drew from his pocket the EMPen. He gripped it in his left hand, with Soul Crook poised in the other.

"You're too early, little brother."

AJ's face was not his own. It was contorted and full of hate.

"He's dead, Ace! Pops is dead."

A bead necklace and dog tags rattled down the steps of the forum to clatter at his feet. Ace picked them up and pocketed them without looking at the tags. "He was a good man and a better soldier."

"He's dead because of you!"

"*Your* blade cut him down. All you had to do was stand down. I warned the Deputy Chief Constable. I warned you all!"

The thick black curtains were drawn aside once more, and three more men in the black and white of Unit One entered Maati.

"You forced my hand!"

AJ was descending the steps rapidly now, his hand on the hilt of that wretched polearm blade of his.

The Major beckoned his little brother with a haughty gesture designed to anger him. At the same time, he removed a cylindrical canister from the rucksack under his arm. With his teeth, the Major yanked the pin and threw it at his brother's feet. As the pinkish smoke burst forth, quickly filling the chamber, he beckoned his brother once more, this time smiling.

"ACE!"

The Major turned on his heels and quickly ran up the forum steps towards the exit at the far end of Maati.

Behind him, he could hear the sound of Unit One's footsteps in pursuit.

"AAACE!"

Glancing back, he could see three of the four agents in pursuit. Ace bounded up the winding stairs three at a time. He tried the latch but found the door to the roof locked. Quickly, he fired twice into the bolt and kicked it open. He could hear panting and footsteps behind. He climbed quickly, his role in the chase very unusual and slightly thrilling. The Major shouldered through the last set of double-doors and out onto the roof. Immediately, he was nearly knocked off his feet by the wind.

From the top of the Horus Bank building, Sun City was nothing more than a colorful mat against the infinite expanse of the Pacific. The wind skirted the semi-walled roof, creating a sound not unlike that of jet turbines. As the Major moved closer to the edge, he could see the warning lights that crowned Rampart's bastions as the great defender descended back beneath the skyline.

Rampart had served its purpose. It had saved Section Seven from the flood water that would have destroyed the lives of the people there, *his* people.

"No more running, Ace!"

You're right about that...

With a grimace, the Major turned to meet Unit One and his little brother.

"It's over!"

872

"The hell it is!"

35: Beast-laid Plans

"The Battle of the 101 changed the unit for a time. After that, we thought, perhaps for the first time really, that if we worked together there was nothing we couldn't accomplish. The feeling didn't last long, though. He showed us just how weak we really were."

- Unit One Sgt. Alec Jefferson "AJ" Moore

Chris and Dice followed AJ as he took flight after the Major. In the fog of pink smoke cast by the Major's grenade, the chamber quickly began to disappear. It was, in pursuing the fleeing Major, that Chris noticed Mason's absence. He turned to find the lieutenant standing in the hall, his eyes wide, seemingly mesmerized.

"Mason!"

"Go on," Mason replied, waving dismissively, "go after him! I'll secure this floor."

It was as though Mason had no interest in pursuing the Major: the target. While Chris thought it strange, it was well within the lieutenant's often bizarre spectrum of behavior. Without wasting another moment, Chris ran for the stairwell entrance after Dice. He climbed the stairs quickly to what he assumed was the roof, and had to pause briefly as shots were fired. He drew his pistol and aimed up the stairwell. A loud boom sounded next.

It did not take him long to place the noises. The Major had shot the lock and kicked the door open.

Strange, he thought. *Why would the door be locked if this is his escape route? Unless, of course, it isn't. Is the Major cornering himself?*

At the top of the stairs, Unit One took a moment to regroup.

"He's stuck unless he has a fucking parachute," AJ said, catching his breath. "But he's not going out without a fight, trust me."

The three of them took a few moments to let the nerves settle. After a moment of silent agreement, AJ nodded and pushed the door open. One by one, they carefully, *tactically* stepped out into the chill, guns drawn.

At the sight of their quarry, Chris had a decent idea what they were in for. His poncho horizontal in the wind, the Major stood in a wide stance, his foot-long blade in one hand and something small and shiny in the other.

"It's over!" AJ screamed.

"The hell it is!"

As AJ looked into the emotionless gaze of his brother, he saw no loathing, only the primal resolve of a beast trapped.

Ace had been his guardian and mentor, his brother and father-figure. Only now, after all this, did it occur to AJ that his brother hadn't been right for a long time. Behind the military code and the dedication to God and country lay the mind of a madman. And it hadn't happened overnight. To AJ's estimation, this was the culmination of decades of neglect. The military had failed Ace. The SDC had failed Ace. And *he* had failed Ace.

Dice lit a cigarette, folding his back to provide cover from the wind. Once it was lit, he pointed at Ace accusingly. "Your men are finished, Major! The entire city is down there, each and every one of them ready to punch you in the dick!"

Ace's poncho snapped wickedly, making it difficult to hear, but worst of all concealing the movement of his arms. "The people have been starved of truth. I would only see them nourished!"

"At the end of a noose?" Chris replied.

"You see only the means, and not the meaning. Soon, we will have unlocked the secrets of the men and women behind the wars. We'll have learned the *true* meaning behind the expenditure of lives innumerable!"

AJ holstered his pistol and poised to draw Deadbolt. Moving slowly, he advanced on his brother. "Couldn't hear you, bro. Sounds like you said: 'I give up and will lay my weapons on the ground!'"

"You joke, even now! I no longer know if that is an admirable exuberance in the face of danger or if you are showing signs of legitimate mental deficiency. Brother! You — most of all — must be made to see my work in its totality.

And, as such, I *cannot* allow you to die. Stand down! Your fight here is finished!"

AJ looked to Chris and then to Dice before turning back to face the man who'd raised him. "Fuck you!"

"When you were just a boy," Ace continued, undaunted, "you'd cry yourself to sleep, mourning a mother and father you never knew. Those nights I sat over you, exhausted, and lying to you about a future that I knew would never come. I told you fantasies about your father. About how he was a successful businessman. Likewise, I told you fantastic tales about a loving mother. I told you they died in an accident, their only regret not being able to see you grow. These were *lies*, necessary only to get you to sleep, that I may snatch a few hours of shuteye. Then, when those sheepherders at the Ministry of Familial Affairs tried to seize you and auction you up like some kind of slave, *I* freed you. No one else gave a damn about you. Only me!"

Ace's words cut deep, but this was how Ace worked. This was but one method behind the machine that was the Major. Everything was a weapon to him, especially words. He would whittle men down psychologically before breaking them down physically. It didn't matter if there was any truth to it, only that it hurt. And it did. This was "Iron" Ace Monroe, the man he'd once heard say, "Kill their will, destroy their resources, kill their families, kill their friends, and destroy the very thing they fight for. Above all else, *KILL*!"

"The truth is, *half-brother*," Ace continued, "your father was a pathetic, useless drug addict, barely human when compared to *my* father. Your father was killed by his own overindulgence and took our mother with him! You see, he washed her away in *his* grief. He was weak! And after that, Mother — a once proud and beautiful woman — destroyed her mind and body with drugs too. If you'd been a bit older, you would remember that in her dying hour she couldn't even remember your name."

"Shut up!"

Ace summoned him with a jerk of his head, even as his arms disappeared beneath the folds of his poncho. "Grow up, boy!"

AJ turned to his partners. "I've got to do this. This is between him and me. But, if he starts to... I don't know, *win...*"

"We've got you," Chris said solemnly, his hair and bandana twirling above his head like a halo.

With a deep breath, AJ took several careful steps towards his brother, the white-hot stakes of the gambit crystal clear in his mind. Ace would not go lightly, and he would most certainly try and kill his friends. And though he'd never faced an opponent he so openly feared, the whole thing came with a sense of inevitability.

The world wasn't cold like some liked to say. The world was hot. Hot and powered by fury. Humans didn't occupy some dying rock of apathy and disinterest, but rather a world burning in the blaze of conflicting interests. A world where no one was right and at the same time no one was truly fit to define wrong. AJ and the only man he loved had not been brought to this by some slight, but instead by a million different decisions over the course of their short lives. In that regard, not only was the fight inevitable, it might as well be destiny.

He's going to try closing the distance quickly. Keep him at bay, make him tired, and then take him out. A couple of butts to the head and he'll go out just like everyone else. Maglet on the belt, secure the wrists quickly. He'll wake up pissed as a cornered fox, but alive.

Here we go!

AJ swung Deadbolt in a wide arc, not firing the blade for fear that he might accidentally kill his brother. The stroke was little more than a feint to garner a response and to that effect, it succeeded.

Ace ducked under the swipe and swatted the metal pole aside. As AJ expected, the Major rushed in to close the distance. He sidestepped a heavy boot and slipped a slash from his brother that would have been fight-ending.

If his brother was pulling punches, it wasn't obvious.

He drove the butt end of Deadbolt into Ace's foot, pinning it there, and held the hilt end to his face as though handing him a mic for comment. He triggered the ejection of the weapon's blade and fired the hilt into his brother's jaw. The sound was wince-inducing. Before the Major could recover, AJ kicked the pole with his foot, driving it up between Ace's legs to strike him in the groin. As it rebounded to the sound of his brother's grunt, he swept Deadbolt up, spun it over his head and slammed the metal end of it atop his brother's head. Ace's knees buckled and he fell forward awkwardly. Somebody catcalled.

On hands and knees, Ace shook the cobwebs loose.

"Give it up, Ace. You're getting old."

Ace held a hand out. "It would seem so. Help me up."

Without so much as a moment's hesitation, AJ took his brother's hand and yanked him to his feet. He knew the instant Ace's iron grip locked down he'd made a terrible, terrible mistake.

Ace snatched AJ's left elbow with his creaking metal hand and gripped his shoulder with his right. Stepping into him, the Major hooked a leg around one of his. With a tug, he was flipping over Ace's shoulder. The force with which he struck the ground was the equivalent of falling from some great height. AJ tried to hold on to Deadbolt, to no avail. The attempt to break his fall resulted only in the pinning of own arm beneath his torso. Ace followed up the throw by landing on him with all of his weight. Unable to shield himself with his arm pinned, AJ could only watch helplessly as his brother slammed the metal fist of his prosthetic arm into his face and temple repeatedly. Eventually, his eyes shut and only the crunching sound of metal on bone filled his head until the black took him.

The Major would kill AJ, of that he was certain. At the risk of losing his best friend, Dice aimed his revolver and shot for the head. The bullet rocked the Major, and blood immediately sprayed down the front of his poncho. He tilted back precariously, like a bronco rider, but remained poised over his fallen partner. The Major's fist, which had been poised to pound AJ's head into burger, stalled and blood streamed from the fresh bullet hole in his cheek.

The Major shook his head furiously like a person struggling to stay awake and drew a pistol from his belt. Dice threw his coat up as the Major fired several shots. One got through and struck his left thigh above the knee. He went to return fire, only to find the Major aiming his pistol at AJ's head.

"Put the goddamn gun down!"

The brief exchange gave AJ the time he needed to break free of the Major's grip. The Unit One sergeant picked up Deadbolt and staggered drunkenly to his feet, blood dripping from his nose and mouth.

While the Major traced his brother's movements with his gun, Dice aimed his revolver at the Major. He felt obligated to tell his partner, "You did good, AJ! All the way up to the part where he kicked your ass."

AJ's head was a throbbing, foggy mess of rage. As Ace allowed him to regroup with the others, he wiped blood from his nose. Blinking, he tried fruitlessly to see with his left eye. He drew Deadbolt and cast its scabbard aside. Pulling punches wasn't going to cut it. As demonstrated brutally, Ace was far too dangerous for that. Taking him lightly was only going to get someone killed.

Even now, the Major stood a good distance from them, checking his watch and aiming his pistol at them. "This is good!" he yelled. "This is very good! It won't be long now. Who's next?"

"You talk too much," Dice replied. "We're not fighting you one-on-one like the villain in a comic book. We're going to hit you from all sides like the villain in a *better* comic book."

"What are you proposing, snitch? Encircle me? Gun me down from a distance like cowards? No! This rivalry means more to you than that!"

Dice scoffed.

"Major!" It was Chris that stepped forward. "Nothing you've said justifies your actions. Why kill Macek? Why hold the people you swore to protect hostage? Nothing you're doing makes sense!"

"This was the only way, Lieutenant! The people have been lied to for far too long. Everything these people aspire to comes at the expense of the people. Libra, the Liberty Day Parade attack, the Consortium, Agency Zero, and even Unit One; these are all pieces in the endgame. The prize being continued domination. The Liberty Day attack three years ago was the catalyst. Everything since has been the careful administration of a plan centuries in the making."

Ace made a disgusted face.

"Haven't you ever wondered why narcotics continue to flow into Sun City despite spending billions on a checkpoint system that spans from here to Brazil? Have you ever wondered why illegal gambling and the sex-slave trade remain rampant, despite the fact that these are the easiest crimes to identify under Libra? Ever wonder why, if Unit One is to be the future of law enforcement, there are only six of you? And why the majority of your time is spent doing TV spots, photo-shoots, and media appearances? Why dress your 'last line of defense against crime' in Skyy Shoes that don't protect the toes, or seat them on motorcycles not equipped with the essentials? Basically, why hire a bunch of fucking kids and a washed-up gangster to be the face of law enforcement? Why, indeed! Other than to achieve one true initiative… to make money! Justice has been productized. And *you* are the products!

"These people and their ilk have built dynasties on the fundamentals of deceit, corruption, manipulation, and subjugation. In my time with them, I have borne witness to machinations of limitless aspiration, and schemes subhuman in their depths. If you don't believe me, you've only to look back three years."

The gun felt alien in his hands outside of the range. Mason moved through the pink smoke slowly, careful to watch his footing. As he crept towards the center of the forum, a dark shape began to emerge.

At first it terrified him, but surely — he told himself — that was the intent. It was a man. Just a man. He wore some kind of mask, designed to terrorize. White patches of skin were bound in a haphazard stitching of thick, black cord. The top of its head was host to an array of antennae, all of them twisting and contorting like the snakes of a gorgon. The sight of this bent creature would have been enough to send Mason running but for two factors. The first being the creature's back facing him, the second being the dossier Mason had read of First Lieutenant Ken Jennings — or "Witch Doctor," as he was called.

Mason placed the barrel of his gun to the back of the fake gorgon's head, and as he did so, the mist parted to reveal Spectus and the access point from which Agency Zero hoped to steal its secrets.

"Unit One?" the man in the mask asked.

"Lieutenant Mason Bruce, Unit One."

"Well, Lieutenant, I'm just about finished here. No need for the gun. I am not armed."

"Is this the 'truth' that the Major speaks of?"

"Aye."

"Have you read it?"

"Enough of it."

884

"And what does it tell you, Witch Doctor?"

"It tells me that we've come to the end of an era."

"'End of an era?'"

"Aye. The Era of Secrets is about to give way to the Era of Truth and nothing, *nothing* will ever be the same. Frankly, it's fucking scary."

"And you've exported this 'truth' to *this* server?"

The man in the mask took his hands from the keyboard. He lifted his hands slowly and removed the mask. Turning, he kept his hands raised. When he saw the black jacket with the white pinnacle, he seemed to breathe a sigh of relief. It was then that Lieutenant Mason Bruce put the pistol to his nose and pulled the trigger.

Ace held his gun aimed from the waist.

"Three years ago today," he continued, "a DPRK general and 'terrorist' known only as 'Changgok' detonated explosives in this very plaza, killing three-hundred-plus citizens. That single event gave the SDC more than enough political ammunition to pass the State Defense Act. And, of course, the State Defense Act, for all its chaff initiatives about curfews and network access restrictions, was really only the vehicle for one thing: Libra! And Libra has since sparked the interest of the political community on a global scale. Just as they knew it would! You see, Libra removed the tattered and already compromised veil of privacy we had, forever.

"I remember thinking at the time, 'The people will not stand for this! First the bombing and now this? Surely they will fight back!'"

AJ couldn't make sense of it. "You're saying the LDP attack was *allowed* to happen?"

"I'm saying that Changgok is a myth, a lazily constructed bogeyman to keep the people of Sun City up at night. It's the War on Terror, version 2.0. They needed another Osama Bin Laden, but I, *we*, pounded our enemies to dust, so they *made* one!"

"Not a myth," Chris replied through clenched teeth. "Just a pseudonym."

Ace's smile was wicked, something worthy of a Halloween mask.

"A pseudonym? For whom?"

Dice dropped his cigarette and stamped it out. "AJ... Sometimes, man, I swear you're dense."

Chris turned to him. "We're looking at Changgok, AJ."

Ace raised his arms. "In the flesh!"

"You killed them?"

"Not my plan! But allowing them, *helping* them pull it off was necessary. Really, it was the only way!"

"You set the bombs that killed all those innocent people?"

"Who else could have done it, brother? Sun City is the most secure police state in the history of the world. Did you really believe that some renegade, and a Korean general at that,

886

could sneak past the SCPD, the SDC, *and* Agency Zero to plant bombs at the biggest event of the year without being caught? And worse, evade the surveillance might of the State for three years?"

"I don't understand!"

"I think you're lying, brother! I don't think you *want* to understand. Did you know that their plan was to keep 'Changgok' at large indefinitely? They wanted to use the myth as a recurring nightmare for the purposes of swaying public opinion."

"You're a hypocrite then, Major!" Chris screamed. "You should have hung yourself! You're just as bad as the people you would persecute. People I loved died on that day. You killed my sister!"

"If you knew they were planning this," Duck asked, "why go along? Why didn't you say something? Or why didn't you enact your sick version of 'justice' right then and there and save three hundred civilian lives?"

"See, brother? These are the questions of merit!" Ace took a menacing step forward. "In 1962, Lyman Lemnitzer, then acting as Chairman of the Joint Chiefs of Staff, signed an initiative to place bombs on civilian flights entering the United States from Cuba. The plan, had the Kennedy Administration not rejected it, would have killed hundreds of US citizens and given the then Council of Eight the political capital necessary to justify a US occupation of Cuba. This instance of treasonous intent was met not with trial and execution but merely

887

temporary dismissal, followed by promotion to the role of Supreme Allied Commander of NATO. And worse; this proposal set the stage for an entirely new culture of political maneuvering: using false-flag operations as justification for war. Wars unending!

"It was my men who fought these wars! It was I!" The Major took another step forward, and Dice fired a round at his feet. Ace didn't even acknowledge it. "You see, the proposal of treason would not have been enough, even today. Had I gone to the media, at best, Macek's career would have been delayed. But if the crime were *allowed* to happen…"

Chris shook a fist at him. "*Made* to happen, Major. *Made to happen! By you!*"

"Now their crimes will be known, and when their seediness is still fresh on the lips of the people. Once we have broken Spectus and released the truths held there, the Council of Eight, the Octumvirate, will have nowhere to hide!"

AJ stepped to meet his smiling brother once more; his words were like a filth that had been thrown into his face. Only one truth was clear to him and it was the oath he'd sworn. "'Those that would maim or kill the people of the State unjustly and with callousness shall be met with swift and absolute punishment!' Ace, you killed those people and you are as much a threat to this city as anyone!"

"I would love to show you just how weak you really are, AJ," he replied, sneering, "but I *cannot* allow you to die!"

"Cut the bullshit, Ace! Enough with your fucking speeches. Why are we here? Why did you bring us up here? Was it really to confess?"

"The truth? Structural integrity. And to protect Spectus!" Ace pointed to his feet. "I see you're wearing the shoes I got you."

"I was trying to be nice, asshole! I don't even like them."

Ace held out the silver device in his left hand. "More's the better!" He pressed a button, and a flash, not unlike the one that had taken his arms that day on the 101, took AJ off his feet.

The explosion shook the roof of the Horus Bank building and sent gravel and debris into the air. In the flash, AJ had vanished but before Dice could run to his friend's side, other flashes erupted, followed by rolling canisters of white smoke that clogged his nostrils and blurred his vision.

Dice crouched and aimed into the smoke, ready to fire. "AJ! AJ, buddy, you all right?"

The shape moved through the smoke low and fast. Dice aimed and fired, but the thing struck him all the same. The first impact caught him in the center of his chest and drove the air from his body. The second came in the form of a rusted metal hand that snatched his neck and hoisted him into the air. Stunned and breathless, he looked down into the glaring, scarred face of the Major.

"You," he growled. "Now that Minowara is dead, we've no use for you. I hereby revoke your deputy status!"

The Major slammed a fist into his gut and tossed him over his shoulder, much like he'd done AJ. It was far less entertaining on the receiving end. Dice struck the ground on his shoulder, and a piercing pain ran down his arms to explode out of his fingertips. He lay in the gravel, dazed, his revolver lost somewhere in the smoke. He tried to call out to Chris in warning, but no air in his lungs meant no sound. He pondered this flaw in the human design as he lay writhing in the gravel.

Boots slid in, shoving gravel into his face, and Dice rolled onto his back, fearing the blade that would end his involvement in everything, really. He looked up and could see Chris and the Major engaged in the smoke. After a moment, Dice took several deep breaths and got to his feet. The smoke was being pulled from the roof quickly by the freezing wind, and soon he spotted his revolver lying several yards away. He dashed for it.

If combat skills were art, the Major's fighting style was block print: aesthetically bland but completely practical. Where Chris had been trained in Muay Thai, Brazilian Jiu-Jitsu, and Judo by traditional instructors who wore *gis* and were bound by ages-old traditions, the Major was trained in CQC: *Close Quarters Combat*. This was the military's no-nonsense approach to turning the body into a weapon capable of neutralizing opposition as quickly and effectively as possible.

The unanswered questions in such an encounter, even behind the emotion of potentially finding justice for his sister and the budding family she'd lost due to the Major's actions, were not inconsequential to Chris.

While CQC was most certainly effective, there were layers of martial arts understanding and intricacies that the military could not impart on the Major. Chris would expose these weaknesses. He would break down the Major, humble him. And then, when the man who had orchestrated the worst terrorist act in Sun City's history lay prostrate, he would find out if he had what it took to enact a true vengeance.

As the mist from the smoke grenade disappeared, the Major's movements became more and more predictable. Chris parried and slipped his strikes with relative ease, careful to avoid the soldier's attempts to grapple. He returned strikes with a heavy focus on leg kicks. He repeatedly slammed a shin into the Major's thighs and calves, until his steps became visibly labored. In doing so, he robbed the Major of mobility and, at the same time, stole the driving force from his punches. As the skirmish went on, Chris' confidence grew.

As the Major staggered, reeling from a counter punch to the gunshot side of his face, Chris dashed in, eager to end the fight. He primed the gauntlet on his left hand, a move that immediately caught the Major's attention.

It's too late! Chris would have told him.

He threw a kick with his right leg, hard enough to force the Major to defend but, in fact, only designed to set up a punch with the gauntlet. Ace blocked the kick, as he'd expected, leaving his right side open. Chris threw a wide, swinging overhand that the Major blocked with a shoulder. The gauntlet fired with a bang, sending metal and blood flying in all directions.

Dice picked up the revolver and winced at what sounded like a gunshot. When he turned to see, Chris and the Major both were still standing and Chris seemed to have him reeling. Flames engulfed an object a few feet away, and he knew it was AJ. He ran over to his friend, fear of the worst kind filling him.

When Dice had come to Sun City, he'd learned quickly that his English, considered excellent by his Minowara friends in Japan, was, in fact, piss-poor by the rest of the world's standards. This made an already difficult transition into legality all the more challenging. When Williams deputized him and granted him the keys to the Sun City legal universe, his inability to communicate effectively soon threatened the move. Sure, he could have used a real-time translation device, but no one, not even himself, would have taken him seriously. Soon, his handlers became scarce and for a time it looked as though he would be unemployed and back on the streets. It wasn't until a guy, whom at the time he would have described as a "flamboyant, loud-mouthed punk," insisted on being partnered with him, that his descent into isolation and ultimately obsolescence began to rescind.

AJ was his friend. And if he was dead, there would be Hell to pay.

"*That hair is pretty strange,*" were perhaps AJ's first words to him. "*The way it sorta scoops up in the back makes you look like a duck. Can you shoot?*"

"*Yes,*" he'd responded.

"*Gotta give it to you, the name 'Daisuke' is kind of bad ass. Mind if I just call you 'Dice' though?*"

For Dice, AJ had been the first Sun City native to not only bypass the linguistic barriers willingly but also proactively dismantle them on his behalf. AJ shared his sometimes-juvenile sense of humor, and together they could turn even the most tedious of duties into something like fun. Over time, a trust, unlike any Daisuke had ever known, formed. More than Raizen, more than Sugihara, AJ was his brother, his *kyodai*.

Now looking down at his friend, his heart hurt.

How much can a man take?

AJ had only been put back together a little while ago and now here he lay, on his side, clutching his legs at the shin, one in each hand.

"You okay, buddy?" he asked, knowing the answer.

AJ clenched his jaw, unable to speak. His cheeks were wet, his eyes wide, smoke-filled, and bloodshot.

He knelt next to AJ, pulling two maglets from his belt. He threw one over each of AJ's scorched shins and tapped them to activate. He kept tapping with his index fingers until

893

the maglets were crunching down on his partner's shins, stanching the flow of blood.

"Fuck, fuck, fucker!" AJ looked up at him with feverish eyes. "How bad is it? I'm afraid to look…"

One foot lay mangled and black, attached superficially by a swath of flesh no thicker than the fat shoelaces he'd been wearing. The other was gone entirely. Dice just shook his head and placed a hand on AJ's chest, pressing him flat to the ground. "Just relax."

"I'm tired, man. I'm so tired of this shit."

"I know, buddy. I know."

AJ looked about, a frenzied expression on his face. "Where is he?"

"Chris has got him."

"Go! I'm fine. Help Chris!"

The Major's prosthetic arm hung limply at his side. With his other hand, he reached into his trousers and withdrew the metallic cylinder he'd used to detonate the explosives he'd somehow hidden in AJ's shoes.

Before he could get a firm grip on the device, Chris slammed a kick into his side, knocking the cylinder free. It struck the rooftop and rolled. Sensing his chance, he pressed the attack, driving the Major back with kicks and punches. Along the way, he primed the only remaining charge: the one in his right knee.

"You're good," the Major told him, spitting blood from a split lip. "You know it was I who'd selected you out of the thousands of candidates the SDC had on deck?"

"That has no bearing on anything."

The Major wiped blood from his mouth with a handful of poncho. "You were a perfect student in the Academy. You had an amateur background in competitive martial arts. You would have made a damn fine soldier. My hope was that you would rub off on my brother, act as a positive influence. Give him someone to compete with. At least until he was ready."

"Ready for what?"

"To *lead*, of course!"

"Well, your brother lays maimed, maybe dead. At your hands, no less!"

"A flesh wound. He won't die. You've no idea of the cloth we're cut from. Unfortunately for you, I've made no place for you in the new world. You were a tool, Lieutenant, chosen only to groom the situation for a time; fertilizer!"

"Do you have any idea how crazy you sound, Major? We can put a stop to this." Chris took a maglet from his belt and threw it down at the Major's feet. The Major kicked it away with hardly a pause.

"You think I'm beaten?"

Chris stood ready, with his hands up, his feet apart.

"You mistake my praise for capitulation." The Major swung the sack from over his shoulder to his side and pulled a pair of grenades out.

Quickly, Chris realized he'd given the Major too much space out of respect, a costly error. Before he could close the distance once more, the Major had already primed one of the grenades. He threw it to the ground hard, bouncing it into the air. Chris braced himself. In mid-air, not five yards away, it exploded. White light replaced everything, and a piercing whine filled his ears. Chris covered up as best he could and waited for the blows or blade that were sure to follow.

The Rampart had fallen, and a stream of red taillights like ants began pouring out of the city from every possible corridor. From ten thousand feet, the thousands fleeing were like blood-filled arteries.

"There!"

"I see it, sir."

The hover unit swooped down on the roof of the Horus Bank building, just in time to see a white flash followed by several smaller flashes that he knew were incendiaries.

Williams unbuckled himself and moved to the open bay door. The scene was chaos, but he could make out the black jackets and white deltas of his men. They lay in disorder, pointing at one another, interestingly enough. The only man standing wore a tattered olive poncho that whipped ferociously in the wind.

"We'd better not be too late!"

Chris' jaw was broken and he struggled to make sense of his surroundings, as footsteps seemed to circle him. The flashbang grenade had left him dumb long enough for the Major to dissect his defenses. Each time the world began to materialize, another blow would connect from the mist, sending him reeling back into the purgatory of sub-consciousness. Any ground won against the Major had been reclaimed fully, and his retribution had been inflicted tenfold in very little time.

Just then, a blow struck the back of his knee and sent him sprawling to the ground. As he slid into the gravel, a boot struck his temple and threatened to end the fight for good.

Chris reached for his pistol but found the holster empty. Instead, the barrel of the semiautomatic pistol he sought appeared in his face. Behind it, like some terrible backdrop, the Major's bruised, bloodied and monstrous face.

He knew the Major wasn't the type of guy to cock the gun and ask for last words.

This is it… I'm sorry, sis.

A bullet barely missed him and sent gravel sailing into the air. The shot had come from behind — behind and above. He turned, but saw only spotlights and the orange flashes of heavy machine-gun fire. Chris covered his head and rolled away as a storm of bullets poured down onto the roof.

From Chris' vantage on the ground, he first saw what was left of the Major's prosthetic arm tear away entirely. The rest of the rounds sent him spinning until even his poncho was no more. Then bullets struck his legs and torso in great splashes of blood and seemed to tear him to shreds until finally the Major's knees buckled and the bullets floored him. The rounds continued, pushing the Major's body for several feet in a hail of high-caliber rounds. Whoever had just killed him was making sure…

The spotlight veered away, and Chris could see an SCPD hover unit overhead. Manning the gun was Deputy Chief Constable Williams. The bullets had ceased, but the barrel still spun, a stream of gun smoke like exhaust pouring from the barrels.

He looked for the Major and saw only an uneven mound of carnage. And yet, though his body lay mangled in a horrific display, a hand still moved, snatching at the air in what could only be silent rage.

36: The Art of Darkness

"The Major sought truth but truth itself is a fallacy. There are only facts, and facts can be rewritten."

- Agency Zero Tech Specialist "Hollow Black"

She sat up slowly, propped on shaky arms. The folding of her abdominals caused her to wretch once more. Bile splashed onto the surface between her legs. She played with the substance, testing its consistency between her index finger and thumb.

Why am I here?

Her eyes burned, even in the meager light. This, too, added to her nausea. The air, unfiltered, stank of mold and death.

Why? Why am I here?

The Agency Zero specialist known as Hollow Black placed her hands on her head and screamed. She screamed until her voice failed, which did not take long.

The light, the smells, the weight... Why am I here? I hate this place.

She rolled onto her knees and tried to stand. Her back creaked audibly, and her legs, swaying wildly like those of a newborn fawn, gave out momentarily. The soldier pitched forward and struck something solid.

Blue light blinded her. She covered her eyes and waited a long time for them to adjust. As she waited, Hollow Black held herself up against the smooth, cool surface of the thing she'd collided with.

I hate this place.

As her vision became acclimated, the blue light grew brighter. She looked up, and things became clearer.

This is why... why I am in this place.

She should have been angry, watching Detective Constable Rena Bryant floating in her immersion vat, but she wasn't. Even as she watched her rival's eyelids twitch, her fingers spasm, and her head jerk from side to side occasionally as the synapses in her brain fired, she felt no hatred.

I could have killed you, Rena Bryant. A million times over.

Hollow Black placed a hand on the tank and could not help but marvel at her own flesh when contrasted to the peaceful, almost angelic expression on Detective Bryant's unblemished face.

Unlike the detective, her own skin was the color of a glacier's base and spotted with sores that looked like black watercolor. Her fingernails had grown long and were now flaking and black. She moved her hand across the glass, tracing the movement of the detective's flowing hair. As she did so, the flesh on her palms smeared away painlessly.

I told you to stay out, Detective, and yet here you are.
Obstinance...

Hollow Black, watching the reflexion of her own
pinwheel eyes in the glass hull of her immersion tank,
connected to select members of her unit over neurotrigger.

[Operation: Bloody Patriot has failed. If you are
receiving this message, you are part of the contingency plan.
Coordinates incoming...]

She hasn't turned yet, the North Korean defector Oh
Jin-ah thought sardonically, watching the Unit One detective
float in her home. *Your body will decay. Your bones will*
become brittle. That will be your toll, but you — like me — will
pay it willingly because you, too, understand that the body is a
vessel for the mind and nothing more. Horse and buggy are no
more. So, too, shall be the body. Libra is the new vessel. You
understand this, Detective Constable, and that is why I won't
kill you like a babe in the crib.

Hollow Black found her scarf hanging in the corner and
draped it over her shoulders, careful to cover her lipless mouth.
She left the room on uneven steps, her arms incapable of
providing the kind of natural sway many took for granted. She
passed the corpse in the corridor with nothing remotely close to
interest in her heart.

As she made her way down the hall, the feeling in the
balls of her feet, in her fingertips, and in the base of her spine
began to return. These new sensations served only to remind
her of how much she'd grown to hate this world. These pangs,

these failings in the design of the human physiology, were non-issues in Libra.

It took too much strength to push open the doors to the stairwell. It took even more effort to ascend the steps into the heart of the SCPD's Thirty-first Precinct. Her hearing returned as she moved through the empty corridors, but all she heard was the squish of her own naked feet on linoleum. Along the way, she stopped, gripping her head, the sensations bombarding her too much to bear. She screamed. She cursed in myriad languages and in code. She cursed what she considered to be the rotten, superfluous underbelly of technology. The maggoty surface upon which Libra had to reside.

Hollow Black left the building and entered into the waning light of day. The sun, like a hot poker, pierced her eyes and stirred her mind angrily. She moaned and cursed some more, covering her eyes with a forearm. Waiting in the meager shade of the precinct's awning, she regarded the world with a palpable disgust.

The 101 stood stalled, as people attempting to flee Sun City barred each other in their idiotic, selfish haste. Above, drones from outside city limits raced across the sky, leaving behind cat-scratch contrails that only served to mask the sun and its warmth. Behind the haze, she could see Section Three and, at its center, the Horus Bank building, where the would-be *Grand Magistrate* was likely leaking out the last of their ambitions in blood and failure.

You've failed, Major... but you still owe me. We still have an agreement and you will not renege. I will not allow it.

After nearly twenty minutes of searing, exhausting exposure, an SCPD hover unit finally descended into the parking lot, albeit at breakneck speed. Its skids carved into the hood of a police cruiser before slamming into the pavement.

Lieutenant Rose Montenegro, the Venezuelan soldier of fortune "Legion," leapt down from the hover unit and ran over. Like a fool, the lieutenant offered an arm or stretcher. Hollow Black declined both scornfully.

Legion's pixie hair was dyed orange now, like their uniforms. She was bruised and covered in what looked like plaster. The soldier looked up at her with a weary expression and began recanting what Hollow Black already knew.

The Major was captured or killed. Spectus had been breached but its contents had not been secured, and so, utter failure was theirs.

"Understood, Lieutenant," she told Legion in a voice she hadn't heard in a very long time.

The brawny woman helped her up into the hover unit where three more Agency Zero soldiers waited. Hollow Black recognized them from the dossiers...

A short, longhaired sergeant from the Philippines named Santos, Alwin; codenamed "Prowler." A former SAS captain named Thompson, Ben; codenamed "Big Game," and lastly, a mohawked gunnery sergeant named Bell, Savon;

codenamed "Peacemaker." They watched her board the hover unit with thinly veiled intrigue and disgust on their faces.

Oh Jin-ah took a seat next to the machine gun, her trousers squishing wet, and buckled in, careful not to damage her flesh more than necessary. Legion climbed in and took a seat opposite, her need for instruction and hope written on her face pathetically.

The material world is a grisly place, Oh thought, *not fit for the mind. It pulls at me, forces me to do and say things... There are rules here that I have no say in. This place is meaningless. Death is better.*

The hover unit began lifting into the air, and the sudden feeling of weightlessness turned her stomach.

We'd do well to end it...

Once they were in the air, Legion leaned in to her. "How fucked are we, Black?"

Your fate is of zero consequence, to me and likely to anyone.

"The Major lives," she said, still finding her voice. "The contingency plan is effective immediately. Concern yourselves only with your roles in that plan. The plan..."

Legion glared up at her but, in moments, Hollow Black could see the soldier begin to waver before her eyes. The orange spirals of her eyes created a sensation of anxiety, by design. Soon Legion, like everyone, was forced to look away.

"I am in charge until the Major returns," the former North Korean information specialist told them. "*If* the Major returns.

"They must come to know you and your capabilities," she thought but inadvertently said aloud.

Deviate from the plan to demonstrate assertiveness. The plan has flaws. Take this opportunity to correct one of them. Orders should be given now, forcefully.

"I will speak," she continued, still mincing thoughts with words recklessly, "and you will listen. Failure to do so means death for us all. Compliance means victory from defeat. Is this something you can understand?"

The best of the Major's remaining inner circle looked to one another in silence. After an awkward few moments of silence, it was the curly-haired ex-guerrilla from the Philippines who spoke.

"Be weird, grey bitch," he said, his fingers toying with the machete on his lap. "We're *all* weird. But, get this straight... We're recovering the Major. Dead or alive, we're recovering the Major."

Hollow Black bore into him with her pinwheel eyes but, to her surprise, the man named Santos seemed immune to her gaze. He stared back with a wild-eyed expression that could not be deciphered for anything other than a steel resolve.

"Satisfactory," she told him, "and part of the plan..."

37: The Setting Sun, part two

"You can't call any of what happened a victory. Not if you're being honest."

- Unit One Deputy Informant Yamazaki "Dice" Daisuke

There would be no moistening of the lips for either of the Minowara men. Likewise, there would be no ceremonial cremation. And so, the past and would-be future of the second most powerful and influential criminal enterprise in Sun City would be burned and buried in the earth, like everyone else.

Whether or not complicating the funeral arrangements of the Minowara had been part of Sugihara's plan, Dice could not be sure. He doubted it, but wouldn't be shocked to find out he was wrong. Sugihara, after all, was nothing if not spiteful.

[How are you holding up, Dice?]

"Ask me later, Rena. The ceremony is starting."

The yakuza of the Minowara-gumi — those still loyal, anyway — stood in neat rows, assorted by rank. The two co-chairmen who hadn't defected stood expressionless, stone-faced. The *waka-gashira*, the lieutenants, the real power in the organization, wept loudly, some tearing at their clothes, cursing, and driving their dress shoes into the earth. The *shatei-gashira*, the individual gang leaders, and their footsoldiers

906

leaned on one another for support, while the wives, girlfriends, and escorts just stared at their feet. It was mostly theatrical: a ritual typically intended for the *new* boss.

All in all, Dice counted roughly two hundred souls, dejected to varying degrees of legitimacy. In the uppermost end of that spectrum was the woman at his side, the heiress.

Omoe Minowara wore an exquisite matte black kimono. Her hair, long and glimmering black, was braided in a complex wrap that pulled the hair away from her hairline in artistic patterns. Her eyes, though large and filled with sadness, were subtly shadowed with black and beige. Her scent, too, was subtle but, even in the cool breeze, Dice thought he caught a whiff of hibiscus.

Though Omoe's appearance should be the last thing on Dice's mind, as she stood next to him, her arm grazing from time to time the sleeve of his blazer, he could not help but be acutely aware of her presence.

Large enough for a decent golf course, the grounds were segmented by meandering trails of sandstone, lined with little ornate lamplights. Date palms and palmetto provided patchwork pockets of shade enjoyed by the deer, squirrels, ducks, and swans that had long since grown apathetic to the presence of man. Above flew the gulls and albatrosses whose shrill cries disrupted regularly the low drone of the priest's mantra.

The weather had been merciful, with fog threatening but still a long way out at sea. Nevertheless, the coast always carried a seafaring chill that cut through an overcoat with ancient expertise. Dice resisted the urge to lend Omoe even so much as a warm arm, lest his level of comfort with her be seen as an affront.

The event would have been large for a common man's funeral, but to see so few in attendance for what was, not a month ago, the most powerful yakuza chairman in the Pacific, disturbed Dice greatly. After all, it wasn't as though the Minowara had up and disappeared overnight. He knew that the men who weren't here were with Sugihara.

The betrayal and the effectiveness of the betrayal made the hairs on his arm stand up. Not only had Sugihara toppled the head of Minowara-gumi, but he did so losing only a single loyalist: a German white woman for whom only one man would weep.

As far as coups go, the Major could have taken a lesson from Sugihara.

Dice wore a generic black suit, white dress shirt, and black tie, as was the custom. He still moved about on an exoskeletal leg brace, thanks to the bullet he had taken from the Major. Beneath the suit, his shoulder was black and blue and bandaged from having to be reset, also thanks to the Major.

A long and tightly regimented row of men and women close to the deceased passed before them in a slowly moving column. One by one, they lit incense over a black candle, three sticks apiece, and placed them in a large mahogany box of ash that stood on an altar before the caskets. After placing the sticks of incense upright, each person turned and bowed low at the waist to Omoe before returning to their place either seated or standing behind them, depending on rank. No one bowed to Dice, but he returned their bows to Omoe crisply, respectfully.

Once the procession of incense had ended, a process that had taken a little more than an hour, the priest assigned the deceased their Buddhist names. Folding the sleeve of his robe carefully, the priest dipped a large brush into a stone bowl of black ink and, with mesmerizing strokes, produced large, flawless *Kanji* characters on white mulberry paper. This would ensure that the dead could not be summoned inadvertently by those using their original names.

Oyabun Minowara, his casket crafted in a cherry-colored wood with gold lining, lay facing north, while Raizen, in a casket of black with platinum engraving, lay with his head to the west in the way of the *Amida Buddha*. Where the caskets would normally rest on dry ice, the bodies only present for the ceremony — to be later taken to a crematorium — today they rested on tinder, and the estate would serve as a crematorium.

Anything else would prove far too dangerous under the current circumstances.

As he looked at the caskets, Dice couldn't help but wonder, *Why the differing orientations?*

Raizen being positioned with his head to the west of his father's held significance, and only Omoe Minowara would know the answer.

Perhaps she's granting Raizen the independence he so desperately sought in life.

As the bodies were lowered into the earth, the moaning from those in attendance escalated accordingly. Grown men fell to their knees and tore at the grass like madmen. Women who probably couldn't pluck either of the deceased out of a photo "fainted" and had to be carried off, so great their sorrow.

For Dice, however, no theatrics were necessary. The gravity of the situation was real, and hurt accordingly. Sugihara, once a friend and brother, had gunned down his wife and friend and, at the same time, orchestrated the downfall of the syndicate that had given him a life, at least for a time...

The priest's chanting seemed to meld with the ebb and flow of the waves below in a kind of melancholy melody. The low drone was picked up by the same wind that sent the ties and scarves of those present flailing like the outstretched and manic flailing of the truly distraught.

The mantra died in perfect unison with the descent of the caskets. When the cranes raised once more, their carriage straps were empty. Even the priest embraced silence. It was in that moment that the finality of it all hit Omoe like a sniper's round. She pitched forward. Dice tried to catch her and couldn't. Where his arm would extend past her waist to break her fall, the bandages and stiffness prevailed. Where he would buckle his knees and place himself in front of and perhaps beneath her, if need be, his exoskeletal brace lagged and reacted far too slowly. Omoe Minowara collapsed onto her hands and knees and a collective gasp from those gathered challenged the coastal winds themselves.

Though his first impulse had been to pull her up, Dice resisted the urge. Rather, he knelt next to her, bowing his head lower than hers until the grass licked his face. When her strength returned, he extended a hand and did not rise. It was excessive, sure, but so were the circumstances. Dice knew that, if the Minowara were to survive, face had to be maintained. Though Omoe Minowara would never truly *run* the organization, she was acting figurehead until Sakakibara and the rest of the syndicate in Japan could come to the rescue. Face had to be maintained. Head to the turf, Dice waited.

"Yama-kun..."

He looked up to find the crystalline shallows that were Omoe's eyes. He opened his mouth to speak, and positioned his feet to stand.

You are not alone, he wanted to tell her.

"Over there!" A voice yelled.

The words startled everyone, including the priest, who halted mid-mantra. The man screaming — a yakuza that Dice did not recognize — pointed, at the same time reaching into his coat.

Dice got to his feet, a chill seizing him in the gut.

They appeared like black smoke. A thick column of men poured onto the estate from directions that were portentous in their own right. They came from seemingly all sides, as though they'd been in waiting since long before the funeral's start. They moved like locusts, like waves of malicious ants in black suits, to converge on one another in a march that would have been thunderous if not executed on grass and sandstone. They descended on the gathering.

At the head of them was a short man, colorfully attired.

Dozens became hundreds, as green fields became black with suits. The intruding force moved toward the funeral like a tsunami, like a tide overdue. So great were their numbers that, in order not to trample the funeral itself, their ranks bowed and bent until finally the funeral was engulfed entirely in a sea of uninvited suits.

The great cry of exclamation that had been slowly building at their approach crescendoed, and now the Minowara were all screaming and falling into one another, drawing weapons.

Daisuke stood stiffly, his eyes never leaving the colorful figure at the head of the army.

The man who'd marched his legion onto the field came to stand over the graves, shoulder to shoulder with the stunned priest, opposite where Daisuke stood. He wore the royal blue jersey of a Japanese minor league baseball team, and neon green cargo shorts. On his head was a mesh trucker's cap and, as he approached, his steps could be heard above the panicked din only for the snap of the flip-flops on his feet. Beneath the cap was a bushel of feathered and dyed hair and an excessively pierced face, etched in boredom. In the man's pale hands was a bag of sour-cream-and-cheddar-flavored potato chips.

Sugihara...

The priest growled something at Sugihara, to which the short yakuza laughed shrilly. With a foot, he shoved the priest away. The elderly man of faith fell to the ground, his robes tangled up in his feet.

"Don't try me, priest! You silly bald wizard!" Sugihara warned, pointing.

The thought of drawing his gun and putting a bullet in Sugihara's skull was almost pornographic to Dice's imagination. In fact, the only thing stopping him was the weight of Omoe on his arm. She, along with the rest of the Minowara, would be massacred if he did so.

Hell, we might be massacred anyway, he thought.

Feeling utterly powerless, Dice watched the man who'd engineered the whole macabre affair make himself comfortable at the center of a thousand sets of warring eyes. Sugihara, tossing the bag of chips in his hand, as though he might find a prize inside, stared back at him with a toothy half-smile.

The priest sat on the ground in silence. The mourners, legitimate and otherwise, had gone silent. Even the gulls, with their nihilistic cries, stifled their nonsense. The only sound to be heard now was Sugihara producing potato chip after potato chip from the colorful bag in his hand. The usurper fed each chip slowly into what looked like a wood chipper of shark's teeth, smiling all the while, never breaking eye contact with Dice. When the bag was finally depleted, Sugihara crumpled it up and tossed it into the grave of Raizen Minowara. Smacking his lips, he dusted his hands dramatically and rubbed his belly.

Before Dice even knew what he was doing, he'd broken free of Omoe's grip and was galloping in his leg brace around the graves to get to Sugihara. At first, Minowara loyalists tried to stop him, and then it was Sugihara's lieutenants. None prevailed as, driven by forces older than mercy, Daisuke would not allow himself to be stopped. Punches were thrown and threats of murder exchanged, but when all was said and done, he loomed over the much shorter Sugihara, the fires of retribution burning wildly, intoxicating.

Though seething, Dice spoke in a measured tone. "Why are you doing this? We were friends. All of us. We were friends."

Sugihara snorted and looked away as if impatient.

"You betrayed everyone who ever gave a shit about you."

"'Gave a shit about me?' Quit talking like you have a clue, Yama-kun. That old fool lived like a king while the rest of us had to scratch and claw to make ends meet. He betrayed us first."

"And Raizen?"

Sugihara pursed his lips and sighed. "Think about it. Do you really think Raizen would have been any different? Worse, he was incompetent and a coward. We'd be licking the Titans' boots under his leadership."

Omoe, with a handful of men at her side, was approaching. Dice held her out of earshot with a hand.

"And Madison?"

Dice stared down into Sugihara's cold gaze, the fingers of his shooting hand twitching in anticipation of the words that would snowball into homicide.

Sugihara ran a hand over his face and made an exasperated sound. "You want to fight?"

"What about Madison?"

"You should have never come back."

It was true but not the complete truth. Dice pressed him. "I didn't shoot Madison, you did. Why? Why betray someone who wanted nothing but to support your ambitions?"

Sugihara waved a hand dismissively. "To hell with you *and* Madison. She knew what I was trying to do and chose you. And look at what it got her, Yama-kun. Face-down in the filth like trash!"

The revolver under Dice's arm left its holster seemingly of its own accord. As it did so, it yanked his arm up and forward to reach out and touch Sugihara's forehead with its barrel.

The sound of guns being drawn and cocked could have been mistaken for a granite avalanche.

Dice made his peace in silence, even as Sugihara picked his teeth with a finger.

Be seeing you soon, love.

"That's enough, Sugihara-san."

915

Dice didn't have to look away from Sugihara to know that Omoe was at his side. The smell of hibiscus this time was unmistakable.

"You've made your point," she continued in a voice that was both melodic and heartbreaking. She placed a slender hand on the gun and lowered it.

Dice allowed her to stay his hand, despite the rage that burned behind his eyes. Taking a step back, as was fitting, he bowed to Omoe respectfully before moving to stand behind her. His hand, still holding the gun, trembled violently.

In a move that Dice would have advised against, Omoe bowed deeply to Sugihara. "Sugihara-san, there will be time for the airing of grievances. All I ask today is that you allow me to say goodbye to my brother and father in peace."

Omoe, still bowing deeply at the waist, could not see the euphoric satisfaction on the shark-toothed yakuza's face, but Dice could.

I'm going to kill you, he swore.

After an obnoxious pause, Sugihara shrugged. "Okie-dokie."

With a flick of the wrist, the usurper signaled for his army to disperse. As the legion of men turned and began marching back the way they had come on a sea of murmurs, Sugihara trailed behind lazily, drunkenly. Before he could get out of earshot, he turned.

"I won't forget this, Yama-kun! You seem to forget. Your bitch may be dead, but you have other friends. Be seeing you!"

Dice holstered his pistol only once the last of the Seidai had disappeared beyond the hill. When they'd gone and the priest was ready to proceed, he lowered himself into the grave of his one-time best friend to retrieve Sugihara's trash.

Climbing back out ruined his suit and brought tears of rage to his eyes, tears that would glimmer in the afternoon sun until the flames of the Minowara funeral pyres dried them.

"Henceforth, the Order of the Sun is no more. Those of you who remain have much work to do to reclaim the glory stolen from you. You will do so as the Order of the Beast. The Elders have spoken and so it shall be.

"Beati sunt qui illustrantur."

- Council Page Bryce Macek

Cedar Medical had done what they could for her, and now she lay beneath the brown sheets in a ward gown of light blue. Her eyes were closed and still; she showed no signs of recovering from the bullet that had pierced her bosom just above the heart. Her hair fell around her face and, for the first time since before they were married, she looked at peace.

Dice gripped her hand, caressing the palm with his fingers. Her hand was cool to the touch, and the tiny hairs of her left arm had turned white. The bracelet on her wrist, just below the maglet that secured her to the bed, read "Madison E Grünewald."

The "E" was for Esmeralda, her grandmother's name.

Williams stood against the wall by the door, and Rena sat in a chair in the corner. Thankfully, they did not speak and had even gone as far as to dismiss the SCPD detectives who'd been guarding the "Party Crasher."

What was the point in guarding a comatose person anyway? After all, the doctors had been very explicit in their grim prognosis.

Chief Williams had been a good friend, as had Rena, and they deserved something. Reluctantly, Dice spoke. "It would be easier, I think," he said, his voice croaking, "if I knew she wasn't in pain."

"She can't feel anything," Rena replied.

"How can you know that?"

Rena looked as though she would respond, but stopped herself.

Williams stood with his arms folded and arched his eyebrows. Since gunning down the Major, he, too, hadn't been the same. The normally candid and outspoken leader of Unit One seemed quiet and introverted of late.

"If she *were* to wake up," Williams said, "she's not on the next plane back to Tokyo. The SDC wants her around until they can confirm that her attack on Kazuo Minowara wasn't at the behest of the Major."

"She wasn't working for the Major."

"How can you be sure?"

He just shook his head. *She was working for Sugihara.*

"I don't want there to be any illusions, *Detective*. No matter how this pans out, her crimes speak for themselves. She's looking at life in Supermax or death at the hands of the next Premier. She is a murderer."

919

Dice clenched a fist. "She's a pianist, Williams. She's a great pianist! She'd just forgotten who she was!" After a pause, he added, "The same way I'd forgotten who I was…"

Williams sucked his teeth in disgust and moved for the door.

"Deputy Chief Constable."

Williams turned to look at him with a tired, remorseful expression.

In the inner lining pocket of Dice's overcoat was a heavy and brand-new badge that represented his full instatement into the State Defense Consortium as a detective of Unit One. It had been his reward for aiding in quelling what the city was now calling 'The Iron Insurrection.' He walked over to Williams and attempted to hand it to him.

"What the fuck is this?" Williams asked, shoving it back at him.

Dice insisted, driving it into the big man's chest forcefully.

"That's a goddamn shame, Daisuke. You've come a long way."

"And this is why I can't."

"What does that mean, Detective? Why 'can't' you serve the people of Sun City? I'm fucking dying to know why you 'can't' do the right thing!"

Revenge. Murder.

Before he could even reply, Williams scoffed. "Do you remember what you said to me when I plucked you out of that holding cell?"

He did.

"You said 'I'm only looking for an opportunity to redeem myself.'"

"I remember."

"Well, being a good person isn't about racking up more good deeds than bad, Daisuke. Trust me when I tell you that no one is counting that shit. We're all struggling and we all have problems. Greed, hatred, envy, and malice; these things exist in all of us. And it's not about letting these things happen and then 'making up for them' afterward. It's about knowing that they exist within you and fighting every day to keep them in check."

Williams slammed a meaty fist into his chest.

"*That's* what redemption is, Daisuke! It's not a collection of acts, Detective. It's a fucking lifestyle!"

Williams held the badge out. When Dice did not take it, the chief dropped it at his feet. "You're not done! Or, if you're really serious, have the fucking decency to resign like a professional."

With that, Williams kicked the door to the room open and stormed out.

Dice looked to Rena, but she just shrugged.

Williams' conversation with Daisuke had left a bad taste in his mouth. As he moved through the busy corridors of Cedar Medical, he considered placing Daisuke under arrest on suspicion of a plot to disrupt the peace. If anything, it would be to protect the man, in case he had ideas of joining Minowara's daughter to fight the man who was suspected of orchestrating the Chairman's murder.

In their brief time together he'd grown quite fond of the rehabilitated yakuza. Dice, in his opinion, had a kind of organic intelligence and the kind of deductive reasoning and logical thinking that couldn't be taught in a classroom.

If you throw this away, kid, I'll never forgive you.

Williams entered the elevator and ordered the patients inside to exit. Once the doors slid shut, he held his wrist to the control pad and selected sub-level three. When the doors opened once more, SCPD officers in body armor, holding assault rifles, greeted him. Though they recognized his face, as he did theirs, they demanded identification, as was their explicit instruction.

It was too easy these days to mimic a person. Past the guards, he made his way down the dimly lit corridor to a set of steel doors.

The room was guarded by two more SCPD officers. He showed his identification once more and allowed a handheld retinal scan to be pressed to his face. Once satisfied, one of the officers swiped a wrist and the door slid open. Williams entered the room, and the door slid shut behind him and locked loudly.

Inside, Lieutenant Mason Bruce sat to one side of the room, looking at his mobile. Opposite him was the blue-haired Corporal Lin. The rookie, who'd driven Pandora up the ass of DAS' prototype mech, was no longer a recruit but a full-fledged member of the unit.

Between the two of them and up to his neck in a see-through medigel tank was the Major… or what was left of him.

Major Ace Monroe's prosthetic arm was missing and his other arm, though bandaged, was locked to the wall by a restraining mechanism designed for holding machines in place. They called it a "Hold-Fast." Inside the medigel tank, nanomachines worked to repair or preserve the Major's organs, keeping him alive. There wasn't much work for them. His right leg was gone entirely and his left leg gone above the knee. A great piece of his torso had been removed on the right side, exposing a lung.

He watched the Major's lung expand and contract, and found it mesmerizing.

"How you doing, soldier?"

"Chieeeef…," a fractured and barely audible voice wheezed. "Whyyy?" The Major's head was down, but his fingers twitched and gripped wildly. "*Why?*" he repeated.

"Why what, Ace?"

The Major raised his head, an act that caused his whole body to convulse violently, splashing nanomachine-infused gel onto the floor. A beard of mostly grey covered his scarred face. His hair had grown unchecked into a mangled and receding afro that was silver at the temples. His face was gaunt, and with the tremendous amount of scar tissue there, it gave him an ancient look, vampiric even. The Major's eyes, sunken and yellow, sought him out for a long time in the dimly-lit room before finding him. When they did, they narrowed, and something of the wolf returned.

"DCC…"

"Major."

Despite being a man literally in pieces, the Major's face twisted into something like a smile. "I'll n-neverrr… understand why the State ssspends m-money caring for convicted fff-felons…"

"Looking a gift horse in the mouth?"

"Merely c-commentinggg on the waste. Futilityyy…"

"You're to *stand* trial for your crimes, Ace."

"Funny… You were always fun—ny…"

The Major's expression was genuinely searching. It was as a child asking a question. "Why n-not just let me die?"

Williams shooed Mason out of his seat and took it. Rotating it so that the back faced the Major, he sat, arms crossed before him. "Your confusion doesn't surprise me, Ace. I think you've made it clear to everyone that the idea of 'justice' is something you don't really get anymore."

Ace cocked his head back, staring down his scarred nose. "J-justice? There's no justice in this world! I fought to—"

"For what's its worth, I'm sorry, Ace. I'm sorry I shot you to shit. I'm sorry I failed you as a colleague, as a brother-in-arms and— and as a friend."

"What are you p-prattling about?"

"I should have seen the signs."

Ace leaned forward, tugging at the restraint with his one remaining arm. "What sssigns?"

"The signs that you'd gone all Section Eight on us."

"I wonderrr w-what you w-will say when my man's f-findings get out..."

Mason looked up from his mobile and stared at the Major for a moment before returning to his device.

"You mean Jennings, the man who hacked Spectus?"

The Major's eyes were wide and his lips trembled. "No namesss..."

"There was nothing on the server, Ace! Nothing!"

"I-impossible! Imposss—"

Williams watched, as Ace's face ran the gamut of expressions. His ruined body shook, splashing more of the life-saving liquid on the deck. "Im—impossible!"

"It was trash, Ace. Whatever was on that server was wiped clean long ago."

"L-lies!"

"Not lies. I would tell you to ask your man, but he didn't survive the siege."

Ace's eyes narrowed menacingly. "You're l-lying! The second lieutenant had ex-explicit instructionsss... He was not fightinggg. You're a l-liar, Chief!"

Mason pocketed his mobile at this and headed for the door. Before leaving he turned. "You know what, *Major*? If you think you're going to get a nice, tidy sentencing and execution, you're mistaken. You've pissed off a lot of *very powerful* people! People who will see you brought low, humbled, disgraced, and humiliated for as long as it takes before you beg for the same death as Premier Macek. I'm going to watch with glee as you rot away in the deepest, darkest cell until your teeth fall out and the only thing recognizable about you will be your mad ravings!"

Mason's face was flushed, his glasses fogged.

"What the hell's gotten into you, Lieutenant!" Williams barked angrily.

Without replying, Mason left, slamming the door behind him.

"I think he's upset," Lin said blandly, his hands folded in his lap, a blank expression on his face.

Williams turned back to the Major. "I'm not lying, friend. First Lieutenant Jennings is dead, dead for joining your insane coup. Whatever was in that database of theirs didn't amount to a megabit of nonsense."

Ace let his head fall slowly. "Liesss..."

"Mason wasn't lying, by the way. The SDC is tossing around ideas for a new form of capital punishment."

The Major's head was hanging now. "I don't care."

"I *do* care, Ace. And I'll do what I can for you, if for nothing other than for old times' sake."

Williams meant it, too. Seeing his former commanding officer like this was difficult, bordering on unacceptable.

Men like this should be allowed to die.

Ace, staring down into the liquid that kept him alive, did not meet his gaze. "You should go."

"Would you like to see your brother, one last time before the sentencing?"

"No."

"Are you sure?"

"I've... I've done enough to him."

"On that, we can agree."

Ace Monroe: lifelong soldier, co-founder of the SDC, founder of Agency Zero, co-founder of Unit One, Commander, Major, veteran, warrior, friend...

"Goodbye, Ace," Williams told him sincerely. "Thank you for everything. Well, not *everything*... Fuck, you know what I mean..."

"Goodbye, Wil—"

And it was then that the Major's expression became blank, void, and truly defeated.

"Goodbye, Chief..."

Williams left Corporal Lin to guard the Major and made his way back to the elevator. His heart was heavy. It wasn't that the Major was all that wrong. In fact, he, too, wondered about the SDC, about this 'Council of Eight,' and about Macek. He, too, had a problem with the influence of money in law enforcement. But, at the same time, Ace's way was flat-out wrong. *Murder was murder.* No two ways about it. And it was that fact that braced his resolution. As the elevator ascended silently, his mobile rang. He tapped behind his ear and took the call. It was his wife.

"Hey, honey. At the hospital, for work. Nothing serious. Yes. I submitted the PTO request this morning. Hm-hm, I can't wait either. We *need* this. Hm-hm. Wait, what?"

He stopped the elevator with a push of the emergency button. It took a few seconds for the buzzing sound to stop.

"But we discussed this! We have a plan! We have a whole fuck — sorry — *freakin'* itinerary!"

Williams leaned against the elevator wall, his knees weak. "What about your sister? She was going to watch... No, I get it, I get it. But this was going to be just us... Maybe we can— you already bought their tickets? You said 'their!' Oh, *both* the kids are coming now?"

He put a hand on the pistol beneath his Unit One jacket. "Great! Yeah! Sure! Hm-hm, Cabo with *both* the kids sounds fucking *wondrous*! What do you mean? My voice hasn't changed, it's the reception. I'm in an elevator. I sound tired? No, I'm fine. Say what? Wait? But they're in Capital City,

928

right? Honey, how is Capital City on the way to Cabo? Your parents? Why do your parents need a vacation, they've been retired for years. How do you vacation from permanent vacation? 'Two days with them?' But my vacation is only..."

Williams slammed his head against the elevator wall, only to find it too forgiving. He needed something harder. Something like concrete, or a landmine.

"That banging sound? I don't know, honey. I think they're doing construction."

After calling in Bryant to relieve him from guarding the Major, Mason sat in a police cruiser outside of Cedar Medical. His hands were on the steering wheel, but he could not settle on a destination. It was still early evening and there was plenty to do back at the precinct but...

I'm tired of playing Unit One.

Spending time with the Major had been the proverbial "straw."

Monroe would suffer. He and Councilwoman Diane West would see to it personally. The Major would be rebuilt, only to tear down once more, slowly, painfully, *publicly*. He could have broken the Major right then and there. He could have handed him total defeat, personally.

"*Yes!*" he could have told him. "*Yes, I'm lying! I killed your man to protect my father's legacy, and the contents of Spectus were far from trash. I have it all,*" he wanted to tell him, "*a mountain of data! All sitting on a drive still spotted*

929

with your man's brain fluids. Everything you suspected and more, far *more!*"

He was certain these words would have broken the Major. And that would have been something to behold. Perhaps, when the SDC — under his direct and very specific instruction — had finished ruining the Major and breaking him down over the course of the next year, he would visit once more. Perhaps he would be the one that strapped the Major's delirious and emaciated body to the chair for lethal injection. At that moment, he would mouth the words: "*You were right, but fuck you!*"

Mason sat staring forward, the car still sitting in the parking stall. He was reaching for the switch to disengage the emergency brake when a call came to him from a secure channel. The channel range was unlike any he'd been exposed to under the SDC. A chill crept over him, and suddenly something like stage fright took him. He answered but did not speak.

[Lieutenant Mason Bruce?]

The voice was grainy, old, and familiar.

[Lieutenant Bruce?]

"I'm here."

[Do you know who I am?]

John Cholish, he thought, but he knew better than to say it.

"I do." He collected his strength, taking a deep breath and exhaling. "I've been expecting this call."

930

[Of course, you have. You are a very bright young man and a true patriot.]

Mason wondered who else might be listening. Were they all listening? Were they gathered somewhere, in some secret chamber, licking the wounds the Major had inflicted on them? He wanted to ask.

[Are you ready to step up and claim your rightful position?]

"I am ready."

[Is the data secured?]

"Yes. I have it."

[Then we should meet without delay. Will you be ready when we summon you?]

"I will."

[Good. On behalf of the Council of Less than Eight, I extend you our deepest condolences. We cannot hope to replace your loss, but we can *help you enact restitution.]*

"I... I thank the Council."

[See you soon, Mason Bruce.]

"Sir."

[Yes?]

"Please call me by my true name."

The line was silent for some time before Cholish returned. *[Very well, Council Page Bryce Macek.]*

The call disconnected. The Unit One lieutenant, son of the deceased William F. Macek, Premier of Sun City, let his hands fall from the steering wheel. A sickening wave of

931

conflicting emotion swept over him. The charade was at long last over, and he would finally be recognized for his efforts. But this recognition, hard earned, would not be shared... with *anyone*. Father was dead. Mother was dead. This realization pulled at the corners of his mouth.

Macek looked around. When he was confident that the lot was clear, he gripped his head in his hands and began to wail.

AJ sat in front of a monitor in the Seventh Precinct with his feet on the desk. He'd spent the last four days filling out reports on the 'Iron Insurrection.' The mountain of work had given him a fresh hatred for his brother, perhaps even more so than the loss of his feet. Rehabilitation was an ongoing process but, after six weeks, he could kind of walk again.

Behind him, Chris typed away, a slow, two-fingered affair.

"You and Bryant on speaking terms again?" Calderon asked.

"Of course! What do you know?"

"I know you were upset by the fact that she decided to honor the terms of her engagement rather than tryst with you."

AJ threw his hands in the air. "Really? 'Tryst!' Are you even using the word right? And look who's talking. I could swear I saw you and your nerdy bandmates topless in an *aggressively oiled* beer commercial just yesterday."

Chris rolled his eyes. "Ministry of Media, pal, not my choice."

"So, when they tell you it's time to go full frontal for Life-long Condoms, you're all in?"

Chris laughed heartily, a special occurrence in and of itself.

AJ picked his jacket up from the chair and slipped it on. "I hope you don't mind if I cut out a bit early."

"I don't care. Half-ass it if you want to. I'm used to it."

"I've been over here filling out paperwork. What the hell have you been working on?"

"I finished my report last night," Chris replied matter-of-factly. "I'm doing agent work."

"Oh, really? Anything interesting?" he asked sarcastically.

"Couple of things, in fact."

"Do tell."

Chris turned his chair around to face him. "Not sure if you were aware, but Thiago Garcia has been missing since before the parade."

"The Fifth Estate guy?"

"One in the same. Well, the protest group and their new leader, in particular, seem to believe he was abducted by Agency Zero."

"No shit? What would Agency Zero want with Thiago Garcia?"

"You *do* know who his brother is, right?"

"I don't know. A lot of Garcias in the world."

"Omar Garcia."

"The MMA fighter?"

"Yup."

"What the hell?"

"Yeah. And, as you must know, Omar has a fight next month that stands to be the highest-grossing event in this city's history. Olympic in scope. We're going to be there to aid in security."

"I don't see the connection."

Chris continued, "Well, the woman who's screaming loudest about the abduction just so happens to be the sister of one recently deceased Luther Gueye. Which segues nicely into another bit of information you might find personally reassuring."

"I'm all ears."

The revelation of Luther Gueye's death at the hands of his brother had not come lightly. In one fell swoop, Ace had destroyed the case they'd built against Luther, while at the same time doing so in such fashion as to make picking up the case all but impossible to prioritize.

"Embedded in Gueye's own neurotrigger," Chris continued, "was a custom program capable of supplanting itself in the neurotrigger of another. Over the network and through basic communication channels, like a virus. And Rena could probably explain it better, but the program was essentially a human killswitch."

"This is Rena's theory…"

"She's a bright one."

"So, Luther made Diedre kill herself."

Chris furrowed his brow. "I guess you could put it that way. Another way to say it would be, he spied on his lieutenants using a program. And when somebody tried to say something he didn't like, particularly his name, they went suicidal."

"Well, shit…"

Chris smiled. "Feel better now?"

"I guess I do. I knew he was dirt."

"You were calling Gueye out when no one else was trying to hear it. Your instinct was right all along, AJ. You should be proud. Damn fine work, Sergeant."

Getting praise from Chris still felt strange. He had trouble thinking of him as a superior officer, though now he was. He waved a hand dismissively. "Thanks. Sucks, though…"

"What's that?"

"Would have been nice to see him in maglets, is all."

Chris nodded. "There'll be others."

"Yeah. Well, I guess I'll see you tomorrow. Have a good night." The door slid open. He picked up Deadbolt from the place where it had been propped next to the door and collapsed it. He slid it onto his belt and gave Chris a 'peace' sign.

"AJ."

He turned.

"I still think about my sister," Chris said, his eyes low. "Every day. And while I blame your brother, I would not let *his* actions come between us. I think of you as a... as a friend for sure. That said, if you need anyone to talk to... well, I'm always here."

"I'm sorry for what my brother did to your family. If I could undo—"

"You gonna go see him?"

It was the first time AJ could remember appreciating being cut off mid-sentence.

"You know," Chris continued, "before the sentencing?"

AJ thought about it for some time, standing in the doorway. He thought about everything that had transpired; of the love and hate that fought for control over his feelings about the man who had raised him. He imagined standing face to face with his brother one more time, and had to admit...

"I wouldn't know what to talk about."

</BW>